HE WHO FLEES THE LION

J. KLEIN-HAPARASH

HE WHO
FLEES
THE LION

Translated from the German by
RICHARD *and* CLARA WINSTON

ATHENEUM *NEW YORK*
1963

Published originally under the title . . . DER VOR DEM LOEWEN FLIEHT
by S. Fischer Verlag, Frankfurt am Main
Copyright © 1961 by S. Fischer Verlag, Frankfurt am Main
English translation Copyright © 1963 by Verlagsanstalt
Kultur und Politik, Vaduz, Lichtenstein
Library of Congress catalog card number 63-17859
Published simultaneously in Canada by McClelland & Stewart Ltd
Manufactured in the United States of America by
H. Wolff, New York
Designed by Harry Ford
First Edition

FOR ALISAH DEUTSCH

*As if a man fled from a lion,
and a bear met him; or went into
    the house
and leaned his hand against the wall,
and a serpent bit him.*

AMOS, V. 19

CONTENTS

LIST OF PRINCIPAL CHARACTERS

Characters who most frequently appear are shown here in
SMALL CAPITALS

BOOK ONE

LUDOVIC (LUTZ) ALDA, landowner in Bucovina
GENERAL BADERESCU, chief of the Second Bureau (Intelligence Service)
ALECU RANANU, lieutenant colonel in the Second Bureau, friend of
Alda
STEFAN (FANICA) ROZESCU, officer in the Second Bureau
Orest DANGHU, "the Blaze," secretary of the Minister of the Interior
DUMITRIU, inspector general of the Sigurantza Generala (Secret Police)
Eusebiu (SEBI) ZERNESCU, inspector of the Sigurantza
Eugeniu (JENICA) Popovici, spy
RADU CANDOMIR, landowner in Bucovina, friend of Alda
ANATOL BILINSKI, Polish refugee
MARTHA VARSANY, Alda's mistress
JOSHUA RUNDBERG, Alda's tenant
KARL RUNDBERG, Joshua's son, friend of Alda
MARGARETA Luceanu
Ioan Luceanu, her husband
AGLAIA (Aia) Odanovici, Margareta's sister

BOOK TWO

Fyodor Ivanovich LAVRENENKO, director of the Electrostantsia in Lvov
Mark Lvovich SAPOSHNIK, deputy director
Pavel Pavlovich MAXIMENKO, *planovik,* (economic planner)
Arkady Samuelovich FEINGOLD, *politruk,* (political adviser)
ANTEK (Antoni Antonich Gorecki)
TADEK (Tadeus Karlowicz Zembrinski)
VASSILY (Vassily Vassilevich Khominiuk)

BOOKS THREE AND FOUR

MIRA LINKHAND, née Rosen
FREDDY LINKHAND, her husband
A. L. LINKHAND, Freddy's father
COUNT VLADISLAV (VLADEK) VORONOVSKI
Count Roman Bolgurski, Voronovski's brother-in-law
Hilda Mermelstein, nurse
Emilian MERMELSTEIN, her husband
Riva Saposhnik
Ruchele Boim, Riva's mother

BOOK FIVE

Inspector Axintie (Puffi) BARBULESCU, attached to the Bucharest head-
quarters of the Sigurantza
STANESCU
STRATILESCU } Cernauti Sigurantza
Countess Agathe Zinnendorf
Count Felix Zinnendorf, her son
Mischa Eisner
Max Duttner } Karl Rundberg's men
Bela Nagy, wholesaler
Fifi Nagy, his wife
Feri Dohany, Nagy's chauffeur
Elsa, Nagy's maid

BOOK SIX

Fyodor Fyodorovich POTAPENKO, party secretary
Sergei Ivanovich TARASHCHENKO, deputy party secretary
Dmitri Alexevich Rudnenko, machinist
DR. LEON FEUERBERG, physician in Lvov
Jeanne (JANINA), his wife
Ignat Ilich Gorbatenko, director
Rudnicki, coachman
Wagner, warehouse supervisor
Natan Kornhaber, chief milker
Ruben Meerblum, supervisor of cheese making

Tatiana (TANIA) Obadieva, cashier
Chalev, head gardener
Benderski, gardener
Yossel Besselmann, Rundberg's business associate
Arye, Besselmann's son

TIME OF THE ACTION: *November 28, 1939 to May 10, 1940*

BOOK ONE

ONE IS CHOSEN

*The urge for truth
and the joy in falsehood. . . .*
GOETHE

A GLOSSARY of Romanian, Polish and Russian words
will be found following the text

THIS EARLY IN THE MORNING—IT WAS BARELY EIGHT O'CLOCK —the lobby was almost deserted; a single man sat in a corner hidden behind his newspaper. It was pleasantly warm in the room, and the deep leather armchair was soft and comfortable. The spy was sleepy, but he did not dare allow himself a nap. He had not called on the Chief for a whole week, and if he brought nothing today, he would be out of a job. He threw an envious and reproachful glance at the man in the corner. A bellboy was bowing before him and saying something. The man nodded his thanks and went to the telephone booth.

The spy stood up, yawning, and strolled toward the revolving door. At the desk he slowed his pace, turned, at first hesitantly and then resolutely, and held out a badge to the desk clerk. It was not his own badge; until he was regularly employed, he had no right to flash it.

Georges, the desk clerk, scarcely looked up. He seemed not to see either badge or man. In the same abstracted way, he pushed a guest registry form across the desk. The spy, twirling his black mustache, read under his breath: "Ludovic Alda, landowner, born 1898 in Aldeni, Bucovina. . . . Romanian? Do you know the man?"

"Don't you?"

"I am asking the questions here." The gray face, haggard from lack of sleep, flushed.

You bastard, if only I dared, how I'd like to . . . Georges thought. But he was under instructions to transmit all requested information to the various branches of the Sigurantza, the Secret Police. In November, 1939, Bucharest was swarming with foreigners—refugees, businessmen, spies.

"Domnule Alda," he said, "is a boyar and a well-known sportsman. He has been stopping at the Union for fifteen years."

"Good." The spy started away from the desk, then paused irresolutely. What now? he thought, as he wandered back to his seat. What am I going to tell the Chief? I must bring him something, no matter what. Maybe I can use something about this Alda, a Romanian who looks like an Englishman. Something funny about him. Something funny about everybody in Bucharest today. I should be able to work up a story.

At this moment Alda emerged from the telephone booth and went to the desk. "My bill, Georges," he said. "And please reserve a sleeping compartment for me in the night express."

"Thank you, Domnule Alda." The tip had been generous, as always. "And—just one moment, please." The desk clerk turned, drew a slip of paper from a pigeonhole, and laid it on the counter, retaining it as if unintentionally. Alda understood; he leaned forward so that his ear was close to Georges' mouth, and the clerk whispered, "That man back there—Sigurantza—asked about you."

"Thank you, Georges," Alda said; it was impossible to tell whether this information interested or in any way disturbed him. He took the slip of paper with the telephone number and strode toward the elevator. The boy was just sliding open the elevator door when a shout—"Hello there, Lutz!"—made Alda turn around.

An officer in the uniform of the Queen Marie Regiment of hussars had called him. Alda went up to him and shook hands. "How are you, Alecu?"

"Fine, as you see."

"Oh!" Alda had been examining his uniform. "Congratulations on the lieutenant colonelcy. Since when?"

"Ages, *mon cher*. Ever since November first. I'm in the intelligence service now, if you care to know."

"You—in the Second Bureau? Not with the regiment any longer—not with the horses?" They sat down at one of the small tables in the lobby.

"When country calls, I must put on fat. Look at this!" He put his hand to his hip and stomach. "Lard, lard, lard everywhere."

"You still look like a stallion, Alecu—thoroughbred, of course."

Alecu Rananu whinnied softly. His friends called him Stallion because of his passion for horses and his habit of scraping his foot and whinnying at the sight of or even the mere mention of women who took his fancy. Alda looked around. "But there isn't a woman in sight."

"So I've noticed. That was just to keep in practice. It's a long time since I last whinnied."

"Are you working so hard?"

"Don't laugh—from eight in the morning till late evening and sometimes all through the night."

"Poor chap. What's it all about?"

"Official secret, of course. But one thing I can say, it's damned interesting." He looked up at the clock. "Listen, Lutz, I'm supposed to take you to the Old Man. So get your coat and come along."

"What do you mean, take me? Who is the old man?" Alda had remained in his seat, although the other man had risen. He looked up at him in amusement, and at the same time glanced at the spy several tables away. The spy hastily, but too late, ducked behind his newspaper.

Rananu sat down again. He moved his chair close to Alda's. "But, Lutz! You wouldn't think of not coming when Baderescu sends for you!"

"Suppose I did think of it?" Alda shook his head. "I can't say I like these new ways. With all due respect, what is General Baderescu to me? Am I his subordinate? Take me—come, come, Alecu." He laughed.

"You are an officer, Lutz," Rananu said seriously, "and Baderescu is not just any general, either."

"Granted. But I am only a reserve officer, and as long as I am not wearing a uniform, I don't intend to let myself be—taken. Have you by any chance been assigned to arrest me, Alecu?"

"Are you mad!" Rananu laughed.

"What does your General want of me?"

"He wants to talk with you. Those are his own words, *parole d'honneur.*"

"Why should he pick on me? And how does he know I am here? I haven't been in Bucharest for four months and got in less than two days ago."

"I told him—if you insist on knowing."

"You?"

"It's really so simple. *'Mon général,'* I said last night, 'may I have tomorrow afternoon off? I've been invited to luncheon, and that sort of thing always stretches out—it's awkward to be looking at the clock all the time.' 'Who's going to be there?' he asked. 'I wouldn't want you getting into bad company.' So I mentioned your name. 'Oh,' he said. 'Alda? Is he in Bucharest? And you're a friend of his? Well, bring him here; I want to speak to him. Tomorrow morning at nine would be best.' " Rananu's voice took on an insistent note. "You know enough about the army to realize what it means when a general makes such a request—and Baderescu no less. And here it is almost nine and we're still lounging around. Come on, Lutz!"

"One moment, Alecu. Why did you tell the General that we were going to be lunching together?"

"Because we are. At Margareta's. She told me that you were in town. And she's invited you, hasn't she?"

"Margareta?" Alda took out the note the desk clerk had given him. "Yes, this is her number. And how does she know that I'm here?"

"Sulica saw you at the bar in the Athenée."

"So he did. Well, I must telephone at any rate."

"You can do that later. After all, you know what she wants. All this is wasting time, Lutz old boy. Just come, as a favor to me."

"All right, as a favor to you, Alecu." He went to the elevator.

The spy was no longer sitting in his corner. He had moved several tables nearer, where he could pick up a few words of the conversation. He already knew who the Lieutenant Colonel was and what position he held, and there had been some talk about General Baderescu. He had what he needed.

The two-story house with the small front garden was much like the other houses on the quiet street. There was no brass plate at the door, and no guard. In the roomy vestibule heavy antique furniture stood on a faded rug. A sergeant came forward to meet the two. He bowed to the Lieutenant Colonel.

"*Bon jour,* Fanica. Tell the General I'm here," Rananu said.

The Sergeant vanished, and they sat down. "I suppose you're wondering about this unmilitary young man, aren't you, Lutz?"

"I am. A Sergeant who greets a Lieutenant Colonel by bowing!"

"This Sergeant," Rananu explained, "is Dr. Stefan Rozescu."

"Of the textile mills?"

"The only son. Our special-missions officer. The entire correspondence passes through his hands. He translates from German, English and Italian. An enormously rich young man, and in addition a highly proficient linguist."

"Very interesting."

"All of us here are fairly well off."

"You're certainly anything but poor, Alecu. How many plum trees do you have now? Do you know?"

"What a question! Sixteen thousand three hundred and sixty-seven. In partnership with my brother, of course. But he lives in the country and has no expenses. So I have to scramble. *Sans blague,* only rich fellows work here. Can't you guess why?"

But before Alda could reply, the Sergeant reappeared at the head of the corridor. "The General is expecting you."

Rananu sprang to his feet. "Forgive me if I go ahead of you— I know my way around here."

Alda noticed the low, wallpapered door only when Rananu opened it. It led into a large salonlike room.

In a niche opposite the door, at a big desk littered with folders, sat General Baderescu, chief of the Second Bureau. He was not in uniform. A blue suit, hardly the height of fashion, clothed his spare frame; his shirt had a stiff, detachable collar, and he wore a cheap wine-red tie. His feet were crossed under the desk; his clumsy, black boots had an old-fashioned look. His appearance was rather that of a village schoolmaster than of a general in an army whose officers were noted for foppishness.

Rananu snapped to attention and saluted him with the obligatory "Long life to you, Domnule General." Alda bowed mutely. The General extended a slender, veined hand that might have belonged to an old woman. Then he gestured to a chair at the left of the desk. "I beg your pardon, Domnule Alda, I must just ask Rananu—here"—he handed a slip of paper to the Lieutenant Colonel—"look the man up." Rananu clicked his heels. As he left, he winked merrily at Alda. Alda did not respond, for he was intent on studying the General.

The man had a narrow head, with thin, grayish-blond hair, parted on the side. His face was pockmarked and of an unhealthy yellowish complexion, but there was nothing disagreeable about it. In fact his light-brown, lively eyes behind their old-fashioned, gold-rimmed spectacles, and the regular, sound teeth in the strongly shaped mouth gave him an engaging appearance. His deep, soft voice fell pleasantly upon the ear. With an amiable squint, the General turned toward his visitor. Alda felt the resistance he had built up inside him beginning to weaken, giving way to a readiness to be obliging. But he forced himself to preserve an air of conventional politeness.

The General opened the conversation: "Well, Alda, what did you think when Rananu brought you my message? Incidentally, thank you very much for coming."

Alda bowed slightly, but did not reply. The General had forestalled him, as though sensing that his visitor was preparing to ask questions of his own. A bit nervously, Alda reached into his pocket for his cigarette case. But the General quickly opened a drawer and placed two packs on the table—one of them American Camels, the other, wrapped in common, thin, paper, Nationale, one of the cheapest Romanian brands. "Please, help yourself. I know you young fellows are partial to these Camels. I stick to Nationale, although they're dreadful, God knows."

Alda gratefully took a Camel—they had become hard to obtain lately. "I was surprised, sir," he said after the first puff.

"And you thought: the old man has a nerve. But your intelligence won the day."

"My intelligence?"

"You said to yourself: If he wants to see me, it won't do a bit of good to refuse, since he can run me in whenever and wherever he pleases. Is that right, Domnule Alda?"

"I don't regard myself as that important. But I was, or rather I am, very curious to know what the Chief of the Second Bureau wants of me."

"Good, excellent. And do you know what would have happened if you had not come at my invitation?"

"Rananu would have caught it."

"Not at all. Rananu was serving only as a messenger. My purpose was to let you know that a rather important matter was involved, and you understood. If you had not come, I would never have sent for you again. Never again. I can only use intelligent people, Domnule Alda."

Old fox, Alda thought, while he looked at the General with a questioning air. "Your praise is very flattering, sir, but I hardly deserve it. Up to this point I have understood nothing at all."

"Patience. You will soon understand everything. This is the third time I have had occasion to spend some thought on you. My opinion of you has steadily risen."

"The third time? I had the honor to be introduced to you many years ago. That was . . ."

"In 1927. The steeplechase for army officers. You rode *hors concours*. A handsome chestnut, as I recall."

"Belami," Alda said. "A magnificent horse."

"At the tough hurdle in front of the royal box the others worked their mounts like jockeys. But you rode so lightly and your aids were so well calculated that in admiring your nerve I hardly noticed your horsemanship."

"There are plenty of good horsemen in our country."

"I know all of them, although I don't have the privilege of belonging to the elite branch of the service. There isn't one of them who has this—uncanny nerve I've seen in you."

Alda waved his hand to imply that the General was exaggerating.

"No, no," the General said forcefully, "it's not a thing to be dismissed with a gesture." He paused and waited. But Alda held his peace. "I've read a good deal about you," Baderescu resumed. "About the lepers' camp, for example. If I hadn't seen you riding, I would have thought the whole business just a publicity stunt. But as it was, I took a different view of it. I knew what was behind it. What decided my opinion of you, though, was your play."

"What does the play amount to? Pure box-office. It made money—that's about the best to be said for it. . . . But you certainly did not ask me here to discuss these things, did you, sir?"

"I want you to know my reasoning," the General countered. "It wasn't the story or the witty dialogue that impressed me, but the logic with which you wove the plot and solved it. Logic and imagination! You are my man, Alda." The General looked Alda straight in the eyes. His face lit up with a cordial smile.

"Your man, sir? I'm glad to hear it."

"You understand me?" The smile had vanished. "You know

what I want of you?"

"You want something of me? At your service, sir, to the limit of my ability. But I really don't know—"

"Are you rich, Domnule Alda?" the General asked abruptly.

Alda looked up. "Rich? I don't know why that should interest you, sir, but if you wish—" The General sat in expectant silence. "I own precisely one thousand acres of good land, fifty acres of well-tended orchard, two fishponds, and about twelve hundred acres of forest, sound, well-grown beech. That's all rented out. In addition I have a fine country house in top-notch repair and a small town house. Also some valuable pictures and rugs, inherited and acquired, and a rather decent collection of snuffboxes. Oh yes, and a half interest in an apartment house. It's enough to live on, sir." As if the General could not have found out every such detail with ease! But compared to Rananu or Rozescu, he certainly could not be called rich.

"That ought to be enough," the General said in a flat voice.

Alda sat very straight. "What do you mean by that, sir?"

"Nothing new, Domnule Alda. You like to gamble. You have often lost more than a year's income at one sitting." The statement was made without a note of blame or accusation; but Alda nevertheless felt himself under pressure. The man opposite him did not say a word without a specific purpose.

"Of course I like to gamble," he said with an easy laugh. "Yes, I have all the vices—horses, cards, gypsies. All things that cost a great deal of money, sir."

"If you love things that cost money, do you love money, Domnule Alda?"

"Good Lord! Since when does a spendthrift love money? Money, and what can be bought for money, are two different things."

"The more I talk to you, the more my theory is confirmed."

"Your theory?" Alda asked with open mockery.

"Yes." The General pointedly overlooked his tone. "And therefore let's get down to business. I will place any sum you like at your disposal. Work for us."

"For the Second Bureau?" Alda asked coldly. "Never. Not for all the money in the world. No!" he added vehemently, and shook his head with excessive vigor. Although the General's offer had not taken him by surprise, he felt that he had not put his rejection of it sharply enough.

"And why not?" the General asked softly.

Alda forced himself to answer calmly. "I do not feel the slightest leaning toward the profession."

"Which is to say that you despise the members of the profession?"

"If a man has no talent for music, does it mean that he despises musicians?"

"A lame comparison." The General snorted. Alda shrugged and looked out into the garden. The General leafed through a folder. Then he cleared his throat. "We seem to have run into a blind alley," he began again. "It was my mistake. I must admit that I expected a great deal from this conversation. But my chief aim was to get to know you better. I knew too little about you. From a personal point of view, this meeting has been very rewarding for me."

"I'm sorry to have disappointed you," Alda said politely.

"Did I say I was disappointed? Do you imagine I thought you would jump at my offer?" Alda made no reply. "It would not have fitted the picture I'd conceived of you. Alda the aristocrat, grandson of the great Neagoe Alda, sportsman, gentleman—do you think I expected you to engage in espionage for money?"

"Then you only wanted to lead me into temptation, sir?"

"Not at all," the General declared. "Such childish tricks don't interest me. It was simply a test. If you had agreed, I would have had some assignment for you, we would have paid generously for it, and I would have revised my opinion about the kind of man Alda is. But as it is, I'm glad. I am delighted that you can't be bought. I don't have to revise my theory."

Relieved, Alda took him up. "I, too, am glad, sir. If another general were in your place—"

"If another were in my place?" Baderescu leaned back in his chair and looked up at the ceiling. "Then you would have received a call-up order, like so many other reserve officers nowadays. Reserve Captain Ludovic Alda would have stayed with his regiment for a week and then been reassigned to the Second Bureau. And the General would then have given the Captain his orders. Wouldn't that have been the simplest and surest way to go about it?"

"No doubt you have your reasons for not having taken that course, sir," Alda said. He felt like an actor playing an uncongenial part.

"Certainly, certainly. In every army, officers and soldiers go to their deaths on orders, and that is how it must be, or the army is no army at all. Discipline and obedience are more important than personal courage or heroism. Our tasks here in the Second Bureau require courage, but not the soldier's courage. They require intelligence, nerve and adaptability—being able to cope with every situation, to see with a thousand eyes and hear with a thousand ears.

Above all, they call for love of country. A man who works for us, Domnule Alda, must love our country beyond all else."

The General had spoken these last words with great intensity. The old fox isn't playacting, Alda thought, looking at the pockmarked face and furrowed brow; he means it.

"Do you really love your country, Domnule Alda? Or are you one of the thousands from the new territories who are still Austrians at heart after two decades, still mourning for the old monarchy, and feeling nothing but contempt for the uncultured Walachians?"

"If you had looked into the history of our family as closely as you have into my personal affairs, you would know better than to ask," Alda replied.

"Your grandfather was a patriot—I know that. I had the pleasure of knowing him, and I revered him."

"I was raised by my grandfather—my parents died when I was three. I am a Romanian, although I was an Austrian officer in the war, sir. A reserve officer."

"Is there such a great difference, whether a man is an active or a reserve officer? In war—"

"Even so, it is not the same. Once the war is over, the reserve officer returns to civilian life."

"There is war in Europe, Domnule Alda. Hannibal *ante portas.*"

"Yes, there is war, and for that reason—" Alda's face had lost its cool, controlled expression. His nostrils quivered, and there was a deeper blue in his gray-blue eyes. "A dangerous trend is developing more and more clearly in this country. People are openly showing sympathy with that megalomaniac murderer. They admire him, or pretend to, and before we know it he'll have dragged us into fighting on his side. It may come overnight, and this country of decent peasants and herdsmen will be turned into a blood-soaked wasteland. All because a few opportunists who set the tone think their time has come. Criminals who want only to further their own interests. Here's another item for your dossier on me, if you want it. It's this: I mean to be on the spot where murderers and oppressors are being fought. But I don't mean to fight for them. Never!"

"Do you think I am an opportunist, Domnule Alda?" The General asked softly.

With considerable warmth, Alda replied, "Certainly not, sir. But you are a soldier who could not desert from the colors."

"Evidently you have theories of your own, Domnule Alda," the General said with a sad smile. "At any rate, you have sized up the situation. Those fine gentlemen are preparing a New Order. Which is to say, chaos. The outsiders who could never get anywhere, the incompetents who never had anything because they were too stupid or too lazy, the greedy who batten on any misfortune—all these boys see a chance to come into their own. And our decent, simplehearted peasants are to bleed for them, in a war which will yield them nothing and which will overthrow all they hold dear. As for us, they'll get rid of us the moment they come to power."

The General fell silent and stared into space. What had they arrived at? Alda wondered. They agreed, apparently, on basic matters, but what good was it? And as though the General had guessed these thoughts, he spoke again: "You are thinking. 'What does he still want of me? If he sees things this way, he must understand my refusal.' Is that right, Domnule Alda?"

"Right, sir."

The General resumed hesitantly, "Is it your way to let things take their course? To throw up the struggle because the other side is stronger than you are? To let the bad cause win because you think the time is not yet ripe for fighting it?"

He raised his head and looked firmly at Alda. "If you were in my place, would you simply wait it out until the new men came in and gave you the sack? Would you let them have it their way?"

"Is there anything you can do to oppose them?" Alda asked hesitantly.

"Oh, that. . . ." The general dismissed the question. "Various things." He paused as if to summon up strength for a final effort. "I will not move from my post—although there may be someone who is trying to oust me. Don't forget that I have carte blanche in money matters. That gives me quite a bit of leverage. And they have to be awfully careful with me, since I'm one of the most popular generals in the army. Moreover, I'm the best of advertisements for their filthy cause. People say, 'If Baderescu is with it, then the cause must be a good one.' "

Alda nodded his agreement. The General had evidently expected a heartier response. When Alda said nothing, he asked directly, "How does it strike you?"

"A dangerous plan."

"Dangerous? For me? Good Lord! I'll be sixty-five soon, and there's no one who will miss me if the worst comes to the worst. If they try to court-martial me, I mean. But we're still a while from that."

"A long while, I should think."

"No, not so long. So far the game is being played for oil and cattle and grain. Soon it will involve the land and the people."

"Are you so sure of that, sir?" Alda asked unhappily.

The General looked at him wide-eyed. "How can you ask? If there is any purpose at all to this war, it must be waged against Russia."

"Purpose—hm. . . . Still and all, there is the Pact. The Germans have simply handed most of Poland over to the Russians. Don't you call that friendship?" He spoke boldly, but with an undertone of doubt. He did not believe what he was saying.

The General was too preoccupied with his own thoughts; he heard only the words and not the tone. "The Pact? That doesn't mean a thing. I know what the Germans think of it—I know with utter certainty. It doesn't matter a damn, as far as they're concerned. But what are the Russians up to? They're important. More important than the Germans. And—you see, I've read everything that has been written about them, both pro and con. It's hard to extract the truth from all those reams of paper—everyone who writes has an ax to grind. What's happened to the Russian muzhik in these past twenty-two years? Are the sons like the fathers? And what does Stalin mean to them? What is the party really—what power does it have?"

He spoke rapidly, with pent-up excitement. "What the opportunists are all counting on is the collapse of the Soviet regime. They talk about it openly. Two weeks of blitzkrieg and the colossus with feet of clay will be finished, they say. But tanks and Stukas won't decide this war—though they'll play their part, God knows. The last word, the decisive word, will still be spoken by the infantryman, the peasant, the muzhik. Everything depends on him, on his will, his spirit." The General's eyes probed Alda's face. "Do you know what I want you for?" he resumed, slowing his pace and dropping his voice. "I want you to go to Russia. There's no one else I can send. You're someone who understands what is at stake and what I need to know. I'm not sending you to spy. I'm not interested in troop strength, weapons, deployment plans. I want to know what they think about the Pact, what they say about it, how the authorities explain it, and how the people—the workers, peasants and soldiers— take the explanations. I want to know what they're like and how they'll behave when war comes. No espionage," he repeated, "although—assuming you go—you run the risk of being caught and so forth. . . ." He fell silent.

Alda scarcely looked at the General. In a low, almost casual voice he said, "I'll go, sir, but whether I can do the job—"

The General showed no sign of surprise. "It's not an easy assignment, Alda, but of all the men I know, you're the only one for it. Have you been in Russia? I know that you have an excellent command of the language."

"I was in Russia more than twenty-two years ago, sir, as an officer in the Austrian Army. That's not much help. The Russians of today speak a different language. But I'll not be going to make speeches. I'll restrict myself to the role of listener, as far as possible. And"—he paused for a moment—"I wouldn't have to go to Russia proper. There are Russians barely twenty miles from Cernauti—workers, commissars, soldiers. Soviet Russia begins in Snyatyn now. A hop across the Ceremus and there you are. It isn't necessary to go to Moscow to find out what we want to know. I speak Ukrainian, or rather Ruthenian, like our peasants of Bucovina and their cousins across the Ceremus, and I think I can move about safely between Snyatyn and Lvov without attracting attention. I know the region very well."

"You'll take it on, Alda!"

"It isn't so very much. But I'm willing, sir. Only I want to state my conditions: I am not a number in your files; I am not going as your agent; I remain a free man. Free in my decisions. When I report back—if I report back—it's not as an employee of the Second Bureau. And, one last thing: I don't want any money."

"Just as I expected," the General said. "But you will have to cross a border where every foot is guarded. On the Russian side, God must help you; but on our side, why needlessly complicate the matter and run a double risk of being arrested or even shot? A scrap of paper without even your name on it, and you'll pass the frontier without trouble."

"I realize I'm not going on a country outing. Let me handle it myself, sir."

"When will you go?" the General asked quietly.

"I'll return home today. I'll need two or three days for settling my personal affairs. I'll have to work out some sort of plan or itinerary."

"God be with you!" The General stood up slowly and came over to Alda, who had also risen. "Alda," he said softly, "don't think I'm glad to have recruited you. If I had a son who was as well suited to this assignment as you are, I'd have sent him." He cleared his throat. "I will be just as anxious about you. And if you should have any scruples about the matter—your grandfather would have approved of it, I'm sure of that."

The General pressed a button.

"Now you will be going to Margareta Luceanu's. Eat well, drink and enjoy yourself. Are you taking the night train?"

"Yes, sir."

Rananu entered. "Is everything in order?" the General asked him.

"Yes, sir," Rananu reported. "I've arranged for him to be here to see you at four o'clock."

"Good. You have leave until ten tomorrow morning. By then you should have slept off your liquor. You've got your car, haven't you, Alecu? Bring Alda his coat and hat and then drive to the passage. Wait there for him."

"Yes, sir." Rananu returned in a moment with Alda's things, clicked his heels, and left the room.

"Come," the General said, "I'll guide you." Alda followed him down a long corridor to a door. "Go across the garden and out through the open gate in the wall. And now, God be with you!" He took Alda's hand and pressed it hard. Then he kissed him on the brow and solemnly made the sign of the cross over him.

The Sigurantza in the capital had many offices. Some of them were located in a five-story blocklike building on a busy boulevard. A watchmaker's shop on the ground floor had been converted to a reception room. An official sat at a desk equipped with a telephone and a register. Beside him sat a police sergeant.

Eugeniu Popovici, known to his friends as Jenica the Gambler, leaned toward the official's ear with an ostentatiously confidential air and asked to have his name sent into Divisional Chief Zernescu. He was handed a card on which a clumsy hand had scribbled a number in red pencil. Ordinarily Jenica received this with a certain discomfort—for it was evidence that he did not "belong." But today he thrust it into his pocket without a qualm, for he hoped that before long he would not need a number.

The first three stories of the building were reserved for that section of the Security Police which dealt with political parties, for the alien registration office, for archives, and other such routine matters. On the fourth and fifth floors were the offices of the "brass." Jenica paused in front of a door on the fourth floor, gathered his courage, and entered. A man sat at a typewriter in the sparsely furnished room. He did not look up as Jenica entered. When Jenica asked where the Chief was, he responded with a silent nod toward another door. Jenica removed his hat, spat into his right hand, smoothed his hair, straightened his scarf, and opened the door.

Zernescu's room had none of that efficient streamlined atmosphere appropriate to the office of a director of the Secret Police. Instead, it was outfitted like a petit-bourgeois parlor at the beginning of the century. In one corner was a stiff-backed sofa upholstered in green plush, while a group of matching chairs clustered around a hexagonal table with brass reinforcements at the corners. The floor was covered by a brightly colored peasant rug, and in front of the desk—which again might have belonged to Grandmother—was a white, rather worn sheepskin to which a poor imitation of a polar bear's head had been attached. On the wall hung two colored engravings in gold frames: The Hunter's Departure and The Hunter's Return.

Jenica did not go up to the desk, but stood at the prescribed distance at the edge of the sheepskin. "Long life to you, Domnule Inspector," he said. Zernescu did not respond to the greeting. He was busy cleaning his ear with a tiny spoon. He suspended operations a moment and seemed to be waiting to see whether the itching would stop or whether he would have to continue. Jenica did not dare say another word. He stood as humbly as a pupil who has learned his lesson but does not know what teacher's mood will be.

At last the Inspector stopped scooping at his ear. He wiped off the celluloid spoon with his thumb and forefinger and tucked it into the upper pocket of his vest. Then he cleaned his fingers thoroughly on a huge blue-and-white-checked handkerchief. Since the handkerchief was handy, he proceeded to blow his nose vigorously. He folded the handkerchief again, replaced it in his pocket, and at last turned his face blankly toward the spy. He scrutinized the man for some seconds, his eyes filled with boredom and contempt. When Jenica's numbed silence persisted, he screwed up his face and said, "Well?" All of Jenica's animation had subsided. He stood like a bird before a snake. The Inspector was obviously enjoying his discomfiture. "Well, are you going to stand there like an idiot? Tell me your lies and don't waste my time."

"No lies, Domnule Inspector, as God is my witness, no lies," Jenica stammered. "It was to do with the *Serviciul de Informatziune.*"

"What the devil have you got to do with the Second Bureau? And which one? The Russian, French or English? Cretin, say your piece and get out. Have you anything to tell me about Poles, Englishmen, Jews? Spit it out!"

"Sir," the spy stuttered, "there's someone staying at the Union who looks like an Englishman. I thought that was what he was and trailed him, but it turned out he's Romanian. Then Rananu came along—you know, the Colonel from the Second Bureau. They talked for a long time and kept mentioning the Old Man. General Baderescu, you know. And then the two of them drove off. I'm sure they went to the Second Bureau, and it must have been important."

"Really? Important? You think so?"

"Sir," Jenica begged, tears filling his eyes, "this man can't really be Romanian. If you saw him, you'd swear he was an English lord or an Austrian count or a German."

"So what?" Zernescu asked in a tone of disgust. "What other dope do you have on him? What's his name?"

"Ludovic Alda."

Zernescu burst into rude laughter. "You dumb pimp. If you didn't spend all your time in low dives and bordellos, you'd know who Alda is. Your ears are stuffed with wax again. Probably they were discussing a horse. That's all those two would talk about. Beat it!"

Broken, Jenica slunk away. It did not occur to him to contradict; Zernescu had slapped him down too often. Out in the corridor, he tried to compose himself, but did not succeed. He would have to bury all his hopes. He no longer stood a chance for a regular job with the Sigurantza; perhaps he would even lose his meager earnings as an occasional spy.

As he trudged toward the exit, a hand was laid on his hunched shoulders. He started, turned around, and saw the furrowed face of the secretary who had been working at the typewriter in Zernescu's waiting room. "Come back," the man said curtly.

Jenica followed him, and sat down on the very edge of a hard bench. It began to dawn on him that the Inspector had changed his mind, that the information was important after all. And as the dismay of disappointment subsided, hope rose. A turning point in his life had come, Jenica felt. His insolent expression returned; he hung his hat on the rack and lit a cigarette with something of the jauntiness with which he had entered the building.

In the next room Zernescu sat brooding. His thoughts circled around two images that appeared, disappeared, merged, blurred into one another. One of them was the hubbub of a fashionable horse show: dignitaries, army officers in dress uniform, beautiful, well-dressed women, fine horses, music. And this scene melted into the other: a prison yard in the Bessarabian town of Balti, near the Dniester, under the merciless glare of the sun. Hundreds of prisoners: Russians, Ukrainians, Jews—or, to sum them up in a word, Bolsheviks. And among them a man just as ragged and dirty as the rest. The picture of the prison yard momentarily covered the scene of fashionable pleasure as a cloud blots out the sun. One face was in both pictures: in one the face of a handsome rider, in the other the face of a tattered man in the prison yard.

What was the name of that man in the Balti prison? Zernescu reached out for the telephone; then he dropped his hand again. It was no use; nobody around the office ever knew anything. He would have to solve the problem alone. He placed his elbows on the desktop, propped his heavy head in his hands, closed his eyes, and meditated. *One* face. Ludovic Alda and—what was the prisoner's name? It was on the tip of his tongue—a simple name. Easy, Zernescu said to himself, take it easy. What had been the situation? The Royal Commissioner had come on an inspection, and had taken several officials from Kishinev with him to help with the interrogations. Zernescu, only a minor functionary at the time, had been along. Men, women, children, prisoners already under sentence and those merely being held for questioning, suspects, refugees from across the Dniester—all had filed into the yard. The Royal Commissioner, a powerful man with umber complexion and tigerish eyes, had paced down the rows of prisoners, the district attorney at his side and the Sigurantza officials trailing behind him. They noted down the names of the prisoners whom the Commissioner designated. That meant interrogation at night, torture, whippings, red-hot irons being pressed into soft flesh.

The man stood at the far left of the first row of prisoners. He had been caught swimming the Dniester near Ocnitza, his clothes in a bundle around his neck. Soldiers had fired at him and missed. Captured and taken to the prison, he denied that he had been on the Russian side of the river. He carried no identification, spoke Romanian, French and German, and alleged that he was a correspondent for foreign newspapers. After twenty years Zernescu could still see the movement with which the district attorney turned to the Commissioner and whispered, "Bolshevik." The Commissioner made his standard gesture toward the Sigurantza officials.

What in the world was the name of that journalist? Good God, I never forget a name!

They had questioned the man, but the real interrogation was scheduled for the next night. The next night, however, the journalist was gone. Simply disappeared into thin air. What was the fellow's name again? He could see the man's spare frame, contrasting so strongly with the well-fed, gross figure of the Commissioner. Suddenly he stood up; the name had come back to him. Gross, of course, Oskar Gross of Vienna. And yet it couldn't be. He tried to picture Oskar Gross in a red hunting jacket, and rejected the image. And then he visualized Ludovic Alda barefoot, in a torn shirt, dirty, with unkempt hair; that seemed even more fantastic. Even supposing that they were one and the same person, he thought, how could I possibly prove it? It's all so long ago, and what has brought it to my mind? Just because this filthy stool pigeon has put a flea in my ear?

He suddenly was filled with hatred for the spy. I'm as much of an idiot as he is! Just because he sees Alda talking to Rananu! All further than the door of the Second Bureau. "Others will have to see this through," he murmured to himself. "Bigger fish." He went to the telephone and asked for the Inspector General. "That's right," he roared into the mouthpiece, "the Inspector General in person."

"What is it?"

"Long life to you, sir. This is Zernescu, Section Four."

"I know. And what do you want?"

"I should like to speak to you personally on an urgent matter, sir."

"Really urgent?"

"I think so."

"Come right over—I can give you a few minutes."

Zernescu heard the click of the telephone. He snatched his hat and coat from the hook and was slamming the door behind him before he had them on. The spy sprang to his feet as he passed, but Zernescu paid no attention. Jenica sat down again on the edge of the chair and sent an inquiring look at the man at the typewriter. But the secretary went on typing impassively.

The lights were on in the large, elegant room with its massive, leather-covered furniture. The curtains at the window were drawn. In front of the long desk stood two easy chairs. With a careless wave of the hand Inspector General Dumitriu invited Zernescu to take one of them. Dumitriu was in his mid-fifties, weary, rather bored; he dressed with extreme care, followed a strict diet, and shunned everything that would remind him of his diseased liver. He sat down opposite Zernescu and leaned his head against the back of the chair, so that he addressed the air when he spoke.

"I assume this is really urgent, Inspector."

Zernescu cleared his throat. "Sir," he began hesitantly, "a piece of information came in an hour ago. In other circumstances I would have . . . but there is something about this—I may be mistaken, yet I think I had better tell you the story from the beginning. Just today Lieutenant Colonel Rananu of the Second Bureau had a conversation in the lobby of the Union with Ludovic Alda. Then both left for the Second Bureau. That was my man's report."

"And?"

Zernescu gave himself a mental push. "There's something funny about Domnule Alda, sir—it's nothing I can prove, and the only evidence I have is my memory, and it's a long time ago. . . ."

"Come to the point, please."

Zernescu pulled himself together. "I once encountered Alda, I believe, in surroundings altogether different from his usual ones.

those boys care about is women, cards and horses.

He picked up the telephone and put in a call to the Sigurantz
in Cernauti. After a minute or two Cernauti responded. Stanescu
the Chief there, answered in person.

"Do you happen to have a file on Ludovic Alda?" Zernesc
asked. "He has property in Bucovina."

"Alda, the horseman? I don't think so, but I'll look. Please hol
the line."

After a short while, the official was back on the phone: "There i
no Alda file, but we have a man here who knows almost everybod
who counts in Bucovina. Would you care to talk to him?"

"Excellent." He waited. After a moment, another voice came in

"This is Detective Sergeant Ciobotariu."

"How do you do. You know Ludovic Alda?"

"Yes, sir."

"What kind of bird is he?"

"A high liver."

"Whom does he know? Who are his friends?"

"He goes around with other landowners. I see him every so
often at a bar, with a lady."

"Political?"

"Not at all."

"Thank you."

Zernescu replaced the telephone on the hook and nodded in its
direction, as if to say that he had known his call would be fruitless.
But something gnawed at his vitals; he could not shake off the
thought that this blind bird Jenica had found a grain of corn. And
he, Zernescu, was condemned to swallow it. So he swallowed it and
began to digest it.

Alda was Alda, not Oskar Gross, the Bolshevik. Rananu had
dropped by to see him, and the two had probably discussed a horse,
a brawl, a card party. Such chitchat might very well drift from one
subject to another, and—suppose that lousy pimp had not been lying
—the name of Baderescu might have cropped up quite naturally.
But if Alda was Oskar Gross and Rananu did not know it, the situation was a lot more dangerous. For what else would Alda be doing
but spying? On the other hand, Rananu, or rather the Old Man,
might know perfectly well who Alda was and might have sent for
him! Then Baderescu could pump everything of any value out of
him, and the Second Bureau would once more have a lead on the
Sigurantza. "I'm not up to this," Zernescu moaned under his breath.
"Holy Mother of God, why do this to me? That goddamned little
rat!"

He paced the big room. He knew that he himself would get no

This was back in 1920, at the Balti military prison. He did not call himself Alda then, but Gross. And he escaped somehow a few hours before we were going to interrogate him. The fellow's looks stuck in my mind, though. I saw Alda at the Horse Show in Braşov. It was the very same face, sir."

"You mean to say you just realized this today?"

"Yes—and no," Zernescu faltered. Rather shamefacedly, he explained, "At the time, I refused to believe my eyes; it struck me as so—"

"Your zeal deserves high praise, but we are often fooled by such similarities. At any rate, if we assume that this man—you said his name was . . . ?"

"Gross," Zernescu interjected. "He called himself a journalist."

". . . that this Gross and Alda are one and the same person, what good is this information? I know Alda myself, though very slightly—my impression is that he is an intelligent, well-bred, pleasure-loving man with expensive passions. No doubt he can afford them. He owns a lot of land, has rich relations and even richer friends. But politics . . ." The Inspector General stood up and took a few steps on the rug, studying the pattern intently. No one, not even Zernescu with his keen policeman's nose, would have realized that Inspector General Dumitriu was thinking very hard. He was not trying to solve the enigma of Oskar Gross and Ludovic Alda. Instead he was thinking it was odd that for the second time today he should have stumbled upon the Old Man.

The Second Bureau was apparently interfering in the affairs of the Sigurantza. Two days before, a man had been arrested in Bucovina. A Jew who crossed the Ceremus twice a week. The Sigurantza had good reason to believe the fellow was working for the Russians. But the Second Bureau had claimed him as one of its agents, and the Sigurantza had had to release him, of course. To make the matter more annoying, the credit for the man's arrest would have gone to the Inspector General's nephew, the chief of the "Flying Brigade." And now this business with Alda—what would Baderescu be wanting of him? Dumitriu did not like the Old Man. He had a deep distrust of men on whom nothing could be pinned. It was going to be difficult to dislodge Baderescu. But this might be a useful lead, a way of finding out what cards the Old Man held. The Sigurantza could use such information.

Zernescu cleared his throat. "An interesting story," the Inspector General said with just a shade of geniality. "Perhaps you're on the track of something there. And was there anything else you wanted to discuss?"

Zernescu felt considerably emboldened. "I only wanted to remind you of the Mariniu case, sir."

"The Mariniu case? Why, that was at least—"

"Sixteen years ago, sir. The trial took place in the winter of 1923."

"Almost three years after the episode. But what makes you bring that up?"

"Do you remember how the foreign press handled it? The stories that were printed?"

"But practically everything the foreign papers said was true. Lieutenant Mariniu was nothing but a criminal." Dumitriu sometimes enjoyed surprising his subordinates.

He succeeded completely with Zernescu. "Yes, but, sir, they were Bolsheviks, you know," he stammered.

"No more than you or I. Miserable Jews fleeing from pogroms in the Ukraine. Mariniu caught them on the Romanian shore, robbed them of everything they had, slaughtered them, and threw their corpses into the river."

Zernescu stared. Could an Inspector General of the Sigurantza talk this way?

Dumitriu seemed to be serenely unaware of his subordinate's consternation. "But all that's over and done with—the man was acquitted. He has a good post today, in the Finance Ministry, I think. Legal adviser, or something."

"That's right, sir," Zernescu said. "As you said, all that's over and done with. It's the newspaper articles I was thinking of. Who could have leaked that stuff to the foreign press? Something tells me that that man Gross was the author of the articles."

"And so your theory is that Gross was really Alda?" Zernescu shrugged. "As I said, it is a highly interesting premise. Thank you for coming to me with it." He considered for a moment. "I'd like to see the man who overheard the conversation between Rananu and Alda. Would you send him over right away?"

"Yes, sir."

Dumitriu extended a limp hand. Zernescu shook it, bowed low, and made his exit. Only as he took his coat and hat from the rack in the anteroom did he realize the significance of those last words. That whoreson, that lousy gutter rat, was being given an interview with the Inspector General. Whereas he had had to wait eight years for the honor.

Zernescu shrugged uncomprehendingly as he walked across the courtyard. He went to the nearest tobacco shop, telephoned his office and had Jenica called to the phone. "Take a cab and come to the Sigurantza Generala right away. I'll be waiting for you at the entrance."

A few minutes later Jenica sprang from the cab. "Sixty lei, sir," he said.

Zernescu handed him a hundred-lei note. "Keep the change and buy yourself some poison with it." But his tone was mild and patronizing. After all, the man was going to see the Inspector General; one of these days he might become someone to reckon with. "Listen now, the Inspector General wants to know about that stuff you reported to me. Don't disgrace me. Go in there and report."

"Long life to you, Chief," Jenica said. "Don't worry, I won't disgrace you."

Zernescu lingered indecisively for a moment. He would have liked to wait for Jenica and hear what had taken place. But that would be beneath his dignity. He had suddenly lost all desire to return to his office, although there was plenty to do. Aimlessly he started walking toward the center of the city.

In the meanwhile Jenica was standing before the Inspector General, relating in detail and with many elaborations what he had seen and heard and pieced together. He could not tell how the Inspector General was taking it, because Dumitriu stood with his back to him. When he was done, the great man turned around and scrutinized him from head to foot. "Well, good. Here. . . ." He took a thousand-lei bill from the pocket of his jacket. "Not because your information is worth anything, but because you know how to keep your eyes open. Next time report directly to me. I'll let Inspector Zernescu know."

Rananu's car stopped in front of a fashionable florist's. Rananu decided on pale pink carnations and Alda on chrysanthemums, Margareta's favorite flowers. "I still haven't called Margareta," he said, and went to the telephone.

"This is Alda. I'd like to speak to Madame Luceanu."

"She isn't here at the moment. Can I give her any message?"

"Just that Colonel Rananu and I will be coming to dine."

"Lutz Alda?"

"The same. Who is this, please?"

"Margareta's little sister."

"So Margareta has a sister? She's never told me."

"Ah well, we haven't seen each other for a long time. I'll tell her that you called, Domnule Alda, and please don't come later than half past two."

"Certainly not. Au revoir."

Alda hung up and looked across at Rananu. His friend was engrossed in the carnations, looking each one over carefully, laying some aside and taking others.

Alda quickly dialed a number. "Hello . . . ? I came to see you yesterday."

"Yes, I recognize your voice. I have a surprise for you. The man has been released, at the request of a government office. I've just found out."

"Ah yes, I knew it wasn't serious. The amount I left with you as an advance could be . . . certainly, thank you very much."

Alda walked very slowly toward Rananu. The news he had just received made him uneasy—that everything had gone so smoothly, and that there had been official intervention. What office? But there was no point worrying about that now; he had nothing to go on.

He told Rananu that they were expected at Margareta's at half past two, and asked about the unknown sister.

"She's been away for many years, studying abroad. A completely different sort from Margareta. Terribly interested in philosophy or psychology—that sort of thing—and a good deal younger than Margareta—no more than twenty-four or -five, I'd say. A pretty girl, but I have the devil of a time making conversation with her."

Back in the car again, Rananu glanced at his watch. "We still have a bit of time. How about driving over to the stable—I want to look to the horses—and then to my house?"

"Fine." To see horses, to inhale the odor of a stable—at the moment, Alda could have wished for nothing better.

Rananu had three horses in his town stable: a creamy white Lipizzaner and two thoroughbred roan mares. The Lipizzaner was ten years old and famous as a dressage horse; the two mares were very fast and noted jumpers. Immersed in the beauty of the animals, fondling them, stroking their necks, the two men forgot all else. Alda, standing between the mares, was the first to recover from his trance. He watched Rananu. No one would have believed him capable of such tenderness as he displayed to his white stallion. At last he stepped out of the box into the aisle and told the attendant to water the horses. When they thrust their noses into the pails with obvious boredom, Rananu looked satisfied. "You're a good fellow, Gitza," he said, taking a banknote from his pocket and handing it to the soldier. Grinning, the soldier took it and replied, "Long life to you, sir."

"I'd like to see the horses exercised," Rananu said to Alda. "Just another five minutes, if you don't mind."

"Nothing I'd like better."

Gitza called two stableboys, who led the horses into the paddock outside. Rananu had each of them pass by him at a trot. He nodded contentedly, then commented with a regretful frown; "I never get a chance to ride. Haven't been mounted once since the hunt at Radu—that's more than seven weeks ago. Patriotic duties, damn it all. . . . Gitza, keep on as you've been doing. Lead the horses around for an hour every day, at a walk. I don't want a soul riding them, not the Heavenly Father himself." With a last loving look he bade the horses good-bye.

At Rananu's house the servant brought them zuica—plum brandy—salmon and olives. While Rananu was changing, Alda called the Union Hotel. He asked to have his suitcases packed and sent over to Rananu's house. Then he sat quietly, drinking zuica, smoking, and trying to think over the events of these past few hours. Rananu's behavior had been rather baffling. His friend had not so much as mentioned their visit to the General, had asked no questions. Rananu was not usually so reticent, and the two of them were very close. Did a man adjust so quickly to the habits of the Secret Service?

The *casa boiereasca,* the boyar's town house on the Piatza Amzei, was a rambling one-story building. Despite its location almost in the center of the city, it was surrounded by a parklike garden. The land was worth millions, but Ioan Luceanu would not sell an inch because his wife Margareta loved the house and garden.

Two servants in national costume—heavy black trousers, wide, three-colored woolen sash, white, full-sleeved embroidered linen shirt, fur-lined leather vest whitened with chalk—took Alda's and Rananu's coats. One of them sped off to announce their arrival to the lady of the house; the other opened the door to the vestibule, whose walls were covered indiscriminately with old English hunting prints, genre paintings by Grigoriu, and cheap reproductions. On the floor, along with old, handwoven peasant rugs, was a large Turkish carpet and machine-made carpeting in garish colors. The china closets, which stood where you would least expect them, contained a mixture of antique French, Viennese and Meissen pieces, and bazaar knickknacks.

The two men had barely time to glance at these things, which in any case they were long since familiar with, when a woman entered the room. "Lutz!" she cried and threw both arms around Alda's neck. She kissed him on the mouth, on the nose, the cheeks, the eyes, so tempestuously that he did not have a chance to catch his breath. In the midst of these demonstrations she suddenly pushed him away. "What an abandoned female I am, without an ounce of pride! Here I am, overjoyed at seeing you, and you've been in town for ages without calling me. You're simply scoundrels, all you men."

"You're right, Margareta." Alda looked fondly at the black-haired, small-boned woman with green, sparkling eyes. Years ago he had been her lover, but their passion had cooled as quickly as it had kindled. A good friendship remained.

Margareta offered Rananu her cheek to kiss. "Good to see you, Alecu. You'll not stop whinnying today." She took their arms, pressing close to Alda. Together, they entered the salon. The walls were covered with dark-red velvet. Scattered on the huge, thick rug were dozens of pillows in all colors, sizes and shapes; there was not a chair or table in the room. Everything, including glasses and ashtrays, was on the rug. From the excessive loudness of the greetings the new guests could estimate the number of cocktails that had already been drunk. "Aia," Margareta called into the noise and smoke, "the men want something to drink."

A slender woman appeared from a corner, holding a tremendous shaker. "Take glasses and sit down," she said.

Margareta rushed out into the vestibule again.

Rananu made the introductions. "This is Margareta's sister Aia."

She extended her left hand. "Delighted," she said, and filled their glasses.

Alda kissed her hand. "What about you?" he asked.

"I've already drunk more than I normally do in six months."

"One more won't hurt," Rananu said. He glanced around and nodded with satisfaction; there was ample reason for whinnying.

A servant announced that dinner was served, and the company filed noisily into the dining room. Anyone who saw this room for the first time inevitably stopped and gaped. Even those who knew what it contained had to overcome stunned disbelief and discomfort before they crossed the threshold.

Ioan Luceanu's great-grandfather, who had entered upon his inheritance at about the time Napoleon Bonaparte reached the peak of his power, had sent one of his serfs to Paris for training in the art of painting. After a year the serf had come along so well that he ventured to paint a fresco on one wall of the dining room. He painted a copy of the Last Supper. But Christ and his disciples bore an unmistakable likeness to Napoleon, Emperor Francis, Metternich, Tsar Alexander, and other princes, generals and statesmen of the time. Victors and vanquished, rulers and subjects, sat peacefully united, in Biblical garments, at the table. Ioan Luceanu—the firstborn of the family were all named Ioan—returned to the city from his country estates, saw the work, and gave the artist an unforgettable whipping. But—thrifty as he was—he let the fresco stand. Successive generations took the cue, and went on decorating the dining room in the same spirit. Walls and ceiling were covered with paintings representing banquets of personalities prominent in some branch of public life. Every generation, it seemed, had tried to outdo the other, and so everything was painted in the most glaring colors. After a century and a half there was scarcely a foot of wall space left unembellished. The effect was dizzying to the mind and painful to the eyes.

Most of the guests knew the room and its strange history. They fortified themselves by going promptly to the big buffet, pouring themselves some zuica to whet the appetite—white or pale-gold brandy, with the fragrance of ripe plums—and helping themselves to the hors d'oeuvres. In quantity and variety there was enough to have fed three times the number of guests. But no one had time to glut himself with delicacies, for the bowls of *sarmale* were quickly brought in—finely chopped pork and chicken mixed with rice and spiced vegetables, wrapped in grape leaves and boiled in cream. Everyone sat down wherever he pleased, and Alda, who had entered the room with Margareta's sister, remained her partner at table. The sarmale was praised lavishly—as etiquette required, and as it deserved to be. A delicious white wine mixed with soda water was served. Romanians do not care for unmixed wine; everyone, from boyar to porter, drinks it with seltzer. It takes effect gradually, and never produces real intoxication. Alda ate with good appetite; the wine was excellent and he was feeling good. He turned to his neighbor, who seemed unwilling to thaw out, and drank to her. "You're much prettier when you smile," he said, and when she forced a smile he added, "Not that way. Take your glass and drink a toast with me. You might look me in the eyes and smile. No reason why you shouldn't!"

She took her glass, but the smile did not appear. "Long life to you, Lutz Alda!"

"Cheers!"

They drank.

"Entertain me," he said. "Pretend I'm an uncle from the country who has just come to town to have a good time. Tell me something—anything you like."

"Gladly. Shall I talk about horses?"

Alda thought he heard a note of faint mockery in her com-

pliance, as if she were classifying him as a certain type of man.
"Horses?" he said, frowning slightly. "I don't imagine that your
studies have left you time—"

"Oh, no!" She checked him vivaciously. "I've always found
time for them, always. In fact I owe my acquaintanceship with you
to a horse. I've known you for a long time, boyar. Though it wasn't
mutual. Do you remember Polka?"

"Could I ever forget her? I bought her from your father.
Polka—that was a long time ago."

"My father would never have sold her; she was my favorite
horse. No, Father had just died. You bought her from my uncle
—and I could have killed the two of you. How I hated you both."

"And the hatred has lasted right down to the present?" Alda
said laughingly.

"It lasted two years anyhow."

"And afterwards?"

"Afterwards? Oh, adolescent emotions." She fell silent. Then
she said hesitantly, "I saw you riding at the concours in Constanza
—on Polka."

"Do you ride often?" he said, changing the subject.

"Here? So far I haven't ridden once. Rananu has promised
to take me with him sometime, but he's very busy, and a young
lady is not supposed to go riding alone, so my relations think."

"Rananu isn't the only man around. There wouldn't be any
shortage of cavaliers."

"I know, I know." She dismissed the notion. "But I don't like
these cavaliers. I'd rather do without riding than feel obligated to
them. They leave you in no doubt as to the price you're to pay
them for their courtesy."

"But there are plenty of young men who would be overjoyed
to escort you. As for the price, you ladies only pay it if you like
to." He was annoyed with her, and she evidently sensed it.

"I don't mean it that way," she said, rather forlornly. "It's difficult to explain just what I mean. Perhaps because I've lived
abroad for many years. Alone, unattached, unsupervised. Perhaps
the way I've lived has made me rather poor company. . . ." And
then, as though retracting anything which may have seemed to be
soliciting sympathy, she added, "But of course that is the sort of
life I prefer."

Alda realized that she was saying these things because he
struck her as an understanding person. But what can I do with
these confidences? he thought; in point of fact, I'm no longer here.
He tried to think of some reply, some banal, meaningless reply
that would prove he was not the kind of person to be entrusted

with her feelings and thoughts. Then he looked into her eyes—dark, warm, big eyes—and with a faint smile he placed his hand on hers.

"I don't usually wear my heart on my sleeve," she said. She shook her head, as though amazed at herself. "Long life to you, Lutz Alda. I wish you'd call me Aglaia."

"Cheers, Aglaia." They sat looking at one another, and no one else existed, although all around them people were disagreeing violently over matters that fled their minds a moment later, and were advocating views not their own.

Two guests entered the room. One of them was a puffy-faced man of about fifty, dressed rather carelessly, but in extremely well-cut clothes. He was introduced as Hilary Hold, an American, representative of an automobile concern in Romania. The man he came with attracted everyone's attention—and evidently meant to. He was good-looking, but his was not the handsomeness that tends to win good will. The even ivory color of his face, the smoothness of his cheeks and the rounding of his brow seemed somehow artificial, as if created with wax and actors' makeup. Only the corners of his big icy-green eyes, the small mouth with its too-well-carved red lips, and the thin, slightly hooked nose seemed alive, and they expressed malice and greed. A white streak ran across his longish, silky black hair. His dress, too, had something peculiar about it, for although some of the other men were dressed rather extravagantly, they produced an effect of distinction. But this man's blue suit, pin-striped with gray and white, was of an exaggerated tailoring that could be taken either as a deliberate striving for originality or as a misconception of what looked well on him. The jacket was too long and too tapered at the waist, the shoulders too padded, the sleeves tight and so short that the cuffs of his silk shirt were almost entirely revealed. On his left wrist he wore an oval watch with a wide gold strap, and on his right wrist a bangle of heavy gold chain.

His name was Orest Danghu. Almost everyone called him Dunga or Dungatu, which means "streak" or "blaze"—in reference to the streak of white in his hair. He was an official in the Ministry of the Interior. People were somewhat circumspect in speaking of his work; he was known to be a man with the highest connections.

Hilary Hold greeted the company with a "Hello" whose heartiness momentarily drowned out the buzz of conversation. He went over to the table of aperitifs, downed a large glass of zuica, ate a green olive, and returned to the table. In gruesome French he apologized to the hostess for his lateness and asked if he might still have something to eat. Those bandits, he said—nodding his head toward Danghu—had worn him out as well as starved him.

Everyone's eyes, however, had been on Margareta as the new arrival bowed to her and retained her hand after he had kissed it. Alda had not known that the Blaze was Margareta's present favorite, but he guessed that fact at once from the sharpness with which the rest of the company watched the pair. But how could Margareta, a woman of taste, possibly be attracted to a man of this type, who was, moreover, many years her junior?

The two new guests were served their sarmale, and the talk resumed. Soon the discussion turned to Hitler and the war. Alda began listening more attentively when the man with the blaze spoke. No doubt about it, the voice suited the fellow—a lacquered voice. Underneath, it was crude and unplaned, and above this roughness was a coating of lacquer. There was something about the voice, about the man's whole personality, that Alda found repulsive.

"Many of us," Danghu was saying, "still do not have a proper attitude toward present-day developments. And yet we can't stand on the sidelines too much longer. The Germans are strong; they're the men of the future. Ridiculous to let sentimentality stand in the way. In politics, you must have concrete aims; sentiments get you nowhere. If we throw in our lot with the stronger side, we will be able to dictate our terms. Moreover, Hitler's ideology has a good deal to commend it. In a way he is preparing the ground for us. First and foremost, he is out to get rid of the Jews, which is something we all applaud. We've had enough of the scum!"

"Really?" It was a woman's voice, low, brittle, husky from alcohol and nicotine, but wonderfully magnetic. The single word, spoken in that voice, captured everyone's attention. Lida Haimovici, "Princess" Haimovici, fixed her shining black eyes upon Danghu. Her ravaged face expressed unutterable contempt and disgust. "Really," she repeated. "Get rid of the scum. And then what will you live on? Are the businessmen you suck up to also included in the program? Because Hitler makes no exception; he'll kill them all, the scum. Scum!" she repeated, savoring the word with a strange masochistic pleasure.

"Why, Lida," the Blaze said quietly, "what are you thinking of? I never dreamed that you would take offense. After all, in political arguments. . . . You know that as far as I'm concerned, people are people." The fixed smile had not left his face.

"People are people," Lida said scornfully. "Tsatza!"

It was amazing; the smile remained, although everyone around the table froze. *Tsatza* can mean "dear," but it also means "pansy."

"It isn't proper to show our feelings in company, Lidutza, even after drinking a bit too much. But we like each other, don't we?"

"Does anyone like you?" she retorted. "Do you like anyone? You like those who pay you. What won't you do for money! The Nazis butcher people out of principle—but you? You'd butcher them for perfume and neckties, for silk pajamas to prance about in when you receive your customers. Who are you trying to fool? *You* say scum? You scum of the scum!" She clutched her heavy whiskey glass as though she intended to throw it at him.

Margareta had jumped to her feet. She placed her hand on the woman's arm. "Please, Lida!" She beckoned to Alda and made room for him. He placed his arm around Lida's shoulders. Danghu's eyes shifted to his face, with venomous fury. But Alda ignored him, though the man was barely three feet across the table from him. "Won't you come and sit with us for a while, Lida?" he said. She stood up obediently and let him lead her. Aglaia joined them, and led them through several doors to the library, a large room with big glass cases filled with books, a wide divan, and a number of leather-upholstered easy chairs. "I haven't been in here for a long time," Alda said. "How pleasant and quiet it is."

"That's right, nice and quiet—at least you don't have to mingle with scum." With perfect grace, as if she were crossing a stage, Lida went over to the divan and lay down. Aglaia put a pillow under her head. "Thank you, Aia. So comfortable. And now some whiskey. Whiskey is the only decent drink. Ring, please, Aia darling."

"I'll go for it."

She returned with whiskey, ice and a siphon. Alda poured. Lida took her liquor straight, as was her habit. "The last hours before the world comes to an end. I'm glad my father didn't live to see it. His grandson—my son—is already a Jew baiter." She said this without bitterness; by that very token, the words sounded the more frightful. Lida drained her glass and held it out to Alda again. He and Aglaia both drank with her. I wanted to enjoy myself, be merry, flirt with attractive women, and here I am sitting and getting drunk, Alda thought.

He looked down at Lida, and realized that she had fallen asleep. Gently he removed the glass from her hand. Aglaia spread an afghan over the sleeping woman. Then they went out to the glass-enclosed veranda.

"Come, Lutz, let's take a walk in the garden. It will do us both good," she said.

"Don't you think we ought to return to the party?"

"Ought to? I'd rather not. But if you wish—"

"Aglaia, if we are going to be good friends, as I hope—"

She turned her face to his. "When we were sitting in there, I believed for one happy minute that we could be real friends." She thrust her hand lightly under his arm. "Come into the garden. I'd like to tell you something, and I know I must hurry." And when he looked at her in surprise, she went on, "I can feel that you're on the point of leaving, not really here at all. You're altogether different from the person who'd been described to me, and different from my memory of you, too. When I heard your voice on the telephone to-day—but what nonsense I'm talking. Come, let's go."

They walked along in silence for a while. A thin mist hung in the warm, humid air. In the yellow moonlight their shadows stretched out over the withered leaves that rustled softly under their feet. The silence became sultrier, more and more oppressive, and Alda felt that it had to be broken. It was not good, not right, he felt; it was a silence that promised too much. He cleared his throat; he had to say something.

"A good idea, this walk," he said lightly. "Clears the head after all that drinking."

"That's why we're taking it." She fell silent again. He didn't want to understand her irony and her sadness. "Lutz," she spoke again. Her clear, warm voice was composed. "Don't be afraid."

"Afraid?" he asked lamely, and thought, She's right, I'm a coward.

"I can feel that you aren't yourself today—aren't the way you are, or can be. You're not really here at all."

It was the second time she had used the phrase, he noted. Did his secrets show so clearly? They were standing on a gravel-strewn terrace in front of one of the house doors. He placed his hand on the knob, and she quickly reached out, as if she wanted to stop him from opening the door. But he turned the knob, and they went in. She switched on a small light in front of a mirror. Her face was pale in the dim illumination, as set as if carved in marble. Only the eyes were alive, for they were swimming in tears. And as he examined her face in the mirror, he saw his own also, saw it with her eyes. Stiff, cold, lips compressed—an alien face. He took hold of her wrist and drew her away from the mirror. "Aglaia," he said, and could not go on. He released her, but she remained leaning against him, and raised her hands to his face. They were cold and trembling, but he could detect the intensity of feeling in her fingertips. Her hands closed around his neck, and their lips met in a brief, savage kiss.

"Come, Aglaia." He took her by the hand and led her down the long corridor to the room where Lida lay, still sleeping. Her lips were slightly parted; there was a smile on her face, which had lost its tormented, ravaged look—as if she were having a pleasant dream.

Aglaia closed the door softly. "The sleep will do her good." She pushed aside a pair of portieres and led the way, switching on the light as they entered. They were in a kind of winter garden filled with potted plants. Aglaia sat down on a bench and beckoned to Alda to join her.

"I don't like Lida," she said, "but her history fascinates me. One wonders how it will end, but at least she has lived a full life."

"One must pay for every good minute in life."

"There are some minutes for which no price is too high."

He nodded. "And Lida has paid—she does nothing but pay."

"She's had everything. Genius, success, love—"

"Do you know her story?"

"Tell it to me, Lutz."

"A regular True Romance: the little Jewish girl who reaches the top in spite of every obstacle, because she's beautiful, witty, charming and a great artist."

"And calculating."

"Lida?" he exclaimed in astonishment. "What makes you say that?"

"Her marriage to Prince Robert Calenare."

"Why, Aglaia! Lida's only passion was the stage. She lived for her acting—only for that, until Robert Calenare entered her life. Then she fell in love, that was all. It was he, not she, who insisted on marriage, because like most men he thought that marriage settles matters, that you then have the woman you love entirely to yourself."

"And then someone else came along—"

"No, only her oldest passion—the theater. It was stronger than love, marriage, even motherhood. Robert refused to understand that, could not understand it. He never could bring himself to accept it and—"

"Why has she stayed in this country? She speaks French and German just as well as Romanian."

"Suppose she had tried elsewhere? As a Jew? She didn't want to believe that she, Lida Haimovici, couldn't recapture the public that had adored her in the past. And now she's been broken by intrigues, crushed."

"Crushed. No husband, no son, no home, and not even art. Nothing but alcohol and cocaine and—" She stopped.

"And men. They're a narcotic, too. And they help her no more than do the whiskey and the cocaine."

"I understand, but still I'm horrified. Perhaps I'm not generous enough. I admire Margareta. So much charity and kindness—she's not like that with anyone else. If you only knew—she spends nights searching for her, brings her back, tends her, talks to her, tries in every way she can to keep her from her vices."

"Yes, Margareta is wonderful. But you've just said it yourself: she has had a rich life. And one really must pay for every good minute." He raised his head, listening. From one of the other rooms came the sound of music. "The radio?" he asked.

"No, Margareta has sent for gypsies."

"Gypsies!" He listened eagerly. "Banica—yes, of course that's who it is!" He leaped to his feet. He held her hand and drew her along behind him; they ran through a number of rooms and corridors and arrived, breathless and laughing, at the salon.

In one corner stood a cembalo. At it sat an old gypsy with the face of a faun. Another gypsy, almost hidden by the huge instrument, was at the double bass, and beside him was a clarinetist. But no one was paying attention to the rest of the troupe, for Banica was playing. When he caught sight of Alda, his face broke into a radiant smile, and without pausing in his fiddling, he made a low bow. Here was his boyar, who understood him and whom he loved. He took a step forward, but then drew back, for he had to finish the piece he was playing.

Alda drew Aglaia over to the table and they sat down. The waiter was pouring champagne; Alda, however, asked for red wine.

"Do you know what we are drinking, Aglaia?"

"Turk's blood—isn't that its name?"

"Yes. And what are we drinking to?"

"To"—her mouth smiled, but her eyes remained grave—"no price being too high."

He looked at her, touched his glass to hers and drank it to the bottom. When the servant began refilling it, Banica appeared before him. "Our songs, yes, coane?"

"Our songs, Banica."

And Banica played as only a gypsy who feels himself understood by a generous boyar can play. The whole company stopped talking. They smiled, with tears in their eyes and lips quivering. Banica's violin sang old herdsmen's songs, the yearning *doină*, the solemn *horă*, the jubilant *"Ciocârlia."* And then another horă, on and on, until the guests could not stay in their seats. They stood up, closed hands, formed the circle, and in solemn, deliberate tempo they danced the old round dance. Rananu called the steps. "To the right! To the left! The horă to the center! The horă stand still!" The music slowed and slowed; the faces of the dancers grew graver. A long diminuendo passed softly into utter silence. But it lasted only for the space of a breath. Abruptly the violin struck up a new tune. The gypsy with the faun's face pounded with all his might upon the keyboard of the cembalo; the clarinet rippled, the double bass moaned. Legs flew, the circle whirled madly, the huge room and its crazed paintings reeled around the dancers.

Margareta, Alda and Rananu leaped into the middle of the circle. Margareta flung her arms around the shoulders of the two men, and the three danced together. The gypsies played faster and faster; the faces of the dancers grew more and more flushed. The music reached a crescendo and then stopped. Exhausted, limp, and happy, the dancers dropped into the nearest chairs.

Alda sat down beside Aglaia again and raised his glass to her. "Let's drink." She mutely obeyed. "Banica," he called out, "play for me: 'It's not my fault that the tavern stands right by the road.'" The gypsy played this and many other favorite songs of Alda's; he knew them from countless parties. Everyone joined in the singing except for Danghu, who sat between two of the ladies, trying to make conversation with each in turn, and seemingly unaware of the uproarious gaiety all around him.

Alda had not once looked at the man with the blaze. But Aglaia was conscious of Danghu's watching them. "I find him disgusting —Margareta's new acquisition," she said.

"Margareta will come to no harm, I'm sure." Alda looked at his watch.

"Must you go soon?" she asked.

"I'll tell you a secret. I mean to take French leave—I have to catch a train."

"Where to?"

He hesitated almost imperceptibly. "Home," he said quickly.

"And you must leave today?"

"I must."

"May I see you off?"

"You may." Quickly he added, "That's very good of you."

"Let's go," she said gravely.

"Stay here for a little while. I'll wait in the vestibule."

As he passed by the gypsy fiddler, he slipped several bills to him.

Rananu was standing in the vestibule. He knows all about it; he knows I am leaving now, and where I'm bound, Alda thought. He felt trapped. "I've had my bags sent to your apartment," he said.

"Would you like me to drive you?"

"No, you stay here and enjoy yourself; I'll take a cab. Would it be all right to ask your man to take my baggage to the station?"

"Of course. He's at your service."

Alda shook hands with Rananu. "So long, Alecu. Have fun and make my apologies to Margareta for leaving like this."

"Will do." Rananu held on to Alda's hand. "Lutz—well, then

—good luck!" He turned quickly and went back into the salon.

Aglaia came up to Alda. "I'll take Ioan's car and drive you there myself."

Alda called Rananu's apartment and asked the servant to bring his bags to the station and give them to the Pullman porter. Then they drove slowly down the Calea Victoriei to the Boulevard Elisabeta, where Aglaia had to stop for a light. Her hands, red in the glow of the signal, lay loosely on the wheel. "When is your train going?" she asked.

"What's that?" It was so plain his thoughts were far away that she didn't repeat the question. Her face tautened; she looked straight out over the steering wheel. The light changed, and she turned right on the Boulevard Elisabeta. Then she stepped on the gas and drove far above the speed limit on the busy avenue. When the traffic thinned out, she drove faster and faster, as if life depended on gaining these instants. In a few minutes she drew up in front of North Station. Alda didn't move. "We're there. Wake up, sir."

"Forgive me, Aglaia, I'm not good company today." He took her arm. The station clock read ten as they reached the platform. "Six minutes still," he said. "One moment—I'll check my bags." He dashed into the brightly lit sleeping car, and was back in a moment. Aglaia was standing in the throng of passengers hurrying to board the train. Her eyes shone when she caught sight of him, but when he jumped down in front of her, she smiled sadly.

"You look so cheerful. You're glad to be rid of me. Is it a woman, Lutz?"

"You want to know so much, Aglaia!" He laughed.

"All aboard! Aboard, please!" the conductor called.

"Lutz—"

"Yes, Aglaia. Good-bye, my girl." Still laughing, he embraced her and kissed her on the mouth. Slowly, the train began to move. Alda jumped onto the running board and boyishly waved his hat. He went on waving as long as she remained in sight.

The train had stopped only for a minute. Alda stood beside his suitcases and wondered why Candomir's chauffeur wasn't there. Then a figure emerged from the mist. "Welcome, Lutz!"

"You've come yourself, Radu?" They embraced, kissed, and then went to the car, each of them carrying a suitcase. "How are Florica and the children?"

"First-rate, thanks. They're spending a week with their grandparents."

"And you came yourself. Where's Rudolf?"

"I'll tell you about that later." He took the wheel, and they drove off. The road was unpaved, full of holes and puddles with a thin layer of ice that cracked under the tires. Certainly no road for a speed of fifty miles an hour. Candomir concentrated upon the driving, and they sat in silence. Alda studied his friend's face: lean, manly, tanned by sun and wind, the dark-brown eyes keen and bold. A hunter's or rider's eyes, under heavy black brows. He looks like a haiduc in his fur coat, with that collar turned up and the fur cap, Alda thought.

The gate to the estate was open, and the car raced up the driveway, past the ruins of the old castle which stood out eerily against the black sky. Candomir stopped in front of the three-story white house, in which only a few of the windows were illuminated. Old Mishu, back bowed, came down the few steps from the front door and greeted Alda familiarly: "Welcome, Coane Lutz." He set about tugging the two suitcases out of the car. "Let them be, Mishu, I'll take care of them," Alda said, and followed the old man into the house. It was five o'clock in the morning and the servants were still asleep. Mishu no longer did much around the house, but his sense of duty forbade his staying in bed when there was no one else around to attend to a guest. Radu Candomir put the car in the garage and returned just as Alda had settled down by the fireplace in the hall, where a fire was crackling. Mishu rolled in the tea cart, quietly as a shadow, and disappeared.

"Now what's been happening, Radu? You were so mysterious on the telephone. What's this about Rudolf? Has he gone and gotten sick?"

"You might say so. He's caught the new sickness."

"The new sickness?"

"Yes. The chief symptom of which is that he refuses to drive Director Regenbogen. He won't drive Jews, he says."

"Rudolf? But he's driven Regenbogen to the factory every day for fifteen years."

"But now Herr Hitler is in power, and Rudolf is a German."

"Come now, you know as well as I that Rudolf is no German. He's a Pole or Ruthenian or one of those mixtures we have around here."

"Rudolf's mother is Polish, his father Ruthenian, and he has just discovered his German identity. 'A Ger-rman man don't drive Jews,' he says. At first I thought he was drunk, although that's not like him."

"What did you do?"

"I cut the saddest figure in the whole affair. When I think of what my father would have done in such a situation! Rudolf probably wouldn't be alive today."

"Yes, when I picture Coane Iancu—"

"Picture me instead, taking him aside and trying to reason with him. But he just stuck to it stiffly: 'Baron, a German man don't drive Jews.' 'Rudolf,' I said, 'you're not a German; you can't put that over on me. I've known you since you were born; I knew your father and your grandfather. All their lives they used to curse the Germans.' 'I feel myself one, sir.' And then he added something that gave me to think. 'That's the order, and please, sir, don't ask any more about it. Either Regenbogen or me.' I wanted to knock him down, and maybe that would have been the thing to do, but all I did was tell him, 'Collect your wages and don't let me see you on the property again.' But what really gave me a shock was old Regenbogen's reaction. 'For heaven's sake, Coane Radu,' he said, 'you haven't gone and dismissed Rudolf? They'll make trouble for you. It isn't worth any fuss. I'll find some vehicle to take me the few miles from the factory, or else I'll walk.' Old Regenbogen with his rheumatism. 'It's just the times, Coane Radu!' He had tears in his eyes. 'Far worse things are happening to the Jews in Germany and Austria than a chauffeur refusing to drive them.' "

"What did you do?"

"I drove Regenbogen home myself, and now my new hunting carriage with the two white stallions is at his door every day and takes him to the factory. I would have hitched up four horses, if I could. As a protest!" Candomir paused and put his hands to his temples. "But I didn't ask you to come here to tell you about Rudolf. It's a more serious matter than that."

"Well, come out with it, Radu."

"For the past few days I've had a guest. Someone you know." Candomir, who had been sprawling in his chair, sat up. "You'll see him in a moment; I hear him coming."

Alda did not recognize the man who entered until he stepped close to the floor lamp in front of the fireplace. "Anatol!" he exclaimed in surprise. "Is it possible?"

Anatol shook hands with him. "I guess it is a surprise for you to see me here, Lutz," he said. "Incidentally, just so there are no slips, my name is now Bilinski. Plain Pan Bilinski." He dropped into a chair. His long, thin face with its weary, deep-set eyes seemed lifeless. It was an overbred, refined, tired and passionate face. His hands, very slender, with long, thin fingers, bespoke strength, although now they lay limply on the arms of the chair.

"Tea, Anatol?" Candomir asked.

"Please. My throat is raw from smoking too much."

Candomir poured for him, and Anatol took a cigarette from the box on the table. Alda gave him a light. Anatol was a collateral member of the Polish royal family, but had served like any other ensign in the Austrian Army, where Alda had met him. It was not so astonishing after all, that he should be here. Anatol was a Pole and therefore—like so many others—a refugee.

"You've just come," he said. "Straight from Poland?"

"He's been through hell," Candomir said.

"No more than others," Anatol demurred. "It really isn't important."

"But he had to leave his wife there."

Anatol's face became a mask of grief. "Yes, I had to leave her there," he repeated in a lifeless voice.

"That's why I asked you to come, Lutz. We must help Anatol." Candomir fell silent, but there was a plea in his eyes so intense that Alda was puzzled. Anatol stared silently into the glow of the fire.

"Tell me the story, Radu. Or better still, you tell it, Anatol."

As though he had awakened from a bad dream, Anatol turned his face toward Alda. "You see, Lutz, I can't help clinging to every hope, but reason tells me the outlook's pretty grim. I saw my wife for the last time shortly before the outbreak of the war. She was visiting relatives in Czeravna. The estate is about a hundred and twenty-five miles east of Lvov. I wasn't able to find out whether she is still there because I didn't dare contact anyone. I had to cross the border. On orders," he added softly.

"What can be done now?" Alda asked.

"Yes, what can be done, Lutz? You know better than we."

"I? Why me?" He had to master a spasm of irritation before continuing. "What exactly did you have in mind, Radu? And you?" He turned almost brusquely to Anatol, who shrugged wearily and spread his hands in a gesture of despair. "You say your wife was in Czeravna at the outbreak of the war. On one of the Pototzki estates?"

"That's right. My wife is related to the Countess Pototzki. When it looked like war, I wrote to her to stay there. I'd joined my regiment, the uhlans, in Lvov. But you know how long we were able to hold off the Germans. And perhaps you already have some idea of the anarchy that reigned when the Russians suddenly moved in— how everyone in any sort of high position was hunted down. It would have been pointless to try to do anything. I wasn't permitted to take any risks because—" His voice dropped away.

"I understand," Alda said. "So you haven't had any news of your wife since the end of August. You also have no idea whether she stayed in Czeravna or went elsewhere, whether she's in the German-occupied part or under the Russians." He ignored Candomir's angry and despairing looks. "Then what's to be done? Make some suggestion, Radu. Or you, Anatol. You've just come from there. How does it look?"

Anatol straightened up defensively. "I'd like to make it clear that the idea of asking you for help does not come from me," he said, with a certain stiffness. Then, speaking slowly, sadly, lamely, he went on. "We'd been married just a year. I've never loved anyone as I love her, and I wouldn't go on living if I knew she was dead. I know now that she means more to me than my country. I hope you understand."

Alda nodded—almost bowed. Here was a test of love, if ever there was one. If a man really loved a woman, would he save his own skin and wait for miracles? Or did he only realize now—when he had reached safety—what perils hung over the woman he loved? Alda was not aware that he had shrugged his shoulders slightly, but Candomir caught the gesture. The three men sat in silence, and the silence of each meant something different. Alda felt that it was up to him to break it. "Lots of situations seem hopeless at first sight and later prove to have a solution. I'll put my mind to it. . . . At what point did you cross the border, Anatol?"

Candomir spoke up for him: "From his description it must have been between Milije and Banila. It was night, and about three hundred yards away he saw a brightly lit small factory. That must have been the Milije distillery. How he reached the highway without being seen is a mystery to me. Then, in a kind of trance, he turned to the right, taking the road that leads to Vishnitza. Without knowing where he was going, he followed a convoy of peasant carts as far as Beromet."

"And since he knew the area, he could easily make his way through to you. I see. But how did you reach the Ceremus on the Polish, or rather the Russian, shore, Anatol?"

Anatol cleared his throat. "My flight must strike you as wild and improbable. I myself find difficulty reconstructing it. If you asked me to explain how I succeeded in getting past the Russian and Romanian border guards, I couldn't. Not now, and perhaps never, I'm afraid."

Candomir threw an imploring look at Alda, a look that said, Have pity on him, don't ask him. Alda looked down at the floor. "Yes," he said, "I'll put my mind to it." He glanced at the clock; it was nearing seven. "But now I'd better lie down for a couple of hours. I've had hardly any sleep."

"Good, Lutz," Candomir said, "we'll lie down, and at nine—"

Anatol stood up with an effort. He nodded mutely to Alda.

* * *

After taking a shower, Alda sat down on his bed. He was still very tired, and so lost in thought that he scarcely noticed Candomir's entering the room.

Candomir sat down beside his friend. "Odd," he began uncertainly.

"Because I didn't get all fired up at the adventure? Did you expect me to leap to my feet and say, 'Think nothing of it, I'll rescue your wife even if she's in Siberia!'? But why are you so involved in this, Radu?"

"Involved!" Radu exclaimed. "Do you know who Anatol's wife is?"

"How should I know? And why should that be pertinent?"

"It is pertinent, Lutz. Highly pertinent," he repeated hoarsely. "And if this project doesn't interest you, then—"

Alda stood up and set his hands on his friend's shoulders. "Well, who is Anatol's wife? Since that's what's eating you."

"Janina!" Candomir whispered almost inaudibly.

"No! Did you say Janina?"

"They were married in Paris thirteen months ago."

"Janina. Good Lord!"

"Now do you understand, Lutz?" Janina was the only woman Candomir had ever loved, whom he would never stop loving, though he had a good marriage of many years' standing, with another woman.

"Does Anatol know about you and Janina?"

"Of course not."

"I'll get her out, Radu."

"Lutz, Lutz . . ." Candomir's voice failed him.

Alda felt a touch of guilt. If Radu knew. . . . Perhaps he would be able to explain everything later—if he carried off the coup, if he came back at all. "There's no point going to sleep now. Every hour is precious. I want to order my affairs as quickly as possible and then—"

"As you think best, Lutz." Candomir went out with springy step. As soon as he had closed the door behind him, Alda rang. He asked the servant to bring him his riding clothes, and to tell the other gentlemen also to dress for riding. So common was it for him to stay at his friend's house that he kept a whole extra wardrobe here. Riding breeches, boots and a leather sports jacket soon lay ready for him. He dressed and inspected himself in the big mirror. The clothes were well worn, and though they looked decent enough when freshly brushed, as they were now, a few days of neglect would transform them into the outfit of an agricultural worker or groom.

Candomir and Anatol, both in riding dress, were already at the breakfast table. Alda put in a long-distance telephone call, asked the operator to call back, and joined them. He and Candomir attacked breakfast with hearty appetites, but Anatol took only a few bites, drank half a cup of coffee, and lit a cigarette. In deference to his state of nerves, the other two hurried through their meal. "As I've already hinted to you, Anatol," Candomir said, lighting his cigarette, "Lutz has agreed to go to the rescue of your wife. If there's any man in the world who can manage it, he's the one."

"My God, how grateful I am to you both! Only . . . I don't know why you should be doing this for me."

"Forgive me, Anatol," Alda broke in to save Radu from saying anything to this. "Sometimes I sound gruffer than I mean to. As I did last night. Besides, I had the feeling that Radu had been representing me as a kind of superman—an impression I like to correct. But let's stick to the business at hand. First of all: have you a photo of your wife?"

"Certainly." Anatol opened a button of his shirt and unfastened a locket from a chain he wore around his neck. He handed it to Alda. Candomir leaned over his shoulder, and both men gazed tensely at the picture inside. After a moment, Alda snapped the locket shut and handed it back to Anatol, who took it abstractedly.

"So Czeravna will be my starting point. Can you suggest someone in the village who could give me information if your wife should no longer be there?"

"A doctor there—by the name of Feuerberg."

"The man would be Jewish, right?"

"Certainly," Anatol said. "Does that bother you?"

"Not at all. On the contrary."

"Because he would be the most trustworthy person there. If my wife were in difficulties, she'd turn to Dr. Feuerberg."

"That's fine. And once I've tracked her down, I'll also need some sign to prove that you sent me, or else she might think it was a trap."

Anatol considered. "If you say I sent you and she seems doubtful, say '*Rêve*' and she will understand. It's a private allusion of ours."

It was lucky that Candomir was standing behind Anatol, for he was not good at dissimulation. Seeing how his friend winced at this detail, Alda could imagine how much self-control it must have cost him not to have betrayed himself so far. Did Anatol really know nothing of his wife's past? Alda had never seen Janina. But he knew all about her from the stories of Candomir. She came from an aristocratic though impoverished family. The two had met in Paris, where she was studying to be a pianist, and as Radu had described her, she was beautiful and extremely proud. She had been a little in love with him, but had been disinclined to leave Paris and abandon her studies. So she had turned down his proposal—and Radu had never forgotten her. Years later he continued to speak of Janina; the passage of time had only intensified his feelings.

The telephone rang shrilly. "It's for me, Radu," Alda volunteered. He headed for the study and closed the leather-padded door behind him.

"This is Rundberg's," he heard a woman's voice say.

"Karl Rundberg, please."

"One moment."

After a brief pause a gruff, sleepy male voice said, "Yes?"

Alda whistled several bars from the opera *Martha.*

"What else?"

"Come along to your father."

"All right."

Alda hung up.

"A good idea of yours, Lutz," Candomir said when he rejoined them. "A little ride will do us good."

"Not so little. We're riding to Aldeni."

"Fine! That's Lutz's estate," he explained to Anatol.

The pallid sun had burned away the last of the morning mist and shown down upon bare trees and brown, autumnal grass. The chief groom was walking two horses back and forth, followed by a stableboy with a third. Candomir pointed to a handsome gray. "I know you'll like him," he said to Anatol.

"Thank you," Anatol said. He approached the horse, rubbed the strong neck, stroked the nose, and after lengthening the stirrups swung lightly into the saddle. All three were ready to start together, Candomir on a high-legged, dun thoroughbred, Alda on a chestnut Anglo-Arabian. They rode at a walk down the wide lane flanked by huge, ancient beech trees. Alda was particularly fond of this part of the grounds. Now, taking farewell, he looked up at the leafless crowns of the trees, which for centuries had shaded the riding path. The trees may go on standing for centuries, he thought, but the time of gentlemen on horseback is coming to an end.

The well-kept grounds passed into woods. The deep, damp autumn leaves muffled the steps of the horses. The girths creaked and the bridle rings tinkled softly and melodiously. Without a word being exchanged, all three chose the same moment to draw up the reins, and the horses began to trot with short, rhythmic steps. In a few minutes the riders gave them their heads and passed into a restrained hunting gallop. Then Candomir said, "Now!" and set a sharp pace. The others stayed level with him. Alda called over to Anatol, "Obstacle!" Peering ahead, Anatol saw the ditch, the dried bed of a brook, and nodded. Now they were close upon it; three pairs of calves touched the flanks of three horses. The animals strained forward and flew in a single line over the wide, deep trench. The men's hands patted the sweaty necks of the horses, praising and reassuring them; snorting, the animals continued on in long, springy strides.

"Wonderful," Anatol said with a deep sigh.

"Fine, eh?" Candomir's eyes flashed.

Alda said nothing.

They came to the end of the woods. Meadows spread out before them, and freshly plowed fields. Candomir took in the view with a searching, affectionate gaze. Anatol's eyes were veiled with sadness. Seeing their expressions, Alda imperceptibly shook his head. As though he had guessed their thoughts and agreed.

They rode over narrow roads, often only footpaths through the fields. Alda kept to a sharp trot; it was still a good twelve miles to his house, and he wanted to be there before the car from town arrived. He rode along without thinking of the two men, who kept behind him, for he was saying farewell. Every inch of this land was dear to him; it was the land of his forefathers.

A serpentine path led through a dense stand of old beeches, pines and firs, winding around and up the hill. There was a wide, still-green lawn, with beeches and elms forming a grove in the center and surrounding a rambling, one-story house. It was in the old Moldavian style, with red Gothic windows and a broad terrace flanked by round red pillars. A solid building, built for eternity, and yet lightly poised above the ground.

"Beautiful, isn't it?" Candomir asked.

"Beautiful," Anatol agreed.

"The taste of the Aldas is famous. My great-grandfather speaks of it in our family chronicle. The Aldas were always special people." Candomir's words sounded jesting, but he evidently meant them in dead earnest.

Two men came from the house. The elder man greeted the party with the familiar air of an old retainer. The younger one, who was barely eighteen, strongly resembled him. "Long life to you," they said with one accord, and the smiles on both faces were identical. "Good day, Gheorghe One and Gheorghe Three," Alda said. "How are things in Aldeni?"

"When the master is here, all is well," the old man replied, and the boy grinned agreement.

Candomir called out a merry greeting to them. Anatol, too, assumed the smile that gentlemen reserve for the faithful servants of their friends and acquaintances. They dismounted, went up the few steps to the terrace, and entered a broad hall. A woman of about sixty came forward to meet them. She wore the peasant costume of the region, embroidered, wide-sleeved blouse, gathered blue skirt reaching almost to the ankles, and a narrow woolen sash around the waist, striped red, blue and yellow. On her head was a white silk kerchief, knotted at the back. "Good day, Zamfira." Alda shook hands with his housekeeper. She replied with dignity, the hint of a smile upon her grave face, "Welcome, boyar!"

She responded to Candomir's handshake with a slight bow. Anatol, too, shook hands with her. Then she led the men into the salon, whose floor was covered with precious old Transylvanian rugs. The Louis Seize furniture seemed lost in the big room. Some heavy upholstered chairs of a more modern style were grouped about the large fireplace, a low, heavy table between them. On the walls hung family portraits: long-bearded men with haiduc caps and boyar cloaks, the broad Turkish saber at their sides; men with bold, defiant and thoughtful faces. Some of them wore the vestments of Greek Orthodox priests; many were in the uniforms of the Austrian Imperial Army. There were women in the embroidered white mantles and artfully folded kerchiefs of the Moldavian boyars, or in Parisian toilette, with strings of pearls and gold chains around their necks, diadems in their hair, and long pendants in their ears. Alda's grandfather, black-bearded, with large black eyes, was the only one of the Aldas in ordinary civilian clothes. Alda's father, blond, smiling, wore the uniform of an Austrian hussar, and Alda himself was there, mounted, likewise in uniform. Anatol cast a rapid, interested look over the portraits, and examined the icons in heavy gold frames. He sat down easily, familiarly; obviously he felt at home in the Alda house because he was among equals. His own house was also full of such portraits, though the dress and the cut of beards were somewhat different. These were the ancestors; and a man's worth was based on his ancestors. That was what his smile expressed. Alda smiled too, but only Candomir was able to decode that smile: until this moment I was only a man named Alda, who had served in a feudal regiment, whom you saw here and there at riding meets, but who nevertheless didn't quite belong. Good Lord, a man who demeaned himself by scribbling, who was friends with all sorts of people! But since he has a house, a large estate, servants, and above all ancestors, you'll forgive him such japes and consider him an equal. Even if he is the sort of fellow people send to pull their chestnuts out of the fire. After all, we aristocrats have to have such people.

Zamfira, followed by a young maid also in the national costume, brought in trays with bottles, glasses and canapés. "Now," Candomir said good-humoredly, "comes a rare pleasure. I'll wager it's been a long time since you've drunk liquor like this, Anatol." For Zamfira had brought the choicest drink of the region, the dark-red liqueur made from the mahaleb cherry.

Anatol rose and turned with studied solemnity toward his host and Candomir: "You two have taught me that there are still men around. I don't have words to express what I feel. I thank you for your readiness to come to my aid." He raised his glass toward Candomir and then toward Alda. They drank.

I will be going through hell and high water to rescue his wife, and he thanks Radu, Alda thought. That means he knows I'm doing it for Radu's sake, and so he must also know that there was something between the two of them. He knows Radu's chivalrous nature, his capacity to sacrifice for those he loves. That's why he came to him. Otherwise, wouldn't it have been more natural for him to have taken refuge with Medwed, his old army comrade and hunting companion?

"Zamfira, we'll dine around two o'clock. Mme. Varsány is coming from the city." Alda spoke rather loudly, to forestall any reply to Anatol's toast.

"Very good, boyar."

"One more minor matter, Anatol," Alda said casually. "Have you some special name for your wife?"

"I've already told you: Rêve."

"Do others ever call her that?"

"No. It's a private name of ours. Her name is Janina."

Candomir raised his glass. "Success!" he said.

"Success," Alda repeated. But he gave the word the intonation of a question.

Zamfira returned to say that the Baroness had arrived. Alda rose quickly and went outside. He saw Martha laughingly bidding the man at the wheel good-bye. "Hello, hello, Martha!"

"Hello, Lutz!"

They stood and looked into one another's eyes, smiling, laughing. He took her head in both hands and kissed her gently on the brow and eyes. "Radu is in the salon, with another guest. I want to have a word with Karl." He signed to the man in the car to wait, put his arm around Martha and conducted her into the hall, where the maid took her fur coat. Candomir came out and greeted Martha with comradely gallantry. "I'll be back in a moment," Alda said, and went outside again. He walked around the car to the driver's side and shook hands cordially with Karl Rundberg. Rundberg's pale, light-blue eyes smiled with sly self-satisfaction; his whole angular face, with the upturned nose and the sunken cheeks grinned rather clownishly. "You worked beautifully and quickly, Lutz," he said. "We can rely on you."

"Platzer?" Alda said. "I hardly did anything."

"I know, I know—the Sigurantza released our most important man out of sheer kindness of heart. Did it cost much, Lutz?"

"Nothing worth mentioning. In fact, I contributed very little. By the time my contact was gone to get in on the game, Platzer had already been released. Some other branch of the government intervened. It's something we have to discuss further. Look: I have a houseful of guests at the moment. Drive to your father's and wait for me there. I'm not sure when I can get away, but don't drive back to town before I've talked with you."

"Won't you be coming to town with me?"

"I don't think so," Alda replied uncertainly.

"All right. I'll be at the old man's." He started the motor. "See you later, then."

"Till later, Karl."

When Alda returned to the salon, Martha was sitting between Anatol and Candomir, and the conversation was flowing freely. She had just emptied her glass. Her face was slightly flushed.

Alda was about to take up his duties as host by refilling Martha's glass. Anatol, however, anticipated him. Suddenly transformed, he sprang to his feet and brought the decanter of yellow apricot brandy. "Thank you," Martha said, and after she had taken a good swallow, "this is the best drink in the world. You've also been in Bucharest?" she asked Anatol.

"Of course. But that is not where I come from just now."

"Pan Bilinski is from Poland," Alda said.

"A refugee?"

"Yes," Anatol said, "a refugee. And Baron Candomir has kindly taken me in."

"How good to have friends."

"It's the greatest thing in the world, madame," Anatol said earnestly.

Alda, who did not find this small talk too enjoyable, asked Martha if she would see how dinner was getting on. She rose at once. Her way of moving was quick and lively, but with an underlying aristocratic control. Her simple black woolen dress with white collar and white cuffs showed faultless taste and a feeling for discreet elegance. Her hair, parted in the middle and combed high to either side, was tawny blond, with golden glints. Her oval face, with its healthy, sun-tanned color, and her probing, questioning blue eyes showed knowledge, experience and yet hope. Martha was an altogether lovable woman, and Alda loved her. The thought of parting from her for an indefinite period troubled him more this time than on previous occasions. She would not ask, as she had never asked before; and as always she would be plagued with speculations, when he left without saying where he was going, or when he would be coming back.

They were sitting over coffee and cognac when a servant called Alda from the room. Alda rose reluctantly and went to the "office" —the room traditionally set aside for conducting the business of the estate.

A tall, corpulent man was waiting for him. He was in his early fifties, and his puffy, sensualist's face with its foppish pointed beard scarcely suited his clerical garb. Alda greeted him with the customary "I kiss your hand, Father." But his tone sounded sarcastic rather than deferential.

"A pleasure to see you, boyar," the priest replied. He was not very acute at hearing nuances. He twisted his Falstaffian face into a smile. "A rare piece of good fortune to find you at home. Ah, you young folks, how you gad about."

Alda offered the pastor cigarettes. Gheorghe, as custom required, brought wine and cakes, filled the glasses, and left. The pastor tasted the wine appreciatively, drained his glass, and with the practiced air of a habitual drinker, refilled it. "Well, boyar, I've come to see you about a domestic matter. You know my Pulcheria —well, her husband, Captain Grigoriu—he would rather like to leave the army, and so Papa—I have only the one daughter, you know—so Papa has to do something for them."

"If I can help in any way—" Alda wanted to keep the visit from stretching out too long.

The pastor cleared his throat, finished his second glass and refilled it once more. "Well, it's like this: Pulcheria still has her dowry, and Constantin, my son-in-law, isn't like the other officers—I mean he doesn't drink and gamble and so he's put a little aside."

Alda knew that Constantin Grigoriu had been commander of a border patrol for four years, and that during this time smuggling between Poland and Romania had flourished.

"Well, the two have been keeping after me to ask—since your tenancy contract with old Rundberg runs out on the first of January—to ask you whether—whether you wouldn't rent Aldeni to Constantin on the same conditions. And if you wanted to throw in the house with all the furniture—you wouldn't have to sell it—we would pay a good rental price."

Alda smoked in silence and gave no sign of his reaction to this proposal. As the minutes passed and he still did not answer, the pastor began squirming about a bit on his chair. He filled his glass again and raised it to Alda with a timid, embarrassed smile. Alda seemed not to notice, for he did not respond to the toast. The pastor finished the glass, cleared his throat, said, "Well now," and did not know what else to say. In spite of his robust nerves, he sensed the tension in the air.

At last Alda stirred. "Well now," he said, "your proposal calls for some thinking over." He had been on the point of saying something else, and wondered at his own self-control.

The pastor felt that the storm had passed over. He spoke again, with renewed courage: "You see, boyar, you must look at the matter in a practical light. Rundberg can't remain in Aldeni. Jews will no longer be tolerated in the country—perhaps not even in the city any more."

"Why not?"

"Good Lord, boyar, don't you know what's going on?"

"What is going on, Your Reverence? Who will presume to tell me how to run my private affairs? I can rent my land to anyone I like—Negro, Jew or what have you."

"That isn't realistic, Coane Alda. What a thing to say! A man who writes for the newspapers."

"For that very reason," Alda said firmly. "Because I know the situation. All those stories are sheer rumor, Your Reverence."

"Are they? I'm sorry to contradict you. I am better informed."

"That may be. It depends on the sources of your information."

"They are the highest, boyar, the very highest, I assure you," the pastor said, filling his glass again.

"And what about your own feelings, Your Reverence? Suppose that is the way the wind is really blowing. Do you think it right to take old Rundberg's livelihood away? He's a friend of yours; you've always lived on the best of terms with him."

"If I don't put in my offer, someone else will, and blood is thicker than water. Old Rundberg is a decent fellow, very decent. A good neighbor, always ready to stretch out a helpful hand—but still a Jew. How can I help it? We must move with the times, boyar, and we priests have our instructions. That is—" He realized that he had said too much and fell silent.

Alda had no desire to press him to the wall. He knew that the priesthood had succumbed too. After all, the worst you could ordinarily say of this pastor was that he drank, played cards and did a bit of wenching. He was too stupid to take part in political intrigues and conspiracies. All he was after now was to get hold of a good thing for his daughter. No sense arguing with him; the times were on his side. On the whole it was rather fortunate that the pastor had come to him just now. He would talk the matter over with Rundberg, and be guided by his opinion.

He rose. "Forgive me, Your Reverence," he said. "I must get back to my guests. Give my regards to your wife and Pulcheria. I'll think over your proposal."

Alda strode rapidly through the grove. He knocked on the door of the tenant house, and stepped directly into the big main room. With its old-fashioned furniture, the heavy old folio volumes in the glass cupboard, the big silver candlesticks and the pictures on the walls, it looked exactly like the living rooms of many old Jews who had inherited their household goods from their fathers and had done nothing to add a more modern note to the furnishings.

Joshua Rundberg and his son sat over the chessboard. Karl stood up, and the old man wanted to stand also, but Alda quickly reached his side and gently pressed him back into his seat. He shook hands with him warmly. Rundberg was a widower; his sister, also widowed, ran his household. She appeared with a tray of wine and small cakes and greeted Alda. Karl took the tray from her hands and filled the three glasses while she withdrew as quietly and inconspicuously as she had come.

"It's good you've come, Coane Lutz," Joshua Rundberg said, stroking his short, almost white, pointed beard. "That is," he corrected himself, "it's always good when you're here, but especially this time. There's a great deal to discuss, and I hardly know where to begin."

"Before you begin," Lutz said, "the pastor came to see me."

"I can imagine why—he wants to lease Aldeni."

"And rent or buy the house."

"So you know?"

"I know."

"And hard as it is for me to say it, I am inclined to advise you to sell the place."

Alda looked at the old man, and then at Karl's grinning face, which seemed hardly to conform with the gravity of the subject. He understood: the two Rundbergs had evidently discussed every aspect of this question.

"Sell Aldeni? Of course I'm not here very much. Still, to sell it—"

"It seems terrible, I know, Coane Lutz. But believe me, it's the best thing. Not that farming is headed for bad times; on the contrary. But your grandfather wouldn't have taken advantage of these good times, Coane Lutz. An Alda cannot make common cause with robbers and murderers. You'll find you'll have nothing but trouble renting the land; the tenants will be the sort of people who want to wring everything they can out of the farm, to strip it bare. Right now everything in Aldeni is still the way your grandfather arranged it. You know that, Coane Lutz. I've always acted according to his wishes and kept the place as he would have liked to see it. If you intend to keep Aldeni, run it yourself. You understand farming—I know that—and you love the place. But don't take on any of these present-day tenants."

He looked at Alda, and when Alda made no comment, continued, "Tomescu wants to buy Aldeni. He offers a fair price. I advise you to sell the place to him. For your own good and for ours."

Alda turned his head in perplexity from the father to the son. Karl nodded, grinning. "We couldn't stay on, in any case. They're out to get us Jews. And not just us—we sometimes hear things that concern others beside the Jews. Sell the place, Lutz, and go to Switzerland or America, far away from this plague-stricken Europe."

"If that's your considered opinion, I'll sell. But I'm not going to America."

"What did I tell you?" Karl said to his father.

"But how are we going to do this?" Alda wondered. "I have to leave tomorrow—for an indefinite period."

"Tomorrow?" Old Rundberg was astonished and concerned. "That's impossible—selling an estate is a pretty complicated matter."

"I have to."

Karl's eyes widened. He suddenly realized where Alda was bound. "Don't ask, Father," he said. "If Lutz says he can't postpone leaving, he can't. We'll have to manage somehow." He fell silent and squinted up at the ceiling. Alda threw him a look of gratitude. Karl had conceived and executed hundreds of dangerous smuggling coups, had never overlooked a detail, always hit on the right scheme. He would think of one now. As he pondered, he wore, as almost always, a rather stupid grin. It was an expression achieved by drawing back his upper lip and exposing his gums. The grin adequately disguised the real intelligence and courage of his lean face with its high, strong brow over which strands of ash-blond hair fell.

"It could be managed," he said. "With a power of attorney. We haven't time for a court order, but we can have the necessary papers drawn up by the notary, can't we? I'll drive Lutz to Cernauti—and we'll have everything settled in an hour. To whom should the power of attorney be given, Lutz?"

"Your father, naturally."

"In the present circumstances that isn't so natural. Father might have difficulties where a Romanian would not."

"Karl is right. I appreciate your confidence, Coane Lutz, and thank you for it, but we must be sensible."

"You handle the sale, no one else!" Alda said firmly to the old man. "Please!"

"Well, then, that's how it will have to be. Get ready, Father. And you, Lutz, come with me right now, as you are. Your guests will forgive you."

The two Rundbergs stood up, but Alda remained in his seat. "No, Karl, I don't feel up to driving to Cernauti just now. Ask the notary to come here. Uncle Stefan will come, as a favor."

"I'll ask him," Karl murmured hesitantly. He was clearly wondering why Alda was unwilling to go to the city.

They walked in silence back to the main house. At the driveway Rundberg nodded his head in the direction of the east. "You're crossing the border, Lutz?"

"What makes you think that?" Alda said evasively.

"I'm asking because I can recommend a good crossing place. Go to my old friend Jivan Bes; the Ceremus flows behind his garden. Between the Five Oaks and the distillery. Jivan is reliable." He waited a moment for the instructions to sink in and continued, "Once you get across—in Snyatyn there's David Kligler, or better still Hersch Birnberg. Yes, Birnberg is better. His house is fairly close to the station—there's a big brown gate; you can't miss it. He knows you."

"How so?"

"Not you, but he knows about the *Uden*."

"The lord?" Alda sounded bitter. *Uden* is a variant of the Hebrew word *Adon,* the Lord.

"You are a lord. I wish all lords were like you. Must you go?"

"Would I otherwise?" Alda put his hand on the door latch. "Now you'd better drive to town and bring the notary."

Rundberg nodded and left. Alda quickly entered the house and joined his guests. By now they had shifted to red wine. "Are we going to see something of our host at last?" Martha asked.

"Do forgive me." Alda bowed slightly in Anatol's direction. "There were some things—couldn't be postponed—"

"Please, don't put yourself out on my account," Anatol said. He assumed a modest deprecating air which was very much at odds with the jaunty mood he had been in when Alda entered. Alda felt called upon not to spoil the enjoyment of his guests and filled his glass. "Ah, that tastes good," he said. "Washes down problems."

"You have problems, Lutz?" Martha asked.

"Nothing worth discussing."

Candomir proposed that they go to see the horses, and off they all went to the stables. Refreshed by the brisk autumnal air and the sight of the animals, they had barely returned when Gheorghe informed Alda that the notary was waiting in the office.

The notary was an old man with yellowish-white sideburns, black-rimmed pince-nez, black tailcoat, striped trousers and highly polished congress boots. His neck was squeezed into a stiff high collar; his black necktie was tied in a huge knot and held in place by a pearl clip. All in all, Stefan Dragomiretzchi looked as if he had stepped out of a book of the fashions of 1900.

Gheorghe came with refreshments. They raised their glasses and drank, and while the notary was savoring the wine, Alda explained the purpose of the trip. "Uncle Stefan," he said, "I've decided to sell Aldeni. Unfortunately I have to leave, and don't know for how long. I want Joshua Rundberg to handle the sale. So he must have full power of attorney."

The notary went over to the smoking table and selected a plump cigar. He trimmed it carefully, took his time lighting it, and sat down again, giving his trousers a tuck. Slowly he puffed the smoke out, watched it rise, and cleared his throat several times. At long last, drawing cautiously on the cigar, he began to speak: "Karl has already indicated what you have in mind. I know you won't let yourself be argued out of it; you're an Alda. Your grandfather was the same way, and in some respects you're very like him." The notary paused and blinked up at the smoke of his cigar. "However, your forebears were people with a strong sense of responsibility. They either ran their estates or they served the government as soldiers, officials and priests. You, on the other hand, have put your freedom before everything else. Now you want to sacrifice your ancestral lands for it. No, let me finish, Lutz! I'm not saying all this to change your mind, but only so that I'll feel I have done my duty. I had the greatest respect for your grandfather, and I feel I must say these things in tribute to his memory." The notary drew on his cigar, and the bright glow made it apparent that he was more upset than he showed. "I know you aren't selling the place in order to take advantage of high land values, or because you can't hold on here. You're trying to anticipate events; you want to be quicker and wiser than destiny. Isn't that it, Lutz?"

"I am selling Aldeni because Grandfather would have done exactly that. It can no longer be the home of the Aldas. And it isn't really that I'm giving it up; it's being taken from me by the times, which are doing away with the traditions of the Aldas and their like."

"Very well, Lutz," the notary said deliberately. "I know it isn't easy for you. I hope and pray that your predictions turn out to be wrong." He rose, went over to the desk and settled himself. From a fat briefcase he took the necessary forms. Karl Rundberg sat down at the typewriter, and the notary began dictating the terms of the agreement.

After the document was drawn up, Alda asked the notary to stay to supper. He himself lingered a moment to speak to the Rundbergs. "Just one more thing," he said. "Whatever money comes in is to be given to Karl."

"Then won't we see you again before your departure?"

"I don't think so."

"Coane Lutz." Rundberg strove to master his emotion. "I don't want to seem to meddle, but—my father worked for your family, you know. He was born on this estate. The Rundbergs here always had the full confidence of the Aldas—I believe they have well deserved it. Before your grandfather's death I promised him that I would look out for you. Forgive me—that was the way he put it."

"You have done so, Domnule Rundberg. You have been a true friend, and a trustworthy estate manager."

"Now, Father," Karl said, "Lutz knows how to look after himself. He doesn't want to say where he's going—you know how he is —but he isn't going to do anything dangerous."

"Everything is dangerous nowadays," Joshua answered in a hoarse whisper. "I know in my bones he's going into danger. But what can an old man do? I will pray for you, Coane Lutz, I will pray for you every day."

Alda extended his hand, and the old man held it fast while with his left hand he reached into the pocket of his jacket. He took out a small black silk cap and put it on. Then he placed both hands on Alda's head. Without pathos, without theatricality, but with the deep fervor of belief, he spoke the ancient Hebrew prayer. When he came to the Amen, Karl, who had covered his head with the palm of his hand, repeated it after him. As the old man lowered his hands, they brushed affectionately over Alda's cheeks. His eyes, looking deeply one last time into Alda's, were wet. Then, without a word of good-bye, he left the room.

Shaved, smelling of English soap and Cologne water, Alda descended the stairs. He entered the salon in a cheerful mood, and his

spirits rose at the sight of Martha, who greeted him with a happy
smile. She had changed and was wearing a green evening dress
whose low neckline revealed the swell of her breasts. The pearl necklace she wore was a gift of Alda's; he had bought it for her in London. She was sitting beside the notary, who was paying court to her
with old-fashioned gallantries. All four had glasses of zuica in front
of them; the straw-covered bottle had been three-quarters emptied.
"You've come just in time," Candomir said, laughing, as he filled
Alda's glass.

"I must apologize for keeping you waiting so long."

"We realize you have important matters to take care of," Anatol
said, and added, in conspirational tones, "I imagine it's all on my
account?"

Alda dismissed this with a polite smile. "Why have I come just
in time?" he asked Candomir.

"Because the old gentleman here is invading your territory. If I
catch his meaning rightly, he has just proposed to Martha."

"I cannot understand why she won't have me," the notary said.
"She is the first woman who has ever turned me down. In all my
many years."

"And you are—" Candomir furthered the joke.

"A mere seventy—in the prime of life."

"And a distinguished figure: doctor of law and philosophy, notary, reserve lieutenant, honorary president of the hunting club, chevalier, holder of various decorations, and so on and so forth," Alda
put in.

"Now, now, that sounds too much like a newspaper obituary,"
the notary said. "But doesn't all that tempt you, beautiful Martha?"

"The chevalier—does that mean nothing to you, dear lady?"
Anatol jested.

"To marry a simple chevalier would be a distinct comedown for
me. I am a Varsany of Lakatty and Menesfalva; my father was imperial and papal chamberlain and a count. I would have every right
to call myself countess, if I wanted to."

Anatol sat up straight. "Your father's name was Árpád, wasn't
it?"

"Yes," Martha replied. "Did you know him, by any chance?"

Anatol seemed not to hear the question. He looked at Martha.
"Your mother was a Countess Larish," he said in an extremely low
voice.

"Why, yes," she said in surprise, and dropped her tone of levity.
Her seriousness communicated itself to the others. "But not of the
main branch. I think the family property was in the vicinity of Cracow. I never knew my mother; she died at my birth."

Anatol avoided her eyes. "Your mother was a Larish! What a small world!" He seemed to lose himself in thought and stopped contributing to the conversation. The others felt constrained, as though it would be bad form to go on chatting as before. Alda did not feel energetic enough to break the silence. Anatol's subdued pathos was playacting, he felt, a way of drawing attention to himself. The fellow was rallying all possible forces to his cause. He already had Candomir, and through Candomir had the promise of help from Alda. And now he was making a play for Martha. Why? Because she was beautiful? Then why was he so impressed at hearing of her antecedents? What were his motivations there? Was he interested in Martha as a woman, or trying to ingratiate himself with still another person "with good connections"? Was he an aristocrat turning to another aristocrat for possible help, or ladies' man making up to a woman?

The air cleared when Zamfira announced that supper was served. The notary led in Martha with elaborate courtesy, and the three men followed.

The round table was set festively with white damask, precious antique china, silver, crystal, and flowers. Martha sat between the notary and Candomir, Alda opposite her, and Anatol between the notary and his host. A maid and the youngest Gheorghe waited on the table. After eating, the five of them went to the library, where Turkish coffee was served. Having drunk his coffee, the notary was ready to take his leave. He stood up, bowed to Martha, shook hands with Anatol, and threw his arms wide in the suggestion of an embrace toward Candomir. Alda accompanied him to the door.

When he returned, the others were sitting in silence, drinking coffee and smoking. Martha soon excused herself, pleading tiredness.

"We ought to discuss your expedition, don't you think?" Candomir said.

"What is there to discuss?" Alda replied. "I shall proceed according to the information I have. Things are bound to take a turn for the unexpected, but how is something we cannot anticipate. But I want to ask you two"—he looked first at Anatol and then at Candomir—"you don't know where I am going or why. If anyone should ask about me, I've gone away without giving any reason or destination. Naturally, I don't expect you to swear to this, but I do want to have your word."

Candomir sprang to his feet and held out his right hand. Anatol did likewise. "It is the least you can ask of me," he said. "If you knew how grateful I am—"

Alda rang. The servant brought more coffee and a bottle of cognac. "Fine," Candomir said. "Courvoisier, hm—the best thing after a lot of drinking. A fitting close to the evening. *Hai noroc, frate—* good luck, brother!" His eyes were filled with tears.

"*Şi la multi ani*—and many years to come!" Alda replied in a loud, bright voice. I would not like to be feeling the way Radu does now, he thought, and began to sing softly, *"Hai, zdrâng, zdrâng."* Candomir sang the second verse, and Anatol soon joined in, although he understood not a word of the old peasant song, which tells in innumerable stanzas and without mincing words of a girl's love affair, from the first rendezvous to the baptism of the child and the subsequent wedding.

When Gheorghe reported that Domnule Rundberg was back, Alda poured the remaining brandy into four glasses. He touched glasses with Candomir and Anatol, but did not drink his own; instead, he took two with him when they went out to the car. "Hello, Karl. That didn't take you long. Here, drink with me," he said. Karl Rundberg, still sitting in the car, greeted Candomir and bowed mutely to Anatol, whom he did not know. He took the glass. "Noroc, boyar!" he said, raising it toward Alda.

"Şi la multi ani!" Alda replied, and they drank. Candomir and Anatol got into the back seat. Alda relieved Rundberg of his now empty glass and went up to Candomir. He placed his free right hand on Candomir's and patted it. *"Are sa fie bine, frate*—it will turn out well, brother," he said. Candomir seized his friend's hand, and on a sudden impulse drew him toward himself. Alda lost his balance; his left hand struck the door of the car and the glasses shattered. He felt something wet on his hand, but ignored it. "Splendid. Broken glass brings luck to pass. We can use it. Go ahead, Karl. Au revoir, au revoir!"

His hand was bleeding rather heavily. "The blacker the clouds, the lighter the rain," Alda murmured, and went into the bathroom. With Gheorghe's help he painted his bleeding hand with iodine and bandaged it. Then he went upstairs.

Martha was already asleep. The glow of the reading lamp cast a golden tint on her tanned face. She lay on her back, her head to one side, her tawny hair falling over the pillow. The strap of her blue silk nightgown had slipped down, revealing the roundness of her shoulder and breasts. Alda gazed down at her with a painful sense of how deeply he loved her. She opened her eyes. "Lutz—" she murmured longingly. "Come. . . ."

Alda was awakened early in the morning by the pain in his left hand. Carefully, he freed his right arm from Martha's embrace, and went into the bathroom. He stripped off the adhesive. The gashes on the palm were already closing, but one deep cut on the second

joint of his middle finger looked bad and was aching fiercely. Such
trifling injuries could turn into major nuisances, Alda knew. He
went quietly to the house telephone, called the stables and asked
that someone go and bring the doctor from the village.

Half an hour later Gheorghe brought him a visiting card. Alda
read: Josif Vendrinschi, M.D., first lieutenant, Reserve Medical
Corps. "The new doctor," Gheorghe said.

"Is Dr. Schmetterling no longer in the village?"

"He's been gone for six months, boyar."

A lean man of about thirty entered the room with affectedly
stiff, military posture, marched rather than walked up to Alda,
clicked his heels before him and bowed. "Dr. Vendrinschi," he said,
raising his heavily pomaded head, which the sharply drawn part in
his hair seemed to divide into two equal halves. "You sent for me."

"Not you exactly," Alda replied very politely, "but Dr. Schmetterling."

"He lives in Cernauti now. I have taken his place." The new
doctor's voice was certainly not likable.

"But I should have been informed!" By an old agreement with
the village, the estate paid half the doctor's retainer fee. Although
the answer was fairly obvious, Alda asked with stressed politeness,
"Do you by any chance know the reasons—"

"Why, boyar, there's only one reason nowadays. There's no place
in the country for Jewish doctors, and it's to be hoped that before
long they'll be out of the cities too. Then we can have our turn."

"Who is we?" Alda asked.

"We Romanians."

"I see, I see," Alda said. He held out his left hand.

It seemed that there were some splinters of glass in the wound.
While the doctor was extracting them, Alda considered the situation.
It was odd, he thought, that the same topic should come up with
whomever one spoke to. But he continued to conceal his anger, and
only read out loud the name on the doctor's card. "Vendrinschi—
what district do you come from? Are you from the Bucovina?"

"Of course," the doctor said somewhat evasively. "My father
and Pastor Domanschi's wife are brother and sister."

So that explained why Dr. Schmetterling had been ousted.
"Then you are a Ruthenian after all, aren't you?" Alda asked quietly.

The doctor flushed. "I am a Romanian, a Romanian army officer,
Domnule Alda," he stammered in some heat.

"I beg your pardon, doctor," Alda said with exaggerated courtesy. "I had no wish to offend you. For me personally there are no
differences. I consider Romanians, Ruthenians and Jews all equal."

"Allow me to differ!" the doctor gasped.

Alda ignored him. He wrote out a check for a thousand lei, about three times the usual fee. "Thank you very much for your trouble, doctor," he said glancing at the bandaged hand. "You treated that very skillfully. Thank you," he repeated. There was no mistaking his meaning; the doctor could go.

They sat at breakfast, and Martha served the invalid with a somewhat mocking attentiveness. Alda told her how he had cut himself, and described his encounter with Dr. Vendrinschi, the Ruthenian who was posing as a Romanian.

"My God, the things people will think of!" Martha exclaimed. "Someone who *wants* to be a Romanian!" Alda overlooked her quip. Martha did not care for Romanians, and he no longer tried to reason her out of this prejudice. "A wonderful idea of yours, coming to the country," she chattered on. "We can ride this afternoon. I'm looking forward to it so. And tomorrow—"

"Tomorrow I'll no longer be here," Alda said lightly.

"No longer here?" Her gaiety vanished. "You're going away, Lutz?"

"On an assignment. I may be gone for a good while. I don't think you ought to stay here. Visit the Zinnendorfs. The Countess will love having you. And Felix is a good fellow; he won't be dangerous to you—I mean to me."

"It would be nice to see Aunt Agathe." She hesitated. "But I'm afraid I can't go there."

He was astonished. "Why in the world not?"

"I—I'd rather not tell you, Lutz," she said unhappily.

"But I must know!" he retorted sharply. "After all, it concerns me too."

"Very well, Lutz, I suppose I'll have to say it bluntly. My relations with Aunt Agathe are no longer what they used to be. Don't misunderstand me—I'm very fond of her; she's still the only person I am really close to, and she feels nothing but kindness toward me—I'm certain of that. Perhaps for that very reason a false note has crept into our relations."

"I wish you would speak more clearly—"

"Very well. Aunt Agathe thinks—in short, she doesn't like our living together."

"She doesn't like it? But what—"

"What business is it of hers? Aunt Agathe isn't narrow-minded. Think how calmly she took it when I became a singer, and went traipsing off on a world tour. In the past such a thing would have been impossible, but nowadays plenty of aristocrats have turned to similar professions; they now enjoy the privilege of necessity, so to speak. And she understands perfectly well that a young woman cannot live like a nun. She's always approved of my friendship with you, because she's very fond of you and thinks well of you. But she makes distinctions. If—she writes—the two of us were off somewhere and met and stayed together, that would be quite all right. Then I'm Madame X and you're Monsieur Y, and what we do is entirely our concern. But she says that to have a public liaison right here on the estate is absolutely wrong; it is—I'm quoting her—offensive."

"Offensive! That's a pretty strong way of putting it. It never occurred to me that she might look at it that way. But what counts is this: how do you feel about the situation, Martha?"

"Do you mean, how do I feel about rectifying it by becoming your proper wife, Lutz? Naturally I've thought about it fairly often. But I've always rejected it."

"Rejected?"

"Does the word bother you? Then let's say, excluded it—as impossible, as something undesirable," she said quietly.

"Might I know your reason?"

She ignored his irony, sat up straight and took his hands, touching the injured left hand very lightly. "Don't misunderstand me. I'd rather not be married to you because I want you to love me."

"And you think the one excludes the other?"

"Lutz, you're not made for marriage. You shouldn't marry, because you can't be a husband; you can only be a friend and lover. Besides, I'm no great partisan of marriage. I don't have a very high opinion of it, even aside from my own sad experience."

"Poor burned child." He moved his chair close to hers and put his arm around her. She buried her head on his shoulder.

"Do understand my meaning, Lutz? People have to be adults before they marry."

"I should think I'm too old rather than too young for marriage —and we are talking about me, aren't we?"

"Lutz," she said earnestly, with deep sincerity, "you're not adult and never will be. Not even at seventy. It's just that that makes you so—so attractive. In other words, I love you too much to marry you."

"You know that's too complicated for me."

"You're not telling the truth. You understand me perfectly well. You don't like marriage either and you'd soon regard it as a fetter. How you would hate to have someone else passing on all your intentions and decisions! Oh yes, marriage is supposed to promote love, loyalty, companionship. But would those things compensate you for the loss of your liberty, for the freedom from attachment which is so vital to you? You would become a silent martyr in marriage, because naturally you would never let your misery show. But I would sense it, and pretend I didn't know, and before long there would be a wall of unspoken resentment between us. We would be unable to reach each other, and both of us would be unhappy."

"How wisely you put things, Martha, and what a talent you have for pessimism."

"It's impossible to be too pessimistic."

Alda stood up and began pacing the room with slow, deliberate footsteps. At last he stood still and began gropingly, "I think you have a false impression of me, Martha. It's true, I am interested in the other side of life. I've searched it out, and never tried to dodge when it searched me out. Because it happens, Martha, that the other side searches out a person." When she nodded, he went on with growing certainty, "And why did it find me receptive? Because I've always been eaten with curiosity about it and about myself. Do you understand that, Martha? If there hadn't been some—this is the only word I can find for it—some psychic or intellectual defect in me which made me unable to resist curiosity, interest—call it sympathy, if you like—I would be like everyone else: sensible. As it is, I'm not and perhaps I never will be. But sometimes I'm powerfully drawn in that direction."

"I understand, Lutz," Martha said.

"And now? I love you. I love you, Martha."

"And you think and hope—" She fell silent and gazed searchingly at him.

"Go on, Martha."

"You hope that it will turn out well, better—is that it?"

He nodded. "It will turn out very well—for the two of us." He put his hand under her chin and raised her head. The tears in her eyes filled him with dismay. "Martha—clever, silly Martha." He took her into his arms. "What is so dreadful about a little bit of marriage? I promise you, I swear by all the saints, I'll be the way you'd like me to be."

"That's what I'm afraid of. I'd rather have you the way you want to be."

"Don't split hairs, Martha. We'll be married; you set the date."

"Then my thoughts, my opinion, mean nothing—your will be done?"

"But, Martha, it's your will too—if I didn't feel that, I wouldn't think of it."

"I know you, Lutz! But you've been warned. I love you, and I'll stop at nothing to hold on to you—as long as possible."

"Even marriage?"

"Even marriage. So we'll be married when you return from—from your mysterious trip."

"You want me to go?" he asked, in surprise and disappointment.

"Absolutely! For both our sakes."

He had hoped that she would exert some pressure on him to stay. But she wanted no sacrifices. He was at once disappointed and relieved. "Very well, then. We'll marry when I return. Write to the Countess and ask her for hospitality until I come back and marry you."

"You are cunning!"

"Don't I have to be?"

He took her into his arms and kissed her. "All your philosophy gone down the drain!" He laughed.

She freed herself from his arms. "If that's what you want to prove by this, you're mean. After all, I'm nothing but a weak woman."

"Thank God," he said, and kissed her again.

Martha and Alda were sitting over martinis when Karl Rundberg arrived. He anxiously inquired about Alda's bandaged hand. Alda explained, but left Dr. Vendrinschi out of the story. Supper was very gay. Alda was in rare good humor, as was Martha, and Rundberg's sarcastic wit furthered their high spirits. Toward the end champagne was served, and Alda said, "Karl, let us drink to the health of my fiancée. Martha and I are going to be married soon. You're the first to hear the news."

"Oh," Rundberg said, surprise, joy and sentiment merging into a grin on his clown's face, "that's glorious!" He stood up and raised his glass to Martha. She extended her hand, and he kissed it, bowing very low.

After coffee Martha withdrew, for it was evident that the men had things to discuss.

"Karl," Alda said, "perhaps you can explain a little episode that has been preying on my mind."

Karl straightened and looked tensely at Alda. "What is it, Lutz?"

"Tell me, Karl, does this man Motje Platzer know me, and does he know about my position in the organization? Does he know that I'm the Uden?"

"What an idea, Lutz! It's out of the question. He's a cattle dealer and has probably done some buying around here as well as in other villages. He'd know that you're the boyar of Aldeni. But that you're the Uden—whatever gave you that idea?"

"I put two and two together. After Platzer's sudden release, it occurred to me that he might have said some things under pressure which would make them think he was more valuable free than locked up. Perhaps they want to use him as bait. That would explain a good deal. Then, another thing: a few hours before I found out that Platzer was free, the desk clerk at the Union whispered to me that a Sigurantza man was on my trail. Can you see a connection, Karl?"

Karl sat hunched up, thinking. "As far as the Sigurantza man goes—everyone is spied on nowadays. You needn't worry about that, Lutz."

"Worry?" Alda shrugged. "The idea of being an accomplice of Motje Platzer isn't very pleasant to me either, but if you walk in the rain, you risk getting wet. What department has an interest in Platzer?"

"The Second Bureau," Rundberg said.

"I don't understand." Alda drawled out the words as if he had barely heard Rundberg's answer.

Rundberg looked down at the floor. His mop of blond hair fell over his forehead, forming a bang that almost covered his eyes. "Platzer works for the Second Bureau," he explained. "He brings information across from the other side. In fact, he is an important man; otherwise headquarters wouldn't have intervened for him."

"And you don't like it, Karl?"

"Not at all," Rundberg said. He brushed the hair back from his forehead. "No, I don't like it at all. That's why I'm calling a halt to our activities at the Ceremus."

"Because Platzer works for the Second Bureau? How does that affect the situation?"

"It affects it very much. Almost all the men who work for us are also agents of the Second Bureau. That's been most convenient, because it means they're covered on this side of the river. A man goes across, delivers our watches, receives his dollars for them, and then picks up a newspaper, or a propaganda pamphlet or some other piece of inconsequential information, for the Second Bureau. That proves he's carried out his mission. No more is asked of him because he can't do more. And still he figures on the books as a paid agent. He never sees his pay, and doesn't ask for it, since he makes enough by smuggling. Around forty unpaid agents on the books—that makes a very nice income for certain parties at headquarters."

"Clear as glass. But why is this bothering you all of a sudden?"

"I don't want to take part in activities directed against the Soviets—not when Jews are in on it. There might be one among them who turns out brighter than the others and actually brings valuable information across. This Platzer business is a case in point."

"I don't follow your reasoning."

"It's this: we Jews shouldn't be working against the Russians."

Alda looked at him in astonishment. "Why so?"

"Well, its fairly simple. In Russia they make no distinction between Russians and other nationalities. The law forbids anti-Semitism and has severe penalties for any anti-Semitic utterances or acts. I want you to understand me, Lutz—to understand my personal point of view, my—you might almost call it—pact with the Russians. This is the present lineup: on one side we have those who are building an unprecedented organization for the annihilation of Jews just because they are Jews. On the other side we have the Russians: a police state, but without racial distinctions. I won't help the former against the latter. To put it bluntly, anybody who works against the Russians—I mean now, today—is working for the Germans. And for a Jew, that's the height of depravity."

"So you want to quit because you think that when your men give the Romanian Second Bureau information about the Russians, you're helping the Germans?"

"That's how I see it. Don't you, Lutz?"

"I'm not so convinced that if there were a war between Germany and Russia, Romania would team up with Germany."

"You can't mean that, Lutz. All you can mean is that Germany and Russia seem to have buried the hatchet. In that case, Russia may not enter the war, and Romania will not be forced to take sides with Germany. That's theoretically possible, of course. But if this war has any purpose at all," Rundberg went on, "it must be waged between Russia and Germany."

Alda made a startled gesture. Strange echo. He had heard the same words only a few days ago, from a person as different as possible from the smuggler Rundberg. Except that both these men were after their fashion, shrewd and experienced—General Baderescu and Rundberg. What about himself? What did he really think of the Hitler-Stalin pact, which had been signed a bare four months ago and had given so sinister a turn to the history of Europe? The Russians had given Hitler a free hand, and although the French Maginot Line still held, what would happen when Hitler had finished dividing up Poland with Stalin and was able to transfer his troops from the East to the West? Was it so unthinkable that the two despots would stick to their agreement, each assuring himself of a sphere of influence and subjugating Europe between them? A wild gavotte of images whirled through Alda's mind. For the past six years he had been risking his life to save people, to help wherever he could. Time and again he had ventured into Germany and German-occupied territory to help those in trouble, to help get people out. He knew the atmosphere of the country, the hypnotizing nature of Nazi propaganda. He knew the ever-repeated slogans, substitutes for a philosophy, which contained the Nazis' aims and ultimate goal: the Bolsheviki, the plutocracy, the Jews. The Reich, which the Nazis identified with the Millennial Kingdom, was to liberate the world from this threefold plague. The Bolsheviki always came first on the list; they were the principal foe. Yet the Russians, who had been ready to march against Germany the year before, when the Nazis threatened to occupy Prague, had spurned England's offer of an alliance and instead made a pact with the Germans. At the moment each of the partners was honoring the agreement and carving up poor Poland on a basis obviously prepared beforehand.

Why, then, was the General—and why was Karl Rundberg, and why was he himself—convinced that war between Germany and Russia was inevitable? For his doubts and objections were merely for the sake of argument. He wanted to hear his own opinion confirmed by men he respected. And from each he heard the same thing: if this war has any purpose at all—. But since when had war ever had a purpose?

"Yes, Karl," Alda said finally. "Perhaps I'm going over there partly out of curiosity. I want to be honest with you: I've promised to go, and had almost made up my mind to stay. I would have had to settle that with myself, and it wouldn't have been easy. But there are certain rules I don't find it easy to break, and keeping a promise is one of the most basic of them. . . . Don't brood about it, Karl," he added, reading his friend's expression. His tone grew more earnest. "If I wasn't firmly resolved before, I am now."

"Good, Lutz," Rundberg said. "If you're determined to, go. Why suddenly lose heart? Here we sit, two old border jumpers, smugglers since we were knee-high, and we invent all sorts of problems just because you want to take a trip across the border. The Commies won't eat you. You're a tough morsel. . . . Let's discuss some business."

"You're right," Alda said gratefully. "Go ahead, Karl."

"You've chosen a good time for your little expedition. Everything's in the clear; we have no goods en route. Your share of the last trip comes to about four thousand American dollars. Shall I transfer the money to Zurich, as usual?"

"There must be quite a bit in that account by now."

"How much have you drawn in the past two months?"

"Three thousand or so."

"That means you have about one hundred and fifty-five thousand dollars in Zurich, not counting the latest four thousand."

"A lot of money."

"We made up to twelve hundred per cent on the last deal."

"And you want to retire from business!"

"That subject is closed for the night. Now: what's to be done with the proceeds from the sale of Aldeni?"

"Send that to Zurich also. How much do you think it will bring?"

"Between sixty-five and seventy million lei. Yesterday the dollar was at five hundred lei in Bucharest. Our friendship with Germany doesn't help our foreign exchange."

"In other words, I don't receive much more for Aldeni—for all that land, standing timber, orchards, the houses and the main house —than for a few cartons of nickel-plated watches?"

"What kind of profit is there in agriculture? At best, given intensive work, seven per cent. The watches were a different proposition altogether. We bought them for around two dollars and sold them for twenty-five. But now that's over."

"Yes, that's over," Alda repeated with a sigh of relief.

"I hope your conscience isn't bothering you, Lutz. It shouldn't. If you had gone into that game only to make money, you'd be a very rich man now. You've employed your money—as my major in the army used to say—in exemplary fashion. I know. If all the rich had used their income the way you do—who knows?—there might be a lot less unhappiness in the world."

"You don't mean that seriously, do you, Karl?"

"Absolutely. Property, money—to live pleasantly and easily— why not? The thing about money is that it mustn't be used for power—all the misery in the world comes from power."

Alda laughed. "An estimable theory, Karl. It was first advanced by a highly intelligent man who was forced to drink a cup of poison a couple of thousand years ago."

"As far as I'm concerned, it's my own idea, and I live by it. So do you, and all those who are like us. We let others share in whatever scraps of power we've managed to obtain. We try to balance things out on our own."

Alda laughed. "Karl, Karl, what a joke." He became serious. "Of course it would be a lot harder without this ethical cloak. We'd find it rather depressing if we had to tell ourselves simply: I'm a smuggler, a lawbreaker."

"I don't say the idea hasn't occurred to me. I guess I'd find it terribly dreary. But I'd view myself as a parasite, as bad, only if the system itself had a moral basis. The Almighty, or God, or whoever else created this world—and who occasionally takes it into his head to destroy it—never created frontiers. Frontiers are inventions of men—from which all the rest follows. There have been smugglers as long as there have been borders, and there always will be as long as borders exist."

"So you're a smuggler by conviction! Then why should the incident with Motje Platzer—"

"That's just it!" Rundberg interrupted. "I'm abandoning an occupation which forces me into conflict with my convictions. That's obvious." He changed the subject. "On the whole, I think it's an excellent idea that you're going across," he said slowly. "Perhaps, when you're there, when you hear what people say and deduce what the Russians are thinking about it—"

"About the pact with Germany, you mean?" Alda asked rather anxiously.

"Hitler and the Nazis in general owe their existence to incessant shouting, to their everlasting boast that they're going to smash Bolshevism." Rundberg fixed his eyes on Alda. "A good thing you're going. You'll find out."

"So you're playing Second Bureau on a private basis, Karl," Alda said. "What good will it do you to know what people are thinking and saying? And who? The common people? That means nothing. The common people have no say. Are they asked?"

"Still and all," Rundberg said, "since you are going, keep your ears open. Any report will be useful: we'll be able to act accordingly."

"In business, you mean?"

"For people of our sort there are more important things than business nowadays."

"How do you mean that, Karl?"

"I'm referring to the people who are less resourceful, less sharp, than we are—those who don't know what to do, where to turn. They'll need us, Lutz."

"What can a few single individuals do for them?" Alda asked sadly.

"A good deal, believe me! We have always fought against the powers that be. Our tricks are our weapons. Those in power aren't always so clever—you know that too, Lutz. Money isn't the issue any longer, but helpless, defenseless people. You understand me, don't you, Lutz?"

Alda did not reply. But his eyes expressed understanding. And assent.

Alda's instructions were brief but comprehensive. The main thing was that Rundberg knew what needed to be done, and would act in his friend's spirit.

"I'd rather not contact anyone on this side," Alda concluded. "I'll get across without help, and manage by myself on the other side too. But for an emergency I should have one or two addresses."

"That's so. I've already mentioned Hersch Birnberg in Snyatyn. And in Lvov, there's Yossel Besselmann, Kilinskiego 8. They know about the Uden."

Later they had tea with Martha. "Karl will drive you to town," Alda said. "Better pack all your things."

At six o'clock the car was ready in front of the house. Martha sat down beside Rundberg. Alda shook hands, and Rundberg said, "Good-bye." His voice was hoarse; in the twilight his grin looked like a grotesque grimace.

"Good-bye, Lutz," Martha said as the motor started. Her hand, waving, faded to a shadow in the autumnal dusk. Alda went back into the house. He wrote a good many letters and put them all into a large envelope for Karl. They would be sent abroad without passing through the censorship. He waited until midnight, and left the house unnoticed.

He wore riding dress, and over it a short peasant jacket and a high fur cap. Aside from a tobacco pouch filled with cigarette tobacco, a package of cigarette paper, and a clumsy flint lighter, he had nothing in his pockets.

At the foot of the serpentines he cut off on the path to the woods. It was misty and very dark, but he could have found the narrow path he was seeking blindfolded. After a half hour's tramp through underbrush, he sat down on a stone. He took out the pouch, rolled a cigarette—his bandaged left hand hampering him somewhat—and sat smoking and thinking. When he started out again, the phosphorescent dial of his steel wristwatch showed fifteen after one. If all went well, he could be across the border by five o'clock in the morning.

BOOK TWO

THE RESCUERS AND THE RESCUED

> But most rulers, my dear friend,
> are bad.
> PLATO: *Gorgias*

YODOR IVANOVICH LAVRENENKO, THE DIRECTOR OF THE LVOV
Power Plant, sat in his office in his overcoat, his peaked
cap on his head. He was a man of about thirty-five, lean
to the point of gauntness, with the head of an ascetic.
The cheekbones in his yellowish-brown face were very high. When
he pondered he closed his eyes, and his face seemed almost lifeless;
his cheeks and temples were sunken, and his vigorous mouth was
compressed to a thin, pale line. His hands, small and scarred, were a
grimy brown and fluttered nervously, while the rest of his body
remained immobile.

Lavrenenko opened his eyes and looked around. For weeks he
had been feeling uneasy. This room was too elegant for him. Only
the portraits of Stalin, Molotov, Voroshilov and Budyenny reminded
him that he was within the zone of the Soviet Union's power. He
hated the massive desk, the big Persian carpet, the heavy leather
chairs and the huge cabinet behind the desk. He longed to be back
in Proskurov, where he had directed the power plant from a little
office with a crude wooden table and unpainted, straight chairs. He
could not understand the comrades who liked or were impressed by
this sort of luxury.

His uneasiness increased as he picked up the sheet of paper on
the desk in front of him and read it through carefully for the third
time. He wanted to check each point, and be sure of where he stood.
For he had learned to think as he had had to learn everything else in
life, ever since he had left his Cossack village at the age of thirteen in
order to join the Reds. In those days he had been far better at riding
and shooting than reading and writing. He had worked successively
in a coal mine, a shoe factory and at a lathe, and at the age of twenty
had been taken from his lathe and sent to engineering school.
Among the first in his class, he became a party candidate, later a
regular party member, and worked his way up rapidly from engineer at the Proskurov plant to director.

He had never returned to his native village and did not know
whether his parents, brothers and sisters were still alive. He had no
longing to see them, no longer felt linked to them by memories.
Nowadays he scarcely ever recalled that as a boy he had gone to
church and crossed himself before icons. His God had been Lenin,
and now was Stalin. Lavrenenko was married. His wife and six-
year-old son had remained in Proskurov; she was one of the heads
of the workers' insurance organization.

Lavrenenko pressed a button, and after a moment Mark Lvovich
Saposhnik, a small, stout man, entered the room. He greeted
the director laconically and sat down. His head was shaped like a
rather oblong melon, widening out toward the neck. His hamster

cheeks formed a sharp contrast to the small mouth with its pursed lips and to the soft, slanting chin. His forehead was high and narrow, his brown, stringy hair unkempt. That gave his face a rather artistic look, which was partly deliberate. His brown eyes were small and deep-set. Saposhnik was almost the same age as Lavrenenko and had had a similar career. Before becoming deputy director at the Lvov Power Plant he had been director of the power plant in Grishino. Here he also directed a foundry and welding workshop attached to the plant, but his present post was nevertheless a demotion. All the same, he had made great efforts to be sent here, for he hoped that the bourgeois doctors would be able to cure his tubercular wife.

He wore a gray-blue suit with an absurdly short jacket. His unpressed trousers were not long enough to conceal the worn tops of his black high shoes.

He waited for Lavrenenko to speak, but the director sat in silence. Only after Maximenko came in did a conversation develop. They talked about the weather, about prospective apartments, about clothing, which could be had at preposterously low prices here. Maximenko, the *planovik* or economic planner for the power plant, was already wearing a blue suit of Western cut. He was an extremely powerful-looking man. His wide, rather flat face with its strong nose and big, sensual mouth, bore a naïve, childlike expression. His healthy dark complexion made his fine, straight teeth look even whiter than they were. His movements were emphatically athletic; quick and spirited, as though he were chasing a ball. He had been the coach and gymnastic instructor at the Dynamo Plant in Kiev, had later worked in the planning bureau at the headquarters of *Ukerkomenergo*. That was the name of the trust which was responsible for all the power plants in the Ukraine.

The talk revolved around trivialities while the three men waited for Feingold. When he entered, smiling, they fell silent. He shook hands with each of them, and tossed his blond hair. His oval face was light-skinned and smoothly shaven. Feingold was slender, broad-shouldered and trim. Under his brown leather coat, still in excellent condition, he wore a gray-checked English sports jacket. Both coat and jacket were open, exposing an embroidered white Ukrainian shirt. He wore it smockwise outside his trousers, and pinched in at the waist by a wide leather belt. Arkady Samuelovich Feingold was thirty-eight, but his face still held the nonchalance and charm of youth. The Party Committee had assigned him to the plant to take charge of political schooling and indoctrination. That was all anyone knew of him. None of them had ever seen him before, or heard of him, nor had they learned anything about his previous career. He always managed to fend off questions without appearing mysterious.

When all were seated, the director removed his cap and laid it on the desk. Running his hand over his close-cropped hair, he began, "A message has come from headquarters today. Because the Lvov plant with its workshops employs almost four hundred workers and office help, it has been granted an auxiliary farm." He fell silent and looked down at the paper in front of him. The others fully understood the implications of his silence.

Saposhnik cleared his throat. "Good, very good," he said.

"*Da.*" The director acknowledged Saposhnik's comment and went on: "The Committee has been informed of the order and will help us secure the necessary land and buildings, provided that we ourselves find what we need and make proposals. For the present, the plant treasury will advance the necessary funds. Once the Committee has confirmed the establishment of the farm, it will be set up as an independent organization and an account opened for it at the Gosbank." The director looked at the paper, whose contents he knew almost by heart. He hesitated, as if searching for a particular passage. "To the amount of fifty thousand rubles—yes, that's it." He pushed aside the rough sheet of yellow paper with a scraping noise. His right hand brushed over his face and lingered at his chin. "Yes," he repeated, and looked around the circle of men. All but Maximenko looked like cats in a thunderstorm.

Lavrenenko, clearing his throat and coughing several times, volunteered the first remark: "There have been a number of experiments with these auxiliary farms in the Soviet Union, but they have not had the desired success."

"Those experiments have cost a number of people their party cards," Feingold put in with a smile. By using this colloquial expression for expulsion from the party, he put everyone a bit more at ease.

"That's just it," the director said. "There have been no new auxiliary farms set up for years."

"They never pay; they always have deficits," Saposhnik said.

"Not only that," Feingold commented in his high, clear voice. "They always lead to quarrels. Everybody feels cheated on the distribution; it's impossible to stick to government prices, and the quotas are never met."

"Then why should we—?" The director appealed to Feingold.

"Ukerkomenergo will not be the only trust to set up an auxiliary farm in the Western Ukraine." This was the new name for the part of Galicia which had fallen to Russia and been incorporated into the Soviet Union after the partition of Poland in 1939. "No doubt the other big organizations have already received word or will be receiving it soon. So the thing for us to do is to get hold of our land and buildings while there are good places available. As close to the city as possible. These farms have little value in practice, but the party expects other values from them." He paused and smoothed out his cap, which he held on his knee. "Namely, propaganda values. We must offer the workers here something tangible. It is winter now, and more than six months until the next harvest."

Abruptly, he shut his mouth and seemed unwilling to say any more. He took the cap from his knee, and with a graceful swing set it on the back of his head. Then he took from the pocket of his jacket an oblong box of Uzbeks and offered the cigarettes around. These Uzbeks were far more significant than oral or written reports. They could be bought in the Moscow shops, but were available only to foreigners or to the *verkhovki,* the leaders. If Feingold smoked Uzbeks, that proved that he was either one of the leaders himself or in close touch with them. Political schooling and propaganda could be handled by any *partinyi,* any Bolshevik, as soon as his own training was complete. It was a job like any other. If, however, one of the leaders was assigned to the job, then the party had extraordinary plans for the Lvov Power Plant. The directors of said plant would be forever sitting in a glass house. A great future awaited them, certainly; but this future would also be extremely dangerous. They would have to accomplish prodigies in administrative and technical work; and while the rewards might be high, their tasks would be very hard.

Saposhnik broke the silence. His lips parted, revealing two rows of large yellow teeth. "If," he said, "the auxiliary farm is intended as propaganda, then the balance of accounts won't be so important. It will always show a deficit. It's impossible to run these things without losses. That is well known, so there's—less responsibility."

"Less risk, you mean," Feingold said. "Less risk for you. That's true."

"For *me,* you're right," Saposhnik said, already regretting what he had said. He knew that these auxiliary farms were managed by the deputy director of the parent organization. That had been the rule when the experiments were first begun in the Soviet. The new assignment made him a much more important person. And so he proceeded circumspectly and without haste, as befitted a proper partinyi. "We'll need forty dessiatin of land with possibly two or three dessiatin of orchard, about twenty milch cows and eight to ten horses. I think we could begin with ten sows and one boar. We'll raise poultry too, and put in good acreages of vegetables, of course. . . ."

"I see you've already dealt with these problems," Feingold said. "What you've listed is the norm for the auxiliary farm of an enterprise with four hundred workers. Have you ever organized a farm before, or been active in the agricultural sector?"

"Neither," Saposhnik hastened to reply. "But I've read about the subject and of course heard it discussed at party meetings."

"Heard about the failures, of course," Feingold said. "So you can learn from previous mistakes. Let me advise you—and I am taking full responsibility for what I say—don't take forty dessiatin, but sixty or even eighty. Headquarters will approve it. Don't limit yourself to twenty cows; tie up as many as you can buy. The peasants—I mean those who haven't been expropriated so far—will be glad to sell when they read the decrees on beef, milk and breeding cattle. Horses will be very cheap too. Buy as many as you can. They will be needed for transportation over short distances. The army will be taking the entire output of motorized vehicles for a long time to come, and the trucks we've found here hardly matter. Buy whatever you can lay hands on. Things are cheap. For the 'natives' a chervonets is still a chervonets, and if they can sell off things they can't use, they'll sell gladly—the fools."

The three men listened with eager interest. Feingold knew what policies the higher powers had decided on. Otherwise he would not have dared to take the responsibility.

"Isn't fifty thousand rubles a bit scanty for developing such a program?" Saposhnik asked.

"Fifty thousand rubles is a lot of money here. At the moment, anyhow. But that isn't important. The authorization states that advances for the work of the auxiliary farm will be approved. There's nothing said of any limit on the sums, is there?"

"No, no figures are given," Lavrenenko replied uncertainly.

"Our power plant has plenty of money," Feingold proceeded boldly, "and takes in large sums every day. It will be quite safe for you to allot whatever money is needed for setting up the farm. The directive covers you as far as the trust is concerned, and the party will make no difficulties. On the contrary. Of course you're going to need verification of your expenditures." He turned to Saposhnik. "Do you know how that's done? I take it you're aware of the regulations on purchases from private individuals?"

"Contracts signed before a notary."

"Quite right. It's complicated but unavoidable. A notarized document will stand up to examination. It's indispensable for the bookkeeping, too. We ought to get started as quickly as possible," he concluded.

"I'll start today. Of course I need some kind of vehicle and—a director for the farm. I'll ask the party. Maybe there's a young man, a member or candidate, who knows something about agriculture."

Feingold, who had started to rise, sat down again. "Look for some native who knows the district and the people. Make him your director."

"Not a partinyi? But this is a post of responsibility. The man will have *stamp i pechat* [stamp and seal]. He'll sign checks, hire and fire people." Lavrenenko spoke with some agitation.

"The ultimate decision in important matters will still be Saposhnik's," Feingold explained. "The director's job will be best entrusted to someone from these parts, if only because of the language, and settling prices. Besides, there's no reason to keep him on forever. Once the farm is organized and everything is functioning properly, he can be replaced by a party man. In general, all the office help and workers of the farm—at least for the present—are supposed to be natives. In that respect"—he turned to Saposhnik again—"you needn't stick to the norms or insist on a lily-white record. At the moment what is needed is work, and workers. Later we can separate the chaff from the wheat—I assure you, in due course that will be done. I must go now," he said to the director. "I'm expected at the Secretariat." He stood up and shook hands with Lavrenenko. "Saposhnik understands what's wanted. Give him a free hand and as much credit as he asks for."

"He'll have it, and the full responsibility too," Lavrenenko said, feebly responding to the handshake.

"This doesn't look particularly tricky to me," Feingold said, shaking hands. "At least not at the moment."

For a while after his exit there was perfect silence. What Feingold had told them in his clear, self-assured voice provided endless material for reflection. His personality and his manner alone marked him as belonging to a realm they had never yet been privileged to approach. It appeared that those who worked in these higher spheres were beginning to veer from their strictly drawn guidelines. What times, what surprises, were to come? A despairing expression crossed Lavrenenko's face. He threw looks of bafflement first at Maximenko, then at Saposhnik. Saposhnik's eyes met the director's expressionlessly; Maximenko shrugged mutely, as if to say that it didn't concern him; he would deliver the quota, whether it was kilowatts or pigs, vegetables or milk. "That *tovarishch*," he said, standing up. He looked down at the floor, then lifted his round head, still without change of expression. "I understand. He wears a

Ukrainian shirt. I'm certain he speaks Ukrainian." Then he too left the office.

"What did Maximenko mean by that?" the director asked.

"I wasn't listening," Saposhnik replied, although he had heard and understood. It was not advisable to talk about Feingold, about his way of dressing or speaking. Feingold was evidently an important man, and walls had ears. "The important thing is that I'll get the funds when I need them."

As he left the room, Lavrenenko observed that he walked on his heels and pointed his toes outward. Like a duck, the director thought. Alone, he tried to put his thoughts in order, and caught himself dwelling on Maximenko's trivial remark. What in the world had the planner meant? He was just going to Maximenko's office when the point came to him. They were Ukrainians, all four of them, even though Saposhnik and certainly Feingold were Jews, and even though the discussion had been conducted in Russian. Fyodor Ivanovich Lavrenenko, the descendent of Ukrainian cossacks, caught himself searching his memory for Ukrainian words, and not finding any. He pulled his cap lower over his forehead and strode rapidly out of his office. As he left the building and walked out into the dreary sleet storm, he murmured two words under his breath: "Western Ukraine." They had a bitter, scornful sound.

"Look around and take a close look at this, *Starshina*," the *Starshiletenant* said. He reached for the water glass, drank it down, belched, and said, "Stefan Stefanovich Nikitin." That was his test. As long as he could reel off his name, patronymic and surname, he was not drunk. He dipped a piece of bread into the mound of salt shaken out on a sheet of newspaper, and put it in his mouth. But then he spat out the bread, reached for a pickled cucumber, changed his mind and refilled the glass from the bottle of 96-proof vodka on the table. He sipped, kept the liquor in his mouth for a while to drive away the taste of the salt, and then let it slide down his throat with a long-drawn-out "Ah!" Once again he turned to his subordinate. The Starshina sat dumbly over his glass, eyes glazed. "Did you look?" the Starshiletenant asked.

"I looked," the Starshina replied. He was very drunk and had great difficulty forming words.

"And? But wait, my dove, wait! I'll help you—you mustn't make mistakes. Here"—he filled the glass—"drink it down."

The Starshina reached for the glass. His throat, his stomach quailed before the fiery liquor; but it was impossible to resist. He let the clear liquid trickle down. A sound came from him, a groan or

shout of joy. Then he gently replaced the glass on the table. The
Lieutenant had watched each of his movements with close attention.
When the Starshina's groping hand reached out for a slice of raw
bacon, he called out, "Stop!"

"Name!" the officer roared.

"Ivan." The answer was low, painful.

"Patronymic!"

"Yakovlevich."

"Surname!"

"Borenko."

His hand fumbled for food again. But the Starshiletenant kept
at him. "All together!" he commanded.

"Ivan Yakovlevich Borenko." Beads of sweat stood on the Starshina's forehead. The Starshiletenant looked around triumphantly,
demanding applause from his hosts. Antek and Tadek manifested
hearty admiration. Vassily smiled. The Lieutenant turned to his
subordinate again, who still sat rigid. The sweat pouring down his
face was the only thing about him that moved. "Look around, look
around carefully, Ivan Yakovlevich Borenko!"

The Starshina's trunk swerved jerkily to the right, to the left,
then returned to its normal position. But his eyes were glazed.

"Did you look around?" the officer asked, his voice tender,
coaxing.

"Lo-ooked aroun'," his subordinate replied.

"And what did you see?"

"Nothing," the Starshina squeezed out.

A smile of sheer happiness illuminated the Starshiletenant's
knobby face. His small, deep-set, gray-blue eyes glowed, his brow
flamed, his tousle of straw-blond hair nodded vigorous approval. He
threw his long arms around the Sergeant's rigid body and kissed
him fervently. "Nothing," he repeated. He turned to the others.
"Nothing. Did you hear that? Ivan Yakovlevich Borenko, Starshina,
my subordinate, friend, brother, buddy, comrade, is sober, cold sober.
He recited his whole name, didn't he? Did he obey my order or
didn't he? You're my witnesses. He looked around the room, and
what did he see? Nothing!" The Lieutenant dropped his head, then
raised it and looked mournfully at the three across the table. "Citizens, I give you my word of honor: the politruk is a pig, a liar. For
weeks he told us stories, nothing but fairy tales. We're going to a
country where there are nothing but capitalists, nothing but *burzhui,*
this liar says to us. It'll be swarming with landowners and manufac-
turers, usurers and speculators. Those bloodsuckers, the politruk says
to us, they have all the best to eat and drink, they sleep in silk beds,
and their houses are full of rugs and pictures in gold frames." He

looked around the room and laughed scornfully. "Where is it all? What have you got here aside from this rickety table and these two broken benches?"

Antek sat looking up at the Starshiletenant; his good-natured brown eyes, upturned nose and boyishly open mouth seemed to be radiating attention and interest. Actually he hadn't understood three words of the Lieutenant's speech. But he thought the time had come to repeat one of the Russian words he had picked up. *"Konechno,"* he said, "naturally." Tadek, who was trying to produce an accommodating smile on his dark, gloomy face, repeated the word because it was his habit to imitate Antek in everything. Only Vassily, who had understood every word spoken by the Russian, was in any position to reply. Although he ordinarily spoke little, he now turned to the Lieutenant. Deliberately seeking his words, replacing Russian words he did not know by Ruthenian equivalents, he said: "Comrade Starshiletenant, of course you're right. But there's another small matter you may not have noticed. Not everybody in this country is a capitalist. For instance, we three aren't. As you know, we are *perekupshchiki,* buyers for the Meat Trust, and we earn a hundred and thirty-seven rubles a month."

"Each," the officer corrected him. He tried to reckon out the total, but gave up. "No matter, but you also have percentages. Is that right?"

"Right," Vassily agreed. "But doesn't a starshiletenant make as much or more than all three of us together?"

"To each according to his performance," the officer said proudly. "Or is any of you going to say that he can do more than a Soviet Russian commander?" He looked slyly around. Antek and Tadek laughed vaguely. Vassily raised his hand to check the Lieutenant. "I only wanted to say," he replied quietly, "that we are not burzhui, not capitalists. We are honest workers."

The officer broke into scornful laughter. "Did you hear that, Ivan Yakovlevich?" He almost choked with laughter. "Honest workers. I'll kill myself laughing. Honest workers! Did you hear that?" He nudged the Sergeant.

"Yes," the Starshina replied, suspending his steady chewing on a piece of bacon. Then he slowly slumped to one side. Since he was sitting on the end of the bench, he found no support and fell to the floor. Antek and Tadek started up, but the Starshiletenant waved them back with an imperious gesture. "No matter, let him lie. He has no culture." He looked around the room, his eyes dwelling on the cracked walls, the dirty cement floor, the cracked, filthy basins, the rickety table. "All this mess. But that isn't my affair. So you're honest workers. Call yourself that if you like. But in your hearts you're usurers and speculators." He looked at Antek and Tadek and met vacant smiles. It began to dawn on him that they didn't understand what he was saying, and so he turned to Vassily, who was selecting a relatively unwrinkled cigarette from a pack of Polish Egypski and lighting it.

"Why do you think that, Citizen Starshiletenant?" Vassily asked in his calm, deliberate manner.

"I don't think so, I'm convinced of it, *Grazhdanin Perekupshchik*. But do we have an agreement, you three and me?"

"We have an agreement," Vassily said.

"And what is it?" the Starshiletenant sneered. "If you've forgotten, I can remind you."

"That would be good. So we know exactly what you mean. I am responsible for keeping the agreement."

"Very good, marvelous!" the officer said. He tore a strip from the newspaper on the table, skillfully twisted a small cone and filled it with makhorka, the standard tobacco of the Russian Army, made out of the stems and ribs of tobacco leaves. He nipped the cone closed at the upper end, put the thin end cautiously into his mouth, and lit it. The Starshiletenant drew the biting smoke deep into his lungs, blew it out with evident enjoyment, and resumed: "I agreed to drive you on five trips, didn't I? Is that right?"

"Right," Vassily said.

"Have we made these trips? Have we loaded your cows, pigs and sheep and brought them here? Have we worked well for you?"

"Not for us but for the Meat Trust," Vassily objected.

"I don't give a damn about the Trust. We unloaded the animals where you said. Some at the slaughterhouse and some . . . But what does that matter? We do our work and we make our little deals."

Vassily waited for the officer to finish.

"We drove a total of one thousand three hundred and twenty miles. Do you think a five-ton truck doesn't use any gas? Are you trying to cheat the Red Army or"—he tucked the charred cone of newspaper into his mouth again and relit it—"or do you think you've paid your share with one or two bottles, a little bacon and a couple of onions? Did you promise to give us two watches after five trips? Yes or no? I ask you, did you promise or didn't you?"

He looked from Antek to Tadek, who were whispering together. Tadek, who understood nothing, was having the situation explained to him by Antek, who thought he understood. The officer looked with contempt at them, and turned once more to Vassily. At least he understood, the *khakhol*. "Then where," he asked with venomous scorn, "are the watches? Two." He raised the forefinger and middle finger of his right hand and brought them to within an inch of Vassily's eyes. "Watches!"

Vassily did not draw back. He looked over them into the Starshiletenant's face. His voice had a note of dismissal and contempt. "Oh, so this is all about the watches? Of course I have them here."

"Of course you have them here," the Lieutenant said scornfully. "Konechno. But where?"

"Konechno," Antek and Tadek repeated.

"I said where are they?" the Starshiletenant roared.

"Here," Vassily said quietly. "Here they are."

The officer stared. Vassily had laid both arms on the table. The sleeves of his woolen jacket were rolled up, and on each wrist something glinted and flashed. On each wrist was a steel watch with black face, golden numerals and yellow, phosphorescent hands. The watches were fastened to his wrists by wide leather straps, the right-hand one a flaming red, the one on the left dark blue.

The surprise was complete. The officer stared raptly at the watches, and Antek and Tadek also showed amazement. The Lieutenant moved his lips. He whispered something inaudible. His whole being was concentrated on the watches. His gaze moved from the red, cracked skin of Vassily's fingers to the wrists, lingered there, moved away again, back down to the wrists, and once more stayed there, magnetically fixed. Antek's eyes sought Vassily's, with an amazed and menacing expression. But Vassily watched only the Russian, who now stood up and bent his head, over the right and then the left wrist. "They're going," he whispered, stunned. "They're going. No doubt about it, they're real watches." With an extreme effort of will, he tore himself away from the sight and looked at Vassily with a doubtful, rather timorous expression. As though his fate, the whole shape of his future life, depended upon this man. The two other men also stared at Vassily. Antek's ordinarily gay and good-hearted eyes expressed a venomous fury, and Tadek's were if possible even fiercer. The silence in the room was palpable.

But Vassily seemed to have sound nerves. The tension of the others apparently did not affect him. He folded his arms. The watches flashed on his wrists. "Grazhdanin Starshiletenant Stefan Stefanovich Nikitin," he began at last in his deliberate, rather laborious fashion, "I forgive you for what you said, since you were mistaken and misunderstood us. You expected us to give you the watches as soon as you entered this room. Perhaps we should have done so. But I wanted to give you both the watches at the same time. Citizen Starshina has gone to sleep meanwhile, and it will be impossible to wake him. Perhaps I will give you one watch now, and we will wait with the other until Ivan Yakovlevich awakes?"

"You are very *kulturno,* tovarishch." It was the first time the Starshiletenant had bestowed this title on Vassily. Up to this moment he had always called him "citizen," to emphasize the distance between an officer of the Red Army and a lowly buyer who was, moreover, one of the "natives." But a man who offered him a watch, and such a watch. . . .

Vassily gave no sign of having understood the flattering salutation. He unfolded his arms and extended his hands to the officer again. "If we're not to wait for the Starshina, please choose. That is your right as commander anyhow."

The officer's eyes swerved only for a moment between the two watches. That was purely a matter of form; in reality he had made his choice the moment he saw them. Hesitantly, hoarsely, his eyes fixed on the watch, he said, "The red one."

Without removing his hands from the table, Vassily fingered the buckle of the watch. It fell to the table with a soft click. He picked it up by the strap and held it out to the Starshiletenant with a light, gracious movement. The officer snatched it as though to save it from some rival. Hastily, he thrust it into the pocket of his short, padded jacket.

Vassily's face, with its rather disorderly, dangling mustache, showed no change of expression. "Should we try to wake the Starshina so that he can also have his watch?" he asked.

The Starshiletenant sat down without answering. He had evidently not heard. He still had to assimilate the miracle of the watch. Vassily appeared to understand. He waited a while before he repeated his question.

The officer sprang to his feet. *"Da!"* he said, in a tone that expressed obedience and subordination. Rather unsteady on his feet, he pushed the bench abruptly to the wall. Then he kicked the Starshina in the backside. The man continued to lie motionless. "Get up, Starshina, get up!" he roared. There was no indication that the man had felt the kick or heard the command. The officer stood looking down at him thoughtfully, his hand fingering the watch in his pocket. "Yes," he said frowning, and looked back at Vassily again. "If you would help me," he asked politely.

Vassily stood up and came over to his side. The officer stooped forward with legs wide apart, firmly gripped the collar of the Starshina's tunic, and with a sudden jerk pulled him up. He then dragged him to the bench by the wall and sat him up. Vassily held the swaying man while the Lieutenant removed his cap, tunic and *gimnasterka,* a smocklike uniform blouse. He unbuckled the wide leather belt from which depended the pistol in its holster, and paused, holding the gun in his left hand. After a moment's reflection he buckled the belt over his own around his waist. The Starshina wore no shirt. A short, sleeveless undershirt partly covered his hairy, muscular chest. With one swift movement, the Lieutenant slung the Sergeant to his shoulder, carried him to the water tap, and asked Vassily to turn on the water. A strong, thick stream shot from the tap. The officer slid the drunken man from his shoulders into his arms, pushed his head under the water, and kept turning the motionless body so that the cold water ran now over his neck, now full into his face. Vassily helped by holding the Sergeant's legs. Soon the man showed signs of life. He groaned, gurgled and moaned, and began to kick more and more vigorously. The Starshiletenant was obviously enjoying himself; he turned his victim's head under the cold water until the gurgling groans became roars, the screams for help of a drowning man. The man struggled so hard that it seemed impossible to hold him. But his tormentor didn't stop until he spoke his first clear words. Then he removed the man's head from under the tap and signaled Vassily to let go of his feet. They crashed to the floor and flailed about for balance. The Lieutenant loosened his grip and the Starshina stood; he staggered, but stood, shaking himself, gaping at his superior. Then he turned slowly away and vomited, gurgling and groaning. When he straightened up, the Lieutenant seized him by the nape of the neck and bent his head low again. "Get it all out of you," he encouraged him, slapping his stomach. Finally he commanded, "Wash yourself, wash your face and head." The Starshina washed, and then staggered around soaking wet, looking for his clothes. When he spotted them, he marched toward them; only his first two steps were unsteady. The Starshiletenant fingered at his collar, removed his neckerchief of gray linen, and handed it to the Sergeant, who dried his face, hands and neck with it. The officer took back the cloth and thrust it into his trouser pocket. He watched as the other man slipped into his gimnasterka and buttoned it. The Sergeant's face grew thoughtful; he looked anxiously around the room. Suddenly he lifted his padded jacket, looked on the bench, under the bench, under the table. Now he was sober and alert. "My pistol," he bellowed. "Where is my pistol?"

"Here, you drunk," the Starshiletenant said, laughing. He handed the weapon to its owner, who quickly buckled on the belt. He jammed his hat onto his tousled hair and reached for his jacket.

"Should we go?"

"What's the hurry?"

"I'm sick of it all, of drinking and—driving." The man's face darkened; he spat in disgust on the floor.

"Let's sit down," the officer said, pushing the bench back to the table and with a gesture inviting Vassily to sit. Vassily took his place at the end of the bench. The Starshina sat down with visible reluctance. The Starshiletenant addressed his subordinate in a tone of pedantic correction. "I have done these men an injustice," he said, "for I accused them of having the minds of capitalists and usurers. But they are honest men and have kept their word. Look here, Ivan Yakovlevich!" He dug his right hand into the pocket of his jacket, drew out his clenched fist, and slowly opened it before the eyes of the Sergeant, who watched with bated breath. The watch with the red strap lay on his palm. He displayed it like a magician.

"What is that, Ivan Yakovlevich?" the officer asked.

"A watch." The Sergeant answered hesitantly, after a long pause.

"Yes, a watch, and this tovarishch has given it to me. For our work. And there is one just like it for you, except that yours has a blue strap. Tovarishch," he said to Vassily, "deliver the Starshina his watch."

Vassily already had the watch in his hand. He held it out to the Sergeant. The man reached out for it slowly, looked at it, held it to his ear and then to his open mouth. "It runs, it runs beautifully." The Lieutenant, too, put his watch to his mouth.

"You are right, Starshina, it runs beautifully. Shall we put them on?" They helped each other. When they were done, they beamed happily at each other.

"Watch, watch, watch!" the Starshiletenant cried jubilantly, waving his left arm in the air.

"Watch, watch!" The Starshina followed his example.

Then they fell into each other's arms and shouted in unison, heads over shoulders, "Watch, watch, watch!"

They sat down again, grave and deliberate once more. "I drink to your health and thank you." The Starshina repeated the sentence like a formula.

"No reason for thanks," Vassily said. "We thank you." He drained his glass. As he set it down, he said with a trace of a smile, "Vassily Vassilevich Khomniuk."

"Right!" the Starshiletenant said happily. "And now we must go, brother." He stood up and slapped the Starshina vigorously on the shoulder. The two men touched their forefingers to the brims of their caps, turned left about face and marched one behind the other to the steps that led up to the door, singing, *"Esli zavtra voïna* —if war comes tomorrow." At the steps they turned around and called in unison, *"Dosvidaniia—*good-bye." Then they bounded up the steps and were gone.

* * *

After their departure the room was very still. Antek swept the bottles, glasses and remnants of food together, cleaned the table as best he could with newspaper, and then propped his elbows on the tabletop and his head in his hands. He smoked negligently, without removing the cigarette from his mouth. Tadek sat down on one of the steps, his big, rather shapeless and black-haired hands resting on his thighs. The powerful muscles of his trunk were outlined under his coarse black sweater. His eyes, set deep in their sockets, were a muddy brown, and very small. His left eye was almost invisible. It was clamped shut, either out of habit or as the result of some injury, and gave to his coarse face an expression of cunning and cruelty. The low forehead and the huge, florid, lobeless ears intensified the impression of brutality and violence, as did the broken nose. A soft, feminine mouth and weak chin accentuated rather than diminished the look of dangerous brutishness.

Vassily sat at his end of the bench and smoked. His attention had turned to a greasy piece of newspaper in which the bacon had been wrapped. It was a copy of *Izvestia*. He started reading a Tass dispatch when the high, chirping voice of Tadek made him look up. Then he went back to the newspaper article. It was about the Russian advance in Finland. There were only a few lines, without commentary, but he seemed to be meditating on the meaning of these lines and not to hear what Antek growled in his direction. Since Antek had spoken German, the words could be meant only for him. Antek would have spoken Polish to Tadek, who knew no other language. He spoke German with Vassily because he understood neither Ruthenian nor Russian and Vassily did not speak Polish. "I was talking to you," Antek said. He scarcely raised his voice, nor did he turn his head or remove the cigarette from his mouth. "I asked you whether you understood what Tadek said."

Vassily glanced indifferently at Tadek and turned back to the greasy newspaper.

"Tadek thinks we ought to beat you to a pulp." Antek's voice held neither anger nor excitement. It sounded light and friendly, and his smile was rather impish. But there was an unwonted earnestness in his boyishly reckless, laughing eyes.

"Tadek wants to beat me to a pulp? But why?" Vassily did not sound especially surprised or interested, and certainly betrayed no sign of fear or anxiety.

"Because you didn't obey my order."

"Obey your order? Who orders whom?" There was no challenge in his tone.

"I give the orders. That should have become clear to you these past few weeks. It's quite a while since we picked you up on the highway. Or have you forgotten that you were almost starving, without a coin in your pocket? Is that right?" And when Vassily didn't reply, he repeated, "I ask you: is that right?" He spoke quietly, the smile appearing and disappearing.

Vassily watched these facial changes with interest. "Yes," he said casually, "that's right."

"We took you into the company. You've had plenty to eat, a roof over your head, and a *spravka*, your working permit from the Meat Trust. The director is my man. He does what I tell him. Is that right?"

"Hm," Vassily agreed.

"We've worked well, made good money. Everything went along fine at the Trust. The director got his share, and goods at government prices besides. Our group was the best. Haven't you had money in your pocket right along? Plenty to eat, drink and smoke? Who fixed it all?" Antek waited for a reply.

"Why all the questions? What are you getting at?" Vassily seemed to be growing impatient.

"You're to answer me, not ask questions. Or else—"

"Or else?" Vassily spoke with an undertone of boredom.

"Or else I'll tell Tadek to beat you to a pulp. He's burning to." The smile remained on Antek's face, but his forehead was flushed red.

"Very interesting," Vassily said. "You give the orders and he does the pounding." His eyes slid toward Tadek, coolly probing. "I suppose you wouldn't have the guts."

"Someone has to do the dirty work. He's good for nothing else, and he likes it. I enjoy watching."

Vassily swung his right leg over the bench and sat astride it. He waited in silence. Whatever Antek might have had in mind, Vassily's display of nonchalance decided him. The smile imperceptibly gave way to an expression of sheer murderousness. *"Na nego!"* he snapped. "At him!"

Tadek rose and started toward the bench. He shuffled, bending his knees at each step, as though his legs could barely support the huge weight of his body. He held his hands in front of him; his mouth was open and he breathed hard. Vassily sat on the bench as if the whole affair didn't concern him. Tadek lunged forward—and snatched at the air. Vassily had sprung from the bench and was standing by the wall. Before Tadek could turn, he had leaped behind his back, into the middle of the room. He stood there, his hands dangling, as Tadek turned and charged him. The hairy hands were outstretched, the stubby fingers curved like claws. A gruesome sound streamed from him, a combination of gasping breathing and enraged moan. Suddenly there was a muted thud. Tadek opened his eyes—both eyes—wide, veered about, collapsed, and remained lying on his face. He lay motionless, a great shapeless log, felled by an uppercut that had landed with perfect precision on that weak chin. Vassily glanced at the recumbent form, then stepped over it, rubbing his hands as if he were washing them. He sat down in his former place, pulled the pack of cigarettes toward him, and searched for a smokable cigarette. Antek, who had not stirred during the brief struggle, sat with an amazed, incredulous smile on his boyish face. "Is he dead?" he asked, without moving his head. He showed no fear, no concern, only a kind of horrified curiosity.

Vassily took his time replying. He had found a broken cigarette, and now cautiously lit it. It sufficed for a few hasty puffs; then he threw the butt to the floor. "Dead? Out for half an hour at most. Maybe he'll come to sooner." He glanced out of the corners of his eyes at Antek. "And you'll take that hand of yours out of your pocket, or the same or worse will happen to you."

"You can box." Antek paused thoughtfully. "You seem to have a talent for lots of things." He ignored Vassily's threat.

"I can box, yes, and you take that hand out of your pocket now. I can handle knifers, too."

"This is the second time in seventeen years I've seen Tadek look like that." Antek removed his hand from his pocket. Vassily walked around the table, gripped Antek's shoulder firmly with his left hand, and put his right hand into the man's trouser pocket. Smiling, Antek did not resist as Vassily put the big clasp knife into his own pocket. Antek went on as if nothing had happened: "That time there were eight of them set on him, with knives and clubs. And today one, two—and he is on the floor." He looked down at Tadek. "And hasn't moved yet." In a tone of almost reverent admiration he added, "It happened too fast for me to see. Where did you learn that?"

"When I worked as stableman for Count Kinsky after the war, there was an English trainer there. He taught me. There's nothing to boxing when the opponent doesn't know how," Vassily replied quietly.

"Kinsky? Was he a Pole?"

"Czech, I think. But the stables were in Austria."

"Were you there long?"

Vassily looked at him in astonishment. Why all these questions? What was Antek getting at? "Two years."

"You learned German there, didn't you?"

"There and earlier, in the army. I served with the Austrians."

Vassily had answered reluctantly, and Antek seemed not to notice. He had dropped his smiling mask and seemed thoughtful and serious, as if he wanted to find out something and wasn't sure what he was hunting for.

Vassily sought a way to evade Antek's questions. As if it had just occurred to him, he said suddenly, "I'd better explain that business about the watches. That was what you were mad about, wasn't it? But I had to give them to the Russians."

"I know why you gave the Russians the watches. Because you promised, isn't that it? You wanted to play the gentleman—or the good honest worker. A promise is a promise, and all that tripe." His eyes probed Vassily's face.

"They kept their word and so I had to keep mine," Vassily said. "Don't forget, I was the one who did the negotiating with them. I made the agreement: five trips, two watches. They made the trips and we took in a nice little profit. Anyhow, the watches were mine, weren't they?"

"Aha, that is it: they were yours. I didn't see it that way. The watches belonged to the company. They were your investment in our business. I'm the chief; I'm the one who gives orders. And I gave an order that the Russians weren't to have those watches."

"But why not? Two watches: that's chicken feed. Why should we cheat the Russians?"

"Why not? They cheat everybody, don't they?" He had abandoned his usual manner of speech. The hypocritical friendliness was gone, and passionate hatred had taken its place.

"Why do you care?" Vassily replied. "They haven't cheated you. They kept their promise."

Antek gave a piercing laugh. "I thought you understood, but you're only another dumb peasant. Where did you say you learned German? Working and in the army. Do you know where I learned mine? In the pen, my friend. Brandenburg Penitentiary. Four years of it. In at nineteen, out at twenty-three. On a pickpocket rap. And you know who taught me that trade? My father, my own father. Taught me right down the line. At three I was begging, at five nabbing stuff at the market, at seven getting into people's houses to pick up whatever I could—'Does Mr. So-and-so live here?' Nobody dreamed a kid would be up to anything. I was pulling my own weight at an age when other kids are still learning their multiplication tables. At nineteen others go to the university or start work in a factory. My university was the pen. I learned all I needed there. When I came out I believed in nobody and nothing, and was afraid of nobody and nothing. And felt nothing but hate, hate, hate. My father lay dying. 'Antek, forgive me. Go for the priest. Give me water.' I didn't move. I let him croak, and before he was cold I started searching the house. I found plenty. Enough to set up a vegetable shop. I bought Tadek too. He belongs to me. Like a dog. He's belonged to me for seventeen years. I'm his master." He stood up, walked around the table and knelt beside the unconscious man. "See if there's any vodka left."

Vassily accumulated two fingers of vodka from the glasses and bottles standing around, and also knelt beside Tadek. "Hold his head," he said, and poured the liquid cautiously between his teeth. Tadek spluttered, swallowed, opened one eye, closed it again, and grunted. When Vassily gave him another drink, he swallowed eagerly. Then he sat up without help, and in a moment was on his feet again. He stretched and with a squealing sound of pain raised both hands to his chin. Clumsily, he began to massage it.

"Tell him the pain will go away in a week or so."

Antek said a few words to Tadek, then turned to Vassily again. "He says it isn't too bad and he isn't mad at you."

"How come?"

"Because I told him so. I told him everything's all right and we've made up again. Because a guy can talk to you." He flashed a swift, sidewise look at Vassily. "I mean, you understand. Or do you?" This time he rested his eyes on Vassily, probing, questioning, searching.

Vassily smiled reassuringly. "I know what you mean. What about your mother? You only mentioned your father."

"My mother? My father sold her, when I was three years old. To a man who took her to South America. She was blond, I think, and had a nose like mine. Sometimes I dream about her. He got eight hundred crowns for her."

"Have you ever heard about her or from her?"

"She didn't last long. Lungs. My father used to boast that he'd pulled off a good deal."

"He sounds pretty bad, your father."

"Bad? While I was with him, I didn't realize what he was like. When he taught me, he wasn't strict. Hardly ever hit me and had a lot of patience. I had decent clothes and a bicycle and money in my pocket—though of course he would always do anything for money. Other things besides steal and sell women."

"You mean he always wanted more."

"No. He never kept it for long. Cards, dice, horses—the more he had, the more he played, and he never quit until it was gone. When he won once in a while, he laughed like a child and gave me all kinds of presents. Always trying his luck; he was always trying to prove he was lucky, and he never did. I thought about it a lot. In the pen. You have plenty of time to think there. That's where I started to hate him. When I came out, I'd made up my mind to kill him."

"Just as well you didn't have to—I mean, that he died of his own accord."

"I suppose so, when I think it over, but at the time I hated him for that too. There was no use killing him when he had only a few hours to live."

"So then you found his dough and bought a vegetable shop."

"Yes, there was dough, in the old hiding place. But I wasn't able to buy the store."

"Why not?"

"You need a license, and the police knew about the four years. They got my picture and fingerprints and the whole file from the Germans. They don't just let you go. The German cop takes you to the border, and the Polish police take over there and see to it that you go back home. And they keep after you: were you here, were you there, were you mixed up in this and that? Of course they couldn't pin anything on me, but it's a while before they let you go— and then they keep an eye on you."

"Did you get your chance finally?"

"Not me. I went to see the police chief. He was smart, right on his toes. 'We've heard that line before. Going straight—selling vegetables—nice cover-up for a fence.' Then I went to a lawyer. 'If you apply to the courts, you'll get your license. But I wouldn't advise you to; it might take forever. Better to buy your shop through a straw man.' So I did that. I bought it in Tadek's name—and the police chief was right. About fencing, I mean. And they never caught us. I'd learned plenty, in the pen and before. They searched the place time and again, but never found anything. Not once. Finally they got tired of it and stopped looking. Seventeen years— Tadek and me."

"So you never had a chance at honest work." There was no blame, merely statement of fact.

Antek glanced at him. "You understand, Vassily, all those cops and district attorneys and judges don't want us to go straight. Just the reverse. They're chicken breeders."

"Chicken breeders?"

Antek smiled. "That's the way I figure it. When a man lives on chickens, he wants to breed them, breed more and more of them. And what are we to the police and the judges if not chickens? They live on us just the way poultry farmers do on their birds. If we weren't there, they wouldn't be needed. They don't want honest men; they want thieves and forgers and burglars. That's their livelihood."

"There may be something to that. But how does that affect you?"

"If a man's a crook and they won't let him get into a new field, then he goes on being one. If only because it's the easiest thing to do. So the police chief was right; I became a fence. Onions and turnips every day, and once in a while, every so many months, real goods. And they never caught me."

"So you liked that?"

Antek studied Vassily thoughtfully before he answered. "Liked it? Sure. It was a kind of game. Slaving away, pushing the handcart around day after day. Haggling with the farmers over a few cents more or less on a bushel. Tending that shop from morning to night, and all the while, in my father's hiding place, there was enough to buy thirty shops."

"Yes," Vassily said, "I can see it was a good life. Eating, drinking and women. With money, you can have a lot of fun."

"If you have fun every day, it's no fun. But once in six weeks or in two months I went on a bender with Tadek, always with Tadek. 'Eat and drink as much as you like, Tadek; take a girl, Tadek; spend as much as you please.'"

"What about you? Did you only look?"

Antek laughed. "Of course not. But I got more of a kick out of Tadek. Especially with women."

"Why?"

"They didn't mind going with me; they weren't out for money so much. But they were afraid of him. So I bought their fear, too. It gave me a kick, to buy their fear."

"And you never liked any one of them enough—you know what I mean—so you really wanted her without paying. For good. That's never happened?"

"Never! I know that game. Saw the whole thing when I was a kid. And the stories I heard in the pen! Most of the trouble in the world comes from women. There are men who live on women. That's their business. I pay for mine. Even those who say they don't want money. If a dame wants to sleep with me, she has to take money. She sells and I buy. That way it's a straight business proposition."

"Oh well, I suppose that has its good side!" Vassily said. "So you went on like that for seventeen years and didn't get sick of it? Always the same thing, you and Tadek?"

"I was right! I knew I was right!" Antek pounded his fist on the table. He stood up abruptly and sat down facing Vassily on the end of the bench. It was obvious that he wanted to say something decisive and could not overcome an unaccustomed embarrassment. "Smoke," he said, pushing a pack of fresh cigarettes toward Vassily. He took one himself and lit it with slow, thoughtful movements. "This is the first time I've ever talked about all this. The first time in my whole life. I can only talk to him"—a slight gesture of his head in Tadek's direction—"like to a dog. He catches the drift; he's as faithful as a dog. He'll kill for me and let himself be killed for me. All well and good. But talk, talk . . . ? He doesn't understand. You understand, and yet you don't say much. When you ask a question, I know you understand."

"Go on talking. A fellow can understand another fellow if he wants to."

"And you want to. That's it. You're right, a man can't go on having the same thoughts and wanting the same things for seventeen years. I looked for other things. Where do you think I looked? In books. It wasn't easy. When you've just learned how to read and write decently in jail, and then not even in your own language! But I learned. Now I can read and write Polish and German. You'd be surprised at all I've read. I couldn't count all the books. Before long the inside of my head looked like my shop, full of roots and vegetables, but I was never able to make a decent soup out of it. Still I went on reading, more and more all the time. I just couldn't give it up. You get into the habit—like drinking. Curiosity, wanting to know things—it can become a regular disease. Then one day I got to know the carpenter. There was a carpenter in the yard where I had my shop, and the carpenter's helper there was an older man. Sometimes he sang at work. Always the same song. In fact, just a few words of it. And he sang it like he was threatening someone with it. So one day I took hold of his coat button and asked, 'Say, boss, what's that song you're always singing?' He looks at me hard and says, 'I'm no boss. Maybe he is.' And he jerks his head toward the inside of the shop. 'I work for him for seven zlotys a week. I suppose you're a boss with your store. That's why you don't like the song. But one of these days it will be sung so loud that all the bosses will find it bursts their eardrums. It's the 'Internationale' I'm singing: 'Arise, ye wretched of the earth.' And now let go of my button, Mr. Boss.'

"I let go of his button, but somehow he didn't let go of me. 'Wretched of the earth.' The words kept going around in my head. Whom did he mean by that? Was I one of them? Anyway, one day after work I asked the fellow to have a drink with me. Over the fifth glass I heard a lot about Marx and Engels, the international proletariat, the treason of the Social Democrats, and just who are the wretched of the earth. By the time we parted, I was his brother and shouted right along with him: 'Death to the bourgeoisie.' We saw a lot of each other after that, and he gave me pamphlets. Later he took me to meetings. Pretty soon I was sure I belonged to them, because we hated the same people. Still, I didn't let myself be taken in; I was nobody's fool. I sounded them out every so often. I wanted to know whether they were honest about it. And except for the fellow travelers and the loudmouths, I found they were. They didn't take me into the party, because I was a storekeeper, not a worker, but they were willing to have me as a sympathizer—that's what they called it. And I shelled out when they needed dough for elections, strikes, support of political prisoners. Not too little and not too much. Hitler was just getting started in those days, and in 1934 most of our chicken breeders were starting to flirt with him. The police started hunting my pals, and sometimes I used to have twenty of them hidden in the house. After a while that died down—it was always on again, off again, with Hitler. Then came the business of the Pact. Hitler and Stalin? Some of the guys grumbled, but most hung on. Still, none of them felt easy about it, and as for me, I wanted to stick a pin in the whole soap bubble. But I couldn't give it up. Because then I wouldn't have had anything left to believe in.

"And then came the First of September. The cavalry rode off to do battle as though tanks hadn't been invented. Those that survived went off to Hungary or Romania and left the country to the Germans. It had hit the chicken breeders all of a sudden that they weren't Poles at all—weren't they really Austrians? And if it hadn't been for Versailles and Wilson, wouldn't they be still? Good old Austria, dear old Franz Josef, beautiful Vienna; they'd be able to get on with the Germans, wouldn't they? Because after all, Germans and Austrians were practically synonymous. And then *bang,* the Russians were here! That was when the running really started. Anybody who had anything or was anything could think of only one thing—getting away; across rivers, over mountains, driving, riding, walking, not stopping until they got to some place where Stalin wouldn't catch up with them. Those who couldn't get out went underground."

Antek poured himself a glass of water. He was hoarse from talking so long. He lit another cigarette. "At the time, you were still in your village on the Prut or the Dniester and didn't see how it was in the beginning. But here we went careening through the streets. Now we were saying that we knew all along it would turn out this way, and nobody'd had any doubts and nobody'd grumbled. Weren't those Russians clever; they got what they wanted without firing a shot, without losing a man. Our saviors! Every time we talked to one of their soldiers or officers, we discovered new miracles. They had an answer for every question and never tired of answering. 'Yes, tovarishch, we've got everything; back home we have plenty. Bread and meat, fat and butter, sugar and chocolate, apples and lemons. And coffee? Coffee too, two plants for roasting coffee in Moscow alone, and don't forget Dneprostroi and the Moscow subway. Clothes? Oho, all you want. You just go right in, tovarishch, into our big department stores, and buy whatever you like. And cheap! No speculator's prices. You buy at government prices, tovarishch—and don't forget Dneprostroi and the Moscow subway. Work? In the Soviet Union everybody must work; who does not work shall not eat, says Stalin. Everyone is given work. As for pull, or dog-eat-dog competition, we don't have any of that. From each according to his abilities, to each according to his merits. Why, tovarishch, we make ten thousand automobiles a day, twenty thousand tractors, a hundred thousand tanks and three thousand planes. Yes, tovarishch, every single day—and Dneprostroi and the Moscow subway.'

"Then there were the songs. Back and forth through the city, from morning to night, in rain and shine, soldiers, platoons, companies, whole battalions, with and without guns, marching and singing: '*Esli zavtra voĭna*—if war comes tomorrow, Katyusha—*Ja drugoĭ stran ne znayu*—I know no other land where the soul breathes so free.' In the beginning it was wonderful, but the mood didn't last. The Russians got down to business. Our people, I mean those in the executive, went running to the party secretariat: this was their day, they thought. They came back like drenched poodles, and pretty soon it was clear that *they* wouldn't be giving the orders. Because their idea of communism was years out of fashion. Marx, Engels, Lenin? On the scrap heap. Now there's only one kind of truth, the be-all and end-all: *skazal* Stalin—Stalin has said. He's said everything. He must be Moses, Jesus, the prophets and apostles, Solomon and Goethe and everybody else who ever said anything worth remembering all wrapped up in one—and of course he's lived a couple of thousand years, because otherwise how could he know and say so much?

"There were quite a few veteran Communists around. They didn't like the way things were going. They had the Communist catechism in their heads, blabbed about criticism and self-criticism, and about all they'd done and suffered for the cause. They told how they'd been beaten in jails, been starved and persecuted, for years. For the cause. The *nachalniki,* the partinye, listened to them, shaking their heads or nodding: 'Fine, very good. Those burzhui, those fascists, terrible.' But that didn't satisfy our veterans, and they kept coming back. Then one day one of the leaders, Verkhovsky, said to them, 'Comrades,' he said, 'we see you are good fighters, the real advance guard. You are valuable revolutionary elements and we have tremendous respect for you and your achievements. But you have to grant, comrades, we must judge you by other standards; must expect more from you than we do from the masses. You're the elite, so you must be guarded from mistakes. Ninety-nine times good and one time bad is a hundred times bad, says Stalin. A real Bolshevik must make no mistakes. And you want to be Bolsheviki, members of the Communist party of the Soviet Union, don't you? Don't you?' Did they! They shouted and cheered.

" 'Good,' the nachalnik said. 'Go to the others in your party and tell them what you've heard. Those who come to the Party Committee tomorrow with credentials from the Polish Communist party will be accepted for special schooling.'

"They weren't all idiots, of course, but several hundred showed up with their red cards. They were told to gather in the courtyard of the former governor's mansion. Then trucks drove in: drivers in uniform, two in each truck. Blue-gray coats, red caps, machine guns slung over their shoulders. NKVD—you get it, don't you?' 'Form rows, march, make it snappy.' Forty men to each truck. Off to the station. Forty in each car. Two men with guns guarding every car. 'Tovarishch, where are we being taken?' No answer. 'Tovarishch, my wife, my child, my mother, nobody knows where I am, where I'm going.' No answer. 'Tovarishch, I have no food, no clothes, no soap, nothing.' Then they finally answered, 'We'll take care of all that.' The locomotive whistled—and off they went.' "

Antek fell silent. Bluish shadows hung outside the windows, which were below street level. A dense cloud of tobacco smoke, mingled with alcohol vapors and smells of food, hovered in layers above the table. From the doorway came gasps, groans, whistles and at almost regular intervals a whimpering sigh. Tadek was snoring. His huge body lay on the steps as if crucified; in the twilight its indistinct outlines made it seem more grotesque than ever.

It grew darker. The glowing dots of cigarettes cast a reddish gleam on glasses and bottles. "So you hate the Russians so much, Antek? On account of the Communists they shipped away? Have you heard from any of them?"

"Just from one, from whom I got the story. He managed to give them the slip near Kamenets Podolski. There the bunch of them were divided up. *Donbas* for some—the coal mines. Others were sent north to chop wood in the forests. I hid the fellow for five days. He was about done in, not so much from hunger, cold, tramping and hiding, as from hate. I never would have believed a man could be so eaten up by fury and hate. But no wonder. A man of thirty who had eight years in the jug behind him. Rebellion, inciting to riot, sedition, all that stuff."

"I see. What happened to him?"

"He rested up and ate till he got his strength back. Then I gave him some rags and ten American dollars and he got across the border, to the Germans."

"To the Germans? But—"

"Takes you aback, does it? Not me. He's gone to help Hitler. That's the way it is. He'll be a professional killer. And if ever a nachalnik or a partinyi falls into his hands, he'll cut him into little pieces."

"Why should a Russian fall into his hands? They're friends now, aren't they—the Germans and the Russians?"

Antek laughed. "Friends! Wait until they get at each other! And they will, as sure as you're sitting here."

"That may be," Vassily said deliberately. "But about your friend who went over to the Germans—do you think that was right?"

"Don't you? What else could he have done, with his hate?"

"He and the others might not have got themselves into a position where they had to hate."

"I don't understand that, Vassily."

"Your friends went to the nachalniki with accounts of all the mistreatment they've endured from the burzhui, the fascists, the capitalists. The nachalniki listened and couldn't make very much out of these stories. Because many of them have suffered worse things, and heard about worse things. Those stories weren't new to any of them; at most, they were a proof that the burzhui haven't changed. Aside from that, they weren't much interested."

"There's something to what you say. What surprises me is the way all of a sudden you can talk so much, and be so smart." He laughed. It was not a pleasant laugh. "You understand the nachalniki too well; you think they were right. I've trusted you; there's something about you that made me think I could trust you, and now—"

"Now I'm no longer the sort of person you thought I was, and you're sorry you told me all this. Is that what you mean?"

"Maybe," Antek murmured.

"You're too hasty, Antek, and too ready to settle a thing with a yes or no. I'm going to explain what I mean."

"Go ahead!" Antek blazed up. "What the hell's stopping you? I want to know all about it."

Vassily frowned; deep furrows appeared between his brows.

But they vanished as he spoke, lightly, easily, and the hint of a smile played around the corners of his mouth. "Don't kick up such a fuss, Antek."

Antek laughed, an honest, liberating laugh. "The way you say that! The way you say that!" he repeated. Then, in a milder voice, "All right, explain it to me," he said.

"You said I understand the nachalniki and side with them, and you're ready to dislike me for it. Because to you understanding and accepting are the same thing. But they are two differect things entirely. It isn't so very hard to understand the nachalniki. A lot of them spent ten, twelve, fourteen years in Siberia. They saw thousands die of hunger, cold, or clubbed to death. That was before the Revolution. Millions more died during the Revolution. Compared to that, what your friends went through in Poland seems pretty small stuff. You may say they're all pulling on the same rope, all want the same thing, hold the same principles. But is that really true? Didn't you yourself say that they talked about Marx and Engels and Lenin and found out that it was all old hat to the partinye? Then suppose the local Communists had been appointed to jobs where theory counted? There's only one law nowadays: *skazal Stalin*. And what Stalin says is miles away from what used to be said. So there'd be misunderstandings, mistakes, clashes, and pretty soon the cry would go up: sabotage, counterrevolution! And then who would be in Siberia? All of them. The nachalniki first of all, because they'd be the ones responsible. Responsibility terrifies them. It always reeks of prison, forced labor, Siberia, death. Why take risks? The reason the nachalniki rounded up your comrades was because they were so persistent. So you still have courage? You believe? Then you'll have to learn the Bolshevik way. First we'll try your strength by work in the mines and forests, and if some of you kick off, so much the better. Men who've put in twelve hours of heavy labor a day don't try to find out whether *skazal Stalin* is always right. Political maturity, submission to the Soviet regime, means being afraid! Your nashalniki had that political maturity. And can you hate a man because he's afraid? Or because he's in such terror that he's driven to teach everyone else to be afraid?"

Antek gave him a searching look. "I don't get it, Vassily. You're a peasant, and then sometimes you talk like a preacher, or like a book. Where the devil did you learn all that? From the horses?" There was distrust and envy, eagerness and suspense, in his question—and also a suggestion that he had fired off a last, carefully guarded cartridge.

Vassily smiled as if remembering a happier time. "Yes, from the horses. If people went to horses to learn, things would be lots better.

If a horse is mean, some man is always to blame. The horse has been treated badly, beaten for no reason; his pride's been offended or his spirit broken. Such horses see every man as an enemy and fight them, avenge themselves if they can. But let someone come along who has patience, who means well by the horse, and the animal will understand. With a good word, a pat, a carrot and a lump of sugar, he can change a vicious horse into a reliable one. That's how it is, Antek."

Antek let this pass. His suspicions seemed to have evaporated. "Look here, Vassily," he said quietly, "I'll tell you why I'm so sour on our Russian saviors. It's not only the business of our own Communists. Taking it the way you do—about their fear, I mean— I might even feel sorry for them. But what disgusts me about them, what makes me sick to my stomach, is their greed and their jealousy. You know our boss. With his broad mug and pig's eyes and his everlasting 'I need, I must.' He speaks Polish pretty well. His parents came from the district of Lodz, they moved to Odessa under the Tsar. He spoke to me on the street one day—that was during the first days of the occupation, and we were still full of enthusiasm. There was another man with him. Me, I was polite as could be, tried hard to understand what they wanted. Then the fat fellow began talking Polish. They were hungry, he said, and there wasn't anything in the restaurants. Oh, I said, if you'll do me the honor, I can offer you a simple meal, a glass of vodka, a glass of beer? They did me the honor all right. I've read about people lost in the desert without water, and then at last they come to a pond. They don't dip up the water and drink it; they throw themselves into it, clothes and all, and gulp and gulp until they can take no more. That's the way those two Russians fell on the food. They stopped not because they couldn't go on, but because there wasn't anything left. Cleaned me right out. Then they belched and said, 'Kulturno.' And they went on saying that when they looked around the apartment. I ask you, my three little rooms; you know the joint. They fingered the tablecloth, they tried the springs on the sofa and examined the curtain material. They looked in the chests and shook their heads in amazement over the clean linen and said, 'Kulturno.' And then they went into the bathroom, and everything was kulturno. But it wasn't kulturno by the time they left. Looked like it had been used by a hundred thousand savages from the steppes.

"And the way they asked questions! 'How many people live in this flat?' and 'Who does this belong to?' and before long I realized they would have liked to move right in and send me to the devil. Luckily Tadek came in with his mother, and they toned down when they saw those two. You know him, and that mother of his with her beard and deep voice—takes some getting used to. So they said, 'Dosvidania,' and our fathead asked me to show them to the main road because they wouldn't find the way alone. You can imagine I led them in a circle; I didn't want them ever finding the way back to my place again.

"But all the way back the fat boy kept nagging at me to come and work for him. He was director of the Meat Trust, he said. Fine work, and he'd show me how I could earn a good living at it. I went and took Tadek along with me only because I wanted to find out whether he was lying. Couldn't really believe a fathead like that would be the director of such a big organization. But he was, and since one job's as good as another and you've got to have a document to prove you're working, we signed up.

"And then it started. Pants today, shoes tomorrow, a shirt next day, and of course a watch, and vodka every day. 'You have everything and we have nothing.' 'You live like lords and we sweat.' 'We starved and suffered to liberate you.' 'I want that, I need that, I must have that'—the same refrain every day. All right, I thought. We didn't have to kill ourselves on the job. Made as much as we pleased; every rag was worth plenty of rubles. The Russians bought whatever they could lay hands on—and when the watches started coming in, we didn't know what to do with the money rolling in. Watches! The smugglers brought them in by the thousands —they know when the market's right. From Hungary, from Romania, cheap French and German watches, and the Russians bought and bought and paid whatever we asked. You'd think they'd found their rubles in the street. We had to pay the dealers dollars for the watches. In the beginning we had no trouble getting them; the little people who'd saved a few hundred were glad if you bought their dollars from them. Because everybody in Poland has dollars; that's been the standard currency for hoarding for ages. But now, with the Russians here, they're scared of keeping them. The official rate is five rubles to the dollar. It rose to twelve, to twenty-five, to sixty! Naturally that meant the watches were more expensive; after a while a lousy Lohengrin or Lorelei brand watch cost a sackful of rubles. It was the same with sewing machines, typewriters, pianos. What a boom! How could I let such a chance go by? Especially when the nachalnik hung on to me like a leech.

"All of a sudden the bottom dropped out. No watches, no dollars, no rags, no rubles—nothing. Trading stopped. Practically everybody had been assigned to work, because it got harder all the time to go out on the street without a spravka. Our organization was built up, and we were told that everybody had to meet his quota. So-and-so much a week, so-and-so much a month. Go out to the villages, buy up cattle and pigs—at government prices, what's more—and deliver them. By then the nachalnik had an apartment, and his wife and three children had come from Russia. Every single day he wanted something else. At last it got too much for me; I put on my best preacher's face and told him that unfortunately he was mistaken if he thought I was the Gosbank; did he really think I could get all those things on my wages and on the commissions I would never earn? Then he gave me the dope. With us, he said, the perekup-shchiki earn all they want. Forty per cent for the trust and sixty for the black market. All right, nachalnik, I can do that too. But how am I going to persuade the peasants to sell for thirty kopeks a pound live weight? And how am I going to bring the animals here? Transport? he asks. Have to see the army on that. The boys want to live too. And the peasants should thank God that they get anything at all. They won't for long, because sooner or later it will all be kolkhoz.

"So is that what I waited for? Just enough to eat, and risking God knows how many years in Siberia? I've had enough of rotten deals, enough of being a thief and a fence. If I wanted to live like that, I could have gone over to the burzhui, gone to Romania, to Hungary. There I could live high on what I have. Is that what I wanted? No, I stayed on here. I waited for them, for a decent life, waited to be a man among men. And what am I? A thief among thieves! Now I'm afraid too, just like them. But still that wouldn't be the worst of it. If only I didn't feel every minute of the time what strangers they are to us, and that we exist only for them to exploit us. And how they envy us! For everything. There's nothing worse than their envy—not even their lies, their *skazal Stalin,* their 'You have everything.' Not even their thinking they can put it over on us again and again. I tell you, I can't stand it; I'll die of disgust."

These last words burst out of him in a scream. When he went on, it was in a lower voice: "I suppose you'll have an explanation for that, too, Vassily. But I don't want to hear it. I don't want to understand any more. Don't even want to try. Never again. You're a decent guy, and since you already know so much about me, you might as well know this: I was wild when you gave the Russians those watches. I wanted to squeeze one more ride out of them. And those were the last watches we're going to see for a long time. They aren't being smuggled over any more. You saw how—"

"No more watches?" Vassily asked, as if that were the principal thing.

"No more watches, I tell you! And they don't give a damn about cash."

"Where do you want a ride to, Antek?"

"To the San, and then across. Tadek's coming too. If you'll come too, I'll be glad."

"You mean you think we ought to go over to the Germans?"

"Why not?"

Vassily stood up, walked slowly over to the door, turned around, came back to the table and stopped in front of Antek. Antek raised his head and looked up at him with tired, sad eyes. "I just have a question I must ask you," Vassily said. "If you were up for execution and were given the choice between being hanged and shot—which would you choose?"

"The bullet's the easier death," Antek said.

"If you go, you're choosing the harder death. That doesn't mean I'm not disgusted with what's going on here. It's possible to understand something and yet feel disgust for it. I'm not trying to bluff you; I want to help you. Now if you want to go, go. I'm staying."

Antek sat and reflected. After some time he asked, "What makes you stay? You weren't building any hopes on them, the way I was."

"I could have got out; of course I could have. But I wanted to see with my own eyes whether they were really so bad, whether they ran things as badly as their enemies say."

"Well, what do you think now, Vassily? Is it like under Hitler or isn't it?"

"No, Antek, different. Their lies are somewhat more attractive."

Antek nearly flared up again, but thought better of it. "I get you," he said. "Rope or bullet." He gave a shrewd laugh.

"That's about it," Vassily retorted.

"Well, I know enough about them, but not about you. So if you stay, I'll stay too."

He stood up, stretched, and reached for a cigarette. "Give me a light," he said good-humoredly. After the first puff he shifted the cigarette to his left hand. "Let's make up, Vassily, and since you're smarter, you be chief." He extended his hand. There was a certain solemnity in the gesture, and Antek flushed with embarrassment.

Vassily shook hands with him. "Not the chief, that's nonsense. We're comrades, Antek."

"Fine. And now let's go get something to eat. We've talked ourselves out."

Both men laughed. They awakened Tadek and helped him to his feet. Then they stepped out into a dark, still, littered courtyard. They passed through a number of yards. In one of them, behind a rampart of assorted trash, was a light. They walked around the huge heap. Between it and a garden fence was a walk of large square slabs of stone, which led to a gate. Antek unlatched the gate and they entered the garden. A narrow path, lined by bare wintry bushes, led to a one-story whitewashed cottage, with bright-colored curtains behind polished windows, surrounded by gnarled fruit trees— Antek's home.

When they entered the small hall, the kitchen door opened, releasing a mixture of appetizing smells. A huge woman stood in the doorway, filling it from jamb to jamb: Panya Jadwiga, Tadek's mother. "You're late tonight," she growled. In one hand she held a lit cigarette, in the other a glass half full of vodka. The men gave her good evening and went ahead into the main room, where the table was already set. Everything shone with cleanliness, smelled of soap and floor wax. Tadek removed his boots and went first to the bathroom. He returned with a scrubbed look, shaved, his wet hair neatly parted. The others had meanwhile polished their boots. Antek came back from the bathroom clad in a heavy red bathrobe over flannel pajamas, feet in felt slippers.

When Vassily came in, freshly shaved, he found Antek explaining the change in plans to Tadek. Tadek kept turning his head to look at Vassily, grinning in spite of his sore chin. He held out his hand to Vassily. Vassily took it, and suddenly it closed like a vise around his own. The pain, unexpected and violent, sent tears to his eyes. It was fairly clear; Tadek wanted to redress his own disgrace, and so Vassily played along, writhing and twisting as though the pain were beyond bearing. But Tadek only squeezed harder, intending to force him to his knees. Suddenly a savage pain flashed through his elbow; he had to let go, and stared dumbfounded at Vassily. Smilingly, Vassily waved a warning finger at him. Tadek felt his elbow, which had stopped hurting. "He's a devil," he piped to Antek.

Meanwhile Panya Jadwiga had filled the soup plates. Crimson beet soup with garlic-flavored meatballs. The men spooned it up rapidly and in silence. Before they had time to catch their breath, plates of pork goulash with cabbage and potatoes stood before them. Their glasses were filled with foaming Okocim beer from Antek's ample old stock. Panya Jadwiga, who had already had her supper before "the boys" came, watched over the table, replenished their glasses and plates, and in between kept sipping at her glass of vodka or puffing at her cigarette. She sat straight, a colossus of a woman, with iron-gray, stringy hair parted in the middle and coiled in a bun at the back of her head. Her forehead was low, her mouth shaded by thin gray whiskers. She seemed to have a perfect set of teeth. She spoke little and never addressed her son by name; she called him *syn*—son. As she filled his plate or pushed a glass over to him, there was a look of belligerent love in her cold blue eyes. She had noticed that Tadek, though he shoveled in his food the same as ever, was having trouble chewing. "Been fighting?" she asked in her low-pitched masculine voice.

"Just a playful tussle, Panya Jadwiga," Antek hastened to say.

"With him; he's all right, Mother," Tadek added in his falsetto voice.

Panya Jadwiga sipped her vodka. "Jujitsu or boxing?" she asked professionally. Apparently there was some basis to the story Antek had told that Panya Jadwiga had once been connected with a circus as giant-woman.

"A little of everything," Vassily said lightly, and displayed his right hand, which was red and swollen. "He has the strongest grip of anyone I've ever come across, has Tadek." He made an effort to speak Polish so that Tadek would understand.

Tadek blushed with childish pride. "Oho!" he squeaked, and patted Vassily's hand as if to prove to his mother that their fight had only been in fun. "He's all right, Mother!" he repeated.

"It's all right for boys to fight if they make up after." She cleared the table and came back with a large plate of fruit. Then she left the room.

The men sprawled lazily on their chairs. Tadek cracked nuts between his fingers and offered them to the others. Antek glanced at the wall clock. "Twenty after seven. We still have time."

"About the passports, you mean?" Vassily asked. "Yes, we have plenty of time. We're supposed to come at nine, and if we're late it doesn't matter much. They work all night anyhow."

"So in two hours or so we'll be Soviet citizens. Our dearest wish is about to be fulfilled." Antek smiled his artificial smile.

"What difference does it make?" Vassily seemed disinclined to more conversation, for he got up from the table, sat down in an old wing chair by the fireplace, and closed his eyes.

For a while the silence was broken only by the crack of nutshells and Tadek's munching. Then there was a grating noise from the hall. Tadek stopped cracking nuts and listened. Vassily opened his eyes. Antek's expression changed from anxiety to vexation at the disturbance. "See who's outside Tadek," he said.

A smooth, polite voice asked in Polish whether Pan Antek was in. Then a man entered the room. He went up to Antek with a smile of intimacy and extended his hand. "Good evening, comrade," he said with a slight bow. "Forgive my disturbing you at this late hour. But we both have no time by day, and the matter is really urgent. Quite urgent." He threw a rapid glance at Vassily.

Antek caught it and introduced Vassily: "This is Comrade Khomniuk, my friend. He works at the Meat Trust. And this is Comrade Mermelstein. Comrade Khomniuk speaks Russian, Ruthenian and German."

"Aha, German? Well, well, that's very convenient. You're Ruthenian, aren't you, Comrade Khomniuk? Probably an old Austrian too? Like all of us, eh?" He laughed vacantly. "But now it makes no difference." With a little bow he turned to Antek again. "I haven't come alone, you see. There are two people with me, close acquaintances, a young couple. They have a request to make of you. No, request isn't really the word for it. It's a matter of business, as it happens. They're standing in the yard. Can't very well let them freeze out there, eh? If you don't mind, I'll bring them in, eh, and then we can discuss everything at leisure, and where it's warm too, eh?"

"By all means." Antek frowned at his volubility. "Ask them in. Though I'm no longer in business. Haven't been doing any for a long while. Tadek, go along with Comrade Mermelstein and show the people in. I'll get dressed."

With the animation of a retrieving dog, Tadek posted himself beside Comrade Mermelstein. With a polite bow to Vassily, the man went toward the door, followed by Tadek, who had the air of escorting a prisoner.

Antek rose and went to the other room for his clothes. Vassily followed him; he also wanted his boots. "I just wonder what the comrade wants with his 'people,'" Antek said.

"You know the comrade fairly well, eh?"

Antek laughed. "So you're saying *eh* already. Of course I know him. He used to borrow money from me. There's a man who always needs ten times as much as he has. Probably he wants money again, eh?"

"That may be. Was he a comrade in the old days?"

"Of course not! He's a lousy crook! I hear them coming. I'll tell you later, if you're interested. But you'll soon see for yourself."

Antek was dressed by the time the outer door opened. Mermelstein was the first to enter the room. Behind him came a young woman, head largely hidden by a vivid kerchief, and a tall young man who removed his hat as he entered the room. Tadek followed. The two were introduced as Comrade Linhan and his wife. Antek played the host and asked them to take off their coats and sit down. But they sat as they were.

Linhan was a man of about thirty, tall and heavy, with a full, pink face and a thin mustache that barely covered his upper lip. Despite that masculine feature, his mouth seemed pretty in a womanish way. His face was rather attractive at first glance; it had an air of bonhomie and gaiety, but this rapidly gave way to indolence and disinterest. His stubby fingers and broad, hairy hands seemed out of keeping with his whole bearing.

His wife was considerably younger than he. She had pushed her green silk kerchief back as she sat down, revealing wavy red hair over a high, pale forehead. Her face was rather long and earnest, and she held her lids lowered, so that it was difficult to tell the color of her eyes. There was a note of masculine firmness about her thin, pale lips. Her raccoon jacket was hip length. Beneath was a narrow skirt, slit on both sides. Her knee-high boots were smart and obviously of good workmanship.

She wore this outfit with an air of going along with the times. Everyone was doing that nowadays, trying to look like Russians and workers. These metamorphoses were all the more grotesque since most of the Russians who had come to Poland had promptly procured good suits, silk shirts, excellent boots and shoes, and they often wore expensive furs. In the early days of the occupation the Russians had been recognizable by their tattered or worn clothing. Now, a few months later, it was the natives who out of necessity or hypocrisy proclaimed themselves by casual or proletarian dress.

Mme. Linhan had nothing casual or proletarian about her. She was dressed like an actress who is trying to represent a Soviet woman on a Western stage. She had created her own version of contemporary Russian fashion, a stylized and becoming way of dressing. It was as though she hadn't seen the Russian women's threadbare coats and jackets, their shapeless canvas shoes with holes in the soles, the red, blue, green and dirty-white berets that sat on their crudely cut or stiffly braided hair. Of course, there were other models she might have thought she was copying: older Russian women who indeed were costumed in boots, kerchief and fur jacket. These women came shuffling along in huge, creased, dirt-grayed men's boots, much too large for them, and often worn over bare feet. When they wore a *shuba,* a fur or fur-lined coat, it had been patched innumerable times, kept in the family for generations, or obtained by chance or barter. They never went out without covering their heads with a shawl of thick wool, inherited from mother or grandmother. How many children had been wrapped in this same shawl to protect them against the biting cold? It had been rolled up to serve as a pillow, stretched on the floor as a sort of sleeping mat when there was no bed. But it lasted, the good old shawl, and could be wound around the head again and again, even though it transformed the head into a shapeless lump and robbed it of all trace of feminine charm.

They were proletarian figures—lumpenproletarians, who, according to the doctrine of the new rulers, no longer existed. Nowadays there could be only workers, peasants and Red Army men.

But Mira Linkhand—Linhan was a distortion which she had silently accepted—wanted to have nothing to do with the proletariat or with the state of the world for which the Soviets were fighting. She was far from all that, and yet so close that for months she had been living in terror: terror that she might have to go back, back to the place she had come from.

BOOK THREE

THE GIRL UP FROM THE CELLAR

Ninety-nine times good and one time bad is a hundred times bad, says Stalin.

IRA LINKHAND WAS NO LONGER A PROLETARIAN, AND NEVER wanted to be one again. She had come up from under, from a gloomy basement hole in the Twentieth District of Vienna. In 1914 the war had uprooted her parents from the ghetto of a small town in Eastern Galicia and deposited them in the capital. There her father engaged in house-to-house peddling, really a form of beggary. All his free time was spent in the synagogue. At last he had nothing left to sell on his peddler's tray. Her mother died of weariness, of a profound distaste for life; her father followed suit a month later; and at the age of six Mira was sent to an orphanage. That was her first stage.

Everything offered her there was a great improvement on all she had ever known. The shapeless smock that covered her skinny little body was neither becoming nor new, but it was clean and not torn. The bed was neither soft nor comfortable, but she had it to herself. The food was not tasty—she had nothing to compare it to in any case—but it came to the table hot, on a plate from which she alone ate. No one disputed her right to the slice of bread. After the hopeless misery of her earliest childhood, the orphanage was an absolute haven, a decisive step forward.

But she soon learned that there were better things still than these elementary comforts. Her instinct led her to the proper means for securing these better things, even within the narrow confines of the orphanage. If you wanted them, you had to be good, diligent, attentive and obedient. She became the best-behaved, most diligent, most obedient girl in the orphanage, and the best pupil in the school. She spent all her energies on pleasing. At first she was naïve and clumsy about it; as she gathered more experience and began understanding people and conditions, she grew more subtle.

At fourteen, almost on the day that her first menstruation took her from the twilight state of puberty to a certain maturity and dignity, she left the orphanage with the best wishes of the directors and a recommendation to the owner of a flourishing millinery shop, Frau Adele Kadisch. Mira learned to be a milliner. With the same conscientiousness she had shown in school, she threw herself into her new job. Softhearted Frau Kadisch gave her not only an apprenticeship, but also a home, which she had never had before. No work was too much for Mira; she did all the errands and never protested, never tired. But she soon saw that hard work was not enough; in this field one had to have personal taste and ideas, and these she lacked. However, she copied as much as she could grasp from those more talented. She never became a first-rate designer, but in a pinch she could substitute for one.

A visit to the movies, at the invitation of one of the other girls, decided her future. The film, produced on a tried-and-true formula by one of the Hollywood factories, spelled out the wish dream of millions of ordinary girls. In the end the boss—young, handsome, courageous and idealistic—married his stenographer and carried her off to his palace, a mansion equipped with the ultimate in American convenience and luxury. Poor Mira, however, was so literal-minded that she came away with the belief that you had to be a stenographer in order to attain to such success.

She was sixteen at the time and knew she was not as beautiful as the girl in the film. But she knew also that her developing body, her gold-tinted eyes, red hair, and long, shapely legs were attractions that counted and that could increase her value. She had heard often enough from her experienced and candid workmates that "some men are wild for virgins because the pigs think they're something if they get there first." That remark had given her a great deal to think about, and she had come to the conclusion that not all men were as honorable as the boss in the film, and that virginity had its practical value. Therefore she would keep hers until she could trade it for something worthwhile. She would be a stenographer like the girl in the film, more efficient, more farsighted, more competent than others, and as an additional gift she would bring the man of her dreams her intact virginity.

Man of her calculations, it was, rather than man of her dreams; for Mira was no dreamer. Consequently she did not attribute to him the face, stature and attributes of the actor in the film. Rather, she saw him as a complex of abilities and possibilities for improving her situation.

The first year Mira saved every tip she received from the women whose hats she delivered, and later she saved her modest wages. Her employer never thought of charging her for board and room. She looked on Mira as a poor, helpless orphan, a fine, hard-working girl who deserved all possible encouragement. Frau Kadisch was a widow who had arranged good marriages for her two daughters. She was an excellent businesswoman and enjoyed a tidy income from her millinery firm, so that she could afford to keep the girl as if she were another daughter. Perhaps she even considered adopting her. But there was something about Mira that troubled her —a feeling that at bottom was distrust. This girl had nothing to give, no warmth, no feeling of any kind. She seldom laughed and never wept, never expressed a desire, never made friends. She simply went about her duties in so quiet and dry a manner that she seemd to fend off any show of motherliness. Yet a child that had grown up in an orphanage must be yearning for a maternal hand, Frau Adele thought. It never occurred to her that for this girl the memory of her mother was linked with perpetual hunger, with misery, dirt and hopelessness.

Frau Kadisch was a motherly person, and all her instincts led her to treat this girl in a motherly way. But Mira, so cool and unreceptive, soon made Frau Kadisch modify her own behavior. When she was alone with Mira, she stayed within the confines of a general amiability which had been a routine manner for her with all her dependents over the years. But when she gave a tea, a coffee hour or bridge soirée for fellow members of the many philanthropic clubs to which she belonged—on which occasions Mira served or supervised the service—her tone to the girl was distinctly warm and maternal. Watching these little tableaux, the good ladies could only conclude that here was a case where Frau Adele was once more showing her heart of gold. And how could these philanthropic and for the most part prosperous women show their admiration except by becoming loyal customers of Frau Adele's rather expensive millinery shop? Thus the old saying about casting bread upon the waters was once more confirmed. Mira might be a rather poor object for affectionate maternal feelings, but she was clearly good for the business. All the more reason to keep her, to be nice to her; otherwise "the child" might come to harbor dangerous ambitions. Consequently Frau Adele asked her daughters henceforth to give Mira their cast-off clothing.

Both daughters responded energetically. And since they were rich and spoiled young women, their offerings were all in excellent condition, came from the finest shops, and were only a little out of fashion.

Mira, practical and sober, took all this in her stride. She said "Thank you" most politely, but showed no surprise. She had simply failed to understand Frau Adele's attempts at kindness. Maternal feelings aroused no echo in her, could not do so, for she had no way to receive emotions. She calculated causes and effects and quickly came to see why she was being given all these things. It was a form of payment, she decided, for the advantages she brought her benefactress.

Nevertheless, these clothes became a milestone in Mira's life. For nearly two years she had been living in an atmosphere devoted to the embellishment of femininity, and the clothes helped her find her own place in it. Intelligent as she was, she had perceived that dress was not only the principal thing in life to vain and empty-headed women, but the weapon of the ambitious. Among the clothes that were given Mira, many turned out not to fit too well, or not to suit her. One of the girls in the shop recommended a seamstress, a Czech who was a genius at alterations. Mira fought a number of hard battles with the woman, and emerged as the victor. Out of every five dresses, three would be altered without charge for Mira; the other two would be sold and the proceeds divided. The arrangement proved profitable to both sides. Mira appeared before the ladies at Frau Adele's parties in ever more charming outfits, and her savings bank—an ancient photograph album with a key—became filled with banknotes.

The hoard was decisively increased by a find she made in one of the many handbags that had been given her: a lipstick case, a compact and a perfume bottle made of a metal that looked like gold. Walking on one of the fashionable avenues of the city, Mira spotted in the shopwindow of a jeweler a set exactly like the one she had found. The clerk had no objection to informing the smartly dressed young woman that these charming trifles had been made by one of the best English goldsmiths and sold for 2,100 schillings. He showed her the hallmark. Mira thanked him and promised to return. At home she found the same hallmark on "her" set. For the first time in her life she had something that represented a sizable value. The valuables must have been left in the pocketbook out of carelessness or forgetfulness. She decided to set a limit of three months during which she would let the pocketbook containing the gold set lie openly with her other things. Then, if neither of the two daughters discovered the loss and started a search for it, Mira would see about selling the pieces.

In these calculations it did not occur to her that she was playing a dangerous game. She never stopped to consider the possibility that the affair might turn out badly, that it could end with police and prison because the act was, after all, a theft. Although she had grown up in conditions which inculcated absolute respect for law and order, Mira herself, perhaps because she had always been such a good girl, lacked all fear—that element which often guides people toward the "ethical" course. She had no morality, sound or unsound; she was as amoral as a predator who has been given nothing but the strength of his teeth and claws, his swiftness and agility, and is set loose to sustain himself by what he can kill. And like the predator, she had no capacity for remorse if she inflicted pain upon others. She had scarcely any concept of suffering, either for herself or for others. She suffered no more than she rejoiced. Her only feeling was discomfort when, waking or dreaming, she was swept by recollections of her earliest years—memories of that atmosphere filled with the smells of hunger, dirt and utter destitution. Such memories came to her in the form of sense impressions. They haunted her, and she would do anything to rid herself from their threatening presence. There was only one way of being sure that she would never again be sucked back into that atmosphere. The richer you were, the more surely was the way back blocked off.

Good and *better* became realities which could be expressed in figures. A thousand schillings were good, three thousand were better. If she could keep the gold things she had found in the pocketbook, she would have that much more capital. It did not trouble her that the losers might be upset over the loss; it equally did not occur to her to interpret this find as a just disposition of providence. She did not tell herself: Frau Adele's daughter is rich and the loss of 2,000 schillings doesn't mean anything to her, while it will help me a good way along. She felt no need for such reassurance. With each day that passed after the find, her certainty increased that she would be able to keep the compact, lipstick case and perfume flask; and out of this certainty emerged the courage to establish an alibi for herself.

Frau Adele usually had her daughters and their families to Sunday tea, and Mira served at table, since both the servants were given their Sundays off. The talk rippled on boringly, no one making much of an effort to be entertaining. These family visits were something of an ordeal for everyone except Frau Adele, who loved to see her daughters. During one of the many lulls in the conversation, Toni, the younger daughter, took out her lipstick and compact and began making up. It was very quiet; the children were absorbed in their *Sachertorte* with whipped cream. Mira looked at Toni's black enameled compact and exclaimed, "What a pretty compact! And the lipstick case matches it. I have a set like that. It looks like gold. It was in one of the handbags. It's awfully pretty, but I'm still too young for such things. I don't use any lipstick and only put a little powder on my nose." She laughed, which was rare for her. While she spoke, she had glanced at each of the sisters to see whether her words aroused any sign of interest. But nothing happened. Frau Adele gave a friendly nod and commended Mira's restraint with cosmetics: "That's very good, Mira." The others smiled for their mother's sake, and the conversation went on spiritlessly. Mira cleared the table, busied herself with the children, and then went to the kitchen to wash the dishes.

Back in her room, she took the cool, smooth pieces of jewelry out of their pouch and held them on her palm. Each one was a different shape, but the same delicacy of line united them, made them a "set," and valuable. To Mira, however, these three pretty toys were nothing but gold, worth so-and-so much, embodying a definite quantity of security. That was Mira's first and decisive encounter with gold.

She tucked the three pieces back into their respective pockets, closed the bag, and laid it on the bureau. Then she read, slowly and thoroughly as she had done many times before, the prospectus of a school which taught typewriting, stenography, bookkeeping and foreign languages.

Next day, shortly after closing time at the millinery shop, Mira sat in the office of the director of the business school, noted for its successful application of modern methods. After inquiring into all details, she signed up for evening courses in typewriting, stenography, bookkeeping and correspondence, and in addition six hours weekly of English and French. She also enrolled for a six-month course, one hour a week, in commodities and currency.

She presented Frau Kadisch with a *fait accompli*. She would not be giving up her work in the shop, she said, but would have to leave every night at six o'clock, because her course began at six-thirty. She had decided to change her occupation because she realized that she could never be a first-class milliner; she had more of a taste for office work. After a semester at the business school, she would be able to help Frau Kadisch with the bookkeeping and correspondence—which, after all, was as important as making hats.

Frau Kadisch accepted all this. As long as Mira did not intend to leave her, she had no objection. In fact, she insisted on paying all the expenses, including tuition and books; and after Mira had been studying for three months, she presented her with a brand-new Underwood portable.

Mira made brilliant progress. She took herself in hand the way an experienced trainer leads a one-year-old filly on a lunge rein. She had no unusual talent. But she did have a singular capacity for work and application. In class she never lost a minute from inattention, and at home she sat for hours over her books and typewriter, learning and practicing. Her Sundays meant ten hours of work. She followed exactly every one of her teachers' suggestions for homework. She drafted endless business letters to Paris, Milan, London and New York. She wrote them in shorthand and on the typewriter, in German, French and English. She typed countless chapters from novels and works of nonfiction. She memorized vocabulary lists and wrote the words down again and again until they were completely familiar to her. She left nothing untried which would help her to gain command of the foreign languages, was constantly on the hunt for French and English radio broadcasts, never became bored listening to radio plays, political, economic, agricultural and scientific lectures, children's hours, advice to housewives —to anything at all.

Her teachers were amazed at the girl, whose achievements far outstripped those of others with far greater gifts. At the final examination, which was staged as a kind of competition, Mira was invincible: she was not only the best among her three hundred fellow students, but she would have excelled girls who had been practicing secretaries for years. With her certificate and the enthusiastic recommendation of the director, she would have obtained an excellent job in a moment. But she had other things in mind. What her teachers thought and said about her was not important; she knew that all this was only the beginning. Gratifying, but still only a beginning.

Although none of the other girls had paid much attention to the course on Commodities and Currency, Mira had thrown herself into it with special interest. While other girls her age were reading novels, going to the movies or playing games, dreaming of love and engaging in flirtations or something more serious of the same kind, Mira brooded over fat volumes on economics, finance and politics. The strange idiom—at first she had had to consult the dictionary to find out even what the words meant—gradually became familiar to her, and soon formed a part not only of her vocabulary, but of her thinking as well.

She had found herself at last. Among all the strange words and concepts, the conclusions and theories, the propositions and instructions, she came to be at home. Stocks and premiums, raw materials and finished products—variable, stable, fluctuating, stagnating, controllable and uncontrollable values—acquired a clear meaning for her. She began to understand what part gold had played in the course of history, why it was advantageous to import certain goods and export others. She grasped the nature of a money economy, the reasons for deficits and surpluses; she understood about inflation, deflation, price stability, security; and in her mind she conducted operations over many countries and across seas, calculating precisely costs, wages, tariffs, transportation and risks. Soon she was familiar with all the major currencies of the world and their relative strengths or weaknesses. And all this she learned after her day's work for Frau Kadisch. No one knew what she was doing; no one hindered her.

She no longer worked in the shop, but only in the office. Without realizing it, Frau Adele had glided into a state that might well be called dependence. Mira never had occasion to make demands; she manipulated matters so that Frau Kadisch anticipated her wishes. For in her simple way this woman drew reasonable conclusions from her experiences with Mira. The girl was proving a blessing; that must be respected. If Mira wanted to take over the of-

fice, which had always been the limping part of the business anyhow, there was no reason why she shouldn't. Frau Adele was too un-
imaginative to foresee any undesirable consequences. Moreover, her
attitude toward Mira had already become a mystic, superstitious
feeling toward a fetish, toward a goose which lays golden eggs, and
which establishes a hold over its master solely through his fear that
it may stop producing.

And Mira truly laid golden eggs. Quietly, unobtrusively, with
few words and a vast amount of work, she transformed the bookkeeping, financing, inventory and correspondence of Adele Kadisch's millinery salon into a model of order, clarity and thrift. It
was all done within three months. Herr Proske, the old bookkeeper
who was longing to retire on pension and had stayed on only for
Frau Adele's sake, began to see that he could leave his duties in
good hands. The girl in charge of correspondence, who worked
half days, was less happy about leaving, since her job at Frau Adele's
entitled her to an elegant hat twice a year. But she too retreated
before the amazing competence of this energetic novice. The books
were started afresh and maintained so that anyone could make sense
of them. Accounts which had remained receivable for years were
turned into cash by polite, terse reminders. The inventory was
cleaned out, stock that did not move sold to shops in the provinces.
Every yard of ribbon, every spool of thread, was accounted for.
Nothing fell under the table, nothing was thrown away, no business
hours were wasted. Mira kept books on everything, wrote the letters,
conferred with the suppliers, kept customers informed of every
change of fashion, attended to the banking and dickered with the
tax collector. After she had been at work for six months, Adele
Kadisch's millinery salon was transformed into an efficient enterprise. A great deal of money came in, far more than Frau Adele had
ever hoped to make; and this fact not only deepened her appreciation of Mira's achievements but also intensified her superstition
about the girl as a bringer of luck. At the end of the year she gave
Mira a bonus of a thousand schillings, a gold watch, and an annual
contract as business manager on a salary of 3,600 schillings. It was
quite a job for a girl barely seventeen.

But this girl neither saw nor felt the exultation of success; she
did not permit herself any sense of self-satisfaction, which might
have led to a slackening of effort. Mira had not been hopeful; she
had simply calculated, and it was neither amazing, admirable nor
gratifying that a careful calculation came out right; rather, it was
something self-evident and predictable. Meanwhile she had not
stopped studying; she now knew far more than was needed to run
a small enterprise like Frau Kadisch's. She spoke, read and wrote

French and English flawlessly, although one would have listened in vain for the special emotional quality that gives these languages their life. For her the words were items she could possess if she could produce them at will. That languages could be used to express grief or gladness, that they could exalt and comfort—of such powers she was totally unaware.

She was unfeeling, inartistic and inwardly uncultivated. She took no interest in anything that could not be expressed in numbers; and what subtlety and slyness she possessed—masterfully hidden beneath deliberate quiet—were the product of an intensive process of thought. To the world she presented the image of a reticent young girl aware of the difficulties of life and armed to meet them. Externally she had been able to "make something" of herself. She looked good, though not especially attractive. Without seeming to primp, she was always clean and neat. For a long time her sole piece of jewelry was the gold watch given to her by Frau Adele. She did not sell the gold cosmetic set after all, nor did she make use of it, for she still did not use makeup. It was listed in her little account book as an article of fluctuating value. Since she scarcely ever spent money, the credit side of this book soon carried a neat sum, accumulated from savings and the sale of her expensive castoffs, but far from enough for her to fulfill an ambition she had already conceived. She wanted to be part owner of the millinery salon. For the present she had to wait, not only for financial reasons, but also because Frau Adele became ill. A serious grippe was followed by complications which necessitated that she stay in bed and limit her activities for some time to come.

After a long rest cure in the south, Frau Adele recovered sufficiently so that she could come to the shop, although only for a few hours at a time. She came and discovered that the business was running beautifully without her. Mira had used the time during which she was in full charge to make certain excellent improvements, and in so doing only confirmed Frau Adele's fatalistic faith in her. Her recent bout with illness had not really made Frau Adele mindful of being close to death—she was only sixty and a woman who enjoyed life thoroughly—but it had roused in her that conventional sentimentality rooted less in ill health than in traditional phraseology. "I felt so bad last night I thought I was at death's door," she would say to her daughters and friends, and would receive the conventional effusions of sympathy. She found she rather liked producing a sensation by saying things like that.

By the time she had recovered, she had mentioned death too

often not to think of a will. The existence of a will would prove how seriously her state and statements were meant to be taken. And an orderly person does not die intestate. She sent for her family lawyer and, behind closed doors as was only proper, acquainted him with her final wishes. The lawyer—interspersing their talk with the usual jokes reserved for well-paying clients—took notes, and a few days later presented her with many covered sheets of legal paper. Frau Adele read the document with childlike respect for the elaborate terminology and legalistic flourishes. But her attention soon flagged as she faced the impossibility of penetrating the thickets of verbiage, and she gave up without bothering to ask the lawyer to explain. It would have seemed like distrust, and she trusted the good man completely. She did not even question him when she discovered a clear error. There—in figures and words—stood 50,000 schillings, and she had meant and said 15,000. "For my dear ward, Mira Rosen, 50,000 schillings." She read the passage through twice, and wondered whether the error would affect any of the other points. But this money was to come from a special fund, the remainder of which would go to charities.

She let the fifty thousand stand.

When the lawyer had taken his leave and the coast was clear, her daughters, sons-in-law and philanthropic women friends did not find Adele in the somber mood that might have been expected after so solemn an act. Rather, she greeted them with a mood of perfect composure. For God had appeared to Frau Adele, had given her a sign, saved her from a mistake, and shown her the right course before it was too late. Naturally that "too late" was far in the future, Adele trusted; but for that very reason the lawyer's error was ideal—an error which in some remote future would make Mira richer and she herself no poorer. For when the time did come— Frau Adele estimated that she had a good twenty years yet (Why not? Her mother had died only three years ago!)—the poor orphan Mira should have the best of everything.

Adele's cheerfulness was no pose. It continued even when ordinary life with its multitude of demands made her forget her recent illness and the joy of being coddled. She forgot her will, too. She might well have lived another ten, fifteen, twenty or more years, had she not been in too great a hurry to cross the street one day. A car driving at breakneck speed ran into her, and her head struck the curb at such an unfortunate angle that she died in the ambulance on the way to the hospital.

If her sudden death was unexpected, the reading of the will provided a number of surprises for all concerned. Her daughters and sons-in-law, who had done some reckoning on the size of her fortune, found that it was far larger than they expected. However much they missed Frau Adele, this was a consolation. And Mira, now in possession of a considerable sum, found herself able to realize her long-considered plan. She had passed the second hurdle in her career. Eighteen years old, equipped with money, experience, knowledge, and an indomitable will, she was able to venture the first step toward independence. And she ventured it. She showed the sons-in-law that she was responsible for the increase in the value of the estate. Would it not be foolish to liquidate a business which their poor dear mother-in-law had been running in name only for the past two years? Rather, this was the time to institute a number of projects she had long had in mind; if this were done, the business would become even more profitable than it had been.

The sons-in-law were convinced. They signed a contract with Fräulein Mira Rosen making her a partner in the firm; she held a 30 per cent share and each of them 35 per cent.

The third stage began well. Mira was entering her nineteenth year. She had a one-third share in a business of which she was the well-paid manager. She was much closer to her goal. It was almost time for the Prince Charming of the film to appear. And so she began preparing herself externally. She invested in her body just as she had invested in her mind. Massage, hairdressing and skin care now had a regular place on her schedule, as stenography, typewriting and foreign languages had had in the past. She became a client of the same couturiers whose clothes she had formerly received secondhand, and she was wise enough to let them tell her what best suited her figure and complexion. As a result, only a few months after she assumed her new role, her appearance changed markedly for the better. She became in every respect a desirable woman. And all her commercial ventures proved profitable. With the investment of relatively small amounts of capital, the value of the firm rose steadily.

During this period Mira struck up a friendship with a French girl whom she had hired for the shop. Angèle was older than Mira and more experienced socially. A pretty brunette who interspersed Viennese dialect with her Parisian French, she was very popular with the other girls and especially with the foreign customers.

Now that she was no longer living at Frau Adele's, Mira had rented a modern three-room apartment near the shop. She offered to board Angèle until she found a place of her own; but the arrangement was so agreeable that she asked her to stay on. And since Mira had no social life, Angèle created it for her. Before long

Mira found herself involved in a whirl of social activities which she accepted rather gladly. For she could learn from them. Mira regarded everything that came her way as a kind of education. Now she learned, because associating with others—receiving guests, being a guest, going to theaters, bars, dances, concerts and museums —was all "part of it." When other people voiced opinions and expressed preferences, she remained silent, but she noticed everything.

Had she been more responsive, she would surely have been a success with men. But she regarded these relations, too, as simply a kind of instruction. Now and then she allowed a man to kiss her; it even gave her a degree of pleasure; but she drew back as soon as she saw the danger of more ardent overtures. To the man her behavior might seem timidity; but in fact it was another form of calculation. She had not yet met the man to whom she could give "it." Give? Rather, exchange it for something of superior value.

Mira shared her apartment with Angèle for two years, and remained untouched in every sense of the word. The business flourished. Mira remained sole manager; the sons-in-law did not attempt to direct things, and in fact learned to trust her as blindly as Frau Adele had done. For it was evident that anything this girl undertook was bound to succeed. The day came, however, when they thought it advisable to introduce her to the former owners of a similar large enterprise in Germany. In view of the impending political changes in Germany, Herr Futtermann and Herr Burger had liquidated their firm and were now looking for investment opportunities. For Mira, they had come along just in time. When they offered to buy into Adele's Millinery Salon, Mira declared that she would only sell the entire firm, and she named a price that stunned her partners. To their further astonishment, after prolonged negotiations she obtained it. After the sale of the firm to Futtermann and Burger she had a capital of half a million schillings or (as she herself was now accustomed to reckon), about eighty thousand dollars, deposited in a Swiss bank. She remained on for several months, managing the firm at a good salary, and then withdrew. Angèle, too, was leaving—returning to Paris to marry a bacteriologist whom she had kept waiting a good many years—and Mira decided to join her. She wanted to look around in the wide world for a sphere of activity commensurate with her abilities.

But Freddy Linkhand entered her life.

It happened on the highway between Paris and Deauville. Mira was on the way to the resort with Angèle and Raoul, Angèle's new husband. Raoul, who could just barely drive a car, had been persuaded into buying an ancient jalopy. When it stopped on the road exactly 91 miles out of Paris, Raoul did not even pretend that he could do anything about it. He leaned against the vehicle with a philosophical air and pantomimed expressively at passing drivers.

Soon a young man stepped out of a flashy convertible with an Austrian license plate, and after a few minutes' examination, declared that the trouble was major and that the car would have to be towed off to a garage, where it would require at least two days' work by expert mechanics. Angèle broke in with the practical remark that in that case she hoped he would haul the car to the nearest garage and take them all on to Deauville. It would be a great favor to two newlyweds and would give him the company of a charming young lady who was also his fellow countryman. Angèle gestured grandly at Mira, who responded with a quiet smile.

Such was the beginning of a gay week in Deauville. Freddy Linkhand took rooms in the same hotel as Mira and her friends.

The proprietors of the hotel immediately assigned the best suite to Freddy Linkhand. There were Linkhands all over the world, and they were all very rich. Mme. Rachelle Linkhand, whose villa in nearby Trouville was famous for its paintings, sculptures and carpets, might well be a relative of this young man. That he was rich was evident at a glance to a woman with thirty-six years of experience in hotelkeeping. The newlyweds were given No. 33, Mira No. 39 on the same floor, and Freddy's suite adjoined it, although it had a separate staircase. For, Mme. Ruchti reasoned, if he was a member of this group and chose to stay at her modest hotel, he was doing so only for the sake of the red-haired girl with the serious face, who was obviously neither a cocotte nor an upper-class girl out on a spree, but an enviably unspoiled and desirable young woman. Linkhand, who was both rich and handsome, probably wanted a girl *pour le coeur*. The rich could afford anything, after all.

The proprietress was not far wrong. Freddy Linkhand was a real Linkhand, one of the very rich ones. Mme. Ruchti judged people with the shrewd eye of a hotel owner. For her purposes and by her lights, M. Linkhand was first-class.

However, this was not the opinion of Linkhand senior, A. L. (Albert Leo) Linkhand. Freddy's father regarded him as a *strop,* which in the language of the gem dealer is a stone that is virtually unsalable because of some defect which cutting and polishing cannot take out: either poor color, or some foreign body imprisoned in the stone. When A. L. Linkhand called his son a strop—only in his secret thoughts, of course, for he loved him as well as he loved his other two children, possibly even better—he had his reasons.

For Freddy was not only stupid, uncultivated and unpolished;

he was also lazy. Boundlessly lazy. He had learned nothing and knew nothing. No private or public school would keep him. In spite of the most attractive salaries, tutors declined to try to teach this yawning, indolent boy who was interested in nothing. As a young man, his education was on the level of a ten-year-old. Although he could speak three languages—he had stayed briefly in various French and English boarding schools and had, as was the Linkhand custom, spent a number of years with relatives in France, Belgium, England and America—his vocabulary in these three languages was as limited as that of a child. His reading matter consisted of detective stories and automobile magazines; it took him three months to wade through a real book. He did nothing and had no desire whatever to work.

Freddy's mother, Mme. Rachelle Linkhand, née van Taagen, shared her husband's opinion of the boy. She might have resigned herself to the fact that he was lazy, uncultured and ignorant. But she could not bear her son's passivity. If only he had turned out a spendthrift, a gambler; if only he had revealed some *outré* passion. But her Freddy had no interest in anything. Aside from his rather clumsy hands and movements, and his conspicuous ears, he was a good-looking young man. But what girl in proper social circles would have talked with Freddy for more than five minutes without starting to make fun of him in the sixth? Mme. Rachelle came from a large family which had turned out generations of money-makers, scholars and artists. She had looked forward to this late-born son with a great deal of tenderness, and had lavished patience and devotion on his upbringing. But he had turned out an utter nonentity. What was worse, the whole huge Linkhand and van Taagen clan was aware of this undeniable fact.

Gustav (G. G.), the older boy in New York, and Freddy's sister Elinor, Lady Godbrooke, in London, would shake their thoroughbred heads sadly when the talk turned to Freddy. They were sincerely sad, for envy was no part of their psychology. They were so wealthy that the extra inheritance which might be theirs because of their brother's inadequacies scarcely counted. And Father Linkhand had too much respect for money and its power for good and evil to leave much in the hands of a lazy blockhead. The time had come for him to think of legacies: the family had recently celebrated his sixty-fifth birthday. Money, however, did not matter much. What did matter was the sense of solidarity which had marked the whole Linkhand dynasty for generations. All the Linkhands in Paris, London, Vienna, Berlin, Amsterdam, Brussels, Warsaw, New York, Buenos Aires, Rio de Janeiro, Caracas, La Paz and Bombay knew about the strop in the family of one of their most prominent members. Not that they would drop him. The family would look after any Linkhand who needed help, even through his own misdoing. That was a tradition already centuries old. But such a case had never yet occurred. If the living Linkhands could have gone for counsel to all the countless dead in their tombs, the founders and ancestors of the dynasty—traders, bankers, scholars, scientists and doctors, Talmudists and cabalists—all those ancestors would have shaken their wise old heads. For *they* knew that even the gods struggle in vain against stupidity, and that in such a case there is nothing to do but accept fate.

Not that Freddy Linkhand had no contact with other people, no friends or no girls. He understood all about the way simple people lived their lives. If, for example, the gardener's helper Alois confided to him that he could not marry his girl because he still needed 525 shillings to buy furniture, Freddy not only realized that furniture was essential for marriage, but also that it took money to buy it. Here was a problem that could be settled with no more trouble than the writing of a check. And so he wrote the check and took pleasure in Alois's pleasure. Marie, the chambermaid, and Leopold, papa's chauffeur, who had patiently taught him how to drive a car, also found him sympathetic to their cares. And they shared their joys with him as well. He was far more at home with them than with the members of his caste.

None of Freddy's relatives and acquaintances, not his parents nor his friends below stairs, would have recognized Freddy at Deauville. For he was an altogether different Freddy, a Freddy in love. In the past the valet Robert or a grateful Alois had supplied Freddy with girls as the need arose. Sex was a convenience; he had never experienced love in any form. His relationship to the opposite sex was like that toward his car. Both were good to have and cost money.

Now Freddy Linkhand was in love. In love with this serious red-haired girl who sat beside him and watched as he steered his car with careless skill. They spoke little, and in simple, commonplace sentences—Mira's low-pitched voice and Freddy's cheerful tenor exchanging simple questions and answers. They did not make conversation; they talked. And what each needed to know about the other was transmitted within a few hours. She learned that he was the son of the Viennese Linkhand whose big house in the city and whose villa in Hietzing were known to all and sundry, whose wealth and reputation were practically a byword. And he knew that she was not from his social class, but a girl who had worked all her life and accomplished more than others who also work. And the ease with which they communicated gave him courage and *élan,* made him soar above himself, changed him into something more than the Freddy Linkhand whom all the Linkhands quietly despaired of.

Angèle, who thought she knew Mira perfectly after an intimacy of two years, found herself confronted by a miracle which had taken place within a few hours. Mira, whom she had observed so closely, whom she knew to be inhibited, frigid, old-fashioned and prudish in her dealings with men, was transformed; she had become a buoyant, youthful, smiling, infatuated Mira.

She was infatuated, because the time for her to fall in love had come. The phantom from the film, the marriageable boss, had assumed flesh and blood, was sitting beside her. Her calculations had been correct; the right person had been found. Now she would do all that had to be done to convert him into a factor in her life, the life she wanted to live.

It all went according to program. Mira and Freddy lay on the sun-baked beach and told each other about themselves, while Angèle and Raoul swam far out into the sea. Freddy saw a young body with lovely thighs and long legs; he did not see the ugly feet which were Mira's cross, because she was wearing bathing slippers. He saw round, full, well-shaped breasts, golden eyes, and genuine auburn hair. A beautiful young woman lay beside him, talked with him, listened to him. Everything was so delightful; and he had done it all alone, not with the help of Robert or Alois. Besides, this girl was not interested in a few hundred schillings, for she had money of her own. Yes, he liked her enormously and wished they could stay like this forever.

Mira saw a strong young man with a broad chest, muscular legs, the face of a lad utterly without cares, well nourished, and untouched by struggle. And she thought, quietly, that she would like to sleep with him even if he were not A. L. Linkhand's son. But since he was, since the boss from the movie had really come to earth, the figures must all square. In the interests of that consistency, he could have "it" only on their wedding night. Not a day sooner. Mira Rosen vowed this to herself during her flirtation (which was no flirtation) with Freddy Linkhand on the beach at Deauville.

Freddy did not get in touch with his mother until the third day after his arrival. Then he called her just after he came from the beach, and said enthusiastically into the telephone, "Hello, Mama, I'm here. How are you? I've found wonderful company. Will I be coming to dinner? No, I'll just drop in; I'll be eating with my friends. Oh, wonderful people, a couple from Paris, a young professor and his wife, and a young lady from Vienna. Charming. Don't be angry, Mama. *Küss die Hand,* Mama! Yes, possibly this afternoon, just for a few minutes. Küss die Hand!"

Rachelle Linkhand was reflective as she set the telephone back on its hook. This was not the Freddy she had left behind three weeks ago in Vienna.

She did not see her Freddy that afternoon. He was on the beach with Mira all afternoon, returned to the hotel, dressed for the evening, and then all four dined together. They had a gay time, and toward midnight they went for a drive, laughing and singing. They drove through Trouville and Freddy said something about a surprise, stopped in front of a villa, but learned from a servant that Madame was at the casino—in Deauville. Mama's villa, Freddy explained as he turned the car. He drove to the casino and invited the others to come in with him and see what it was like. They did not even pause at the "small tables." Freddy led the way to the *cercle privé.* "Linkhand," he said to the attendant at the portieres, and the four were allowed in.

Mira found herself in a scene straight out of the movies. Well-dressed ladies and gentlemen, superbly poised croupiers, low voices, the quiet click of *jetons.* At the "highest" table sat eight men and two women; one of these was Freddy's mother, in a simple black dress of matte silk and no jewelry except a string of black pearls.

"Greetings, Mama," Freddy said, walking up to the table. Mme. Rachelle stood up, saying, *"La main passe,"* and turned to her son. He stooped to kiss her hand, while she rapidly and discreetly surveyed his friends over his bent back. With a mother's and woman's instinct, she had instantly realized that her son was interested not in the brunette but in the red-haired girl who stood there rather stiffly. A lady? No, but certainly no adventuress either. But Freddy— what *had* happened to him?

There was no time for questions. Rachelle had already placed a hand celebrated for its beauty on her son's arm and was being introduced: Mme. and Professor Tornier of Paris and Fräulein Mira Rosen of Vienna. She paid a compliment to Professor Tornier that was really meant for his charming wife, remarked to Mira in German that she was pleased to meet her and had never before realized that such lovely red hair could be found in nature. Mira responded with a smile she used to keep for her finest clients, and with a somewhat masculine bow. (Mme. Rachelle was sure: no, not a cocotte!) Then she turned to her son, the perfect understanding mama, and said in English that she liked his friends. She excused herself then;

unfortunately she had to go back to the table and give the poor devils she had robbed a chance to recoup their losses. Would they all come to tea at her home the next day, at five o'clock?

The tea at Mme. Rachelle Linkhand's fulfilled its purpose admirably. On the one hand it displayed the wealth and splendor of the Linkhands, and on the other hand it provided the hostess with information and some surprises. Information about Mira Rosen of Vienna, and surprises about her son Freddy, so transformed by love that his mother scarcely knew him. And this shy, monosyllabic Mira, who turned out to be a self-made girl, was certainly no gold digger. Rather, she was inexperienced with men. She had fallen in love, only God knew why, with that silly son of hers.

At seven-thirty, while the two couples were back at the Maison Ruchti changing for dinner, Mme. Rachelle was making a telephone call to Bad Gastein, where A. L. Linkhand was taking his annual cure. Mme. Rachelle told her husband of the latest developments. She gave exhaustive answers to his matter-of-fact questions. By the time he hung up, A. L. Linkhand was as *au courant* as if he had been present.

After dinner he took his evening walk. This time it served for mental rather than physical digestion.

A. L. Linkhand could trust his wife not to exaggerate or distort anything. If she said something was so, then it was just so. His son Freddy was in love, and the girl was in love with him. He had made up his mind, some time ago, that there was little chance of his son's marrying. Now this premise had to be discarded. It was a fundamental rule with the Linkhands to consider all the aspects and consequences of an event. Under normal circumstances, the family would have had some say in Freddy's choice of a bride. They would have decided on some suitable girl from within their circle, and introduced her to the young man. But Freddy's defective intelligence had ruled that out: no girl of good family would want to be married to him. Now a girl had appeared who was not too impossible socially—but would it not be tempting providence to couple *two* strops? What would be the result of such a union?

Of course, not every affair needed to turn into a marriage. There were instances—though rare—within the family, in which such episodes had been brought to a harmless conclusion by the surest of all means, money. In Freddy's case that possibility could be kept in mind, and things allowed to take their course for the present.

A. L. Linkhand returned to his hotel and telephoned the most solid and discreet detective agency in Vienna. Its director asked no unnecessary questions, but listened closely as he took down A. L. Linkhand's instructions: "Everything about her, from birth and further back. Don't spare expense—work thoroughly—and quickly."

Sixteen hours later a courier brought him a sealed envelope filled with many typewritten sheets which contained all the data the most experienced investigators in Vienna had conscientiously collected about Mira's twenty years of life.

On the same morning that the investigators were ferreting out all the facts of Mira's biography from the basement in Brigittenau to her present holiday in France, and setting down on paper the tiniest details of what they found, a decisive scene in that life was taking place on the Deauville sands.

Mira had spent half an hour swimming with Freddy on a lonely stretch of beach. Then they had lain close together, but not too close, in the sun. They talked little. Something began to cast a shadow over their glorious carefree mood. Two days hence Mira was going to return to Paris.

Freddy, who had not had many desires in his life (and who had hardly ever desired something that was not instantly fulfilled), suddenly found himself up against a wall of unsatisfied desires. The girl at his side was mentioning plans in which there was no place for Freddy Linkhand. He would soon cease to exist for this girl. That much was clear to him. But to do anything beyond that, to oppose these plans, try to dissuade her, was something he did not even consider. Fleetingly, it occurred to him that he might also go to Paris—there were Linkhands there too—in order to be near her. But he had been dependent on his family all his life, had never made a decision on his own, and could not bear the thought of having arguments with them over such a thing. This was the first dilemma of his life, and Freddy's habitual nonchalance vanished before it. He was in love, saw the object of his love disappearing, and protested against this danger with a naïve, pained and rather plaintive question: "But what about me?"

Mira turned her head and looked at him. She knew he meant it, and replied, "I'm sorry, too."

Both fell silent, Mira waiting and Freddy in a state of perplexity that might have mounted to despair if such an emotion had lain within his capacity. "I wish awfully we could stay together," he said.

Whereupon Mira, who had been waiting for this cue, played her trump card. She raised herself on one elbow and looked straight at

Freddy. "I've made no secret of my life," she said. "I'm twenty now and I've worked for my living since I was fourteen. It hasn't been easy. Whatever I've accomplished means more to me than if I'd just stepped into a set of circumstances. I don't have very much money, but I can increase it; I'm completely independent; there's no one in the world I owe any accounting to, and I can make my way anywhere. That's one thing." She paused, for she was not used to talking at length. And Freddy, who had never heard such things in all his life, stared at her in admiration. Then she went on: "You're the first man I've ever felt I wanted to belong to. I know you want me too, and there is really no obstacle to a so-called friendship. But I have my views on that. Maybe they're out of date, but I have them. I wouldn't sleep with a man unless I was married. That's what I've always thought, and that's the way it's going to be. I can't marry you. I wouldn't be a proper wife for a Linkhand. So it's better for us not to think about that. We still have two days; let's enjoy them. It's been a lovely week and I'm grateful to you for it. But in three days we'll go our separate ways and I hope we'll have happy memories of each other." She had spoken in German; now she added in English, "Very, very sorry." Then, obeying an impulse foreign to her, and with a very creditable imitation of passion, she threw her arms around him, pressed her body close to his, and kissed him long and ardently.

What she'd said was simple and clear; anyone could have understood. But Freddy Linkhand did not. Although he had listened with the closest attention, he could not follow her line of reasoning. And even if some of it might have remained with him, the embrace and the kiss, the contact with this alluring body, wiped away whatever had penetrated to his brain. He was left only with a fierce craving in his blood, an intense desire for this body that was momentarily so close to him. He could not yield to the desire; Mira abruptly pulled herself away.

"So you want to go away from me, forever?"

"I think it's best."

"I don't see why. If you kiss me, you love me. How can you want to leave me if you love me?"

"Because I can't play around like other girls you've known. I've told you frankly. The man I belong to is going to marry me."

"Then why don't we get married?"

"Because a Linkhand would have to marry a girl from his own class."

"But you're much nicer than all the girls I see around, a thousand times nicer." There was an interval while Freddy thought with all his might and main. Then, as if hit by a flash of lightning, he announced, "Of course we can marry—even if everybody throws a fit. I have money of my own from Grandma van Taagen—seven hundred and eighty thousand, or eight hundred and seventy thousand—or millions—I really don't know exactly."

"Of what? What kind of money, I mean?" Mira asked, her interest aroused against her will.

Freddy put his finger thoughtfully to the side of his nose. "Oh, you mean what currency? No, not schillings. Francs or dollars, one or the other, I'm sure."

Mira had to shake her head. It was touching, terribly sweet, she thought to herself—but she did not know what to make of it. A man who didn't know the amount of money he had, who didn't even know in what currency—she would never have thought it possible. Were these Linkhands so rich, or was her Linkhand such a . . . ? She did not finish the thought, but promptly decided for the first alternative. If things worked out, she would clear up the uncertainty, she thought.

For the time being, she stuck to her attitude of renunciation. "I don't have to foist myself on any family, and I never would want to. Make a lot of trouble between you and your parents and relatives—no, please, Freddy, put it out of your mind. I like you, very, very much, and I don't want to make you unhappy. Do you want to marry me?"

"Absolutely positively." Freddy loved such expressions.

"Then you'll have to fight. No one can say a bad word against me. The little capital I have I've made by honest work. Don't forget that, Freddy. I'm not ashamed of having come up from nothing, absolutely nothing. Without a father or mother or anyone to help me. You're the first person I've ever spoken to about this. And now —you're a man; act like a man!" She stood up and went into the water. Freddy sat where he was, watching her. He was moved by her legs, her thighs and her shapely hips; but more than that, he sensed that here was the woman who was meant for him, who would be his salvation. He was conscious of her strength, of the power she already held over him; he felt that from now on his life was bound up with that strength.

Almost at the same time that A. L. Linkhand received the dossier from the Viennese detective agency and began studying its contents (File S/11345 A. L. L. re M. R. No copy!), Freddy entered his mother's boudoir. "Nice weather today," he said after kissing her perfumed hand. He slumped into a chair before the open bay window and stared into space. Mme. Rachelle took a cigarette, inserted it in a long ivory holder, lit it, and sat down opposite him. She reached out and lightly patted his cheeks. Freddy's face brightened. Mama was in good humor; apparently she was content with him. Now she smiled as if she understood that something was on his mind and that he needed help.

Freddy blurted it out straightway: "Mama, I'd like to marry Mira," he said. "May I?"

Mme. Rachelle was scarcely surprised; she had been bracing herself for something of the sort. After the briefest of pauses she said, "I think your Mira is a very nice girl, and a very competent one, too." She sounded natural; she did not try to convey anything in her tone. There would have been no point. She knew her son as only a mother could. But hitherto she had never dealt with a Freddy in love. That was unexplored terrain. She knew, though not from her own experience, that lovers were unpredictable. Hence it was well to proceed with caution.

"So you agree with me!" her son said eagerly. "Tell me, Mama, what objection would there be to our marriage? Why shouldn't I marry her?"

With anyone else Mme. Rachelle would have advanced a number of arguments. But not with this son of hers. Instead she asked, "When is it that a man marries, Freddy?"

Freddy didn't know the answer. He shrugged.

"All the Linkhands—I can't list them all, and if I add the van Taagens, there are a great many—all of them, if they weren't attending some university, would have been in business at your age. Each one would have his job, would be doing something, counting for something. And then when a girl—from his own circle, of course—came along and he told her 'I want to marry you,' naturally he could. He'd taken on an obligation and he was able to meet it. Do you understand me, Freddy?"

"I'll meet my obligations too," Freddy said.

"On Papa's money?"

"Why not? He has plenty."

"Freddy, you don't understand money because you've never earned any. You'd do better to ask your girl. It seems—"

"Mama," Freddy broke in, and he was suddenly a new Freddy, "Mama, when you speak of Fräulein Mira Rosen, please don't say 'your girl.' I don't like that."

"Forgive me, Freddy, I—" Mme. Rachelle was breathless.

"You know," this strange new Freddy went on, "if somebody came along and said about you 'that Linkhand woman'—in the same tone that you refer to Mira—I wouldn't like it either. Mira isn't the kind you say 'your girl' about. She isn't that kind of girl at all, Mama. On my word of honor, she isn't."

What a pity, Mme. Rachelle thought; I wish to God she were. Aloud, she said, "My dear boy, I didn't mean it that way at all. I have great respect for Mira. She's serious, capable and hard-working, and young as she is, she's created a position for herself that any man might envy. That's just it."

"Mama, you haven't said everything. She's decent, understand. No funny business with her."

Mme. Rachelle ignored the vulgarity, but she understood, and again thought, What a pity. But she did not want to quarrel with her son right now. Why say no when the thing still hung in the air? What would A.L. have to say? What attitude would he take toward—the girl? She caught herself and corrected the phrase in her mind. Freddy was right. This young woman was no sweet, soft, cuddlesome thing, a cute plaything for a rich man's son, who would subsequently depart with a tear in her eye and a check in her purse. Not this girl. This girl knew just what she wanted. She had her plans.

"Freddy," Mme. Rachelle asked with a gentleness that perfectly concealed her grim thoughts, "what does Fräulein Rosen say about your plans? I assume you've spoken with her."

"This morning, Mama. She told me what she thought. I followed every word she said, but later I couldn't remember. I know this one thing, though; she likes me, and I love her and don't want to give her up. I don't want to give her up, Mama. I want her!"

Mme. Rachelle saw his forehead getting flushed and the tiny bubbles forming in the corners of his mouth. She heard his voice breaking and knew that any word or expression of opposition might throw him into one of those tantrums of his which she so intensely feared. Taking his head in both her hands, she drew him close. "Don't, Freddy, don't. No one has said no. Your parents aren't going to deny you. We want you to be happy, Freddy, my silly little boy. But we must take a close look; we must know whom we are receiving into the family. We are Linkhands, after all!"

"She doesn't care about that."

Rachelle could not help laughing, and Freddy joined in her laughter. He was relieved; it was going to be easy to win Mama over.

"Really not?" Rachelle asked, still laughing.

"Really, Mama. Now I remember what she said." He thought hard. "Something like this: 'The little I have is the result of honest work and counts a hundred times more than money you've inherited or had given to you.' Something like that. Do you understand it, Mama? Is it true?" Timidly, he added, "Please explain it to me, Mama."

"That's splendid—she believes just what Papa and all the Link-hands and van Taagens have always believed. That a person must work. Why is Mira Rosen so proud? She's worked for what she has. If you, for example, were earning your own living—I mean this only theoretically—you could marry Fräulein Rosen today and nobody would have the right to say anything about it. Why is it you don't do anything, Freddy?"

This question, asked so often, should have made him cross. But he replied readily enough, "I get no fun out of it, Mama. What for? I can't force myself. Work is disgusting."

"But Freddy—" She was genuinely distressed.

"You strike me as so odd. You Linkhands and van Taagens with your self-importance and your talk about work. If Alois or Leopold works, I can see why. They have to, or else they'd go hungry. But otherwise, what for? I can live very well without working."

"Do you think Mira would like you if she heard you talking that way? She's a person who has worked all her life."

"Mira likes me, I know that." He brooded for a moment. Then he said—and his mother could scarcely believe her ears—"If Mira insists on it, though, I'll go to work for her."

This was the miracle. Now Rachelle fully grasped what love meant, what it could do. She needed no further proof. This was full defeat. She would say to A.L., It's hopeless to fight against a superior power. All that parents, brother, sister, relatives—all that blood, tradition, teachers, schools, examples, arguments and promises—had not been able to accomplish over the years, a Fräulein Mira Rosen, bobbing up from God knew where, had done in five short days. Your son is ready to go to work. Understand, A. L. Linkhand, your son is willing to work if this girl Mira asks him to.

A. L. Linkhand skimmed through the dossier once, and then read it twice more with extreme thoroughness. He now knew more about Mira than she herself. The dry report was a novel that moved him deeply, the picture of a life that made him shudder and stirred him to profound admiration. This girl Mira Rosen—whose real name was Miriam Rosenbaum, but she did not know it—had been found, delirious and half-starved, at the door of the orphanage. She was then six years old. Still feverish, she had stammered out her name; it had been only partially understood and entered in the register as Mira Rosen. Why should anyone be particularly care-ful about the name of a foundling—especially in the year 1918, when everything was in total confusion? This girl had not been blessed with any glorious gift, and yet she was a phenomenon, one among millions.

A. L. Linkhand, philosopher, brooder, wise man and skeptic, understood this girl, and he also understood that she would be vio-lently drawn to the opposite pole of her own existence. Others, hard-boiled and cynical, might conclude out of hand that Mira Rosen wanted to marry Freddy Linkhand because he was a Link-hand. A.L. knew better. Certainly calculation was an element, for with Mira Rosen everything was calculation. But she was evidently attracted to stupid, lazy Freddy. For she herself was clever enough and hard-working enough for two.

She had no family whatsoever, no relatives of any kind. Her reputation was spotless. From her physical description and photo-graph, she was not bad-looking, and there seemed every reason to think that she could be taught good manners. *Savoir vivre* could be acquired—aside from certain fine points which only a highly restricted group was conscious of. Of course, a few stubborn traces of a proletarian or petty-bourgeois background could not be entirely eliminated; still, they could be made to seem originality—given suf-ficient wealth. But this was all trivial compared to the sterling qual-ities of the girl in question. As A. L. Linkhand looked at it, *she* would be the giver and the Linkhands the gainer in this match. To be sure, once the first glow wore off the marriage, the girl would realize what a simpleton she had taken into her bed. Still, in regard to bed—that might balance out a good deal. Perhaps his son had a special talent in that direction—the boy must have *some* gift. And if children came along, they would be Linkhands—with valuable new blood. . . .

A. L. Linkhand had had his light supper in his living room as usual, and was drinking a glass of mineral water when the tele-phone rang. He was in a mood of rare good cheer as he picked it up. He was looking forward to the conversation with Rachelle, to her clear, still youthful voice.

"Freddy has just been to see me. The boy—"

"Is in love."

"You already know more than I do?"

"Everything."

"And?"

"I have no objection."

"A.L.!" Rachelle screeched, reverting to a bad habit which she had conquered years ago. Then, as though to make amends for this gaucherie, she asked in an especially soft voice, "To a marriage, you mean? Freddy and this girl—this Mira Rosen?"

"Exactly. We've drawn the grand prize, Rachelle."

"What have you had to drink this evening, A.L.?"

"Pure mineral water, Rachelle, as usual. Once I've explained it all to you, I'm sure you'll see it my way. But for the present, just remember this: where we sit is always the top of the heap."

"That much I follow. When is this wedding to take place?"

"First of all there must be an engagement. They don't have to know what tack we're taking. Leave it all to them, you understand. Freddy . . . he may surprise us, after all. Be nice to the girl. I know you can be charming if you want to. Believe me, this will do Freddy a world of good."

"I agree with you on that, and I begin to see your reasoning. Have patience with your Rachelle, A.L. You'll be satisfied with me. I'll call you tomorrow at this time." She changed from German to English: "Bye-bye, old man."

"Sweet dreams, and a long, long *passe* at chemin de fer, my girl."

To any other girl, all that took place in the months between departure from Deauville and the wedding in Vienna would have been a dream. Or rather, that is what she would have called it. Mira had never had any faculty for dreaming. And she had no time, for she needed to have all her wits about her to cope with the polished kindnesses showered upon her by all those many Link-hands, van Taagens, Digenmans, Reynbleks and what nots of the far-flung family. She had to keep herself well in hand, remember every little thing she saw and heard in order to avoid crude blunders. She made the effort to adjust to this milieu not only out of pride and vanity, but largely for the sake of Freddy's father, the only one of the whole tribe who understood her from the first, and whom she understood. Very soon she was linked to him by a sympathy that was a new emotion for her, and that did her a great deal of good. Here was a man! Such people really existed! What balm it was when he talked to her. He always had something new and interesting to tell her. Only now did she begin to understand fully what commerce, business, money, really meant. She began to grasp the whole network of interrelationships, to see what a powerful instrument the family-linked business of the Linkhands was. She learned the history of that business back to the founders, whose activities, as early as the beginning of the eighteenth century, had brought them into contact with monarchs, statesmen, generals,

princes of the church, oriental potentates, scholars and adventurers
—with men of importance throughout the world.

Precious stones—the diamond, clear as water or shimmering
with bluish, rosy, yellow or greenish light; the emerald, with its
mysterious warm green glow; the ruby, ranging from darkest red
like coagulated human blood to lightest, noblest pigeon-blood
color; the sapphire, with shifting blues like the summer sky at noon
or a tranquil mountain lake at sunset—these stones were the medi-
ators and messengers, the connecting links between families. They
had held the scattered members of the clan together over the centuries, had formed them into a whole. And although the Linkhands
had taken part in all the other important commercial activities of
the world, the stone—it was always spoken of in the singular—was
the symbol of family unity. Trading in it was tradition.

Certain rules and commandments had been handed down from
ancester to ancestor, from father to son. A Linkhand did this and
did not do that. These customs had come to be factors in the business world. Experienced brokers on all the exchanges of the
world knew the usages of the Linkhands, and reckoned with them.
The family also had a written code which was passed on from
father to son, and used in correspondence on important affairs—it
contained signs borrowed from the Hebrew, Arabic and Chinese
scripts. There was also a familial language, a fluent mixture of
Germanic, Romance and Slavic words, that was employed for telephone conversations. There were handwritten vocabulary lists and
exercise books for this language, and all the Linkhands learned it
in their youth when they spent their apprenticeships—this was the
ironclad rule—visiting with relatives all over the world. Similarly,
each of them had a perfect command of at least three and usually
five modern languages. A Linkhand could be recognized less by
external appearance than by certain specific details. There was the
way they held their heads, with an almost imperceptible sidewise
tilt. There were their vigorous, strongly veined hands, with the
peculiarly mobile thumbs and forefingers of their left hands.

Almost all the Linkhands were good-looking. They tended to
be above average height, well proportioned, and with an earnest,
thoughtful cast of features. This was true whether they belonged to
the fair—often extremely fair—type of the Netherlands branch or to
the dark South American type. They were never careless in their
movements or their dress. They never let themselves go. Outbursts
of temperament in the presence of others were simply foreign to the
Linkhands. They thought rapidly but talked slowly, and never said
too much.

The Linkhands had a wide variety of hobbies. But one private passion was common to them all. It was an almost shamefaced partiality for one particular gemstone which was not their stock-in-trade. They all dealt in diamonds. But the Paris Linkhand collected sapphires, the Antwerper rubies, the New Yorker semiprecious stones such as amethysts and topazes. A. L. Linkhand, head of the Viennese branch of the family, collected emeralds. Emeralds of rare colors or rare cuts, emeralds with histories that could be traced back for centuries. His was a collection not only rare but also so valuable that, as one of his brothers—half jokingly, half seriously— had said, it was a luxury that not even a Linkhand could afford.

Therefore all the Linkhands were surprised to see Mira wearing the Thirty-three. This emerald of exactly thirty-three carats was one of the finest in A.L.'s collection. Cartier's had set it so ingeniously that scarcely any of the platinum was visible; the fabulously beautiful stone seemed magically suspended against Mira's marble-white skin on its infinitely delicate chain. It created quite a sensation among the ordinarily cool-headed Linkhands when she appeared with the gem. There had been some muttering in the family about this wholly unknown (some said in whispers, "obscure") Mira Rosen who was marrying the only worthless member of the family. But if she wore the Thirty-three, she was someone to be considered, not just a girl who had been found for Freddy because no one better would marry him.

That bit of display made the congratulations warmer and more personal than, possibly, the members of the clan really meant them to be. The effect of this cordiality upon the betrothed couple was hard to determine. Freddy beamed steadily, like a six-year-old who has received a set of electric trains for Christmas. Mira drew her thin lips into a smile which each of the relatives interpreted differently—as uneasy, cold, meaningless, challenging or triumphant. In reality Mira was only dazed. She did not yet understand her duties, did not know what she would have to pay for this next-to-last step on the way to her goal—or rather, for this burning of every bridge that might have led her back to the misery of her distant past.

At the engagement party in the salon of the Meurice some hundred persons sat down to a regal dinner. The Linkhands loved pomp at their family festivals, and even the most fastidious of that fastidious lot would have had no cause to complain of the setting, the service, the cuisine and the beverages. When A. L. Linkhand, who sat at the fiancée's right, tapped lightly on his champagne glass and rose, the hubbub of conversation stopped abruptly. Under the bright light of the crystal chandeliers, the faces that surrounded the vast table were earnest and intent—especially the faces of the men. A. L. Linkhand was practically the senior member of the family, for J. B. Linkhand in Zurich was eighty-three, completely paralyzed from the waist down, and he no longer exercised authority. What they all expected of A. L. Linkhand was not a commonplace toast, a few witty or whimsical remarks followed by a call for a cheer for the couple. What A.L. had to say about this marriage would be important, and most important of all was the information he would give them about this young woman Mira Rosen.

A.L. spoke in French. After a few well-turned phrases, he went straight to the heart of the matter, as he knew they expected him to do. He spoke with a proud and joyful confidence: "My dearest kinsfolk, it only seems that we are breaking with Linkhand tradition in presenting you with what might be called a fait accompli. Who knows better than I what it means to be a Linkhand? Who prizes it more highly? I know what tradition means to us, what we owe to it. Therefore I want to tell you that as a father, A. L. Linkhand thanks God out of the fullness of his heart for having vouchsafed his child the miracle of love, and that as a father he hopes for the blessing that this miracle will bring."

He felt a kind of awe, he went on to say, before the miracle revealed in Mira Rosen's life from her birth to this present moment. Mira had received none of the gifts of the Muses; she was neither a singer nor an actress nor a dancer, whose talent only needed training for it to be a source of wealth. Denied the loving care of either father or mother, she had received to equip her for the hardships of life only certain qualities of character: industry, determination, honesty and courage. And if, barely twenty, she could already look back upon successes that experienced and mature men might be proud of, she owed her rise to these capacities alone, to her seriousness, her will—in a word, to her own work.

"And therefore, when I hung the Thirty-three around Mira Rosen's neck on this day of celebration, it was by no means as the gift of a loving father, but as a distinction—a decoration, if you like —a tribute from a man who knows what work is and who esteems it."

Applause followed, chiefly from the younger members of the family. The women were especially moved; the older men clapped lightly with a note of impatience.

A. L. Linkhand waited until the applause had subsided. He had removed his hands from the table, and his left thumb had closed upon the forefinger, as if he were holding the stone between his fingertips. With this characteristic Linkhand gesture, he continued: "And now A. L. Linkhand the businessman wants to say something that concerns all Linkhands. Mira Rosen, who will soon be Mira Linkhand, was not made for the life that Linkhand women have led for generations and lead today. I do not mean this as a criticism of them. Our ladies have fulfilled their obligations; they have given us not a whit less than they promised—they have always given more. They have enriched our lives, have added to the joys of living when things went well and have been a staff and comfort in times of stress. They have made ideal wives, friends, mothers. Mira will be all that, for she loves our Freddy. But beyond that, with a temperament like hers, she will be irresistibly drawn toward the business affairs of the Linkhands. I understand such a personality, and I am not going to block it with a wall of outmoded prejudice. I hope you trust my judgment of people." He straightened up, looked around the circle, and seemed to be winking at each of the older Linkhands in turn. "I, A. L. Linkhand, with forty-eight years in business behind me, solemnly declare to you: the House of Linkhand will have reason to be proud of its newest associate, Mira Rosen."

Now the older Linkhands were the ones to applaud and laugh, a relieved and liberating laugh.

A.L. knew that he had won the important battle. He knew, too, when it was time to stop. "And so, if I now ask you to drain your glasses, I want you to drink above all to the welfare of the bride, Mira Rosen, who will soon be a Linkhand. She is already my daughter, in my heart, before God and before everybody." He gently raised Mira to her feet, embraced her and kissed her on brow and cheeks.

There followed the usual confusion of outcries, laughter and touching of glasses. The servants poured fresh champagne. A. L. Linkhand led the final cheer for the couple. P. R. Linkhand of Warsaw said in Hebrew, *"Mazal uvrakhah"*—luck and blessings— and stepped on a crystal plate wrapped in a damask napkin. Everyone thronged forward to congratulate the couple and the parents, and the orchestra began a polonaise, which then shifted to a slow waltz to give the older people the privilege of the first dance.

Twelve hours later those Linkhands who had not been present at the engagement party were thoroughly briefed by telephone on all the important details of the new marital alliance and on the unusual personality of the prospective bride. By next day every Linkhand knew what A.L. expected of his daughter-in-law, and that he had given her the Thirty-three for an engagement present.

*   *   *

The wedding took place in Vienna that fall, and was celebrated with Linkhand elaborateness.

Mira spent the period of her engagement in a way few other girls would have done. She had little time and less patience for all the preparations for the wedding. Fittings had been arranged for her with dressmakers, furriers, shoemakers and other craftsmen, designers of worldwide reputation; she went to these dutifully, but she let Mme. Rachelle and various aunts and cousins assemble her trousseau for her. She herself sat in A. L. Linkhand's office and learned. She applied to this new world of business the same determination and concentration that had stood her in such good stead barely five years before in the commercial school. And she grasped everything. She made a point of never missing a remark, never interrupting an explanation. She took in everything her mentor had to tell her, and as soon as she was alone, she began to absorb it and put it to use. It seemed as though all she had needed for the perfection of her mental techniques, for the fullest development of her commercial abilities—which always quested after remote goals and, once these were attained, still remoter ones—was this association with A.L. He poured out his knowledge of the business practices of almost three centuries. She admired him, but would never have attempted to express what she felt for him, for it would have sounded false. They soon knew each other well because they had one thing in common: they were both people who did not imagine and did not hope; they calculated.

These lessons occupied the months before the wedding. After the honeymoon, Mira's traveling apprenticeship began, and continued for a year and a half. The plan, worked out to the smallest detail, was a model of Linkhand methodical thinking. In London Mira was to have a famous plastic surgeon correct the flaws in her hands and feet. After the operations she would have to remain in bed, but this time would be put to good advantage, for Lady Whisten would spend two or three hours a day with her, acquainting her with the manners of the society in which she would henceforth move. As soon as Mira was able to get about again, this theoretical instruction would be supplemented by practical experience. An hour a day would be devoted to riding and an hour to tennis. The afternoons would be reserved for the Stone. Nachum Fish would be her teacher—he had already been informed. Mira and Freddy would live with I. C. Linkhand, at whose home Mira would meet important people and obtain insights into commercial relations with India. She would also exchange ideas with her brother-in-law Lord Godbrooke, who was something of an eccentric but had launched a number of remarkably important projects of late. A.L.

himself would introduce her to Sir Frederick Wertheimer, whose company controlled more than 80 per cent of the world's raw diamonds.

After six months of corrective surgery, Mira's hands and feet were still not beautiful, but they were no longer unsightly. She conducted herself in society exactly as did the other Linkhand women, but without possessing their inclinations or their passions. She displayed no preference for any of the branches of art, but she also did not make a fool of herself at social or sporting events. She was a creditable horsewoman, although she never developed any feeling for horses. Riding gave her no pleasure, let alone happiness; but she soon became conscious of the usefulness—the relaxation and liberation—of such exercise, and went riding for the same reason that others take tonics. Her feeling was the same toward tennis. On the other hand, she got on very well with Milton Godbrooke and gave him some astonishingly simple suggestions which won his immense respect and the gift of fifty shares apiece in each of his two newly established companies.

When A.L. came to London, he heard from the Linkhand women that Mira was doing very well and that Freddy was a new person; but the remarks of the men were more significant. From them he gathered that they admired his daughter-in-law and envied him for her. Ordinarily taciturn Nachum Fish, whom the Linkhands acknowledged as the authority on the treatment of gemstones, became loquacious when A.L. asked him about Mira's progress. Not only was she now familiar with every phase of splitting, sawing and polishing the stone; but given a little practice, she would be able to do the work splendidly herself. Mira Linkhand already had an "eye," Fish said. She could "see" the stone, distinguish all the nuances of colors, and had a remarkable faculty for calculating the weight of the polished gem from the appearance of the raw stone.

A.L. introduced her to Sir Frederic in a highly characteristic fashion. A.L. wanted to obtain a virtual monopoly on a certain type of diamond for a period of two years at a price set in advance, and offered to take any quantity supplied independently of the fluctuations of the exchange. Sir Frederic was unwilling to make any such commitment, but on the other hand he did not want to offend A.L. He had offered 50 per cent of the production for two years, over and above the quotas already assigned to the Linkhand cutters. But A.L. was not satisfied with this. He filled Mira in on the details of the affair, and shortly before the appointed meeting telephoned Sir Frederic to say that he unfortunately had to take the plane to Zurich in an hour—the senior Linkhand had called him.

Mira Linkhand would represent him at the negotiations; whatever arrangements she made would be satisfactory to him.

Sir Frederic repeatedly tried to trip Mira up, only in the end to capitulate to her superior knowledge of the facts, her sober business sense and her impeccable logic. That same evening she called A.L. to report concisely on the progress and the outcome of this skirmish. Old J. B. Linkhand was delighted by the whole thing. He could only exclaim, when A.L. gave him the gist of Mira's report, "A Linkhand woman! Or no, a Linkhand man. You've done capitally, A.L." By which he meant not the London deal, but the acquisition of Mira. He wanted to meet her; as soon as her London apprenticeship was over, she must be brought to Zurich. J.B.'s will had been made long ago, but it could always be altered. With this in mind, Freddy and his young wife stayed a week in Zurich instead of the planned three days. They then moved on to Paris. They remained there six weeks, then spent three months in Amsterdam, two in Antwerp and four in New York. On their return trip they stopped off in Warsaw and finally in Berlin, already overclouded by the Nazis. Mira could read the signs of the times, and counseled the Berlin Linkhand, R.O., on ways to rescue a good part of his property. Her circuit completed, she returned to Vienna, where she took up her work with such energy and precision that she enormously increased her reputation in the family.

In Vienna Mira's desk was in her father-in-law's office. No one was surprised by her presence any longer; she was regarded as an established factor. She had her place in the firm and in the family; she was a Linkhand. She struck everyone as a pretty, healthy woman on the best of terms with her husband Freddy (he too had formal names; his business letterheads read A.G.—Alfred Gerhard —Linkhand). Mira was also a wealthy woman in her own right. She had her own bank accounts in Zurich and New York, and received a certain percentage on all large deals which she conducted. A. L. Linkhand had handed her a sizable check for her negotiations with Sir Frederic—and on the whole her apprenticeship had proved extremely profitable. Back in Vienna, she inaugurated a program for manufacturing industrial diamonds on a larger scale. The finished products were dispatched from Holland and Belgium directly to G. G. Linkhand, A.L.'s eldest son, in New York. Sales of industrial diamonds were fairly insignificant and barely covered the costs of production; large stocks were accumulated and stored. This was an enterprise aimed at future profits; but the Linkhands were soon the leaders in the field, virtually without competition and the only group operating on a large scale. Essentially the business was an experiment based on certain political and economic insights of Mira's. It was financed by A.L. and A. G. Linkhand in Vienna and G. G. Linkhand in New York. The Antwerp and Amsterdam families also participated and took charge of the technical side of the operation. They were not especially enthusiastic about producing industrial diamonds, since there was no great demand. But on the other hand, there was also no need for large investments; the plan was Mira's, which meant it had been thought through carefully and was probably well founded. And, finally, goods are goods; if no demand existed, it would have to be created.

In 1937 Mira was the most esteemed if not the most popular woman in the Linkhand circle. Aside from her dark origins, the other women had nothing to say against her. If occasional catty remarks were dropped about Mira's lack of background and taste, the men would stalwartly come to her defense. It was a case of Linkhand solidarity; Mira stood on the same plane as brothers, sons, cousins and nephews. All the Linkhands had benefited by her vigor and efficiency; they were united to her by the firm ties of business, and such ties had far more validity than the foolish snobbism of women. In the Linkhand families, men set the tone. They made the deals and determined the nature of commercial affairs. No Linkhand could doubt the paramount importance of this aspect of life. Mira was a full-fledged member of this business world; hence, she was invulnerable. The women, consequently, avoided running her down—the more so since Mira's conduct as wife and housekeeper was irreproachable. Although the small fires of her first infatuation had long since burned themselves out, she was quite fond of her Teddy bear (a pet name she employed only in the bedroom). He was to her what decent, stupid, healthy girls often are to men who engage in demanding brainwork. Freddy provided her with physical relaxation; he calmed her nerves. Erotically Freddy was an egoist—he was not primarily concerned with giving joy to his partner, but with the satisfaction of his own needs. However, he was proficient at the uncomplicated kind of love play which had not changed since their wedding night. Mira, in her turn, did not ask much of a love partner; she therefore gave no more thought to this matter than she did to her husband's intellectual inferiority—whose full extent she very soon realized. She had to be clever and industrious; Freddy could afford to be stupid and indolent. He had reached his goal the day he was born. And after all, one breadwinner in a marriage is sufficient. In this case the usual roles of man and woman were reversed. Besides—and this was very important —she could justify her advantageous marriage this way. She had long since brought in as much as a very rich bride might have brought as a dowry to a clever and industrious Freddy. She never even bothered to compare her husband with other men, for she wanted him just as he was. For—although this was a thought she repressed—if Freddy had not been what he was, she would never have become a Linkhand.

Mira saw the political situation solely from the economic standpoint. She regarded Hitler's anti-Jewish measures in Germany as a warning to Jews everywhere, but that was about the extent of her emotional involvement. In this she differed sharply from the other Linkhands, who felt genuine grief over the harassment and humiliation of their coreligionists. The Linkhands extended every possible help to Jews fleeing from Germany to Austria. Mira, too, made sizable contributions; but of far greater importance than her money was the organizational talent she devoted to this cause. She succeeded in finding jobs for a great many refugees in Europe, or in providing them with the means and the credentials necessary for emigrating overseas.

But in the summer of 1937 it was still possible to live in Austria in Linkhand style—although precious paintings and statuary, as well as the priceless emerald and carpet collections, had all been shipped to New York. Mira also advised that the country villa, with its spacious park, be sold, and the family make do with the town house. Rachelle Linkhand spent ten months of the year in restless peregrinations between Paris and London, New York and Vienna; but A.L. and his daughter-in-law sat at their desks every day and managed their business. They were at their desks on the first of July, 1937, when A.L. was due to depart for Bad Gastein— to do his month's penance, as he jovially expressed it. The chauffeur was due to arrive for him at three o'clock. It was eleven o'clock in the morning, still time to look over the day's mail. Mira would stay on at the office until July 15 and then take her vacation at Trouville with Freddy. Rachelle was going to Brighton. They would all meet again in Vienna on September 1.

Mira was checking the bank statements of the preceding month when her father-in-law interrupted to hand her a letter. The Warsaw Linkhand—with characteristic frugality, he preferred to write rather than telephone—was asking A.L. to receive a certain Count Voronovski and to arrange the purchase of two emeralds from him. The stones were family heirlooms, but they could be had at a bargain, since the Voronovskis, with whom he was involved in a troublesome affair over forest rights, were in straitened circumstances and their daughter was to be married soon and needed a dowry.

The Warsaw Linkhand also asked A.L. to provide the Voronovskis with imitations of the emeralds, so that no one would know the family had had to part with the stones. For of course everyone would expect the Countess to wear the emeralds at her daughter's wedding. In a postscript P.R. asked that the commission be credited to him.

Mira read through the letter and handed it back to her father-in-law. She screwed up her mouth slightly in an inquiring smile.

"Paul's problems—counts, woods and emeralds," A.L. said. "He'll never forgive me if I leave today without seeing the Count. And yet this forest affair is going to cost him a pretty penny before it's over."

Mira knew something about the matter, for she had heard it discussed in the family. At present it was the subject of a lawsuit between P. R. Linkhand and Countess Voronovska on one side and the Polish government, or rather the army command, on the other. Where emeralds were in question, it was quite natural for P.R. to appeal to A.L. in Vienna; but Mira was not too fond of the cautious Warsaw Linkhand. "You shouldn't postpone your departure on account of this, Papa. If you feel that I don't know enough, I can ask Brandmann to take a look at them."

"No, no, I can rely on you. But still—I wouldn't want to bother with them unless they were really something out of the ordinary. And then—that business of supplying imitations. We'd have to get them cut by someone who really has a feel for it."

"Perlberg of Antwerp is here visiting his daughter; he called yesterday. He'd do it as a favor to us."

"Old Perlberg cutting glass!"

"He won't mind too much—it's only a matter of a couple of hours for him. I assume they are cabochons."

"What makes you say that?"

"Because P.R. would have mentioned it if they'd been cut differently. And since he says they're very beautiful in color and the two together must weigh a hundred to a hundred and fifty carats—"

"Wait, wait, you have a head on you! Cabochons, right. In a moment I'll tell you the whole story." He went rapidly to a case lined from floor to ceiling with books. "What was that Count's name?"

Mira glanced at the letter: "Count Voronovski. The first name is Vladislav."

"Here it is." A.L. carried a heavy volume over to the desk. It was an encyclopedia of all important gems that had ever been in the possession of the Linkhands—a privately printed book with illustrations and drawings. He leafed through the pages. "Here, Vienna, 1815—the year of the Congress. Two Asiatic emeralds, sold by Saul Linkhand to His Excellency Count Mieczyslav of Voronovski at Voronovka, so cut that when put together they form an egg and set so that they can be worn singly as earrings, together as a necklace. Chain of ducat gold with small emeralds as links. Model: wedding ornaments of Francis I. The two large stones weigh 107.3 carats, the chain weighs 319 grams, fine gold, and the small emeralds, beautiful Indian gems, total 27 carats. His Excellency paid 115,000 gulden, 75,000 in good gold and the rest in notes. You can subtract the notes—Polish counts never paid theirs. But I imagine our ancestor—not directly; he was the Amsterdam Linkhand's great-grandfather—made his profit on the 75,000. They would have been worth around 60,000. Deduct 5,000—no, too much, 3,000—for the chain—the count will want to keep that—and there remains 57,000 gulden. In today's money and reckoned in dollars—Jews and gentiles, the Poles are all alike in reckoning in dollars—that would be about 45,000 dollars. A man has to make a bit of profit—there's also P.R.'s commission—so offer him 30,000 and go to 33,000 at the most—oh well, since it's a count, 35,000. That—as Morgenbesser, the old crook, used to say for forty years—is my last word."

"All right, Papa. That simplifies it. All I need do, then, is make sure they're the same stones and come to terms with His Excellency the Count."

"Don't say Your Excellency to him," A.L. remarked, clearing his throat. "That's only for subordinates. You're his equal. Just say Count—Count So-and-so, or plain Count." He gave the lesson a jesting twist. "Incidentally—haven't I told you that we Linkhands are also counts?"

"You're in fine fettle today, Papa," Mira said with a somewhat forced laugh. "Lady Whisten briefed me on every last petty title in Europe." But she knew he enjoyed telling her these little things, and so asked, "How did the Linkhands come by their title anyway?"

"That," A.L. said, "is another story about a Polish lord and a Linkhand. It was Rafael Linkhand of Prague who provided August the Strong with a splendid pearl set for his mistress: tiara, necklace and bracelets of the choicest rose pearls. You can read about it in the book. That was about seventy years before Count Voronovski bought those emeralds from us. Rafael Linkhand had sunk a great deal of money in the set of pearls and was proud to be presented to the King. The King was extremely affable and had his high-bosomed mistress try on the jewelry in the Jew's presence. They were all three delighted by the way the pearls suited her. So perfectly that the lady kept them on and withdrew. Naturally our ancestor went straight to the treasurer for payment, and to help the treasurer speed matters along, he presented him with a gift worthy of his standing, a gold tankard. But Rafael brought nothing back from Prague except a document in Latin elevating Rafael Linkhand and all Linkhands related to him by blood to the hereditary rank of counts. We are the Counts Levarenka—don't laugh! But old Tomas, Rafael's father, when he saw the document, called in his younger son Michael, who was a scholar, and had him translate it word for word. Then he asked, 'Are you sure there is nothing in it about eight thousand doubloons that the King owes us?' When Michael said that there wasn't a word to that effect, old Tomas took a pen and wrote on the back, 'Cost eight thousand doubloons, but isn't worth it.' The original document is in Paris. Here is a facsimile of it." He took a sheet of parchment from a drawer.

"It means a lot more to be a Linkhand than to be a Count Levarenka," Mira said matter-of-factly. She had not fully understood the story. How could kings take pearls without paying for them, and how could they raise Jews to nobility? She had to think that over. "Has any Linkhand called himself by the title?" she asked.

"Just one wanted to—your brother-in-law Gustav."

"Gus? G.G., the hundred-per-cent American?"

"Yes. That was in 1915. He was barely eighteen and wanted to join the Imperial Uhlans—an aristocratic old regiment. The title of Count helped him there, and of course baptism, too."

"But how could he? How stupid that is. And Gus—Gus is so smart."

"Too smart, my dear, too smart. We did our best to make him drop the whole idea. But no—he would volunteer for the army and petition the Court Chancery to recognize his status as a noble. Luckily I had one thing to fall back on: that the original document was in Paris, and we were at war with France. All in all, I managed to stave off the step for a year. By then the uhlans were no longer mounted troops, and it was no longer such a rarity for Jews to be reserve officers. And then when the war was over, a title like Count Levarenka simply became comical. But the real counts, the great lords who held their titles for eight hundred or a thousand years and more, you know—they had something. They were buyers. Magnificent buyers when they had money, and a source of marvelous things when they were short of funds. The Jews needed the great lords to become rich, and the great lords needed the rich

Jews when they were in financial straits. Many a time the grand-sons of the lords paid the grandsons of the Jews debts their grand-fathers hadn't settled. They were as good as their word, the real lords. The Linkhands dealt with the great lords for centuries, with barons and counts, princes and dukes, kings and emperors. In those days they were truly royal merchants. Today we're all ped-dlers and—call it what you like, my daughter, I call it profiteering. In 1914 the kind of business that was really noble ceased to exist."

Mira was totally devoid of any strain of sentimentality, particu-larly in business matters. Her answer to A.L.'s lament was a com-monplace. "Times change, Papa," she said and stroked his hand.

"You're right, Daughter. So, when the Count comes, you know what to do. I'll look in on you after dinner, before I leave. So long."

After A.L.'s departure, Mira stayed in the office to attend to a number of matters. The large room with its immense, deep rugs, its walls lined with books, its steel filing cases and the huge safe, which took up half of one wall, was warm and familiar to her; she felt good sitting at her desk, over her work. She reread P.R.'s letter once more, made a note in her tiny handwriting 30-35, in the upper right-hand corner, and filed it away. She studied the description of the gems in her father-in-law's book—one emerald, it appeared, was a shade lighter than the other; that would be useful to force the price down—and replaced the book on the shelf.

She had forgotten emeralds and counts and was immersed in her next task when the receptionist announced a caller, Count Voronovski. "Send him in," she said.

Mira was expecting an elderly gentleman. The man who en-tered was young and strikingly handsome; he would have made a perfect count in a film. Mira became so intent on studying this representative of a species entirely unknown to her that it took a moment for her to remember who and what she was. Above all, that she was involved in a business relationship, and that she was taking A. L. Linkhand's place. This meant that she was a business-woman in her office, and the man was a count—one of those great lords who, as her father-in-law had explained just that afternoon, disposed of precious possessions with hardly a qualm when they needed money. She rose from her chair, and extended her hand. "Mira Linkhand," she said as he bent over her hand. "I'm repre-senting my father-in-law. Our cousin in Warsaw wrote to us. Please sit down." She gestured somewhat awkwardly toward one of the leather easy chairs which stood by a small round table. Boxes of cigars and cigarettes, and a massive silver lighter, were arranged invitingly on the table.

With a natural gesture of polite gallantry, which was expressed not so much by arm or hand as by his whole being, he allowed her to precede him. Mira, normally entirely blind to a business associate's exterior, observed the movements of this man she had known only for a minute, watched his few steps to the conversation nook with keyed-up attentiveness. When they sat down, she felt the relaxation of tension as a physical thing, and sank with relief into the big, soft chair with its high back and wide arms.

She pressed a button under the tabletop. The attendant appeared, and she gave him an order. With a gesture that felt strange to her, she invited the guest to smoke. He took a cigarette and gave her a light. Mira, who could not make conversation, asked the Count whether he had had a good journey, whether he knew Vienna, when he had seen her cousin. The Count replied in rather clumsy German, fumbling for words; but he was polite, well-bred, as he had been taught to be from earliest childhood. Mira did not care what he was saying or how he was saying it; she hardly noticed his grammar or his accent. All she wanted was to hear this low, masculine voice, rather hoarse from issuing commands or drinking. The Count was an officer—why, certainly, *gnädige Frau* —in the cavalry. Naturally, a Polish nobleman is always a cavalryman. An uhlan, of course. He was attached to Warsaw's Uhlan Regiment No. 5. And even sitting down, he clicked his heels as though this red-haired Jewess without any of the airs of good breeding were a superior officer. In fact, he regarded her as a kind of superior, since she had made it plain right at the beginning that she was acting for her father-in-law. A great deal depended on this moment. Everything. Namely, his sister's trousseau. For although Marenzia's dowry would be paid as soon as they won that suit (damn it all!) over the forest, she couldn't very well be allowed to move into the palace of the Princes Bolgurski in her chemise, so to speak.

He had reached this point in their conference when Charles arrived, pushing the portable bar. "Madame, a Meukoff? Monsieur too?" Charles filled their glasses, left the cart within reach, and disappeared. Mira had profited by this little interlude to recall Lady Whisten's lessons. She drank to the Count, raising her glass slightly —and it did not even occur to her that she was coquetting. But the Polish Count, far from inexperienced in such matters, promptly concluded that the red-haired woman was smitten with him. In the present situation that could be an advantage.

"*À votre santé!*" he said, and drained half his glass. It was up to him to broach the real subject of their meeting. Mira waited, in a most obliging state of mind. But he took his time. She imagined he was acting from embarrassment and inexperience in business matters; even for businessmen it was often hard to make one's proposition and to strike the right tone. But Count Voronovski, aware of his attributes, had decided to guide the interview in a certain direction. That should not be difficult for him. He knew women; it seemed to him still too early for attack, and so he decided to keep to an easy trot until the signal for the gallop was given. It would be given by her, he felt sure. She had the command now—assuming that she really represented her father-in-law in all respects, including the evaluation of the gems. The money was all that counted. He finished his glass, took a Pall Mall from the box, lit it, and cleared his throat.

Mira was familiar with that clearing of the throat; she had heard it innumerable times as the prelude to important negotiations, even on the part of experienced, not to say hard-bitten, men. Evidently this present conversation was of great importance to the man sitting across the little table from her. And so, seeing him struggle with the difficulty of beginning, she did what she had never done before. She surrendered the certain advantage that another's uncertainty yields, and met him halfway: "Our cousin writes us"—at this point she herself cleared her throat, not so much because she was embarrassed as because she was trying to conceal the struggle of two personalities within herself: the one that had existed up to fifteen minutes ago, and this new one which was wholly unfamiliar to her, and which threatened to seize control—"that you have certain objects you intend to sell. They fall within our line; rather, they are a hobby of my father-in-law. Emeralds, are they not?"

The Count reached into his breast pocket, unfastened a safety pin intended to foil particularly daring pickpockets, and took out a small package wrapped in red silk. He spread it open on the table, revealing the two emeralds, artfully set in matte gold.

Instantly, all Mira's coquetry vanished. She was herself again. She examined the stones and the setting; they were those described in the book. She went to her desk, as if the Count were just any broker, and took out a magnifying glass and scales. In a few minutes she had detected the difference in the color of the two stones, and had more or less determined their weight, although they were in the setting. She had reached the point at which it was usual to ask: And how much do you want for them?

Neither the stones nor the artistic setting meant anything to her. She had no feeling for beauty, only for figures. Emeralds were Papa's business, or rather, he would keep these for his collection.

One of them was of rare perfection; the other was also very fine and suffered only by comparison with its twin. As she knew Papa, he would sell the "weaker" stone for the best possible price and keep the "stronger" one, which she judged was worth a good thousand dollars or more per carat. Now she was sober again. A figure sufficed to recall her to reality. The Count, who had followed her to the desk and was standing beside her, watching her examination of the stones, did not know what to make of the expression of composure and sober gravity he observed in her face. He no longer saw the inept blandishments of a woman who would be easy to handle. This was a regular Jewess; her keenness awoke when money was at stake.

At this point Mira looked up at him, into a face turned thoughtfully and anxiously toward her. For the first time in her life Mira felt sympathy. Sympathy in the true sense of the word. She suffered along with this man, for she misread his feelings. He was looking the way he did because he had concluded from the closeness of her examination and her changed expression that she had found fault with the stones, that she would offer a low price, or would not want them at all. She, however, thought he was distressed at having to sell gems that belonged to the family. "What are you asking for the stones?" There was nothing encouraging in these words, and certainly not in the tone, although she was prepared to pay—to pay far more than the sum which her father-in-law had set.

But Vladislav, Count Voronovski had never before dealt with a woman so inexperienced in love and so experienced in business. He couldn't understand this red-haired woman.

"Well, you see, madame, it's this way. We are selling the gems because we need money. A certain sum," he hastened to add. "And if we get that, very good. If we don't get it, the whole business has no point."

"And how high is this sum?" Mira asked.

"I think," he said, taking courage, "we need a hundred thousand. Or—" He wanted to leave an avenue open for negotiation; perhaps that was asking far too much.

Mira straightened up abruptly. No, she thought, the emeralds are not worth that. She calculated in her head. Even if she figured the better stone at fifty thousand, the weaker one could not possibly come up to it. Seventy thousand was a good price, and she herself would buy them for eighty thousand only because—but for God's sake, what was ailing her? How could she possibly justify such a price to A.L.? And above all, why did she want to accommodate this man to the tune of such a sum? She heard herself saying,

"No, Count, I think you are asking too much. We know what the stones cost. We wanted to offer an acceptable price approximating their value."

The Jewess wants to bluff me, the Count thought. What impertinence: we know what the stones cost! He repressed various replies which verged on the impolite, and decided to be aristocratically, condescendingly calm: "You can scarcely know that, madame. The gems have been in our family for two hundred years."

"Exactly one hundred and twenty-two years. They were bought in 1815, right here in Vienna, by Count Mieczislav (she stumbled a bit over the name, of course) Voronovski, along with a chain made of gold and small emeralds. They were bought from a Linkhand."

The Count was stunned. "Yes, with a chain. But Mama doesn't want to sell it," he managed to say. He no longer sounded condescending.

"I'd very much like to help you out. For us, it is not a major matter. But please understand—you are not a businessman. If—" She had wanted to say that if only the details of the transaction could be kept from the Warsaw Linkhand, she would pay what he asked. She was baffled, and fell silent.

Perhaps, the Count thought, I was stupid and asked too much, and she's embarrassed over how to refuse me. What will become of Marenzia's trousseau now? Mama said we should get at least fifty thousand. "You're right, madame," he replied placatingly. "I'm inexperienced in business." He gave a slight, respectful bow. "In that case I must rely upon those who are. If a hundred thousand zlotys are too much, how much could we get for the stones? I'm asking only out of curiosity."

Slowly, so that she would not show her astonishment, Mira turned to him. He noticed for the first time that her eyes were gleaming like gold, that her mouth, which had seemed so hard, was smiling softly, tenderly. He could not unriddle the smile, but he understood her words: "We will buy the stones. It is a sentimental matter on both sides. You need the money for an important purpose, and the Linkhands will be glad to have these stones that once belonged to members of their family. We will pay the hundred thousand zlotys." She was still smiling as she turned back to the desk. The smile meant this time: What an idiot you are, Vladislav, Count Voronovski! And she pitied herself because she, Mira Linkhand, had fallen in love with this idiot.

But her methodical mind kept emotions at bay. This was a business deal, and a very good one at that. A.L. would make a large profit from this stupid uhlan whom she felt sorry for, which she really should not. No, she must not. "How do you want the money? And where?" she asked matter-of-factly.

The Count evidently did not understand the question. "Well, I think, I mean, there's no difficulty. I give you the stones and you give me the money. And—there's something else very important. I don't know whether you've been informed. Pan Linkhand in Warsaw knows—knows all about it. . . ."

Mira reflected for a moment. "Oh, I understand, the imitations. Yes, at once." She lifted the receiver; he heard her saying, "Try to reach him." Then she turned to him again. "I'll give you a draft on the house of Linkhand in Warsaw for a hundred thousand zlotys."

"Draft? What exactly is that, madame?" He was too well-bred to *show* distrust, especially to a lady, but he was sure something was amiss. First she said the price was too high for her; then she agreed to pay it, and now. . . . The Jewess has some trick in mind, he thought. I'll go to the Warsaw fellow with my draft and he'll make a fuss about it, for why the devil should he pay in Warsaw for something they've bought in Vienna? No. The soldierly frame of this descendant of knights and cavalrymen stiffened. "My idea is that you give me the money here," he said firmly.

Mira was very patient. If at all possible, she would humor the man's whim—what else could it be? But where was she to get hold of a hundred thousand zlotys in cash in Vienna? She pondered only for a moment, then recalled the broker on the Berggasse who in times past had conducted financial transactions for Adele Kadisch—illegal transactions in foreign exchange. The thought flashed through her mind that a Linkhand did not stoop to such dealings. But she put that thought aside. After all, it was a Linkhand principle to please the client. She preferred not to recognize the true reason, her eagerness to gratify this man's whims, to make him like her.

Before she could reply, the telephone buzzed. It was Perlberg. He spoke Dutch, and Mira replied in the same language. Perlberg was reluctant to work during his vacation, and particularly reluctant to undertake the kind of job being asked of him in this case. But she soon convinced him that they needed him. He would be doing an immense favor to A. L. Linkhand, who had been his employer for forty years, if he would undertake this discreet bit of work. Couldn't he drop by for a moment right away? Yes, she would wait for him in the office.

She hung up and was about to call the money broker when the long-distance telephone rang shrilly. Lord Godbrooke calling from Belgrade. They conversed in English. He would be taking the plane for Vienna in fifteen minutes. Could she have the car waiting for him at the airport? He would be with them for supper. Was Papa already in Gastein? He had an interesting matter to discuss with Mira. So long.

Now Mira called the broker. The fat man's asthmatic puffs and groans rattled in the receiver. Who? Linkhand? A. L. Linkhand? Cash? What for? A draft—surely. Any amount Frau Linkhand wished. But cash? Not a draft, bank notes? Impossible—who dealt in such large sums of zlotys! When would it be wanted? As quickly as possible? Today? There was a pause during which only snorts could be heard over the telephone. Three minutes passed. Then: "At three groschen above the day's quotation and a hundred dollars commission, I'll do it for you. By half past nine this evening."

"Fine," Mira said. "Take my phone number and call me when you have it."

"You'll have the zlotys at half past nine this evening," Mira reported dryly. She did not know whether to wonder more at her strange client or at herself for getting herself involved in illegal transactions simply to satisfy his foolish whim. The whole business was not worth it. But was she still thinking about business at all?

Perlberg was shown in. The cutter, bald, in his sixties, wearing steel-rimmed glasses, came up to Mira's desk with a murmured greeting. She extended her hand, and he shook it rather unceremoniously. He was not in the best of moods, for gem cutting was not uppermost in his mind at the moment. Rather, he was in Vienna to discuss more vital matters with his daughter and son-in-law. He wanted them to join him in Holland. His son-in-law was in the trade too. He could start work in Amsterdam any day. Could work quietly there, without having to fear that Hitler would come and clamp down on the Austrian Jews the way he had clamped down on those in Germany.

Perlberg was far from a poor man. He had his handsome *"huisje,"* five large, comfortable rooms, his savings, and one of the best incomes in his profession. He had sat at the grinding wheel for over forty years, and his masterpieces had won prizes at exhibitions. There was, for example, the famous miniature gem weighing barely a hundredth of a carat, with all sixty-four facets in incredibly precise proportions—visible only under the magnifying glass, of course. Now he was here at the request of A. L. Linkhand's daughter-in-law not because this was a chance to make some schillings, or because he felt himself a subordinate. He had come because he knew the trade, with its frequently obscure and mysterious affairs, and was therefore ready to help out in an emergency. He knew that many rich people wore imitations of their genuine jewels and kept the real ones in the safe. But a high-ranking professional like Perlberg did not bother with imitations—however artfully they might be cut. True, he had worked for years at the leather-covered wheel for colored gems. He was as much at home with them as with diamonds. But glass—no, he had never yet cut glass. Only A. L. Linkhand could make such a demand upon him.

Catching sight of the emeralds on the table, he reached out for the one closest to him, and with an instinctive gesture took out his folding magnifying glass. Going to the window, he weighed the stone in his palm, let it roll so that the light fell upon it from different angles, at one point held it low so that it was out of the direct rays of the sun, then raised it so that the sunlight streamed full upon the gem as he examined it. Only then did he fit the magnifying glass over his right eye; his left eye remained wide open. "Good," he said finally, and reached for the second. Finally, placing both stones together and examining them together, he muttered something in a language that the Count did not understand. No, it was not Yiddish; he had heard that often enough in Poland. The red-haired woman nodded and answered briefly. The cutter had said, "Much better, almost flawless; the first is fine too, but the color isn't quite as good." And Mira had replied that they were aware of that, and what did he think about the possibilities of recutting? "Can be done without much loss in weight," the cutter replied.

"Well, we'll put our minds to that after A.L. has seen them," Mira said. "At the moment the question is the imitations."

"Tough, tough, troublesome because of the shade of difference in the colors. I'll have to hunt around for the glass. I'll come between ten and eleven tomorrow with samples."

"When can you have it done?" Mira asked. "There's still the question of having them set."

"If I find the glass today, and if the wheel you have here is all right—I'll have them ready by tomorrow at this time."

Mira turned to the Count to explain. "Herr Perlberg kindly agrees to make the imitations. It's a difficult task, since the stones are not the same color and probably differences in cutting will appear when we take them out of the settings. That part of it, too, must be left to an expert; when settings are as old as these, they are easily damaged. Herr Perlberg is an artist in his trade; I'm certain he will do splendid work."

The Count looked perplexed. Had he understood her to say different colors? What was up? Was she trying to make a fool of him? Like that business about a draft on old Linkhand in Warsaw?

He didn't understand financial transactions, but he wasn't color-blind. There were two emeralds. Not the same color! What the devil was the difference? Another of those funny tricks. Aha—and why was he not to receive the money until half past nine? What was this woman playing him for? He went up to the desk, picked up the stones and studied them. "I must say, madame, it is hardly possible to be mistaken about this—one stone is just like the other."

He turned his head sharply at Perlberg's bleating laughter. The cutter ignored his glare. He went over to the table in the corner, took a small black cigar from one of the boxes, lit it, and to add insult to injury, picked up one of the tall whiskey glasses and with deliberation mixed himself a half-and-half.

"You see, Count," Mira said, "there are differences among gems that the ordinary person doesn't even notice, but to the expert they are most important. For instance, I could show you twenty diamonds. Look as hard as you liked, you'd see no differences in the color. And yet these invisible differences, which every person in the trade would see, account for the differences in price. Sometimes one stone will have twice or three times the value of another. Nothing that you need worry about. In the case of your stones there is also such a difference; that is why one of them is reckoned as more valuable than the other. But what interests you is the total price, and that is not affected. The price is settled. Still—I'd like the imitations to be so good that only the magnifying glass would reveal that they are made of glass."

The Count looked rather dashed. He did not fully understand what the red-haired woman had said, but he could sense that she meant well by him. Had she not met him on the price? That meant at least five thousand for him. Suppose he tossed two thousand or so into the maw of his creditors; that would leave him three thousand clear. With that he might be able to buy Major Jaskulski's five-year-old horse, Captain, after all; the horse was fast now and promised to be faster. Ah, if only they would win this lawsuit! Then Mama would not have to sell the gems, and the whole mess and embarrassment about the glass wouldn't be necessary (crude of the Jewess to rub that in; no, she certainly was not a lady).

"I see that, madame, since you explain it so well. When will Herr Perlberg be done with his work? Ah, if only that suit of ours hadn't dragged on so—all this wouldn't be necessary."

Mira saw that he was unhappy again, and could not bear it. "One thing at a time. I've been intending to look into that matter. It occurred to me that there was another line of approach aside from the course your lawyer has taken. I will speak to my cousin about it."

"Thank you for taking an interest. But I think the root of the trouble lies with these—democratic judges. Out-and-out Bolsheviks."

"It may all turn out well for you," Mira said reassuringly. "But we'll speak of that later. . . . Mijnheer Perlberg." The cutter slowly approached the desk, cigar in his mouth. "I'll be here from nine o'clock in the morning. If you should need me earlier, telephone at the house before eight. Between eight and nine I can't be reached." She had spoken German so as not to exclude the Count. "One more minute, since you're here. Tomorrow you'll surely be too busy. There is one matter—" She went to the safe, turned the combination and opened the huge door. Then she returned to the desk with an envelope. The Count saw figures written in pencil on both upper corners of the white envelope, as Mira laid it on the table. Perlberg opened it and glanced inside, or rather smelled it. "Springmann's work," he said.

"Right," Mira said. "But there are four of them that are no good. Papa says it's the stone; I think they were burned in cutting."

Perlberg sat down in her chair. Mira stood behind him, looking over his shoulder. The Count started to his feet to offer her his chair, but she signed to him, shaking her head, to remain seated. Perlberg casually spread out the white paper. It was a fairly large square; on top of it lay a thin layer of greenish, transparent paper, and then a layer of absorbent cotton. Embedded in the cotton—the Count had to stop himself from displaying by sound or movement anything like plebeian surprise—were diamonds, a quantity of diamonds almost the size of hazelnuts. The full light of the afternoon sun fell upon them so that they shone with an incredible unnatural, scintillating brilliance.

"Nice batch," Perlberg said. Folding back the upper part of the paper, he read the figures: 45 and 273. "Sixers," he growled as if talking to himself. "Nice work, just the colette. Springmann's old fault. But otherwise good, very good." He reached for his magnifying glass again and examined all the stones; then, with astonishing swiftness, he picked them up one after the other and inspected them once more, turning the stones between his thumb and forefinger. The Count watched his movements with close attention. Mira's face, too, was earnest and full of suspense. Perlberg had at first laid aside five of the forty-five gems—Voronovski had counted them. Then, after studying one closely for some time, he assigned it to the larger pile. "These four are the culprits," he said, looking them over once more. "Spoil the whole batch. I'm of your opinion, Frau Linkhand—burned." He laid the stones on the balance. "So—

twenty-five point three—we might try; they may turn out very good. Not as good as these—" he indicated the larger heap—"but white. They'll lose something, but may make good five-caraters, good. I'll take them back with me to Amsterdam."

"Fine," Mira said. "And now would you please pick out the best of the good ones? I need an especially fine stone."

Perlberg returned to the gems with complete absorption. In a few minutes he had selected the stone. He placed it on the balance. "Just five point seventy-six," he said. "Crystal, I call it; someone else would say blue-white—a hundred per cent flawless. So." He laid it aside.

"Thank you ever so much, Mijnheer Perlberg. We'll see each other again tomorrow."

Perlberg stood up. "Good-bye, Frau Linkhand." He turned to the Count: "It was an honor, Your Excellency—and there are greens and greens."

The Count had stood up; he said, with a considerable measure of respect, "Very pleased to have met you," and bowed.

Then he and Mira were alone. She took from the drawer several small envelopes, put the four stones set aside by Perlberg into one, writing 25.3 in the left-hand corner and 4 in the right, the single stone into a special envelope on which she wrote 5.76 and 1, and then replaced the rest of the batch in its original envelope, correcting the two figures 45 and 273 to 40 and 242.94. While she was doing all this, she talked to the Count. "Where are you staying, Count?"

"That's a matter of custom with us, madame. At the Klomser. The Voronovskis always stay there when they come to Vienna."

"Yes, of course. Is it a nice hotel?"

"Well, you know, it is perhaps not so comfortable, but old. My grandfather—"

"I understand. Do you have—forgive me, I don't want to be indiscreet—do you have other business in Vienna? Because it will take one or two days before the imitations are done and set. It is work that takes great skill. But then they will hardly be distinguishable from the genuine gems."

The Count laughed. "Then I don't understand why people pay so much for the genuine article. If there's no difference—I mean, if no one can tell."

Mira looked at him. There's a good deal you don't understand, my handsome young man, she thought. You might consider that if your great-grandfather or whoever it was had bought his wife glass instead of emeralds, your sister would be without a trousseau.

But she said, "It isn't so simple a matter, Count. Gems are not for adornment alone. It would go too far afield if I tried to explain. . . ."

"I know, I know," the Count hastened to say. "There are other things involved." He let the matter rest there. But he was thinking: the reason precious stones exist is that Jews can make a profit on them. But this time we've outsmarted you. You won't get rich on Mama's emeralds. If only I had the hundred thousand in my hands. He glanced surreptitiously at the wall clock. It wa six twenty-five. He could only hope that there would be no slipup.

Mira's gaze followed his to the clock. She wrapped the two emeralds in their scrap of red silk and carried them, together with the diamonds, to the safe, which she locked. The Count watched her actions with mixed feelings. Now his emeralds were in the safe and he did not have his money yet. Oh well, let her try anything. The cavalryman's mentality of the Voronovskis took possession of him momentarily. Half past nine, she had said. If that money is not in my hands by ten o'clock at the latest, then there'll be hell to pay, my roan filly with your colors and carats, your drafts and your safes. The conception of Mira as a filly sent his thoughts in another direction. God knows, he mused, she really isn't bad. Good face, straight teeth, nice eyes, and that hair. Waist pretty good, though maybe a shade too large around. But those legs! Her hands, though —common, not a trace of the thoroughbred!

Mira left the safe and came over to him. "It is rather late, Count, and you haven't yet said whether you have other business in Vienna."

"Not much. Perhaps I'll drop in at the Embassy. The Ambassador's wife is a cousin of mine. And then I have to see a saddler— I have his address here. I don't know whether you're interested in these matters—those old Viennese saddles, you know—if I could lay my hands on one of them—"

"Perhaps I could find one for you. I ride too, and we have heaps of tack around at our place. Left by my brother-in-law, who now lives in New York."

"Oh," he exclaimed, "you ride!" This was something quite different. If she rode, why then. . . . All the women of his acquaintance—that is, the ladies, of course—rode, some of them quite decently, with courage and good form. But they knew nothing about carats and drafts. Whereas here was this woman who tossed around hundreds of thousands and no doubt understood more about these things than he would ever understand . . . and at the same time she rode! She understood horses. Why hadn't she said so at once? And he was no longer Vladislav, Count Voronovski;

he was a handsome, fearful, happy boy who had found a playmate in a strange, foreign and incomprehensible world.

"I'm no great shakes as a rider, I'm afraid. I did have an excellent teacher in London. But I'm afraid I've never got much beyond a leisurely trot."

"The English," he said scornfully. "Horribly conservative. Way outdated. Using the curb on top of the snaffle! Who rides that way nowadays? The Italian style is the modern one, gnädige Frau. You have good horses?"

"There are two in the stable at the moment. Mine is Irish, six years old, I think. A—a sorrel—is that what you call it? His name is Happy."

"Irish—a hunter? A genuine hunter?"

"Probably. My brother-in-law, Lord Godbrooke, gave me the horse."

"Imported from England! Then he must be a genuine hunter." He pronounced the term reverently, like a believer speaking the name of a saint.

Mira suddenly felt an unwonted closeness to horses. For they had helped her see this man as she wanted to see him. In his element. How he suddenly glowed with enthusiasm! How handsome he was. She wished intensely he would take her into his arms and kiss her. They were standing so close together; why did he not feel what she wanted?

But Count Voronovski, whom his friends called Vladek, was not thinking about the woman; his mind was on her horse. "I wonder if I might have a chance to see your Happy, madame," he asked.

Mira, abruptly brought back from wanton and alien thoughts, composed herself. "Why certainly, I go riding every morning at eight. When I drive to the stable tomorrow—it's over toward the Prater—I'll pass by the Klomser and pick you up."

"That would be perfectly wonderful! Thank you ever, ever so much, madame. *Ich küss die Hand.*" He took her hand and raised it to his lips, and Mira felt a foretaste of what she longed for.

"I shall take my leave now, madame, and—"

"Do stay a few minutes more, Count; I'd like you to meet my husband. I'll call him, and while we're waiting, let's have another cognac. Or rather, I'll send for tea. A late hour for tea, but we're dining late tonight. My brother-in-law is coming from Belgrade and—if you have nothing better in mind, why don't you eat with us? And then you can take your zloty right with you when you go." She did not wait for his reply, but picked up the telephone and gave Charles the orders.

In spite of the prospect of tea, the two drank another Meukoff and smoked. Voronovski enjoyed the American cigarettes and the cognac. It warmed him, and loosened his tongue. He was just pouring himself a second when Freddy came in. He went up to the stranger with his unvarying, engaging smile. If Mira sent for him to come to the office, it was usually because she needed his signature. Today he was being asked to have tea, which was not generally served in the office. He had had his tea long ago, but if Mira wished it, he would have another. He noticed that Mira was in higher spirits than usual; she must have done a bit of extra-special business. Papa had said something at lunch about a Polish count, he recalled. This was probably the one. Freddy balanced his teacup skillfully, stretched out his leg, and smiled warmly. He smiled even more cordially when Mira said, "We have some business with the Count; he is staying in town for a few days and will be our guest tonight. Milton is also coming."

"Great, that's really great," Freddy replied.

The Count thought Freddy a very nice fellow—and moreover felt a keen respect for him. If his wife engaged in such stupendous transactions, what must her husband do! He compared this healthy, tranquil, smiling Linkhand with the serious, formal, deliberate P. R. Linkhand of Warsaw, with his old-fashioned, patriarchal courtesies. Evidently there were differences between Jews and Jews as there were between Poles and Poles. With Jews like this you could get on pretty well.

Mira interrupted the Count's humanitarian cogitations. "We'll call a halt to this session, gentlemen. I have my household duties, you know. You'll want to change, too, Count. We dine around nine. You'll take the Count to his hotel, won't you, Freddy?"

The Count was thrown into confusion. His only civilian suit was the one he had on. He had, of course, not taken his uniform on this business trip. There was no one in town from whom he could borrow evening dress; he didn't know a soul in Vienna. He had made that remark about the Ambassador only to impress.

"Madame, my dear Herr Linkhand, I'm afraid I shall have to renounce the pleasure and honor of being your guest tonight. The suit I'm wearing is the only one I have with me. My civilian clothes are all back home on the estate; I use this suit only for more or less forbidden outings in Warsaw. Otherwise I always wear uniform. Year in, year out. And I didn't think to bring a uniform with me. On a business trip, you understand."

"Of course," Freddy said. "That's a filthy shame."

Mira understood; she understood perfectly. She had not been born a Linkhand, and until the age of seventeen. . . . But she

wanted this man to spend the evening; she wanted to see him, to
hear his voice. "That's certainly no reason for us to lose the pleasure of your company, Count," she said. "Besides, you would have
to call on us later tonight in any case. I also want to have a talk
with you about your lawsuit. So let us do as our friends in England
always do. If my brother-in-law were not coming—he's a bit odd
about these matters—"

"Oh yes," Freddy said, "he can be a pain in the neck, I tell
you." He liked this Polish Count. Thank God, here was a man
who did not go on talking eternally about business.

"Freddy, go up with the Count and let him try on one of
Gustl's dinner suits."

"Fine." Freddy was pleased. "Come along; the English always
do this kind of thing. If I ever visit your castle—"

The Count allowed himself to be persuaded. He felt that he as
good as had the hundred thousand in his pocket now—if only Lord
Brother-in-law did not put in his oar. Why a lord, incidentally? Ah
yes, in England it was possible; even Jews were lords there. And
he did not necessarily have to be a Jew. A fortune like the Linkhands' could attract even a Christian lord—even a Polish count.
Ah yes, the Count mused as he followed Freddy up the wide staircase to the private apartments, there are Jews and Jews, and Jewesses and Jewesses. This red-haired Jewess had her eye on him; he
felt sure of that.

Freddy led his guest to the rooms his brother had occupied before moving to New York; Gustav still used them when he came
back on a visit without his American wife. Before he opened the
right closet—there were half a dozen, filled with clothing for all occasions—Freddy tried four. Finally the dull black of cloth and the
gleam of silk lapels indicated that he had found the right one. "Ah,
here we are, Count, we'll have it in a moment." He pushed several
jackets back and forth along the rod. "Here," he said, "try this one."
It turned out that his guess was right. The jacket fitted. So did the
shoes, seamless, of black patent leather, and the black silk socks,
and the shirt of white Japanese silk. From another wardrobe
Freddy took pajamas and slippers and led the way into the adjoining room. There he waved cheerfully to the Count and took his
leave.

As he dressed, Count Voronovski mused. Here was a vast
stock of clothes and shoes belonging to a fellow whose home was
in New York—where undoubtedly he had far more. The Count

had been born at a low ebb in his family's history, when his father had already overburdened their only source of wealth, the land, with mortgages. His father had gone on spending freely on horses, women, cards and drink, but had never had money for barest necessities. Count Vladislav was poorer than the sons of some small tradesman or official. In the past the family had gone on living in their palace, though the rooms were gradually denuded of the furniture, paintings, rugs, porcelain and silver bought, inherited, or won by the pillage of previous generations. Eventually, all went to the creditors in partial settlement of debts. Finally, after Count Jozef's death, his widow had to move, with Vladek and his younger sister, Marenzia, from the few remaining habitable rooms. The reason, the Countess always pretended to her friends, was that the Russian border was too close. Which would have been believable if the family had had another home. As it was, she was fortunate in finding a place for herself and her children with one of her deceased husband's aunts—and she was taken in less for the ties of kinship than for her talents as housekeeper, companion and mentor of this aunt's grandchildren.

For Vladek's mother Elizaveta, daughter of a Russian prince who had perished along with his whole family in the October revolution, had enjoyed an education of the finest aristocratic type. She was a great lady and remained so even when reduced to a position of dependence upon the miserly, petty old relative who lived with her daughter, son-in-law and grandchildren in a rambling old castle. Still, the Count's mother had taught not only her employer's grandchildren but her own children all she could teach them. By the age of twelve Vladek knew everything a young nobleman must know. Without excessive difficulty he passed the entrance examination for cavalry school, became a second lieutenant at twenty, and only recently—at the age of thirty-one—had risen to the rank of captain.

His mother went on bearing her lot, without prospects and without hope. Marenzia, who was not only beautiful but artistically gifted and socially graceful, would probably have been doomed to the dreary life of a spinster if the existence of the Voronovski forests and the suit in connection with them had not brought her to the attention of eligible bachelors of her class.

The suit had come about in the following fashion.

As a result of the bankruptcy and suicide of a local businessman, a number of promissory notes made out by Vladek's deceased father, Count Jozef Voronovski, came into the possession of P. R. Linkhand. The notes gave the possessor certain rights to parts of a forest that had once belonged to the Voronovski estates. P.R.

inquired about the value of the papers, and found his fears confirmed. The name of the debtor was evidence enough that the sums could not be recovered. Nevertheless, being the soul of order, P.R. had his lawyer inform the widow and children that the notes given long ago to So-and-so were now in his possession, and hence he and not So-and-so was the creditor. He had no hope of collecting; the notification was merely a matter of form.

The Countess took counsel with her son in Warsaw, and the two decided to tell off this Jew who had the temerity to remind them of debts they had never made—all the more so since the forest in question was by now probably on Russian rather than Polish soil.

Apparently it was not so easy to gain access to this Jew—he lived in a fine house on one of the best boulevards of the city. This was enough to indicate that this Jew was different from those they had previously known. When they were finally shown into the office, they found themselves confronting a well-dressed, aristocratic-looking gentleman who heard out their protests with the hint of a smile and a measured gesture suggesting that he was well aware you could not get blood out of a stone. The lawyer's letter was only a notification, not a request for payment, he said. However, since he had acquired shares in this forest as security for a substantial sum, he was interested to know where the forest was located, and if it still existed. For the rather carelessly drawn-up receipts merely stated, "The forests belonging to Count Jozef Voronovski in Voronovka, specifically the lots between the white stone and the ruin." Could the Countess or her son throw some light on these details, which might have some relevance for him as a businessman?

P.R. asked this merely as a matter of form, for he did not hope for much help from these people. He had been born and grown old in this part of Europe (formerly Russian territory and now part of Poland). He spoke Russian and Polish, and he knew people in general and the aristocracy in particular. These were nobles. They had to be judged by other than the usual standards. All they could say was that there was such a forest; they had no idea of its present situation. In the days of Vladek's grandfather it had all been Russia, and after the war Voronovka had been only fifteen miles from the border. To which country the forest belonged now . . . the Countess really did not know. Another man might have grimaced in disgust. P.R., who knew the aristocracy and its traditional vagueness about practical details, merely remarked that he thought it necessary to find out, and that if any information useful to them turned up, he would let them know.

* * *

The Countess returned home, and Count Vladislav continued with his military duties. To the family's surprise, however, the matter did not end here. It soon began to appear that their unknown property might be their salvation. Three weeks later, P.R. asked them to come to see him and informed them that the forest existed, in all its former vast extent, and that the whole of it was on Polish soil, although in places it ran to within five miles of the Russian border. Moreover, it appeared that nothing stood in the way of marketing its lumber. The firm of P. R. Linkhand would, of course, not place any liens upon the income thus derived, for that would be in violation of the firm's principles. He was sure they would be able to come to an amicable arrangement, but only after the family was receiving appreciable sums from exploitation of the timber. At the moment it was important, and essential to the interests of both parties, to make sure that the rights of the Voronovski heirs were reestablished on a sound legal basis. For that purpose he recommended a specialist in such affairs, an attorney named Dr. Manfred Lipowski.

P.R. had spoken at some length, and the Voronovski heirs had listened with strained attention. But they understood little more than the fact that suddenly some highly valuable property had fallen from heaven upon them. Only the rules which had been drilled into their caste for centuries and had passed into their very blood prevented the three aristocrats from hurling questions at P.R. As it was, the young officer only asked his mother in French for permission to put a few questions to Pan Linkhand.

"The forest, then, exists?" he asked.

"There is no doubt about that," P.R. replied.

"And my mother, my sister and I are the owners of the forest. If we like, we can sell it?"

"Certainly," P.R. replied. "Once the formalities are settled, you can do whatever you like with it. Naturally"—P.R. cleared his throat—"the portion mentioned in the promissory note, from the white stone to the ruin—my people have already made a survey —becomes your property, so to speak, only after the sums already mentioned have been paid."

The Count partly comprehended this. "You mean, that section belongs to you? Very well. We would not repudiate what you have in black and white and what our father, God bless him, signed. But a forest has many trees. Suppose you keep your part and we sell the rest of it."

P.R., as has been said, knew counts. It would be utterly pointless to attempt to explain to this young man that he was not the owner of the section in question, that it had only been signed over as security (worth six times, perhaps ten times, as much) for sums advanced to the late Count. It could be sold, the debt could be liquidated and there would still remain a sum tremendous by the family's present standards—after sale of only that one section, which represented but a fraction of the total property. He did not intend to wring a substantial profit out of a possibly dubious mortgage by fleecing three inexperienced people. The Linkhands did not take advantage of the helpless. P.R. Linkhand had the reputation of being cautious and stingy, but he was honest; he not only acted honestly but thought honestly. He must therefore attempt to explain to these three people what was involved, for he saw prospects for a transaction on the Linkhand scale.

He turned to the Countess once more. "The property involved is large, very large," he said. "A beech and oak forest, with stands of pine. It's area has been estimated at fifteen thousand acres, and it may turn out to be even more. It is, however, twenty-five miles from the nearest railroad station. Transportation of the timber by horse-drawn wagons and trucks would be not only expensive but terribly time-consuming over the bad roads of the region. The forest can be profitably exploited only if sawmills are erected right on the property, and if a narrow-gage rail line is laid to the nearest railroad station. Is that clear?"

All three nodded, although they could not imagine being embroiled in such undertakings.

"It is obvious," P.R. continued, "that you are not in any position to direct such work, since a project of this sort calls for a good deal of technical and managerial knowledge. Also a certain financial structure would have to be created, for which both experience and the backing of large sums of money would be prerequisite. One must learn how to do business just as one learns how to fight battles." P.R. smiled paternally across the desk at the young officer. "Therefore, my dear Count, you must look for a partner who will bring into the business what you lack: experience and money."

The Count thought he understood what Pan Linkhand was getting at. "And where will we find this partner? Would you, sir, care to be our partner? You have experience and—"

"And money, you were going to say, Count?"

"Haven't you?" the Count asked, surprised and disappointed.

"Let us assume the conditions for a partnership exist. However, you really ought to consider the whole matter carefully. For instance, you should make inquiries about my firm. Suppose, then, that we meet again tomorrow."

But a brilliant idea had occurred to the Count. "How would it be, sir, if you relieved us of the whole problem? I mean, if you made an offer to us for the whole forest. Right now, on the spot. You buy the forest. Then you can do whatever you like with it."

His mother and sister nodded almost imperceptibly. Their clever Vladek had spoken from their hearts.

But this Jew who looked like a cardinal appeared unwilling to seize an opportunity that ninety-nine out of a hundred business-men in his position, Jews or Christians, would have jumped at. P. R. Linkhand declined it for various reasons, in which prudence and morality played equal parts. He did not try to tell his reasons to the Count, his mother and his sister, for they would not have understood. Instead he adopted a tone that he very rarely employed in business dealings:

"You see, my dear Count, my dear ladies, by birth and educa-tion, by tradition and by the tasks our country has assigned to you, you are very remote from the profession of the businessman and financier. I too am bound by traditions that go back at least three hundred years. If I were to accept your proposal and offer you some price, no matter what it was, I would be breaking with my traditions. The value of such a property cannot be estimated at a first or even a second glance. To make an offer in such circum-stances would be either foolish or crooked. We Linkhands are not foolish, nor are we unethical." He turned directly to Countess Elizaveta. "Countess, your daughter and your son are good-looking, healthy young people who belong to a noble family. They will marry, and you will have grandchildren. You must see to their fu-ture. As a businessman who knows the values of things, I advise you not to sell the forest. Rather, assure yourself, your children and your grandchildren a fine life, a life without cares."

That was something the Countess could follow. The man spoke convincingly; he used choice language, and he spoke of a life without cares for herself, her children and grandchildren. That was the decisive factor. She did not think or dream beyond neces-sities: shelter, food, clothing. She did not count on large sums, had not counted on them for the past twenty years. In fact, she had done very little reckoning in her life, although at the moment she was much perturbed by a particular calculation that went running through her head: how the sum of two zlotys, which was all she would have left after buying their return tickets, was going to maintain two persons in Warsaw for the next two, if not three, days. Vladek? It was the twenty-second of the month; he had probably been charging his cigarettes for the past week. But at the moment this awkward problem in arithmetic was thrust into the background. She extended her right hand to P.R. with the gesture she had learned—and taught—was the one used for equals, and as

P.R. stood up and bent over her hand, she said, "I will discuss the whole matter with my children. Rest assured, we are glad to have made your acquaintance and—we trust you." And when the solemn moment had passed: "It is rather complicated, I must say; we had not expected to be staying overnight, or even several days, but—*les affaires sont les affaires.*" She rose.

P.R. asked her to stay a moment longer, and begged the Count to have a few words with him at the far end of the room. There, not in a businesslike tone, but in that of a benevolent elderly friend, he offered to be of assistance until the project began to yield tangible profits. Undoubtedly the Count would have certain expenditures he had not counted on, which could easily swallow up the pay of the entire officer corps, let alone that of a first lieutenant (which Vladek still was at the time). In any case, whether the family decided to go into business with the house of Linkhand or with someone else, he was glad to be at their disposal.

Count Vladislav had never been made so magnanimous a proposal in his whole life. He could only click his heels and stand at attention as if he were in the presence of his colonel.

P.R. picked up the telephone, with an apologetic bow toward the table at which the ladies were sitting, and spoke softly into it. A man in a dark coat slipped through the door, bowed, laid an envelope on the table in front of P.R., and vanished. P.R. said, "Here, Count, for initial expenditures. Ten thousand zlotys. Would you be good enough to confirm this, for the sake of order." With one hand he pushed the receipt toward him, with the other handed him the envelope. The Count signed and slipped the envelope into his pocket. "I think that is all," P.R. said. With an imperceptible frown he had noted that this Count, poor as he was, differed in no wise from all other nobles; he pocketed the money he had received without counting it.

Thus it came about that the Count and his family, whose situation had taken an outward turn for the better as a result of the unlooked-for shower of money, sat one day in the offices of P. R. Linkhand, Warsaw, and signed documents presented to them by four lawyers: powers of attorney, statements, acknowledgments, petitions. The transaction had begun. And after the heirs' title to the property had been legally established, after a staggering inheritance tax had been paid, the Society for the Development of the Voronovski Timberlands was set up and incorporated.

The house of P. R. Linkhand figured in none of the many official documents. A separate contract, drawn up between P. R.

Linkhand and the heirs, assigned to P.R. a participation of 51 per cent. Advances to date, and investments that would run into seven figures, were the basis for this arrangement. The expenses for the various phases of the business passed through the Countess's hand. She paid them as representative of the family, for her son, as an army officer, could not participate officially in a commercial enterprise. The Countess signed all the checks. As far as all authorities were concerned, the Voronovski family were the owners of the new firm. Only the stock exchange knew that P. R. Linkhand was behind it. But that did not matter, once the business was under way.

The Countess and her daughter took up permanent residence in Warsaw, occupying two rooms in an excellent small hotel. P.R. had discreetly asked the Countess how much she would need for her maintenance in Warsaw, and after a hasty calculation she had said one thousand zlotys. That sum came to her in monthly installments; it permitted her an easy though not luxurious life, since two hundred of it went to her son.

News of the altered fortunes of the Voronovskis circulated swiftly through the most exclusive salons of Warsaw's aristocracy. People reminded themselves of former friendly relations and ties of kinship; the Countess and her daughter were invited out, and the invitations were accepted since the Countess expected that she would soon be able to reciprocate. Thus the Countess learned from members of her own caste what a magical aura hung about the name of P. R. Linkhand. The respect that was shown to her, she realized, was due less to her and her late husband's irreproachable family tree than to her association with P. R. Linkhand, the nabob. That, too, provided the proper frame for her daughter's extraordinary beauty. Naturally a number of suitors appeared, handsome men with great names and noble, expensive passions. But all were up to their ears in debt. Prince Roman Bolgurski was the notable exception. The Voronovski family were much impressed by his qualifications. He owned considerable land, operated an excellent stud and could boast of an estate with well-kept grounds and a palace equipped with modern conveniences. Hence he was a fine match for Marenzia who, as soon as the seed sown by P. R. Linkhand began to sprout, would possess a considerable dowry in the form of a sizable current income.

Prince Roman Bolgurski typified the solid and trustworthy type of modern landed proprietor. He understood agriculture and was not easily duped by his farm managers, stewards and tenant farmers. Thirty-five, stocky but far from fat, with somewhat sparse, dark-blond hair, an open, intelligent face and large blue eyes, he

spent ten months of the year on his estate, saw to everything himself, and had scarcely any debts worth mentioning. He liked to
drink with the young men of his class, gambled somewhat, but
knew when to stop, and had had a fair number of love affairs. He
spent six weeks of every year traveling abroad and two to three
weeks in Warsaw, before the spring work began. He had a handsome house in a quiet, elegant street of the capital, all of it rented
except for three rooms which he reserved for himself. He had fallen
in love with Marenzia; she liked him too; and there was no obstacle to the marriage.

The Countess would have liked to marry her daughter with
pomp and circumstance, with all the ceremony to which a rich
bride and heiress was entitled. But she did not have the means and
did not want to borrow (though in these early stages of new-found
glory she could easily have found creditors), because she knew only
too well the consequences of debt and the suffering debt could
bring. Pan Linkhand had congratulated her on her excellent choice
of a son-in-law, but apparently had not realized that a mother in
such a situation needs a great deal of money for her daughter. A
family affair that could run into money had nothing to do with the
business—whose costs, moreover, were far higher than had been
expected.

In spite of its good Polish and aristocratic front, the enterprise
was an affair of the house of P. R. Linkhand. Consequently, no one
else could put his fingers in the pie. Financial circles took their revenge by dropping various hints in certain quarters. The owners of
the land through which the narrow-gage railroad would have to
pass took cognizance of the unique situation, and quadrupled the
normal selling price. Those who owned sizable parcels of land
did their best to organize the small owners behind the same policy
and under the ancient banner of anti-Semitism. The campaign was
effective—all the more so since there was little love for Jews in Poland. That had always been so, and now anti-Semitism had become
virtually a matter of honor. For was not Poland on the best of
terms with Germany? Did not Göring go hunting with Count
Potocki, and was not Colonel Beck a regular visitor to Berlin? What
was all this about a buffer state—what an ugly phrase, another in-
vention of Jewish journalists. The Germans needed the Poles. Were
not the Poles destined to fight on Hitler's side against the Bolsheviki and the Jews? And wasn't this new outfit being run by Jews?
The Voronovski family? Now, really! Since when did counts make
a profit on Jews and not Jews on counts?

Such was the popular view, and it may be assumed that P.R.
had taken it into his calculations. As long as the firm formally be-

longed to the Voronovski family, however, he expected to have comparatively little trouble.

When the small owners presented him with their inflated prices for land that had been virtually worthless only the day before, he countered by the application of tried and true methods of financial operation. There was scarcely a farm in that part of the country which was not more or less heavily in debt. Through a bank that practically belonged to him, P.R. obtained possession of long-over-due mortgages and notes. The mills of justice, lubricated by keen lawyers, began to grind. Suddenly the enterprising property own-ers were in urgent need of money to meet these obligations. Shortly afterwards, several newspapers in the capital made it known that the Voronovski heirs were applying to the authorities for permis-sion to rebuild the one wretched road in the area, and transform it into a wide paved highway on which ten-ton trucks, such as were used in the Canadian woods, would transport the lumber from the Voronovski sawmills. The news items tipped the balance; the alarmed landowners hastily settled at reasonable terms, and the way was open for preliminary work to begin.

But trouble arose from a new quarter.

In the Ministry for National Defense sat a Lieutenant Colonel who was not a count, not of the aristocracy. All that was known of this Lieutenant Colonel Karinski was that he was an unusually com-petent officer who was regarded as highly ambitious. But he never tripped over his own ambitions. For he had a way of ascribing his successes to his superiors and of praising them until they began to believe that the credit was really theirs. In consequence he had a good deal of influence over the generals under whom he worked.

One night at supper this Lieutenant Colonel read a newspaper item about the plans for paving the highway. He read it again at breakfast, went straight to his office, took out his maps and began plotting the location of the Voronovski woods. He made measure-ments, wielded the compass, calculated, and at eleven o'clock ap-peared before his General with an accumulation of material which, he hoped, would win him eternal laurels.

The General, who was a count, at first wanted to know nothing of the matter. But his subordinate convinced him that the heirs of Count Voronovski were not really involved here; the person who would be affected was a Jew, the shamefully rich Linkhand. Link-hand was, to be sure, enormously cunning, but not so clever that a patriotic Pole could not see through him.

Before the day was out, the General had signed the devastating document addressed to the directors of the Society for the Develop-ment of the Voronovski Timberlands. In concise military phrases this document stated that the cutting of timber in the sector where these lands lay was banned for reasons of national defense, according to Public Ordinance Number So-and-so. Violation of the ordinance would incur the penalty of such-and-such fines and imprisonment for so-and-so many years.

P.R. perceived that this unexpected assault was directed against himself rather than the Voronovskis. On the other hand, if the cited ordinance really did exist, he must be prepared for a hard and protracted legal struggle in which his prospects for success depended upon a change in the political situation. Long conferences with his lawyers ensued. The legal experts came to the conclusion that the state had the right to issue such bans, but that no general could do so on his own. Thus the order could be contested on formal grounds, but the chances for success. . . . And they dropped into a meaningful silence.

P. R. Linkhand had often been pitted against the government in the courts. He knew that if the state took anything from a citizen, it had to pay compensation. He therefore informed the Ministry for National Defense that the directors of the company intended to fight with all the legal means at their command for the right to develop the woodlands. The Countess signed this letter without apprehending how close she was to her former and so recent condition of want.

The Voronovski case naturally created a great sensation. P. R. Linkhand had invested a fortune in the company, and he was determined to save it and, if possible, to save the whole transaction. Under his keen direction skillful lawyers brought suit, brought a horde of suits. Their and P.R.'s agility kept the Countess's head above water in society. For people concluded from all this legal activity that all was by no means lost. The Voronovskis might no longer expect a huge fortune, but they would almost certainly obtain some compensation; otherwise old Linkhand would not be throwing so much good money after bad. Who else was paying for the army of lawyers, for the enormous legal costs? Certainly not the Countess, although she seemed in comfortable circumstances. Marenzia still looked beautiful, dressed well, and Roman Bolgurski was evidently thinking of no one but her. Why hadn't the couple married yet? What were they waiting for? The Countess still had the emeralds she had worn at Marenzia's engagement—old people remembered having seen them around the neck of Vladek's grandmother. If the woman had been able to keep such a necklace, she was certainly not poor!

But when a year passed and the engagement had not yet terminated in a wedding, the time came for the Countess to part with her necklace. Bolgurski had made his impatience plain. He loved Marenzia and wanted to be married as soon as possible. Marenzia wanted to also, although she knew very well where the shoe pinched. She understood that it would be terribly painful for Mama, really impossible, to let her marry without a trousseau. But there was the necklace, after all. It should be worth enough for a decent if not opulent trousseau and a respectable wedding. Since Roman had said that he was willing to wait for the dowry, there was no reason to delay any longer—all the more so since it had been settled that Mama would move into her new home with her.

The family finally agreed that the emeralds should be sold and the proceeds used for the trousseau and wedding. If anything remained over, mother and son could divide it. But they had no idea of the market value of the necklace. They vacillated between optimism and pessimism, one moment guessing too high, another too low, until Vladek asked his mother to draw up a list of what would be needed for Marenzia. After considerable figuring, they decided that they could not manage with less than fifty thousand zlotys.

But before the Countess finally parted with the jewelry, she wanted to consult Pan Linkhand. In the secret recesses of her heart she hoped for a different, a miraculous, solution. Perhaps this noble man, who must feel that the legal tangles would soon be unsnarled, and that the Voronovskis were worth their weight in gold, would understand a delicate hint?

P.R., however, was in no state of mind to go on helping this family. They were costing him too much already. With his undeviating formal courtesy, however, he examined the necklace and advised the Countess to show it to his cousin in Vienna. The Viennese Linkhand would buy the stones and surely pay a good price for them.

This was how it came about that Vladislav, Count Voronovski, carrying a suitcase stamped with monogram and coronet but containing no more than two sets of underclothes, socks and handkerchiefs, landed in the Hotel Klomser in Vienna, entered the house of Linkhand conscious of the great weight of his responsibility, concluded a highly favorable transaction, and found himself invited to supper and provided with the attire necessary for such occasions in the *grand monde.*

With boyish exuberance he showered, rubbed his hair with strange and splendidly perfumed lotions, and combed and brushed it carefully. Coal-black, his hair looked like a polished helmet above his clear brow, which was pale where it had been protected from the sun by his cap, the traditional *konfederacka,* and deeply tanned where it had been exposed. His head was narrow, high-bred, emphatically masculine; his nose rather large but straight except for an almost imperceptible bend high up on the bridge; his chin strong and as sensual as his mouth, whose slightly upturned red lips exerted an unconscious charm whenever he smiled or laughed. As he stood naked before the bathroom mirror, his trunk hairless and muscular, his waist narrow and lithe, with long, strong, lean cavalryman's legs, slightly bowed from much riding, with small feet and slender, well-groomed hands, it was easy to understand that he pleased women.

But if he thought himself a conqueror because he had already had a good deal of success with the ladies, that was an error into which men of his type could easily fall. He had not conquered; he had been taken. He reacted to women out of inclination, gallantry and chivalrousness toward their wishes, but only as long as they aimed at what he could give, at purely physical relationships. He was incapable of anything beyond these. He had no subjects for conversation, serious or merry; he read seldom and knew little. He was a soldier, and he took his occupation seriously, would have loyally followed any flag to which he had sworn an oath. His ideal was fighting itself—fighting on horseback; he could scarcely imagine any other kind of combat. Horses meant everything to him. His poverty did not permit him to own one of those thoroughbred, expensive creatures. But he was not bothered by a desire to possess them; rather, he rejoiced in the sight of them, was stirred by the mere fact of their existence. He simply wanted to ride them, and train them. His vast knowledge of horses had not been acquired by study; he knew no anatomy or pedigrees; but his instinct was good. And although he had the highest regard for fine horses, he loved all horses without exception.

Since it would still be more than an hour to supper, he lost himself in a photograph album which lay on a small table, and which showed not only horses but riders, mostly in uniform: officers of the old Austrian Army. Here was something far more important and far more interesting than emeralds.

Meanwhile Mira had instructed the cook to add an English as well as a Polish dish to the menu. Then she telephoned her father-in-law in Gastein. As was usual with her, she came straight to the point. "I've bought the stones," she said.

"Are they good?" A.L. asked.

"Perlberg has seen them. He says one is good, the other still better."

After a brief pause: "How much?"

"That depends on how much you reckon off for the five-point-seventy-six diamond from the big set."

"I understand—a swap. But won't the set suffer?"

"Perlberg is taking the bad ones to Amsterdam for recutting. He says he can fix them."

"In that case I would think seventeen hundred per carat for the five-point-seventy-sixer."

"That is, about ten thousand for the stone? O.K. What should P.R. get as a commission?"

"Is there room for a thousand?"

"Plenty of room. Then—one moment, Papa—in that case the emeralds have cost us in the neighborhood of twenty-seven thousand one hundred."

"Not bad. A good deal cheaper than I figured."

"I could have bought them still cheaper—by exactly the amount that the diamond costs. But you understand: we Linkhands want our profit, but not our clients' loss." (This was a favorite phrase of A.L.'s.)

"You're my good girl."

"Thank you. One more thing, Papa. Do you know much about P.R.'s forest deal?"

"Just what he told me about it a few months ago. He's stuck with it, and it's costing him a good deal of money. I don't recall the exact sum, but I rather think he's not very hopeful about it."

"How would he take it if we—A.L., A.G. and Lord Godbrooke—wanted to go in on it?"

"He's a businessman, and if he's pessimistic he'll want to salvage whatever he can. Naturally his suspicions will be aroused if we make him an offer. But why should we go into it? P.R. has lived his whole life in that part of the world. He knows local conditions better than we do. If he has no hope, why should we sink anything in a bad deal?"

"Because it isn't a bad deal. I told you that months ago. Would you do something for me, Papa? Milton is eating with us tonight, and the Count too. Please telephone P.R. and tell him that the emerald affair is settled and that the commission has been credited to him. And at the same time ask him whether he'll take us in on the timber deal."

"Isn't that a bit too hasty, Mira?"

"You're right, Papa, it is, but this is one time when haste is called for. As I said, Milton is here—and the Count too."

"But he's just a figurehead; he hasn't anything to say."

"He would have, if he is made to understand the role he will have to play."

"Well, all right, it doesn't cost anything to ask. I'll broach the matter cautiously. If he's agreeable, he'll call you tonight. Good luck and thanks. My regards to Freddy and Milton—and the Count too!" He laughed. "Enjoy yourself, Mira."

As Mira dried herself after her bath, she grew more and more thoughtful. She wondered about the adventure on which she was embarking. First of all, there was the matter of the diamond. She had been toying—even while she was still in the office—with the idea of giving it to the Count as a wedding gift for his sister. The best of forty-five stones. She had not mentioned it, in order to give herself a chance to change her mind. Now it was too late for that.

She slipped out of her bathrobe and stood naked in front of the big mirror. Would she please him as she was now? What would happen, what would become of her, if he disdained her, if he did not want her? What use would money, property, work, ambition be to her after that? Could all that help her quench the despair at having this first—this only—wish of her life go unfulfilled? For hitherto she had wished for nothing personal, only set her heart on this or that material object.

She went up close to the mirror and looked at her eyes, which shone with an ardor she had never seen before, at her mouth, whose hard lines had within a few hours taken on a tender softness. She saw and recognized the change, and rebuked herself. She must regain command of herself. No one must see what was going on within her. Desire creates strength, and increases existing powers; but wishing enfeebles. Was she strong enough to switch off her will? Strong enough to become weak? She did not know, because for the first time in her life she was being overpowered by an emotion that she had only observed in other people, or at the theater, the movies, in novels. She had dismissed it as imaginary. Now, in a few hours she had discovered that such emotions were real, that she could long to be embraced, caressed, taken; that the mere thought of it made her giddy, and that she was helplessly running counter to self-interest because for once her actions were not being dictated by the will, but by an emotion which had sprung up mysteriously and gained irresistible power over her.

For how was it possible that she, Mira Linkhand, should toss ten thousand dollars into the lap of this young man whom both her father-in-law and the Warsaw Linkhand dismissed as totally without importance? It wasn't true that she was doing so out of any sense of business ethics. That was a pretense, all right for A.L. and perhaps for his cousin in Warsaw but not for her. Her real motivation, she knew, was a senseless urge to help the Count; and that was why she was planning to interfere in the timberlands project.

She wanted to free him from his financial predicament, offer him the chance to live as he wished, to live like a count. What else could she, Mira Linkhand, do for him? Pour out her feelings in tender words? Mira had no capacity for that; all she had ever done was reckon.

From the small safe in the wall she took her ruby jewelry—an immense pigeon-blood ruby shaped like a teardrop and suspended from an antique necklace of small rubies, a wide bracelet set with rubies, and earrings of the same workmanship as the chain. Then she rang for her maid.

Freddy, who had already dressed for the evening, was bored. He paid a call on the likable Count, and found him absorbed in the album. "Excuse me," the Count said—he was still in shirt-sleeves— "these things are fascinating. Here's Emir the Second—there was a famous horse—and Buccaneer and Dawn, and that one is Maestoso the Third."

Freddy had slumped into a chair. He smiled benevolently. "Get into your duds, and we'll go down and have a cocktail," he said.

The Count sprang to his feet. "Oh yes, forgive me. You know, when I see horses, even just their photos—" He picked up the jacket and looked puzzled. "Uh . . . I think this suit has something missing."

"Something missing?" Freddy asked.

"The—the vest, if you don't mind."

"Nobody wears them any longer. Gone out of style."

The Count was profoundly impressed by this revelation. "You understand, Herr Linkhand, I'm not exactly up on civilian dress. But if people don't wear a vest any longer—where do you put your watch?"

Freddy looked at him. "Watch? Like this one?" He extended his hand from the long cuff and showed the matte gold wristwatch with its black leather strap.

"No, like this one!" the Count said, taking a heavy gold pocket watch from his vest pocket. He owned a wristwatch, but it was a serviceable cheap one and fit only to be worn on duty. His friend Lolek had lent him this heirloom for his trip. A coat of arms, a coronet and an intricate monogram in Cyrillic letters, formed of tiny diamonds, adorned the big gold lid.

Freddy was much struck by it. "Just like Uncle J.B.'s in Zurich," he exclaimed. "But this one is much prettier. Does it play, too? J.B.'s makes music. That's a fine piece you have there, Count. Let me have a look at it."

The Count was embarrassed. He snapped the watch from its gold chain and handed it to Freddy. Throughout his trip to Vienna he had been nervous about the possibility of its being stolen by some pickpocket. He watched anxiously as Freddy opened the lid, looked inside, and finally closed it again and returned it. "No music, a pity. Still—awfully nice. But no pockets to put it in. Let's go over to my room and I'll fix you up with one."

In Freddy's room they stood for some time over a small chest that was filled with wristwatches and pocket watches of various shapes and makes and precious metals. "Here," Freddy said, "this one ought to suit you." It was a solid gold calendar watch which showed all divisions of time from the second to the year. Freddy explained everything down to the hand in the center, which moved between two semicircles and was supposed to show the phases of the moon. "I don't understand that, don't know what it's for. But look." He pressed a knob that protruded from the watch's side. A thin hand began moving around the face, and when Freddy pressed another knob it stopped running. He pressed the first knob again, and the hand snapped back to its starting point.

"A stopwatch!" the Count exclaimed. In his whole regiment there were only two people who had them, both of nickel, and big pocket watches.

"That's right," Freddy said, laughing, "but I've got nothing to stop with it. I'm no sportsman. And then—all those hands! Tell you what, Count, give me the pleasure of keeping the watch for a memento. You can't go riding with that big watch, can you? This one's a lot better on horseback, isn't it?" Laughing, he strapped the watch to the Count's wrist. "It has a black strap, too. Doesn't quite do for a sports watch, but fine for tonight. Milton, my brother-in-law Lord Godbrooke, has eyes in the back of his head, and he'd have fits if he saw a fellow wearing anything but a black strap with evening dress. But let's go down now; it's ten minutes to nine—time to toss down a couple of cocktails."

The Count was speechless. He stood lost in contemplation of the magnificent product of the watchmaker's art in his hand, which was being offered to him. How? Why? Here stood this friendly, well-spoken, generous Herr Linkhand giving away a watch which— God only knew what such a watch was worth. An anxiety that had oppressed him since his boyhood settled down upon him. Had he the right to accept it? Could he ever repay his host for such a gift? "I really don't know how I've deserved so much kindness, Herr Linkhand. It really won't do, you know."

"But why not? Look here, Count, I like you. You don't keep talking about transactions and money—you like horses, the way my brother Gustl does. Why make a fuss over a stopwatch? You can make use of it; I don't ever. Why not let me have the pleasure of giving it to you, eh?"

And so the Count decided to oblige this charming fellow by accepting the watch. Perhaps, he thought, he would offend him if he did not accept it, or offend against the laws of hospitality, sacred to every Pole (guest in the house, God in the house!).

"Thank you very much, Herr Linkhand, for your gift. I hope I shall be able to repay you. You are right; we must drink to this!"

They did so at the bar, lubricating their mutual esteem with several martinis mixed to perfection by Charles. Mira found them talking with heartwarming congeniality. Her salmon-pink evening dress and ruby jewelry set off the color of her hair, which swirled about her head in an artful cloud, but which was carefully arranged at the sides so that her small, beautiful ears were completely visible, accentuated by the earrings. The two men sprang from their hassocks—or rather, only the Count did; Freddy stumbled and did not rise to his feet as surely and gracefully as the athletic Count. In any case Mira had eyes only for the Count. "Welcome to our house, Count," she said, extending her hand for him to kiss. She asked Charles for a highball. "Milton has already arrived; we'll be able to eat soon."

Lord Godbrooke came up to the bar. Tall, gaunt, with a sallow-complexioned, long face, somewhat bulging forehead, and gray, intelligent, rather bored eyes, he was forty but looked older. His hair, heavily sprinkled with gray, was parted carefully in the middle. At Mira's suggestion they all spoke French because the Count did not speak English and Lord Godbrooke did not care for German. Lord Godbrooke sipped his martini, and Freddy and the Count gradually paired up, which suited Milton, for he had a great deal of news that he wanted to discuss with Mira.

Charles, who had gone out after mixing Lord Godbrooke's drink, returned a few minutes later to call Mira to the telephone. It was the asthmatic money broker, announcing that a Polish package was at her disposal and that, as Frau Linkhand might note, it still lacked four minutes of the agreed deadline. He went on to say that it had taken some doing, and that if it had not been for the Linkhands—. Mira interrupted his gasping asseverations to ask him the price, and how he wanted his money. "Sixteen thousand one hundred dollars, including commission, and if possible Zurich or New York."

"Very well," Mira said, feeling a moment's gratification that she had calculated correctly. "Could you deliver the package to my house?"

"Certainly."

Mira informed Charles that someone would soon be dropping by. The caller was to be shown into the library. She took checkbook and pen from her bag and made out the check. She had scarcely rejoined the men in the bar room when Charles came to say that a gentleman was waiting to see her. As she went to the library, leaving Lord Godbrooke politely discussing horses with the Count, it occurred to her that she was doing something altogether improper for a Linkhand. By involving herself in this unsavory manipulation, and actually meeting her accomplice face to face, she was committing a grave infraction of the guiding principles of the family. For it was dangerous to deliver oneself into the hands of such operators, and doubly foolish to do it in order to gratify the whim of a young man whose very existence had been unknown to her twelve hours before. She was glad of the dim light of the library; she could hope that the money broker would not recognize her as the girl who used to call on him some years ago, in the interests of Frau Kadisch.

The fat man showed no sign of recognition as he rose ponderously and handed her the bundle of bank notes, wrapped in tissue paper, bearing the imprint of a Silesian bank. "Counted it myself," the man puffed, and took her check. With "An honor to be of service to you," he made his way out the door. Mira counted the notes, and carefully rewrapped them in the tissue paper. Even if the fat man kept silent, the affair was still full of potential embarrassments. What did the servants think? What if the talkative old butler dropped a remark to A.L.? If her father-in-law asked her about it, what could she tell him? She sighed and shrugged fatalistically. She had felt compelled to act as she had done. Now she need only give the Count the package. It was five after nine, time to return to her guests.

Freddy had refilled the men's glasses, and Lord Godbrooke, splendidly dissimulating his impatience and boredom, was answering the Count's questions about Irish hunters. Not only did he have important business matters to discuss with Mira, which this Count would probably interfere with, but he was also feeling increasingly hungry. Ah, there she was at last. All those shades of red, Lord Godbrooke thought. No, she would never learn the finer points of dress, capable as she was in other respects.

She handed the Count his envelope. The evening had been so lively that he had actually forgotten the money. With a bow he thrust it into his breast pocket. He felt certain that everything was in order. No need to look or count; he was dealing with gentlemen, that was plain.

At that moment Robert opened the portieres and announced that supper was served.

The supper wound to an end toward eleven o'clock. They moved to a large, pleasant room full of easy chairs and low tables for their coffee and cognac. Godbrooke contrived to take Mira aside and explain in detail the affair that had brought him to Belgrade. She promised to think it over. Now it was her turn to air her proposition. She indicated cautiously that, assuming that P.R. was willing, she intended to look into the timberlands business. In broad outline she described the matter to Godbrooke, and explained the circumstances that had brought it to a standstill. There were, she indicated, ways to start the ball rolling again. Once launched, it would be a tremendously profitable venture. Lord Godbrooke was not especially keen on doing business with P.R., but Mira reasoned him out of this.

She was on the point of suggesting a new project to Godbrooke, which might easily be combined with his Yugoslav deal, when Charles called her to the telephone. With a gesture Lord Godbrooke would have found unforgivable in any other woman with claims to good breeding, Mira beckoned to him to accompany her. That would surely be P.R., she whispered, and scurried off toward the telephone with an air of triumph he had never before observed in her. Which led him to the conclusion that she thought the timberlands deal a particularly good one.

He followed his sister-in-law and found her already discussing the matter with P.R. She was explaining that Lord Godbrooke and A.L. would come in, if her idea proved workable. Would P.R. send her a memorandum on what legal steps had already been taken?

P.R. was hesitant at first. Then, concerned about keeping down the length of the long-distance call, he hastily agreed to send Mira what she wanted, asked about the emeralds, and hung up.

In those few minutes a decisive step had been taken. This was the beginning of a business enterprise to which Mira Linkhand would devote all her knowledge and ability, all her prudence and cleverness, audacity and unscrupulousness.

"How long will you be here, Milton?" she asked.

Dear Mira could sometimes be *too* direct, Lord Godbrooke thought. No hostess was supposed to say that sort of thing. "There are several other matters I want to discuss with you, Mira. Difficulties have cropped up with that business in Yugoslavia."

"All right, we'll talk about them right after lunch tomorrow."

"Can't you make it tomorrow morning?" Lord Godbrooke asked with some disappointment.

"No," she replied, with more energy than seemed appropriate. "I've already made appointments for the whole morning—things that can't be canceled." She had set aside the morning to be alone with the Count. That was more important to her than any business discussion. "But we'll lunch at one, and right afterward we'll sit down together and discuss everything. Will that suit your plans, Milton?"

"All right, Mira. And now, if you don't mind, I'll be getting to bed."

The Count took his leave shortly after. Freddy drove him to his hotel, and they parted as the best of friends. By the time Freddy returned, Mira was already asleep. Or at least she seemed to be. In reality she slept little that night. For the first time in her life she longed for a man.

The man for whom she longed sat in his old-fashioned hotel room, the watch and the fat envelope of zlotys on the table before him. His one thought was that he would be able to buy the horse, Captain. Now and then he started the hand of the stopwatch and then made it snap back. The money and the watch had made him happy. He fell asleep without being troubled by any longing.

Next day Mira was back at her desk in A.L.'s office, reading the mail. She had read all the letters through, had gone over some of them twice, but not a word had remained in her head. Finally she gave up and stared dreamily into space. She no longer knew herself; she was an altogether different Mira from the woman who had sat in this chair twenty-four hours before. She was in love, and her love was returned. Had she not been kissed by the radiant young count? Had they not fallen into each other's arms, drawn by an irresistible force, when he helped her out of the saddle on a quiet stretch of bridle path lined by ancient trees?

Passionate love had had no place in Mira's life hitherto. She had known nothing about it, and now it had attacked her by surprise, and she found herself defenseless. Her world of figures, of combinations and speculations, of work and self-improvement, excluded personal feelings. Now she was shaken by love, by longing, by the desire to inspire passion. Her drive to success had consumed all her energies. Her will had suppressed the instincts which existed within her as in any other young woman. Freddy Linkhand had become her husband, and she had found pleasure, and perhaps a certain amount of physical release, in his arms, but never rapture or delirium. And she had not fastened her desire on any other man because she had not known there could be anything beyond this tepid satisfaction.

Now her time had come. Her destiny had begun to unfold. She had the same feelings, the same wishes, as any other young woman who experiences love for the first time. She wanted to be alone with her beloved, anywhere, to shower him with tenderness, to serve him in every way.

Her reverie was shattered by the ringing of the telephone. Perlberg had come with the samples, accompanied by Loewe, the goldsmith. She had to talk with them, give instructions; the business of everyday dispelled dreams and sweet unrest.

Count Vladislav Voronovski, however, sat in the breakfast room at the Klomser, a cigarette in his lips, a glass of vodka before him, the packet of bank notes in his pocket and the gold stopwatch on his wrist, and was happy. It had been beautiful riding in the Prater. The two horses, Mira's and the old stableman's horse, had been magnificent. The tack, too, was first-class. So were the riding breeches that Freddy had lent him, again from G.G.'s wardrobe. The big roan he had ridden was no longer young, but perfect in his gaits and temperament, and Mira's horse was actually a genuine Irish hunter, with all the marks of finest breeding. She sat her horse well, having clearly learned from good teachers; her riding fell short of having real class, but as she herself had said, it would do.

And so they had ridden for half an hour, walking and trotting the horses. Then they'd had a brief canter and stopped to rest by the old trees. There he had kissed her—or she him; who could say precisely? At any rate, they had got along famously, although at first they had both been rather clumsy about it. Who could teach him anything about women? Hadn't he seen from the first that the redhaired girl had an eye on him? Why not? Vladek thought. I've no objection. She's damned good-looking in riding clothes. Wellgroomed, too, from top to toe, and what a perfume her skin and hair have. He smiled and raised his glass to himself: Cheers, Vladek, you handled that very well.

Count Voronovski was highly content with himself, and remained so. He became Mira Linkhand's lover, and she performed wonders for his cause. Even skeptical P. R. Linkhand, who tended to mete out praise in small doses, fully acknowledged her accomplishments. An English company became an official partner of the Voronovski family—a company whose directorate was studded with dukes, lords and sirs—and within a bare four months the society had won its suit against the Polish Ministry of Defense. Affidavits signed by prominent experts attested that the heavily wooded area was a handicap to national defense rather than an advantage. The government itself ought to see to its removal, rather than oppose those who were attempting to clear it. Long before the beginning of the new year a host of woodcutters were putting up their shacks, sawmills were roaring, and the new branch railroad was delivering lumber to the freight station.

At the end of January, 1938, Mira returned to Vienna from Warsaw. She had a prolonged, somber conversation with her father-in-law and persuaded him to liquidate his affairs in Austria. She herself took charge of the liquidation, securing the best-possible conditions. A. L. Linkhand and Rachelle took up residence in Zurich. An Italian concern bought their town house and offices in Vienna. When the German troops paraded into Austria in March, the Linkhands suffered virtually no losses. But A.L. often shed tears in a quiet corner of his new house in Zurich. He had lost his country, and his daughter-in-law's farsightedness did not console him for that. At the time of the Anschluss she herself was fortunately in Warsaw—accompanied, as she was on all her travels, by Freddy. The Polish timberlands business was proving enormously profitable. By a whim of fate, the former Voronovski palace in Warsaw was for sale at just this time. The company bought it. Part of it was set aside for office space, and a part was turned over to the Voronovski family as their residence, for they could now afford to live in real style. The Countess had her permanent home on her son-in-law's estate, but she spent the winter months in the capital. Her parties soon became famous in Warsaw, as her son's horses were famous throughout the Polish cavalry. He had five of them, and was constantly competing at meets and winning trophies. He was happy with his horses, and with Mira. Yes, with Mira too. Now he could live like his ancestors, and Mira had made it possible. Aside from horses, he had no expensive passions. Naturally he gave parties for his fellow officers occasionally, but he did not hold open house for them, for it would have been disagreeable to them to be unable to repay hospitality. As for women, the only woman who mattered to him was Mira. He loved her. At first he had taken up with her out of mingled cynicism and curiosity, for she was of an alien race, not at all a lady, and consequently the very opposite of his conception of a woman and mistress. But soon gratitude had driven away these other feelings. Moreover, her aroused passion had evoked an equally strong response from him. He was too young, healthy and naïve not to respond to it, and in his relationship to

Mira he became, for the first time in his life, the ideal lover. She brought him pleasure, and drew hers from him. Nothing intellectual —no exchange of opinions and ideas—linked them. They were held by the strongest of all bonds, that forged by sex, by irresistible drives. When they were separated, the craving to be together came not from their minds but from their bodies. Their skins longed for the other's touch; their blood was fevered with recollection; and their love-making, though often hasty, became the celebration of a mystery.

Mira had had two private rooms furnished above the offices. As a matter of course, she and Freddy lived in P.R.'s home. But she frequently had to work late—and thus she contrived to enjoy stolen hours with Vladek.

The two were dependent upon one another, but this dependence was no torment, no burden; it was a pleasure intensified by secrecy. An ideal situation was achieved, and Mira's long training in prudence stood her in good stead. While others were present, she made good use of the somewhat stiff forms of courtesy she had once learned from Lady Whisten. At business meetings, when Vladek's signature or formal consent was needed, she never betrayed their intimacy by a look or a gesture. And, of course, Freddy's indolence was highly favorable to the love affair. Even if the thought of a relationship between his wife and another had occurred to Freddy, he would have rejected it as something uncomfortable and troublesome. He did not observe any change in his wife's conduct toward himself, for he was not the man to observe such changes.

Mira's relaxed air, her softness and gaiety—which had replaced the coldness, angularity and sometimes cranky humorlessness that had characterized her—was attributed to her ever-greater successes in business.

The ninetieth birthday of J. B. Linkhand of Zurich was the occasion for a celebration on a grand scale. All the Linkhands of Europe and overseas assembled. On the fourth of April, 1939, a resplendent company gathered in J.B.'s great house. The formal congratulations were delivered in the morning. To spare his strength, grown-ups and children filed quickly past J.B.'s wheelchair. For the festive dinner, the entire family gathered in the Hotel Baur au Lac. A.L. delivered the toast to the nonogenarian, and there crept into his words sorrow over the recent events in Europe. A few days previously Hitler's troops had invaded Czechoslovakia.

In such circumstances it was difficult for the celebrants to summon up much gaiety. But the muted mood changed somewhat when Mira Linkhand, about half an hour after her father-in-law's speech, struck her glass and in her customary terse fashion invited all the businessmen among the Linkhands (for many of them were scholars, artists, scientists and doctors) to a conference at J.B.'s house at ten o'clock in the morning next day. The acclaim that greeted this invitation proved to A.L. that the prediction he had made at his son's engagement had been more than fulfilled.

At precisely ten o'clock in the morning the Linkhands assembled in J.B.'s huge dining hall. They took their seats promptly, each with a sheet of paper and sharpened pencils before him. Boxes of cigars and cigarettes, lighters and ashtrays were scattered down the length of the table. The curtains were drawn, the electric light turned on. At five after ten a servant wheeled in J. B. Linkhand. The upper end of the table had been left free for his wheelchair. Then the servant left, and the Linkhands were among themselves.

J.B. opened the meeting. "I want to thank you, especially those of you from overseas, that you have spared neither time nor trouble to come in person to congratulate the eldest Linkhand on his birthday." He put on his glasses and his glance wandered up and down the table. "It's good of you," he added in his feeble but distinct old man's voice. "That is really all that I have to say. It seems likely that I shall soon be called to our fathers. I shall die in peace when my time comes, because I know that our family is united, and strong in its unity. But now I ask you to give all your attention to our dear Mira. She has something of the greatest importance to say to you." J. B. Linkhand removed his glasses and laid them on the table in front of him. He gazed at Mira, who sat opposite him, to the right of her father-in-law and to the left of her brother-in-law, G.G. of New York. In all this gathering of Linkhand men she was the only woman.

Mira stood up. This was something new. In the past she had always spoken from her seat, her eyes fixed on a sheet of paper on which she had noted cue phrases and figures. Her voice, hoarse and low, had sounded as if it came from a machine, without rises and falls, without emphasis on important words and phrases. If what she said had not invariably been sensational, her speeches would have been soporific.

But now an altogether changed Mira confronted them. There was none of the tension which had formerly made her face rigid and her movements wooden. She was controlled, sure of herself. Her glistening, golden eyes looked around without constraint at all these men who had long since come to acknowledge her as an equal business partner and inaugurator of new projects, a power in the family and the world of finance. Mira's voice was still low and hoarse, but it was no longer inhibited and expressionless. There was a mysterious, alien force in it.

"Our senior has said that I have important matters to propose to you. If I, who am one of the youngest, not only in years but also in membership in the family, bring this problem forward, I do so because to my mind it is high time—it is the eleventh hour—to discuss it and make a decision. My proposal is: liquidation of all Linkhand and associated enterprises and all property on the continent of Europe. I propose we transfer all Linkhand capital to the United States and to certain Latin American countries. I propose that new firms be established in connection with the existing ones in the hands of the overseas members of our family."

Linkhand discipline was proverbial. At all family meetings the supreme law was to let a person finish what he had to say. But what they were now being asked to listen to seemed to a good many of them intolerable. Some were not only disturbed, but offended, outraged—they would have liked to stand up and leave the room. Why, one and another of them thought, what does this outsider think we are? How dare she give such advice to the Linkhands, who are Europeans? Fathers, sons, brothers, cousins, in-laws—from Europe and overseas—whispered to one another in various languages, so that the senior Linkhand had to tap his pencil firmly on the table. There was instant quiet. "Please go on," he said to Mira. And she continued as if this murmur of protest had not occurred.

"I know that many of you here are shocked by what I propose. I am aware of the reasons. The Linkhands are rightly proud of their European tradition, which was created in the course of centuries and has survived wars and revolutions. Moreover, the family has always emerged from such upheavals stronger and more famous than before. The businessman, the entrepreneur, must know how to profit by every situation. Wars and revolutions create such new situations, and often can be turned to better account than normal times. But this war toward which Europe is moving will destroy not only Europe but all traditions. It will be waged by traditionless people, by the enemies of tradition, the enemies of the spirit and culture of Europe."

The Amsterdamer called out, "Oho!" and the Parisian, ordinarily one of Mira's warmest supporters, said loudly, *"Bêtise!"* The Antwerp Linkhand made a gesture intended to convey that these were exaggerated phrases. Many others indicated by gestures that they were not in accord with her.

But she remained undeterred. She gave herself barely a minute's pause. "Let me tell you how I have come to my conclusions. There is always time for you to say no after I have spoken. Perhaps the events in Austria might not have been conclusive, but what hap-

pened two weeks ago in Czechoslovakia banishes all hope. Hitler
has Prague. He has captured Czech heavy industry, has taken it
over without having to shed a drop of blood. By dint of such bloodless victories he is now able to put into the field the largest and
best-equipped army in Europe. The English, who in the past could
always be counted on to defend the balance of power in Europe,
have made it plain that they want no war. This has come through
most clearly in their refusing an alliance with the Russians, who
recognized the full extent of the danger and wanted to take action.
Today Hitler is practically the master of Europe. And Hitler is our,
the Linkhands', greatest enemy. For we are Jews, and rich. He may
turn against the West or against the East without serious opposition.
He will do the one or the other within the foreseeable future, and
will kill and plunder the defenseless everywhere."

"O la-la," said the elegant Parisian Linkhand. His two sons and
three sons-in-law, reserve officers in the French Army, wore sarcastic
and hostile expressions. With each passing minute they liked this
woman's candor less.

But Mira went on. "I am not appealing to the Linkhands as
Europeans or as patriots, or even as Jews, but I am appealing to them
as businessmen, entrepreneurs, financiers, who must balance the
chances for profit against the predictable risks. What do we lose
when we transfer our sphere of interest from Europe to America?
We will find there the necessary support among our relatives. We
will not be poor relations, for we will be bringing money, a great
deal of money. We can afford the same good things as most Ameri-
cans, and more. And who could prevent us from conducting our
lives in keeping with the traditions of the Linkhands?" The Amsterdamer cleared his throat audibly and looked across first at the
Warsaw Linkhand and then at A.L. and J.B. But neither responded.
"Have the American Linkhands broken with tradition? Wherever
we are, there the Linkhands will be—except in a concentration
camp or—"

This was too much for the Amsterdamer. None of them, not
even J.B., the senior, had ever seen such an episode at a family conference. He slapped the table with the palm of his hand and exclaimed, "Now really, I must say!"

J.B. was about to call the Amsterdamer to order, but Mira asked
him to let J.J. have the floor. She herself turned to him: "Yes, Uncle
J.J.? What would you like to say?"

J.J. remained in his seat. "You have overlooked an important
point, my dear niece," he said. "Linkhand solidarity. Where there is
room for one Linkhand, there is room for a hundred. Holland is not
large, but it has space enough for every Linkhand in Europe, if

things should ever come to the pass you are trying to describe."

"Or Belgium," said M. D. Linkhand of Antwerp, who was eager to demonstrate his solidarity with J.J. They conducted many deals in common.

"What makes you so certain that Hitler will not march into Holland or even Belgium?"

"Why that's preposterous!" J.J. said. "Holland? What would he be doing in Holland? Ridiculous!"

"Ridiculous!" the Belgian echoed him.

Mira turned to P.R. of Warsaw. "Paul, would you answer a question for me?"

"Certainly," P.R. said, with some surprise. He had already settled the matter for himself. He would go. Her arguments had convinced him, as well as what he had seen of her business acumen in Warsaw.

"What did Herliczka of the Wittkowitz works say in our Warsaw office a bare four weeks ago?" Mira asked. "You remember, we began talking about Hitler, and I asked him whether people in Prague were not afraid that Hitler would occupy all of Czechoslovakia."

P.R. spoke into the air, without looking at Mira or any of the others. "I remember exactly. He said, 'Ridiculous!' And then he repeated it more emphatically: 'Ridiculous! Utterly out of the question!'"

Mira did not pursue the matter, did not attempt to deepen the effect produced by P.R.'s quotation. "I know," she said abruptly, "that my way of doing business has not been approved by some members of the family. These quick transactions of mine were not in keeping with Linkhand tradition. But you have realized that business must be adapted to the times. For Jews all types of business, quick deals included, are coming to an end in Europe. It is no longer the place for the Linkhands. Of course we hope that Hitler will not remain master of Europe, but he will be master long enough to annihilate us. And who can ultimately destroy him? England? At the moment there's no sign of anything of the sort. Is France—unarmed, inwardly disunited and splintered, largely corrupted—the future savior? Hardly. So Europe must look to Russia. But we Linkhands may not even place our hopes there. For what have we to expect from the Russians, we and our like, whom they regard as the most dangerous enemies of their system?" Mira bowed her head for a moment, raised it, and looked searchingly, challengingly rather than appealingly, up and down the length of the table.

"I am not speaking this way to impose my will on you, or because I am frightened," she continued. "I am not thinking of my personal safety. I have told you this because I consider it only right to give you my opinion of the situation. That is my opinion, my advice; it is, if you will, the expression of my gratitude to the Linkhand family."

Mira sat down and took a cigarette. G.G. offered her a light. It was very still in J.B.'s dining room. Most of the men were smoking, staring into space or up at the ceiling.

In response to a gesture from J.B., A. L. Linkhand rose. In the expectant silence he spoke briefly: "I do not want to add anything to Mira's arguments and proposals, but only remind you of the rules we have always observed and which, with your approval, we will observe now. In conferences over important affairs of the Linkhand family, a two-thirds majority has always been decisive. Each of those present has a vote. My question is: Are all participants in the family council agreed that we shall hold a vote on Mira Linkhand's proposal? Will those in favor please raise their right hands?"

Everyone raised his right hand.

A.L. continued: "I am pleased to see that we are unanimous in regard to the formal aspect of this decision. Remember, too, that whichever way the majority decides, all members of the family without exception are bound by that decision. There is no appeal. The vote will take place in this room at six o'clock this evening." He sat down. J.B. asked G.G. to ring.

The servants appeared, drew the curtains back from the windows so that the spring sunlight streamed into the room, and served sherry and caviar on toast. Not a word was spoken concerning the preceding debate and the impending vital decision. A.L. had reminded them of their time-honored procedures, and the Linkhands knew how to maintain them. They would have six hours in which to discuss and confer, each with his group, each with his following; but all would unconditionally obey the will of the majority.

The balloting was open, as was the custom of the family. The youngest voter, the twenty-six-year-old son of the London Linkhand, E.X. (Edwin Xavier), read the names from a list, a copy of which lay before J.B., the senior. At his side sat A.L., formerly of Vienna, and P.R., Warsaw, who were closest to him in age. J.B.'s checklist was subsequently filed with the family chronicles—one of the most important documents in that large collection.

Each person, as his name was read, stepped before the group of three and stated, "I am familiar with Mira Linkhand's motion and am for [or against] it." Of the hundred and three participants, eighty-eight voted for Mira's motion, including J.B. and, to everyone's surprise, P.G. of Paris. P.G.'s sons and sons-in-law were against the motion, as were the Amsterdam and Antwerp representatives, but their sons and sons-in-law were for it. All the overseas Linkhands were for it, as was R.O., formerly of Berlin; but his sons and sons-in-law, who had already settled down in Switzerland, voted against it.

P.R. of Warsaw announced the result of the vote: 88 in favor, 15 against.

Mira rose and earnestly thanked those who had voted for her motion. She fully understood, she said, the sentiments of those who had been opposed. Even if the future proved her wrong, she asked them all to believe that her action had sprung solely from the desire to save the family, to preserve it. "If there is ever again a Europe in which there is room for the Linkhands, nothing will prevent us from returning, just as nothing can prevent us from being Linkhands and working like Linkhands in our new countries." Then she informed them that she had already worked out detailed plans in regard to liquidation and departure.

The entire group set about studying Mira's plans, and carrying out the necessary arrangements. Those plans were masterpieces of commercial strategy; Mira had not left the smallest item out of her calculations.

For the next ten days Mira worked furiously, and performed new prodigies of strength, circumspection, diligence and foresight. The Linkhands soon knew not only when they were to leave Europe —on the fifteenth of July, aboard a ship of the line Lord Godbrooke controlled—but also that comfortable houses would await them at their destinations and some sketches for congenial as well as profitable work.

J. B. Linkhand, the senior member, had voted for Mira's proposal, but it seemed out of the question that he himself would emigrate. Nevertheless he too made all the necessary arrangements. He explained that he intended to leave Europe because his home was his family, and only in proximity to his family would the short time he had left of life hold any meaning for him. The sale of his home —the house had been built in 1723 and continuously occupied by Linkhands—was a symbolic act intended to demonstrate to any Linkhand who might be wavering that J.B., the oldest of them, who had least to fear, was ready to sacrifice all that linked him emotionally and practically to Europe, were that necessary to prove his solidarity with the family.

* * *

By April 15 all the visiting Linkhands had left Zurich. Mira remained for a few days more, at her father-in-law's request, to rest from the prodigious amount of work she had performed. But her longing for her lover became acute—all the more so since she no longer had anything to distract her. She was glad that she had arranged to meet Godbrooke in Warsaw on April 23. Certain projects would have to be wound up, not only the lumbering interests. The Linkhands had made highly profitable contracts in wool with textile mills in Lodz. Now they would have to withdraw from these enterprises as unobtrusively and on as favorable terms as possible. Mira would, of course, do all in her power to speed the liquidation, but—she had already hinted this to her father-in-law—she would not be able to travel with the family; she would follow them several weeks later. A.L. accepted her reasons. "You're a true fighter Mira. The first in any advance, and the last in the rear guard," he said, patting her hand.

"Thank you, Papa," she replied. "That's the way it should be. If you're content with me, then I'm happy."

A.L. gave her a searching look. "Do you mean it that way, Mira? The way you said that?"

Mira looked up. "I don't understand your question, Papa. Haven't I always been sincere in what I say to you?" Of all the members of the family, the one she felt really close to was her father-in-law. Toward him she felt gratitude, respect, fondness, and she wanted him to know it.

A.L. did not care to reveal the many perplexities that had arisen in his mind since he, and particularly his wife Rachelle, had noticed the changes in Mira's personality: the new softness, the new appeals to emotion. He confined himself, in answer, to a paternal, old man's banality: "What are you thinking of, Mira? You are and always will be my darling, brilliant girl. No, no, I don't doubt your sincerity, and never did. I think I've proved that. But I want to be sincere too—" He paused, groping for words.

"Yes, Papa, say it," she said gravely and quietly.

He took the plunge. "Look, Mira, I'm old. Gustl and Ellie can take care of themselves. My one concern is: what will become of Freddy when I am no longer here?"

Mira was honestly taken aback. She did not like to, did not want to, think of the possibility of A.L.'s death. "What puts that into your mind, Papa?" She laid her hand on his in a tender gesture that struck him as strange in her, but that gave him pleasure. "What an idea! Look at J.B., who's twenty years older than you are!"

"Only eighteen, Mira. But never mind that; I was speaking of Freddy. He loves you very much, Mira. As far as he's cap—I mean—

he's deeply attached to you."

"I know, and so am I to him." She meant that, as she said it. She was attached to Freddy. She was accustomed to him, owed a great deal to him, and he did not interfere with her, not even . . . Mira felt sudden alarm at the possibility that her carefully guarded secret love had been discovered. Her mind began working feverishly. She must not let A.L. think anything of the sort. She must convince him that it wasn't true. "What do you mean about Freddy, Papa? What's troubling you?"

He looked at her. Could he have offended her? She seemed hurt; she had withdrawn her hand from his. He took it back. "Don't be upset, Mira," he said tenderly. "Troubled? No, you could hardly call it that. I'm not troubled. But I am a little concerned. You're a young, beautiful, wealthy woman. A desirable woman. Understand me right, Mira. Temptation will come to you, and—to put it bluntly—I'm afraid that someday you might leave Freddy. Then he would be very unhappy."

"Papa!" Mira was utterly amazed. Not at what her father-in-law had said, but at the way he had said it. For now she was certain that he knew. But instead of reprimanding her, his kindness was intensified. Was he not begging her, imploring her, not to leave Freddy? She searched his face. There was no anger or indignation there, only an anxious plea. What, how much, did he know? Perhaps she could dispel his suspicions, prove herself innocent. Everything must remain as it was. She wanted to keep everything: the Linkhands and Vladek. "Papa," she repeated with a degree of agitation that her father-in-law had never seen her exhibit before, "whatever put such thoughts into your mind? What does all this mean?" She wanted to force him to lay his cards on the table. Then the game would be easier. Perhaps she could still win it by a bluff. Perhaps she could hold him to a draw. Unfortunately she did not have full control of herself; she could not help letting A.L. see her nervousness.

But he misinterpreted it. He thought that Mira was offended and upset because his doubts had done her an injustice. "Please understand me, Mira," he said softly. He sounded placating rather than accusing, and Mira breathed easier. "The others, Ellie and Gustl, have everything. Happy family lives, fine children, joy in their work. Freddy has only you. You are his life, and that's why I am worried." His voice was very feeble, almost a whisper. "Worried that someday, if you should—" He stopped.   .

Mira understood this time. He was concerned solely for his son and his son's happiness. That was the major point in his contract with her. He had just reminded her of that. He was not accusing her of any breach of contract, only trying to prevent her from committing one. As soon as Mira perceived that, she found it easy to reply, "I don't know what makes you think of all this, Papa, but—I hope you know me well enough—well enough not to be worried. . . ." She studied him intently as she spoke. No, he didn't know. "I see that you're troubled, Papa. You have no reason to be. I promise you that I will never leave Freddy. Not to my dying day!" She held out her right hand, and he took it in both his hands.

Relieved, touched, glad, he said, "I believe you, Mira!" For these were the words he had wanted to hear. He was reassured, as a father —and as a businessman. Mira had spoken honestly and given her handclasp. Could there be a stronger proof of sincere intention among businessmen?

While the Linkhands in Western Europe went ahead with their arrangements for emigration, according to Mira's plans, and while their relatives overseas made preparations for their reception, Mira herself took charge of the last part of the tremendous task: liquidation of the Linkhand interests in Southeastern and Eastern Europe. Within barely seven weeks all the work was done in Yugoslavia, Greece and Romania. With Freddy she flew to Zurich, and from there issued comprehensive reports, inventories and audits to the various members of the family—all of whom expressed their gratification. That girl Mira—she really *was* unique.

There remained one last country, which was as Mira had planned it: Poland. Here was the vast lumber export business which had grown out of the Voronovski timberlands. Hundreds of square miles of additional woodlands had since been acquired; vast quantities of lumber were being exported via Gdynia to all the ports of the Middle East and thence to all the hundreds of installations the world over where the British were erecting barracks. In accordance with Mira's logical system, Lord Godbrooke directed all these activities, from forest product to finished barrack; and, likewise on Mira's advice, the Voronovski family had been taken into the whole business, more or less as the official representatives of Polish capital. Their percentage of the profits was almost insignificant to the company, but of considerable importance to them.

Marenzia Voronovski's husband, Prince Bolgurski, was the only one among these Polish nobles who had some conception of the vast scale of the business. Fortune had smiled upon the Prince. He had found himself a lovely wife from one of the best families in Poland—who, moreover, had turned out to be rich, very rich, not only in zlotys but even on the dollar scale. It was inevitable that the

Prince was thrown into contact with Mira, although all the negotiations with the Voronovski family ostensibly were carried out by P.R.
The Prince quickly realized that this woman was a key figure in
the English company headed by her brother-in-law Lord Godbrooke.
The wedding gift for his wife, that beautiful and incredibly costly
diamond which had been given to her in the name of A. L. Linkhand of Vienna, had provided him with much food for thought.
The Prince understood that in comparison to the vast sums at the
disposal of this company, his own financial operations were on an
extremely small scale. But he also realized that for reasons he did
not understand, the Linkhand interests were benevolently disposed
toward his relatives, and therefore presumably toward himself. And
he thought it only wise to take some advantage of this link.

The consequence was that one day he telephoned Mira and
asked for an appointment.

Mira, who had spoken to the Prince three times in all, was surprised, but gave no sign of it. She asked him to come to her office
around five o'clock, if that was convenient.

The Prince came straight to the point. He wished to invest his
own and his relatives' capital in an industry closely connected with
agriculture. What he had in mind was the establishment of a sugar
refinery on one of his estates, which happened to be situated close
to an important railroad junction. Was Mme. Linkhand familiar
with the refinery in Khodorov and did she know how profitable it
was? He was convinced, he said, that the factory he wished to build
close to Warsaw would certainly be even more so. He was also
thinking of a large, electric-powered mill; there was plenty of room
for both on his property.

While Mira listened attentively, the Prince explained the project in more detail. But he was hesitant about the most important
point, he said. He was not very familiar with the procedures for
financing such projects. He was prepared to commit all the funds at
his disposal, but of course that would not be nearly enough. Could
Mme. Linkhand give him any suggestions? How did one go about
borrowing from a bank, issuing stock, or even interesting foreign
capital?

While her caller was speaking, Mira had been thinking intensely.
Not about the Prince's project, but about his personal qualities
and how she could best fit them into the plan that for some time had
been vaguely taking shape in her mind. By the time he finished,
she knew how to approach the matter.

"Your plans are good, *mon prince*," she said, "and have a sound
practical basis. They would not be difficult to carry out; it is easy to
obtain money for a promising venture. After all, finance capital exists

to promote industry and trade. But capitalists are cautious, have to be so, and the first question they ask themselves is whether the times are favorable for establishing new enterprises. A sugar refinery or a mill is not like a forest which can be cut off in a given time. You might call the latter a destructive process. Such enterprises as you project, *mon prince,* are constructive, which means that they are established with a view to a long future. The times we are living in are not favorable to new building. Europe is restive, troubled, and the capitalist takes that into consideration above all else. Believe me, most financiers are fearful of what will happen to their already existing investments at home or abroad if events in Europe go on developing in the direction they have taken."

Her caller was listening with deep and intelligent attention. She offered him a cigarette, took one herself, and while they smoked she continued. "I don't know whether you have sounded out any foreign financiers as yet, or what answer they may have given you. But the companies with which my family is connected would not be interested in your project—good and substantial though it is—because unfortunately the times are too uncertain."

She fell silent and looked across her desk at the Prince. She could have answered him far more succinctly, she thought, but for her eagerness to win over this amateur with his timid, small-time ideas— to win him over and use him for her plan.

He sat in silence, thinking over what she had said. Finally he spoke up, slowly and hesitantly: "So you think, madame, that there will be a war?"

"What I think scarcely counts. But the fears of other persons, far more prominent and cleverer than I, do. I know the general mood in Europe."

"But Poland—"

"You see, *mon prince,* as a foreigner, I am really not entitled to express my opinion. You are a patriot; I have no right to suggest to you that your country may be involved in a war just like any other country in Europe. You would naturally reject such an idea for psychological reasons. But the capitalist must be prudent. That is his first, his highest, duty."

The Prince looked at Mira. The plans he had cherished, had counted on, were evaporating. He had already put them out of his mind. What this woman was saying was of far greater importance. The capitalist must be prudent! Was not he himself also a capitalist, though a modest one? Was it not his duty to save his own capital? "Forgive my taking so much of your time, madame," he said, "but I must ask you another question."

"Certainly, please do so." The fish had taken the bait; she was pleased with herself.

"You have some idea of our—I mean, of my wife's and her relatives'—reserves. Of course they are nothing compared to the sums with which you operate—"

"Don't say that, *mon prince;* they are considerable. Moreover, your reserves will be a good deal larger when the lumber business is liquidated—and liquidation is imminent."

"How, then, can we protect this capital?"

"Would you like my advice?"

"If you would be so good," he said meekly.

"You see, *mon prince*—" Mira checked herself, forced herself to appear matter-of-fact. "I naturally cannot say to you: do this or that. At most I can tell you: If I were in your position, I would transfer everything I possess to a country which, within the limits of human foresight, will not fall under Hitler's power. The safest country, of course, is America.'

The Prince started back. "What do we have to do with America? I don't quite understand. You mean to say I should transfer the money, or that perhaps I myself—America? I hardly think I shall ever go there even on a visit, and certainly my family would not." He had suddenly become tense, embarrassed, and was obviously sorry that he had raised the question.

Mira had been watching him closely, and knew what was going on in his mind. Her statement had been intended as a trial balloon. Now she was certain that the Prince was not the man for America. "I know that many members of the Polish nobility have a horror of America. I don't quite understand it—you in particular, since you are interested in agriculture—"

"America is out of the question," the Prince said, his face and voice plainly expressing his distaste

Mira shrugged. "You asked me for advice, and I can only give the advice that seems good to me. As I have already said, that is what I would do if I were in your place. But there is also Switzerland, as a kind of compromise. It is in Europe, and yet not so threatened as other countries—although of course we can only judge that by past experience." She was anxious not to offend the Prince. If he was trying to act like a businessman, it was because he did not share the feeling usual to his class of being above considerations of money. He wanted to have more; he was more practical and sober than his fellow nobles, and he was willing to make concessions; but his prejudices were the same as theirs, and any departure from these prejudices struck him as sinful. Very well, then, my aristocrat, you don't want to go to America, but you're worried about your money; you're not as dense as the others and you're willing to grant that things can easily go wrong here in this little corner of the world. If not the Russians, who terrify you, the Germans may very well gobble you up. You don't feel easy, and it would be a pity about all that money, wouldn't it? I want you out of the country, and you don't know that, and still less do you know the reason.

"You see, *mon prince,* now you've misunderstood me. You regard my proposal about America as, at the very least, disrespectful. I spoke only as a reasonable person who draws his conclusions from studying the times. If I have offended you, forgive me; I didn't mean to."

The Prince hastened to assure her that he did not feel offended. But she must understand that even with good reason a man could not simply pick up and leave the land where his fathers and fore-fathers had lived.

She was well aware of that, Mira said, but she also knew that it was wrong to cling too obstinately to the past at the cost of the future. Living people were more important than faithfulness to tra-dition. The Prince's wife was one of the loveliest women that she, Mira, had ever met. She understood that a child was on the way. In that case, wasn't the future just as precious as the past?

Roman Bolgurski turned his light blue eyes toward Mira. For the first time it entered his mind that his beautiful, beloved Maren-zia, and the child soon to be born, might be in danger. The idea appalled him. This red-haired Jewess would know how he could go about saving them. "Then what would you suggest, madame? Aside from America, of course. That is really out of the question."

"Move your wife and your mother-in-law to Switzerland. Buy a small house there, six to eight rooms, not in a big city, and live with them there until the situation in Europe is clarified. Deposit your money in Swiss banks, or better still, the major part of it in American banks. Later, perhaps, I will be able to make suggestions to you on how to use it—profitably."

"I'm grateful for your advice. But my property, the land, the house, the stud farm, everything—"

"Sell it," Mira said.

"Sell!" The Prince was shaken. But he composed himself and said with dignity, "I am afraid we do not look at things in the same way, madame."

"Of course not," Mira said coolly. "But you asked me for advice, and I have given you the best I have. Perhaps, when you consider the whole matter and talk it over with your family, you'll come to a firm decision. In these times decisiveness is all-important. I shall be glad to help you wherever I can."

"Thank you, thank you very much," the Prince said. His indignation had subsided. After all, this Jewess knew no better. How could she understand the feelings of a man like himself had for the place of his birth?

"You're most welcome. I certainly hope you prove to be right, *mon prince,* rather than the pessimists," Mira said. She was confident that he had taken the bait. You and your class, with your mystic attachment to your land, she thought. It's all right to drink your income up, throw it away on women, gamble it away, but when it would be rational to sell your land, you're too noble for that.

The Prince rose. "Once again, my thanks to you. And if I may come to see you again—"

"Certainly, certainly. You're welcome at any time. However, I'll be leaving tomorrow and won't be back before the end of the week."

The Prince bowed. No sooner had he gone than Mira went up to her unofficial office and pulled the shade halfway down—her sign to Vladek that the coast was clear for a rendezvous.

After Mira had settled affairs to her and her associates' satisfaction, there remained little more for her to do in Poland. If she had wanted to, she and her husband could have left Warsaw with P.R., his wife, and his youngest, still unmarried daughter; she could have accompanied all the Linkhands on the ship taking them from Europe. One extra spurt of effort, and she could have taken care of the final details. But she was in no hurry. She had carefully constructed an obstacle to her departing, and she would remove it only when she cared to, that is, only after the Linkhands were all out of Europe.

There was Vladek, whom she could not part with, whom she had somehow to take with her into her new country and new life. She knew she could not sway him by the arguments that soberer people found compelling. That was why she had tried to be helpful to Prince Roman Bolgurski. If he left the country with Vladek's mother and sister, his example would, it seemed to her, make it easier for her to overcome Vladek's moral and patriotic scruples.

She was very pleased with herself when, several days later, Prince Roman Bolgurski requested another appointment. She arranged to see him next morning at ten'clock. The preceding evening she had spent a few glorious hours with Vladek. He was in a joyous mood because his brother-in-law had sold him his best horse, the stallion Slim. "Think of it, Mira!" Vladek crowed. "The sire had blood by Eclipse and the dam is out of Kinsczem. He'll be nearly seven at the next Olympics. Guess who'll take the military and the jumping prize there? Your Vladek!" His lovemaking was more passionate than ever. Mira's senses reeled. In the blissful trance of weakness that followed, she even forgot her plans, which left no room for her lover's horses or his riding triumphs.

How she loved him! But for that very reason, she was bent on holding him as she held everything she had achieved in life.

When Freddy came for her in response to her telephone call, she was back at her desk, sitting lost in thought. She knew what her caller would be telling her, on the morrow: that he had turned her advice over in his mind, and was ready to follow it. And once he and his family were out of the country, she must set about persuading Vladek to leave. That would not be easy. But what would her life be without the happiness that had flooded her barely half an hour earlier?

As she had expected, the Prince was anxious to apologize for having taken such an obstinate line at their first meeting. Madame must understand that he loved his country and the soil on which his forefathers had always lived and worked. But he realized that his supreme duty now was not to expose his family to danger. He had talked the whole matter over with his wife and her mother. As it happened, the situation was particularly favorable at the moment. He had medical certificates to the effect that his wife needed a lengthy stay in a Swiss sanatorium because of an infection of the lungs—the danger was all the greater in view of her advanced pregnancy. Her mother would naturally want to be with her in this difficult period, and of course he did too. Fortunately he had excellent connections with the Foreign Ministry, through a cousin. He had therefore been promised a post at the Polish Embassy in Bern. He had had no difficulty finding customers for his stud farm, and in fact, had sold it very advantageously. The harvest was excellent, and he already had a serious offer for his house in Warsaw. Arrangements were virtually completed for leasing his land and farm buildings for five years. "Of course," he concluded, "the fact that all this has gone so smoothly speaks well for the optimism of the buyers. Perhaps you are being too pessimistic, madame. Though by now I, too, take a pessimistic view."

Not so foolish, Mira thought. You're quite right, lordly scion of the aristocracy. She replied with a serious and considered air, "I *am* pessimistic, and my attitude has an absolutely tangible and logical basis. We too have liquidated our assets, not always at a profit and not only in the Eastern countries, where the danger seems the greatest, but in many Western countries as well. Our pessimism is a pure matter of business; it is founded upon political events which threaten not only the economy, but also some people's lives. Still, it is quite understandable that others should see the picture differently.

I had no choice but to give you the same advice I would give myself. Since everything has worked out so well for you, you aren't taking any financial loss. What's more, you've managed admirably to preserve appearances."

The Prince caught the innuendo and flushed a little. But he asked meekly enough, "If I may trouble you a moment longer—how am I to go about transferring the funds from all these sales to foreign banks—not to speak of the much larger sums which, you say, are due to my wife's family?"

Mira explained the procedure. She gave him the names and addresses of two reliable brokers. She would help him with further details later, she said. She was flying to London on July 13 and would be back by the eighteenth, or the nineteenth at the latest. They agreed to meet again on July 20, and the Prince took his leave, courteously thanking her for her trouble.

The *Blue Ocean* had been refitted, and could now well be called a luxury liner. Lord Godbrooke, at any rate, had not spared expense; he had had the vessel refurbished from stem to stern and installed every imaginable convenience for shipboard life. There was more than enough room for the two hundred and twenty-seven adults, one hundred and thirteen children and eighty-six servants who were accompanying their employers on this family voyage. By the day before departure they were all on board, already living in their staterooms and eating in the dining halls. The Linkhands left the Continent—to which only a few months before they had felt linked by indissoluble bonds—happily and easily, conscious that they were making the right choice.

When Mira appeared on board, accompanied by Freddy, she was greeted with joyous acclaim. She had arranged matters for all their safety and assurance. She had vanquished many difficulties and had loyally, wisely and conscientiously put the affairs of the Linkhands on an excellent footing. And now this remarkable woman was remaining behind to make sure that even their household effects were safely transported across the seas to the new homes of the Linkhands. P.R. stood up at the farewell dinner in the dining room of the *Blue Ocean* and said all these things. His words were greeted with loud and heartfelt applause. Mira thanked everyone, wished them a good voyage, and promised, "Au revoir in a few weeks."

The *Blue Ocean* set sail at 7:35 Greenwich time on July 15. All the passengers were gathered on the deck, even J.B. in his wheelchair, to wave to the few who were remaining behind: I. C. Linkhand of London and his numerous family, Lord Godbrooke and his wife and children, Mira and Freddy Linkhand.

Mira returned to London for a last conference with her brother-in-law. Lord Godbrooke had a few suggestions to make; he approved of everything that Mira had already arranged or was about to undertake. He was content, highly content, with the results of the past several years. Mira would need no more than three weeks to wind up matters in Poland and then leave from England for America.

After talking with her brother-in-law, Mira telephoned her old teacher, Nachum Fish, and arranged to see him next morning in the gem-cutting workshop where she had first received instruction. She had with her a raw diamond of 114 carats. It would do splendidly as a pretext for this visit. Freddy was still sleeping when she took a cab to Whitechapel, where Fish had his shop.

Fish, who had not seen her for years, received her with pleasure and respect. He led her into his office, a tiny area partitioned off by walls of glass so that he could keep his eye on his whole shop. The hum of small motors, the scratching of the diamonds on the revolving wheels and the singing of the gem cutters were assurance that not a word said in his office would reach the ears of any eavesdropper.

Sitting on his stool, silk cap pushed to the back of his head, Fish gazed at the diamond as though his eyes could probe its interior—although he had known for decades that every sizable raw diamond revealed its true qualities only after splitting, and often only after undergoing the first phases of the cutting process. Mira watched his lean face with its almost white mustache and felt her guess confirmed: he was the right man. "*Na ja,* yes," Fish said—though forty years a British subject, he still dropped into the Yiddish of his childhood and boyhood—"you know as well as I—"

"I wouldn't say that, Mr. Fish. I wish I knew half as much as you do." She flattered him with conscious intent.

The old man opened the door. "Fingermann!" he called. "A good cleaver—let's hear what he says," he explained.

Fingermann entered in shirt-sleeves and apron; with his ascetic face and long, reddish hair, he looked more like an artist than a workman. "What do you say to this?" Fish handed him the stone. Fingermann examined it under the magnifying glass. "I think we could start here," he said, running the nail of his little finger along one side. "But I'd have to study it for a while."

"Right," Fish said. "Will you do it?"

"Of course," Fingermann said, laying the diamond on the scale. "If we're lucky, we'll get one thirty-carat piece out of it, maybe more. It could make a fine stone, fourteen to sixteen carats, and quite a few excellent smaller stones. I'll know more tomorrow." With a nod, he left the office.

"Is that all right with you, Mrs. Linkhand?" Fish asked.

"Fine. I'll come back tomorrow around noon. But there's something else on my mind. I need your advice and your help, Mr. Fish. I must get a young man out of Poland. We need him. Of course he can't obtain a passport. The young men are being mobilized now."

For a moment Nachum Fish pretended not to understand. Then he said, "I don't know how you know, but I can swear to you by the Torah that I don't do it for money. I have—good contacts." He paused and looked at her. "The man who needs the passport is a Jew and in danger?"

Mira quickly snapped open her bag. She took a small envelope out of it. "Here, look at him," she said with an easy smile.

Nachum Fish only glanced at the passport photos. They were not very clear; Mira had had them made in London from a photograph of Vladek. In any case, Fish could not judge faces as well as he judged diamonds. "What languages does he speak?" he asked.

"Polish, Russian, German, French, and of course Yiddish," Mira replied smoothly.

"I'll talk to my friend. Tomorrow, when you come by at noon, I'll let you know about the stone and—"

"Thank you very much, Mr. Fish." Only after she was outside did she permit herself a sigh of triumph.

When she left London on July 18, she had tucked away in her handbag, where she usually carried her checkbook, a splendid, genuine Belgian passport with a variety of useful visas, in the name of Josef Wandermann.

On July 20 Prince Roman Bolgurski reported to her on his progress in winding up his affairs. He was very pleased when Mira praised him for his efficiency and circumspection. He had bought all the Swiss francs he could, and was continuing to do so. There remained only—.

Mira understood. The sum in question, she said, would be available only after the new owners took over the Voronovski properties. She would then have the money transferred directly to the Bolgurski account in Bern. No reason for the Prince to delay his departure.

But the Prince did not quite see it this way. He must take up his post at the Embassy by August 3 at the latest, and he was anxious to have all such matters out of the way before he left Poland. He hoped madame would understand.

Madame did. She refrained from saying what she would have liked to say: that Prince Bolgurski's distrust was as petty as it was ridiculous; the Voronovski forests would have yielded the family not a penny but for her intervention. But she restrained herself and said only, "Then we still have almost two weeks. I'll see what I can do."

Problems seemed to resolve themselves of their own accord. She had been negotiating for some time with a group of financiers over the sale of the timberlands, sawmills and transportation facilities, but had postponed signing the final agreement in order to have a pretext for remaining longer in Warsaw. Once all that was settled, she no longer had any business in Europe, and certainly not in Poland. Ever since the German demands for the Corridor had become more and more insistent, her brother-in-law in England was increasingly nervous and impatient. She must therefore close the deal.

Now, however, the head of an institution officially attached to the Ministry of Trade hinted to her that the government was interested in buying the property. The opportunity seemed too good to let pass. As soon as the deal was settled, Mira reported the state of affairs to London. At the same time she told Prince Bolgurski that he could have the Voronovski family's share of 89,000 pounds sterling deposited wherever he liked. Gratefully, the Prince gave her the name of his Swiss bank. Mira promptly telephoned the order for the deposit to Lord Godbrooke. But for the sake of regular procedure, she sent letters to Countess Elizaveta Voronovska, to Princess Marenzia Bolgurska and to Count Vladislav Voronovski, informing them that the sum deposited to Prince Bolgurski's account in the Swiss bank was in settlement of all claims of the Voronovski family; would they kindly confirm by signing copies of the letter.

Only the Prince understood the implications of the letter, and winced at the rap on the knuckles he was receiving in payment for his petty distrust. The Princess and her mother assumed that the letter and the signed copies were mere formalities; they were too involved in preparations for their departure to pay attention to such matters. The Count signed the receipt without a thought. He had some forty thousand zlotys in his money box. Let his brother-in-law worry about all that other money, and Mira, who was always looking out for him. How often she had proved that! If Mira had not entered his life, would he ever have been able to own a horse like that stallion Slim? For the past two years he had been living the proper life of an aristocrat, and it never occurred to him that maintaining his horses cost far more than his regimental commander spent on himself and his family, that their feed alone amounted to more than his total salary. He didn't think about it, but Mira did. These were all important elements in her plan. Everything was ready; she had even bought his ticket on the ship that was to take him from Gdynia.

She went ahead and conscientiously arranged the transfer of all the company's property to the new owners. She gave herself ample time, considered every detail. On August 18 Lord Godbrooke informed Mira that the payments had come through. Nothing more remained to be done. Mira asked him to book passage for herself and Freddy on a good ship sailing from Southampton to New York.

By August 20 she was ready to reveal her plans to Vladek. His ship was due to sail in two days. She had not only booked passage for Josef Wandermann, but she had a sizable sum for this ficticious Belgian to take with him—enough for a comfortable life until they could be reunited.

But on the twentieth the shade remained at half mast in vain. Vladek did not come. The next morning she learned that he was off with his regiment on maneuvers, and wouldn't return till evening. A day had been wasted.

She had a very early supper with Freddy and asked him to drive her back to the office. He might go to bed early if he liked, but she had a great deal to do. This was her last evening of work in Europe and there were a number of matters still to be settled. She would take a cab home, she said. As always, Freddy complied without protest.

At half past eight Vladek arrived—bathed, shaved, smelling of good soap and Cologne water—showing no sign of the strenuous exercise of the past two days. For him many hours in the saddle were no strain, but a pleasure. He took her into his arms, and for over an hour they were too absorbed to talk.

When they lay side by side, tired and blissful, Mira broke the silence with a word that scarcely seemed to suit the situation. "A pity," she said. She sounded intensely sad.

Vladek turned lazily toward her. "What's a pity, my filly?"

She turned to him and put her arm under his neck. "A pity that I must leave you, Vladek."

"You're leaving and you'll be back. That's how it's been all along."

"When I go this time, I won't be back. Not for many years, perhaps never."

"Oh, come now. That's impossible; I won't permit it. You can't leave, I won't let you. It's too nice with you."

"I know, I know, but my whole family is gone. There's no one and nothing here to hold me. Except you, Vladek."

"Then stay with me and don't think of such foolishness. Leaving? What for? Why should you?"

"Why do you think your people have left Poland?"

"But that was something different. My sister has this lung trouble. Mama had to go with her, and Roman was sent by the Foreign Ministry."

So they had told him that story too, and he had swallowed it! Mira could feel her anger rising. Her job would have been far easier if he had known the true reason, she thought. "And you believe all that?" she asked, unable to suppress the scorn in her voice.

He sat up and looked down at her. "Don't you?"

"How can I, when I know the real reasons?"

"And what are they?" He sprang from the low bed with such force that the springs sang. "Don't look at me that way, Vladek," she protested. "Have you ever known me to tell you anything but the truth?"

"All right, all right," he retorted. "Will you kindly tell me what you're imagining?"

"What I know, what I know for certain. Prince Roman Bolgurski has left with his family because he, too, considers the situation too dangerous, because he's afraid there will be a war, and he wants to protect the lives of himself and his family—"

"Enough!" he interrupted in a rage. "I cannot listen to such rot. Besides," he added scornfully, "I'd like to know how you claim to be so certain of this."

"Very simple. He came to me for advice, and I advised him to the best of my ability. He is an extremely sensible man, your brother-in-law. He has all your money in his account—a fortune. If he invests it properly, he'll be very rich someday."

"Yes, yes, yes, money, money and always money. What kind of idiot do you think I am? Are you trying to tell me that a man like my brother-in-law, a reserve officer, a man of the highest nobility, is scared stiff of a war that hasn't even come yet, and just because he might lose his money? If that's what you think, you're very much mistaken, madame."

"You're getting needlessly excited and not behaving like an aristocrat. I was certain that the Prince had informed you about his various talks with me. He came to see me frequently during the past few weeks, and I helped him a great deal, especially in arranging the transfer of the money to Switzerland. And I did it all for your sake, only for your sake, Vladek. Because it wasn't just—just a favor."

"Forgive me, but when I hear such charges—" He was still worked up, still incredulous.

"How could I suppose you knew nothing about it? Wasn't it

reasonable to assume that you had been told about your brother-in-law's plans?" She calmed him with a gesture and went into the adjoining room. Returning with a briefcase, she took a sheet of paper from it and handed it to him. It was her letter concerning the recent transfer of money. He read it, word for word, but understood it no more than he had a few days before, when he had signed it.

"All right," he said, "but what has this to do with their leaving?"

"Vladek," she said, "you don't understand anything at all about business. Your brother-in-law has all your money in his hands."

"And you think he's going to take it away from us—is that it?" he flared.

"Not at all. If I had thought that, I would have protected you and your mother. You can depend on that."

"So then—you admit he's an honorable man."

"Of course. But only to the extent that he has no intention of robbing your mother or you."

"Well, then—"

"But he ought to have told you. About his departure, the purpose of it, and especially what he has in mind to do with your money."

"I have been told about his departure and the reason for it."

"He told you the same thing he told his acquaintances and the people at the Ministry. In all sincerity, Vladek, did you ever before hear anything about your sister's having trouble with her lungs?"

The Count looked crestfallen. "That sort of thing can flare up all of a sudden," he said lamely.

"In that case, I can reassure you. She's healthy as a horse. Do you want a certificate tomorrow saying that you have weak lungs or a bad heart? I'll buy you ten of them."

"You mean such things can be bought the way you buy rolls at the bakery?"

"There aren't many things that cannot be bought, Vladek."

She saw that he was angry, but she didn't care. There were ways to placate him. "I know you're upset. But the truth must be spoken and you must be man enough to bear it. I was sure you knew what your brother-in-law had in mind, and that you'd agreed to it."

He opened his mouth as though he wanted to roar, to shout some insult, to vent his rage; but he closed it again and shook his head, and confined himself to a contemptuous wave of the hand. "You're crazy, that's it," he said coolly. "You're a fool."

"You are the first person who has ever said that to me, but perhaps it's true," she replied quietly. "Nevertheless, you might give this fool your answer to a single question. What are you going to live on now, Vladek?"

He looked at her, with an air rather of superiority than astonishment; but gradually his face drained of color. Then the old expression of submissiveness returned. In matters of money she was superior to him. If her question was justified, it was better for him to be meek. He succeeded in forcing a wretched, tentative smile. "I no longer have any money, Mira?" he asked. His voice was as tentative and wretched as his smile.

"As far as I know"—she reckoned mentally—"you ought to have around forty-three, perhaps forty-four thousand zlotys."

"Not quite forty thousand."

"If you're lucky and another horse as fine as Slim comes your way, you'll have almost nothing left. But suppose you hang on to the forty thousand. If you manage to be economical, that will last for five or at most six months. And then, Vladek—can you live on your salary?"

He looked down at the floor. "I suppose I'll write or telegraph my brother-in-law, and he'll have to send me money. It's mine; he won't deny that, will he?"

She shrugged. "I don't know. But writing or telegraphing won't be as easy as you think. Understand, Vladek, he had no right to send either your money or his out of the country. It's illegal to do so. If you want your money back, or only part of it, you'll have to answer some highly unpleasant and embarrassing questions. Would you want to do that, Vladek?"

"No." He shook his head sadly. "Then I have nothing left."

"But you have, Vladek. In Switzerland, in the keeping of your brother-in-law. Your Mira has seen to that. It's down in black and white that it's yours. Enough money to live like a gentleman."

"But you yourself say I can't bring it back here. So what good is it?"

"If your money cannot come to you, that doesn't mean that you can't make use of it." She saw that he did not understand and tried to phrase it so that he would. Taking his hand and fondling it, she said, "Listen, Vladek. I'll make it clear to you, and perhaps you'll realize that I am no fool. I knew very well that your brother-in-law was smuggling"—she felt him wince at the word and attempt to withdraw his hand, but she had chosen the word deliberately and was prepared for his reaction; she held his hand fast and went on quietly—"your money as well as his own and your mother's. But could I imagine that he was doing so without your consent? Am I a fool because I drew the only sensible conclusion: that you, like your relatives, were sending your money out first and then intended to go yourself?"

"Forgive me," he said, crestfallen. "You're not a fool—I just blurted that out." He took her hand and kissed it. Then he sat down on the rumpled bed and drew her down. She put her arm around his neck and pressed him close.

"I'm not angry with you, Vladek darling—"

"What can I do now, Mira? You're clever—can't you advise me?"

"There is only one thing to do; I've already told you. You must leave, rejoin your relatives and your money."

"But I can't do that; I'm not a civilian. I wouldn't be able to get a furlough or a passport. Don't you know what's going on? We're on alarm status. We may be sent away tomorrow or tonight, any moment. The Seventh has already left—yesterday."

"Suppose you did have a passport, Vladek; suppose you could leave?" Her heart pounded. He must say yes, she thought; inwardly, she commanded him to say yes.

"Don't talk nonsense, Mira. If I had a passport, if I were the Emperor of China—if, if—" He laughed unpleasantly.

"Vladek." She held him tightly. "I can get you out of the country."

He did not reply, and remained quite calm. She knew that he was thinking, and forced her heart to beat more quietly. He must not see how keyed up she was. When he freed himself from her embrace, not violently, but with a gentle, determined movement, she let him go. He stood up and took a step, then turned around to face her. "What did you say, Mira? I did catch the drift, didn't I? 'If you had a passport'—and then 'I can get you out of the country.' Did you say that?" He was altogether changed. His face was gray, and beads of sweat quivered on his upper lip. She saw him filled with a fury, a hatred, that had nothing in common with his ordinary, occasional fits of temper, which she could always placate with a word or a gesture. She had never seen him like this, seething with rage, breathing hard.

"I want only what is best for you, Vladek."

"I want only what is best," he mimicked her. "You—" He gritted his teeth audibly. "Listen to me now. I'm not Vladek to you—I am Count Voronovski. And I wish I had always remained that to you. Then you would never have dared say anything like that to me, you filthy, stinking Jewess." He took a step toward her, towered over her. "What is the Jewess daring to propose to Count Voronovski? That he desert. A Polish uhlan officer whose forebears were officers. My grandfather set his dogs on you Jews for the fun of it. He could shoot you. How right Hitler is—the whole lot of you should be slaughtered. Ah!"

Mira raised her head. She looked into his eyes and saw hatred, murderous hatred. She sat still; only her fingers clamped convulsively shut, her nails dug into her palms. She wanted to assure herself that she was awake, that it was true, that these incredible words roaring into her ears and penetrating her brain came from his mouth. These horrible words were spoken by Vladek, her beloved Vladek, his eyes flashing a murderous hatred. She was not afraid of him. She was horrified by something she could scarcely bear to face, a torment to her thoughts. She saw her father, the beggarly peddler, and the dog that belonged to some nobleman—its owner must have looked like this man Vladek who stood barely a step away from her. The face she had caressed a thousand times was now utterly alien, the face of someone she had never known, but had only feared in nightmares.

She commanded herself to wake up; her fingers relaxed, and she heard herself saying quietly, deliberately, "Hitler makes no distinction; he'll kill them all, Jews and Poles alike, even if they're noblemen and ride on horses like the Count's Slim. Your Excellency has a good memory for his fine ancestors and a bad one for Jews and Jewesses who have made him rich. If it were not for the Jewess, Your Excellency would be a beggar and would have no Slim." She stood up, took the receipts from the table, and quietly slipped them into the leather folder. As she did so, her hand felt something smooth, cold and metallic. She did not know what it was; then she remembered: a cigarette case made to look exactly like a pocket pistol. She had bought the toy in London as a present for a friendly customs official, and had forgotten to give it to him. She did not take it out, but tucked the folder under her arm.

The Count watched her movements with sullen, brooding fury. It was not clear whether he had grasped what she had said, whether her words had affected him. He seemed to pay attention only when the name of his horse was mentioned. A brief light flickered over his grim face. "Yes, Slim," he said in a clear, high voice. "Slim—I wouldn't give a hair from his tail for a hundred thousand red-haired Jewesses."

"I know," Mira said coolly, her hand gripping the toy in the folder. "I know. His Excellency the Count had better go back to the stable with his horse." And then slowly and deliberately she said, "Get out, you bastard."

She had spoken the words in English, though she did not know why. He did not understand, but the contempt struck him like a blow. "What did you say? What did you mean?" He took a threatening step toward her; she stepped rapidly aside, evading him. The folder, tucked under her left arm, was pressed close against her body; she held her right hand hidden inside it. Now she repeated what she had said, using the coarsest Polish expressions she had learned in the year and more she had spent in the country.

"I said that His Excellency should get the hell out of here—this minute—or else"—she drew the smooth toy from the briefcase; it rested in her hand, cool and reassuring—"or else His Excellency will never ride Slim again." She held the thing in her hand, then slowly lowered it, with assurance, as though she had handled weapons all her life.

The Count stared at her; he took a step backward, then another, and then he was at the door of the room. His eyes remained fixed on the weapon; he did not look into her face. "Mira," he said hoarsely, "you wouldn't—"

"I would," she said coldly. "His Excellency has no right to threaten a defenseless woman, even if she is a Jewess. There is a great deal of money in this folder, important documents as well as receipts for smuggled foreign exchange from His Excellency and His Excellency's noble family. Such dealings in foreign exchange, Your Excellency, are punishable by two years' imprisonment. Reason enough to attempt to burgle the Jewess's office at night."

He retreated; she followed him step by step, driving him before her, hurling each word into his face. As he went down the stairs, she called after him three words, the foulest insult she had heard on the streets of Vienna as a very small girl: *"Drah di, Strizzi!"* Then he was gone.

She closed the door and turned the key twice in the lock, turned it mechanically with her left hand, her right hand still holding the pistol. Then she looked at the toy and tossed it on the desk. At the impact the lid sprang open and cigarettes rolled over the top of the desk. A pity I didn't show him what he ran from, she thought, and lit a cigarette. His Heroic Excellency was scared stiff. An army officer who can't even tell a toy from a genuine gun! But perhaps it was better this way. Every Jewish woman ought to have a pistol with her these days, and use it when anyone insults her!

Her hands dropped to her sides, and she stood rigid. It was as if she heard a voice speaking within herself. What was it saying? Of what was it reminding her? She did not fend it off. What do you want to say? she thought. That I myself am at fault, that I took him for myself, bought him because I wanted to have him, because I loved him? Can that be love, when the mouth that has been passionately kissing you shouts "filthy Jewess" at you five minutes later? When the eyes that held all the happiness in the world for you can glare at you with murderous hatred? Did I want just to save his life, which otherwise will be in danger? Was I so anxious for him to go on leading his pleasant, easy existence? You're lying to yourself, aren't you, Mira? It wasn't for his sake that you went to all that trouble. You wanted him for yourself, for the pleasure you found in his arms, for your own lust, Mira. That's why you calculated and speculated, why you reckoned and lied, why you made him rich, so that he could have a house, live in comfort with servants and horses, so that he would be happy. Because when he was happy you were, but you were concerned only with your own happiness, Mira. You wanted your own happiness. Yet isn't that love? What else is love if it isn't having and holding the happiness you feel in someone's arms, in your breath mingled with his? Feeling your skin take in life from his. Isn't that love? What else is it?

She still stood in the same spot, listening to the dialogue of her inner voices, pondering. No, there was nothing left. Nothing at all. No longing, no desires, no wishes, no happiness. Nothing at all for Mira Linkhand who had taken a Count for her lover. The Jewess and the Count. It did not exist; there was no true bridge, no tie between the two. She should never have forgotten that. The chasm remains; it is self-deception to think that it does not; and if one tries to pretend otherwise, one is quickly brought back to the truth.

She twitched, she shook herself; she spewed forth the disgust that was choking her, and then felt cleansed and saddened. No, there is no room in my life for love, she told herself. I do not understand love; I understand only figures, calculations, business and money, credit and debit. That's all neat and clean. Figures are good; you can see them on paper, keep them in your head. They don't deceive you. Figures are money, and for money you can buy anything. Almost anything. I'd better stick to money, to business, to the Linkhands. That's where I belong.

"Over," she said. She tidied her hair, powdered her face, put on lipstick, and sat down at the desk. Good, she thought, so it's over. She pulled open the desk drawer, glanced rapidly through papers, threw many of them into the fireplace. She propped the folder on the desk. The passport fell out of it, the good Belgian passport in the name of Josef Wandermann, with Vladek's picture. She did not open it; she did not want to see the picture. It followed the papers into the fireplace. But she put the receipts back into the folder, together with the money, the neat packets of pounds sterling, dollars and Swiss francs. The letters of recommendation which she had for him—which were to insure him a warm welcome abroad, find him friends—flew into the fireplace. The fire flared up, and the heavy rag paper of the passport twisted and curled as though trying to defend itself against annihilation. But it resisted in vain. With her ruler Mira poked it deeper into the flames, added more paper, and the passport turned to ashes. Passport and picture, dreams, hopes and— two hundred good English pounds, which the passport had cost.

That was a figure, three figures. Mira was back in her element. But even as she reckoned, she heard a roaring motorcycle draw up in front of the house, and a course, loud man's voice calling, "Captain, Captain, come quick!" Another, so familiar and so alien, so beloved and so hated, called back, "I'll be down right away." She heard doors slamming, light, hastening footsteps, clink of spurs on the steps and on the pavement outside; then again the roar of the motorcycle. It was gone. They had come for him. But she took the toy pistol, collected the cigarettes, put them back into their container, closed the lid and replaced the toy in her folder. Then she telephoned for a cab and went to rejoin Freddy. By tomorrow at this same time she would be in London, and two or three days later on the high seas.

So she reckoned, but fate crossed up her reckonings.

The landing at the airport in Lvov was a poor one. There was a great thud, and the passengers were knocked about, thrown across each other. There was a great deal of screaming, cries of terror, cursing and complaint in various languages when the plane finally came to a standstill. But one person neither screamed nor moaned—did not utter a sound. That was Freddy Linkhand. The young doctor who was called to the scene quickly diagnosed concussion of the brain, with possible minor fracture of a bone in the skull. He recommended immediate transfer to a hospital, preferably to the Hera Sanatorium, a modern institution noted for its topflight surgeons.

Would it be dangerous for her husband to travel? Mira asked. Suppose she chartered a plane from Lvov to London?

The two doctors at the sanatorium threw each other a brief but significant glance. That glance signified that in the first place their estimate of the fee had been too low, in the second place this big fish must not be allowed to swim away to London, and in the third place—but the elder doctor put the third consideration into words. Of course they could not keep her from taking this risk, but as a doctor of thirty years' experience, who had treated hundreds of such cases, he could never approve. It would be sheer recklessness, especially in view of possible injury to the spinal column.

A telegram informed Lord Godbrooke in London of the accident and its possible consequences—a telegram and not the telephone because it was now August 23 and telephone connections between Poland and England were not available to private individuals. The lines were all taken up, carrying conversations which might decide the destinies of millions of persons.

For on August 23, 1939, a pact had been signed in Moscow. That treaty was between Russia and Germany, but it was of burning interest to the whole world, and to Poland and England in particular. Although a number of its points were made public, the most important articles of the pact went unmentioned in official announcements. Nowhere was there any suggestion that the two foes had agreed on the subjugation and partition of Poland.

While Mira bore up under a terrible burden of grief, guilt, fears and doubts, precious days passed and her husband did not awaken from his coma. Reports in the press and over the radio indicated more and more plainly, more and more pessimistically, that war was unavoidable unless there was some last-minute miracle, unless the aims of the German dictator suddenly changed. Mira did not believe in miracles; she accepted the situation as it was and only hoped for a little more time. The disaster was clearly irrevocable. Had she not foreseen it months ago and guided all her calculations, plans and decisions accordingly? But what good was her knowledge while Freddy lay still, without a word or a movement?

Her first telegram to Godbrooke was unanswered; to the second she received a reply—late in the evening of August 31. That telegram expressed the greatest anxiety and urgently advised her to escape to Romania or Hungary. Mira had thought of this herself, and did not wait for the morning. The doctors reported that Freddy's condition had not worsened, although it was hardly improving; Mira therefore made arrangements to remove him that same night to Romania. She would accompany him, and Freddy's careful and devoted nurse, Hilda, agreed to go along with the patient, provided that she might also take her child.

On Nurse Hilda's advice, Mira tried to rent an ambulance, and when that proved to be unfeasible, she was prepared to buy one, despite the fantastic prices being asked for any vehicle. She had come to an agreement with a garage owner for a 1926 model, and was at the garage learning how to handle the unusual gearshift, when a sergeant accompanied by ten soldiers entered the garage and commandeered all the vehicles in the place for the army. All the protests of the owner, and the pleas of the two women to leave at least the ambulance, were in vain; the garage was stripped clean.

Disappointed and exhausted, the two women returned to the sanatorium toward four o'clock in the morning, and learned that the patient had shown signs of returning consciousness. That was one blessing at least, but it did not forward Mira's plans for escape.

The morning of September 1 ended any thought of traveling with a sick man. German tanks rolled across the borders and German planes dominated the skies over Poland, skies that were gloriously cloudless. Splendid weather favored the German military operations; tanks and troops advanced almost unhindered.

On September 3—the day that France and England declared war on Germany—a bomb fell on the sanatorium, though it was plainly marked with a Red Cross flag. But, the damage was slight.

Mira and Nurse Hilda knew quite well what would face them when the Germans arrived. Yet Mira did not consider, even in a fleeting thought, abandoning Freddy in his helplessness. She would do all in her power to save herself, but not alone. She had entered into a contract with A. L. Linkhand, a binding contract, sealed by her word and a handshake. It could not be broken, in any circumstances. She would keep her agreement, cost her what it may.

Freddy was alive, and with each passing day it became more apparent that he would survive. Hilda was the only one who tended him; the rest of the staff had vanished. The young doctors had joined their regiments; the older ones had fled. The nurses, too, were gone, some to assignments with the troops, most of them to safety across the border. Although the sanatorium had been officially declared a reserve military hospital, no wounded soldiers arrived, and there was no one to receive them if they did. Hilda was new to the place; she had not worked for the past ten years, not since her marriage.

When it became apparent that the building was a target of bombers, Hilda suggested that they would be safer in her house. With the assistance of several men, they transported Freddy the whole distance on a wheeled stretcher, the kind used to move patients about the corridors of the hospital.

Freddy suffered a relapse. He ran a high fever, was delirious, cried out in pain. Hilda gave him injections and administered sedative pills. A terrible night was followed by an equally terrible day. Mira spent almost thirty hours at Freddy's bedside. Hilda was out on various errands. Sofia, Hilda's daughter, played until she was tired, had something to eat, and went to sleep. By the time Hilda returned, Mira was so worn out that she could scarcely stand. Hilda urged her to go to bed, brought her a cup of tea and gave her two pills. Mira did not awaken until the following morning, when the sun's rays fell through the blinds. She was dazed, and felt as though she had lead in her head and limbs. Every movement was an effort. She called out to Hilda, to Sofia, but there was no answer. The only sound was Freddy's low moaning from the adjoining room. Pulling herself together, she went to him, walking with heavy, uncertain steps. She gave him his medicine, washed him and changed his bedding, and took his temperature, which had dropped to 100°. Then she went to the kitchen to prepare some breakfast for him and herself.

On the kitchen table lay two envelopes. One was addressed to

Mira Linkhand, the other to Emilian Mermelstein—Hilda's husband who had recently been called to army service. Mira took the letter to herself, and forgot her physical discomfort in the wave of foreboding that swept her. She read:

> If you had a child, you would understand me. As it is, you will think ill of me for running out on you and making off with your money. I have made my escape with some people who were willing to take Sofia and me with them. There was no use including you in our plans, since your husband is in no condition to travel. I needed a large sum of money for our flight, so I took money from your bag. What I left is not much, but it should last you a while. In addition I am leaving you the house and garden and all the furniture. It is your property, as the bill of sale accompanying this letter will prove. If my husband turns up, show him the bill of sale and give him the letter. The house was my property, or rather my daughter's, inherited from my mother. Forgive me and try to understand me. God help me and you and your sick husband.
>
> Hilda Mermelstein.

Hard days followed for Mira. Any other woman would have given way to tears of hopelessness. Not Mira. Her present task was above all to restore Freddy to health, and to that she devoted all her forces. By now, the twenty-first day after his accident, his temperature was normal, he suffered scarcely any pain, and he could talk with her. Soon he was on his feet and able to walk slowly about the room, with Mira supporting him. She had moved her bed into his room and was with him almost every minute of the day. There were stores of food in the big pantry: flour, hams, bacon, all kinds of preserves, sauerkraut and pickles. The garden was still supplying fruit and vegetables. The weather remained warm, and Mira lived in the house with Freddy without seeing a soul or hearing a strange noise. All the surrounding houses seemed to be deserted; as far as she could see, no smoke rose from the chimneys. Planes no longer appeared in the sky; no explosions could be heard. Everywhere was deathly silence.

The Germans are probably very close by now, Mira thought; perhaps they have already reached the city. But Freddy was making such rapid progress now that in a few days they might be able to hide out, or perhaps try to make their way to the border on foot. Mira explained the situation to Freddy in simple language. She told him, as if he were a child, what had happened and how they must act if the Germans should appear. She gave him regular lessons, repeating them until he had learned them. She also packed a knapsack for the two of them, and hid it in the garden. She had very little jewelry with her, but she did have a watch with a broad platinum band set with diamonds—it had cost some five thousand dollars. She had this, at least, to fall back on, for Hilda—whom she thought of without resentment—had left her only two hundred and twenty-five dollars and three five-pound notes. She took tender care of Freddy, was calm and steady.

Then one evening there were footsteps on the porch. A knock at the kitchen door. Striving to seem natural, Mira opened it. A man in uniform stood there. "Hildusia!" he called out.

"No," Mira said quietly, "Hilda is not here any more. Come in." Emilian Mermelstein had returned home.

From Mermelstein Mira learned that the war in Poland was already over, and that not the Germans but the Russians had occupied Lvov. This surprising turn of events, obviously the outcome of previous agreements between the Russians and Germans, at least removed the danger of being put to death on racial grounds. Mira had cause for other fears, almost as bad, but at least she was granted a breathing spell. She needed time to restore Freddy to health and to build up his resistance in preparation for the hardships to come. They had a roof over their heads and some money, or rather the equivalent of money—enough to carry out a plan of escape when the time came.

She had to include Emilian Mermelstein in her scheme. She would certainly need someone to help her, and she wondered whether it might be this man, who now sat, washed, shaved and in a decent civilian suit, at table with her and Freddy. In choice language—he spoke excellent German—he told his adventures in the war.

While Mermelstein talked, Mira had an opportunity to study the man. He was about thirty-six. He had a rather longish face, with fleshy, now sunken cheeks, and a big, sensual mouth. It was an extraordinarily mobile face, full of folds and wrinkles, but looked good-natured enough. It would have taken a sharp observer to see that Mermelstein was not the good fellow he pretended to be.

He was not, not by any means, and could never keep up that pose for very long. His pretense had the sole aim of obtaining advantages for himself—and was not often successful. He always followed the same pattern. If he succeeded, all very well; if he did not succeed, he threw up the game and looked for a new group with which to ingratiate himself. He had no vocation, although he had tried countless jobs. He had no skills and little knowledge. What he did possess was an innate agility, polished by experience and routine, and an impudence and mendacity which could be dangerous. For he often veiled his intentions in deliberate self-mockery. In fleeing, his wife had escaped from years of painful servitude to him. Her marriage had been a prolonged torment. After the first few weeks of marriage he stopped taking the trouble to be agreeable. A satanic inclination to spice lust with physical abuse soon came to the surface, and transformed their marital relations into hours of horror for Hilda. She had not fled only from the Germans.

He was not especially distressed about her flight. What mattered was the letter she had left. Not her childish whinings about theft, betrayal, repentence, forgiveness and sale of the house—ridiculous! What his mind fixed upon was one phrase in the letter: "Madame Linkhand, who is very capable and very rich." This was something to hold on to. At which point Mermelstein's intellectual activity ceased and another interest stirred, a purely animal instinct. Of course the husband was around, and not bad-looking; but he was convalescing from an illness. The husband was a nuisance, but no real obstacle, if she wanted to. And why shouldn't she? She was a healthy, highly feminine woman, and who gave a woman what she needed? Her legal husband? His brains were addled and he'd go on being that way for quite a while, it seemed. A woman was a woman. If a man were on hand, and one who had a way with him—why not?

Weeks passed. Mermelstein was out in the streets from morning to night; he took the bearings of the troubled times. He stood on the sidewalk when the singing crowds marched past; he listened to the propaganda, and came home in the evening to report what he had learned. Later he sold rags, clothes, shoes, underclothes—a few of the things his, the larger part of them Freddy's and Mira's belongings. He brought back rubles, quantities of rubles, and yet these were only a fraction of what he had received for the goods. He profited heavily from the Linkhands, who never left the house and even ventured into the garden only at night, for a breath of air. Mermelstein exploited the situation, played on their fear of attracting attention, invented stories of sudden arrests, and among these lies strewed tales of how he had struck up acquaintance with important persons, of connections he was making which would ease his life and theirs.

Those were weeks of doubt and insecurity for Mira. Her plans had perforce to be based on Mermelstein's stories. Quite by chance this man had entered her life. By now he was part of it, although she did not like him and did not trust him, for now and then she saw that he was lying. To make matters worse, the man was trying to seduce her. He snatched at her hand or arm whenever he could; he kissed her if opportunity offered. Sometimes he came creeping into the kitchen, and she felt his clammy, avid lips on the back of her neck. She fought him off, she told him off in no uncertain terms, although the sensation itself was not altogether unpleasant, and awakened desires for something. No, not that again, and certainly not with this creature!

One name kept cropping up with increasing frequency in Mermelstein's stories: Saposhnik, a big nachalnik, a powerful man and his friend—Mermelstein had procured various articles for him, had done him favors. He made much of his relationship to this nachalnik, representing it as a genuine friendship. He made mysterious allusions to previous political activities, in the course of which they had come to know each other.

And then Mermelstein himself became a nachalnik—Saposhnik saw the value of this man who could get hold of everything, and appointed him buyer of materials for the small factory attached to the power plant. Mermelstein's spravka now bore the word "nachalnik." He was a chief in his department. He had, it was true, no subordinates, but on the other hand he had only a single superior, Saposhnik, who taught him the nature of his work in half an hour. It was simple enough, though time-consuming and involving endless running around. Mermelstein had to obtain coal and other fuels, lead, copper and other metals, either from state organizations—which had little of anything—or from private individuals who still had stuff stored away.

Mermelstein came home and strutted around as if the whole city's supply of electrical power depended upon him alone. He let it be understood that he was working himself to death. The weight of responsibility upon him was enormous, and a single false step might send him to prison or Siberia. Once again he played on the feelings of the Linkhands by telling stories of all the foreigners who were being arrested and shipped off to camps in Russia's far north, or across the German border. They were lucky to have him for a protector, the more so because he was chummy with the great nachalnik Saposhnik.

Mira tried to understand exactly where they stood. The worst of it was that though she guessed that Mermelstein's stories were mostly lies, it was evident that they contained a grain of truth somewhere. But could she dare to discount most of what he said? A mistake could be fatal. She did not trust assurances of friendship and boasts of how useful his connections could be. But on the other hand she was sure that he could harm them. She had no illusions about the Russians. If they discovered who she and Freddy really were, they would not kill them, but they would send Mira Linkhand back to the lower depths from which she had risen.

A week passed and still another week, and then her difficulties began to mount. It began the evening Mermelstein came home with the news that there was going to be a house-to-house inspection, with everyone registered for the distribution of identity cards. *He* had nothing to fear; his papers were in order, and he held an important job. He would receive his Soviet identity card. "But what about you?" he asked with pretended concern. "What documents can you present? And you aren't working; that's the worst of it."

Mira knew that he was showing off and trying to worry her, but she was also afraid that it might be partly true. It was important not to show any fear. "Of course we have documents. The best. English passports."

"Fine! And when do you intend to leave?" he asked spitefully.

"Whenever it suits me," she replied.

"And where to?"

"That's my own affair. You grill me as though you weren't a nachalnik at the power plant, but an NKVD man." She smiled as though she meant this as a harmless joke. "If you're as fond of us as you say," she continued, "you ought to tell us what to do, instead of frightening the wits out of us."

Instantly he was puffed up, swollen with self-importance. "Of course I'll do everything in my power for you. But the situation is anything but favorable at the moment. If you had German, Austrian or Czech documents, it would be easier, of course. As Jews you could claim right of asylum; otherwise you'll be deported across the border before you can count to five. *I* might be able to arrange things so that you could renounce your citizenship. Then you could be enlisted in the labor program and become Soviet citizens. It won't be easy, but it might be done, must be done. Yet as things are—" He broke off and seemed to be thinking hard. "No," he said finally, "I can't very well say you're English. That would finish you."

He fell silent again and waited for a question. But it didn't come. Mira was trying to decide what was true and what was false in his story. She had no clues but the sound of his voice, the look in his eyes. That wasn't very much to go by. Mermelstein felt called upon to elaborate. "If you say you're English, they'll find out in a few hours—given the good relations between the Russians and the Germans—who you are and what you were doing in Poland. Then you'll be suspect as English citizens and capitalists. Both. And there's always the question of espionage. Russia isn't very friendly with England nowadays. No, you're in a bad fix," he said with an unconvincing show of concern. If only we did have genuine English passports, Mira thought.

She did her best to seem unruffled. "Maybe we are in a bit of a fix, as you say. Have you any ideas? What can we do?" She succeeded in producing a smile that was both appealing and trustful.

"Now we understand each other again! Just give me a chance to think. We're friends, aren't we? For a friend, I'd go through hell and high water."

When one had a friend like Emilian—Milo—Mermelstein, one didn't need an enemy. He stooped to the crudest tricks of melodrama to unnerve the Linkhands. He saw faces at the windows, shadows behind trees. He heard noises in the night, and liked to speak in whispers for fear of eavesdroppers at the keyhole. An entire spy system seemed to have been organized solely for the purpose of watching him, the house and the couple he was sheltering. He was constantly warning them of what would happen if they were discovered. Siberia awaited them, frightful tortures, death before a firing squad. Most of it was incoherent nonsense, Mira decided, but it was disturbing and demoralizing.

Even Freddy grew gloomy, although he hardly understood what Mermelstein was telling them. Freddy saw Mira discouraged and perplexed, and that was enough. In his sluggish mind and heart a spark kindled.

Braggart, malicious fool, Mira thought, listening to Mermelstein. What are you after? What's behind all this? No, I can't go on this way; my nerves can't stand it. How am I going to get rid of this damnable liar, this devil!

But she pulled herself together. She couldn't go to pieces. She kept herself firmly in hand, looked after Freddy, and never let Mermelstein find her alone for a moment. For six days she hadn't stepped over the threshold, just stared through the window into the garden where the trees were bare and the branches creaked in the winter wind. Rain fell, snow fell. It was wet and gray. Mira's thoughts were dreary. She could not make a decision.

Then Nachalnik Mermelstein came home transformed, beaming, happy, carrying a huge bundle. He unpacked vodka and liqueurs, a bottle of champagne, canned salmon, *pâté de foie* and caviar, chocolate—a magnificent assortment of delicacies. He swaggered, singing, into the kitchen, fetched plates, glasses and silver; singing and whistling, he set the table. He threw his arms around Freddy, kissed him on the forehead, danced around Mira, snatched at her hand and kissed it, poured vodka for them all. "Eat, drink and be merry, for tomorrow we die," he bellowed. "No, on the contrary, we'll begin to live. A fine life, a glorious life, a director's life. Cheers!" He drained his glass, and the other two drank with him, encouraged but still on their guard. "What has happened, Mr. Mermelstein?" Mira asked, forcing a smile.

"Not *Mr.* Mermelstein," he corrected her, laughing. "Comrade. Or rather, *Tovarishch Director.* Yes, yes, Director Mermelstein at your service, comrade. But first let's drink up and eat all these good things. Cost a fortune, a month's salary or more, but what the hell? I'll tell you all about it over the champagne. It's good, it's better, it's best, hooray!" He poured the champagne, clinked glasses with them. For once there seemed to be some substance to his boasts. For as he nonchalantly inhaled his cigarette and puffed out the smoke with a grand air, he handed Mira a folded sheet of paper. "Here, comrade, you can understand this much Russian."

Mira, who had learned enough Polish and Russian by now to read the newspapers, saw that the document was a certification that Emilian Oswaldowicz Mermelstein had been appointed a director with extensive powers. It was a real document, stamped, sealed and bearing three signatures. She handed it back to him and said with a forced air of rejoicing, "Congratulations."

And Freddy, while he washed down a huge piece of pastry with a hearty swallow of cherry brandy, extended his right hand across the table and said, "Congratulations, Comrade Director."

"Don't congratulate just me, congratulate yourselves," Mermelstein answered. Then he sketched his plan. As full-fledged director of a Soviet enterprise—and by the by, he was the first native in the whole area to be given such a position, he said—he had the right to hire and fire workers. He would take them both on. For instance, he would engage Mira as—but what exactly could she do in a business?

"What kind of business is it?" Mira asked.

"A farm. A huge farm which has to produce enough to feed the hundreds of employees of the power plant."

Mira said she was an excellent bookkeeper. Did he know what kind of bookkeeping the Russians used? But be that as it may, she could master anything that had to do with office work. Anything at all.

"Fine, fine, I'm sure you can," Mermelstein said. "You'll be my right hand. I don't know anything about agriculture myself, but Saposhnik says a director only needs to know how to organize and direct." But what about Freddy? What could he do?

Perhaps Freddy could be a chauffeur or something to do with cars—or work in the warehouse? He was a businessman, of course, but it might be best not to mention that. He needed the type of job that would not call attention to himself.

"We'll work out something," Mermelstein said. "Anything for

my friends. You see what's involved, don't you? Once you're working, you get a spravka. You know what that is: the best document in the Soviet Union. That's proof that you're part of the labor force, that your older documents have been examined and are in order. With a spravka that your friend, Director Emilian Oswaldowicz Mermelstein, will make out for you, you can receive a regular identity card." He raised his glass to Mira, drained it and added, "You understand what I am doing for you."

"Like a true friend," Mira said. "We won't forget it."

"I hope so!" He looked at her with moist eyes. What she read in his face sickened her, for she knew that he would follow her into the kitchen. It was horrifying; she did not want him, she found him disgusting, and yet she was helpless.

Was there no one to protect her from Mermelstein, from his repulsive lust? She looked around the room as if seeking a rescuer, and her glance fell on Freddy. He had mixed a drink consisting half of the sweet cherry liqueur, half of champagne, and was downing it cheerfully.

She had never seen Freddy drunk before. And that strained, searching and yet completely absent expression on his face was new to her. What was the matter with him? What did he mean, getting drunk this way? She bent over him, saying softly, "Don't drink so much, Freddy. You'll have a headache. That's enough now—you aren't really well yet. Hadn't you better go to bed?"

"Bed? Yes, Mira." He stood up and walked rather waveringly to his bed. Mira helped him undress and tucked him in.

"Have this pill—otherwise you'll wake tomorrow with a splitting headache. And now sleep tight."

"Yes, Mira, good Mira," he said tearfully. She bent over and lightly kissed his brow. His bed stood close to the wall, almost in darkness, but she saw there were tears running down his cheeks. She stood there a moment, thunderstruck. It was better to pretend that she hadn't noticed. If she asked Freddy what was the matter, what could he say? And Mermelstein sat in the same room, watching her with a mocking smile. But why was Freddy crying? Because he was drunk, or—? She went to the window, closed it, slowly went back to the table, and stood still. "I'm very tired," she said.

"The dishes have to be washed," he said, not looking at her.

"Not tonight. I'll do them tomorrow."

"Come along to the kitchen," he said in a sharp, crafty voice. He had narrowed his eyes to a crack; they were almost closed, embedded in the tiny wrinkles and folds of his lids. "Come along," he repeated, opening his eyes. They were not blue, but green. Like a tomcat's, Mira thought, and shook herself.

"I don't want to."

"What's that?" he snapped. She remained standing quietly, looking down at him. He had regained his composure and smiled, an unctuous, hateful smile. "You haven't picked a very good time for not wanting to."

She understood the threat. "All the same," she said, shrugging.

He stood up, scooped up his cigarettes and matches from the table, stretched and yawned. "You put too high a value on what you've got," he said. "I can do without it."

BOOK FOUR

THE HOUSE

*What is true of outer
circumstances is true of inner:
there is no more effective
consolation than utter certainty
of inescapable necessity.*
SCHOPENHAUER

OT HAVING SEEN MERMELSTEIN FOR TWO DAYS—HE LEFT very early in the morning and came back late at night— Mira grew uneasy. She began to regret that she had repulsed him quite so sharply. Last night she had lain awake, haunted by a thousand anxieties. What if, in his offended vanity, he denounced them? What was he planning? She decided to stay up and talk to him.

But there was no need. Early in the afternoon she heard footsteps and voices on the veranda. She recognized Mermelstein's voice; the other was that of a stranger. From a distance it sounded as if the men were talking German; then she realized that it was Yiddish. The door to Mermelstein's room opened and closed. Endless minutes of silence followed, until again she heard the footsteps and voices. The two men were going through the rooms, stopping in each one for a short while.

Mermelstein spoke Yiddish poorly; he groped for words and eked out his vocabulary with Polish and multilated German. The other man spoke fluently. Although Mira's first language had been the Yiddish idiom spoken in Galicia, the part of Poland in which she had been born and to which fate had now cast her back, she had tried to repress the language along with all memory of her awful childhood years. She had banished the language from her memory even before she began her fight for a higher life. Only in the past two years in Poland—by which time she was already so far from where she had started that there seemed no danger of returning there—she had begun once more to use the language when it would help her in her business dealings.

The sound that came to her now, in strange articulation—nasal, drawn out—was not the idiom in which successful Jews told jokes among themselves in Vienna, London, Antwerp or New York. Nor was it the language used in business dealings in Poland. It reminded her of something long forgotten and frightful. The tone—that choppy, peremptory, sly, overbearing tone—conjured up inescapable and horrible memories. She not only heard that voice; she smelled it. It was the very air of desolation, that miasma of helpless poverty, hunger, sickness and dirt. It conjured up a frightful vision of gigantic tentacles reaching out to grasp her and drag her down once more to the place she had come from.

Now the footsteps were in the small hall. One more step! Mira froze in fear. The door opened, revealing the smugly smiling face of Mermelstein. He ushered in someone in a long, wide, exceedingly expensive fur coat with an otter collar, topped by a cap of the same fur. Between the collar and cap Mira caught a glimpse of large yellow teeth and puffy hamster cheeks. The wearer of the coat greeted her in Yiddish: "Good day. My name is Saposhnik." A finger was thrust out of the much too long sleeve and touched to the cap. Mira recognized the coat and cap. They had been Freddy's only a few weeks ago, and this fact made the grinning hamster seem harmless and familiar to her. She said smilingly in her low voice, "I am Mira," —she half obliterated her surname—"and this is my husband." She gestured toward Freddy, who stood up slowly and bowed. "Do sit down," Mira said in Russian.

The visitor disregarded the invitation. "You speak Russian?" he asked eagerly.

"I can hardly say I speak it—that would be an exaggeration. But I can make myself understood." The fluency with which she said this belied it.

"*Nichevo*—it doesn't matter." Saposhnik threw a reproachful glance at Mermelstein. He tugged at the buttons of the fur coat, took it off, and the cap, and tossed both onto the couch. "Hot," he said. "These rags put you in a sweat." Again he glanced angrily at Mermelstein, casting the blame on him for the heat, for the rags that were too warm to wear indoors. Now he stood before them in a blue suit that had also been Freddy's not long ago. But what Saposhnik was wearing bore only the faintest resemblance to the suit that Poole's of London had delivered to A. G. Linkhand. A clumsy and harried tailor had altered a masterpiece into something that scarcely resembled a suit for a gentleman. Without thought for proportions, the extra length in sleeves and trousers had simply been lopped short. On Saposhnik's stubby frame, the suit looked like a clever and original costume for a comedian. Moreover, the discreet dark-blue cloth contrasted glaringly with the orange pullover he was wearing, and the deep gray of the coarse, unironed and no longer quite clean flannel shirt, and the necktie of broad red and white stripes.

This necktie proved that Saposhnik had courageously and publicly declared himself on the side of progress and culture. For there were two factions in the Soviet Union, whose slogans might have been "Down with the Tie, Symbol of Bourgeois Parasitism" and "The Tie is the Sign of Civilization, Progress and Culture." Usually those lucky enough to own ties wore them with aggressive pleasure. Naturally the wearer of a tie had to belong to one of the so-called intellectual occupations. Saposhnik, thanks to Mermelstein, was now the proud owner of three of Freddy's former neckties, and had already become so adept at knotting and wearing these symbols of progress or reaction that he was constantly feeling his tie to make sure it was as it should be.

"I see that you are surprised at my speaking a little Russian," Mira said lightly.

Frowning, Saposhnik looked down at his fingernails; they were short and ragged, as if they had been cut with a dull instrument. "Why should I be surprised? It's a language like any other, though much richer and more beautiful, don't you think?"

She disregarded the challenge. "And more than two hundred million people speak it. An important language."

"Important—that's right. But important for whom and for what?" He was quizzing her as though it were a catechism.

"We learn a language either because we like it or because we must," she said soberly. "It is very good to know many languages, helps advancement. Don't you agree?"

"Every language you speak makes you that much more of a man. You know who said that?" The urge to quote was irresistible, although he was aware that in quoting this he was falling in with the idea she had just expressed. He counterbalanced this by setting her this fresh question.

"A very wise man," she replied.

"But who?" he insisted, and when she looked at him questioningly, he came out with it: "Stalin said it." Her ignorance, he implied by his tone, was inexcusable.

"Then I was right," she replied, smiling.

"To a certain extent," he said crossly. "But—one must know what one learns a language for."

She looked at him uncomprehendingly. "Who must know?" It sounded as if she were asking the time; the question was put so thoughtlessly and casually. There was not a trace of slyness behind it, or any indication that she took all this with the proper seriousness.

Saposhnik found himself at an utter loss. He could not think what to answer, and covered his embarrassment by sitting down at last. In a game both participants must know the rules. In the game of "We Communists know everything" each person had his part, and each had to stick to it. There were rules for who should ask the questions, and the answers were also fixed by rule. This woman did not understand the game; she asked instead of answering. "Dialectics?" The thought flashed through his mind. Perhaps she was a party member from way back, one of those stalwarts who foolishly imagined they had prepared the Revolution because they'd risked a few beatings or short prison sentences? His eyes probed her. The unbecoming cambric smock, the kerchief, and the felt shoes might have belonged to a so-called "revolutionary," but not the face, which was intelligent, energetic and attractively feminine at the same time.

This was a woman who had worked, had had a goal. She was someone who had acted, not just talked, and if she had acted, he ought to have had a dossier on her, not only the vague information supplied by this toady Mermelstein.

But Nachalnik Saposhnik was not here on official duties; he was here on business of his own, which he dearly wanted to carry through successfully. And Mermelstein, who was ordinarily useful, had failed to tell him of a single point which could be a fateful hindrance to his plans: the fact that this Mira What's-her-name spoke Russian. For if she found a hair in the soup that Saposhnik intended to serve her—and she did not look as though she spooned anything up without looking at it closely—he might find himself in trouble. She would not keep her mouth shut; she would talk. And since she talked Russian, she would be heard and understood.

Saposhnik had a high opinion of Mermelstein's talents. In this time of universal scarcity, Mermelstein could obtain things. He had found the land and the buildings for the auxiliary farm. Everything was going swimmingly. But in this matter that so deeply concerned Saposhnik personally, he had pulled a boner. He had omitted from his report a highly important fact—that this red-haired woman, who did not at all look like a *burzhuika,* also spoke Russian.

Saposhnik was interested in the house, the little house which Hilda Mermelstein had left to Mira to make up for all the money she had gone away with. The document she had left behind was rather more symbolic than legal in nature. Mermelstein would certainly have contested it, if he had thought it expedient. But in the present situation he preferred not to appear as an owner. As he saw it, possession of a house would be a blot upon his character and hinder his advancement in a system hostile to private property. But he had promised his superior Saposhnik that he would get the "mansion" for him, the pleasant one-family house with a garden all its own.

Ever since his arrival in Lvov, Saposhnik had been searching for an apartment for his family. The house was ideal. Saposhnik had left his family behind in Grishino: Riva, his wife, and his two children; thirteen-year-old Raia and six-year-old Boris. There they also belonged to the fortunate few who lived in a one-family house, although theirs could not compare with the house that he had just finished inspecting. It did not belong to him, but to his mother-in-law, who lived with them. Unfortunately. For Ruchele Boim, Riva's mother, was the volcano on which he danced, the minefield he was forced to traverse daily.

Upheavals and revolution had passed this old woman by without making the faintest impression upon her. She refused to take notice of them. She neither rejoiced in these political changes nor feared what they might bring. Her whole life had been passed in an atmosphere of oppression. She was steeped in the atmosphere of the ghetto, and she knew all the means that the ghetto employed to hold its own against pogroms, robbery, abuse and extortion under the tsars. But even this knowledge had not helped when the armed bands of Petliura swept through the Ukraine in 1920. Ruchele had seen her parents, brothers and sisters, husband and children slaughtered. They thought they had killed her, too, but she had survived her wounds, along with her daughter Riva, the only one of all her blood left to her. It was almost a miracle that they recovered. By then the Reds were at the helm.

Riva, aged thirteen, went to school and learned whatever the party doled out to the youth. By the age of fifteen she was virtually engaged to Mark Saposhnik. He was the son of a cobbler and had lost his parents in the same pogrom in which Riva's family had been killed. Like ten thousand other orphaned boys, he had followed the Reds, and like them he had become, in spite of his puniness, a tough, embittered fighter against reaction. He married Riva before he was sent to the engineering course in Kiev. She worked in the Grishino sugar refinery—hard physical work she was not fit for, since she had never been strong after her ordeal.

Her mother Ruchele, however, sat in her old place in the street market and traded. It was the same place she had occupied "ba Nikolai," under Tsar Nicholas, and had held on to for decades by dint of regular payments to the *pristav,* the police chief. Her husband had been a Talmud scholar, and all the duties of feeding and clothing her family had fallen on her shoulders. Under the Reds as under the Whites, she sat there and trafficked in the same goods: sunflower and pumpkin seeds, fruit, cheap candy and cookies, mirrors, pocketknives, combs. Her activities were limited not so much by the laws as by the increasingly painful shortages of everything under the new regime. Soon there was nothing left to sell. She resorted to the most impossible methods of providing their livelihood. But she provided that livelihood for years. Riva's tiny wages scarcely counted.

After Mark Saposhnik had completed his education and had found work in Grishino, he moved into her house, and when little Raia was born, her grandmother took charge of her, for Riva went back to her work almost immediately after the birth. But Ruchele went on selling things; she could not stop, even though private enterprise grew more and more dangerous, and although she was caught and fined again and again. She cursed the Soviets as she had cursed the Tsar's officials; she grew craftier, but she went on buying and selling. There was no room in her old head for the idea that she might be endangering her daughter and son-in-law. When Mark Saposhnik tried to explain that he was no longer just the cobbler's son but a state official, a comrade of the nachalnik of the militia, of the judge and the district attorney, she only asked why he didn't use his influence and position to obtain protection for her, instead of keeping at her to give up her little business. She despised him, as she despised all his comrades in the party. All that bunch could do was to play melodies about the glorious future. Did all that stuff help you fill your belly? And people like that had nothing better to do than prevent honest traders from earning their bread!

At such times she used to praise the days *"ba Nikolai."* Curses, blows, pogroms—such hardships were natural to the lives of Jews; God wished it so to test His chosen people, so that they would be ripe for the coming of the Messiah. Nowadays everything was topsy-turvy. Overnight Jews had become nachalniki and were neither Jews nor nachalniki. They not only denied God; they blasphemed Him with scurrilous verses and songs: "Don't wait for the Messiah, he's dead; you've got your Messiah, he's Red." That might be bait for some fools, but not for her, not for Ruchele Boim, the daughter and widow of famous Talmud scholars.

The old woman's constant grumblings got on Mark's nerves, of course; but for the sake of his wife and child he held his peace and nursed his grievances. Besides, the old woman not only did all the work in the household; she also found ways and means, thanks to the connections in the city and surrounding countryside that she had built up over the years, to obtain food and other things that had disappeared from the market. But relations between husband and mother-in-law remained impossible; and after Riva bore a son, the basic tension developed into outright hostility.

Ruchele Boim, daughter and wife of scholars in the Lord, found it inconceivable that her grandson should not conclude the covenant with Yahweh symbolized by circumcision. And Saposhnik, partinyi, nachalnik and convinced atheist, was horrified at the thought that his son might be the object of this sinister and painful ceremony which would leave behind an ineradicable sign of one parent's reactionary principles.

Ruchele Boim proceeded along the path ordained by God. She ran back and forth through the small town, made an appointment with the mohel, the man whom the Jewish community regarded as worthy and capable of performing the operation, issued invitations to the minyan, the needful number of ten Jews, in mysterious ways procured two bottles of vodka and baked an enormous gingerbread

—in short, did everything that was proper. But her son-in-law frustrated all her plans, and nothing came of mohel, minyan, vodka and gingerbread. For while his mother-in-law was out on a business call, Saposhnik drove up in the horse-drawn sleigh of the municipal fire department, and before Riva—still weak from childbed—could raise any objection, the whimpering newborn son was wrapped in an eiderdown and whisked away. The sleigh, driven by a reliable and close-mouthed fireman, dashed out of the town and did not return until four days later. Without the baby and without Saposhnik. The nachalnik sent his wife brief notes informing her of his welfare and place of residence, which he changed fairly frequently during the years of his absence. But concerning her son she was told only that he was in good hands and healthy, that he was thriving—even though uncircumcised—and when the time was ripe, he would return with his father.

Riva, who had returned to her job at the sugar refinery and was devoting her little free time to her small daughter, knew quite well what was meant by "when the time is ripe." As long as her mother lived, she would not see her son or her husband again.

But he came nevertheless, impelled by love and concern, only four years later, despite his mother-in-law. He had just returned from an assignment in Novosibirsk and reported to the party secretary of the province. At the secretary's office he ran into a comrade from his home town who told him that Riva had been ill for the past half year. Tuberculosis, it appeared, with no hope of recovery. Saposhnik, who had proved his worth in various capacities for years, was able to arrange to have himself assigned to Grishino, where someone was needed for the post of director of the power plant. He recovered his small son, who had been given into the charge of an old friend and wartime comrade, Vania, who was head of a kolkhoz.

During the railroad journey back home he had time to study little Boris. The boy differed not one bit from millions of other peasant boys. He talked, moved and sat just like one of them, a living proof of the theory that all men are alike at birth and become what they are only through the effects of upbringing, education and example.

How strikingly true that was Saposhnik learned after he entered his mother-in-law's house, tugging his son along by the hand. The boy took no notice of anything, gave no response to his mother's tearful caresses or to his sister Raia's joyful greeting—the girl was mentally far beyond her years, but had hardly developed at all physically. He also ignored his grandmother's black looks. He stood mute, stiff and sulky in the strange surroundings, and it was some time before he even moved his eyes to survey the walls. The obligatory portraits of the heroic fighters for The Cause, dead and alive, were nothing new to him. But two other pictures caught his eye, and he stepped closer to these. The crude prints represented Moses complete with horns, carrying the tables of the law; and Adam, Eve and the serpent. These obviously stirred his interest. He stared at them in some perplexity for a while. Then he took two steps toward the wall, fell to his knees, touched his forehead to the floor, raised his head, crossing himself several times, and with practiced fluency murmured the Lord's Prayer. Then he stood up, bowed, and stepped backwards from the pictures, repeatedly crossing himself.

All three adults were horrified by this demonstration of piety on the part of the four-year-old. Riva, his mother, turned toward the wall and wept; in the course of years tears had become her habitual release. Saposhnik stood stunned. But Ruchele, the sorely tried grandmother, kicked her tattered slippers from her feet, sat down on the floor, and began a bone-chilling lament, rocking back and forth. It was plain to all that she was sitting shibah.* She knew that the prescribed ritual did not extend to grandparents and grandsons. But Ruchele acted out of despair and hatred. She was bent on showing this apostate son-in-law that his son was dead to all Jews, and that he was to blame.

But Raia, the ten-year-old girl, laughed loudly at the preposterous movements of her new brother, caught the boy by the hand, and rushed him outside so that he could show this new game to all the other children. Saposhnik, however, grew deeply thoughtful. Evidently his little boy had grown up under the supervision and influence of his friend's mother-in-law, and that woman was as wedded to her old superstitions as Ruchele was to hers. These were unfortunate situations with which reason could not contend. One faint comfort remained: his Boris would soon learn to adore other pictures than the dead gods and their apostles. There were enough portraits of living apostles, and still more of the mustachioed, mysteriously smiling god who was just as jealous and vengeful as the ancient deity of the Jews, and for whose glory as much blood had flowed as for the crucified newcomer whom the Christians worshiped. To children pictures were pictures; it did not matter what was represented; they learned quickly to admire and adore.

Saposhnik stayed on with his family. The few hours that his work and the party left free he spent at the bedside of his wife. He played with the children. He loved his family and would gladly

---

* From Hebrew *shibh'āh*, seven: the seven days of mourning after a death, which the relatives spend sitting on the floor and lamenting. In the case of a member of the family who is converted to Christianity, the shibah lasts only an hour.

have devoted his whole soul to them if he had had the time. But he had none; the regime did not allow exceptions. He had a right to certain things as a nachalnik and a Soviet citizen. Doctors came to look at Riva and gave her what medicines were available. As a rare distinction and sure proof of his good position in the party, his wife was sent to a tuberculosis sanatorium in the Caucasus. She returned after a stay of three months strengthened and looking better, but within a few weeks she had relapsed. Nevertheless, she clung to life. She lay in bed, hot with fever, bathed in sweat, gasping for breath. Her eyes, her black, gentle, velvety eyes, sank deeper and deeper into their sockets, and her cheekbones became more and more prominent. The children were not allowed near her; her mother sat beside her bed, mutely giving up her place only when Saposhnik came to spell her.

A year passed, and still another. Ruchele Boim's gaunt figure was bowed as though she bore a heavy burden; white hairs thrust their way from under the edges of her dark-brown, moth-eaten wig, and the whole wig shifted every time Ruchele adjusted her kerchief. She no longer railed at Saposhnik; she spoke only to her daughter, scarcely ever to her granddaughter, and never a word to her son-in-law or grandson. She had cast them out of her heart. Nowadays Ruchele gave alms, for she had money, much more than anyone imagined. Ruchele Boim was rich, in fact. Her son-in-law guessed this, and the knowledge upset him; it alternately frightened him and reassured him. What if the old woman were caught—she had often been suspected—and her secret resources discovered? What would be his predicament, after having lived for so many years under the same roof, in a common household, with a speculator? What party judge would believe that he knew nothing of this wealth or its sources? Was not failure to make a denunciation in itself a serious crime? The slogan was: every worker must be a Chekist. And if he did denounce the old woman—how often had he not considered it, harried by his conscience, by his conception of his duty as a Bolshevik, suffering intensely from the inner conflict?—if he did, and Ruchele Boim were arrested, transported to a prison or a camp, and her money confiscated, what then? It would be the death of his wife, whom he loved every bit as much as he had twenty years ago, and for whom he suffered. Moreover, the household would not run without this close-mouthed, busy, cunning old woman. For even though she hated him, she upheld them all. In her mysterious ways she provided everything, obtained the strengthening nourishment an invalid needed when his salary could not cover such luxuries, or when money simply could not buy things because they could not be found in the shops.

When he applied for a post in the newly occupied zone, and was assigned to one, and when he had looked around a bit in his new surroundings, for the first time in his life it seemed to him, convinced materialist that he was, that perhaps after all something like happiness existed—that happiness described by the mendacious, sentimental writers of past eras, those corrupters of the people. For here in Poland there was everything a man needed, and it could all be bought for rubles. Food, clothing, furniture—absolutely everything. Like his comrades, he became accustomed to exchanging fictional values for solid realities, and again like them, his conscience was not troubled by this fraud. If his good Marxist conscience ever stirred, it was quickly reassured by the readiness with which his superiors extended huge advances, long-term loans, to the party members, to make it easier for them to buy. A crackling torrent of paper money, huge packages of chervontsy (ten-ruble notes), showered down upon the party faithful, and they could live like kings.

In such a situation a man like Mermelstein was worth his weight in gold. He could rustle up all sorts of commodities, and cheaply, too. Up to now he had not failed; why should Saposhnik have doubted his story about the house? Of course there might be some hitch to the matter, but Saposhnik was ready to take care of that with all permissible means, and if need be, with the aid of some adroit dialectic.

As he had gone through the house, he had been seized by a recklessness that was quite new to him. He had looked at these many rooms with their big windows, filled with substantial furniture. He had looked at the bathroom with its stove for heating water, its porcelain tub and gleaming faucets. As he looked at all this, he thought of Riva and his children. Poor Riva would certainly get well in a house like this. His children would have the garden to play in. And even if his dreadful mother-in-law, his enemy and the foe of all progress, had to come along to rule the roost, she would be rendered relatively harmless, for she would not know her way about in this country.

He had entered the kitchen repeating a saying of Stalin's to himself: "Difficulties exist to be overcome." He entered with a pleasant smile that sprang from his hopeful thoughts; and he had no sooner started talking with the woman Mira than he no longer felt like smiling, for it developed that she spoke Russian. His happiness changed to gravity, and to a feeling of fury at Mermelstein. He hid these feelings under the convenient mask of "We Communists know everything." And now it appeared he could not meet that simple question: "Who must know?" Because there was no answer to that question—or rather, because any answer could easily become a trap. No, he thought to himself, Mermelstein is a fool for telling me it would be easy, and I am a greater fool for believing him.

But difficulties existed to be overcome. He passed over her disconcerting question and turned to the matter of work. "You understand that we intend to use you as bookkeeper?" he said to Mira.

"Yes?" she said interrogatively.

"As such you will be responsible for the administrative work, as Tovarishch Mermelstein is for the technical work. Your functions differ, but you will share the responsibility. You will keep the books, help work out the budget, control the income and outgo; you will know whether there is money available for purchases, and you must give careful thought before you authorize any expenditures."

Mira managed to repress her smile. "I will do my best, of course. I used to be a pretty good bookkeeper. Of course, the functions you mention did not all come under the work of a bookkeeper. What type of bookkeeping is used in Russia?"

"Don't say Russia, comrade, say Soviet Union," he mildly reproved her. "Our own, of course—Soviet bookkeeping. I'm no specialist in it, but I can explain it to you in its broadest outlines. May I have a sheet of paper?" He took out a recently acquired fountain pen—as ardently desired by Soviet brain workers as a watch by every Soviet citizen—and prepared to write.

He had not gone very far before Mira grasped that Soviet bookkeeping differed in no way from the American system. But she let him finish his explanation, and did not correct his mistakes. When he was through, she showed him by an example that she had understood him. "You have the idea," he said, carefully dissimulating his surprise at how quickly she picked up these complicated matters. "And once you're actually doing the work, you'll have no trouble." He had observed that she also wrote Russian but not easily. She formed the letters slowly, with evident deliberation. But still and all, among so many illiterates she was a rarity. "Good, very good." He turned to Mermelstein and asked him in Yiddish whether he had the seal and stamp with him. Mermelstein replied that he did, whereupon Saposhnik carefully tore a sheet of paper in half and began to write. Mira guessed that he was making out a spravka.

"What's your name again?" he asked. "Mira, I know, but your family name and father's name?"

"Father's name?" Mira searched her memory. In vain. She did not know what her father's given name had been. "Isak," she said hastily, at hazard. "Mira Isakovna."

He wrote down both names. "And the surname? Linhan, isn't it?"

She did not correct him. It was a name as good as any other, and the unknown Linhan was certainly better than the too-well-known Linkhand, which might be fatal in this situation. If the thing were ever brought up, she could allege a misunderstanding. Saposhnik signed, stamped and sealed the document, and called Mermelstein over to the table, who traced his name underneath it in Russian script. Then Saposhnik handed it to Mira. "Now you are a part of our labor community. You will no longer be wasting your abilities in the service of capitalism, no longer devoting yourself to the interests of parasites, but to those of the community and therefore of yourself. I congratulate you, Mira Isakovna!" In addressing her by name and patronymic, he was expressing intimacy, confidence and equality.

"Thank you," Mira said. "I will work well."

"I am sure of that," Saposhnik said. "Your husband is a chauffeur, I understand. Does he know Russian?"

"Not a word." Mira was tense; it was all-important for Freddy to receive his spravka too!

"What kind of cars does he drive? Passenger or truck?"

"Both," Mira said.

"For the present the job is only theoretical anyhow. In our whole auxiliary farm we have only a single truck, and the driver spends more time repairing it than driving it. But your husband can find some work on the farm. Perhaps in the storehouse, or the stables, or the gardens. It will work out. He's a worker: I can see that by his build." He glanced with a touch of envy at Freddy's broad shoulders, and then at Freddy's hairy hands with their rather stubby fingers. Freddy's nails had not been manicured for months. "And by his hands. There's a man who knows what work means."

"Of course," Mira said without irony, and Saposhnik made out a spravka for Alfred Arturovich Linhan, *magazinshchik*—warehouseman. A warehouse attendant was more or less in the same wage category as a milker or coachman, which meant there would be no complications if Freddy were ultimately to shift jobs.

Mira took the document and thanked him. "There's only one difficulty," she said. "My husband is still recovering from a severe injury. He won't be able to do heavy work for a while."

"So Comrade Mermelstein has told me. He will not have to. By the time things start rolling here, he will be healthy as a horse." Saposhnik spoke good-naturedly. He was now the couple's superior. Both could be forced by law to work, and their place of work was eight miles from their house. "A pity that you will have to lose so much time, especially at the beginning, until you make better arrangements," he said.

"Lose time—in what way?" With her deep experience in negotiations, Mira had noticed the perceptible rise in Saposhnik's satisfaction. The man could not be so pleased only because he had hired two employees. Something else was involved. She was alarmed.

"You have to be at your job at eight o'clock," he explained. "As for your husband, he must be there at seven, and in summer at six. From here, I mean from this place, it is about eight miles to the farm. It may be that after a few months or even weeks there will be transportation available. But for the present there isn't any. That means a daily walk of sixteen miles. For people like us, that wouldn't matter. We've done harder things in the past. But I don't think you will find that easy to get used to. Walking four or even five hours a day."

Why was he bringing this up? She studied him, marked his every intonation; her brain registered every turn of phrase. She had to know what he was getting at, for she could not believe that he was genuinely concerned about them, that there was not something hidden behind this concern. Something harmful to her and to Freddy. What was it? But she must keep her head, must defend herself shrewdly from the unknown assault. "Of course it's not very pleasant," she said quietly. "But didn't you say that you and the other"—she hesitated, for she had never before used the word—"comrades have done much harder things? If we must walk, we'll walk—nichevo." And she really succeeded in producing a smile, a gay smile, and that breezy "nichevo" at the end!

Saposhnik sagged. He felt that the game was lost. This woman was too clever for him. He would not get the house. Still, he must play the game to the end. "That's fine, comrade! That's the real Soviet spirit! We need people like you. You understand that work comes first. But just because you have the right spirit, I want to make things easy for you." He broke off. If he was not careful, he would lose the whole game shamefully, at once.

"Easy?" Mira asked in her level, cool tone.

He colored. "Well, you see," he blurted out, "a capitalist entrepreneur wouldn't worry about such a matter. He would think: let her get up at dawn—that's all right with me, and what do I care that she has a three-hour tramp after work, when she's tired and hungry, just as long as she delivers her quota of labor for my money—that's the way the capitalists think. They know that they can always get another wage slave. But we don't look at it that way. 'Man is the supreme value,' Lenin said. And we act on that basis. Your energy is important to us. What that also means, of course, is that your energy doesn't belong to you alone, but to the community. You must therefore economize on it. That's why, in your own interest of course, I want to propose something to you." He felt a certain twinge of conscience at the phrase "in your interest." But he suppressed it. He was pleased with the way he had put the matter.

What did he mean, this puffed-up hamster with all his boring rhetoric? You won't catch me that way, she thought. But what was he getting at? Damn it all, let him lay his cards on the table. "What you say is very true, comrade—what should I call you? Comrade Director?"

"I call you Mira Isakovna, don't I? So say Mark Lvovich to me. That's the practice between people who understand and have confidence in one another. You have confidence in me, haven't you, Mira Isakovna?" Saposhnik had no sense of humor.

Neither did Mira. "Of course I have," she said. But at the moment she felt something that in the past had been alien to her: fatalism. I don't know what you're after, Mark Lvovich, but I have no choice; I have to go along with you. She propped both elbows on the table and rested her chin on her hands. This brought her face close to his, and he found himself looking into her eyes, which gleamed with gold flecks. A shiver ran through him. Ah, you ought to stay here in this wonderful house, stay with me, you fine woman; what happiness that would be. That would be life. It was hard to dispel the thought, to crush the intense desire. He was left with a feeling of sadness. Mira caught the flicker of melancholy in his face, which extinguished his assumed look of superiority, and suddenly thought that he meant well, meant to treat her well.

He pulled himself together, put aside dreams and wishes, although a moist gleam remained in his light brown eyes. "You understand, it depends entirely upon you to choose as you will," he said, and paused for a moment. "I am thinking only of your convenience. At the farm there are, if I remember rightly, twenty-one houses in all. They're not as big as this one here, but each has a little plot of ground. Millions of people would be overjoyed if they could live in such houses. They all have at least two—some as many as three—rooms. You could pick out whichever one you wanted. Any necessary repairs would be attended to at the farm's expense, of course. That is, at the expense of the state, since they're all nationalized. In any case, you see—"

"Not quite." Mira still did not know what he was getting at, but she felt reassured; here was a man, not a nachalnik but a man, who wanted something of her which she could give. But why was he telling her all this about those houses in the village?

He was tired of beating about the bush. With a good imitation of composure he explained, "You could pick one of these houses and then you'd be living right across the street from your place of work. You could be at work in five minutes at most. That's what I'm suggesting. If you're interested, you could drive out there with me tomorrow and look at the houses."

"That sounds like a good solution," Mira said. Apparently he had some reason for wanting her to live out at the farm. And why not, if the house was habitable? Was that the trap? "Are they really in good condition?" she asked.

"Oh," he said, breathless with suspense, fear, hope, "they are excellent houses of stone. Only here and there they have a window missing, or a door. We will have them fixed up in a few days." He turned to Mermelstein. "Put it down on the agenda. A survey to be made of all the houses belonging to the farm, and a list drawn up of necessary repairs." He turned back to Mira. "They will fix them up very nicely [he said *kulturno*]."

Mira nodded. "Do the houses have light and water?" she asked matter-of-factly, although the presence or absence of these conveniences would not have influenced her decision.

"Light of course! Don't forget you belong to Ukerkomenergo. Everything is ready. Tomorrow they are starting on electrification. The water, however, will take a while. The pipes will be laid as soon as they are available. We've already put in our requisition order. But there are fine wells near every house, and—" He reflected for a moment, and then said resolutely, "You will have water in the house, all you need. I guarantee it."

"That sounds wonderful. When does the work begin?" Mira asked. She was not really interested. It was a small thing to have to live without comforts for a few weeks. The important thing was that she now had a spravka, and that she would be getting away from Mermelstein by moving out of this house.

"You agree, then? You're very sensible!" He took a deep breath. Now came the crux of the matter. He looked down at his hands. "And what will you do about your house?" Had he sounded casual enough?

"With my house?" Mira asked slowly. For the moment she forgot to watch him closely; this had come as a surprise. But of course, the house did belong to her! Or at least she had paid for it, willynilly. But what court would ever recognize the legality of that ridiculous scribble Hilda had left her? How could she explain her ownership? Was it wrong for her to own a house? And why should he be interested, unless he were laying some sort of trap for her? She must not be a property owner, that was it! Probably all this questioning was part of their system.

"What do I care about the house?" she said. "One house is like another. The main thing is to have a roof over your head, and work to do." That sounded matter-of-fact, plain and to the point.

His head turned abruptly. "So then . . . ?" He almost gasped the words.

"So then what?"

"I mean"—he brought it out timidly— "I mean, it's your house, after all. Something has to be done with it. . . ."

"Yes, yes. Of course, of course." She had to give herself time to think. "But I can't live in two houses. If I move to the village, then—" She could not go on. Let him finish the sentence, damn it all. Let him say what she was supposed to do. She would not put her head in the noose.

"You can't live in two houses, right you are. That's good! Ha-ha-ha." He roared with forced laughter.

She ignored that. She smiled as Lady Whisten had taught her to smile when conversing with a gentleman—and for a pleasant moment Saposhnik surrendered to her charm and quite forgot why he was here. "You see, Mark Lvovich," she said finally, "I'm not familiar with Soviet laws and regulations. Please advise me. After all, you know all these things."

Saposhnik forced himself to remain calm. "As you yourself say, you cannot live in two houses. In the Soviet Union only very few people are permitted to own two houses. Only special people who have devoted themselves to the service of the community. They aren't, as you might think, people in high government posts, but writers, composers, painters. In addition to their regular residences, the state grants them a summer cottage in the country, in the mountains or by the sea, where they can draw inspiration from nature for works of art. But most of us must be grateful if we are allotted a single dwelling."

"I understand," she said hypocritically. "I certainly wouldn't ask for more. One is plenty for me."

"This is your own house," he went on, calm now, sure of victory. "You therefore have the right to sell it. In fact you must, since you are not allowed to rent it—there are special laws about that. Here, in this new territory and on a private basis, you can sell, with your furniture. Then you will have money not only to outfit your new house, but also some left over. And for your personal advancement, it would be better that instead of owning a house you live in one that you rent from the state."

Aha! Mira thought. The trap was closing. She was really terrified. "Mark Lvovich," she said hesitantly, "you understand all these matters far better than I do. So please give me advice. All I want is to have things right. Right with the laws and right with my work." She looked squarely into his face and smiled. In all her life she had never smiled that way, for her whole soul was in that smile, all the anxiety in her soul.

But Saposhnik did not see the anxiety. If anyone was to be anxious, it was he. But suddenly the old familiar emotion, anxiety, had given way to tenderness, an urge to make good, an altogether impermissible, forbidden feeling of penitence. For years Saposhnik, the Bolshevik, had labored to kill his soul, his wishes, his longings. A vast system of dogma told him that he must try to smother all feeling in himself. And now, in spite of all, he was experiencing a miracle of inner resurrection. Not that he was aware of it. As he turned to Mira, his puffy cheeks suddenly seemed deflated, his brow was furrowed, his dark-brown eyes gleamed with despairing gladness and gratitude. He was sniffing as if he could barely hold back his tears, and Mira suddenly realized that he was not her enemy, not a cunning, dreaded foe playing a cat-and-mouse game with her. Here, rather, was a man well disposed toward her, who was ready to help. Yet she still could not count on him; she did not understand the reason for his kindness, and so she remained on guard. And she let Nachalnik Mark Lvovich Saposhnik—for the moment not a nachalnik but only the cobbler's son from Grishino—she let him talk. Speech burst out of him like a waterfall that plunges over cliffs and ravines after the spring sun has released it from the grip of ice.

Mira heard the story of a life that she knew well, for she had lived it. What are details, when the general picture remains the same? He had scrounged in garbage heaps for potato peels and onion skins, had snatched bones from dogs, stolen swill from the pigs. Did Mira know what a pogrom was? Had she heard of the Black Hundred or the Petliurovtsy—*Bei zhida, spassai Rossiu*—kill the Jews, save Russia? Could she imagine what it was like for a fifteen-year-old boy to see parents and brothers butchered, his home and workshop drenched with blood and smeared with the excrement of the murderers? Did she know about the stench of decaying corpses, how the memory could turn the heart to stone? Did she know about sight and smell becoming one, forever inseparable and unforgettable? And what it was like to go on living while remembering horror, memory becoming the lash that sent a boy to join the ragged bands of the Red soldiery? A boy so puny that he could scarcely shoulder a rifle, but marching in heat and frost, his body clothed in rags, barefoot, hungry and thirsty. You fought, killed, were wounded; you were one among thousands, a fighter for the Revolution, for The Cause, for Progress, the enemy of all those who made pogroms or tolerated them. Did Mira understand these things? That The Cause could, must be, the greatest thing on earth? That you must be on guard against anything which might endanger it? The Cause was all, the only precious thing in life.

And suddenly the eloquent orator, the Bolshevik, the Nachalnik Saposhnik, for whom The Cause was all, who spoke of it as a priest speaks of God, single-minded and inexorable, suddenly he became meek Mark Lvovich who talked on in low, faltering tones about his wretched little house in Grishino, his sick wife Riva, the children and the infernal mother-in-law. Now the party had assigned him to this new place; he wanted to send for his family and—the thought had just come to him—and if Mira Isakovna did not want to or could not keep this house, perhaps it would offer a perfect solution.

Then he fell silent.

"That would be splendid, Mark Lvovich," Mira said. "I mean, if you could arrange the whole business. You understand, all I want is to have it settled. And what you've told me—all those terrible things—I understand, because I too have had a frightful childhood." She had never spoken a word to anyone about it, had always repressed and pushed away memories of her early childhood. They had been ballast, obstacles along the road she was determined to follow. That road was to lead her far away from all those horrors. But now the moment had come to talk about them; now it was good, it was highly in her favor that her past had held the filthy basement and the orphanage and her work for Frau Kadisch. So she told her own story in her low, hoarse but clear voice. Naturally she said nothing of the years of her successes, the position she had won, the vast fortune she had accumulated for herself and others. She mentioned no names, named no places, spoke of no travels. It was easy to decide what to describe, what to conceal.

And so they were quits, these children of the slums. For he too had revealed and concealed as he thought wise. That smile of Mira's, misinterpreted by Saposhnik, had melted the ice within him, but only partially. Reason, the discipline practiced for years, the routine that had become a part of his psyche, had set limits to self-revelation. And so the confession had turned into a propaganda speech, a peroration that was the expression of his own petty-bourgeois desires for a decent house and nice furniture.

If the house had represented anything of value to Mira, she would have seen what Saposhnik was after the moment he mentioned it. But as it was, the house was something she would much rather be rid of than keep. She had acquired it by default, and felt relief that she could unload it on him.

All this circumlocution had wearied her, but it had proved useful. She did not care whether this nachalnik was doing her a favor, or she him. At least she had made a "connection." Now she had only to build on it, strengthen it, and so establish a position which would resist attack—especially the attacks of this repulsive fellow, Mermelstein. As soon as she began on her job and they saw what she could do, she would be able to hold her own. With these people, every other word was *work*, and that was fine. She had confidence in her ability to work. For the present, her one great weapon in the impending struggle was this ability. Was it the only one? She leaned forward, and in all deliberation looked straight at the nachalnik. He turned toward her, and their eyes met. "Mark Lvovich," Mira said softly, "at this moment I am back where I was as a six-year-old. There is no one on earth to help me. Please teach me, show me what must be done, what is permissible and what is not. I need guidance, Mark Lvovich. May I come to you and ask you for advice, for help, for protection—may I do that, Mark Lvovich?"

"Mira Isakovna, every Soviet citizen is honor-bound to help a person who works well and means well. And I want to help you. I'll teach you, show you—warn you. In a week you'll understand everything, and in six months I, Mark Lvovich Saposhnik, will be able to bring the party a new candidate—Mira Isakovna Linhan!"

"In six months! Can one become a party member so fast?" In six months she would be either with the Linkhands or dead.

"You only have to desire it and to apply yourself, Mira Isakovna. You are the material from which real Bolsheviks are made. Intelligent and serious."

"I'll do my best, Mark Lvovich. When would you like to take over the house?"

"As soon as you're installed properly in your new place, not before. What will it cost—I mean, with the furniture?"

Mira felt pressed again. She obeyed a sudden inspiration. "You see," she said, "that really doesn't matter very much now. You must know about the price. I mean, the state fixes these prices, doesn't it? You must take it at the official price. You've already promised me you'd take it, Mark Lvovich. It will certainly do your sick wife worlds of good. The rooms are big and dry and there's lots of sun. The garden is beautiful in warm weather; she can lie in the sun, and the children can play. . . ." She warmed to the theme.

Victory all the way down the line! he thought jubilantly. "I'll come for you around noon tomorrow. Then you can choose which house you want and I'll arrange for the repairs. As soon as you've decided, we can go to the notary and draw up the agreement. By then I'll know what the right price is for such a piece of property. Agreed?"

"Excellent," Mira said.

"I'll go now." He stood up and shook her hand vigorously. "Keep well," he said, in a low, affectionate voice. His eyes sought hers, but dropped almost immediately. Freddy had made a movement. Maybe the big, silent bear is jealous, he thought, and extended his hand. "Dosvidania, Tovarishch Linhan." Freddy stood up and made the kind of bow his governess had trained him to perform at age five. Saposhnik sniffed with embarrassment and looked around at Mermelstein. He slipped into his fur coat and put on the cap. "I don't ordinarily wear clothes like these. I bought them for my wife," he murmured, as he shambled out of the kitchen. Mira accompanied him as far as the veranda door. "Good luck, Mira Isakovna," Saposhnik said.

"The same to you, Mark Lvovich."

He jumped down the three wooden steps. As he turned the corner of the house, his way of walking, encumbered by the enormous coat, resembled a grotesque dance.

The village had been a settlement of German peasants whose ancestors had come from Swabia. The land had been passed on from generation to generation, and not only the land, but the founders' industry, perseverance and love of order. The settlement had flourished. Its fields, gardens, houses and outbuildings were testimony to loving care and practical intelligence. Now the former owners had emigrated back to Germany. By agreement between the Soviet Russian and the German authorities, they had taken their movable goods with them, and had received payment in money for the land and buildings.

The Polish and Ruthenian peasants from the vicinity of Jiusefovka had stripped the houses of doors, windows, barn gates and various other items sorely needed on their own premises. They had done a great deal of damage to the village and made scarcely any improvement in their own homes.

Mermelstein, scouring the countryside for land for the auxiliary farm, had come across this abandoned village. Saposhnik had quickly settled the formalities of taking possession. The power plant's farm would include two hundred acres of excellent tillage, fifty acres of orchard and vegetable gardens, twenty-one solidly built houses, a number of barns and stables. Once the needed repairs had been made and livestock bought, the hiring of the working force could begin. Saposhnik had arranged for the electric power line to be put through to Jiusefovka. The farm would therefore have light and power, and it was high time that Mermelstein set about obtaining implements, livestock, and workers. He tried, but his powers as a procurement agent seemed to have deserted him. It was well nigh impossible to get hold of animals and farm equipment.

One day Saposhnik spoke to Mira about how badly things were going. She quickly realized all that was at stake for him. He had to establish the farm, or he would be out of this job, and would, moreover, have to answer to the party for his failure. And he was her one source of protection at the moment. It was therefore vital to her to put the farm on a good footing.

She set herself to studying the whole problem. She had long talks with Saposhnik in which she familiarized herself with Soviet practices. It soon became clear that the key to the situation was to find ways to evade rather than to keep to the strict regulations—for Saposhnik himself admitted that these regulations were completely unworkable.

In the meantime Saposhnik had bought Mira's house—at a ridiculously low price—but he had not yet paid for it. The large advances from the party had suddenly stopped. Rumor had it that various high functionaries sent out from Moscow on inspection tours had reported that the *nachalstvo,* the occupation officialdom, were living on a scale of luxury incompatible with Soviet conceptions of simplicity. Mira had no thought of pressing Saposhnik for payment. The house had served its purpose—it had put this temporarily influential man under obligation to her. Already, moreover, she had replaced Mermelstein in Saposhnik's confidence. Saposhnik could not drop him, but he treated Mermelstein with contempt. Since Mermelstein was thoroughly incompetent where real work was called for, he was now idle and useless.

According to the terms of her agreement with Saposhnik, Mira was selling the house with all that was in it. Now her own place in the village was ready, but she had nothing in the way of furniture and household gear for it. Three days before the deadline for moving, she found herself without money, and with nothing left to turn into cash except her diamond bracelet. It occurred to her to pry a few of the small stones from the bracelet, to sell them. But where? She found herself forced to ask Mermelstein to find her a buyer— she knew no one else to ask. Mermelstein was deeply insulted that she refused to entrust the diamonds to him. But feeling sure that he would make something on the transaction, he brought her to see Antek.

* * *

"You'll have a glass, won't you? Can't hurt in this cold." Antek signaled to Tadek, who hurriedly put glasses and two bottles, one of vodka and one of vishnevka, on the table. He added a plate of ginger cakes—Yadviga always kept a supply of these on hand. Only Mira and Freddy took the cherry brandy; the rest drank vodka. Mermelstein drained his glass at once, and held it out promptly for refilling. "Yes," he said, "it's easier to talk after a drink." He turned to Antek: "You're a busy man, so I'll keep it short. In case you don't know, I'm now director of the power plant farm. The comrade here is the bookkeeper, and this comrade"—he indicated Freddy—"is the warehouse man."

"All that has nothing to do with our business," Mira interrupted. "I'd like to ask you, Herr—what was your name again?"

"Gorecki," Antek said politely. He too spoke in German.

"Well, Herr Gorecki," Mira said, deliberately avoiding the "comrade" that Mermelstein had used with such emphasis, "I have four small stones to sell." She took from her bag an envelope which she handed to Antek. He was firmly resolved not to buy diamonds, no matter how cheap they were, and certainly not in the presence of Mermelstein. But his instinct to be polite to a woman checked any brusque rejection. He opened the "envelope" which Mira had made of a sheet of white paper and looked at the four small diamonds with no particular interest.

"Pretty," he said. "But I'm afraid I must disappoint you. Comrade Mermelstein has misinformed you—we haven't seen each other for a long while, so it's not surprising he doesn't know. I've given up business dealings. I don't buy and don't sell. Except cattle. All three of us are buyers for the Meat Trust—my two friends and I." He gestured toward Vassily, who thoughtfully twirled his mustache and stared into space, altogether disinterested in the conversation, and toward Tadek, who sat with Freddy, steadily refilling his glass and clinking glasses with him.

Mira pricked up her ears at the mention of buying cattle. For the moment she forgot the real purpose of her visit. "What did you say you buy? Cattle? Is that true?"

"Certainly. We drive around the countryside twice a week, buying. For the Meat Trust, of course."

"So then there are cattle for sale. Milch cows, too?"

"We can get anything we want, and milch cows are easier than beef cattle because the peasants are obliged to deliver a certain quota of milk, and they don't want to."

Mira looked over at Mermelstein. He was steadily downing

vodka. If Antek said he wasn't interested in the diamonds, then there would be no deal, and hence no rake-off for old Mermelstein. Conversation, for its own sake, did not interest him. It didn't seem to occur to him that if others could obtain cattle, he could too, and that if he did not, someone else would. Mira looked at Vassily.

"Are you a specialist in cattle too?" she asked him.

He stopped stroking his mustache and replied politely, "Well, yes, I know something about cattle. Why are you interested, Frau—"

"Linhan," Mira said quickly. "I'd like to have a serious word with you two." She turned to Antek again, who was still holding the envelope. "So you don't want to buy the stones. Would you by any chance know someone who would? I need money—so they can be had at a bargain."

"I'm very sorry," Antek said, handing the stones back to her. "But I really can't give you any hope. There's no demand at all. Who would buy diamonds now? The Russians? They don't know anything about gems; they do without such things. The natives? What for? Besides, people aren't buying anything at all nowadays, from what I hear. Except food. You understand—"

"I understand," Mira said absently. "But what does a person do when she needs money, as I do right now, for example?" She smiled nervously, and bent her head in anxious perplexity. When she raised it, she found herself meeting Vassily's eyes. He was looking at her with more interest than sympathy.

"Yes," he said deliberately, "it's not easy. But it depends on how much a person needs."

She looked closely at him. "I don't know whether the sum I need would strike you as a lot or a little. I'd say—about five thousand rubles."

Vassily turned to Antek, who gave a lightning toss of his head at Mermelstein. Vassily said no more. Mira, too, had understood. Mermelstein wasn't the kind of man you let know anything about your business. She changed the subject. "I'm interested in what you said about buying cattle. Perhaps you could give us a few tips."

"Gladly," Antek said. But the atmosphere was not conducive to sober discussion.

Freddy and Tadek had been sitting on the sofa with the bottle of vishnevka between them and glasses in their hands. Freddy was saying to Tadek, "Listen, now, listen close, and I'll teach you a jolly song."

"Konechno," Tadek said. He hadn't understood a word.

"All right, listen: 'Hussars, uhlans, dragoons, the light and the heavy, the whole damned cavalry'—come on, sing along. Once more: 'Hussars, uhlans, dragoons—' "

"*Ja jestem taki zimny Dran!*" Tadek sang falsetto an old Polish hit song.

"Now, none of that. '. . . *dragoons*'—dasnidanya, don't be so dumb," Freddy bleated. "Come on, once more: 'Hussars, uhlans, dragoons, the light and the heavy, the whole damned cavalry—blood must flow, red Turkish blood'—ha!"

"Ha-ha-ha," Tadek chirped, slapping Freddy's thigh in time to the music. They were real pals and understood one another perfectly.

Antek had turned his chair and was listening to them, smiling. The noise had roused Mermelstein from his stupor, and he raised his glass and drank to the two of them. Laughing, Freddy looked over at Mira.

Mira turned away, shaking her head, but not angry. She shrugged—no sense reproving a spoiled child. And she threw a glance of apology at Vassily, who was watching Freddy with close attention. He appeared not to see her look. "Herr Linhan," he said, "I know that song. Let's sing it together." He placed both hands to his mouth as if he were blowing a bugle. "Mount!" he commanded.

"Yes!" Freddy said, delighted.

Vassily blew another signal. This time it was Freddy who issued the command: "Charge!"

And then the song rang out in harmony: "Hussars, uhlans . . ." on to the end. But it no longer sounded like snatches of a silly song Freddy had droned out in alcoholic monotone. Vassily's face wore an absent expression, and on Freddy's was an earnestness Mira had never seen in him before. She and Antek were strangely moved by the song, which had lost all its childishness and rang out with solemnity and majesty.

"Oh," Freddy said, "he can do it! That's how it should be sung! Yes, that's the way. How do you know it?" he asked Vassily. He spoke clearly and soberly. His childish, drunken gaiety had vanished.

"I served in the cavalry in Austria."

"Were you with the Emperor's uhlans—an officer like Gustl?" Freddy asked. His eyes filled with tears.

"No," Vassily said, smiling. "I wasn't an officer, but I was an uhlan."

"Then you must have known my brother Gustl—"

Mira intervened before Freddy could pursue his questioning. She spoke no louder than usual, and without sharpness, but firmly: "Enough, Freddy, forget these old stories. It's time for us to go." She threw a look of apology at Vassily and Antek, and stood up.

"Yes," Vassily said, "we must go too, now. To collect our identity cards. If you wait a moment, we'll go together. Get ready, fellows," he said to Antek and Tadek.

Mira extended her hand. Vassily pressed it rather more firmly than was necessary. She understood that he had something to tell her. He released her hand and looked around at Mermelstein. He had dropped off into his stupor again. In a low murmur Vassily said, "We'll have the money for you at five o'clock tomorrow afternoon. Come just with your husband."

Mira thanked him with a look, and nodded quickly. Before she could say anything, Antek and Tadek rejoined them in their outdoor clothes. They stood with Mira and Freddy while Vassily went into the adjoining room. He returned in a lambskin jacket and high fleece cap. Tadek dislodged Mermelstein from the chair. "Everyone going home now," he squeaked.

Mermelstein rubbed the sleep from his eyes and looked around vacantly.

They parted in the yard.

The issuing of the identity cards went swiftly. There were three windows, and behind each sat a militia official who took the spravka and the photographs, asked a few questions, and entered the data on an official form and on the card. The photograph was pasted to the card, stamped, and the recipient signed the card and the official form. Whereupon spravka and identity card were handed over, and the Soviet Union had acquired a new citizen. A good many of the men were directed to a table along the side wall, at which an official sat making out military cards. This, too, was quickly taken care of. The official entered the data from the passport in a small book, asked the man's branch of service and rank, and within ten minutes the new citizen was also a member of the Red Army Reserve.

When Vassily reached this table and had replied in his mixture of Russian and Ruthenian to the question about his branch of the service, he heard someone behind him say, "Cavalry, that's fine. A rider!" He turned and found himself looking into a smiling, strikingly handsome face. "Yes," the man said, "cavalry." He spoke pure Ukrainian. "That's a service for you!" He took the military card from the official's hand and read the name: "Vassily Vassilevich Khomniuk." He restored the document to Vassily, who tucked it into the outer breast pocket of his woolen jacket, along with the identity card and spravka. The other man watched his movements. "That's right, Vassily Vassilevich, keep it buttoned. Don't lose it," he said gaily. "It's a great thing to be a Soviet citizen. You should be pleased!"

"I am pleased," Vassily said deliberately. "Once you have an identity card, you know where you belong."

"Certainly," the man agreed. "You're already working, aren't you?"

"I have always worked," Vassily said. He scrutinized the man —a bigwig, by his appearance. The man stood squarely, legs wide apart in sleek polished boots and breeches with those comic puffs high up on the thighs. His brown leather jacket was open and he wore his cap at a jaunty angle on curly, golden hair.

"So a man should," he said, laughing and exposing two rows of gleaming teeth. "What are you working as now?"

"A Meat Trust buyer."

"So you've gone from horses to cows! Quite a comedown for an old cavalryman."

"Work is work. You can't always choose what you want to do."

"Why not? With us you can. A man gets simple work only if he knows nothing. What would you like to work at? What are you best at?"

"I'm content with my work. We three"—he gestured toward Antek and Tadek, who were standing side by side, waiting for their military cards to be filled out—"work together in a group."

The nachalnik—he was obviously that—glanced at the pair. "Poles, aren't they?" he asked. "Do you speak Polish too?"

"Not much. I'm Ruthenian, but we get along pretty well, and our director seems to be satisfied with us."

The man took a flat box from his pocket and extended it toward Vassily. "Smoke?"

"Thank you." Vassily carefully took a *papirosa* from the box, and produced his lighter. His new acquaintance looked benignantly down at the cheap lighter as he bent to light his cigarette from it. Vassily took a deep puff. "Good, very good. That's fine tobacco," he said. "Thank you very much."

"Nichevo," the nachalnik said. "We smoke what we can get."

"Indeed," Vassily said after a pause.

"Now tell me, what's your real occupation?" the blond man said suddenly.

"I've worked with horses all my life," Vassily replied slowly.

"Racing horses too? I mean, thoroughbreds?"

"Mostly with thoroughbreds."

"Were you a jockey or breeding them?" the other man asked eagerly.

"I was a jockey for a while, but then I got too heavy and worked in the stables. But excuse me—my comrades are waiting. I must go now." Tadek and Antek had received their documents and were looking over at Vassily. "We live together and have to get up very early, Comrade Nachalnik."

This didn't seem to trouble the other man. "Let them wait a little longer." He beckoned to the pair, who approached with some uncertainty. "Wait on the bench," he told them. "I have something to discuss with Vassily." And while Antek, who guessed rather than understood what had been said to him, drew Tadek along behind him toward the bench, the nachalnik turned to Vassily again. His face wore an immensely friendly smile: "Vassily Vassilevich, you like working with horses, don't you? I know a good place for you. They aren't thoroughbreds, of course, just work horses. But horses are horses, and not cattle, eh?"

"Horses are horses, Comrade Nachalnik, but I can't just throw up my job."

"That will be arranged. The power plant is setting up a farm now. Not a big affair, just eighty dessiatin of land; fruit and vegetables, milch cows, and there are supposed to be twenty horses. You will be the *starshi koniukh,* the chief of the stables, there. You'll have the drivers under you and a chance to show what you can do. Not for the parasitic capitalist landowners but for the people. Pretty good, eh?"

Vassily beamed. "Do you mean that seriously, Comrade Machalnik? I'll come, of course I'll come, if the Meat Trust lets me go. But —don't you need gardeners on the farm? My friends here—they're fine workers. They can do anything." He nodded in the direction of Antek and Tadek.

"Of course we need them too. The three of you go to the Meat Trust first and . . . wait a moment." He disappeared into the room behind the windows.

Antek sprang toward Vassily; Tadek followed more slowly. "What does he want of you?" Antek asked.

"I don't really know," Vassily replied soberly. "But at the moment all three of us have new jobs. On a farm. You two are going to be gardeners and I'm—chief of the stables."

"What about the Meat Trust?"

"He'll take care of that. Lucky we're getting away. I've been wondering how we were going to. It makes you nervous, having one foot in jail all the time."

"I don't give a damn. One thing or another—it's all the same. How did he know that we're gardeners?"

"I told him so. You'll learn. I know enough about gardening to help you out. It's good work; you'll see."

Antek looked at him wide-eyed. "You mean to tell me you just up and said I was a gardener, just like that?"

"Well, I wanted us to stay together."

"That's rich. But—"

He didn't have a chance to finish. The nachalnik returned with an envelope from which he took a sheet of paper. "What are your names?" Antek gave his and Tadek's names. The nachalnik entered them on the form. "So, now you go to the Trust, give this letter to the director, receive your discharge, and report to the office of the power plant." He turned to Vassily. "Ask for me there. My name is Feingold. And now, good night."

The three walked home in silence. Once they were home, Tadek threw open a window to let the smoke and alcohol smell escape, as he did every evening. He added wood and coal to the stoves, cleared away the bottles and glasses, and made up the beds. Then he closed the window and sat down in the armchair near the stove. Vassily and Antek remained sitting at the table. Antek waited, but Vassily seemed lost in thought. He sat stroking his mustache and seemed not to notice Antek's inquiring looks. At last Vassily raised his head. "Yes," he said slowly, "it will be better this way. I'm glad to be out of that thievish business. You know, the pitcher goes to the well too often. . . ."

"We won't be any better off, Vassily. With these guys you're always going from the frying pan into the fire. Who knows what this nachalnik has in mind? There's something fishy about it, changing a man's job just like that, at ten o'clock at night. There must be a reason for it; he must be out for something."

"I don't look at it quite that way. With the director of the Meat Trust, we were already accomplices. He had us in his power; we had no choice but to steal. This boss is new. He can only ask us to work. If he makes crooked propositions, we're just innocents who don't know what he's driving at. Yes, Antek?"

"Maybe." Antek reflected. "You're right, Vassily, it's bound to be an improvement. But how did he come to ask you?"

"By chance—I hope. He gave me a cigarette, seemed pleased to learn that I'd been in the cavalry, wanted to know this and that . . . and then he said under the new setup everyone gets the kind of job he does best, and so now I'm starshi koniukh and you two are gardeners. I can manage horses all right, but what about you two and gardening? Oh well, it's still winter."

"Don't get conceited, Vassily. I'll handle the gardening just as well as you handle the horses, you can bet on that." He laughed so boisterously that Tadek, who had almost fallen asleep in the big chair, woke up and joined in his laughter. Antek turned to Vassily again: "It just so happens I'm a trained gardener! Comrade Starshi Koniukh, bring me a couple of hundred loads of horseshit at once!"

Antek roared with laughter. Tadek laughed till his eyes filled with tears.

Vassily looked at Antek in surprise. "How's that?"

"Simple enough. What beats me, though, is how you hit on the idea. Tadek knows something about gardening too. As for me, I worked in a nursery for almost four years. For eighteen months I was chief gardener."

"Where? When?"

Antek stopped laughing. "In the pen, Vassily, that's where. I'm a damned good gardener, I tell you. As a matter of fact, I often used to think that maybe Tadek and I should start up a nursery garden somewhere near town. But I was always afraid it would remind me of jail. Now it doesn't matter. What's the whole country if not a jail?"

"Better not look at it that way, Antek. You make your life too hard. Be glad you're getting work you like. And I'm glad the three of us will be staying together. Tomorrow morning we go to the Trust and get our discharges. Then at nine we're due at the power plant to report to Comrade—what was his name again?—Feingold."

"Did you say the power plant? The farm belongs to the power plant? Oh, God—didn't you hear what that stinker Mermelstein said? Do you realize that he's our director now? And the red-haired chick's the bookkeeper, and the big guy with his cavalry song's the warehouse man. Can you figure it out, Vassily?"

Vassily listened in astonishment. He had paid no attention to Mermelstein's boasts. Now he recalled what had been said. It wasn't a pleasant prospect, to work under the orders of that man. Could it be that they were going from the frying pan into the fire, after all?

"Antek," he said finally, "even if Comrade Mermelstein really is director of the farm, we'll manage him. The woman's all right, I think. If we three stick together, Mermelstein can't bother us. He'll dance to our tune. Does he know anything about farming?"

"He doesn't know anything about anything; he's just a lousy small-time crook. I've known him for years. He's always sucked up to people with money and done dirty work for them. Once he—"

"I don't want to know the details. But how did this Linhan woman come to be connected with him? Do you know her?"

"No. But she's not from around here; you can see that. She must have run from Hitler. And her husband's just a big baby."

"Yes." Vassily smiled. "A baby. Do you have any money in the house, Antek?"

"What do you need money for, Vassily? But of course I have. You haven't touched your share yet."

"That's fine. I need five thousand rubles."

Antek threw him a quick glance. "You can have ten thousand if you like. You want it for—" He hesitated.

"Yes, I promised it to the woman."

Antek shook his head wonderingly. "You're a queer bird, Vassily. Why do you want to give that woman five thousand rubles? You like her that much? Have you any idea how long a starshi koniukh has to work to earn so much money? You can't afford it; look for a cheaper dame." He laughed coarsely.

"You mistake my motives, Antek—you can believe me or not, as you like. She's in a spot, and I promised—not really on her account, as a matter of fact."

"On account of the cavalry?" Antek laughed. "What was that silly song, Vassily?"

"The song, the silly song. . . ." A shadow passed over Vassily's face.

"Well, as you like. You can do what you please with your dough. But look out for Mermelstein. If he smells easy money, he's after it. That's one reason I wouldn't touch the diamonds."

"I realized that. I told her to come tomorrow afternoon, and not with Mermelstein."

"That's better. The woman has a head on her."

BOOK FIVE

HOWL WITH THE WOLVES

*Yet it seems that men have a
slightly corrupted nature,
for they were not born wolves,
they have become wolves.*
VOLTAIRE

I T WAS LATE ON A STORMY JANUARY NIGHT IN THE YEAR 1940 and Octavian Pradescu, officer on duty of the Sigurantza Generala, had all but dozed off in his office. Suddenly his telephone was ringing. He had barely lifted the receiver when a voice babbled, "This is Protopopescu, pharmacist, Cotroceni, Strada Independentziei 14—you have that? Something's up in Number 17, the house that belongs to Senator Mandrescu. A big gang there, I can hear them talking Russian—some kind of conspiracy. The bandits are up to something—revolution! Send a strong force. I've already called Inspector General Dumitriu—he's a good friend of mine—unfortunately can't get him. Be quick and you'll catch them all!"

Pradescu knew the house in question and knew moreover that Senator Mandrescu had been away for months. It was also true that the Inspector General was out of town, and that the pharmacist knew the Chief. To arms!

He immediately dispatched two heavy trucks: police armed with pistols and carbines, gendarmes equipped with repeating rifles, hand grenades and tear gas—altogether a hundred men, not including the officers. Three cars of Sigurantza officers led the raiding party, and in a few minutes had reached a side street about thirty yards from the suspect house. Lights were blazing all over it, as they could see in spite of the closed shutters. A cordon of heavily armed men quickly surrounded the place. They decided to break in at once, without warning. The two side doors were battered open, the front door smashed, and a horde of police poured into the rooms.

It became clear at once that this was no band of revolutionaries, although the gendarmes—brave but naïve peasant boys unfamiliar with the phenomena of urban life—did not know quite what to make of the scene. For the house was teeming with a good many more or less naked men, the younger ones garishly made up and wearing wigs, so that they might have been taken for girls had there not been convincing evidence to the contrary. The gendarmes and police were quickly sent out while the Secret Service men remained with the "revolutionaries," who were frantically trying to dress and having trouble finding their own clothing.

The commander of the raid, a certain Inspector Barbulescu, might have settled the affair to everyone's satisfaction—to the satisfaction of the authorities and the persons implicated, that is—by deciding that he had burst in on an innocent dinner at which the guests had simply drunk too much. But some very high government officials happened to be in the party, and this cast a different light on the affair. It was one thing to be obliging, but Barbulescu was an experienced and intelligent officer. Being obliging to ordinary citi-

259

zens was one thing, but being obliging to important people often landed a man in bad trouble. And so he chose to be nothing but a proper official doing his duty.

He therefore pretended that he did not recognize any of the guests, and summoned the vice squad. Within fifteen minutes a number of dignitaries, coat collars turned up as high as possible, accompanied by a mob of giggling and screeching queens, were being crammed into a patrol wagon and taken to the nearby precinct house.

Needless to say, all the participants in the "symposium" were as free as the breeze an hour later. The whole affair was hushed up. But a few whispers leaked out, and the curious story of the frustrated revolution was soon making the rounds in high society. A number of resounding names were mentioned, including that of Orest Danghu the Blaze, recently appointed Secretary General in the Ministry of the Interior.

Danghu was not very popular. His meteoric rise was the subject of numerous rumors. A position such as Danghu occupied at the age of thirty-one could scarcely be reached without excellent connections and patronage from the highest quarters. But where did the patronage come from, and where did he himself come from? There was no boyar family by the name of Danghu; there had never been a Minister, Archimandrite or General Danghu. Obviously, then, no father, cousin or uncle had paved the way for him. To be sure, his collaboration with certain groups had helped him in the latest stages of his career—the groups that were interested in a close alliance with Germany. But how had this unknown got into the Ministry in the first place?

Danghu had been poor when he entered the Ministry of the Interior. Now he lived in a five-room apartment in the finest quarter of town, kept a cook and other servants, and drove a big German car. He undoubtedly had money. That was not too surprising, for the Ministry of the Interior was a fine source of income in these times. One could make a pretty penny just from visas and temporary residence permits for foreigners. And who could object? After all, the Jews could afford to pay plenty, and in dollars.

With money comes influence. By now he seemed to be the most important man in the Ministry. He could mobilize the criminal police, the secret police and the gendarmerie by pressing a button. Men twice his age, grown gray in service, trembled before him. No doubt about it, he was the man of the present, and still more of the future.

*   *   *

About a week after the incident on the Strada Independentziei the Secretary General called in Inspector Barbulescu. The Secretary General showed no embarrassment at having been caught in such a situation by his subordinates. He had been in excellent company, with men of the finest names. A touch of perversion was quite *comme il faut* in such circles—more so than ever, in view of the new political currents. But this fellow Barbulescu had presumed to turn the whole group over to the vice squad—that was sheer impertinence. The Blaze looked forward to this confrontation with Barbulescu—he enjoyed making men cringe before him.

The big, fleshy Inspector showed no fear. His full, florid face was not a shade paler than normal. He carried himself well, as if he were coming to be lauded, not to beg for his life, the Blaze thought. You wait, my friend, you wait.

He let Barbulescu stand before him for five full minutes while he leafed through the newspapers. Then he turned and scrutinized him from head to foot. "Well," he said, and his voice had no trace of its habitual unctuous mildness; it was rude and harsh. "Your inspectorship has really done a fine job—that's outright Bolshevism. The only places where we can use Bolsheviks is in the penitentiary or the salt mines. You may take your choice."

Barbulescu stood at attention and didn't flinch. The Blaze, who had perfected the technique of the stare, fixed his eyes on the Inspector's forehead as though trying to see through to the brain. Then his gaze moved slowly over face, body and hands down to the tips of the victim's shoes, seeking the familiar signs: the flutter of eyelids, the quiver of lips, clenched hands, sagging knees. Nothing of the sort. The Blaze was dismayed. He felt like a singer who has suddenly lost his voice on the stage. If this insignificant Inspector wasn't afraid of him, didn't fear his rancor, then what was all his power worth? So the Blaze shouted, "You're supposed to recognize your superiors! You goddamn stinking fool, what did you think you were doing?"

"I acted exactly in accordance with the regulations," Barbulescu said with utter calm. "That is the way you wanted it, or otherwise you would not have telephoned, sir."

"What would I not have done? Who telephoned? What telephone call? Are you mad or drunk? I'm having you locked up this minute!"

That was it—the man had gone out of his mind from sheer funk, the Blaze thought. Why else the complacent smile? Of course, the man had gone clear off his rocker.

But Barbulescu's next words, spoken with smiling equanimity, dispelled this theory. "Lieutenant Pradescu was informed by telephone that a revolutionary meeting was taking place in Senator Mandrescu's house. The raid was made on the basis of that call. Obviously that is exactly what you wanted, sir." Barbulescu's smile spread over his face. "An alarm is an alarm! Lieutenant Pradescu has been in the service for twelve years. Right from the start I thought there was something fishy about it. What would Bolsheviks be doing in Mandrescu's house? Naturally we quickly realized that it wasn't a—hm—meeting of revolutionists."

"Then why the devil didn't you clear out at once?"

"For a moment I wanted to do that, but then I realized that you had meant the whole thing differently, sir."

"*I* had meant?"

"I saw through the whole affair," Barbulescu continued with his smug smile. "You yourself telephoned. In the first place, to test how well a general alarm functions when you aren't on duty; and in the second place, to show the gentlemen from the other Ministries that duty is duty. I mean, of course, you naturally gave no warning to the other gentlemen of what was to happen. But me—within two minutes I saw the whole plan! That's why I made believe I didn't know the gentlemen, and why I seemed not to recognize you, sir."

It was beginning to dawn on the Secretary General that this fat man was either extraordinarily stupid or fantastically cunning. Either he believed what he was saying or he had invented this version of the affair. Not a bad version either, although it had certain holes and weak spots. At any rate, it was usable—officially or unofficially. The Secretary General turned his handsome face toward the Inspector, the hint of a smile in the corners of his mouth. "You're a sly dog," he said appreciatively. "How long have you been in the Sigurantza?"

"All my life, sir—since 1913," Barbulescu said, standing at attention once more.

"I take it you've not expressed your opinion on the affair to anyone?" Danghu asked sternly.

"I beg pardon, sir, but I had to make an oral report to the Inspector General, because otherwise I'd have had to do it in writing. I explained that the affair was simply in the nature of a drill, and it's just as well that the other Ministries know everything runs like clockwork in our department. That we act without fear or favor. A brilliant idea of yours, if I may permit myself a comment, sir."

Dumb or cunning, Danghu thought, the man is worth his weight in gold. I don't really give a damn what people say, but still it's better to have it served up this way. "No, not a bad idea, if I do say so myself. But on the other hand, if you've seen though it, others must have also. So I must have made some mistake. Think about that, Barbulescule." The diminutive was affectionate.

"I already have, sir. I've got the whole thing figured out."

"Let me hear it," Danghu encouraged him.

"You don't really have to be concerned about what the public thinks so long as the people who matter know the score. Still, you never know what fantastic stories may be concocted. For that reason I think it better that the public should find out what really happened. In the first place, there's the propaganda value. The Sigurantza, the gendarmerie, the police—everybody at their posts in case of need, incorruptible. And secondly, from the social point of view —it could be left open whether the gentlemen from the other Ministries knew about it or not. Let people draw their own conclusions, eh?" Barbulescu spoke with real enthusiasm; it was evident that he had given the matter thorough consideration.

Danghu looked sharply at him. All his doubts had vanished. The man was all right. What his real thoughts were—the devil with that. The main thing was that his version was highly savory. "Then what would you suggest, Barbulescule?" Danghu asked, and managed to sound as if he knew the answer in advance, that it was bound to be precisely what he himself had in mind.

"Ah, coane, I can see you understand." "Coane" sounded sweeter to Danghu's ears than the highest title. It was the word used to address members of the old aristocracy, and Danghu's supreme ambition was to be called coane, not domnule. "The thing must be made public in the right way, by roundabout methods."

"Yes. Do sit down—why are you standing? Here." Danghu indicated the chair in front of his desk.

"Thank you, sir." The Inspector spread his bulk in the upholstered armchair. "I figure it this way. Not one of our newspapers—"

"Newspapers?" Danghu asked slowly. "I didn't count on newspapers. Besides, it's already too late by now."

"Please give me a hearing, sir. I've been in this trade almost thirty years, and I think it will work out well. We must put one of the left newspapers up to it. Let them raise a rumpus about having the men—the policemen and the gendarmes, I mean—haled out of their beds late at night, in cold and stormy weather, just for one of these practice alerts. Let them yell about cruel orders. Only as much as we like, of course—what else is the censorship for? Once the article's written, it won't be printed until you've approved it, sir. Let them say you're a tyrant, that you have no consideration for the men—"

"Ah yes, and then?" Danghu was beginning to see.

"Then," Barbulescu explained, "when they've finished running off at the mouth, *our* newspapers will have their turn. All of them. You know, coane, with press conferences, official explanations and all that. Fatherland and civilization and tradition and defense against Bolshevism. In the end the whole thing will be just one more subject for political argument: is a practice alert of that kind in no matter what weather and at any hour of the day or night permissible, useful, good, or not? Everything else is beside the point, forgotten, never happened."

"You are a thought reader, Barbulescule." The Secretary General stood up. "That was exactly what I had in mind."

The Inspector rose. He straightened to attention once more. "I am most happy to be of service to you, sir." He bowed, and Danghu waved his hand in gracious dismissal.

Barbulescu lumbered along the corridors and down the stairs, responding genially to the snappy salutes of lesser officials and patrolmen—they all knew him. Portly but erect, he tramped to the Hotel Athenée-Palace. There he went to a telephone booth and made a lengthy phone call. He emerged from the booth as poker-faced as ever, although he was thoroughly pleased with himself. Barbulescu never showed his emotions. But he had cause for satisfaction.

The new Secretary General, aside from being a pansy and perfumed like an old whore, was a moron. But better dumb than smart. A smart man would never have swallowed all that guff. A smart man would never have let himself be caught in lace underwear with a lot of fancy boys in their birthday suits. A smart man in such a position would have quietly piled up the money and married a girl of good family. If he liked boys better, what the devil—but not out in the open like this fathead. Salt mines, eh—who are you sending to the salt mines? Fat Barbulescu? You'll have to get up a lot earlier. I've watched dozens like you croaking on the manure heap since 1913. You're riding high because the Germans are backing you. But you need me, you streaked, pasty-faced gypsy's brat.

"The old man," said Lieutenant (since January 1) Stefan Rozescu to Lieutenant Colonel Rananu, "is in full uniform today. Hung all his tinsel on him. Two rows all the way across to his armpit and one around his neck. What does it mean, Alecu?" When Rozescu was alone with his friend, he ignored the difference in their rank.

"A little rendezvous with some gentlemen from Germany."

"Where?" the Lieutenant asked. "Surely not here."

"At the War Minister's home. Eleven-thirty. Both of us are going, too. Stand up and let me look at you. I'm responsible for you.

. . . No, you're a hopeless case; you'll never look like a soldier. Yet you're neat enough in civilian dress. The trouble is you look like a civilian even in uniform. How do you do it?" Rananu laughed.

"And you, Alecu, always look like a soldier, even in civilian dress. How do you do it?"

"I don't do a thing. It's just that I am a soldier."

"There you are. It's just that I am a civilian. A convinced, incorrigible civilian."

The Lieutenant Colonel grinned at him. "So you are. And so you can remain." He abruptly changed the subject. "How old are you, Fanica?"

"I became twenty-six yesterday."

"Yesterday? Without a word to anyone? Or wasn't I refined enough for your intellectual friends? You won't even invite me to a glass of champagne! All the same—*noroc si la multi ani.*"

"Thanks, Alecu, thanks. But I didn't celebrate, and I asked my parents not to make any fuss. We can drink the champagne whenever you like. Tell you what, Alecu, come and have dinner with me today, after the circus. Then you can have a decent drink to wash down your botheration and—" Rozescu broke off.

"Say it, Fanica. I know what you mean. Disgust, isn't it?" Rananu looked at Rozescu, who had sat down at his desk and seemed to be hunting for something among his papers. "Don't you agree, Fanica, that it's one lousy stinking mess we're getting into now? I don't understand the old man."

Rozescu responded to Rananu's searching look. "That's it, Alecu," he said gravely. "The old man. He's an enigma to me."

"To you? How long have *you* known him? What about me? You're not a soldier, Fanica—you can't really care. But I am, and for me the old man has always been the model of a soldier, of a patriot, of a decent man. And now he's teaming up with that rabble. I don't understand it, Fanica. Can you explain it?"

Fanica bowed his head. "I would understand if he went along with the Germans to keep the country out of the war. Any means would be legitimate for that. But going along with the Germans means the opposite. War, Alecu. A war we're bound to lose!"

Rananu seemed ready to take exception to this. But the ringing of the telephone interrupted their talk. He lifted the receiver. "Yes, sir!" he said. "Right, sir." Then he beckoned to Rozescu. "The old man wants us. Come on. Straighten up a little." He tugged at Rozescu's blouse and shoulder strap. Then they went, their spurs clattering on the bare flagstones of the hall.

General Baderescu sat in full plumage, as Rozescu privately called it. The furrows on his brow did not smooth out and his rigid bearing did not relax as he signed to the two men to take seats. He indicated a newspaper before him on the desk.

"You marked a passage here in red," he said to Rozescu. "Why do you think it so important?"

"Beg pardon, sir, I marked it not because I thought it so important but purely for—for reasons of information."

"What do we care what the *Facla* thinks of the Sigurantza's alert? Incidentally, sheer rot, the whole idiotic story."

"That's just it, sir," Rozescu said.

"What do you mean, Rozescule?" the General asked tensely. "What concern is it of ours what these parlor Communists think about the alert? Although—"

"No doubt you've wondered why the article passed censorship, sir," Rozescu said casually.

"I did. Aha, I see. Logical thinking, Rozescu—bravo!" The General smiled, then broke into hearty laughter. "A first-year cadet could figure out what will follow the article."

"It hardly matters," Rozescu replied quietly.

"How do you mean that?" the General asked with apparent indifference. When the Lieutenant took his time about answering, the General looked at Rananu. "What does the child mean?" he smilingly asked.

"He's a very wide-awake boy, sir," Rananu said.

The General turned. "And you, Alecu, have no doubts? Aren't you the least bit skeptical? You don't worry about a thing, accept everything?"

"I don't know what you mean, sir. Officially, of course, I share the opinions of my superiors. I've learned to do that and have done it for more than twenty years. It's very comfortable, sir."

"You aren't that way, Alecu. I know you; otherwise I would never have taken you away from your horses. I brought you in here because I need men like you. Not just Lieutenant Colonel Rananu, but Rananu the boyar. And you must give an honest answer to my question."

"To an honest question if you challenge Boyar Rananu, sir."

"That is to say, you suspect me of having something nasty up my sleeve, eh?"

Rananu rose to his feet more slowly than was his habit. "Sir, before you sent for us, Lieutenant Rozescu and I were having a talk about you. Yes, about you, sir. And we found that we were both wondering about the same thing, and didn't like it. Yes, sir, didn't like it, even if you degrade me for it. But you spoke to Boyar Rananu. You see, we cannot understand your going along with the Germans, sir, and we're feeling pretty sick about it. I would never have said that to any other general, sir, but I do say it to you."

"Palace revolution!" the General thundered. Then he was silent. The two officers stood at attention before him.

When the General broke the silence, his voice was very low. "This isn't the time for lengthy explanations—not yet. But since you've ventured to talk to me this way, you must draw your own conclusions. I think you know what would have happened to you if . . . Sit down," he said smilingly. He took out his big, heavy gold pocket watch, a gift of the deceased King Ferdinand. "It's nine twenty-five. You have two hours, which you will use—you too, Rozescule—to change. Tunic, dress boots, cartridge belt, fur cap with plume, white gloves. Help our philosopher a bit, Rananu; see that he does us credit. And then, I have a special request. Would you, Rozescule, ask your father—or is that your mother's province? —to lend us the parade coach." He meant the Rozescu Rolls Royce; there were only three in the country. "Say the old man has personally asked for it. And, Rananu, before you go, telephone the Second Guards Regiment and ask them to send the fat Corporal who's a taxicab driver in civilian life. I want him in parade uniform. We're going to present ourselves like characters in a Hollywood musical."

"Very well, sir," Rananu and Rozescu said. They rose uncertainly, in doubt whether to take their leave.

The General pretended not to notice their indecision. But then he said something after all. "Boys," he said softly, "it's not easy for me. I need my friends and their trust, now more than ever. Do you understand? I count very much on your confidence in me, your blind confidence. There are things which cannot be said, may not be said. Only this much: whatever you see, no matter what appearances seem to indicate—the 'old man' is still the old man. More so than ever now when you, with some justification, are doubtful of him." He resumed his ordinary official tone. "You, Rananu, will be my adjutant at the conference. Among the participants will be the Minister of War, the Secretary General of the Ministry of the Interior, the Inspector General of the Sigurantza, and a certain General of the elite troops"—he glanced at Rananu, who nodded his understanding—"you two, and myself. That is the Romanian side, so to speak. The German side is represented by Colonel Baron von— I've forgotten the name, something with 'bingen' or 'dingen.' He served as a captain in the last war, was assigned to the intelligence service during the occupation and is an expert on Romanian affairs. Unquestionably he is Chief of Intelligence now, and his competence is attested to by the fact that he has picked out the most corrupt and subservient among us. He is a"—the General cleared his throat— "partner not to be despised. Then there are three other men, civilians, who will remain in the background, but are not to be taken lightly. You, Rozescu, will be my secretary and interpreter. I shall understand only Romanian or French. You must be very alert and talk very slowly. I'll need a great deal of time to consider my replies. Among the Germans, only the Colonel, the chief, speaks French. The others all speak Romanian. But they will probably speak only German for the same reasons that I shall speak only Romanian. That is about all. Dismissed."

"Did you understand, Fanica?" Rananu asked as they sat in Rozescu's small Vauxhall, en route to the Rozescu villa. Rananu had instructed his servant to bring his dress uniform there. He felt he should supervise his young friend's dressing.

"Don't you?" the Lieutenant asked, an unusually prankish smile playing around the corners of his mouth.

After the conference, General Baderescu and Danghu—the Blaze—left together, followed by Dumitriu and Rananu, with Rozescu bringing up the rear. Secretary General Danghu had to strain to keep pace with the General's military stride. "There's a highly important matter I should like to discuss with you, General," he said. "It concerns one of your men. Dumitriu has the file with him. We have some valuable information which I think will also be useful to you. Since we are now—"

"Whom do you mean?" the General interrupted brusquely.

"Alda, General."

"Alda?" the old man asked. "Alda? Why, he's dead."

"So you know too, General?" Danghu's exclamation sounded jubilant. "Were you informed of the details?"

"What details? I was at the funeral myself. That must have been—one moment—in 1917. The Bucovina was occupied by the Russians and—"

Danghu stopped in his tracks and stared at the General in dismay. The General took another step forward, then stopped, visibly impatient.

"Whom are you speaking of, General?" the Blaze asked.

"There is, or rather there was, only one Alda. That was Neagoe Alda, the boyar of Aldeni, a great nationalist and patriot who died twenty-three years ago. Your report comes a little late."

Danghu laughed—a giggling, superior, malicious laugh. The General involuntarily gripped the hilt of his sword. "I don't mean him, General, but Ludovic or Lutz Alda." The Blaze waited tensely for the effect of his words. He might have waited forever; he had missed the one moment when the General lost composure.

"Ludovic, Lutz?" the General asked without interest, and took a half step forward. "Oh yes, the writer and jockey. Right, he's a— one moment—a nephew or grandson of old Alda. Yes, yes, but—"

"Then you don't know Lutz Alda, General?" the Blaze asked, disappointed but still trying.

"Possibly I do know him, but not well enough to remember him. His—er—literary achievements are not so overwhelming, and I don't take an interest in horses. Drinking, cards, and women— good Lord, those things belong far back in the past for me. But didn't you say he's dead? Peace to his ashes."

"But he is one of your men—or was," Danghu said impudently.

"My men? You mean you think that Alda is or was my agent, Domnule Danghu?"

"If he didn't work for you—I mean for the Second Bureau— then he was a Bolshevist agent. There are only these two possibilities."

"Communism is the business of the Sigurantza, Domnule Danghu," the General said. "Our business is military intelligence. Of course I'm grateful for any suggestions and assistance, but I'm in a great hurry today. Lieutenant Colonel Rananu handles these outside matters. Rananu!"

"Yes, sir."

"Secretary General Danghu, or rather Inspector General Dumitriu, wishes to inform us about a certain matter. Stay here with Lieutenant Rozescu, find out what this is all about, and report to me whatever you think important."

"Yes, sir!" Rananu repeated, saluting. The General put his hand to his cap and went forward toward the stairs, leaving four men standing with mixed feelings. They were still standing in silence when the General reached the steps, turned as though he had forgotten something, and called, "Lieutenant Rozescu!" Rozescu tucked his sword under his arm and trotted forward. With an indifferent expression, as if he were issuing some minor order or reproof, the General said softly, "Rananu must show no surprise, only disbelief. Alda is his personal friend, nothing more." In a loud, stern voice he added, "Dismissed."

When Rozescu rejoined the group, Rananu asked, more to break the embarrassing silence than out of real interest, "What was wrong this time?"

"My tunic is too long, my collar a quarter of an inch too short, my sword hangs down too far, and in general I'm a disgrace," Rozescu said equably.

"I could have told you that," Rananu said rather too loudly, and laughed. "But, gentlemen, we have business—I'll find us a room where we can sit down without being disturbed. Excuse me a moment." He brought his hand to his plumed cap.

"Shall I help you, sir?" Rozescu said.

"Very well, come along," Rananu replied, and they left Dumitriu and Danghu alone.

As soon as the two were out of earshot, Danghu whispered vehemently to Dumitriu, "Rot, sheer rot; the old man hardly knows Alda exists. You're getting old, Inspector."

"What makes you think that, sir?" Dumitriu asked with an undertone of scorn.

"It was clear as day. His only association with the name of Alda was with the man's grandfather."

"Secretary General Danghu," Dumitriu said angrily, "General Baderescu would not have become chief of his department if he did not at least have a certain skill in masking his emotions. I might add that the investigation of Alda has nothing to do with the service; you are undertaking it on a private basis, sir." The Inspector General's face was green.

Danghu had no time to relish the man's obvious discomfiture, or to counter with one of his feared replies, for the sound of clinking spurs warned them that the two officers were returning. They had found a room in which they could confer. As soon as they were seated, Dumitriu produced a number of typewritten sheets of paper from his attaché case. He wanted to forestall any introductory remarks by Danghu, and therefore put on his glasses and began reading aloud:

Eusebiu Zernescu, Chief of Division IV of the Sigurantza Generala, submitted the following report on November 28, 1938: Ludovic Alda, landowner from Bucovina, was today observed talking at length with a high-ranking army officer in the lobby of the Hotel Union. He then drove away with this officer. Said Alda has long been under suspicion of being a correspondent for revolutionary newspapers. Zernescu has personal knowledge of the fact that many years ago Alda, under the alias of Oskar Gross, was arrested as a Bolshevist agent and held in the prison of Balti, from which he escaped. It has further been established that Alda has published various articles in foreign newspapers defaming the name and honor of the Romanian nation. A past such as this disqualifies him for association with an officer who occupies an important post in the Secret Service, unless this service is employing him as an agent.

Danghu looked across at Rananu, who had not removed his plumed cap, but had pulled it so far down over his forehead that it

touched his eyebrows. He sat with his sword between his outspread legs, gazing indifferently down at the hilt. Rozescu, too,
seemed bored. Dumitriu continued in a low monotonous voice:

The Sigurantza has deemed it advisable to discover the facts
about Alda. It was determined that on the evening of the day in
question Alda went to Bucovina, and that two days later he vanished. Here follows the statement of Pastor Domanschi:

"On the afternoon of November 29 I called on Boyar Alda at
his home and asked him to rent his property to my son-in-law,
Reserve Captain Grigoriu, since the contract with the Jew Joshua
Rundberg expires on January 1. Alda replied that he was about to
leave on a trip, that he would do as he pleased and rent his property to—his own words—a Negro, a Jew, or anyone he liked. He
is very seldom in Aldeni and permits the Jew Rundberg to admin-
ister all his business affairs. He has an immoral relationship with
a Viennese woman! When I later inquired about renting, I was
informed that Aldeni, as the property is called, had been sold to
a certain Domnule Tomescu, and that the sale had been arranged
by the Jew Joshua Rundberg, who was provided with a power of
attorney."

Tomescu, former magistrate in Bucovina, later a lawyer, refused to give our investigators any information whatsoever. It
proved impossible to question the former tenant, Joshua Rundberg, since he emigrated to Palestine two weeks after Alda's disappearance, taking with him his sister and two grandchildren.

Rundberg's son Karl, a salesman for foreign textile firms, ad-
mits to having spoken to Alda on the evening of November 30.
His story is that Alda told him that he was leaving, but did not say
when or mention any destination. This, according to Karl Rundberg, was his usual practice; he had been arriving and departing
unexpectedly for more than twenty years. As for the woman with
whom Alda cohabited, Karl Rundberg could only report that she
had left, that he did not know where she had gone, and that she
is Alda's fiancée. Her name is Martha Varsany.

The local physician of Aldeni, Dr. Josif Vendrinschi, states
that early on the morning of November 30 a carriage and team
sent by Alda took him to the manor house to treat the landowner's injured hand. In addition to a number of small cuts, there
was a serious injury to the middle finger of the left hand. The
doctor had to remove a rather large splinter of glass. Evidently
Alda, after some heavy drinking, had crushed a goblet in his hand.
This, at any rate, was how Dr. Vendrinschi accounted for the
accident, and Alda did not deny it. While attending to the injury,

the doctor had some words with Alda concerning the Jewish doctor Schmetterling, whom Dr. Vendrinschi had replaced. Alda indicated that he was quite irate over Schmetterling's removal, and offensively said to the doctor, "I regard Romanians, Ruthenians and Jews as all equal."

Grigore Posteuca, a private in Border Guards Regiment No. 7, states that he was standing guard the night of December 1, in the vicinity of the village of Serafintza, about four miles from the Polish, now Russian, township of Horodenka. It was about three o'clock in the morning when the figure of a man suddenly loomed up in front of him. The soldier tried to raise his rifle, but was prevented from doing so by a blow in the face. The man, who wore a short fur jacket, a fur cap, and high boots, seized the guard's rifle. As he did so, Posteuca observed that his attacker's left hand was bandaged. This man attempted to hurl the rifle some distance with his right hand, but the weapon was caught in a bush about twenty feet from the scene of the struggle. The attacker ran off with great speed in the direction of Horodenka. Posteuca was able to recover his rifle in time to send a bullet after the fugitive. The man collapsed, but he had already reached Polish, or rather, Russian, soil. Posteuca is a forester in civilian life and the best shot in his whole regiment. He has won many medals for sharpshooting. It was, however, impossible for him to check the body because the Russian guards answered the shot with a volley lasting several minutes.

The Inspector General replaced the papers in his attaché case and removed his glasses. Rananu placed his hand over his mouth to conceal a yawn, but he did not succeed; his mouth opened so wide that tears started to his eyes. "Exciting story," he said, still yawning. "How does it strike you, Rozescu?"

The Lieutenant shrugged; his smile expressed utter detachment.

Dumitriu showed no change of expression. Danghu, who had watched the scene with keen suspense, gave a baleful look at the Inspector General when it became apparent that Rananu was completely unaffected by the report.

"Well, then," Rananu said, raising his sword and standing up, "thank you for the information. It's not quite complete, by the way. The officer who met Alda at the Union was myself. He happens to be an old friend of mine. If you want to know where we were afterwards, why don't you ask Secretary General Danghu?" He jerked his head rather disrespectfully toward the latter. "We were all at a party at Luceanu's home. As for Alda's being a Bolshevik, that's sheer nonsense."

"Alda is your friend, Lieutenant Colonel," Danghu said. "No doubt that affects your judgment. Certainly you cannot deny that his mode of life is a strange one."

"Strange to whom?" Rananu asked coldly.

"To me, for example," the Blaze replied, trying hard for a show of aristocratic urbanity. "I have no reason to doubt Inspector Zernescu's statement. The man has been in the service for many years. Moreover, the report contains the testimony of various unimpeachable witnesses. Your friend has slandered Romania abroad and expressed his so-called democratic principles with repugnant cynicism. Oh well, he has been taken care of at last and cannot do any further harm. But if I were in your place, Lieutenant Colonel—"

"Stop!" Rananu said sharply. "In your whole collection of hypotheses the last one is the boldest. You cannot be in my place, Domnule Danghu. Never! Certain qualities are lacking. So long as I am here in an official capacity, I must sit by and listen to all sorts of morbid fantasies. But since you go so far as to attack the honor of my friend, you must be prepared to take the consequences that are customary in the circles you have only recently entered. I am prepared to defend the reputation and the honor of my friend Ludovic Alda and his fiancée, Baroness Martha Varsany, with any weapon you wish to choose. Keep that in mind, Domnule Danghu." The Lieutenant clicked his heels and touched two fingers to the brim of his cap. It was a salute in general, for he looked at neither Danghu nor Dumitriu. Rozescu repeated these movements—with a good deal less military briskness but with considerably more cosmopolitan superiority. Then both left the room, spurs clinking. Danghu and Dumitriu had remained seated—Danghu's face frozen in an expression of hatred and vindictiveness.

"Domnule Dumitriu," the Blaze said, "you will be well advised to write your resignation. Today. I shall present it to the Minister with my warmest recommendation. You are an empty barrel, bringing your idiotic reports. As for this fool Rananu, I'll pay him back when the time comes. He'll stumble under my wheels. I'll crush him like that!" He made an exaggerated gesture.

"Very well, Domnule Danghu," Dumitriu said. "You are clumsy and have exposed yourself. I don't care why you were after Alda. But if you wanted to pay him off for something, you should have used bigger guns and waited until you had him in your power, or remained content with the story of his death. You don't yet understand how to cook your private stews on the fires of political power. That's an art which has to be learned. Just as handling pistols, cavalry sabers or foils has to be learned. Which I urgently recommend you set about doing." Dumitriu rose and stalked out of the room.

Danghu seethed with fury. Minutes passed before he could think at all. But still his thoughts circled around Alda; the man had entered his brain like a poisoned arrow. Alda, with his cool, bored look, who ignored him as if he were of no account whatsoever. How he hated him!

Why was this haughty Lieutenant Colonel so sure of himself? Why did he think Alda wasn't the man with the bandaged hand who had attacked the border guard? Why had that cagey Lieutenant Rozescu, who had more money than a hundred men could count, smiled so sardonically? Did they know better? If so, why? How? Was Alda working for the Second Bureau after all? Was the old General playing a double game? Not possible. The old man had come to the secret conference, had proved his good will, had demonstrated that he was convinced as a soldier, as a strategist, of the Germans' superior power. Absurd—it all had nothing to do with Alda, and Alda had no connection with the Second Bureau! Alda was Rananu's personal friend and drinking companion. The Boyar Alda and the Boyar Rananu—jockeys, drinkers, gamblers, whoremongers, boyars. That was all there was to it!

But suppose, as Zernescu claimed, Alda and that man Gross were the same person? Suppose he was the fellow who had escaped from Balti prison and later sent reports on the Mariniu trial abroad? Would anyone except Gross or Alda have been so well informed, have known so many of the details? He had spent months prying around the Dniester region, on both sides of the border. Was that the sort of thing a boyar did?

Was this Alda a real boyar at all? He wrote newspaper articles and plays, fraternized with Jews, was up in arms because the Jews were being chased out, and sullied the honor of his own country. Suppose Alda were a Bolshevik. Suppose he was working for the Bolsheviki, betraying his country to them. Suppose he had now gone over to them completely, after having spied on everything in Romania, not only the army, the political parties, the new tendencies and the new men, but also the Second Bureau. Suppose Rananu had supplied him with important material, knowingly or unwittingly, and suppose that General Baderescu also. . . .

Danghu stood up. That's all nonsense, he thought, but it can be put to good use anyhow. I'll give you some nuts to crack; I'll show you who Danghu is. I'll duel with you all right, but in my own way, with my own weapons and by my own rules!

Then he strutted out of the room. The attendant helped him into his fur coat, nipped in too much at the waist, with a far too wide seal collar. Before he entered his car, he telephoned Inspector Barbulescu, who might very well be Inspector General of the Sigurantza by the morrow.

Toward evening General Baderescu, Lieutenant Colonel Rananu and Lieutenant Rozescu were again sitting together. Rananu had made his report; Rozescu had answered an occasional question from the General. Then the General had lapsed into a long silence.

Suddenly his gaunt frame stirred, and his face relaxed. The two young officers saw him smile. He reached for the receiver and asked to be connected with Secretary General Danghu. Holding the receiver at his ear, the General winked mischievously at the two of them. Then, still smiling, he spoke in his silkiest voice: "Yes, this is General Baderescu. How are you? My officers have just reported to me. Yes, the affair is of the greatest interest to me—no, not personally, officially. For months—no, much longer—I have been on the track of a certain case. It is not impossible—rather, I am quite sure—that this represents a find of tremendous importance. Yes, I am most grateful to you for your thoughtfulness. Really, most grateful. I'd very much appreciate talking this over with you. Tomorrow? Could you possibly make it today? And could you bring Inspector Zernescu—yes, and the gentleman who made the investigation in Bucovina? For—let's say—seven o'clock. Could that be convenient? Excellent. Where? Wherever you wish. Of course. You're heartily welcome! Agreed then: at seven o'clock here. And please bring the dossier with you—yes, it is, if I'm not mistaken, an extremely important matter. The country will be grateful. *La revedere—cu toata stima,* with my respects—Secretary General!"

The General set down the telephone and looked at Rananu and Rozescu. "That's how it should be handled, not as you did it. However, I can't help being pleased with you for giving this—this"— the General fumbled for a suitable epithet, couldn't find it and continued, shrugging—"Danghu his comeuppance. Bravo, Rananu, you behaved like an officer and a boyar. Still, that was hardly the way a Chief of Department N of the Second Bureau should conduct himself. Just as well to have him scared stiff of you, though—and he is; I know the type. But he'll take his revenge. And we cannot afford to waste our time on this kind of private warfare. So I'll let him have his lollypop and hope he sucks it for a long time. A pity you two can't be present; it would be most instructive to you." The

General looked at the clock. "Six-seventeen. All right, boys, you have leave until ten o'clock. Use the time to pack your bags and change to civilian dress. You're both taking a trip. To Cernauti, on the train that leaves at one o'clock in the morning. Send Major Burda to me before you leave. He'll receive our guests. Leave me your number so that I can reach you; you must stay together. Further instructions here at ten o'clock. Where will you be?"

"At Luceanu's, sir. Is that all right with you, Fanica? You can talk philosophy with Aglaia and I'll play piquet with Ioan."

He wrote the telephone number on a sheet of paper, which the General tucked under a file. "Hm," the General said, looking squarely at Rananu. "You and Lutz Alda were close friends, and yet you don't seem to be the least bit concerned or grief-stricken."

"Sir," Rananu answered, "I've known Alda for more than twenty years. I grant you he's crazy as a loon. But even if I saw him tramping down the Calea Victoriei waving the red flag with hammer and sickle, I'd still—"

"I understand. But why are you so sure?"

"Didn't you yourself say, sir, that friendship depends on mutual trust? As for this story about his reported death—" He glanced at Rozescu.

The General understood the look. "Rozescu will have to be briefed about the other aspects of the affair. But not till ten o'clock. Our philosopher deserves our confidence; he has confidence in us. Go now, and if it's any comfort, Alecule, I don't believe in that fabulous shot of the border guard's either. All right; dismissed!"

Rananu and Rozescu arrived almost simultaneously, each in civilian dress, and each bearing two bouquets of flowers. Aglaia prepared an English tea in the nearly round room with the Biedermeier furniture. The surroundings—the warmth, the whole setting—seemed eminently conducive to good cheer, and yet nothing like a cheery mood arose.

Rananu kept thinking that this was where he had last seen his friend. In what an exhiliarated mood Alda had been! He had urged on the gypsies; he had danced. What if the border guard had really shot someone, and that someone had been Alda? Would not he then be responsible for Alda's death? Hadn't he given the Old Man the tip, suggesting that Alda could be enlisted in underground work? A sadness settled upon unsentimental Rananu, and he made no attempt to fight it off. They all stopped talking and sat there glumly until Margareta could no longer tolerate the funereal mood. "What the devil has got into you? Why are we sitting around like a star collection of bores? I was so glad when you said you were coming, hoping things would cheer up around here. It's been dreary enough the past few days—"

Aglaia broke in nervously. "If you think they have to know, you'd best leave it to me."

"You're right—I can scarcely put two words together to make sense. You tell them."

"All right." Aglaia took a moment to master her embarrassment. "Ioan has been terribly upset for quite a while. There's been an unpleasant scene about this—this man Danghu."

"Danghu?" Rozescu said. "Everyone seems to be tangling with that man just now. What happened?"

"Ioan is sick of it all. . . . You remember, Alecu—the day Alda was here? The quarrel with Lida—that disgusting affair."

"Of course I remember," Rananu said gravely. "I agree with every word Princess Haimovici said. But what has that to do with Ioan?"

"Well, Ioan is generous. He knows we sometimes have rather mixed company in the house, and he realizes that the mice will play when the cat's away. In any case, he's a good-natured and easygoing tomcat. But he thinks that any high jinks we may go in for should be among equals, not in the presence of all kinds of scum."

"I second that too," Rananu said. "By scum he means the Blaze, and I second that first and foremost."

"It seems Danghu went around telling his cronies that he's attended a party at the home of a well-known boyar and the goings-on there were no better than at a common—"

"Whorehouse." Margareta completed the sentence.

"How lucky our grandfathers were!" Rananu sighed. "They could have killed such a creature and there wouldn't have been a soul in the country to protest."

"And today such a creature is Secretary General in the Ministry of the Interior and—let me finish—spreads the tale that a certain lady withdrew for hours with an obscure and seditious character for purposes of—"

"I understand," Rananu said.

"Nice of you," Aglaia replied. "You also must know who he meant. Your friend Lutz Alda and me."

"He has some sort of obsession about Alda," Rozescu said softly, for the first time showing interest in the conversation.

"Don't be so intellectual, Fanica," Rananu chided. "Go ahead, Aglaia."

But Margareta interposed excitedly, "He also goes around telling people there isn't a woman in the whole lot he hasn't slept with. I happen to know for certain that he never has with Nelly Bidevocici, Aglaia or me. Besides—"

Aglaia cut short the discussion of this highly interesting point. "All this is only gossip, after all, and Ioan would simply have let it run its course. The trouble is that the affair has resulted in serious financial losses for him."

"How so?"

"I think I can explain that," Rozescu intervened. "My father told me about it. Ioan was involved in a business deal with the Germans; that was why he was in Berlin in November and December. He was selling them wine. I don't remember how many tens of thousands of gallons. When the terms of the contract were settled, Ioan sent orders from Berlin to buy all the wine that could be had. He put the Germans' advances and all his available capital into the deal. His agents here bought and bought, and naturally the price of wine went up. But Ioan, who had a number of other transactions to attend to in Germany, instructed them to go on buying. Then he came back, took title to the huge stocks of wine, cellared it, and got everything ready for delivery. I suppose he was counting on a substantial profit. Then the German buyers came here and criticized this and that. I don't know the technical terms, but the upshot was that the Germans weren't satisfied with anything, refused to take the wine, and now Luceanu is sitting on vast stocks of wine that he bought at prices far above the normal market."

"And?" Rananu asked naïvely.

"Don't you see, Alecu? It was Danghu who fouled up the deal. Why otherwise would Ioan be so angry with the ladies?"

"Danghu? What has he to do with wine?"

"He's the Germans' principal liaison man here in Romania, and he must have told them some cock-and-bull story to upset the deal. Under ordinary circumstances the thing to do would have been to square matters with him *per capiendam benevolentiam,* but—"

"What's that again?" Rananu asked.

"Greasing the palm," Aglaia translated.

"Why, he takes baksheesh like a tourist guide," Rananu said.

"In this case his revenge is worth more to him than money. Besides, he's counting on bigger gains. He'll sell the Germans wine himself, through intermediaries. You can depend on that, Alecu," Rozescu said.

"So that's it," Rananu said, downcast. "But do you mean to say that it all goes back to Princess Haimovici because she made that scene? Is the Blaze out to get Ioan for that?"

"I don't think it has anything to do with Lida, or only indirectly with her," Aglaia said. "Ioan's heard a thing or two. Danghu is aiming at Alda. The whole business started with him."

"Lutz Alda?" Rananu was perplexed. "But he isn't even around. Besides, Danghu's seen him only once in his whole life, so far as I know."

"You're right, Alecu, only once, at our dinner party. Alda sat beside me all the time, you may recall. He asked who Danghu was, and I gave him a brief summary of Danghu's career."

"What the devil happened between the two?" Rananu asked.

"Nothing," Rozescu replied. "Nothing at all."

"Then why this feud? Does it make sense to you?"

Rozescu lit a cigarette. "I don't know either of the people involved," he said. "Nevertheless, I'd say, on the basis of general human knowledge, that these are two men who are destined to hate each other. Everyone speaks and thinks about Alda in the same way; everyone trusts him, everyone is his friend, everyone is fond of him. With Danghu it's the exact opposite. Aside from a certain perverse sensual curiosity that some women—and, as we know, certain types of men—feel for him, everyone dislikes him, finds him repulsive, contemptible. Alda embodies one principle; Danghu embodies the opposite principle. They *have* to hate each other; it's a necessary condition of their existence. Alda would never give vent to his hatred, or only in an extreme situation, because taste, reason and his whole ethical outlook direct him to keep out of the way. Danghu, on the other hand, is restrained neither by reason nor ethics; he's simply too cowardly to kill as long as his antagonist can defend himself. But he will seek every opportunity to stab an enemy in the back, to drop poison into his cup—figuratively speaking, of course."

"I must say, I don't really understand it," said Rananu, who had been listening skeptically, but with intense interest. "Maybe—"

"I find Dr. Rozescu's theory highly suggestive," Aglaia said. "Danghu has power—and it looks as if the Danghus will soon be coming to power everywhere in Europe. And because he is a parvenu, it's not enough for him to know that he is powerful. He has to show his power to prove it to himself and others, again and again. The Danghus are even more dangerous in practice than in theory. They not only want to eliminate the men they hate; they destroy anyone who fails to see the sort of persons they are. Yes, Fanica is right."

"Why don't we eliminate him first, finish him off?" Margareta cried. "What kind of men are you? How did men take care of a cad like that in the past? Challenge him and send a bullet through his head at six o'clock some morning in the woods of Baneasa, or cut him down in the gymnasium of some barracks. Ah, once upon a time men were men," she lamented, with a look at Rananu.

"Take it easy, Margareta," Rozescu said. "Rananu and I, and no doubt a good many other chaps in Bucharest, have thought of that. But Danghu would never be caught fighting a duel—instead he'd have your house searched, and find subversive letters among your correspondence. He'd have you sent to Jilava or Ocnitza after being beaten half to death by his jailers. And even if he could be disposed of one way or another, a new Danghu would come along. These are their times, the times of the Danghus."

"Are we really as far gone already as Germany or Russia?" Margareta asked with honest horror.

"We are well on our way, Margareta," Rozescu replied.

"Yes," Margareta said, "since the debacle with the wine, Ioan says so too. I didn't take it seriously. Now he says—"

"You know how he loves metaphor," Aglaia interrupted. "As he puts it, you either howl with the wolves or you're eaten by them. Do you agree?"

"Another way is to pretend to howl with the wolves, and then eat *them* up, when chance offers, Cousin Margareta," Rozescu replied.

Ioan Luceanu came into the room. He was rather short, with a bit of embonpoint and a likable round face with a close-cropped mustache. Smiling, he shook hands with Rozescu and Rananu. "Your father, Rozescu, has just given me the kind of lecture permitted only among members of a family."

"What about?" Rozescu asked.

"Business, highly unpleasant business. Oh well, we'll live through it."

They sat down to dinner, but Ioan did not pay proper respect to the artful hors d'oeuvres and took little of the grilled sirloin. Instead, contrary to his habit, he drank down a large glass of zuica at one draft. Margareta threw him an anxious look. In all the many years of their marriage she had never seen him this way. He had always been good-natured, gallant, complaisant, and made it a point never to bring his business problems home. She was sincerely fond of Ioan, who had allowed her complete freedom. His troubled mood was unusual and disturbing.

"Have you seen the evening papers?" Ioan said, with a preoccupied air.

"What's up now?" Rozescu asked.

"The usual rot, but there is one thing they were all discussing at the club. An article in the *Patria* in answer to the article in the

Facla about that alert a week or ten days ago. You know what I mean, the story of that midnight raid on a group of suspected Reds who turned out to be—"

"Didn't I tell you?" Rozescu said to Rananu with a gratified air. "I can guess exactly what was in the article, although I haven't read it. Something to the effect that practice alerts are useful and necessary, a sign of readiness—"

"That was the drift. I can't understand it—no one gave the matter a second thought. What idiot would worry about that aspect of the matter?"

"No one has. It's all a hoax. The Blaze arranged it to cover up his—forgive the word—swinishness. He's turning his little session with the boys into an affair of state."

At that point a servant called Rozescu to the telephone, and when he returned to the table, the subject had been changed. Rozescu attempted to return to the theme again over the cheese and fruit, but Margareta had them all adjourn to the parlor for *turceasca,* Turkish coffee. Spirits remained heavy and the conversation seemed unable to get off the ground.

Rananu wanted them to leave, but Rozescu demurred. They had another hour to kill, he whispered; the General had ordered them to stay where they were until he telephoned again. He found a pretext for accompanying Ioan to his study.

"Forgive me, *Nene* Ioan, for butting in on your affairs, but Father told me about your problem. If I guess right, he has refused to help?"

"Yes," Luceanu admitted. "I was counting heavily on your father. Apparently he won't come to my aid. It's not the money he's concerned about; there isn't any risk, as he perfectly well knows. But he won't back me because—"

"Because you've been doing business with the Germans. He can't forgive the Germans for the way they killed my brother twenty-three years ago. I suppose you can remember Iancu—I hardly do. I understand he was a real Rozescu."

"Of course I remember him. They shot him for nothing, Fanica, for absolutely no reason."

"Exactly," Rozescu said, a cloud passing over his clear, young face. "And Father hates them. You see, I'm not the proper sort of heir, not really a Rozescu, not a boyar or a businessman, you understand. With all his fondness for me, I'm a disappointment to him. The older he grows, the more he detests the Germans. Forgive him for—"

"I bear him no grudge. I didn't want to put any pressure on him anyhow, even without knowing why he felt the way he did. But after all, Fanica—what does business have to do with personal feelings?"

"Well, Father takes a different view, and we have no right to try to change his mind. Not that we ever could. Besides," Rozescu added smilingly, "he's so rich that he can afford the luxury of forgoing good deals if they offend his principles."

"I know that," Luceanu said. "I assure you, I didn't find it easy to ask for his help. But I had virtually no other choice." He had spoken quietly and sadly. Now he added with a flash of sudden anger, "Riffraff like Danghu ought to be killed like mad dogs, Fanica, believe me! I came pretty close to doing so."

"Come, Ioan, you'd only ruin yourself, and to no purpose. Another of the same type would take his place, no better. If things don't change fundamentally, the riffraff will soon be in the saddle everywhere. But we've discussed this subject quite a bit tonight. The main thing is: what exactly is your situation?"

"Don't think for a moment that I'm insolvent. I'm temporarily under great pressure. I have turned the Germans' advance—four million marks, in goods, of course—into money, have put all the reserves I had into the deal, and in addition strained my credit. I own vast quantities of wine, yet don't have a monopoly. The big jobbers wouldn't sell to me, partly for reasons of speculation, partly for reasons similar to your father's. I can't sell the wine all at once, either—not in the domestic market—you see why, even though you're no businessman. To do that would be to bring about a disastrous drop in prices. I can't obtain credit from the banks, not even an extension on my notes, although I have offered all sorts of property as collateral. They're simply afraid to lend, and the Jews in particular are terrified. Usually they wouldn't hesitate for a moment to give me as much money as I need; ordinarily my credit is excellent, and with good reason. But under present circumstances—"

"How much do you need to get out of the pinch, Nene Ioan?" Rozescu asked tersely.

"A million dollars," Luceanu said.

"If you had it, would the wine belong to you? Or could they continue to pressure you, and force you to sell it at a loss? Would you be free from all obligations to the Germans and the banks?"

"Yes, Fanica, but what's the good? I can't raise it. The value of Lucesti with the mill and the distillery, not to speak of the pig farm and my dairy farm with almost a thousand Swiss cows—" With the pride of the husbandman he was evidently on the point of listing all his agricultural assets.

"I know, Nene Ioan, I know. Every child in Romania knows. So if you had the money, you'd be out from under, and could do what you liked with the wine. What's it worth, anyhow?"

"What it's worth and what it cost are two different matters. It cost more than twice what I owe. But I certainly won't be able to get that much for it unless—"

"You will. That's why I want to go into this as your partner. Do you think I'm asking all these questions just to pass the time? Listen, Nene Ioan, I'll give you—rather, I'll obtain for you—the million dollars. How much is that in our money?"

"Oho, it sounds ghastly: half a billion! But forgive me, Fanica, how can you . . . ?"

"You'll see. In twenty-four hours you'll have paid off everyone. The only condition I make is that you consult me as to whom you sell the wine to. When the time comes, let me arrange that; I have *something* of the Rozescu spirit in me, you know."

Luceanu looked at him incredulously. "Don't take it amiss, Fanica—I don't really know your . . . but a million dollars is five hundred times as much as a million lei. Haven't you forgotten that?"

"Certainly not, Nene Ioan. In ten minutes—it will take me no longer than that to write the letter—we'll be partners in the wine business. I'm going on a short trip tonight, you see, and it may be several days before I return. Once I'm back, we'll go on buying all we can get hold of. But slowly. You'll do the purchasing, I'll keep in the background, even"—he cleared his throat—"even if Ilie Rozescu should ask you, which he probably won't. Now let me write the letter. May I have a sheet of paper without letterhead, please?"

Shaking his head, Luceanu gave him some paper. Rozescu wrote quickly for a few minutes. "You know the Banca Helvetiana don't you? Do they know you there?" he asked Luceanu when he was finished.

"No. Whose transactions do they finance?"

"Ours, for example." Rozescu laughed. "Here's what I've written: 'Dear Herr Stürzli: Will you please place five million Swiss francs at the disposal of my associate Ioan Luceanu and charge to my account. Kindly see to it that the sum is available to him for withdrawal in lei within twenty-four hours. Sincerely yours, Dr. Stefan Rozescu.' That's all there is to it, Nene Ioan."

"That's all there is to it," Luceanu repeated, dazed. "And if I really do receive the money tomorrow or the day after—"

"You will," Rozescu reassured him. "I am leaving tonight, on an official mission. Tomorrow evening I'll telephone Aglaia, not you. If everything's worked out, have her tell me that Margareta feels well. If something has gone wrong, then she must say that Margareta has a cold. If so, I'll take further measures. But don't worry, Nene Ioan. We're partners now."

"Why are you doing this?" Luceanu asked. "You're not a

businessman; you have no idea how long you may have to wait for settlement. Although, of course, if I don't *have* to sell, I hold a commanding position."

"There you are. Even a philosopher can see that. I want to earn money on the deal, big money. That's why I'm doing it."

"Come, don't give me that. What do you need money for?"

"I will need a great deal of money, Nene Ioan. We all will. So it's agreed. The only proviso is that I tell you whom to sell to."

"Certainly, certainly." He took the precious letter and put it away in his desk. Then they rejoined the company.

Rananu hailed them excitedly. He was bursting with curiosity, but asked no questions. "I've read the article," he said. "It's weird. And there's another interesting item. Inspector General Dumitriu of the Sigurantza has handed in his resignation on account of ill health, and his probable successor is a certain Inspector Barbulescu. What's behind this? At one o'clock this afternoon Dumitriu was well enough to be head of the Sigurantza and by evening he's not. And who is this Barbulescu?"

"Barbulescu," Luceanu said. "A big fat man. You must know him, Alecu. But no, he's quite a bit older than you are. If he's the one I'm thinking of, he's from your village, Ranesti—the son of Vladimir Barbulescu, who was the pastor of Ranesti for so many years."

"He had five sons, all of whom were big and fat. Was one of them with the Sigurantza? Yes, that's right, the name in the newspaper is A. Barbulescu—I remember now. Puffi, of course! Bravo, Inspector General of the Sigurantza—so we're come to this!"

"Why?" Rozescu said. "What's wrong with him?"

"A *baksheeshar*—he'll sell you whatever you ask. So far he hasn't had much to sell, but now . . . oh well, he fits in with the whole crew."

"The Blaze is his superior," Rananu said. "I imagine he fixed it up. Dumitriu is something of a gentleman, after all. Some of Danghu's tricks must have stuck in his throat. So he had to go. The Blaze—yes, he's behind it."

"*Ceterum censeo,*" Rozescu remarked.

Rananu looked irritated.

"I mean that wherever we turn, we stumble over Danghu," Rozescu explained. "So Barbulescu is corrupt?" He turned to Luceanu.

"The story was that he worked for the Germans during the 1916-1918 Occupation," Luceanu said. "Nothing could be proved against him, but he wasn't allowed to rise in the service."

"So now his time has come. He's the right man. For the Germans and for the Blaze as well. And he'll take bribes?"

"Why do you make so much of that?" Luceanu asked in surprise. "As if that were anything new or rare in our country! Who doesn't take what he can get, especially nowadays?"

Rozescu was spared a reply, for a servant called him to the telephone again. When he returned, he beckoned to Rananu. "We must go, Alecu."

"Already? What a pity," Margareta said. "Things were just beginning to liven up. Shall we drink one more cognac?"

Luceanu poured; they clinked glasses, and Rozescu said, before he drank, "Ceterum censeo!"

"I gave Danghu to understand that his information coincides with certain facts we have unearthed," the General said. "He could hardly keep from shouting for joy. The devil only knows the reason for his grudge against Alda; it's really peculiar, the way he hates him. Incidentally, at least three-quarters of the story is sheer balderdash. Zernescu is the only one to be taken seriously. What he reports has some substance. It might be true; it fits in with the picture I've formed of Alda. Confidentially, if I were a journalist—it was a rotten affair, you know. That fellow Mariniu was a beast. And instead of sending him off to dig salt for the rest of his life, they let him off scot-free and tried their best to hush the matter up. It suited them at the time. They knew Mariniu was a mass murderer. But all that was long ago, and no one would be able to prove anything against Alda—assuming that he was the author of those exposés. The point is dangerous for him only in connection with the pattern the Blaze has constructed. We have to lead Danghu off the trail. I've indicated that I think he's right, but that I must investigate in my own way, and I've asked him to collaborate with me—to instruct the Cernauti Sigurantza to assist the army in this case. Without his authorization, I said, we cannot question nonmilitary persons. You will make use of that assistance—naturally. And now listen closely. We have important work. First and foremost: we must rescue Alda's fiancée. You must find out where she is, and we must get her out of the reach of this beast. If she should fall into the hands of Zernescu, for example, or another of his caliber, God help her! We certainly owe that much to Alda. She must be warned and hidden away—if she's in the country, of course. And in all likelihood she is in the country and has no idea where Alda has gone. Who is she, incidentally? You know her, Alecu?"

"Only casually, sir. She's a charming woman and sits a horse splendidly, in the old Austrian style, of course."

"That tells me everything I need to know. Sits a horse splendidly—that's a really brilliant characterization. Alecu, Alecu!" The General shook his head.

"She speaks French and English flawlessly, is a first-rate pianist and one of the most charming women I've ever met," Rozescu put in.

The General whirled around.

"Then you know her, too, Rozescu?"

"Yes. She was a Hungarian baroness. I knew her family. Then I once saw her sing in a London nightclub. She didn't notice me. She was pianist and singer with a well-known ensemble of Hungarians. She's quite a woman."

"Well, they may try to link her with Alda's subversive activities!"

Rananu shook his head. "We must work fast. But where can she be? If she hasn't crossed any of the borders legally—and she hasn't— you can depend on the Sigurantza for that—then she's here in the country, and it's sheer oversight that she hasn't yet been ferreted out. Maybe she went across with Alda?" he concluded dubiously.

"Then the border guard Posteuca would have reported it," the General said.

"Sir?" Rananu cried out, in a scarcely military manner.

Rozescu, too, did not conceal his surprise. "You mean you believe that the man at the border, the man with the bandaged hand—"

"Was Alda? I hardly doubt it. But my feeling is that the border guard's account doesn't entirely hold water. Listen closely, boys, because this is what I am sending you to the border for.

"First I want to explain a few things to you, Rozescu. You've probably realized that Alda has gone across to the Russians. But he's doing this unofficially, that is, not as an agent and certainly not as a paid agent, just as a favor to me. At his own request he's not entered on any of our books. He went at his own risk, and I'm confident that he will return. During his absence, therefore, we must guard his interests. Danghu must have no pretext for attacking Alda legally. The report you two make must cover him completely. You're going to interrogate the border guard Posteuca within an inch of his life, in the presence of Sigurantza officials. Question him kindly, seem to be inclined to believe him, but at the last moment trip him up. Arrange that Sigurantza men be present at all your investigations." The General cleared his throat. "But if you can manage it—" He glanced down at some notes he had made. "Karl Rundberg— hm—he might know where Martha Varsany is. . . . Who is Alda's best friend, Alecu?"

"As we were remarking today, everyone who knows Alda is

his friend. But his closest is Radu Candomir. You know him, sir?"

"Very well, for more than twenty years. I used to visit Cando-mireni often when his father was still alive. But do you know him, Alecu?"

"We're even related, through his wife. She's a Mirbescu."

"Relationships of that kind don't count. The question is, will he tell you anything if you ask him for information? I assume he doesn't know where Alda's gone. No one knows but us. But why did he sell his property? Struck his tents, so to speak. Radu Cando-mir may know the answer to that, and also what happened to the money. To pay debts? Did Alda have so many? You understand, none of that is the Sigurantza's business. And don't forget you're be-ing watched all the time. Be especially careful with telephone con-versations. The Blaze doesn't trust either of you. You scared him today with your heroics, Alecu, and he'll knife you if he can."

Rananu smiled at the General. "Are you trying to terrify me, sir? Incidentally, I wasn't joking. If I get him within twenty paces of my pistol, I'll finish him off without a twinge of conscience, sir."

"Do you think he'll stand up to you with a gun in his hand? Not a chance—he's much more likely to fire one at your back. I've had to deal with all kinds of scoundrels, and this type is dangerous."

Rananu raised his eyebrows. The seriousness of the situation seemed to dawn on him for the first time. "I'm a soldier, sir. I do my duty wherever it lies. Give me your orders and I'll carry them out. What would really make me happy"—he smiled—"is for you to order me right now, 'Shoot the goddamn bastard down like a dog.'"

The General looked at him long and thoughtfully. Then he said softly, "We must defend ourselves as best we can: with intelligence. It's always best to dodge a snake before you crush its head. We must wait for the right moment. Lads—I hope you both realize that we're playing a nasty and dangerous game."

"Then we must howl with the wolves for a while," Rananu said, meeting the General's eyes.

"There are four of us now—with Alda. I wish he were here now," the General said, and he was no longer a general but an anxious old man.

Rananu's and Rozescu's train had a longish wait at Ploesti. Rozescu excused himself and took a cab at the station square. From the few words they exchanged, the cab driver was firmly convinced that his passenger was one of the many English engineers who worked in the oil fields; he could tell by the accent. The cab stopped at a house inhabited exclusively by Englishmen. Rozescu paid the driver, entered the house, but left it by a rear door. As he hurried through the garden, he heard the cab drive away. He made his way through several more gardens and stopped in front of a small private house. Only two windows were illuminated. Rozescu whistled a signal; a window opened and a man's head appeared. Rozescu said in English, "It's me, Danny; let me in quickly."

"Be right with you."

A moment later he was sitting opposite Danny Linton, his chum from Oxford.

"What's up, Steve?" the Englishman asked.

Rozescu looked at his watch. "Danny, I only have a few minutes. Do you have your car here?"

"Of course."

"Then suppose you drive me back to the station, and I'll tell you about it as we go."

In silent assent Linton led the way and put on his coat. In the car he waited until Rozescu, who sat beside him, collar turned up high as if he were shrinking into his coat, began to speak. They drove slowly through deserted streets.

"Listen closely, Danny, and ask questions only if you must. Do you know your man from the intelligence service—I mean, do you know him well enough to speak to?"

"Old Oxford man," Danny said.

"Fine. It seems there's some kind of pact between the Germans and the rotters who plan to sell our country. At any rate, they've come to some understanding already."

"They have, have they?" Linton said softly.

"Tell your man this: they can be got at with money. You understand, everything worth knowing can be bought. It's important—if only because of the oil."

"Naturally."

"I'm going to give you two names. One of them is Barbulescu. Have you got that, Danny? By tomorrow he'll be Inspector General of the Sigurantza. But even if he doesn't get the appointment— he's to be had."

"Barbulescu," Linton repeated.

"Danghu is the other man—have you heard of him, Danny?"

Linton nodded, and slowed the car. "I'll see that our man gets the information. But don't you think he knows all that?"

"Perhaps, but I think we should make sure."

Linton looked at his friend. "All right," he said, "I'll pass the tip along. Barbulescu, Danghu." He repeated the two names, which sounded strange and comic in his pronunciation.

Rozescu looked at his watch. "Let me off now, near the railroad station. Before you stop, glance in the mirror to make sure there's no one behind us."

Linton nodded. A few minutes later Rozescu, collar still turned up high, strode toward the railroad station and into his waiting train.

Inspector Stanescu, chief of the Sigurantza in Cernauti, thoughtfully replaced the telephone on the hook. He had just heard from Bucharest. What a piece of news! Dumitriu cashiered! Not that he was going to weep for him. But who was coming to the top now—by God and all the saints!—Barbulescu inspector general. Stanescu had gone to school with him; he knew the man. But he'd endure that as he had endured so much else. Everything was upside down nowadays. Lucky he had only two years to go before retirement on pension—and he had his nest pretty well feathered too. Both daughters well married, and his son would soon be finished at the university; he'd find a place for him. He would sit down and write his application for early retirement on the spot if it were not such a pity to miss out on these glorious boom times. They were all raking in cash as never before. Every petty police chief was a ruler in his own domain, making his own regulations, and pocketing the proceeds of the general confusion. Baksheesh. No, not so much from Romanians; they weren't the ones who forked over. But what were foreigners and Jews for? The foreigners who for the most part were Jews, and the native Jews who had been declared foreigners. But his thoughts were wandering; he must concentrate on those instructions from Bucharest. Plain enough: the Sigurantza was to place its men at the disposal of B II for investigation of a case. However, he was being asked to keep a close check on the Second Bureau's men and their methods. A precise and strictly secret report was to be delivered to the Inspector General's office. Which meant, Stanescu knew, that the Cernauti Sigurantza—or rather, the personnel assigned to this case—would also be under surveillance. . . .

It was a lovely winter night, clear and cold. Only a few steps took Inspector Stanescu to the liveliest street in the city, the Strada Iancu Flondor, formerly Herrengasse, as Cernauti was formerly Czernowitz. From the theaters and movie houses people were pouring into the cafés and restaurants.

In front of the Café Europa—no longer de l'Europe, as it had been in Austrian days—stood several sleighs, their drivers muffled up in shapeless fur coats that reached to the ankles, their feet in equally shapeless leather or felt boots. Stanescu took a seat in the first sleigh and drew the fur robe over him. The driver started up his horses, and then inquired, "Police headquarters?" He spoke German, though with a pronounced accent, for he was a Jew. Stanescu answered, "Yes," and with tinkling bells the sleigh moved forward at a fast pace.

The sleigh stopped in front of police headquarters, and the Inspector dismounted. The driver raised his whip, wished his passenger "long life," and had already started when Stanescu called him back. "Wait a little, Moschku!"

The horses stood still, and the driver turned toward the Inspector, his movements so impeded by the fur coat that it looked like a slow-motion film. His name was not Moschku but Schajeh, but he did not correct the mistake, for he understood its implications and was by no means pleased that his gratis passenger (when had a police or Sigurantza official ever paid a cabman, let alone a Jewish cabman?) was keeping him still longer. He therefore waited in silence.

"Here's a hundred lei," Stanescu said. "Drive to Lieutenant Ciobotariu's and bring him to headquarters. Tell him I'll be expecting him in my office. You know who I am?"

"How could I not?" Schajeh felt uneasy about the hundred-lei note; it gave rise to a conflict in his soul. Should he take it or refuse it? "Chief, I'll drive for you anyhow, without pay," he said in broken Romanian. "Really."

"Take it and be off."

Schajeh took the note, dropped it into his coat pocket, said, "Long life to you, Chief," and drew on the reins.

By the time he returned to his stand, it was one o'clock in the morning. Ciobotariu had scarcely been pleased at the interruption of his night's rest and the prospect of going out in the biting cold, and had enlivened the drive to headquarters with a steady stream of curses. By now Schajeh had lost the best part of the night—the custom from cafés and restaurants. There remained only the bars. He decided to drive to the Hummingbird Bar and wait for fares there. Perhaps he would still be able to pick up something so that there wouldn't be too big a hole in his night's earnings.

But the night turned out more remunerative than Schajeh had ever hoped for. He drove down Strada Regele Ferdinand at a deliberate trot, and caught sight of a man striding rapidly along on the sidewalk. Schajeh reined in his horses and called out in German, "Going home, Herr Rundberg?"

Karl Rundberg was coming from a bridge game. It had brought him no distraction and given him no pleasure. He was feeling rather bad and wished he were already home, although there too for many weeks he had not enjoyed the peace and quiet which his house had hitherto afforded, and which he urgently needed as a counterpoint to a life of constant excitement. The cabman's shout startled him out of dismal thoughts, and he headed toward the sleigh, responding warmly to Schajeh's greeting, for they were old friends. When the sleigh stopped a few minutes later, Rundberg took a five-hundred-lei note from his pocket and waited for the cabman to make change. "I have only three hundred-lei notes," Schajeh said. He had jumped clumsily down from the box, removed his mitten and was digging in the pocket where he kept his money. "But here, this one with the torn ear"—a corner was missing from the bill—"ought to count for three. Or even for thirty. Take it and have it framed, Herr Rundberg. In twenty-one years this is the first time a Sigurantza man has ever paid. . . . Maybe you have a cigarette, Herr Rundberg?"

Rundberg held out a box to the cabman and took a cigarette himself. Suddenly he no longer felt in the least like going home. And he knew why. The mention of the Sigurantza had given him a cue to what it was that had been bothering him. He had been worrying ever since that flatfoot who wasn't a real Sigurantza man had been walking around the neighborhood asking about Alda. He had bribed the fellow over to his side, but so far he'd received no explanation of his interest in Alda.

"Hm," he said, entering into the cabman's joke. "Who gave you the hundred lei?"

"The top dog of the force, Stanescu—but I had to drive all the way to Rosch."

"What was Stanescu doing in Rosch?" Rundberg asked. He had time to reflect while the cabman explained in elaborate detail. Then he said, "Lucky you're here, Schajeh. We'll drive to the Iron Bridge."

Schajeh showed no surprise. He swung up onto the box while Rundberg once more crept under the fur robe, and while the sleigh glided along, both driver and passenger mused in silence. Schajeh's thoughts were simple and pleasant. Rundberg was a good customer; the drive to the Iron Bridge and back would bring at least three hundred lei. Schajeh believed in the justice of fate. A saying of his grandfather's came to him: An hour before dawn it is still night.

But Rundberg's thoughts were neither simple nor pleasant. Stanescu had sent for his Lieutenant in the middle of the night, and Rundberg wondered why. He instinctively connected this fact with the snooper's questions about Alda. He could think of no good reason, and yet he couldn't banish his uneasiness. He decided to find out why Ciobotariu had been called by his superior in the middle of the night. That was something tangible and rather simple he might easily find out.

Schajeh turned to his passenger. "Where do you want me to stop, Herr Rundberg?"

"In front of Eisner's tavern," Rundberg said.

"It's closed already." Schajeh pointed the butt of his whip at the house.

Rundberg didn't reply. He got out of the sleigh and said, "I'll be half an hour or so, maybe more. You'd better drive into the yard. Perhaps you could feed your horses, but take their bells off."

Rundberg tapped lightly with his fingernail at a window at the far end of the wing. When the light was switched on, Rundberg was waiting at the door, which promptly opened. A stocky, broad-shouldered man in a long nightshirt led him to a comfortably warm bedroom, where he promptly crawled back into bed and reached for his cigarettes. Mischa Eisner fixed small, shiny eyes inquiringly upon his visitor. His features would have been those of a good-natured giant, had not his big jutting chin given his whole face a menacing expression.

"Mischa," Rundberg said, "you must get dressed."

"Now? What's up?" Eisner began throwing on his clothes while Rundberg talked.

"Stanescu sent for Ciobotariu tonight. They're probably in conference right now."

"So?"

"I think it has something to do with the Poles. Maybe new instructions have come through. All along the word's been that they'll be put into a camp or deported. They might be sent away to-morrow, and then it'll be very hard to—"

"I understand," said Eisner. He splashed his face with water from a basin.

"I may be mistaken," Rundberg said. "But in any case we'd better know what's going on. You think he'll tell you?"

"I can try," Eisner said, pulling on a sweater. He reached for his jacket. "So far he's told me everything I wanted to know. Do you suppose he's still at headquarters?"

"He was there with Stanescu forty minutes ago. It seems to me if the Chief is there now, so late at night, and sends for him—you understand, Mischa—it must be something big. Even if it isn't about the Poles, we ought to know," he added hesitantly, meditatively.

"Uh-huh." Eisner lit another cigarette.

"I have Schajeh outside. If you catch the Lieutenant, where will you drive with him?"

"To the Hummingbird," Eisner said.

"Fine. I'll go to the Corso. They'll still be playing there. I'll stay until you come. Mischa, you must find out what they discussed tonight. Do you have enough money?"

"As much as I need for him. I'll pump him, never fear. My method never fails. First a few bottles of wine, then a few double cognacs. When he's floating, I have the band play 'Ana Lugojana.' That makes him sentimental and he tells me all his troubles. After all, we're pals."

When Eisner's light went out, Schajeh untied the horses' feed-bags and led the team out of the yard. Rundberg and Eisner stepped into the street to find him already ensconced on the box. Eisner called out a greeting. "A pleasure, Herr Eisner," Schajeh replied cheerfully.

"To the Corso," Eisner said.

Ten minutes later they drew up in front of the café. It looked closed for the night, but Schajeh knew that gambling was still going on in the back rooms. Only Rundberg got out and Eisner stayed under the robe, but that was also quite in order.

"*Lav diburim*—no talk, Schajeh," Rundberg said, and turned toward the rear entrance.

"Of course, Herr Rundberg."

Eisner asked the cabbie to stop in front of the church opposite police headquarters.

The narrow room was filled with clouds of smoke. Men stood around a long table covered with a much-patched green cloth. They had chips on the table in front of them, or held them in their hands, and tensely watched the fall of the card. Only two cards fell at a time, one to the left and one to the right—one for the bank and one for the players, one for me and one for you. The game was called *nashi-vashi* (which in all Slavic languages means "ours-yours"): the simplest, fastest, most exciting and most dangerous game of chance in the world.

This was no casino, no international meeting place of gamblers who were strangers to one another. Here everyone knew virtually everything about everyone else. All knew that the banker, a man rolling in money, had begun his career as a procurer in Argentina. He had traveled there with two women, had returned to Cernauti with a third, to whom he was properly married. With the money he had made he opened a brothel. After several years of lucrative business he had liquidated this enterprise and retired to private life. And everyone knew that the man who sat facing the banker was his cousin, who had had the same kind of start but fewer opportunities, and now lived in the shadow of his rich relative, earning his rather expensive keep as the latter's secretary.

Adolf, with his pimp's head and small, deep-set eyes, crooked, cruel, hazel eyes which never looked straight ahead and never to the side, but seemed to be staring eternally at his own bulbous, wide-nostriled nose and huge mouth; Adolf, who wore silk underwear, the gaudiest and most expensive neckties, suits of English worsted cut by the best tailors; Adolf, who went about in a cloud of perfume and who used his big, shapeless, doughy hands with manicured fingernails for nothing but shuffling cards, laying out cards and counting money—Adolf was the autocrat of the realm of nashivashi. His reign was uncontested and inviolate, for he was "covered." He enjoyed—for a high price—the protection of the secretary of the criminal police.

When Rundberg entered the room, the *changeur* signaled to a "small" *pointeur,* who stood up and made room for him. Rundberg, lost in thought, sat down without noticing. The changeur leaned forward, laying a handful of chips on the table before him. "Fifty thousand, Domnule Rundberg?"

Rundberg nodded. The changeur stepped back to a table on which a bottle and glass stood. He poured himself a drink, made change, and threw a brief look of satisfaction at the croupier. Rundberg was a "good" player who could lose large sums without a whimper.

Adolf shuffled the cards and laid them on the table for drawing.

"What's the limit?" Rundberg asked.

"No limit," the croupier said; Adolf had kicked him under the table.

Then the banker laid out the cards: a seven on the left, a jack on the right. The croupier took in the stakes on the seven, paid those on the jack. Rundberg alone had three thousand on it. Six thousand now lay there, and Rundberg added four more chips to the thousand, making ten thousand in all. After three rounds a jack turned up to the right again.

"Ten thousand paid," the croupier said, calling the pointeur's attention to the fact that he was entitled to withdraw the money. "Anything said?" he asked. After a win the pointeur can say, "Not betting," or "One round passes," which means that the next two cards count neither for the bank nor for the pointeur.

"Yes," Rundberg said, and pushed a heap of chips that lay before him, thirteen thousand in all, to add to the twenty thousand that lay in the jack's square. A nine turned up on the left, a king on the right. The croupier took in, paid out. Then it went on, an ace left, a ten right, a ten left and a jack right. "Thirty-three thousand," the croupier said.

"A nice take," said a man with a shiny bald pate, a round face and merry brown eyes. "In five minutes. But now pack up and go; it would be a pity to lose all that money. And you'd have to lose. The cat brings home by evening birds that sing too early in the morning."

"I have no chess partner, so I must play nashi-vashi," Rundberg said. "You're right, though."

The dealer no longer lost time cutting and recutting the deck; he dealt the cards out quickly, and while he showed the last to the players, his croupier—whose scholar's spectacles did not improve a face marked by all the vices—said in a low but penetrating voice, "The game goes on. Nine of hearts at the bottom. Place your bets, gentlemen; anything goes."

Rundberg was still lost in thought. The routine "Can we go on?" of the croupier recalled him to the game. "Yes," he said, and without counting, pushed a pile of chips onto the jack's square. After three rounds the jack fell to the left.

"A knave's a knave," the bald man, Max Duttner, said scornfully.

"Yes," Rundberg said, "a knave's a knave." This time he pushed a larger number of chips over, and this time the jack fell to the right. The croupier counted: "Twenty-eight thousand." He tossed out six green chips and took back two yellow ones. "Stake's paid; anything said?" Adolf slammed two cards down on the table—a queen to the left and a jack to the right. "Fifty-six thousand," the croupier said, paying out eleven green chips and one yellow one. "Stake's paid—anything said? Nothing said." To the left a nine, to the right a seven; to the left a seven, to the right an eight, and then: to the left an ace, to the right a jack. "One hundred and twelve thousand," the croupier said.

"Pretty nice," Duttner said. He had only one chip left in his hand; he had put a great deal of money on the lost ace. Nevertheless his whole face was beaming; even his bald pate seemed to take part in the smile. "God must be sleeping when a pointeur wins."

By five o'clock in the morning, when Eisner came up to the gaming table, Rundberg had won two thousand five hundred dollars and more than four hundred thousand lei. Eisner took ten thousand in chips from the changeur, lost them in two rounds, and waved the man aside when he offered more. "Enough for today; I have no time." He drank his black coffee in rapid sips.

Schajeh was waiting outside. "To the steam bath?"

"It wasn't about the Poles," Eisner said, when he was seated beside Rundberg in the steam room. "It was about your *puriz,* your landowner."

"Our landowner? Who do you mean?"

"Cut the comedy, Karl. As soon as Ciobotariu opened his mouth, I caught on. You probably knew all along they were after him. But I'm always glad to help you out, you know. There was talk about your father, as well, and I'm afraid about you, too."

"Tell me the whole story, Mischa."

"Officers from B II are coming today on the Bucharest Express. They're going to hold a little investigation in collaboration with the Sigurantza. They want to find out where Alda has disappeared to and what happened to the money for Aldeni. There was also some talk of a woman. One chap from the Sigurantza Generala, Stanescu, with Stratilescu and Ciobotariu from our local Sigurantza as recorders, and those officers from the Bucharest office of B II, are to be the investigating commission. That's all I know."

"Good, Mischa—thanks."

"Don't be silly—what reason have you to thank me? But what's all this about? Are they likely to be rubbing your nose in the dirt?"

"I'm kosher. They can't touch me. But what do they want of Alda?"

"Ciobotariu doesn't know either; he cursed their guts. After all, Alda's a boyar, he said. It's not the first time they've gone poking into his affairs. There was another inquiry back at the end of November, from Section Four; he himself gave them the information. Told them Alda was all right, completely nonpolitical. Karl, what really is up with Alda? Where is he?"

"Where is he? Where has he always been? You know how it's been for the past twenty years—come and go, come and go again.

"You're on good terms with him. Didn't he tell you anything?"

"Why do you ask? Suppose I am on good terms with him and he told me where he was going and didn't want me to tell anyone. He didn't run away from the Sigurantza. Alda isn't a puriz—not like other *prizim.* He has a good heart. For all. Ever since this— *yemach shmo!* May his name be extinguished!—came along, he's helped hundreds of people. Many Jews. He did hint something to the effect that the Germans were after him. Perhaps someone recognized him—in Bucharest. Alda's been in Germany, often; he's brought out a great many people. Maybe. . . ."

Eisner looked across at Rundberg. They were sitting close together on the marble benches. There was no one else in the heated chamber. The two men made an odd pair: Eisner, hairy, with huge chest and powerful shoulders, his chin jutting forward like a threatening wedge, beside Rundberg's smooth, lean boy's body. His chin was resting against his chest; his soft hair covered his eyes, and around the corners of his mouth was a sad, forlorn grin.

"If you aren't involved in the business and he's safely away, there's nothing to worry about," Eisner said. He was perplexed; he had never seen Rundberg so dispirited.

"Not exactly. If they catch Alda out on something, he's done for when he comes back. We must give the thing a twist—if you know what I mean."

"I don't entirely follow. Do you mean—they may find out that a certain suspicion of theirs is right?"

"That's just it—they have no definite suspicion. Why is B II so interested in Alda all of a sudden? They aren't sure. All they know is that there's a man around here who's neither fish nor fowl." Brusquely he looked up and met Eisner's eyes. "Mischa," he murmured, "Alda is our chief—he's the Uden."

Eisner leaned back. Very slowly, until his back touched the smooth wall. He stretched his legs far forward and braced his heels in the gutter that ran along the stone floor, as if he had to give firm support to his mass of muscle and bone before he let his mind work. "The Uden?" he whispered. "So he's the Uden?" He whistled sharply. "Oho, the Uden! Then he's our—yes, then, Karl—" He jumped to his feet and stood in front of Rundberg in all his massiveness. "What are we lolling around here for? This is serious. If he's the Uden, we must get him out of this fix. Have you a plan, Karl?"

"Plan? Yes, I have. . . . I've thought of one just this minute. I'll need the whole gang within the hour. Round the fellows up. Everyone must be in his place before the Bucharest Express arrives. There'll be some hot work." He drew a heavy sigh. "I hope this works out."

The Bucharest Express arrived almost on schedule. As Rananu and Rozescu stepped down from the Pullman, they were greeted by Major Tarnovietzchi, chief of B II, D 6. Two soldiers took their baggage while the Major, who was acquainted with the two officers, steered them to the waiting sleighs, one of which was for their baggage.

The sleighs were already negotiating the steeply rising street that led to the center of town when Inspector Zernescu, who had got out of a second-class car, was met on the platform by Lieutenant Ciobotariu and promptly led to a sleigh. They drove to the home of Inspector Stratilescu, where Zernescu was to stay.

Eugeniu Popovici was met by no one. He emerged from the single third-class car of the train, carrying a flimsy leatherette satchel, and slowly made his way toward the exit. He was chilled through and very hungry. He had not dared to enter the dining car because he wanted to remain unobserved by the officers of B II and by Zernescu as well. Once more he was traveling on a special assignment direct from Secretary General Danghu.

Popovici had succeeded in keeping out of Zernescu's way. He was terrified of him—a fear that had its root in the many slaps he had received in the past. Even now, in the jubilation of having at last achieved the definite position he had so long dreamed of, that terror was still with him. But now he had a right to use his badge, and what was equally important, he had his regular monthly salary and could count on picking up a little extra.

He was an altogether different Jenica today, especially when the specter of bygone days, Zernescu, was out of sight. As soon as his old Chief vanished, he strode more rapidly toward the exit, swinging the red satchel in his gloved hand—the gloves were yellow leather and brand-new; his coat was gaily cut and, though secondhand, was in top condition; he wore the brim of his dark-blue felt hat pulled dashingly down over his left eye. But he was not yet a real detective and in fact had learned very little about his trade. A more experienced dick might have given some thought to a man who had boarded the train two stations before Cernauti and, after looking the car over, had taken a seat facing Jenica. After offering his neighbor a cigarette, he had initiated a conversation revolving about the variation in climate between the capital city and this northern corner of the country. Jenica had been sufficiently impressed by the good fur coat, the Persian lamb cap, and the heavy gold cigarette case filled with the most expensive brand of cigarettes, to reply politely. Yes, when he had left Bucharest tonight, the weather had been extremely mild, whereas here it felt like Siberia. Both had laughed heartily at this joke. A few minutes later, after a polite good-bye, the stranger left the car, walking forward through the train toward the engine. He got off as soon as the train came to a halt and was at the exit by the time other passengers were just leaving their compartments.

A few minutes later the newly hatched agent entered the long, wide passageway behind a mass of straggling passengers who hid him well. Jenica peered ahead to see whether Zernescu was still in sight; he neither looked back nor to the side, as Zernescu himself would certainly have done. Had he done so, he would have noticed that his acquaintance with the fur cap dropped a newly lit cigarette at the exact moment that Jenica passed by him.

Jenica noticed nothing of all this, for his attention was entirely taken up with a very well-dressed and good-looking woman who was studying him. He hesitated, extricated himself from the crowd, and looked questioningly, smilingly, at the lady. At this, she took a step closer and asked with some embarrassment, "Excuse me. Would you be Director Jeleriu?"

Jenica now realized that he was not the object of love at first sight, but he was not going to lose this chance to make the acquaintance of a charming woman. Smiling suavely, an altogether different Jenica from the worm Zernescu had known, he replied, "I am a director, but unfortunately, to my great sorrow, my name is not Jeleriu. Permit me, *conitza*—Popovici is my name. Of the Ministry of the Interior." He bowed, and with a gesture which he had seen and analyzed, he whipped off the yellow leather glove from his right hand—a gesture intended to suggest to the lady that she offer her hand.

Which she promptly did, with a ladylike and for that reason no less alluring smile. "Doamna Professor Sandescu," she said.

Naturally Jenica kissed the perfumed hand with its vivid red fingernails, at the same time bowing gallantly. "Did the Director know that you were expecting him, conitza?" he asked.

"That's just it, he did not," she replied shamefacedly. "I don't know him and he doesn't know me either. It's about . . . I wanted—"

"I see. I can only repeat that I am terribly sorry not to be Jeleriu. I would be glad to do anything for you, conitza!" he assured her.

She threw him a glance full of gratitude and promise. "Then I must say I'm sorry too. There are not many men so gallant. What can a poor widow do? All this trouble and running around to offices! And yet I'm in the right. If you knew my case, Director Popovici—it's simply hair-raising!"

Jenica puffed out his chest. "Perhaps I can be of assistance," he suggested. "In the Ministry of the Interior we have our connections, you know. You understand, one hand washes the other."

Professor Sandescu's widow gave him a half-dubious, half-hopeful look. "Would you really look into it?"

Jenica put his right hand—now gloved again—to his heart. "I would and I will, conitza. So help me God! But what is it about?"

"That can scarcely be explained in a few words," the pretty widow answered. "When are you free, Director Popovici? It almost seems that you've been sent by heaven."

"My time is my own," he answered grandly. "No one gives me orders. I can see you at your convenience."

"Well, Director," she said timidly, "if you wouldn't consider it an importunity, I live at Number 11, Strada Gradinelor. One moment." She took a card from her brown leather handbag. "If you please, here is my name and address and—if you would do me the honor—come today for lunch."

The card read: Doamna Aurora Ignatiu Sandescu, and gave the address and telephone number.

"Thank you, I kiss your hand," Jenica said gallantly.

Inspector Stratilescu was a bachelor. His household was run by his elder sister, whose husband had vanished without a leave-taking some twenty years before, carrying with him a sizable sum from the cashbox of the company in which he had held a prominent post. He had also made off with a female neighbor. From then on Alexandra had detested all other women. She had contrived to nullify all her brother's marital projects. He was a good deal younger than she was, and she played the part of a mother. It was she who decided that he should enter the Sigurantza instead of joining the army. In the Sigurantza you could always "make some coin," whereas that was true for the army only under certain limited circumstances. Dragos Stratilescu had quickly learned how to make some coin, but never how to hold on to it. Women and cards were expensive passions. But Sandra contrived to put away some tidy sums, keeping them out of reach of her spendthrift brother, no matter how pinched he was. His house was always clean, in perfect order, and his sister set a good table. For Sandra thought a good deal of food and drink; there her parsimony stopped.

She had known her brother's old friend and colleague, Inspector Zernescu, for many years and thought well of him because of his sound attitudes and thrifty ways. She greeted him pleasantly, showed him his room, and fixed him a good breakfast. Then he bathed, and after telephoning the Chief of the local Sigurantza to announce his arrival, lay down to catch up on the night's sleep he had missed. He did this so thoroughly that the neighbors were alarmed.

When Dragos Stratilescu came home for lunch, his guest was well rested and in excellent appetite. Sandra produced an array of national dishes that would have delighted any gourmet's heart, and Zernescu piled into them to show his appreciation of the cooking. Afterwards he and Stratilescu sat over the turceasca and talked. Although his friend was interested in various subjects, particularly in the new state of affairs in Bucharest, the dismissal of Dumitriu and the impending appointment of Barbulescu, Zernescu's particular mission in Cernauti appeared to leave him cold. It seemed that his old colleague did not take his guesswork in the Alda case seriously, and that only his sense of what was proper behavior toward a guest kept Stratilescu from making outright fun of him.

Now, Inspector Zernescu thought highly of his old friend and envied him his professional perspicacity and his cosmopolitan manners. He did not like being treated flippantly, attempted to prove that he was right, and became more and more heated. Before long he had laid all his cards on the table—which was precisely what Stratilescu was after. For only a few hours before, in a quick talk with Max Duttner, Stratilescu had learned that this affair could be a gold mine for him.

Now Stratilescu had the whole story at first hand. To his credit it must be said that he was not merely pretending to be skeptical but actually meant it when he heard Zernescu out and said, with an ironic smile, "You are not trying to tell me that you believe this movie script, Sebi. I've been in this game for twenty-one years. But you can count on me to help you all I can." He yawned and stood up. "I'd better take my nap. Didn't have much sleep last night."

"One minute, Dragos—just a moment. What do you mean by 'movie script'?"

Stratilescu winked and looked at his old friend in amusement. "You don't seriously expect me to swallow all that, Sebi?"

"All what?" Zernescu replied with rising choler.

"This wild fantasy that you fellows in Bucharest are trying to make a case of. Alda—I ask you—Alda a Bolshevist agent, Dniester, B II, shot at the border—the devil knows what else. Well, have it your way. If you think you can make a piece of change on it, that's your affair. But don't try to fool me. Orders from the top office to investigate? All right, I'll investigate. Day and night. What else am I here for? But let me tell you this: if the Blaze or even Barbulescu are in on this, you won't see a red *ban*. When there's grabbing to be done, they lead the way. Barbulescu! Why, I remember a time when he'd take twenty lei."

Zernescu wore a rather vapid look. "Dragos," he said, "you're mistaken. There's no business involved in this at all. This is an honest-to-goodness case."

"No business for you, you mean. You've gone and sat down with a bare ass on the hot stovetop. If there's anything to collect, the Blaze and Barbulescu will see to it. . . . Why do you think Dumitriu has resigned, eh?"

"How should I know? I won't shed any tears over him; he never had a good word for anybody."

"Right. But he's got a good head; you know that as well as I do. He simply didn't want to get screwed. Look, Sebi, I haven't any interest in this thing. My only concern is you. We've known each other quite a while and we're pretty good friends. Don't imagine that the Blaze or Barbulescu believe such rot. Their whole idea is

that there's something to be got out of this. And you'll serve them
well—as a floor mat, understand. If the thing misfires, they'll simply say, Oh, Zernescu thought he had a good lead; he's an experienced officer, so we had to investigate. If it turns out to be a fizzle,
what have they lost? Who'll be burned? You. And why should
you take the rap, when there isn't even a chance of your making any
profit on the case?"

"It never crossed my mind to make a profit," Zernescu said.

Stratilescu shrugged in a manner that expressed an equal measure of disbelief and incomprehension.

"I was and I am certain that Oskar Gross and Alda are one and
the same person, and that he is a subversive. I had to report that."

"You can't convince me," Stratilescu said. "That's just about
the craziest theory I ever heard. Look here, Sebi, there are just two
possibilities. The first is that you've stumbled over your own feet;
it will turn out that you thought you were firing at a target and
were only breaking wind. In that case Danghu has a fine pretext for
sending you to guard the salt mines. But let's assume, just for the
sake of argument, that Alda *is* a subversive. In that case you let him
go about his business for years without saying boo. How much harm
he could have done in all those years! Always associating with high-
ranking army officers, statesmen, the best people, always traveling
around. If that should be so, Sebi, then you're really in the soup."

Zernescu's forehead was beaded with sweat as the force of the
argument bore down upon him. "That goddamned pimp!" he
moaned.

"Who do you mean?" Stratilescu asked.

"That bastard Jenica who started the whole thing. He saw Rananu of B II and Alda talking together. That was what set me off."

"Who is this pimp Jenica?"

"A stoolie, the shabbiest I have, or had. Now he's a full-time
agent; decent boys wait six years for promotion, but this one—"
Zernescu trailed off and brooded until Stratilescu prompted him
impatiently.

"Well, what about him?"

"On special assignment to the Ministry of the Interior—conducting an investigation, if you please. That pimp, that low-down
gambler, that thief. He was the guy who collected all that tripe about
Alda's disappearance, sale of his land, being shot—I hope he croaks."

"Take it easy, Sebi. Easy does it. First of all, why does the Ministry of the Interior send a subordinate official to conduct an investigation alone, and why didn't this agent report to the local inspector's office?"

"Did I say they sent an official? They sent a pimp, a sonofabitch. He wasn't appointed an agent until he came back. He was nothing, a lousy stoolie who got five hundred lei if he brought in a scrap of worthwhile information. Which he did one out of ten times."

"And solely on the basis of what this Jenica—what's his last name . . . ?"

"Popovici."

"Solely on the basis of what he brought back, you and the men from B II, a lieutenant colonel among them no less, and we all, inspectors and a chief inspector, are supposed to set up a solemn investigating commission?"

Zernescu shrugged. "I didn't send him. The Ministry did—that is, the Secretary General."

Stratilescu stood up. Every trace of amusement and sarcasm had vanished from his face. He was furious and wasn't trying to disguise it. "Then I, Dragos Stratilescu, say that the Blaze can go to hell. I'm not having any part of it. What does the lousy bastard think he's doing? You mean to tell me you'll play along with it, Sebi? Do you know what it means? We might as well be in Russia. Worse, far worse. If you ask me, that new agent has been sent here on special assignment just to keep tabs on us, Sebi. Stanescu hinted something of the sort, though not directly. He said we'd better keep our eyes open. He knows Barbulescu of old."

Zernescu raised his hand feebly, then let it drop in a fatalistic gesture. "I no longer see what's what."

"You've certainly got us into a mess, Sebi. I think Danghu is laying for us all; he'd like to get rid of us and bring his own men in. He's setting a trap."

"I can't figure it out," Zernescu said honestly.

"You'll see soon enough. But there's no time for lengthy explanations now." Inspector Stratilescu, who usually made a point of preserving a certain superior air, was in a state of high excitement. He rushed to the telephone and called Stanescu, although he knew that the Chief was taking his midday nap and didn't like to be disturbed. What he said was couched in phrases which any eavesdropper would have found unintelligible. The upshot was that Stanescu asked Stratilescu and his guest to come over to his house at once.

They had sat over their late lunch at Major Tarnovietzchi's until nearly five o'clock in the afternoon. Rananu waited almost to the end before asking the Major to get in touch with the Sigurantza for him. The officials in charge of the investigation were to be called to a meeting at nine o'clock, he said.

The Major received these instructions with military bearing. He felt ill at ease both in his uniform with its high collar and gold braid and in his own skin. General Baderescu considered him a capable officer. He had done a fairly good job in building up his organization. His agents crossed the Ceremus with fair regularity and brought back the information they were sent out for. But their reports had been much sparser of late. Tarnovietzchi explained this by the fact that border crossing was getting more and more dangerous. He had not been particularly overjoyed by Rananu's news that the General intended to allocate more funds to him. Secretly he had hoped that headquarters would not endorse a higher budget, for then he would have had a plausible excuse for failures. If the Lieutenant Colonel should happen to question one or another of the agents and learn that none of them had received a single *ban* of late, the Major would find himself in serious trouble. The Old Man had no sense of humor about this kind of thing. Then all would be up with his hopes for promotion and transfer back to the regular forces. In fact, he would be through with the army—and Major Tarnovietzchi had been a soldier since 1917.

Contrary to etiquette though it was, the Major had been unable to suppress a smile as Rananu explained the nature of the investigation. And when Rananu directly asked him his opinion, he answered frankly that he thought the charges against Alda were preposterous. In the first place, he had known Alda from boyhood; his father had been pastor in a village near Aldeni. Alda couldn't be a Red; he was a boyar, a gentleman. And in the second place, if there had been any such incident at the border as the Lieutenant Colonel described, it would have been reported to him immediately. That was the duty of the officer in charge. And even if the officer had been so forgetful or neglectful of his duty as not to report it, he, the Major, made a visit to the border at least four times a week (which was scarcely true) and would certainly have heard talk of it.

Rananu did not seem displeased by this opinion. They were going to look more closely into the matter, he said. The entire commission—the Major would be included—was to go to the spot and check up on the border guard's statements.

Rananu and Rozescu walked the short distance to the Palace Hotel. Rananu—as he informed the Lieutenant with a hint of a whinny—proposed to have tea with a lady whom he had met in the hotel lobby. Rozescu was going to look in on the university library. He would be back around seven o'clock, he said.

Rozescu got into a sleigh and asked to be taken to the university. He settled down in the library with a volume of Kant and took notes on the "Observations on the Sense of Beauty and Sublimity." After half an hour of this, he took a map of the city from his pocket and located a street close to the university buildings. He returned the volume of Kant and left, pausing in the shelter of the entrance to scrutinize the street in both directions. It was very cold and the street was almost deserted. Rozescu turned to the left, rounded a corner, crossed a quiet side street and mounted the steps of an old house. He entered a dimly lighted corridor with doors at either end. On one door, just to the left of the stairs, was a plaque: KARL RUNDBERG, WHOLESALE YARNS. Rozescu raised his hand to knock, but hearing voices, he turned to the door at the other end of the corridor, which read: KARL RUNDBERG, RESIDENCE. He pressed the bell button. A woman of about thirty-five opened the door and asked him in formal, bookish Romanian what his desire was.

Rozescu suppressed a smile; he bowed and introduced himself: "Permit me, madame, Dr. Stefan—"

"What does Your Excellency wish? I am Doamna Paula Rundberg."

"Then I am at the right place," Rozescu said. "I should like to see Karl Rundberg."

"He is in the office," the woman said. She was small, rather plump, with coal-black hair and highly intelligent and alert violet eyes.

"Yes, but I do not think he is alone."

"You have the wish to see him alone?"

Rozescu fought back the urge to laugh, and adapting to the woman's style, said with emphatic politeness, "If you could aid me to do so, madame."

"Please enter."

They came into a room furnished in solidly bourgeois style, in which a girl or young woman with a thin, pale face and old-fashioned coiffure sat knitting.

"Klara," Rundberg's wife said in German, "tell Karl a Dr. Stefan from—"

"Bucharest," Rozescu said, to indicate that he understood German. This fact appeared to reassure Mrs. Rundberg.

By the time Karl Rundberg appeared, Rozescu was having tea and conversing pleasantly in German with Paula Rundberg. Rundberg eyed the guest narrowly as the stranger shook hands and gave his name. "Dr. Stefan? What can I do for you?" he asked.

"I should like some information from you. Of a business nature. I represent a large firm."

"Which one, may I ask?"

"At the moment, that . . . You understand, Domnule Rundberg, I should like to know whether you are in a position to take over the agency for Bucovina and Bessarabia." He sat down and drank some tea from the thick glass. Rundberg took a turn about the table and sat down facing him. His wife slipped quietly out of the room. She never participated in business conversations.

"Hm," Rundberg said, lighting a cigarette. "What do you really want, Dr. Stefan?" He spoke neither ironically nor challengingly.

Rozescu gazed straight into Rundberg's face. The grin troubled him. It didn't seem to match the kindly eyes and the high, clear forehead. "Stefan is only my first name," he said. "I am a doctor of philosophy, and my family name is Rozescu. The name is fairly well known to you, I think, Domnule Rundberg?"

"Very well known, Dr. Rozescu. Very." His grin widened. "Ilie Rozescu." He wagged his head. "I am greatly honored. May I assume that you are his son?" Duttner was in Rundberg's office at the moment, and now he found his guess confirmed. Lieutenant Rozescu was indeed a scion of the millionaire's family. But what had he come here for?

"I am not calling on you as a representative of the Rozescu manufacturing interests, nor as a scholar, but as Lieutenant Rozescu— of B II. You know what that is, do you not, Domnule Rundberg?"

"What would I have to do with military intelligence?"

"I intend to explain," Rozescu said. "Naturally I cannot ask you to drop your guard; that would be a stupid request to make of anyone. But some two weeks ago you spoke with a—let us call him an official—and gave him certain information about Ludovic Alda."

"I have nothing to add to what I have already said, Dr. Rozescu," Rundberg said. "The man in question—"

"I don't know him. I'm here on an independent assignment. It is not even strictly for B II." He broke off. "Perhaps it will be helpful to you if I tell you that Lieutenant Colonel Rananu, who will be heading the investigation here, is a very close friend of Alda's, and that he is convinced that all the charges against him are untrue and—"

"I can hardly be of help, Dr. Rozescu. Perhaps if you would tell me what you're interested in, or better, ask me direct questions, I'll answer them—if I can."

"That's just it. I want you to feel that you may answer them without reserve. My mission is to help Alda. You see, he has an enemy who, unfortunately, is extremely powerful."

"Who'd be his enemy? Do you know Alda, Dr. Rozescu? No decent person could be his enemy!"

"This isn't a decent person. Not at all. He's a devil—a stupid devil." Rozescu spoke with emotion, and Rundberg was almost persuaded that the emotion was genuine. But might not the slight, scholarly Lieutenant be acting? After all, he must have certain gifts in that direction, if he was connected with B II.

"What are your questions, Dr. Rozescu?" he said soberly.

"Good, I'll ask them. Have you any knowledge, or can you recall, where Alda was during the months of July to October, 1920, Domnule Rundberg? That might be most significant."

"The summer of 1920? So long ago? He usually spent his summers in Aldeni. One moment—1920!" Rundberg reflected. Aha —that was it. Alda had not appeared in Aldeni until late that autumn. Now he knew what they were after. The pogroms in the Ukraine, of course. He had discussed them with Alda, and Alda had taken off. But where had they dug up that old story? "I'm quite certain that Alda was in Aldeni at the time—yes, dead certain. Oh, of course; on November 4—the date sticks in my mind—there was a steeplechase at Count Scaglieri's in Cadunesti."

"Good, very good. Where did you say the steeplechase was?"

"At Count Mastino Scaglieri's estate."

"That was in November, so naturally Alda must have trained at Aldeni from about July on, I assume? He always took his riding very seriously, did he not, Domnule Rundberg?"

"Certainly, Dr. Rozescu. You know the Jewish high holidays, New Year, the Day of Atonement and the Feast of Tabernacles— they're always in the autumn, September and October, and I spent them with my parents. My mother was still living then—I wasn't married yet. I watched Alda school his horses. I can even tell you the name of his horse, Frumos—a white horse, white as milk. He was a gift of Baron Radu Candomir."

"You have an excellent memory," Rozescu said gravely. "That's first-rate. Since you mention Baron Candomir—did he also take part in the steeplechase?"

"Of course. He would certainly remember."

"Did he by any chance train with Alda?"

"He will certainly not have forgotten that, Dr. Rozescu."

"I hope not," Rozescu said, in a detached tone of voice and without looking at Rundberg. "Who else could we call on as witnesses? I mean, who else could confirm that Alda took part in the steeplechase and, more important still, that he was here training beforehand?"

"All the gentlemen who were present—and old Gheorghe. He's still at Aldeni, working for Domnule Tomescu, the present owner. Gheorghe was in service under Coane Alda's grandfather."

"Good, very good. That's all highly interesting, Domnule Rundberg. Now I must know: what made Alda sell his estate?"

"He was badly in debt, Dr. Rozescu."

"It would be useful if there were some proof that debts were paid off afterwards. That's only a detail, of course, but one which would carry weight."

"I myself could name at least ten businessmen to whom my father paid out sizable sums. Of course there were a number of other creditors, but my father would know the whole list."

"But your father has left the country, has he not?"

"He could furnish you with whatever data you want. In three weeks at the latest."

"I don't think that will be necessary. Your father arranged the sale, and the new owner took possession after Alda left. Is that right?"

"Yes, that's right, Dr. Rozescu," Rundberg said, his eyes sad.

"You were very close to Domnule Alda, weren't you?"

"We grew up together. I'm a few years older than he is, and there is a difference between a Jew and a boyar, but Coane Alda never made me feel it."

"I understand. Did he speak to you about his departure?"

"He mentioned it. He traveled a good deal."

"So I've read. In the agent's report."

"Now I understand. Then the gentleman who came to investigate was from B II—"

"No, Domnule Rundberg, he was not from B II. He was—just sent here. He wasn't even a proper agent at the time."

"To tell the truth, this man Popescu or Popovici—"

"Like master, like man—an old proverb. Popovici is a henchman of Alda's enemy. He has no connection with B II."

"Nevertheless B II is launching this investigation only on the basis of the collection of lies this fellow Popovici brought back."

"They weren't all lies, unfortunately. That's the worst of it, of course. You understand, the Second Bureau had to proceed, because it didn't receive the information from Popovici but from a person in high position. It's our duty to investigate even if the situation is not as this gentleman imagines."

"May I ask who this enemy of Alda's is, Dr. Rozescu?"

"Secretary General Orest Danghu of the Ministry of the Interior."

"Aha, that *is* a high position. And a dangerous one!"

"Yes. But we are doing our best to work in the other direction. There's another matter. Popovici brought the report—B II doesn't put any stock in it. And the Secretary General doesn't either, much as he would like to."

"Yes?" Rundberg asked, seeing that his visitor was still temporizing.

"You see, word has come in that a man whose description fits Alda was shot at the border some time after midnight on November thirtieth. A man whose left hand was bandaged."

"Bandaged—his left hand? Then—" Rundberg's brave efforts to sound unruffled were suddenly inadequate.

"It could, of course, be pure fantasy, based on the doctor's testimony."

"Yes, that's possible . . ." Rundberg said lamely.

"What would Alda have been doing at the border, eh?" Rozescu asked casually.

"Yes," Rundberg repeated, conscious of having revealed his agitation, "what would he have been doing at the border?"

"But where can he be now? It has been established that he didn't cross any of the frontiers—legally, at any rate."

"Then he's certainly in the country. After all, he has no way of knowing that he is being looked for. Perhaps no thorough search has even been made for him."

"That seems to be the case. Secretary Danghu prefers to have it that way. But I suspect that a search is really on for Alda and his fiancée. She, too, has suddenly vanished."

"What do you mean by that, Dr. Rozescu?"

"Those are the words used in the report. There's no doubt that she'll be looked for, and if she's found, she'll have a rough time of it. It would be much better if she were not found."

"I understand."

"Good, very good. I shall try to keep in touch with you. Perhaps I'll be able to pass on some useful information—especially about the bandaged hand. I know you're concerned."

"I'm grateful to you, Dr. Rozescu."

"Not at all. It has been a pleasure, Domnule Rundberg." Rozescu stood up and shook hands with Rundberg.

They all took him seriously, whether they knew him or not—Eugeniu Popovici, who shortly before had been Jenica the Gambler, and who had achieved far more than he had ever hoped for: the position of government agent on a fixed salary, directly under the Secretary General of the Ministry of the Interior. But Jenica took himself more seriously than anyone else did. And so he held forth at the lunch given by the entrancing widow Sandescu—Aurora—in his honor. For it turned out to be quite an affair. Important personages with their wives were among the guests, and he was introduced, as Director Eugeniu Popovici, to a General Manager Munteanu and a boyar, Filievici, to whom the others spoke alternately in German and Romanian, addressing him as Herr or Domnule or Baron. Baroness Filievici was extremely elegant, aristocratic and aloof, although her necklace and bracelets did not seem quite so magnificent as those of the general manager's wife—who was younger, blonder, a good deal more appealing and more approachable. Jenica had to absorb a great deal very rapidly; he pieced out what he could from the general conversation, for as yet he had had no chance at a tête-à-tête with his hostess.

The gay, jovial, worldly and obviously very rich general manager went to the sideboard and poured the drinks. The beverage was not the usual zuica, although its color was the same. It smelled different and tasted different. Or rather, it did not taste, it burned; it seared throat, gullet and guts. Ah yes, in these parts people drank whiskey instead of zuica, Jenica recalled; and although it was only three times as strong as his accustomed drink, it took his breath away. His eyes filled with tears. But the others, including the women, had drained their glasses and helped themselves to some of the warm hors d'oeuvres. And while they nibbled, that devil of a fellow Munteanu had filled the glasses again. "I suppose you aren't used to our spirits, Director Popovici! I know, people from the capital drink zuica. Won't do in this climate of ours, though. Strong drink is what we need for our kind of winter. The second glass goes easier, slides down like oil."

Jenica would have liked to decline. He felt the eyes of the ladies upon him; they waited, holding their glasses. Fingering the diamond on her earlobe, Mme. Munteanu said, "Don't press the gentleman, Victor; perhaps he has to be careful about alcohol. You know, Bucharest people—"

That was too much for Jenica's pride. He tipped his glass, gulped, choked, and quickly gobbled down a morsel of warm, buttery dumpling. In two minutes he felt blissful. He had withstood the ordeal by fire; his stomach was inured now. What could wine with 12 or 14 per cent alcohol do to you after you'd drunk 80-proof whiskey? Not a thing, Jenica thought, as he let the wine run refreshingly down his throat.

And so he ate and drank, and his glass was never empty, and Jenica held forth. He purveyed big-city gossip, political and unpolitical, about women he had never seen, whose houses he allegedly frequented; he mentioned well-known men by their first names, spoke of their habits and vices—in short, he was at home everywhere in the great world. The floor was his; everyone listened enthralled, laughed at his jokes, admired him; he was the center of attention, the hero, and meanwhile he drank. White wine, golden wine, red wine during the meal, and over the coffee cognac and liqueurs mixed, as they were served him.

"Ah yes," General Manager Munteanu said, "that's the way it is in the capital. I go to Bucharest pretty often, but you have to have the right connections. What good is money if you spend most of your time with the peasants in these mountains?"

"Right you are," the Baron agreed.

"Yes," Munteanu resumed, "I've made up my mind that if what everyone is saying is true—"

"You can depend on that, sir. I know what you mean, and we are going along."

"Forgive my doubts, Director Popovici—but I'm highly skeptical. I own a newspaper too—not that it goes in for politics; it's more of a trade paper, specializing in lumber export—that's my field."

"I follow you, Domnule Munteanu. But my field is—" The Director of the Ministry of the Interior lapsed into significant silence.

"Oh, pardon!" General Manager Munteanu said. "I certainly did not mean to contradict, and I have no doubt that you are much better informed. But we are not sure, you understand. . . ."

The Director of the Ministry of the Interior did not understand, but would never have admitted it. "I understand, and I, Eugeniu Popovici, the right-hand man of Orest Danghu—I need not tell you what that means. . . ."

A respectful silence settled upon the circle. Munteanu turned to their hostess. "Aurora, my dear, you certainly are in luck. What a connection! My respects. Orest Danghu! Yesterday and today all the newspapers have been full of him."

"Oh yes, the alert," Jenica said nonchalantly. "Well, yes, I do have some influence over him, for he needs me. There are, you understand, certain gentlemen who must—"

"I suppose you are here on an assignment from the Ministry right now," the Baron blurted out in his provincial Romanian.

The general manager favored the landowner with a reproachful look. "Such questions are best not asked, Bruno. It stands to reason that so high an official would not travel out here to the sticks for pleasure. If that were what he was looking for, he'd go to Sinaia."

Everyone laughed.

"I can well believe that!" the hostess exclaimed. "When I win my case, I'll go to Sinaia too, but not alone. I give you my word on that."

Here was another reason for a round of toasts. The glasses were emptied, and promptly filled again. "Ah yes," Munteanu said. "Connections are everything."

"Ah yes," the Baron said profoundly, taking a sip of cognac. "Everything."

The Director of the Ministry of the Interior also drank his cognac and told a few stories to illustrate the principle that connections were everything. The principal actors in these stories were always Secretary General Danghu and himself. He had only to go to the telephone to obtain anything he wanted from Danghu, that is, from the Blaze. Yes, that was what he was called among his intimates. A handsome, polished, and a very rich man—that was the Blaze for you. Yes, yes.

"Of course a man must be worthy of such a connection, Director Popovici. The Secretary General must know that he can rely on you," Munteanu said earnestly.

"Naturally," Jenica agreed without false modesty. He strengthened himself from his freshly filled glass. "Naturally. Precisely the reason he's sent me here. I was here once before, somewhat more than a week ago, to investigate. A top-secret affair, let me tell you. My specialty is working alone, without any help. Found out all we needed to know. And now a whole commission has come here on the basis of my information—colonels from B II, chief inspectors from the Sigurantza. All on orders from the Secretary General. And I am supervising the investigation."

"Here in Cernauti, in Bucovina! Why, Director Popovici, I can scarcely believe that. A top-secret political matter, you say? But we are all loyal and patriotic citizens here." Munteanu sounded offended. The Baron stared thoughtfully into his glass, and the women were chatting about something that seemed to amuse them enormously. They looked as if they had lost all interest in the subject.

Eugeniu Popovici was upset. What a nerve this man Munteanu had to question the one item of truth he had spoken today. "Sir," he said sharply, flushing, "I said that I was here investigating a top-secret political matter, that there is a whole commission here to look into it, and that I will or will not approve the commission's work. It depends entirely on me. I am here on special assignment." Jenica spoke rather thickly, stumbling over his alcohol-numbed tongue.

"No reason to take offense," Munteanu said, and suddenly he was no longer respectful; he employed that tone of insolent courtesy which most plainly expresses doubt. "No reason at all. I wasn't doubting your word. I was only saying that as a native Bucoviner and a good Romanian, I can vouch for the people in these parts."

"In Bucharest we know all about your native Bucoviners and

good Romanians," Jenica's rash, drunken tongue retorted.

The general manager's face grew somber. "Director Popovici, I am a Romanian, an officer in the Reserve and the head of a hundred-per-cent Romanian organization. Ask around about *Mountains and Woods*—that's the name of my newspaper—if you please. I am a Romanian to the core; wherever you cut, Romanian blood will flow!" He stretched out his arm in an extravagant gesture. "I cannot permit such an insult to the Romanians of Bucovina. If you were to say that Ruthenians, Poles or Jews may not be loyal—very well. But the Romanians of Bucovina are to a man patriotic and loyal—I repeat."

"And I tell you that it is poppycock. Director Eugeniu Popovici of the Ministry of the Interior ought to know."

"In that case, sir—" Munteanu reached into his breast pocket and took out several bundles of brand-new bank notes. Five, six, still more. Jenica could not count them so quickly. But he saw the bundle that was placed on the table before him, and he saw the denomination on the band—fifty thousand. He stared at it hypnotized. "Here," he heard Munteanu saying, "here is fifty thousand—a trifle, nothing at all. But you need wager only five hundred against it. A hundred to one, Director Popovici: if you can give me the name of one Romanian of Bucovina who is disloyal, you've won the bet. I know them all. I'm not only a businessman, remember; I also own a newspaper."

"Sorry, very sorry, you've lost your bet," Jenica said, pocketing the fifty thousand. Now the money was in his breast pocket, and he looked at the general manager, the taciturn Baron and the women. But none of them showed the slightest excitement; they all behaved as though fifty thousand didn't mean a thing. "Do you know Ludovic Alda, boyar, reserve officer, sportsman? Alda, born in Aldeni? He is a Bolshevist agent, has direct connections with Moscow. Been one for years. Right now the matter is being investigated, and I'm checking to see that the investigation is conducted properly. Now you know the truth, Domnule Munteanu, and you, Baron, and you, my dear ladies."

Whatever Jenica the Gambler may have expected, he was bowled over at the storm of laughter that broke out. The proud general manager who had argued so energetically laughed as Jenica had never seen anyone laugh before. The Baron, who had scarecely spoken a word, the aristocratic, aloof Baroness, even the hostess, whom Jenica was already calling Aurora in his mind—all of them dropped every bit of reserve. They laughed unrestrainedly; they roared, giggled, screeched, bubbled over with mirth.

"That was well turned"—Munteanu spoke for them all—"a

marvelous joke. Ah, the wit of Bucharest. Another joke like that and I'll be carried out on a stretcher. Bravo, Director Popovici!"

"What joke?" Jenica snarled. "Who's joking? I'm in dead earnest!"

The others laughed again, though not quite so hard.

"Now, that's enough," the hostess declared. "I'll ring for coffee."

"No coffee," Jenica said rudely, mouthing his words. He was dead drunk by now. "No, nothing. Take care, you don't know who I am! The boyar is a Bolshevik, I said, and the Blaze knows it and Zernescu and Barbulescu, and Dumitriu, he's dismissed; I arranged it all." By now Jenica had so identified with his part as director that he no longer knew who he was. "Yes, I arranged it," he repeated. "Yes." He retched and let his head droop. He felt just awful.

Munteanu took charge of him. He propelled him across the room and down the corridor to the bathroom, and there he left him to his rebelling stomach.

Munteanu returned quickly, placing his finger to his lips. "Pretend nothing has happened, Rusia," he said to the professor's widow. He spoke in German. "Have you a sedative? He must sleep. So far everything's gone well. When he comes to, he won't remember. We're not through with him yet; he musn't leave before a messenger comes from Karl. We'll keep him here."

"What do you mean, here?" Rusia asked. "Not here in my apartment?"

"Where else? We'd already decided that."

"Nothing's been decided. I won't stay alone with *him*."

"He won't hurt you, Rusia."

"Won't hurt me? He'd strangle me and clean out the apartment. I know the type."

"What can we do? They're counting on your keeping him."

"You know I never fail you. If you'll stay—all right. But alone—never."

"No, Victor, that's really asking too much of her," Munteanu's wife said. "And what would be the sense? He'd leave tomorrow, in any case. We can put him to bed. If he gets up sober, we can play cards with him, and then—"

"You're right, Gina. He has all that money—he wasn't so drunk as to give it back." Munteanu looked at his watch. "Nearly six. We must put him to bed. When he wakes up, we'll keep him at cards as long as possible."

"Do you want to win from him? Your own money?"

"He'll win to his heart's content," Munteanu said. He was unable to continue, for Jenica returned to their midst. Green in the face, with eyes watering, hair tousled, necktie disarranged. The Director did not look good and he smelled even worse. He dropped onto a chair and remained there, sitting dejectedly, with bowed head, hands in trousers' pockets. At a sign from Munteanu the hostess approached him.

"You seem not to be feeling well, Director Popovici," she said tenderly.

"Not well at all," he whimpered.

"All night on that train and drinking a bit too much."

"Too much train ride." He tried to lift his head, but failed.

"Why don't you lie down now? Let me give you a bromide, and in half an hour you'll be in fine fettle again."

"Yes, lie down," Jenica moaned.

He drank, though reluctantly, a water glass full of a milky liquid, and then the two men led him into the room beside the bath. They settled him on the sofa, and he fell asleep almost as soon as his head touched the bolster.

"That wasn't provided for in the program, but it isn't bad either. While he sleeps, we can amuse ourselves. Poker?"

"But on the level!" said the Baroness. She was the wife of Bruno, Baron de Filievici, who ran a small farm, all that was left to him of the wealth he had inherited from his father and lost, largely in playing nashi-vashi. His chief occupation was being a member of the Rundberg organization—for his property lay on the former Polish border. His wife Mary, a blond Sudeten German, had been forewoman in a textile factory before she married.

"Fine, let's play to pass the time," Mme. Munteanu said.

"I'm with you," Aurora agreed. Her life had been varied, to say the least; she had been a children's nursemaid, a waitress, a nightclub hostess, and had ended by marrying Professor Sandescu, the celebrated magician. Of course the title of professor as well as a number of decorations had been bestowed upon Sandescu by himself. His magician's tricks and props had proved useful in smuggling, with the result that he had formed close ties with Rundberg. He had been forty years older than his wife and in due time had died, leaving her a sizable fortune. Rusia—who changed her name to Aurora after she became a Romanian citizen—had kept up the connection with Rundberg. She had long proved herself a useful and quick-thinking member of the organization.

The Baron was not minded to play in the same game as his wife. Besides, he didn't really care for poker. The only game that really held him was nashi-vashi. He picked up a German newspaper—he was Ruthenian by birth—and began to read. The others sat down around the table for an honest game of poker.

All the members of the commission turned up at Major Tarno-vietzchi's office with amazing punctuality. The Major was there to receive Stanescu, the Chief of the Sigurantza, who arrived accompanied by his adjutant, Lieutenant Ciobotariu. At their heels came Inspectors Zernescu and Stratilescu. They had barely exchanged views on the increasing cold when Lieutenant Colonel Rananu and Lieutenant Rozescu entered. A soldier served the turceasca. The Major invited the group to take seats at the oblong table. A brief, courteous dispute arose between Chief Inspector Stanescu and Lieutenant Colonel Rananu as each tried to assign the other the chairman's seat. Rananu won this little contest, and Stanescu, honored and gratified, took his seat at the head of the table. Rananu sat at his right, Zernescu at his left, Stratilescu beside Rananu, Rozescu across the table, and Lieutenant Ciobotariu beside the latter. Major Tarnovietzchi sat at the far end of the table, facing the Chief Inspector.

"Gentlemen," Stanescu began, taking from his briefcase a number of typewritten pages, "here are your copies of the communication I have received from the Ministry of the Interior." He signaled to Ciobotariu, who took them and distributed them to the members of the commission. All were marked *Secret*. "Lieutenant Ciobotariu will read the report aloud. Please compare your own texts. Then we will proceed."

The Commissioner read aloud the report that Dumitriu had read to Rananu and Rozescu the day before. Rananu asked for the floor.

"Gentlemen," he began, "before we proceed, I should like to make a statement. The man whom we are commissioned to investigate is or was my friend. I have been on the best of terms with him for over twenty years. He is a captain in the reserve and comes from an illustrious Romanian family. He was raised by his grandfather, the famous patriot Neagoe Alda, for his own parents died in his infancy. Although all my personal feelings resist belief in the charges against him, as an army officer and patriot I am obligated to look into them. Hence I shall take part in this investgiation solely in my capacity as an officer and patriot. I cannot be Ludovic Alda's friend if he is a traitor to his country, and if he is that, I can only hope that the bullet of the brave border guard struck him. But if we should discover that Alda is still living, but has betrayed his country—if he is still going about his treacherous business and dares to appear here again, then, gentlemen, I shall make short work of him. I myself would be the first to send a bullet through his heart."

The impact of these words was plain to see on the faces of everyone in the room. "You have spoken like a true Romanian, Colonel," Stanescu said. "My admiration for you is all the greater because I can sense the personal sorrow that lies behind your words. For us, too, the case of Alda is a difficult problem, for we are all reluctant to believe that such a man would be capable of betraying his country. For that reason we wish to conduct the investigation with the utmost conscientiousness, and make sure that truth triumphs."

All seemed agreed and all seemed impressed—each in his own fashion and with his own mental reservations.

Rananu broke the silence. "First of all, let us reassess the testimony of the border guard Posteuca. I suggest that our first step is to go to the border."

The single-car train which was to take the commission to the border arrived at the railroad station in Cernauti at 9:43. Among the few passengers who got out of it was Max Duttner. He moved as rapidly as his bulk permitted toward the exit, sprang into a sleigh, and begged the driver to hurry. The horses took the rise that led to the town at a sharp trot. They slowed to a walk only when they got to the Piatza Fântânei (why it was called that, no one could say, for no fountain had ever been seen there), the entrance to the Jewish quarter. At this point three sleighs driven by soldiers met Duttner's hired sleigh. He recognized Stanescu, Stratilescu, Ciobotariu and the Major, and his alert intelligence instantly concluded who the others must be, and where they were going. A pity to waste the time, boyars, he thought; there's a cold wind blowing in Serafintza. He chuckled to himself. There was a touch of malice in his smile.

His round face was still beaming when he delivered his report to a relieved Rundberg. "I went straight to Gershon Hermelin and had a talk with him. Because he should have known about any such incident. But he didn't know a thing. Still and all, I waited until Private Craciun turned up—he's our man. I talked to him about this and that, didn't want to come straight out with it and tell him what it was about—and then he began of his own accord, complaining that business has dropped off in the last two months; money's getting scarce and why don't we give him little jobs any more. At which I said that business wasn't safe any more. In the first place three men hadn't come back, and in the second place a soldier in his own platoon had shot and killed someone on November thirtieth. Then he said, 'Domnule,' he said, 'if I didn't know you were a

decent sort, I'd give it to you straight and tell you that you're looking for the horseshoes of dead horses. There hasn't been anybody
shot at this part of the border. I've been stationed here since the first
of September. There's been some shooting, it's true, but nobody's
been hit.' And he crossed himself three times like a priest over holy
water and swore that what he said was God's honest truth. I felt a
lot better hearing that, and was able to think out my questions more
clearly. Gershon brought wine and salami, and we ate and drank;
but the thing was on his mind, and he asked me how I came to hit
on the thirtieth of November and said he could check on what happened on that date, because he keeps the platoon's records. He got
up before he'd even finished his glass and brought the book. There
I read with my own eyes: from six o'clock in the evening to six in
the morning on November thirtieth—*fără evenimente* [no incidents].
The report was signed by Craciun and First Lieutenant Virgil Popovici—you know him too, Karl. So I said, 'Brother Craciun, you're a
good fellow; you know how to keep your mouth shut. Nose around
your platoon a bit and find out who told that cock-and-bull story
about a man's being shot here on the night of November thirtieth. If
it isn't true, maybe we can fix up something; there are people who
want to take goods across and we could bring some things from
over there.' In short, his mouth began to water and he toddled off.

"I played casino with Gershon, lost three games—cost me three
thousand—and then Craciun came back with a border guard. 'This
is Private Posteuca,' he said, and we invited the fellow to sit down
and eat and drink with us. And then, slowly, inch by inch, the whole
story came out. It seems that somewhat more than a week ago a
brother or cousin from Bucharest called on Lieutenant Popovici,
the commander of the squad. The Lieutenant was not especially
overjoyed at the visit. He plied his guest with food, wine and cigarettes, but when the guest wanted to stay overnight, the Lieutenant
balked. It wouldn't do, he said; this was a border area and if there
were an inspection, *vai de capul lui*—he'd be out of luck! So the
cousin had to leave, and the Lieutenant sent him back in a sleigh.
As it happened, Posteuca was the driver. They got to talking, Posteuca and his passenger; it's a good hour's drive to the station, and
there was a long wait for the train besides. You see, the Lieutenant
had told the guard to wait and make sure that his passenger took
that train. So they went to the tavern near the station. The man from
Bucharest said the Lieutenant was his brother, on the strength of
which our good Posteuca ordered round after round of hot zuica.
When the fellow started saying what a big shot he was in Bucharest,
Posteuca started boasting on his own account: that he's a forester
in civilian life and a sharpshooter and altogether the best shot

in the whole regiment, and how he's always having to tangle with the Bolshevist spies, and how one took him by the throat and he, Posteuca, sent a shot after him on a foggy night and hit him at seven hundred feet. The guy from Bucharest asked whether that wasn't the night of November thirtieth-December first, and since the guard didn't care one way or another, because the story was pure imagination, he asked how the devil he'd known that. Oh, says the guy from Bucharest, I know a lot more than that: that Bolshevik of yours had a bandaged hand; and at this point he ordered another round of zuica, so Posteuca said yes. And because the town clerk of Serafintza happened to come into the tavern at that moment and was wearing a high fur hat, a short fur jacket and boots, Posteuca went ahead and described the Bolshevik as also dressed that way. And then he said he shot the Bolshie dead and the Russians started firing back. Why not? The man from Bucharest was leaving anyhow, and he couldn't be such a big shot as he said or the Lieutenant wouldn't have sent him packing. So that was that." The grin spread over Duttner's face all the way up to his bald pate, and Karl Rundberg grinned back. The two of them laughed long and heartily and were still laughing when Victor Munteanu came barging in on them.

"You seem to be having a good time. I've done my laughing for today." And he recounted the events of the past few hours and Popovici's present sound sleep.

"You mustn't let him out on the street before noon of the day after tomorrow, Victor," Rundberg said. "He could ruin everything."

"So I gather. When he comes to, Rusia will phone me here. She'll manage to hold him at least till I come back. Then we'll try to get him involved in a card game."

"What will you play?"

"Poker. He comes from Regat, where they all play poker."

"That ought to keep him busy. If he plays through the night, he'll be dead tired by tomorrow morning. But keep him with you when you leave. Take him to a hotel and then—"

"How long do you plan to keep this guy in protective custody?" Duttner asked, laughing.

"Don't laugh, Max. Once he's on the loose, he can make plenty of trouble."

"He won't make any trouble, Karl. I have an idea."

Duttner outlined his plan.

Adolf was keeping the bank. He laid out the cards, one to the left, one to the right, one mine, one yours. But he was scarcely looking at the table. He was feeling dull, uninterested, for this was no real game, no good players, nothing but tinhorns, punks without any nerve. They wanted to play as long as possible with a few chips, and quit as soon as they won. Adolf wasn't even taking in enough to cover expenses. Where was Duttner? Where was the Baron? Where was Munteanu? Where were the boys with money? And where was Rundberg, who had bled the bank so heavily yesterday? The deal was over. As he shuffled, Adolf stole a look around the circle and observed that at the whole table the bets didn't amount to 5 per cent of what the bank had lost yesterday.

Adolf lazily shuffled, cigarette in the corner of his mouth, and laid the cards in the middle of the table for the start of the deal. But before the croupier could begin his litany, the waiter entered the room and beckoned to Adolf. He stood up and the croupier took his place; the changeur took over the croupier's job. As Adolf hurried from the room, he caught the words "Queen of hearts at the bottom. Place your bets, please; everything goes."

In a kind of storeroom, heaped high with cans, bags and boxes, a man was waiting for him, the worn velvet collar of his thin coat turned up high. He was Nyaf (*Knafel*—dregs); that was the only name anyone knew for him. Without any change of expression on his starved-looking face, he whispered, "At Sandescu's, Grădinelor 11, big game. A man from Bucharest is keeping the bank. The Baron, Monteanu, Duttner and Rundberg are betting. A few strangers and some women I don't know—huge stakes. I've already had eight hundred in expenses," he appended.

"I'll take care of it," Adolf said. "Right away." He left the storeroom. Nyaf followed him. "Wait at the other door for me; you'll get your money." Adolf showed no excitement. He was relieved at having found the answer to the riddle. This was a matter he'd soon take care of. Tomorrow they'd all be doing their betting here. What kind of Bucharester, though? Since when had the Bucharesters taken to playing nashi-vashi?

Jenica had watched just one deal and recognized it. He liked this game better than poker. At poker you needed an assistant to take the gulls, whereas with his game you just marked a few cards. Jenica the Gambler had a quick enough eye to recognize where they lay, so that he could play them or let them pass. He would place his bets cautiously, he resolved, not too high and not too low. He had a good-sized stake; he would win two or three cards a deal, and when he'd accumulated a bit of a pile, he'd use his winnings to take over the bank. Because then, then he could work efficiently. Then he could make the passes, place his marks—an enormous advantage over these gulls. The new arrival, that Jew with the bald head, seemed to have a wad of money. He tossed twenty or thirty thousand down on a card and laughed whether he won or lost.

The Baron, too, and the three women, played lightly and for high stakes. He should be able to win half a million, if not a full million, here—easy as eating bread and butter. (Apropos eating, that had been a marvelous supper. *Grătar*—good, grilled, sharply spiced meat, and all those pickled things along with it, and then that first-rate beer!) Jenica was feeling great and had forgotten the afternoon's fiasco—all the more so since no one reminded him of it. Everyone had been respectful, Domnule Director this and Domnule Director that, and the professor's widow, his Aurora, had thrown him tender glances full of sweet promises. But that was not to the point now; this was the time for business. He could rake in enough to hold him for a long time to come, and all his old instincts were marshaled to that end. In his excitement he had quite forgotten that he had come to this delightful city where everything turned out so well for him on a special assignment—for the Ministry of the Interior.

He had taken over the bank, at the urging of the others, and was laying the cards on the table. The bets were made, and he began turning the cards up. Left, right, mine, yours; and in each rectangle lay a great deal of money. The scene was perfect; every confirmed nashi-vashi player would have been in seventh heaven. Suddenly the bell rang.

The cook, who had just served turceasca, went to open the door, and fifteen seconds later a slim, ruddy-complexioned man in the black uniform of a ranking police officer stood in the room. Behind him, carbines in their hands, were two patrolmen. "In the name of the law," the officer said, "you are all under arrest. No one move!" He didn't say this; he roared it. He was famous for his roaring, was Secretary Rosariu of the criminal police; famous, notorious and feared, according to the persons involved. Everyone froze at the sound of that voice. The women sat numbed; the men—Duttner, Munteanu and the Baron—had leaped to their feet, but now stood rigid. And Jenica, the Director of the Ministry of the Interior, at whom all were staring as their savior, who could arrange everything with a word—Jenica sat dumbfounded, with a look of utter fatalism. For this had happened to him all too often; he had been arrested innumerable times. Jenica the Gambler had been through it all; he knew the whole story. That was how it always ended. Gone the glory, gone the beautiful dream.

"Ladies and gentlemen, come with us," Secretary Rosariu said somewhat more mildly, in his rough Bucovina Romanian. Where-upon a babble of protest arose, especially among the women. The loudest of all was the professor's widow, Aurora, but she appealed not to the uniformed representative of the state, but to her guest of honor, who stood on a far higher step in the bureaucratic hierarchy.

"Speak up, won't you, Domnule Director?" she screeched.

Rosariu looked sharply at the person in question. He was an old hand, had risen from the ranks. If Rusia, whose whole career he knew well, but who had never before come into conflict with the law, addressed this fellow as a director—when Rosariu would have taken him for a pickpocket or a confidence man who preyed on peasants—if she referred to him for help against himself, the power-ful head of the criminal police, he'd better find out who he was. "What kind of director?" he inquired. In a much moderated voice, of course.

"You'll get yourself into hot water," Rusia said. "Domnule Di-rector Popovici is from the Ministry of the Interior. He is a con-fidential agent of Secretary General Danghu."

"I'm only doing my duty," Rosariu explained, insuring himself against possible trouble. He was no longer roaring; his voice had be-come quite dulcet. He looked at the Director and said very politely, "May I see your credentials, Domnule . . . ?"

But all the courage had drained out of Jenica. Faced with the uniform and the carbines, he was no longer the Director of the Min-istry of the Interior. He could play that part to gullible women and dull provincials, but not to the police. Now he was once more Jenica the Gambler, who always had some black mark against him and therefore was always afraid. A fine castle in Spain had collapsed, and he was buried under its ruins. What good were his genuine creden-tials and the badge he had in his pocket? Could he dare to show it? What was an agent against a headquarters secretary, and how could he explain his presence here in particular and in the city in general? Had not Inspector Barbulescu impressed him with the necessity of remaining in the background? And what about the Blaze? Could he refer to those two? They would drop him like a hot potato, if any inquiries were made. Jenica saw a black future before him. More-over, he was completely shamed before Aurora, and the other ladies and gentlemen, who were looking at him with undisguised dismay.

Rosariu, that excellent policeman, saw that his first idea about this bird had been the right one. He was once more his formidable self, as he bellowed at the top of his voice, "We'll take care of all this at headquarters."

* * *

Sleighs were quickly forthcoming from the village authorities, and they set out for the border. Everyone was well wrapped in the huge fur coats that Major Tarnovietzchi had borrowed from the Tenth Regiment of light cavalry. At their destination First Lieutenant Virgil Popovici reported to Major Tarnovietzchi, as he had been instructed to do by telephone. Although he couldn't make out what special case the commission wanted to investigate, he dutifully led them on an inspection of the guarded point at the border and then warmed them up in his headquarters with mulled wine and hot zuica. Two tables were placed together for the members of the commission, and the interrogation began. It proceeded far more circumstantially than the easygoing investigation that Max Duttner had conducted with Craciun and Posteuca some hours before—but the results were exactly the same.

The facts in the case remained what they were: a bit of boasting, inspired by an excess of zuica; the key points of the tale had been put into the mouth of the border guard by the man from Bucharest. He had lied, and Posteuca had repaid him with lies. Ciobotariu scribbled notes; Rozescu took the testimony down in shorthand. The pages filled rapidly with questions and answers; but the result remained the same. By and by the members of the commission had no further questions to ask of Posteuca.

Lieutenant Virgil Popovici was once more called before the examiners.

"Do I understand that you are related to Domnule Eugeniu Popovici, Lieutenant?" Rananu asked. The others, especially Zernescu, listened with sharpened attentiveness.

The Lieutenant looked sheepish. "I beg your pardon, sir, but it isn't my fault. He's my stepbrother—we had the same father. I've never been in touch with him. Unfortunately he is—"

"Why did he come to see you?"

"Because he had no money for the return trip. I gave him a thousand lei and sent him back right away."

"Why so fast?"

"Because he causes trouble wherever he goes. He borrows money, defrauds, cheats at cards. I've never had anything to do with him since I left home at fourteen and entered the military academy. He's a real no-good, sir, and has done time more than once."

"Thank you, Lieutenant."

Secretary Titus ("Titi") Rosariu settled with the other gamblers quickly enough. They were all people from town. They realized that an affair of this sort would cost something to straighten out, and made no fuss about it. The women were quickly released. Rosariu didn't want to make a big stink about it; that wasn't in his interest. There was a pretty sum in the leather bag; to the Secretary, that was what mattered. The interrogation developed into a friendly conference and ended in a horse trade. They finally agreed on a division of the spoils: one-third for the Secretary, two-thirds for the gamblers.

But there remained the problem of the man from Bucharest, who sat apathetically on a chair in the anteroom, under guard. Who was he? What all the others had said was sheer nonsense. Director in the Ministry of the Interior—ridiculous! Here, if you please, was the official register of the Ministry of the Interior for 1940. All the officials were listed, the higher ones with photos and brief biographies. Where was there any Eugeniu Popovici? Popovici, yes, there were even three with that name—but no director and no Eugeniu. And were Duttner or Munteanu trying to tell him, Rosariu, that they'd believed the fraud?

"It seemed a little odd to me," Munteanu said. He and the Secretary were old friends. "We can't blame Rusia—I mean Doamna Professor Sandescu—for being taken in. She was too eager, I guess, hoping for help in her inheritance suit. But I was suspicious from the very beginning. This man is a cardsharper, no doubt about it."

"Do you want to appear as a witness, Victor?" Rosariu asked, winking.

"What do you need me for? Open the bag, Titi; the cards are in it. If they're all right, let him go, or hold him until Bucharest reports on him. But if they've been marked, turn him over to the court, because then you've got proof that he pretended to be a director and struck up acquaintance with people in order to take them to the cleaners."

Secretary Rosariu reached for the leather bag which lay at his feet like an obedient dog. He found six marked cards.

The next step was to count the money. There was a total of 365,000 lei. That made 120,000 for the Secretary, 240,000 for the victims of the wicked cardsharper from Bucharest, and 2,500 apiece for the two patrolmen. A fair division.

"What are you going to do with the Director of the Ministry of the Interior, Titi?" Munteanu asked.

"With that bird?" The Secretary yawned. "Not a thing, at the moment. I'll just lock him up. In the afternoon Laurentiu will question him. I'll look at the file tomorrow, and then make up my mind." He pressed a button and told the policeman who entered to put the fellow behind bars.

The three of them stepped out into the street together. "It's gotten to be four o'clock by now," Munteanu said. "What do you say we kill one more bottle?"

"Fine," Duttner said, and Rosariu let himself be persuaded.

The idea of spending the night in Serafintza had no allure for any of the members of the commission. All were in favor of returning to the city by the first train, at three forty-five in the morning, and Lieutenant Popovici soon rounded up three sleds and a great heap of robes. The night was extremely cold, but with the robes and their borrowed fur coats they reached the railroad station only half frozen. The train was there, beautifully heated, and second class was clean and comfortable. Before they knew it, they were back in Cernauti. All were hungry by then and decided to get themselves something to eat. Afterwards they would hold a brief session in the Chief Inspector's office and draw up the program for the afternoon; it was obvious that all of them would want to sleep through the morning.

At Stratilescu's suggestion, the commission went to the Eremitage, the only place open at that hour. They were received by the white-haired waiter Osias, who placed them at the big table just off the dance floor.

At several of the other tables sat women who proceeded, when so many men entered, to renovate their makeup and assume the smiles proper to their profession. The Eremitage was in no way different from innumerable other establishments of the same type. The female performers, though advertised as internationally famous singers and dancers, had the subsidiary duty of luring the clients into drinking as much as possible. Their hopes rose upon seeing this group of well-dressed and evidently substantial men, for as a result of the intense cold it had been a slow night at the Eremitage.

But Osias, white hair parted in the middle, pencil tucked behind his ear, was more pessimistic. Although he included all of them in his obsequious bow, he turned to the big man in black uniform with his question: "What shall it be, coane?"

"We want a good meal and your best wines," Rananu said. "Rozescule," he told his subordinate, "you do the ordering for us." And then he turned his attention to the women.

Rozescu considered the menu and ordered for the party pâté de foie, Wienerschnitzel, salad, compote and chocolate cake with whipped cream. He asked for a good Martell, to warm them up, to be followed by a wine that the wine card—not too credibly—listed as Cotnari.

As Osias trotted off with the order, he had feelings similar to those of Schajeh, the cabman, the night before. The proverb was familiar to him too: It is still night an hour before dawn. He signed to the orchestra leader, and the first bars of Enescu's *Romanian Rhapsody* sounded.

The way to the kitchen led through a tunnel-like corridor. On both sides of this corridor were curtained booths, in one of which Secretary Rosariu, Munteanu and Duttner sat over champagne with three of the women, the most prominent of whom was the singer Marioara. She was the star of the program and had a regular "friend" for the month of her engagement—an official of the Internal Revenue Office who enjoyed a very high income, as he was in charge of the collection of liquor taxes. He left a great deal of money in the nightclub and with Marioara. She was worth it, for she was not only a good singer with a large repertory of Romanian and Russian folksongs and gypsy airs, but she had a good deal of insight into human nature and was, on the whole, an excellent purveyor of those illusions which always find plenty of takers.

Stratilescu hoped to see Marioara and perhaps arrange a rendezvous with her. He could not hope to compete with her official lover. He might acquit himself in looks or other significant masculine qualities; but financially he was out of the running. A Sigurantza man didn't have a chance against a Treasury official. But limited though her time was, Marioara managed to set aside a few hours of romance for the gallant Inspector. After all, he knew the rules and never came empty-handed.

Osias brought the bottle of cognac to the big table, uncorked it, poured, and then—a sign of special confidence—left it standing for his new guests. Then he went into the booth, whose inmates were cloistered from the rest of the nightclub by the corridor and the curtains, and busied himself at the table. He cleared the ashtrays and gave Marioara a sign that she alone saw and understood. And so, when the last notes of the *Romanian Rhapsody* had died away, she stood up and sauntered down from the musicians' dais. Assessing the company at the big table with a quick glance, she murmured a word to the first violinist. In a moment the pianist was playing the introduction of the song hit *"Trenule, Trenutzule"*—"Train, Dear Little Train of Mine," one of the star pieces in Marioara's repertoire. She followed this with *"Tzarancutza*—The Little Peasant Girl"— and then with a French song, *"J'attendrai,"* which was in vogue. Meanwhile the company had been served with food and wine. Their spirits rose, even Zernescu's, and they applauded every selection with great enthusiasm. Marioara, having found a receptive audience, moved nearer to the table, and sang one song after another. The applause grew more fervid, and along with it sounded Rananu's whinnying.

The party was now in full swing. Osias exchanged a questioning look with Rozescu, who replied with an almost imperceptible blinking of his eyelids, and the flow of liquid cheer went on unchecked. But the beverage changed. Rananu invited Marioara to sit down at the table. Champagne foamed; the stag party changed into what Osias called a "real crowd." Ciobotariu and Zernescu downed the champagne like water, and the Major, who knew that the two officers from Bucharest would pay the check, kept up with them— all the more since he was greatly relieved at the turn things had taken. The others were equally sanguine; Stanescu and Stratilescu were pleased with the results of their investigation, and Rozescu was glad to see Rananu in such good spirits. He knew the reason, of course: there was no longer any question of Alda's having been shot. He himself drank heartily, although he was by no means able to keep pace with the others at the table.

There would have been no cloud upon the gaiety if Secretary Rosariu of the criminal police, seated in his booth, had not remembered Marioara. As long as she was singing, he accepted her absence. But now he could no longer hear her, and she hadn't returned to him as he expected. He grew impatient, for he had caught fire. After a good many glasses of champagne, he was seeing the world in a rosy light—all the more since the singer had earlier shown herself amenable to his unequivocal suggestions. Unfortunately, he did not understand the mentality of such women, who would never say no as long as champagne was flowing. But she had already abandoned all thought of keeping her word. These other men were much more to her taste. Above all, here was Stratilescu, whom she knew and appreciated; were it not for the liquor-tax collector, he would certainly have become her protector. As it was, he was a good candidate for second place, which meant a good deal where so desirable a female as Marioara was concerned. But he would be staying in town, and the others were strangers, men from Bucharest; she had seen that at once: the big, manly officer in black whom they addressed as Colonel and the slender, refined Lieutenant with straw-colored hair whom even his seniors treated with marked respect. Ah yes, he would be the one for her, someone for the heart. For there was a tiny corner in that celebrated organ that sometimes proved more powerful than reason, calculation, hard-boiled experience. He sat facing her, smiling, his smooth, youthful face flushed by champagne, laughter and good humor. When people spoke to him, he answered civilly in a choice, polished but never prolix manner. A fine fellow, a decent boy, a darling lover, Marioara thought, and felt a stirring in that tiny corner of her heart. Meanwhile the orchestra was playing her tango: *"Te Iubesc"* ("I love you"), and while she sang the refrain with great expressiveness, she looked across the table at the young man. He answered her look politely, amiably, but not at all tenderly or with any signs of kindling. And precisely this disturbed Marioara, who was accustomed to the frequent and open expression of desire. This cool courtesy demanded nothing, promised nothing. She rose, still singing, and repeating the last words of the refrain in a speaking tone, bowed just as the music ended— bowed with great flourish to the handsome boy, saying, "Since none of the honorable gentlemen has asked me to dance, I take the liberty—"

Lieutenant Rozescu stood up—not too quickly—thanked the lady for the invitation, put his arm around her, and danced the slow French waltz the orchestra had begun. Osias, with his infallible attentiveness and understanding, switched the dance-floor light to blue. It only dimly illuminated that area, and would certainly have provided opportunity for certain preliminaries if Secretary Rosariu's policeman's eyes had not penetrated the dusk. "Doamna," Rosariu roared, "I had invited you, you know," and he took a step toward the couple as though he intended to separate them by force.

The Secretary could have chosen no worse moment to establish his dubious claims. Marioara had just settled into the young man's arm and brought her cheek to within a fraction of an inch of his. At their next turn they would touch, and Marioara knew the reaction, could already feel the sweet, prickling sensation—when the blare of Rosariu's stentorian voice broke the enchantment. Instantly the yielding woman turned into a spitting tigress. She stood still, without freeing herself from Rozescu's arms, and snarled at the disheveled police office. "If you're drunk, go home to bed; don't molest strangers."

Marioara knew she could risk that, for she was Stratilescu's protégée, after all, and as an inspector Stratilescu stood many rungs higher on the ladder of the official hierarchy than a headquarters secretary. Moreover, he was Sigurantza! An ordinary policeman would never dare tangle with a Sigurantza man.

Rosariu, however, was entirely unaware of the presence of high officials in the Sigurantza. For a fraction of a second the insult took his breath away; then he inhaled deeply and roared again, "Doamna Marioara!" At that moment all the lights went on, including the spotlight on the orchestra's dais, its white cone of light directed at the large table. At the same time the musicians played a resounding fanfare. Stunned by the noise and the light, and still more by what the light revealed, the Secretary stood gaping. But he pulled himself together, drew himself to attention in the old Austrian style, facing the table of the big brass, and then hastily made off for the booth, where Munteanu and Duttner were innocently carousing with the two singers. All four of them had gone on drinking at a formidable pace, and they greeted the Secretary with loud and joyful cries, without noticing his consternation.

Rosariu hastily emptied a glass, refilled it, and was beginning to reflect on the possible consequences of this little scene—for he had a good many enemies. But he could not think the matter out, for Osias pulled aside the heavy curtain, bowed politely and said, "Domnule Secretary General"—in good old Austrian fashion he always upped the rank of patrons—"Inspector General Stratilescu wishes to see you."

Rosariu started to his feet, but Stratilescu entered and asked him not to put himself out. The Inspector knew Duttner and Munteanu from Adolf's gambling establishment; he greeted everybody jovially and sat down at the table. A full glass was immediately placed before him.

"Rosariu," the Inspector began after sampling the beverage, "if you would do me personally a great favor—"

"But of course, of course, Domnule Inspector," Rosariu hastened to assure him.

"Then apologize to Marioara. After all, she's an artist, not a streetwalker.

Rosariu's face flamed with embarrassment. "Certainly, Domnule Inspector, at once! I'm terribly sorry."

"Don't apologize to me." Stratilescu smiled suavely. "I've already forgotten the whole thing. But you insulted the lady in the presence of other gentlemen—there are some very important persons from Bucharest, you see—and now she's in tears. It's a pity to spoil everyone's fun."

Rosariu's ardor toward Marioara had been completely repressed by his desire to placate the high society in which she was currently moving. He outdid himself in assuring the Inspector that he would instantly. . . . Stratilescu took another sip from his glass and with a cheerful wave of his hand rejoined his party.

Rosariu went to the washroom, combed his hair and straightened his necktie, buttoned his tunic properly, and proceeded with dignified bearing to the officials' table, where he said his little piece to Marioara. Coaxed by Rananu, and induced by a glance from Rozescu, Marioara softened and with a magnanimous smile extended her hand to the Secretary, who had no choice but to kiss it. Then he turned to Chief Inspector Stanescu and excused himself further:

difficult case, worked all night, under tension. The champagne had made Stanescu more than usually forbearing, and he invited Rosariu to sit down. For lack of any other subject, he asked the Secretary what kind of difficult case he had been working on.

"It's always the same story, Domnule Chief Inspector," Rosariu said. "One of these Bucharest characters wormed his way into a decent house; the lady is a widow. He gave himself out as a Director of the Interior Ministry and fleeced the entire company at cards. With marked cards."

Stanescu's question had been put out of pure politeness and carried with it no obligation to listen. But Zernescu, a policeman to the core, had heard Rosariu's words, and his normally slow-moving mind was soaring on champagne-induced flights. He sought connections and found them. "What is the fellow's name, Domnule Secretary?" he asked.

"He refused to show his credentials, but he'd told his victims that he was Eugeniu Popovici, personal friend and confidant of General Secretary Danghu. Probably the name is just as false as his other statements."

"One moment!" Zernescu bellowed so loudly that the whole nightclub subsided into dead silence. The music stopped abruptly in the middle of a beat. "Where is this Director of the Interior Ministry right now?" he asked in a somewhat lower but still formidable voice.

Rosariu, terrified that he had made another misstep, became quite abject. "I'm sorry, Domnule Inspector. There is ample evidence of crooked gambling—"

"I asked where he is!" Zernescu thundered, in his most professional manner.

"In jail," Rosariu whispered, "but I can—"

"Waiter!" Zernescu turned to Osias, who had come rushing up at his shout. "Bring the biggest bottle of champagne and two of the biggest glasses you have, on my account. Quick!" Bottle and glasses were produced almost instantaneously, and the champagne foamed into the glasses with magical speed.

"My name is Zernescu, Sebi to my friends," the Inspector said, raising his glass and saluting Rosariu.

"And mine is Rosariu—Titus Rosariu, Titi to my friends," the Secretary said, dumbfounded. They embraced and kissed, the orchestra played a fanfare, and everyone cheered so loudly that Munteanu and Duttner emerged from their stall to discover the reason for all this jubilation. They captured Osias, who had witnessed the whole scene, and the waiter—as ebullient as the party because of the enormous increases in the check—briefed them hastily: "There was somebody named Eugenius or something, an Interior director, swindling at cards. And Titi caught him and now they're happy. This is the life, I tell you, this is the life!"

Zernescu was filled with new vigor. "Gentlemen," he said when the general gaiety had subsided somewhat, "we were intending to settle on our program for this afternoon. It's high time we moved on to the Chief Inspector's office. But first I'd like to ask my friend Titi to drive over to the jail with me. Waiter!" He had ordered a bottle and wanted to pay for it. Osias reached his side, but so did Rozescu. "Domnule Inspector," he said gently, "I must beg you to leave this matter to me. It was a great honor to me to be your host, believe me!" And he bowed slightly to Zernescu, who responded with a much deeper bow—to Ilie Rozescu's son!

Osias had the check ready—an imposing column of figures. His conscience was not entirely clear, for he had not only reckoned up the prices exactly as they stood in the wine list (an outrage when dealing with officials of the Sigurantza and police), but had also thrown in several bottles of champagne that hadn't seen the light on this particular evening. The young man, however, paid no attention. He only looked at the sum, 24,700, and wrote his name across it. "Please come to the lobby of the Palace at two this afternoon," he said politely. "I'll settle with you then."

"Thank you, thank you very much, coane," Osias said, although that scarcely expressed his true feelings. He turned away with a despairing expression. Duttner observed it.

"What's the matter, Osias?" he asked.

"I've been had. Food, drink, champagne, and at the end—this!" He pointed to the signature. "I should run after him to the lobby of the Palace? My luck!"

Duttner took the check from Osias's hand. He read the signature, Dr. Rozescu, across the total.

"Here, Osias," he said, "is twenty-five thousand. You needn't go to the Palace. I'll wager that the young man will be your first patron this evening, and will attend to the bill. Not to speak of the baksheesh! If only the two of us could take in this much every night! You don't have to pay me back unless you collect."

"From your mouth into God's ear—you're a nobleman, Domnule Duttner!" Osias exclaimed. That was his highest compliment. He pocketed the money and the check. Duttner then paid his own score. Munteanu was fast asleep. No wonder—this was his second straight night! Duttner awakened him. They were alone; the girls had gone to their dressing rooms. So had Marioara, who was just slipping into her fine fur coat, a present to her from the tax collector. But she wasted no thoughts on the coat, which all the other girls were madly envious of, or on the giver. She was thinking of the slender, well-bred young man. Marioara had fallen head over heels in love once more.

"He's quite good-looking, your acquaintance," Countess Zinnendorf said. "What's his name and where does he come from?"

Martha walked nervously back and forth. "I've only seen him once before," she said. "He was a guest of Radu Candomir's; his name is Bilinski and he's a refugee from Poland. He also visited Aldeni before Lutz left. It seems he knew Father, and Mother too. But what he wants here—" She didn't finish the sentence.

"We won't be on tenterhooks long, Martha. He'll be coming down soon. You think it has something to do with Lutz?"

Martha nodded mutely. She had tears in her eyes.

"Come here, Martha."

"Yes, Aunt."

Martha came over to the chair, and the Countess stood up and took the girl into her arms. "What's wrong with Lutz? I've not asked you until now. You've been here for two months, and not a single letter, no news at all. What's Lutz up to, Martha? Why are you in such despair?"

"That's why, Aunt Agathe. I'm frightened, and longing for him. Two months!"

"But where is he? He must have told you where he was going." She shook her head. "It's really very strange; he must have told you," she repeated.

"No, Aunt Agathe. It's my fault. He wanted to give up his trip. I knew in my bones that it was something very dangerous. But I didn't want him to give up something he was bent on doing, and now—"

"Don't be frightened, Martha. You can depend on Lutz. He comes through thick and thin. Felix was telling me, when they were in the regiment together—"

"If only he were here now."

"When he comes back we'll celebrate your wedding, Martha— a real old-fashioned wedding, not one of the skimpy modern kind."

Martha smiled amid her tears. "If only he were here now," she whispered.

Felix Zinnendorf entered the room, lean, stooped, his thick gray hair parted on one side, his sunken cheeks deeply grooved, his dark eyes peering through thick glasss. He greeted his mother and cousin with a distracted nod. "Janos tells me we have a visitor. Who is it?"

"A gentleman named Bilinski. You recognize the name?"

"Bilinski? There are many Bilinskis."

The Countess looked at Martha. "All I know is that he's a refugee from Poland," Martha said.

"Aha, then he's an acquaintance of yours, Martha. You know him through Lutz, I take it?" the Count asked. "Where is he living now?"

"He was staying with Radu Candomir—has probably come directly from there."

"I see—a long trip. Mother, Molly still won't take food. I'm afraid its something organic. Would you like to look at her, or should I send for old Miklos?"

The Countess didn't answer; she hadn't even heard the sad news about her favorite brood mare, Molly. Her son found this most perturbing. Martha, too, seemed changed. She wasn't her usual serene fun-loving self; she was nervous and seemed to have been crying. What had happened? Was the guest responsible?

There was a knock, and a trim, aristocratic-looking man entered the room. He bowed to the Countess and Martha and then, in a slightly different manner, to Count Felix. "Count Zinnendorf?" he said. "My name is Bilinski." He addressed the Count in German.

"Delighted. Welcome." Felix Zinnendorf came forward to meet Anatol, hand outstretched. He gestured to a chair. "Let's sit down."

He had scrutinized the guest carefully, and it seemed to him that he had seen him once before. But the name Bilinski meant nothing to him. He rang. Janos and two maids brought trays with bottles, glasses and platters of ham, smoked fish, radishes, scallions and green peppers, attractively arranged.

"Do have some of this," the Countess said. "You must certainly be hungry and we don't dine until two o'clock."

"I'm afraid I shall not be your guest for luncheon. The Baroness, too, may not be present." He bowed to Martha. "Apparently we are both supposed to go to Arad—at the request of Karl Rundberg."

Martha gave him an apprehensive look. He pretended not to notice, and also ignored the surprise of the others. He drank half of his glass of barak and took a slice of paprika ham. "What is it all about?" Martha asked nervously. She found his mysterious manner totally unnerving.

He frowned slightly; but when he began to speak, he smiled urbanely. "Early yesterday morning a letter from Herr Rundberg reached Baron Candomir—with whom I am staying."

"Rundberg is a good friend of Lutz's, to put it mildly," Martha explained to the Zinnendorfs.

"Yes. And Herr Rundberg advised me to come here at once

and take you to Arad, to a Herr Nagy."

"Why? What has happened?"

Anatol told the story of the investigation. Martha listened in breathless suspense, which now and then gave way to open trepidation. Anatol's skeptical, superior manner upset her.

"A wild story," the Count said when Anatol had finished.

"What do you think of it, Martha?" the Countess asked.

"Of course I shall go," Martha said, rising. "You'll lend us the car, won't you, Felix?" She turned to the Countess, struggling to remain composed. "And if anyone asks, please say that Lutz came for me. Will you do that?"

"Of course," the Count said, and his mother nodded.

"What can Lutz have done, for them to be after him?" the Countess asked.

"He hasn't necessarily done anything," her son explained. "What we've just heard is enough. They suspect him. Whether or not they can harm Martha on that account, I don't know; but in any case it's better to keep out of their way." The Count, whose family had been settled in Transylvania since the Turkish wars and had been Magyar for the past two centuries, German name to the contrary, had had ample opportunity to study the workings of the political police during the past two decades.

"I'll get ready," Martha said. "I want to leave at once."

Anatol nodded his approval and Martha swiftly left the room.

"Herr Bilinski," the Count said, "how do you happen to know Lutz Alda?"

"I don't know him very well. We've seen each other very little since 1918. I first met him in the Rosenhügel Convalescent Hospital, in Vienna."

"What regiment did you serve with, Herr Bilinski?"

"With the Windischgrätz Dragoons," Anatol said.

"Bilinski—in the Windischgrätz Dragoons? I knew most of them—" The Count looked sharply at Anatol. "I know two Bilinskis. They were in the uhlans; one a lieutenant in the Eighth and the other a captain in the Fourteenth, but—"

Anatol smiled. "Bilinski is an assumed name," he murmured.

"Would you care to explain that?" the Countess asked sharply. Their caller looked every inch a man of breeding, and she had a weakness for masculine good looks, but the superior tone in which he seemed to disassociate himself from any intimacy with Alda canceled the favorable impression she had formed of him. She began to be concerned about Martha's undertaking this journey with a stranger.

Anatol bowed low. "As you command, Countess."

Count Felix took a step closer. "Mama, Herr Bilinski is a refugee; he no doubt has his reasons. It's enough that Candomir and Lutz and Martha vouch for him. But"—he turned to his guest—"if you don't mind—I happen to know for certain that no Bilinski served in the Windischgrätz Dragoons."

Anatol smiled modestly. "My Christian name is Anatol. My real one. The Baroness can confirm that, if she happens to still remember it, for I spent only a single day in Alda's house. The day before his departure."

"Then it's all right, Mama; Martha is under the protection of this gentleman."

The Countess was relieved. Felix had obviously placed the man, though only by reputation. She was glad to be able to feel that her first impression had been correct.

Anatol bowed. "You were unquestionably right to be concerned, Countess. But what's in a name? When I leave this house, my name will no longer be Bilinski, but Alda. The times force such disguises upon us, Countess."

"That's true," Count Felix agreed. "As I understand it, however," he added, "you are Alda only here. Only to the servants. Have any of the servants aside from Janos and the two girls seen you?"

"I don't think so."

"One moment." The Count rang, and Janos promptly appeared.

"Janos, Baron Alda"—the Count indicated Anatol—"arrived at ten o'clock and left with Baroness Martha toward two o'clock. You served at second breakfast and lunch. Tell Juliska the same. Does she know Baron Alda?"

"No, sir, she's been here only two months."

Anatol guessed rather than understood what the conversation was about, for the Count and his servant spoke Hungarian.

The Count expected Anatol to go to his room to prepare for the journey. Instead, their strange guest lingered after Janos had left. "Do you know Rundberg?" he asked.

"No—why do you ask?"

"Because," Anatol said smilingly, "you seem so obedient to his instructions."

The Count looked up. "Why not? My cousin leads the way. We know that he is Lutz Alda's friend."

"It's odd, some Jew pipes the tune and we lords dance. You see, I happen to have met Rundberg. To be frank, he didn't impress me as any overpowering personality. A Jew like thousands of others, I'd say."

"Even if I thought that were so, and even if he weren't Lutz Alda's friend, as my cousin and Candomir both tell me, I would accept the advice of a Jew in such a case as this—blindly."

Anatol threw him a look of astonishment. "I don't see—"

"For psychological reasons, so to speak. Precisely because he is a Jew. His race has a keen instinct for danger. But for that they would no longer exist. I have never seen Rundberg, but I know him, know the type; I mean, the kind of Jew he is."

"That's true, every aristocrat has his Jew," Anatol threw in.

"The Jew he deserves, sir." The Count could not refrain from giving these words an edge. He stood up. "But the subject is inexhaustible and this is not the right moment for it."

Stefanie Nagy lifted the receiver, quickly and energetically as she did everything. "Fifi," she heard her husband's somewhat tremulous voice say, "we have a guest for lunch."

"Is that all your news?"

"Almost."

"What does *almost* mean?" Fifi asked sternly.

"The rest at lunch."

"Who is it who's coming?"

But Bela said, "My love," and hung up. Fifi glared at the receiver as if it were responsible for her husband's insubordinate behavior. She slammed it on the hook, and was on the point of calling him back to find out more. But that would have been the wrong thing to do. Better to save her splendid anger for when she was face to face with Bela.

Fifi hopped into the kitchen. She could no more cure herself of hopping than she could cure her husband of his various vices. In fact, the hopping didn't bother Bela nearly so much as his wife's habit of proceeding from bedroom to bathroom on her hands every morning. She would dive out of bed into a handstand and parade off that way, without letting her feet touch the floor, and would return in the same acrobatic manner. Then she would do a bridge and the split, and end her circus—as her husband called it—with a few entrechats. From these morning exercises she apparently drew the energy she needed to bear up under his vices. These were nicotine, alcohol and women. When he was home, she could keep him in line, but on his travels he was on his own. Therefore before and after every trip she gave him a tongue-lashing about his infidelities, although she must have known—especially in recent years—that they couldn't be very serious. He was twenty years older than his wife; she herself was forty, though no one would have guessed it.

She had long shown her mettle in other realms besides calisthenics. She was the daughter of a tenant farmer and had been only a child when she discovered that her elder brothers weren't content with just the income from farming, but they also transported goods over various discreet paths, and those goods ended in Bela Nagy's storerooms in Arad. Later she took part in these enterprises. In this way she met not only Nagy, but also Rundberg, Duttner and Eisner. Nagy had just divorced his first wife at the time and was thoroughly enjoying his regained bachelordom. He played the cavalier almost like a genuine Hungarian magnate of the good old days. He was the scion of a well-to-do family, and had inherited a sizable business after his father's death. But because a man can never have too much money, he became one of the principal buyers of the silk which the Rundberg organization was then importing from France without paying the staggering customs duties. Fifi's brothers, and later she herself, delivered the goods to Nagy for Rundberg.

Nagy had begun by attempting to seduce the girl, and ended by marrying her. Neither of them had ever been sorry, although they often lived on a war footing for weeks at a time. The older he became, the more he grew attached to Fifi and the more he appreciated her not committing any "follies"—which would have distressed him more out of vanity than out of any deeper feelings. He himself, of course, committed follies; that was inborn, he couldn't help himself. But he lived in terror of his dynamic, youthful wife. With advancing age he became more and more henpecked, and she increasingly tyrannical.

When, toward noon, a bouquet of roses arrived with a card containing only the words "from Tarzan," Fifi knew who her guest was, and was delighted. She greeted Mischa Eisner cordially. After lunch Mischa explained the purpose of his visit. Fifi was very glad to do her part. Rundberg had asked it—that was enough. The lady in question would arrive accompanied by a man who had no relationship either to her or to the organization. Fifi made her arrangements accordingly. The lady would have a room on the ground floor, the gentleman on the second floor. Fifi gave the kitchen help instructions—and waited for the arrival of her guests.

There was a large selection of books and magazines on the night table beside Martha's bed. The reading lamp was on. She saw pictures but didn't know what they represented, read words but didn't understand their meaning. She switched out the light, lay in darkness, and was afraid to close her eyes. If she did, she heard his footsteps more distinctly, footsteps as plain as the words he had spoken to her on the drive through the snow-covered countryside. From Szalonta to Arad he had spoken English, so that Jeno Barinay, the big peasant boy at the wheel wouldn't know what he was saying. There had been none of the coolness, superiority and aristocratic haughtiness of the morning, and none of the mystical, unhappy-warrior mood of the time she had first met him, in Aldeni, as Lutz's guest. All during the ride he had been a man in love, despairing, obsessed. But she too was no longer the woman she had been only this morning; and nothing at all was left of her who had bidden good-bye to Lutz Alda when he set out on that journey into the unknown—into adventure and danger. The stranger's words had penetrated into her, had hypnotized her and made her defenseless.

She sat bolt upright and looked at the door through which she would have to pass. Slowly, she thrust one foot forward. The second followed; both felt for the slippers that stood beside the bed; her hands reached out for her dressing gown. But her feet did not slide into the slippers, her hands did not grasp the robe. She remained sitting on the edge of the bed as though she had to gather strength for the movements which she had unthinkingly performed a thousand times, but which now meant something final, definite. If she climbed those stairs to him, whose pacing footsteps were exerting this spell upon her, there would be no turning back. Lutz! her heart cried within her, and racking sobs took her breath away. Where are you? Are you alive? She called out his name and did not know it. She fell back into the bed and buried her head in the pillow.

Weeping, she did not hear the soft, tentative knock at the door. She did not notice that someone had entered the room, come up to her bed. But she felt the hand that caressed her, tenderly, lovingly.

Fifi held Martha in both strong arms. "It will be all right," she said. "Everything will be all right. He'll come back."

"Yes, he will come. But stay with me."

Silently, the two women sat together, and their tears flowed. Finally Fifi smoothed the pillow, straightened the blanket, brought milk and a pill. Martha swallowed the pill, drank the milk, and soon fell asleep. Fifi shifted the lamp so that its glow would not disturb the sleeping woman. She sat down at the foot of the bed and remained for a long time looking at Martha, who was breathing deeply and calmly like a convalescent. The footsteps could no longer disturb her. But they made Fifi nervous, and her nervousness gradually mounted to anger. She did not like the man who was pacing the floor upstairs. How he had acted at dinner! As though he were doing Bela and herself a favor to sit at their table. A handsome man, and distinguished, undoubtedly a nobleman. Fifi had grown up in the country—she knew magnates, counts, barons. The nobles were men like others. This one was not stupid; she could see that. He was secretive, taciturn and proud. When he said thank you, he might have been conferring a decoration on them. No doubt the noble lord did not like Jews.

Again Fifi looked at the sleeping woman. She stirred, and her face worked; she moaned softly. She's suffering, Fifi thought; even in sleep she can't escape it. How can I help her? She looked thoughtfully around the room, and suddenly paused. Above her the footsteps sounded again, now slow and dragging, now hasty and harried. Why didn't the man go to bed? How long did he intend to keep tramping around his room? That sound of pacing must be disturbing Martha. Fifi sent Elsa, the chambermaid, up to the guest's room to politely request him to be quiet.

Elsa returned with an apology from the guest; he hoped the Baroness would soon feel better. Fifi thanked the girl and sent her off to her room. Then she remained sitting for a while by the bed. Martha had grown calmer since the pacing had ceased. Fifi left the door between her room and Martha's open, switched out the light and for a while listened to the sleeping woman's breathing. It was now quiet and regular. Then she herself fell asleep too.

Next morning—Martha was still sound asleep—Fifi asked in the kitchen, "Where is Elsa?"

Ilona came from the same village as Fifi; she was fifty and had been the family's cook for the past fifteen years. She turned her florid, healthy face toward Fifi. "Elsa won't be able to work today," she said.

"She isn't feeling well?" Fifi asked, concerned.

"Feri gave her a beating."

"A beating? What for?"

"He caught her, the slut," Ilona said with satisfaction. "I always told you what kind she was. Now she's had it. If I hadn't stepped in, Feri would have killed her."

"Killed her!" Fifi exclaimed in horror.

"Yes, and well she deserved it." Ilona turned back to the stove.

"What happened, Ilona? How could the girl have smuggled a man into the house?"

Ilona came to the worktable. She laid a piece of peppered bacon on the chopping board and began cutting off thin slices with a long, narrow-bladed knife. "It wasn't a case of smuggling anyone in," she said, obviously relishing the situation.

"Who was it, then, for heaven's sake?" Fifi asked nervously.

"The gentleman upstairs," Ilona said, arranging the sliced bacon on an oval plate.

"No, that's impossible!" Fifi cried out.

"Why not? By night all cats are gray." She pushed the plate to a corner of the table and began slicing sausage.

"I'd better speak to both of them." Fifi ran down the corridor to the servants' quarters and slipped quickly into Elsa's room. The girl was sitting up in bed. As her mistress entered, she put down the mirror in her hand. The poor thing was almost unrecognizable. Her wan little face was puffed and bruised. Her lips were swollen and showed wide, bloody cracks. Her big black eyes were almost invisible, so swollen were the lids. Elsa had been with the Nagys for the past two years, and had been "going with" Feri, the chauffeur. They expected to marry after he had saved enough to buy a truck.

Fifi drew a chair up to Elsa's bed. "How do you feel?" she asked. "Shall I send for the doctor?"

The girl tried to shake her head, but couldn't. Fifi had suffered many an athletic scrape and bruise, and knew quite a bit about such injuries. Feri's hard fist had given Elsa a nasty pounding. It would be a while before the girl looked like herself again. She ran her hands over Elsa's back, chest, shoulders and arms and determined that nothing was broken. "Happens in the best of families, Elsa. In a few days you'll be your own pretty self again." She went to the bathroom for bandages, salves and iodine, and to the kitchen for some slices of beef to be used for medical purposes. Soon the girl's mistreated face was quite out of sight under its bandages, like a prizefighter's after a bout. Fifi gave her patient two pills, bedded her down comfortably and left her.

In the garage the big Nash stood covered with grime and splashed mud. Ordinarily Feri loved to keep things spruce. Fifi knocked on the door of his room and entered. He lay dressed on his bed; the floor was littered with cigarette stubs and the air was gray with their smoke. He hadn't even heard the knock, and turned his head toward the door only when the latch clicked. Abruptly he sat up and started to his feet. "Stay where you are, Feri," Fifi said. She had come to give him a bawling out, but thought better of it when she saw his face. This was no longer the young, cheerful, good-looking boy she knew. His face looked old, despairing and bleak, and there was a bitter, hate-filled twist around his mouth. He sat with his head bowed and his hair tumbling in matted strands over his forehead. This wasn't an unruly boy who needed a scolding, or someone you could cheer up with a kind word—though Fifi searched her mind for something soothing to say. "I'm terribly sorry, Feri," Fifi said, and felt as if she would burst into tears.

"Yes, ma'am," Feri said hoarsely. His head drooped again.

"Don't let it get you down, Feri. You're not the first it's happened to. Better now than later. You're young and good-looking. You find yourself another girl. They aren't all like Elsa."

"Elsa," he repeated slowly. He looked searchingly at his mistress. "It's all the fault of the gentleman. I should have *killed* him."

"And what would have been the good of that, Feri? Is a thing like that worth a twenty-year prison sentence? Of course, if you'd beaten him up a little instead of Elsa—"

"I did. More than a little, I think. But that was letting him off easy."

"You beat him up, Feri?" She could not have said whether she was horrified or delighted.

"Are you worried about the gentleman, ma'am?" he asked spitefully, and Fifi shook her head vigorously. "Because I'm not done with him yet. If he crosses my path—" His eyes burned.

"Feri, would you do me a favor?"

"You needn't ask me, ma'am—I'll leave. I'll leave, right now. I'll settle up with the gentleman some other time; he won't escape me. You don't want me making trouble here, isn't that it, ma'am?"

"Of course not, Feri, certainly not. That's nonsense about your leaving. The gentleman doesn't matter a thing to me. I'm just thinking of your own welfare. Go stay with your parents for a week, in Deva. Have a good talk with them, go on a drunk, forget it. When you come back, you'll see things differently. Then the man will be gone and Elsa—"

"Elsa . . . ?" He swallowed.

"Do you feel bad about Elsa? I thought you liked her so much. How could you have treated her that way?"

He shrugged in perplexity. "I just saw red—we were supposed to be married at Easter, ten weeks from today. She couldn't help it. If that goddamned . . . hadn't come round her—God only knows how he buttered her up. I feel I'll never be able to touch her again. Best thing for me would be to leave right now." He reached for his cap. "Forgive me, ma'am." He bent over her hand and touched it with his lips. Then Fifi heard Feri's footsteps on the pavement of the yard. The big gate slammed shut, and she went back into the house.

The sound of a closing gate startled Martha out of her sleep. She opened her eyes and looked around the room. Yes, she was still here. The beastly dreams could no longer torment her; the horrible images had dissolved. She rubbed her hands over her forehead and eyes, recalled herself to wakefulness, to reality. How good it was to be awake. She sprang out of bed, let the shade snap up, opened the window. Light and air poured in. The bare trees stood wet and glistening; the winter sun had melted the snow on the branches, and thin rivulets of water were flowing down the tree trunks. As if spring were really on its way, Martha thought, and she filled her lungs with the air that played about her face and chilled her body under her thin silk nightgown. Air is good, and water too. Martha ran into the bathroom adjoining her room. She did not sing, as she usually did when she bathed; instead she thought about Mme. Nagy with her doll's face and the broad nose that didn't fit this face at all. Mme. Nagy, whom her husband called Fifi. Martha repeated the name to herself, smiling. But she promptly forbade herself to smile. No, this woman was no one to smile at in any kind of patronizing way. How good she had been to her, how she had comforted and sustained her, and suffered and wept with her. Good Fifi. Fine, strong Fifi.

When Martha reentered her room, breathless, teeth chattering, wrapped in the heavy bathrobe, she saw her hostess closing the window. "You'll catch cold, coming back into a draft after your bath," she said with stern solicitude.

"Good morning, Mme. Nagy," Martha said, crawling rapidly under the blanket.

"Good morning. I was looking in to see whether you'd starved to death yet."

"Not yet, but I feel so hungry! Might I have bacon and eggs and a huge pot of coffee?"

"Would you like to have your breakfast brought in here, Baroness? I'll see to it at once." She went to press the button—then withdrew her outstretched hand. "I'll bring it myself. We're short on help today."

"No, no! I'll be ready in a few minutes. And, Fifi, call me Martha. We're friends, aren't we?"

Fifi took Martha's hand. "I'll be a good friend to you, a dependable one. My first name is Stefanie."

"Stefanie?" Martha said, touched. She embraced her. "Mayn't I call you Fifi, as your friends do?" She sprang out of bed. "I'll be dressed in a moment." She went into the bathroom, leaving the door open, and Fifi told her what had happened—for the matter was very much on her mind. She didn't mince words, and gave her frank opinion of a gentleman who allowed himself such liberties with servants. It was fortunate that she could not observe the effect of her story upon Martha, that she could not see the alternating expressions of shock, rage, bitterness and revulsion. But Martha could see her own face in the mirror, and that helped. It would be a long time before she could come to terms with this experience. But she returned to the room with a normal smile, and the movements with which she completed her toilette were calm and self-assured. "I had no idea that he was this way. Yesterday was the second time in my

life that I've seen this Pan Bilinski. He came for me at Baron Candomir's request, and brought me to you. Candomir is my fiancé's
friend. If the gentleman chooses to get involved with chambermaids,
he must run the risk of being beaten by the chauffeur. That's his
affair. Come, let's go down, Fifi darling." She put her arm around
her hostess, and there was inordinate gratitude in the gesture.

Bela Nagy was waiting at the breakfast table. When they entered
the room, he stood up and bowed chivalrously to Martha. "I kiss
your hand, Baroness; please be seated." He held the chair for her;
then he said to his wife, "Ilona can serve. Pan Bilinski sends his
apologies. He won't be down today; he isn't feeling quite well."

"This is Domnule Eisner, called Tarzan—Karl Rundberg's
friend," Fifi said, introducing them.

Martha stood up and shook hands with the stocky man. "I'm
delighted to meet any friend of Karl's."

"Baroness," Eisner said, "by far the safer thing would be for
you to stay here. My instructions are only to fetch the gentleman.
I'll go up to him now and then drop by once more before I leave."
He bowed and went up to the room on the second floor. He knocked
and went in without more ado. Eisner knew what had taken place.
He had met Feri shortly before his departure, and had heard the
whole story.

"Sir," he said, "we are leaving for Candomireni in two hours.
Please get ready. Our train goes at one-seventeen."

"I won't be going; I'm sick and don't want to be disturbed." The
body whose outlines were visible under the blanket remained motionless. Nothing could be seen of the man's face but a strand of
dark-blond hair.

"You're not sick, sir, and even if you were, you would have to
leave," Eisner said quietly.

There was no answer. Slender, aristocratic fingers clutched the
edge of the blanket and drew it up high, hiding even the hair. Eisner stretched his neck as though his collar were too tight, and a sigh
broke from him. His anger rose, and at the same time a worry that
he would lose control of himself. He lit a cigarette and drew a
chair up to the bed. Sitting there, silently smoking, he reflected. The
Polish nobleman had to leave. Rundberg wanted it that way, and
in any case it was too dangerous for the Nagys to keep him in the
house. Eisner continued to smoke quietly, and after he had crushed
out the butt in the ashtray, he said very softly, "Pan Bilinski, there's
no sense to it—this game of hide and seek, I mean. A pity to waste
time. We must leave on the one-seventeen train. Get up; I'll help you

with your packing." He fell silent and again waited a while. "We
have a Pullman for the whole trip. I'll take care of you." Again he
fell silent and again there was no answer. Mischa had been patient
long enough. He grabbed the blanket with both hands, pulled it off
the man, and tossed it on a chair behind him. The inert body came
to life. The nobleman sat up instantly, with the result that the com-
press fell from his face and revealed glittering, greenish, hate-filled
eyes staring out of mottled, swollen lids. And through puffed, bloody
lips came a venomous snarl: "Goddamned stinking filthy Jew!"

Mischa would have liked to feast his eyes a bit on Feri's work.
But the nobleman's imprecation robbed him of the necessary calm
—he was surprised by the surge of feeling that went through him.
What did the whole business have to do with Jews, he wondered,
trying to regain his poise. "My dear sir," he said, "the young man
who put you into this condition is not a Jew at all. He is a Hungarian
and Catholic." He spoke slowly, and allowed a smile to creep over
his ordinarily wooden face as the man gave a hysterical screech, and
buried his battered face in the pillow. Quietly, he went on: "Rundberg has telegraphed. You must leave here, leave the city, leave
Transylvania. He sent his telegram without having any idea of the
latest development. I mean this little mess with Feri. Filthy brute,
that Feri—simply goes ahead and takes a swing at a noble as though
he were another chauffeur. And he isn't satisfied yet; he'll kill you
if he gets the chance. These Hungarians are a fiery lot, aren't they,
sir?" he asked smugly.

Haughtiness and superiority vanished from the swollen face,
and gave way to simple plebeian fright. "Let him try it; I'll go to the
police."

"That is precisely what we want to prevent—interference from
the police. You too wouldn't want that, would you, sir?" Mischa
felt that he was on the right track with this difficult nobleman. "The
best thing would be for you to leave here as quickly as possible. He
won't pursue you; he doesn't know who you are or where you come
from."

"Bandages," the gentleman blurted.

"What for?" Eisner asked naïvely.

"Bandages, plenty of bandages, if I am to leave."

At least he had brought the man to this point. "All right, we'll
get you bandages," Eisner said. He went into the other room and
sent the servant Jozsi down for bandages. Bilinski had meanwhile
slipped into his dressing gown and gone to wash up. When he returned, heaps of bandages of various widths and lengths lay on the
night table. With considerable skill and care, Bilinski put on the
dressings. Like a professional, Eisner thought, when nothing could

be seen of the man's face except two narrow slits for his eyes and a hole for the mouth barely big enough to accommodate a cigarette. He completed his toilette quickly, and then began to pack, assisted by a taciturn Jozsi. Eisner meanwhile sat smoking in the adjoining room. He stayed there until Jozsi came to report that the gentleman was ready.

"Is there anything else you want to do here before we leave?" he asked Bilinski.

"Would you tell the Baroness I'd like to see her? I have something very important to say."

Martha's immediate impulse was to refuse to see the man. But she suppressed that impulse quickly. However much she rebelled against the idea, she said calmly, "Very well, I will be expecting Pan Bilinski here." That was the sensible course, after all. The sexual escapades of a man she scarcely knew were his own affair. She had been forced by extraordinary circumstances to accept the hospitality of strangers. These same circumstances had made a certain Pan Bilinski her escort. For her he was and remained a gentleman who had done her a service and had, in fact, incurred certain risks on her account. Since she was a lady, she owed him a courteous good-bye.

She therefore completely ignored his swathed face. "I understand you are leaving," she said. "Bon voyage, then, and many thanks for what you have done for me."

"Not worth mentioning." The voice was muffled by the bandages.

"Ah no! Once more, my warmest thanks."

"A pleasure," he said punctiliously. "Before I leave, there is something I wish to tell you." Though muted, his words sounded altogether conventional."

"Yes?"

"This—this silly story"— he indicated his bandaged head (like a snowman in a thaw, Martha thought involuntarily)—"seems to have been taken more seriously than it deserves."

"Taken seriously?" Martha shrugged uncomprehendingly.

"Yes, by all these Yids. That scum's overjoyed whenever they can trip up someone of our sort."

"I'm sure I don't know what you mean; and certainly not what bearing this might have on me. And—may I ask you to be a little more careful of your language?"

"Excuse me." He gave the hint of a bow. "To come to the point, then: I would not like this incident to be talked about." He said this indistinctly, but in an imperious tone.

Martha was tempted to laugh, but she spoke soberly: "I can well understand, but I don't know what I can do about it. In any case, you'll be leaving here."

"What people here may say is a matter of total indifference to me. But I don't want Baron Candomir to hear of it. I don't want that at all."

"He certainly won't hear it from me, and the others don't know you or Baron Candomir."

"The man who's come for me—I don't know his name—obviously has had his earful. He will tell Rundberg and so Baron Candomir will hear it. I don't wish that!"

Martha, repelled and alarmed by his hysterical excitability, remained cool by great effort. "I don't know how I can prevent it, but I think that if you speak to Mr. Eisner—that is his name—as man to man, he will appreciate your position and be discreet."

"That's impossible. I can't talk to these Rundbergs or Eisners as man to man, nor can I ask discretion of such types. . . . No, I can't talk with them about it."

"Really not?" Martha put on a naïve and astonished tone.

"No. And I wouldn't care to."

"And so I am to ask Mr. Eisner? Well, I owe you a good turn. I'll talk to him."

"Through your friend Alda you belong to that Rundberg crowd. Those people will obey you sooner than me. All the more so if you tell them that I know where Alda is and can make use of that knowledge. Nothing can happen to me, but a great deal can happen to him. I hope you see what I mean, my dear Baroness."

"No," she said, shaking her head. "I don't see what you mean at all." She had heard only the hatred and scorn, but had not grasped the sense of his words.

"It's very simple. The Sigurantza is on his track, and I will help them, for I know where your—where Alda is to be found. Information for information, you see. If this stupid little episode is bruited about, I will bruit about what I otherwise would have kept to myself."

"Aha—now I see. Yes, I see just what you mean. Though it's strange that Alda should have taken you into his confidence. . . . But that isn't the issue now." She took a long puff on her cigarette. "You have the stronger weapons. I shall do whatever lies in my power. And now I think—"

"Yes, permit me to take my leave, my dear Baroness." He bowed. Too low. Then, as he straightened, he added, "A pity—but when a man is madly thirsty, he drinks water. What good is it to know that champagne tastes better? You understand? Drinking champagne used to be your profession, I gather."

Martha looked at the man. She was not angry, not even indignant, only repelled, overwhelmed with disgust. She had to turn her head away; she could no longer listen to the arrogant voice coming through that white mask. In the movement with which she bade him go, there was the kind of repugnance with which one waves away an annoying insect.

When Eisner came down to see her before leaving, she was calm and composed. "Domnule Tarzan, I have a favor to ask you," she said. "Please listen closely; it's very important."

"I'm listening," he said. He looked at her with his button eyes. The sight of her gave him pleasure, and this feeling was printed all across his rough-hewn features. Delight and a comradely readiness to help. Martha understood this face; it cheered her and restored her confidence. He was a link in an indestructible chain.

"This Pan Bilinski is—you understand—he is highly irritable, extremely nervous. Do not leave him alone at any time on the trip, and don't allude in any way to the—the story. He doesn't want it discussed at all, and if his wishes are not met, he can harm us. I mean Domnule Alda—do you know him, Domnule Eisner?"

"Yes, certainly he is—Karl Rundberg's friend." Mischa had changed his mind in mid-sentence, for it had occurred to him that the lady might be better off not knowing that her fiancé was the Uden, the chief.

"Yes, he is Rundberg's friend. As I say, Pan Bilinski is in an extraordinarily excitable—an almost irresponsible—state of mind. He has threatened to betray everything to the Sigurantza if anyone tells Baron Candomir about the incident."

Eisner's hands clenched with an audible cracking of the knuckles. Martha had seldom seen such fury as those clenched hands expressed, nor had she ever encountered such an act of will as that by which this great hulk of a man controlled himself. "Betray? Sigurantza?" That was all he could say, and he brought out the words in a low whisper.

"Unfortunately there was no misunderstanding him. It may be he only meant it as a threat. But we can't be sure of him. I'll give you two letters, one for Rundberg and one for Baron Candomir. And you—you will keep a grip on yourself, won't you, even though it's hard?" She smiled at him, a warm, comradely smile.

"I can keep a grip on myself if I must." He smiled back.

"I can see that. I'll dash off those two letters." She looked at her watch. "You still have more than an hour. You plan to drive straight from here to the station, don't you?"

"Yes, I have my luggage here. But—" He went to the window and opened it. The paved courtyard showed no trace of snow; it was smooth and dry. Eisner looked up at the sky. As he closed the window, he said under his breath, "No help for it." He turned to Martha. "Under the circumstances we'd better not take the train. It would be too much of a risk. With that bandaged head he'd attract attention. And we don't want any questions. We'll drive."

"With the roads as they are? They will have gone all to pieces in this thaw. Suppose you have car trouble on the way—"

"I'm a pretty good driver and I know something about muddy roads. The roads are less dangerous than that fellow—and if he wants to sound off about anything, he can try sounding off to me."

Martha went to her room to write her letters and Eisner reviewed the situation with Nagy. It was dangerous to take the train, he explained. "Let me borrow the car, Bela. If anything happens to it, we'll pay the bill."

"Of course Tarzan can take the car," Fifi said before her husband could speak his mind. "Don't worry about any bills. That's the last thing to consider in such an emergency."

"But Bilinski is under the weather, and to risk such a drive at this season . . . ! It isn't any pleasure by train, let alone by car on these roads. At very best it will take you three days. I think you're exaggerating the need for caution. After all, he is a gentleman."

"There are gentlemen and gentlemen. Including his type— threatening to sing to the Sigurantza! Take the car, Tarzan, and smash it up if you want to. I'll gladly give you the goddamned thing, for Alda's sake," Fifi said.

When Bela Nagy was left alone with his wife he sat looking thoughtfully at her. At last he said, "How long must a man live with a woman before he really knows her, Fifi?"

"A long, long time, Bela *bacsi*." She put her arms around his neck and planted a kiss half on his upper lip, half on his mustache. "It's never too late to start finding out."

Inspector First Class Axintie Barbulescu sat in his office, plagued by doubts. The business wasn't working out as it should have. It had been hard enough to sell the idea to the Blaze in the first place, and now he was raising a fuss all over again. First he'd been scared of a trap, and when the Inspector reasoned him out of that and made it clear that it could only be a profitable deal, that stacks of money practically lay on the table before them, the man had started getting jittery about the Germans. If the Germans ever caught them at it— himself and Barbulescu—they would make hash of them. He knew those Germans. And suddenly he'd lost his nerve completely. "No, I won't do it," he'd screeched. Money was one thing, but risking your neck was another.

Domnule Secretary General was exaggerating, Barbulescu had said; after all, the Germans were not at home here; they wouldn't come into it at all. And besides, a hundred thousand pounds sterling—well, not quite that; after all, Barbulescu himself would need his rake-off—a sum like that was worth going out on a limb for. And the way he, Barbulescu, had it worked out, the devil himself would never catch wind of it. How much time would they need for the whole business? Half an hour! And who was going to betray them to the Germans? The English, say?

They had talked and argued, considered their plans from every angle, and yesterday the Blaze had finally given him the green light. Everything was settled: where, how, when. And now, three hours before the decisive interview, the report from the Cernauti Sigurantza on the Alda case (what an idiocy that whole thing had been!) had come in, and the Blaze was beside himself. They'd found out nothing, nothing at all! As if Barbulescu had not known that in advance. A huge file full of papers, and the whole thing simmered down to nothing. Barbulescu, of course, had not read the file; who gave a damn about such rot? The summary signed by Stanescu and Zernescu had been enough for him. But the Blaze! He had thrown a fit, had howled with rage. They'd all been bribed, he swore. The swine, corrupt to the marrow of their bones. He'd show them—to jail, to the salt mines with all of them, the thieves, the traitors, the Jew-lovers of the Sigurantza and B II! They all should be stood up against the wall, every last man of them!

Barbulescu had waited until the storm subsided. And after a while the madman calmed down, lowered his voice, and asked the Inspector to go over the bloody case, to see whether he couldn't find some gimmick with which they could hang that goddamned bastard Alda. And Barbulescu had puffed out his chest and said, "Trust me, coane. I'll find a way." He eked out this hollow assertion with some choice abuse of Alda, a technique which seemed to have a good effect on his superior.

Then, just when he had Danghu buttered up again, the devil himself had to bring in that official with a letter from the Cernauti magistrate's court: an inquiry about a certain Eugeniu Popovici who seemed to be an accredited agent of the department but who'd been impersonating a director of the Ministry of the Interior in order to cheat a group of honest citizens at cards. That really threw everything off. The answer to the court was sent off posthaste, by telegram, and in nothing like the form suggested by the official. Far from it! Danghu replied that the man in question had wormed his way into the force by a pack of lies. He was an individual who had repeatedly come into conflict with the law, and represented a menace to decent society; such a scoundrel should be made an example of.

Hoping that the Blaze had vented all of his spleen on the poor wretch whom he was consigning to at least a year in jail, Barbulescu cautiously returned to the important subject. That only excited Danghu the more, and a flood of insults, accusations and curses poured over the Inspector's head.

Barbulescu had retreated. Now he sat racking his brains. His hopes for a grand coup, the biggest coup of all, were shattered, annihilated by a hysterical idiot, a fool of a pansy. All right, to hell with the inspector generalship, you madman! But the money! If I only had my hands on it, you'd not see me again, you and your whorehouse of a Sigurantza!

But if nothing was to come of it, he would have to let the boys know. Order above all. He could not send so important a man on a wild-goose chase. Who knew? Perhaps another chance would crop up. Barbulescu reached for his hat and coat, intending to go to see the liaison man. Naturally he wouldn't tell him that the balloon had burst. He would say there was a temporary delay, that perhaps tomorrow or the day after. . . . As he stood considering this, the Inspector's telephone rang. Secretary General Danghu spoke crisply: "I'm leaving about two o'clock today, will be back by evening. I must report to the Minister in person. No, he is still confined to his bed. Would you please call on me this evening. La revedere!"

Barbulescu hung up. Aha, so you can't bear to give up the money after all! But just wait. Better not take it into your head to try to cheat me. Twenty-five per cent, not a *ban* less, or you'll have a surprise coming!

He had reached this point in his reflections when a clerk came in and handed him a letter. Barbulescu read it, reached for the telephone to report to the Secretary General, and then drew his hand back as if he'd been stung. No, Puffi Barbulescu was not going to be such an idiot again. The news that Alda was driving around the country with his fiancée would send his boss completely off his rocker. The money, the money! Danghu was capable of letting everything slide while he went after his obsession again. No, my friend, Puffi is going to call the play this time. We're going to collect those pounds sterling! When that's over, you can go back to your crazy fantasies. Business first.

In any case, the letter was addressed to him personally. He pocketed it. After all, it could just as well have arrived after the Secretary General had already set out to see the Minister, who was ill at his country home.

By two o'clock Barbulescu was back in his office. If all had gone well, the Blaze would soon have the money in his briefcase. A pleasant thought, ruffled only by this news of Alda's appearance in the country. If he knew Danghu, the man would set an army of sleuths on Alda's trail, and once he tracked him down, would get himself involved in a war that he would inevitably lose. There were no real charges against Alda; moreover, he had friends, followers, relatives, who would come to his defense. The Blaze was not strong enough; he would only make more enemies, a whole clique who still had enough power to knock the props from under a contemptible secretary whose sole support was the Germans. No, my man, we've had enough of Alda for the time being. Keep your shirt on and let your good friend Puffi tell you what to do.

The inspector rubbed his hand. A fortune at one stroke! And perhaps the Blaze would also bring back the decree appointing him inspector general, since he was paying a sick call on the Minister and only had to ask to have the order signed. Not that this visit was the real purpose of his trip; that was only an alibi Puffi had slyly cooked up. For next to the Minister's country estate was the house in which the deal would be concluded.

But this letter, now—wait! Wasn't B II in formal charge of the investigation at the moment? Of course. Let the Old Man play with the Alda case; he had time for such silly games. He didn't need money. All right, Old Man, I'll send you the report; just as well to do you a favor once in a while. Because you're not exactly fond of me. We both know that. Ever since the time I worked for the Germans, back there during the war. But now you're dancing in the same horă. What a combination: the Old Man and that dog, the Blaze. Better for you to handle it than that crazy pervert; you're an old pro, anyhow. And if there's a slipup, better for you to take the rap than my boss. Yes, my friend, this report goes to you. I need the Blaze for more important things.

The General laid the last page of the report on top of the stack of other pages. He shook his head, reached for the telephone, and called Rananu and Rozescu to his office. When they entered, he wasn't sitting at his big desk as usual, but pacing the floor. He responded distractedly to their salutes.

"Yes," he said, moving toward his desk, "what more can I say than that it's a good report—too good." His smile faded. "You've done an excellent job, boys, and I hope the Secretary General is satisfied. But I have a number of questions. Whichever of you knows the answers, please reply." The General looked down at his pad. "How often have you spoken to this man Karl Rundberg?"

"Just once, when he was questioned. A funny-looking fellow—that is, when you first meet him. The longer you're with him—" Rananu paused, seeking the words to describe the impression that Rundberg made on him. The General waited, and when he didn't go on, turned to Rozescu.

"And you?"

"I've seen Domnule Rundberg three times and spoken to him twice, once alone and once in the presence of Domnule Candomir," Rozescu said quietly.

"Tell me about each occasion in turn," the General commanded, paying no attention to Rananu's surprised expression.

"Once I called on him at his home, taking all precautions not to be seen, and the second time I met him by chance. He was then accompanied by Domnule Candomir."

"By chance?"

"So it would seem."

"Tell me about this second meeting. That was . . . ?"

"Right after our recent trip to the border. There's nothing about it on the report. When we got back to town, we were hungry and thirsty and went to a nightclub. We had a fine time there. An incident occurred which seems to me worth mentioning, but which isn't strictly part of the answer to your question, sir. To put it briefly, when we got up to go and I was about to pay the check, I found I didn't have enough cash on me. I therefore only signed the check and asked the waiter to come to my hotel in the afternoon. He didn't come and—"

"He didn't come?" The General showed astonishment. "A waiter who doesn't come to settle a check?"

"I was surprised at it, too. I didn't want to seem to be running out on him, so I went to the nightclub around eight the following evening. The place appeared deserted, but for the waiter; such places don't come to life until much later. But when he went to get the bill, and I looked around, I observed Rundberg sitting with a gentleman I didn't know."

"And that was Candomir?"

"That's right, sir."

"I take it you worked on Candomir just as you had Rundberg before?" the General asked.

"I wouldn't exactly say I worked on him, if you'll permit the correction, sir."

Rananu spoke up gravely. "I beg pardon, sir." He waited until the General gestured to him to go on. "Permit me to ask the Lieuten-

ant a question. Lieutenant, this is the first I have heard of your
meeting Domnule Candomir. Why did you not inform me?"

Rozescu stood up. "I beg your pardon, sir. Your reproach is
justified. I intended to report to you. But it seemed to me the
better course to omit a report for the time being—for psychological
reasons."

Rananu was angry, and Rozescu's words did nothing to placate
him. He didn't notice the amused expression on the General's face.
"Leave psychology out of it and explain your conduct!"

"As you wish, sir. I'll try to, sir. At our first meeting with the
Sigurantza men you carried out your role splendidly—if you don't
mind my making a judgment—splendidly. You were strained, and
the effect was marvelous. Because you were being perfectly honest,
sir. The whole performance was genuine. By showing your own
doubts, you persuaded the others of your sincerity. That was correct. But if you had known that Domnule Candomir—who was, so
to speak, the witness for our side—had been primed, you wouldn't
have waited so tensely for his replies; you wouldn't have been in
doubt. In other words, you would have been sure of the outcome,
and the others might have sensed that, and so taken it into their
heads that the witness Candomir was not altogether innocent. The
Sigurantza men are inclined to be skeptical anyhow."

"I don't quite follow," Rananu said, throwing a look at the
General.

The General nodded to him. "I follow him, and you too, Alecu."

"Perhaps he's right," Rananu admitted.

"Well then"—the General pursued his questioning—"you sat
down with Rundberg and Candomir and talked with them. Did
you speak of Oskar Gross on this occasion?"

"Yes, sir. Then Domnule Candomir went to the telephone to
let someone know that he would be home a little later than expected."

"Did you give Rundberg the tip?"

"What tip, sir?" Rozescu seemed astonished.

"This one." He picked up the report and read:

INSPECTOR ZERNESCU: Do you know a man named Gross?
WITNESS RUNDBERG: I know thirty or more people by that name.
ZERNESCU: Is one of them an Oskar Gross from Vienna?
WITNESS: No.
ZERNESCU: Think it over. Have you never heard the name of
    Oskar Gross, supposedly of Vienna, a journalist by profession?
WITNESS: Heard? I've heard the name.
ZERNESCU: When? In what connection?
WITNESS: I prefer not to say. It is a family matter.

INSPECTOR STANESCU: You must answer every question to the best of your ability. We'll have none of that! You cannot refuse to say. (*To* ZERNESCU): Continue, Inspector.

ZERNESCU: What do you mean by a family affair? What family?

WITNESS: The Alda family. I heard about it by chance.

ZERNESCU: Come out with it, now. What is the connection between the Alda family and Oskar Gross?

WITNESS: I cannot talk about that. Coane Alda wouldn't like it.

ZERNESCU: So, Alda wouldn't like it. By any chance because he is himself Oskar Gross?

WITNESS: Coane Alda? What are you talking about? No, of course not. He certainly isn't, Inspector! Coane Alda knows nothing about Gross!

INSPECTOR STANESCU (*to the witness*): Sir, you cannot withhold testimony. (*To* ZERNESCU): Excuse me, Inspector. (*To the witness again*): This is not a private chat. Tell us what you know about Oskar Gross.

WITNESS: Very well, Domnule Chief Inspector. Oskar Gross is a kind of brother of Coane Alda.

ZERNESCU: What do you mean by a kind of brother? Come out with it, now, and speak clearly!

WITNESS: All right, if you must have it. Oskar Gross is a son of Alda's father, who died in an accident in 1900.

ZERNESCU: What's that?

WITNESS: You want to know how Baron Alda died?

ZERNESCU: No, how Oskar Gross is his son.

WITNESS: A natural son. Baron Alda, who was Ludovic Alda's father, was an officer in the Australian hussars, and in the days before he was married he naturally had a mistress in Vienna, and she was the mother of this Oskar. Old Baron Neagoe, the boyar of Aldeni, found out about it, and after his son's death he took care of Oskar. I've heard from my father that he sent money to Vienna regularly.

ZERNESCU: The woman's name was Gross?

WITNESS: No, Gross was her husband's name. He came from Romania, from Botoshani, and he married the woman and adopted the son. They lived in Vienna. In 1925 the husband died and the woman and her son left the country. At the time, Frau Gross wrote to my father saying that she no longer needed the money the Baron was sending, because her husband had left them a sizable fortune, and they were emigrating to Tampico. That was the story as I heard it. My father discussed the matter with me because he did not know whether we ought to tell Coane Alda.

ZERNESCU: And what was your decision?

WITNESS: We decided that Coane Lutz did not need to know about it.

ZERNESCU: So you think that Alda knew nothing at all about the existence of Oskar Gross?

WITNESS: Nothing whatsoever.

The General, who had been reading in a low voice, looked up. He fixed his gaze on Rananu. "What's your opinion of that, Alecu?"

"A wonderful solution, sir. The man on the Dniester was not Lutz Alda, but Oskar Gross of Vienna. No wonder Zernescu made a mistake. After all, since they were sons of the same father, a resemblance would be only natural."

"This marvelously simple solution was just what Rundberg had in mind. And what do you think, Rozescu?"

"That Alda was the man at the Dniester, and when he was caught he gave himself out to be Oskar Gross. In other words, he knew that Oskar Gross existed and used him as an alter ego. And Karl Rundberg was not—let us say—being strictly candid when he asserted that Alda had no idea of his half-brother's existence."

"Both explanations are possible," the General said, leafing through the report. He didn't say what he thought: that Oskar Gross had never existed at all, or that if such a person existed he had had nothing to do with Alda's family or with the Dniester. Alda must have been caught at the Dniester and given his name as Gross, and Rundberg had invented the complicated story of the illegitimate son only after Rozescu had spoken to him of Gross, Alda and the Dniester. He had cooked up a good tale, correct to the smallest detail. The adoptive father was even a Romanian, which would explain why Oskar Gross of Vienna could speak Romanian. The story of Alda's half-brother who had emigrated to Tampico and then returned to Vienna to become a journalist, of all things, was a neat follow-up to the story of the training before the steeplechase. All that conveniently accounted for the time Alda had really been in Balti, or whatever that town in Bessarabia was called. Candomir had told that story, and Rundberg had no doubt planted the whole thing. Perhaps he had also planted the testimony of the border guard Posteuca and of Lieutenant Popovici. The General turned to Rozescu again. "Did you," he asked, "let Rundberg know of the rumor that Alda might be the man who was shot at the border?"

"I mentioned that," Rozescu said quietly. "He was quite shaken when he heard the detail about the bandaged hand. Sincerely shaken and overcome by sorrow."

"And when did you tell him that?"

"An hour and a half before we left for the border."

The General's next question perplexed Rananu. "What do you think of the testimony of Chaim Eisner?"

"Chaim Eisner?" Rananu asked. "Which one was that?" He appealed to Rozescu.

"The old man, one of the creditors."

"Beg pardon, Domnule General, but twelve men and one woman were paraded before us. Alda's creditors; all Jews. It's hard for me to recollect their names, which are so different from the ones I'm used to in my part of Romania."

"Quite natural. Well then: Chaim Eisner, sixty-nine years old, innkeeper and real estate broker. He says, as do almost all the others, that Joshua Rundberg, not Alda, was their debtor. Listen to this." And the General read:

CHIEF INSPECTOR STANESCU: Did you know who the money was for?

WITNESS EISNER: For whom does a tenant borrow money if not for his boyar?

STANESCU: Answer the question as it was asked. Did you know who the money was for?

WITNESS: Of course. Why should an old man like Joshua Rundberg need money?

STANESCU: That means, then, that you lent money to Rundberg because Alda guaranteed the loans by giving his property as security?

WITNESS: I never met Coane Alda. Rundberg's word was good enough for me.

STANESCU: Then why did you press for payment? If Rundberg was good for it then, he would still be good for it. You people forced Alda to sell. First you practiced your usury and then you robbed him of his property.

WITNESS: No one practiced usury, and no one pressed. As long as Joshua Rundberg was the tenant, the loans were secure. But Rundberg wanted to emigrate to Palestine, and who was going to guarantee the loans then?

STANESCU: What do you mean? The estate was there, and Coane Alda would surely have paid just as his tenant had done. If he had wanted to default, Rundberg would also have had to default.

WITNESS: Nobody said anything about defaulting. An Alda never defaults. I knew Baron Alda—may he rest in peace—the present Alda's grandfather. But politics were different in those days.

STANESCU: Explain that!

WITNESS: Alda went in for politics against the Jews. But he is a coane; he wouldn't want people to say he was against the Jews because he owed them money. So he met all his debts and nobody can say his political beliefs were on account of money.

The General put down the paper. He pushed his glasses up to his forehead and rubbed his eyes. "Well, boys, what do you say to that?"

"The persecution mania of an old Jew," Rananu said. "Who would ever believe a word of that? It's all nonsense."

"Do you think it's nonsense too, Rozescu?"

"I think it's a trick, sir. That old man Eisner is quite an actor. A pity you didn't see him, sir, with his big nose and gray beard—and those eyes!"

"I can imagine him," the General said ironically. "You sketch a lively picture. I know him. I've known him for years, so to speak."

The General sat lost in thought for a while. "Good," he murmured softly, "very good. But how he arranged all that in so short a time—*that's* what I'd like to know."

Rozescu was about to make some comment when the interphone hummed. The General lifted it. "Yes, at once," he said, hanging up. "There's a man from the Sigurantza outside. See what it's about, Rozescu."

"Yes, sir."

The Lieutenant went out and in a moment returned with a letter. The General confirmed receipt, for it was addressed to him personally. When Rozescu came in again, the General was already reading it. As he read, expressions of astonishment and alarm passed over his features. "No," he muttered when he had finished, and he began rereading the letter. Then he dropped it to the table as though his hand no longer had the strength to hold it. With an effort he stood up and went to the big general-staff map on the wall. Every cart path and brook in the entire country was marked on that map. The General studied it, seeming to calculate, and then returned to his desk.

"Yes," he spoke at last, in a shaky, old man's voice. A vast disappointment was expressed in that single word. "Yes," he repeated, and cleared his throat. "Alda didn't go across; he's in the country."

Rananu sprang to his feet. "What's that you say, sir?" he exclaimed. There was nothing military in his bearing.

"But that's impossible," said Rozescu, who had also stood up. He was more upset than either of the two had ever seen him.

The General shrugged. He nodded toward the letter on the desk in front of him. "There," he said softly. "Read the letter aloud, Rozescu."

And Rozescu read:

I have the honor to transmit the enclosed report, which reached me by special messenger two hours ago. Since B II is conducting the investigation of the Alda case, and since, moreover, Secretary General Danghu is away at the moment, I think it advisable to place this report in your hands as quickly as possible. With the hope that I may have done you some small service, I am,

Sincerely yours,
A. Barbulescu,
Inspector First Class

Rozescu laid aside the covering letter.

"Sit down, now," the General said. "It'll confound you. Here philosophy won't do us any good."

Rozescu sat down and read the enclosed report:

To Inspector First Class Axintie
Barbulescu, Acting Inspector General.
Esteemed Sir:

In pursuit of the investigation of the whereabouts of Baroness Martha Varsany, it has been determined that she is a niece of Countess Agathe Zinnendorf, and that she stayed as the guest of the Countess at the estate of Satul Turnului, 25 miles from Oradea Mare. The estate is the property of Count Felix Zinnendorf. On the 30th of the present month, around noon, Baroness Martha Varsany departed with her fiancé, Domnule Ludovic Alda of Aldeni, Bucovina.

Sincerely yours,
Aurel Tudoratu,
Inspector.

The silence was painful. Rananu broke it at last with a tormented exclamation: "No, I don't understand that!"

"But I think I understand it," Rozescu said hesitantly. "Yes." His voice became firmer. "Yes, I understand." He looked at the General.

"What do you understand, Rozescu?" Barbulescu asked.

"That's Rundberg's work again, sir."

"Unfortunately it isn't—I've figured it out. Too short a time. No, Rundberg is out of this. I'm afraid the old man with the beard

—Chaim Eisner—was right. Our friend is a secret supporter of the Germans."

"Who?" Rananu exclaimed. "Who? Lutz Alda? But, sir!"

The General looked at him. "What do you *really* know about him?"

"Oh, not now, sir. Did Lutz Alda offer to cross the border into Russian territory?"

"He did."

"Then he has gone, and if they haven't caught him, he is still there. For if he were back, you would be the first person to see him. Without a doubt. This"—he indicated the letter Rozescu was still holding—"is sheer smoke screen."

"Why are you so sure, Alecu?" the General asked.

"I know Lutz Alda. I would pledge my head for him."

"If you're wrong about this, it may well cost someone else's head," the General said very slowly. "And you, Rozescu, what's your opinion?"

"I don't know Alda personally," Rozescu replied. "But three men who have known him almost all their lives trust him unconditionally: the Lieutenant Colonel, Candomir and Rundberg. In spite of certain differences largely superficial, two of these men are very much alike, and excellent judges of men. You don't know the third, sir."

"Oh yes, I know him," the General said gravely. He quieted Rananu's exclamation of surprise with a gesture.

"So much the better," Rozescu said. "Then you know that the man Rundberg loves is not Alda the cavalier, the sportsman, the generous and kind friend, nor is it Alda the intellectual. His attachment is to Alda's true nature, to Alda simply for his qualities as a man. Hence his daring, his devotion, his throwing all his intellectual and physical resources into the fight, as this report makes clear. For we've already agreed sir, that the investigation took the turn it did entirely by Rundberg's manipulation. Old Eisner's testimony is part of the script that Rundberg wrote."

"You mean that Rundberg cued him to represent Alda as a Nazi?"

"Certainly. The Sigurantza suspects him of being a Russian agent. What better way to overthrow this theory than to suggest that Alda, like so many others, is on the German side? To the Sigurantza people, that's a good deal more plausible than that a boyar like Alda should be a Bolshevik."

"That may be, may be." The General mused. "Press that light switch near you, Rozescu; I want to examine your hypothesis in bright light. You must admit that when I draw a connection between those three points, I arrive at the Nazi theory, too. First the sale of the property, then old Eisner's testimony, and now this!" He indicated the Inspector's letter.

"This," Rozescu said, "may be easier to explain than many another factor in the case. I'm dead certain, sir, that Rundberg planted this thing, too. Just as there had to be an antidote for the possibility that Alda is working for the Russians, so there had to be another antidote for the assumption that he has secretly left the country. If he was in Satul Turnului, he is in Romania, and with that the whole flimsy structure of circumstantial evidence collapses completely. The Sigurantza, or rather the Blaze, was happy to think that Alda had vanished into unknown parts. That, after all, is the chief evidence against him."

"Right," the General said. "We conclude then that Alda isn't in the country but Rundberg wants the Sigurantza to think so. Or —" The General paused and shook his head. "No, I'm afraid I can scarcely follow this Talmudic ingenuity."

"I admit, sir, that it isn't easy. But if you had talked to Rundberg and gotten some impression of his character, you'd see it, sir," Rozescu reassured the General. "As it is, you know him only from the documents, sir."

"Rundberg, Rundberg and Rundberg again!" the General exploded. "You'd think he was a wizard and prophet, not to speak of his other qualities."

"He is an organizer, sir, a leader," Rozescu maintained firmly.

"We have no choice but to assume that Rundberg anticipated the course of events," the General mused, his fixed stare returning. "Or else, alerted by the appearance of the spy, he kept in touch with Bucharest and therefore knew that the commission was coming to Cernauti and what its task would be. But even if I were to accept all that, your theory of Rundberg's having established a fictional presence of Alda in Satul Turnului doesn't satisfy me." The General shook his head. "No, it's out of the question. No one would dare."

"Would dare what, sir?" Rozescu asked. "Why not?"

"Who would attempt to deliberately fool the Sigurantza this way? If they find out, whoever planted the story could be in the very devil of a mess. They're artists at smashing anyone who trips them up. And that's hardly a secret, especially among Hungarians. They've tangled with the Sigurantza before."

"Felix Zinnendorf is a Hungarian, but he'd take his risks with the Sigurantza if there were any chance of helping Alda," Rananu said firmly. "He's a captain in the Reserve, and he raises horses. Oh, not to my taste—first-class animals, but nothing much to look at. Still—"

"Tell me about his stable some other time, Alecu. At the moment I want to know what motive Count Zinnendorf would have for helping Alda. That's important."

"Because he owes Alda a debt of gratitude. I have the story from Zinnendorf, not Alda. It was during the war—Alda came to his rescue, cut him out of a trap."

"Aha, in that case . . . thanks, Alecu. Good, I'll accept that, although we ought to check on it. Perhaps, Alecu, you could do that. Go and talk to Zinnendorf. He knows you're Alda's friend."

"I don't think the Count would give out any information even so," Rozescu spoke up. "Or rather, he'll stick to his story, that Alda has been there. It would only stir up the Sigurantza's suspicions if Rananu turned up at the Zinnendorfs'. To my mind it's better if we let this version stand. Let them look for Alda—they can't find him, after all, even if they want to."

"You sound so sure," the General said. "As if there were no other possibility."

Rozescu flushed. "Excuse me, sir, I was only expressing my opinion. I've devoted a great deal of thought to this affair. I may be mistaken on certain points. But I should like to say this, with the greatest possible emphasis: If fate should ever give me a friend in need, I would wish it were a man like Rundberg."

"That," the General said, meeting Rozescu's eyes, "is possibly the strongest argument of all. All right, boys," he said in a lighter tone, "let us hope that we don't hear anything new to upset our latest theory. Karl Rundberg of Cernauti has won all down the line. Let's end this discussion; it's late and we're tired." He placed the file and the letter in the safe behind his desk. "Who will drive me home?"

"I, sir," both men said simultaneously.

"Nice to have a choice. I'll ride with you, Alecu, and you"—he turned to the Lieutenant—"may ask for something else. As a consolation prize, so to speak."

"I would have done so anyhow, sir. May I have leave for tomorrow morning?"

"Granted, Lieutenant."

Ilie Rozescu was a tall, distinguished-looking man with the head of an ancient Roman. His sharp, intelligent features, his piercing dark eyes, his imperious voice, and his firm gestures bore out the picture. He was a lord in his realm, powerful and unbent at seventy-seven. When his son entered, he strode toward him, embraced him and kissed him on both cheeks. Only then did they shake hands.

"Stefan," the father said bluntly, "it's time for us to talk about various matters that concern not only you, but us, your parents. You know how I feel about your course of life. I recognize that you must take the path you have chosen, and I'm proud of you." He puffed on his cigar. "I want to remain proud of you, Stefan. And we —your mother and I—are afraid that—"

"Papa," Stefan said, "forgive me if I interrupt. I know what you want to say. If you hadn't brought up this matter, I would have."

"Then you know what I'm referring to?"

"Yes, Papa. You don't like my working for B II because a rumor has it that General Baderescu is making a pact with the Germans."

"Exactly. Although the word *rumor* is a bit too weak. It's a proven fact."

"You mean the interview with the Minister of War."

"In which Rozescu's son in parade uniform and Rozescu's Rolls Royce took part."

"The Minister of War is the General's superior, and the General is Chief of Staff of my department. We—the General as well as Rananu and myself—are soldiers who obeyed an order. The meeting lasted barely twenty minutes, and not a word was spoken having anything to do with politics. Those twenty minutes at the Minister of War's don't mean a thing, Papa."

"Are you trying to make a fool of me, Stefan?" Ilie Rozescu asked sternly.

"Why, Papa! I only want you to understand what it was all about. Please believe what I say and don't hamper me, but help."

Something in his son's low voice both reassured and alarmed Ilie Rozescue. "I'll do everything in my power," he said. "But speak out, explain. Trust me."

"The General, as far as I can see, wants to give the impression that he's allying himself with the Nazis. He is fundamentally their opponent and regards an alliance with them as a disaster for the country."

"What does he hope to accomplish, then?"

"The General hasn't spelled out his intentions. Yet Rananu and I—and another man who isn't in the country now—are more or less in on his secret. It's a case of howling with the wolves, for the time being. Perhaps he hasn't any specific plan, unless it is to cross up the others. I've learned a good deal lately. I know a few languages and then I understand something about people, can follow their trains of thought better than some others do. . . . I try hard. . . ."

"Stefan." Ilie Rozescue spoke very gravely. "This game of yours is extremely dangerous."

"Don't worry, Papa." Stefan laid his hand tenderly on his father's, which was gripping the arm of the chair tightly. "Prudence and clarity of mind are good guards against danger. I must stick to my job; that I am sure of. And I am acting as you would want me to, Papa."

"My recommendation would be for you to resign your commission tomorrow. I would see to it that you never again returned to the service. Stick to your studies, Stefan. Go away, if you wish—though I find it hard to propose that. We're old, Stefan, and you're all we have."

"Papa, Papa, I'm not an adventurer. There are greater things at stake. Imagine that our country were at war, and I were just any lieutenant in command of a platoon, like a thousand other lieutenants. What would you think of your son if he deserted? However much you loved him, you would despise him." Stefan Rozescu stood up. "The war against civilization, against freedom, has begun. I am in the fight, Papa."

"I'm frightened for you, Stefan." Ilie Rozescu rose to his feet with an effort. He placed both hands on his son's shoulders. "The Nazis—from all I've heard and read about them, and seen of them—I hate them. I don't fully understand what you have in mind, but I do see that it is directed against them. That will have to satisfy me. If I can help you—"

"You can, Papa. You can very well. Especially by helping Baderescu. He mustn't be isolated—socially. He comes to the club to play bridge once a week. Invite him to play. Avoid all discussions of politics, but if any of your friends—I know they're all more or less against the Germans—should raise accusations against him, try to make light of them. At least try. But don't discuss the General with anyone who isn't absolutely reliable; be sure of anyone you take into your confidence. That's one thing you must do, Papa."

"That's not difficult. I know discretion. What else can I do?"

"Later on we'll need money, Papa."

"It's there whenever you ask." The old man was smiling again. "I hope you'll be content with me, Stefan." He took his son's arm and they went out to the vestibule. "I can't go to sleep yet; I'd like to drop in on the club for an hour." He looked at his watch. "A quarter after ten. Dionisie will be in bed by now."

"I'll drive you over, Papa."

"That's good of you."

* * *

Stefan Rozescu hadn't intended to enter the club, but he caught a glimpse of Luceanu's car, so he took up his father's proposal. As they halted before the big mirror in the anteroom to straighten their ties and hair, and Ilie Rozescu studied his son, he could not repress a smile. What have I really known up to today about this big, handsome boy, he thought, except that he's my son and prefers reading books to making money? Here he stands beside me with his fair hair and brown, dreamy eyes, not a bit Romanian in appearance or temperament. Quiet, earnest, poised, my flesh and blood and not at all like me. How good for a father to be able to trust his son, and to have his son's confidence.

Ilie Rozescu put his arm around his son's shoulders, and thus they passed by the usher in his green tailcoat trimmed with white braid who opened the door admitting them to the commodious room with its big, wide, easy chairs drawn up to low tables. There they sat, the generals, senators, ministers, landowners, industrialists of Romania: the suave and the crude, the clever and the stupid, the rich and the scions of old families fallen on evil days. These were the men with ancient names that everyone in Romania knew—the boyars, linked to one another by a thousand ties of kindship and intermarriage.

All of them knew Ilie Rozescu, who now entered with his son. They knew him, his name, his life, his work, his achievements, fortune, habits, virtues and defects. And whether they loved him or not, whether they were his friends or only pretended friendship, they all called out greetings to him. For Ilie Rozescu was the richest of the rich, the most successful of the successful, and—this counted for much—had one of the oldest and finest among the good old names. Ilie sat down to play bridge. His son went into the small gaming room where, a servant had informed him, Luceanu was playing.

Around the table sat Luceanu, Rananu, and two men whom Stefan did now know. Beside Rananu sat a very old gentleman, kibitzing. As soon as Luceanu caught sight of Rozescu, he put down his cards and joyfully held out his hand. "Welcome, Fanica, wonderful to see you." He turned first to the old gentleman and then to the two other players: "This is Dr. Stefan Rozescu, Ilie's son."

There was an exchange of bows and handshakes.

"Come, sit down beside me. I want to look at you from close up," the old gentleman said in a squeaky voice. He took a glasses case from his pocket and fussily exchanged the glasses he was wearing for another pair. "Even a blind man can see the mistakes this boy Rananu makes, you know. I don't need my reading glasses for that. So, you're Ilie Rozescu's son. Oho, oho, you're not a Rozescu, not a trace of it. You're—wait a moment, wait a moment, I've seen you before; yes, I even have a portrait of you. If you had a goatee and longer hair, much longer, and wore a blue coat and a *lavallière* around your neck—hm? You're Ovidiu Bobescu, yes, that's it, your grandmother's father."

"I know," Rozescu smiled. "There's a portrait of him in our house."

"Ovidiu—Ovid, the poet of love," the old man said. "But Ovidiu wasn't; no love poems for him. Abolition of serfdom, introduction of the Code Napoléon—those were his hobbies. I remember well, yes—I was a good deal younger than you are today. Ovidiu Bobescu—oho, that's a long, long time ago."

"Take a look at this, Nene Hector—what can I do with this card?" Rananu interpolated. "No need to brush him up on history. Fanica knows all that. He knows much too much for his age. The main thing now is this."

Old Hector Rozetti changed glasses again and looked at Rananu's cards. "Try playing *sans à tout,*" he said.

"On your say-so—sans à tout." Rananu made his bid.

"*Contra,*" the next bidder said.

"*Tout à tout.*" Luceanu, Rananu's partner, raised the bid.

"Also contra," the fourth man said.

"This is going to be quite a game," Rananu said. Luceanu and Rananu won. "The first round I've won today," Rananu said. "You've brought me luck, Fanica." He sighed. "Last round, fellows; I must be on the job early tomorrow; can't sleep till noon like the rest of you. As soon as I start winning, I have to go to bed." He whinnied softly.

"We all come out even," Luceanu said, reckoning. "See you again day after tomorrow. Long life to you, Coane Hector. So long, fellows—I'm supposed to call for my ladies at the theater," he added as they sauntered over to the bar for a nightcap. Rananu had joined them. When he caught sight of Rozescu senior, he exclaimed, "Coane Ilie is here. I want to say hello to him."

"He'll be delighted," Alecu said. As soon as Rananu had left them, he asked Luceanu, "Everything under control, Ioan?"

"Perfect," Ioan replied, beaming. "A wonderful fellow, that banker Stürzli. In two days everything was fixed up. The wine is ours, Fanica! And what particularly pleases me is that I was able to give them back a large part of their goods—razors, sewing machines, and enormous quantities of watches. You get the idea— if you won't take my wine, I won't take your junk. Now let them see how they can dispose of their stuff."

"They'll find takers for it, Ioan," Rozescu said thoughtfully. "But we'd do best to give them a wide berth. We must go on buying, and it would be a good idea for you to get in touch with people who don't want to do business with the Germans."

Rananu returned, followed by an attendant with a message for Luceanu. "Two ladies wish to speak to you," he said.

Luceanu looked at his watch. "Good Lord! Tell them I'll be with them in a moment." And as the attendant sped off, he said to Rananu and Rozescu, "Now I'm really late! Margareta and Aglaia are here. Come along with me, fellows—if I go alone, I'll catch the devil. Damn it all!"

"So you want us to be lightening rods, you henpecked husband," Rananu said, laughing. "Come along, Fanica, we must save him."

Margareta was waiting in the ladies' parlor, nervously tapping her foot, while her sister was examining the pictures on the walls. In the dim light of the room, Margareta did not even see her husband, who came in cowering behind Rananu's massive frame, and her delight at seeing her two friends was so great that she forgot she was out of temper. She responded to their greeting in her usual vivacious fashion, holding out her cheek for them to kiss. When she spied her husband, she waved in a friendly manner. "Oh, how nice!" she exclaimed. "Aia, look! Alecu and Fanica!"

Aglaia turned and approached the group. Rozescu detached himself from the others and went up to her. "Hello, cousin," she said gaily, extending her hand.

He kissed it gallantly. "My dear coz. . . ."

"Thank you for the flowers," she said.

"Flowers? I didn't send you flowers. I should have, but I didn't get around to it."

"It wasn't you? Who else can have sent me flowers without a note or a card? I don't understand." She frowned thoughtfully.

"You must have other admirers, Aglaia."

"Not to my knowledge—really, I have no idea. Who could it possibly be? Besides, they were my favorite flowers, violets." She looked at him. "Admirers? I don't like the word, Stefan. It sounds so—no, I don't like 'admirers.'"

"Then I won't use the word but will nevertheless go on admiring you."

"I won't stop you." She rejoined the others, who had meanwhile sat down.

"You all must be hungry," Luceanu said, "and I myself have had scarcely any supper."

"There's no hour of the day when I can't eat," Rananu

agreed. "If it weren't for the strict regulations here—you know, ladies aren't allowed into the dining room."

"Oh, that can be arranged," Luceanu said. "And the food here is ever so much better than at any restaurant. Would that be all right?" He appealed to the ladies. When they agreed, he pressed a button. An attendant appeared. "Call M. Gaston," he ordered. The manager of the club appeared, a Frenchman who looked like a grand duke and behaved with the dignity of one. Luceanu explained what he wanted.

"I think," Gaston said, "that if I have the table set in the small *cabinet,* it would not be such a formidable breach of regulations. We can make an exception now and then. I'll send word as soon as we are ready." He strode out of the room with the bearing of a majordomo.

Rananu sighed enviously. "I'd give five hundred plum trees if I could wear a cutaway as Gaston does," he said mournfully.

"On the other hand, he can't ride as well as you," Rozescu comforted him.

"Salt on my wounds, Fanica. I never get around to riding these days, parole d'honneur. For the past three nights I've dreamed of horses. They look at me so reproachfully, like abandoned sweethearts, and weep tears the size of this." He clenched his fist to represent the tears wept by his dream horses. The others laughed. "Ah yes, I don't have it easy like certain philosophers: 'General, may I have leave for tomorrow morning?' 'Granted, Lieutenant.' Who knows what dusty tomes you'll pore over while I—"

"I shall not be poring over dusty tomes, but riding, if that's any comfort to you," Rozescu said.

"Riding? You?" Rananu was beside himself. "And that's what you ask for leave for! Why don't you take your Cousin Aglaia along, you egotist?"

"That's what I'd like to know, Stefan. Why don't you take your cousin Aglaia along?" Aglaia asked sternly.

"Really, why don't you take her with you?" Margareta screeched.

"You certainly should take her with you if you can," Luceanu chimed in with his gravest expression.

"Behold me humiliated and in despair," Rozescu responded, his face utterly serious. "Although I have a good excuse." He spoke directly to Aglaia. "I haven't ridden once since I had the good fortune to make your acquaintance, *ma chère cousine.* Nor did I know that you rode, and besides I would never have ventured to hope that you would care to ride with me. But if that should be the case—"

"It is the case, *cher cousin,*" Aglaia said.

"Then we'll ride tomorrow—provided that I can find a horse worthy of you. But wait—I know a chivalrous officer who has a white horse that would put all the other horses in the country to shame. I shall appeal to him. Domnule Lieutenant Colonel—"

"The devil take you—Pluto? Gladly, why not?" Rananu found it hard to dissimulate; it drove him wild to think of someone else's riding his favorite horse. But he could find no plausible reason for refusing. Pluto, he agreed, would be brought to the Rozescus' home at nine the following morning. Nor did Rozescu display any special enthusiasm. For although he would happily have gone riding with Aglaia at any other time, on this particular morning he would have preferred not to have anyone along.

The richest of the rich lived along the boulevard. Their houses stood in great gardens to either side of the perfectly straight avenue that stretched on for miles. A double row of trees separated the smoothly paved, luxuriously wide automobile road from the riding path and the sidewalk. In the front gardens of the magnificent villas blue pines and dark-green cypresses extended their luxuriant branches toward the blue-gray sky.

Though it was February, a warm wind was blowing and the boulevard was bare of snow. The pavement, over which the powerful automobiles purred swiftly, lay as gray and dry as the sidewalk. Only the riding path was black and moist, although it was not muddy, for the soil had a good admixture of sand and fine gravel.

Aglaia and Stefan met few riders. It was still too early in the year and in the day. But those they did encounter slowed their mounts and took time to look at the couple, for they made a sight to gladden a rider's heart and eyes. Aglaia, in an elegant black riding costume with white trim, boots of dull patent leather, her black, narrow-brimmed soft hat pressed down firmly on her black hair, sat her horse wonderfully. Pluto was a milky white with a curled mane, his tail like a white banner, ears forward, neck beautifully arched, prancing forward steadily, nobly obeying the curb rein, ignoring his much younger companion Amurath, who was inclined to foolery. Amurath was a gleaming coal-black with a bobbing little head, his eyes darting playfully sidewards, snorting and chewing on his bit, prancing along beside Pluto as if the rider seated upon him were not a gentleman such as one might encounter in Hyde Park or Richmond, but a sheik riding into an Arabian Nights adventure.

"I'm so grateful to you for this outing, Stefan," said Aglaia as the horses dropped from a trot to a walk. Her pale face was suffused with color and her black eyes flashed.

"I'm glad you're enjoying it, Aglaia," Rozescu said. "You ride beautifully." He took the reins in his right hand and with his left patted Amurath's neck. As he did so, he glanced quickly at his watch. It was twenty-five minutes of ten. Linton would surely be on the way by now. But how was he going to communicate with him? They had almost reached the end of the boulevard. There were no longer any houses, only small taverns whose habitués were drawn from the many stables in the vicinity. The racetrack was fairly near.

Amurath raised his head and whinnied, as he always did when he saw or scented horses. Replies came from the stables. Then, just in front of them, behind a white Mercedes-Benz with a Berlin license plate, Rozescu caught sight of Danny Linton's black Austin. "Let's take the path to the right, Aglaia," he said, raising the reins. He's bound to see me, even though I'm not able to talk to him, he thought, as they resumed their trot. Soon they reached the edge of the woods, and went into a canter. Aglaia cried out with pleasure as the pace quickened. She leaned forward and sang an accompaniment to Pluto's soft, rhythmic leaps. Amurath was all fire; every nerve in his body was burning to break into a full gallop; but he was held firmly by his rider's thighs and remained alongside his better-trained white companion, who conscientiously and unswervingly held his gait, as human patience had so well taught him.

"Oh, Stefan!" Aglaia exclaimed as the horses fell back to a walk. "How I've needed that! Everything is gone—my bad humor, my discontent, the ghosts. Those flowers came again this morning—I don't like such surprises. But now—"

"Fine," Rozescu said, laughing. The fast ride had done him good too. The sight of the happy girl heightened his joyous feeling and reconciled him to the situation in which she had unwittingly placed him.

They turned left into a forest path. Rozescu glanced at his watch. Almost a quarter past ten. If only Linton would wait. He glanced at the small shed where they had arranged to meet. There was nothing in sight, but Amurath raised his head and whinnied—a sure sign that there was a horse nearby. They approached within twenty paces of the shed. Amurath whinnied again. Rozescu felt certain that Linton must be there. He's seen us coming and has hidden; that means he doesn't want to be seen. Which must mean that he has something important to tell me. Quickly, covertly, Rozescu reached for his left stirrup strap and with a swift jerk pulled the end out of the buckle. Aglaia, looking silently and thoughtfully ahead along the path, did not see his action. Relieved, he felt the strap lengthen. A few yards before they reached the shed, the stirrup fell to the ground. "Bother!" he exclaimed.

"What's happened, Stefan?" Aglaia looked over at him.

"Oh, nothing important. Something wrong with the stirrup."

He stopped his horse and sprang from the saddle, drawing the reins over Amurath's head. "It's dropped off. I'd better go back for it." He tugged at the reins, but Amurath didn't stir.

"I'll find it, Stefan," she said, and was about to turn.

"No, don't bother, Aglaia. I'll manage by myself. But you'd better ride on or I'll have trouble with Amurath. He has his whims." Again he pulled at the reins, but Amurath braced his forefeet against the ground like a mule and refused to move. "Arabian training; he won't budge. Please, Aglaia, take the right-hand turning up ahead, and I'll catch up with you."

"Very well," Aglaia said obediently. Rozescu transferred the reins back over Amurath's head again. To the horse, this made the difference.

Amurath followed his master as obediently as a dog to the spot where the stirrup lay. He watched as Rozescu picked it up; then he raised his head, pointed his ears and whinnied. Softly, insistently, there came a whistled signal from the shed. Rozescu looked around and saw no one. Aglaia must already have reached the turn in the path. He walked behind the shed, followed by Amurath. Bushes reached up to the tumbledown wall. Linton was standing under the overhang of the roof, keeping his horse pressed up against the building.

"Hello, Steve," he said. "I'm holding my horse's mouth shut to keep him from neighing."

"Hello, Danny—stay out of sight. There were obstacles I didn't reckon with." He refastened the stirrup. "Any news, Danny?"

"Plenty. Last night I saw the Oxford man. Seems to have arranged everything yesterday. Said thanks for the tip; it was just what they needed to know."

"So you think it's already in the bag? They've sold the information?"

"Why would he have come otherwise?"

"Well, it's in your hands now, anyway. You'll hear from me, again, Danny. If Alice asks you for an appointment, I'm that Alice. Stay around here for a little longer. So long, Danny. Come, Amurath."

He swung into the saddle, pressed the horse's sides lightly, and Amurath flew forward. In barely a minute Rozescu caught sight of the white horse. He tempered his pace and rode up to Aglaia's side.

"Sorry, Aglaia," he said.

"Everything all right?"

"Fine."

They trotted; the woods ended and to the left of the road a broad, level field opened up, with a wagon path crossing it. They galloped along this path until the stables and boulevard came into sight once more. Then they let the horses drop to a walk.

"Good old Pluto!" Aglaia patted the horse's neck.

"Don't let Rananu hear you calling Pluto old. He'd never forgive you. Pluto is like wine, he says; the older he grows, the better he becomes. Rananu's infatuated with that horse."

"Does that strike you as odd, Stefan? I suppose you've never been infatuated, with a horse or—"

"Infatuated? Do you lose your heart to horses?"

"Oh yes, Stefan. To horses . . . and others." Her laughter sounded forced.

"Your horse must have been worthy of it, Aglaia," he said agreeably.

"Oh yes, Polka. . . ." She fell silent.

"Polka? I've heard of her. Yes, Bucur's out of Polka and by Belami. Alda's best horse, Bucur. Was your mare Polka by any chance Bucur's dam?"

"Alda bought the mare from my uncle. That's a long time ago. By the way, how is Alda? Where is he? Has Rananu heard from him?" she asked, busying herself with the reins.

"Alda? Somewhere in Transylvania. He's supposed to be staying with relatives of his fiancée."

"His fiancée? Alda's engaged?"

"Has been for a long time, but now he's said to be serious about marrying."

"Serious about marrying. Yes, marrying is a serious matter."

Only a single car now stood at the entrance to the Nasta stables, the white Mercedes, and next to it was a tall man, hatless, in riding clothes, who stood admiring the horses and the riders. Suddenly a jerk passed through his body, his heels clicked, his right arm shot up; but the artificial rigidity quickly dissolved into a courteous bow, and the angular fascist greeting became a cordial waving of the hand.

Rozescu concealed his discomfort at the familiarity of the greeting. He recognized the man, but at their meeting in the War Minister's office he had exchanged only a few words with him.

When he turned his gaze back to Aglaia, he was alarmed. Her face was deathly pale, her black eyes staring vacantly, and her hands, suddenly too feeble to hold the reins, were resting on the saddle. Her pale lips twitched. "Aren't you feeling well, Aglaia?"

"Not at all well, Stefan," she replied falteringly.

"Don't give way, Aglaia; hold on just another minute. Here, we're already there." They turned into the yard of a small tavern. "*La Jocheul*"—The Jockey—was written in black letters on a green sheet-metal signboard.

A young man came running up to hold the horses. Rozescu sprang from the saddle and went over to the side of Aglaia's mount. "Come, put your arms around my neck—easy now."

The tavern keeper appeared on the veranda. "The conitza is not well, I see. Here, the left-hand door, this is a quiet room. Perhaps the conitza would like to lie down on the sofa for a bit. I'll bring a zuica at once. Or cognac. Yes, cognac."

Aglaia dropped on the sofa. Rozescu pushed a cushion behind her back, removed her hat and gloves. He held her ice-cold hands in his and rubbed them. The proprietor reappeared with a large tray, two bottles of cognac, a siphon, a plate of anchovies, olives, white bread and butter. "The best medicine!" He half filled one of the big glasses. "This will help you, conitza. This is good for everything." And he promptly vanished.

"Here," Rozescu said. He held the glass out to her. She tried to raise her hand to take it, but could not. "Aglaia!" he exclaimed anxiously. He put his arm around her, supported her and brought the glass to her lips. She swallowed, with an effort at first, then more rapidly and eagerly.

"Good," she said very softly. She closed her eyes and leaned against him. They sat in silence for a while. Then she opened her eyes. "Good," she repeated, and sighed. "More cognac, please, Stefan, and a cigarette." She tried to smile. "Some women can't take the warm wind. The wind brought too much to me all at once today." She reached for the glass, which Rozescu had again half filled. "Drink with me, Stefan." She touched his glass and drained hers to the bottom. "I suppose you think I'm hysterical, Stefan?"

"Oh no, I was just frightened for you, Aglaia. But now you're better, aren't you?"

"Better, yes." Her eyes filled with tears. "No, worse, Stefan. I'm as unhappy as a woman can be."

"I don't want to press you for confidences, Aglaia," Stefan said timidly. "But if I knew what was troubling you, perhaps I could help."

She shifted to the chair facing him and looked into his face, into that smooth, clear youthful face with the dreamy eyes.

"The mystery of the violets is solved," she began. "The man who stood in front of the white automobile, who started to give the fascist salute, he must have sent them."

"But he is—"

"Baron Hartzfeld, a Baltic German. Until two years ago he was my friend, sweetheart, fiancé, whichever term suits you better, Stefan. He made a Nazi of me. Yes, a Nazi. We were supposed to be married, until—"

"Until?"

"It's very simple: Alfred Rosenberg wouldn't allow it. Inferior race. I'm not a Semite, to be sure, but a Slav on my mother's side. My mother was Russian. And in my father's case, too, it wasn't clear whether he was Romanian or Slavic. In any case, general and lieutenant governor though he was, a man by the name of Odanovici was obviously inferior. Another German might have risked it, but not Hugo Hartzfeld—he belongs to Rosenberg's intimate circle and believes fervently in the 'Myth of the Twentieth Century.' "

"I just can't take all this nonsense seriously, Aglaia—all that's rot. But Baron Hartzfeld—I suppose he loved you deeply?"

"Loved me—perhaps he loved me. For more than two years I thought so. I believed in him and in his cause, too. What won't a woman believe when she's in love with a man? Yes, I was in love with Baron Hartzfeld, who finally informed me by letter that he deeply regretted being unable to follow the impulses of his heart because of higher considerations, questions of race, stock—oh God!"

"How did you meet him in the first place?"

"Through Vova—Prince Vladimir Krupenski, who was a student with me in Zurich. A few days before his finals, Vova told me that after he received his diploma he was going to Russia. That was his native land and he belonged there, he said. He would work for the Bolsheviki—why not? And I was really a Russian—would I marry him and come with him?"

"Of course you didn't want to and he went alone."

"Yes, he went, but not to the Soviet Union. He went off with a rich American woman who'd met him in a nightclub."

"Poor Aglaia. That was painful for you, wasn't it?"

"Not really. And if so, it was only wounded vanity."

"But you haven't told me how Baron Hartzfeld came into the story."

"Well, Vova brought him to see me—in Zurich—that was before all these other things happened. It seemed that the Baron was in Switzerland to propagandize among the exiled Russians—the White Russians, that is. He hoped to win them to the Nazi cause by emphasizing that Hitler was an arch-foe of the Bolsheviks. The first evening Vova and Hartzfeld were the best of friends; by the next evening Vova was already bored; and by the third meeting he was making fun of Hartzfeld's doctrines. Hartzfeld parried his remarks with perfect courtesy. I was impressed by that. He's very urbane as well as good-looking."

"So he is. If he hadn't been, he wouldn't have been picked for his mission."

"What do you mean by that?" Aglaia asked, frowning.

"Baron Hartzfeld was on tour for Rosenberg. What would serve Rosenberg's purpose better than for him to take up with a beautiful young woman from the circles the Nazis wanted to convert—does this hurt you, Aglaia?" Rozescu interrupted himself.

"Please go on, Stefan. You mean he was only obeying instructions?"

"At the beginning, undoubtedly. It's only natural that he should have fallen in love with you later, Aglaia."

"You mean you also think he loved me?"

"How could he help himself? But a man like that is incapacitated for love. He let Rosenberg call him off like a dog. Rosenberg probably was no longer counting so much on the Whites, or else your connection with them wasn't close enough for his purposes—after all, you're only half Russian, a Romanian citizen, not one of the permanent exiles. You aren't especially interested in freeing Russia from the Bolsheviks. You would make a nice mistress, perhaps, but marriage with you would have put a useful man out of the running. So I think your racial 'inferiority' was a convenient pretext. Rosenberg simply ordered Hartzfeld to break relations, and Hartzfeld obeyed. They rewarded him with higher and more important assignments."

"Ugh, how rotten they all are!" Aglaia trembled with disgust.

"Better not generalize, Aglaia! And besides—be honest—you were happy with him for a long time."

"I was," she said sadly.

"That's a great deal. You ought to cling to that part of it."

"I've come to terms with it, I think. For more than a year I haven't thought about Hartzfeld as a woman thinks about a man she loves. And, Stefan"—she stared at the table—"I didn't collapse because of him. It was something else."

"Yes, Aglaia?"

"I was more upset by your news that Alda has a fiancée and is going to be married soon. Yes, that was it." She reached for her glass and finished it.

"What is there between you and Alda?"

"Between me and Alda? Nothing at all is between us." She sounded very definite. "Only"—her voice dropped to a whisper—"only that I love him, love him terribly."

"And does he love you too, Aglaia?"

"No, he doesn't. Not at all, not that much." She snapped her fingers. "That's just become clear to me—I'm nothing to him at all."

"Permit me a question: have you known him a long time?"

"Known him? Good Lord, I've seen him only three times in my life! The first time was when he bought Polka. I was very young then and he came to see my uncle. I don't suppose he even saw me. I decided that I hated him because he'd taken Polka away from me—I was barely fourteen at the time. And then I really fell in love with him in Constanza, two years later, at the riding meet. He rode Polka and I was in the stands. Again the thing was all on my side. And then I saw him again last November, at Margareta's party. You know about that, the scene with the Blaze and Lida—that disgusting story."

"Yes, and did anything happen between you?"

"Happen? He came into the room and I felt as if all these years I had been doing nothing but waiting for him."

"And?" Rozescu asked tensely.

"He was restive, preparing to leave, not really there at all. He was very polite, very friendly, rather avuncular and also a little clumsy. He held me away. Now I know why. I suppose he didn't want to be unfaithful to his fiancée."

"Yes," Rozescu said gravely, "he is a gentleman. I scarcely know him, but I know a great deal about him, and it all fits in with what you've told me. He had to behave that way, exactly that way. Because you were serious, and he knew he couldn't meet you on that ground. He couldn't because he is a man of honor. Of all your experiences with men, the one with Alda is the best. It should prove to you that he respects you."

"Respects—you don't know the first thing about women, Stefan!" Aglaia said angrily. "Those are outmoded ideas."

"If you would have a bit of patience, you would see that your view, on the contrary, is outmoded. You let yourself be governed by emotions that don't suit these times at all."

"What do I care about the times? I'm unhappy. What has that to do with the times?"

"A great deal," he said earnestly. "Haven't the times caused you to suffer? Haven't you been the victim of the times? What else was the episode with Hartzfeld if not one more of the many ugly situations in an age in which the tune is being called by a few brutal desperadoes? They used you, as they use millions of others. Why do you think Hartzfeld has been sending you flowers? And why did he greet you so warmly today?"

"Oh," she said, dismissing the matter, "sentiment, that's all.

He's here, happens to have discovered my address, perhaps even went to the trouble of finding it, and thinks it would be a nice gesture to send me violets, which he knows are my favorite flower. And when he sees me, why shouldn't he greet me? After all, we didn't part on bad terms, only out of 'higher considerations.' Perhaps he even still loves me a little."

"And what about you, Aglaia? Are you quite sure of yourself? Not a bit of sentiment, not a bit of love?"

"For Baron Hartzfeld? You really know nothing about women, you philosopher! I love Alda, even though he's involved with someone else and doesn't want me."

"I believe you, Aglaia, and it's a good thing, too. Your feeling for Alda is your best protection against this man Hartzfeld, who has his eye on you again, who wants to use you once more, just as he did before. Does it hurt you when I speak plainly?"

"Go on. How can I possibly be hurt any more?"

"I think Baron Hartzfeld has simply been ordered to resume contact with you, and through you to reach Romanian society. You are a number in the Nazis' files. They are orderly people, and the Baron is nothing if not self-confident. He has great faith in his magnetic personality. The Nordic hero will have no trouble making a fresh conquest of the Slavic female."

"He'll soon learn!"

"What will you do, Aglaia, if he approaches you again?"

"I won't receive him. And if he writes to me, I'll send his letters back unopened."

"May I suggest a better strategy? I would advise you to change roles with him. If the Baron has used you for his ends, do the same; let him pay his call, be friendly but unapproachable. No longer a student in love, but an experienced woman of the world. A seductive, difficult, desirable Aglaia, altogether different from the girl he knew, just as he's now a different man to you. Flirt with him, keep him dangling with half promises, confuse him."

She smiled. "Can I do it?"

"Of course you can. Lead him along and remain cool. The more you fend him off, the more ardent he'll become. The chief thing is: are you ready to do it?"

"Ready? What woman wouldn't be? We're a vengeful sex, Stefan. If I only knew what purpose it would serve . . . and then you have to remember that Ioan is not very fond of Germans. I won't be able to have him visit at the house."

"I'll clear that with Ioan."

"Yes, you can. Ioan looks up to you—there's something about you, God knows what it is." She looked at him searchingly.

"And, Aglaia—you'll be doing this for a purpose. Not just on a personal basis, but to settle a score."

"I'm beginning to see the drift. You've enlisted me as a kind of agent—am I right? You really are a romantic, Stefan!"

"No, not a romantic, an enemy of the Nazis. Not on emotional grounds, but rationally and by conviction."

"If you like. But there's one thing I don't understand—forgive me for bringing it up, but people all say that your General is a Nazi sympathizer."

"People will say a similar thing," Stefan replied with an almost imperceptible smile, "if relations between the house of Luceanu, or rather between Aglaia Odanovici and Baron Hartzfeld, develop as I have foreseen. Everyone will think that Aglaia Odanovici is a Nazi sympathizer."

"And what do we do about that, Stefan?"

"We let them think it. In certain circles sympathy with the Germans is the fashion, and so you are falling in with the fashion. You have an important assignment, Aglaia, and the talent to carry it out. You'll do your best, won't you?"

"My very best, Stefan," she said softly, extending her hand to him.

When Rozescu sat down at his desk in the office, Aglaia's voice still sounded in his ears. They hadn't been parted an hour before she had telephoned because she had news for him. Violets had come once more, this time with a note. Aglaia had promptly invited Hartzfeld to tea that afternoon. Rozescu could not suppress a pleased smile. Rananu, who sat facing him, whinnied softly. "Your ride with Aglaia seems to have been very enjoyable," he said.

Before Rozescu could reply, the General called them in.

"Boys," he said, "we're not finished with the Alda business, not by a long shot. I've just had a visitor, here in the office."

"Not the Blaze, sir!" Rananu exclaimed.

"That would have been the crowning glory. No, Barbulescu came to see me, in deepest secrecy and in a state of consternation. Danghu is raising the roof. Today he read the report thoroughly, for the first time, and then the report that Alda is in the country. He was furious. What business did Barbulescu have passing the word along to B II before he himself was informed? To make it short, he ordered Barbulescu to transmit an order to all the inspectors and sub-inspectors of Transylvania to arrest Alda and his fiancée and bring them to Bucharest headquarters."

"And has Barbulescu passed on the order?" Rozescu asked.

"That's what he came to see me about. He doesn't want to. It seems he did everything he could to dissuade the Blaze, but the fellow can't be reasoned with."

"But the Blaze has no authority to order their arrest, sir!" Rananu burst out.

"No legal authority, you mean. To a man like him, that's the last consideration. But to come to the point: he cannot reach Alda, but he can very well reach Alda's fiancée. Sooner or later he will lay his hands on her, and then God help her! Who knows what those torturers will wring out of her?" The General lapsed into silence. Only his hands, nervously tapping the desk, betrayed his feelings.

"What about Barbulescu?" Rozescu asked.

"He wanted my advice and my backing. He doesn't like the whole affair. As far as I can see, he hasn't been bought, although for a moment I thought it possible that here was another example of Rundberg's influence. But there are too many arguments against that. Something else seems to be operative. He's afraid that Danghu will get himself into a jam, and carry his subordinate with him. Barbulescu isn't stupid; he perceived long ago that Danghu was concerned only with gratifying his vengeance, or his hatred. But Alda, Barbulescu says, is not just anybody. He therefore wants to hold back the order for the arrest of Alda and Baroness Varsany as long as possible—in the interval he wants me to try and bring Danghu to reason."

"May I suggest, sir, that Danghu won't be reasoned with on this one subject," Rananu said. "Even if you could find some telling way of putting it to him. But he isn't the final authority in the Ministry of the Interior. If the Minister were to declare the case closed and bar any further investigation—"

"The Minister is sick," the General said. "Recovering from an operation. Danghu is acting for him."

"If you were to call on him, sir—after all, he can't be so very sick, since he has the Blaze in for conferences—and could persuade him to cancel the investigation for, let's say, tactical reasons—"

The General reflected. "Not such a bad idea. I see no other way out. I must try, anyhow; ideas will come to me. Yes, if Danghu were isolated, without the apparatus of the Sigurantza, he couldn't cause much trouble. If I can only do it! Who will drive me?"

"Let me, sir," Rozescu said.

"Good. It's your turn anyway." He looked at his watch. "Half past three. We'll be back in two hours. Alecu, you take over for me. If by any chance the Blaze should call, I'll be back at the office by six o'clock."

* * *

A few minutes after four, Rozescu's car stopped in front of the Minister's country home. It was still fairly new, situated at the end of a new, unpaved driveway and separated by a large garden from the only neighboring house, also a villa in the cottage style. As he got out of the car, the General told Rozescu, "I'll go in alone. If I should need you, I'll send out for you." He tucked his briefcase under his arm and went to the door. Rozescu began to turn the car. He backed slowly as far as the next house. There the car stuck in the soft, deep gravel. Rozescu got out to study the situation. As he did so, his glance fell on a brass plate engraved with the name of the house's owner: Archibald Whitecliff. He murmured the name under his breath as he got back into the car, stepped hard on the gas pedal, and succeeded in pulling out. Shortly afterwards, when he was once more parked in front of the Minister's house, the General emerged and walked slowly toward the car. He sat down silently beside Rozescu, and did not speak until they reached the highway. Then he said only, "Nothing doing."

"The Minister refuses to call off the investigation?"

"I did not ask him directly, but he made his attitude clear before I really mentioned what I wanted. He isn't so ill. He's letting the Blaze have things his way out of what seems to be a sort of funk. He's given the Secretary General full powers and, far from disavowing him, is ready to back him to the hilt. What's more, there's the chance that he'll tell Danghu of my intervention, sooner than have the Blaze hear of it from some other source. And then Danghu will have a dangerous weapon in his hand."

"Yes, if the Minister tells Danghu and Danghu realizes we must have got wind of the order for arrest. . . . Have you any further data on this curious partnership, sir?"

"Until recently the Minister was swamped with debts; now he is well-to-do. He hasn't had that house long, either. Nor does he seem to feel very much at ease in it."

"I see." Rozescu stepped on the gas and drove at rather high speed through the suburb. "Well, the visit was a mistake, sir, but we had to try it, and now the danger is all the greater. They're sure to track down Baroness Varsany pretty soon. I hate to think of what they'll put her through. You can't expect a woman to resist those methods very long. If she tells them anything at all, the whole thing will unravel; they'll find the way back to Count Zinnendorf, to Rundberg—" He broke off. After a minute of silence, he said, "We must prevent that, sir."

"Can you think of any way to do it, Rozescu?"

"Our first step would be to urge Zinnendorf to hold firm and to get word to Baroness Varsany to remain in hiding. He may have some means of communicating with her without necessarily knowing where she has gone."

"We can try that, though there is scarcely time enough. And even so—do you think he'll stand up to their third degree? It's not only a question of moral integrity, but of physical stamina. What's your second idea, Rozescu?"

Rozescu stared straight ahead as though he hadn't heard the General's question. He glanced at the car's clock. It read 5:05. They had already reached the city; in another ten minutes they would be back at the office, holding a council of war and finding no solution. Rozescu turned off from the crowded Calea Victoriei into a side street. He drew to a stop near a taxi stand. "One moment, sir." He jumped out of the car and raised the radiator. "Breakdown," he called out. "You'd best take a cab; I may be quite a while fixing this."

Without a word the General got into a cab. As soon as the cab vanished around the corner, Rozescu took a pair of overalls from the trunk and changed his clothes inside the car. When he took the wheel again, he looked like an auto mechanic. He made his way down several streets and drew up in front of a secretarial bureau. Entering, he explained to the girl in charge, speaking broken Romanian mixed with German, that he had something to type.

"I'm afraid we have no one here who can type German."

"That won't be necessary, thank you. I only wanted to have the use of one of your typewriters."

In five minutes he had typed his message and placed it in an envelope. The girl took the payment without looking up from her book. When Rozescu stepped outside again, the streetlights were already on. He drove through side streets to the church on the Piatza Amzei. There he stopped. When his clock read 5:35 he drove slowly past the Luceanu home. The gate was closed, and through the bars he caught sight of the white Mercedes. He drove around the first street to the right, then turned right once more into a small alley, and stopped halfway down it. This alley skirted the wall of the Luceanu garden. The spot where Rozescu stopped lay in almost complete darkness. He looked around; no one in sight. In a moment he was on top of the wall and had jumped down into the garden. He walked rapidly along a path covered with damp leaves. The house emerged from the misty dusk; the driveway lantern cast a yellow glow upon the light gray pavement, so that the white car looked golden. So you've driven up in a golden carriage, my handsome Hugo, like the prince in the fairy tale, Rozescu thought as he came out of the shadow of the bare trees. He scurried up to the side of the

car. Wearing his driving gloves still, he opened the unlocked door.
A book lay on the seat beside the wheel. Rozescu opened it. It was a
German edition of a novel by Anatole France: *The Red Lily*. He
smiled. It wouldn't please your Führer, let alone Rosenberg, to know
that you read Anatole France, he thought. He leafed through the
book, and in spite of the poor light his eye was caught by one sentence: "Conquerors seem to me without exception like madmen."
Grinning, he tucked the letter into the book at this spot, leaving the
edge of the envelope showing plainly.

"If it were done when 'tis done, then 'twere well it were done
quickly," he quoted, grinning. But his grin disappeared when he
drove up to the B II office and saw, parked behind Rananu's Buick,
Danghu's black Horch.

Rananu was not at his desk. Rozescu picked up the telephone.

"Yes?" he heard the General's voice say.

"Reporting back, sir. May I see you?" he said with an unusual
insistence.

"Will you come to my office, Rozescu," the General replied.

Rananu was already there. But the center of the scene was the
dapper figure sprawled in an easy chair, legs crossed and his entire
posture breathing insolence.

"Please be seated," the General said softly. "Secretary General
Danghu would like clarification on certain points in the report of
the investigation."

"Clarification from B II?"

"Yes," the General said. "The Sigurantza was, it is true, equally
represented on the commission—in fact, there were more Sigurantza
men than ours—but still we have no objection."

"Very well, sir. As far as I recall, Lieutenant Ciobotariu, who
kept the minutes for his agency, had virtually the same text as I did.
We compared our copies before they were signed by the members
of the commission."

"Contradictions carefully eliminated, that is," Danghu said
disdainfully. "We know that trick. We'll investigate the case without
B II, although this department has made every effort to tie our
hands. That you, General, want to see my chief, over my head, is a
clear sign, clear and—compromising."

Rananu took a step away from the window where he was standing. His movement was so threatening that the General threw him a
look commanding restraint. Then the General smiled engagingly.
"If you would care to elaborate on that, Secretary General Danghu
. . ." he said.

Danghu cleared his throat. The others could feel him searching
for biting phrases. But all the while he kept an eye on Rananu, who

stood speechless and stiff, in prescribed military posture. Rozescu gazed at the General with a calm, assured expression, as if to say, "We are here, we can support you. Show no weakness."

The pause lasted a long time. The General's smile changed, became haughty and mocking. "Well then, let us terminate this visit, Domnule Danghu. I am content with what you have concocted so far. Moreover, our time is limited; we have a great deal of work to do."

"What's that . . . ?" It was a growl of fury.

"I have made myself clear. B II is not interested in your plans and places no value on your opinion. Lieutenant Colonel Rananu, see the Secretary General to his car."

Danghu sprang to his feet. He gasped, choked. His carefully combed hair was suddenly disheveled, so that the white blaze dropped across his forehead. "You wait! I'll take care of you, all of you—you're hand in glove with that Communist Alda! You're all Bolsheviks, all of you, traitors, selling the country!"

Rananu, who had stepped very close to Danghu, drew his arm back, fist clenched. The General called out, "Don't!" and the arm dropped. Rozescu, who had taken no part in the confrontation, now stood up and without looking at Danghu said quietly, "We have looked into the matter of who is selling the country, Domnule Danghu. And we have arrived at some strange conclusions. You will be hearing more about this." He about-faced and said to Rananu, "Permit me, sir, to undertake the duty of escorting the Secretary General to his car."

Rananu stepped back. His face was white, his forehead damp.

Danghu looked frantically from one to the other. His lips quivered, and he seemed far from threatening.

Rozescu followed him to the anteroom, where a corporal helped him into his coat, and from there to the car. He was about to step in when the Lieutenant inquired casually, "By the way, do you speak English?"

Danghu sagged. Rozescu left him and returned to the General and Rananu.

"What made you turn on him that way, Rozescu?" the General asked.

"Self-defense, sir. Harrying him, accusing him, using the same methods he uses. If necessary, falsely accusing him, for all I care."

The General eyed Rozescu sternly. "You had nothing special in mind?" he asked.

"Only my feeling that the man is corrupt the same instinctive way some people are musical, and he can have no scruples because he believes in nothing. He sells whatever he has to sell."

"So you think he has sold something—it would seem so from his reaction. But haven't you rather messed things up for us?"

"If he has reason to fear us, he may try to make a pact with us. Or else he'll follow tried and true practice and shout, 'Stop thief!' A test of strength, sir."

"A pact? With him? Never. Besides, we would never know what we were getting into. A test of strength? Hm. Take this down, Rozescu: 'To the Attorney General. Request immediate issuance of arrest and search warrants against Orest Danghu, Secretary General in the Ministry of the Interior. There exist strong grounds for believing that he has betrayed important state secrets, especially relating to the military, to a foreign power.'"

The General signed the letter and said to Rananu, "Take this to the Assistant Attorney General. He will make no difficulties. I myself am going to the Ministry of War. A test of strength, eh!"

A few minutes after nine o'clock two automobiles stopped in front of the fine house which was the residence of Secretary General Danghu. A line formed rapidly: three army officers as advance guard, then two detectives, and behind them the military Provost Marshal and the Assistant Attorney General. Completing the procession was a hatless and coatless man in a shabby suit.

Major Burda of B II pressed the doorbell. The door was opened almost instantly. "Here already?" an elderly servant said. "Thank God—I just this minute telephoned. There." He pointed to a half-open door. Lying on the rug in front of his desk was Secretary General Orest Danghu. The white streak of hair had fallen over his face, half concealing a round black hole in his forehead. The Blaze was dead.

To all appearances Danghu had committed suicide. But the party of investigators soon determined that he had been shot. The murderer had made only a cursory attempt to make the death seem a suicide. The shot had been fired from a distance of about six feet. The pistol lay nearby, but its factory stamp and number had been filed away.

According to the servant, a man he had never seen before had rung the bell, and as soon as the door was opened had pushed him aside and stepped in. The stranger had said something to the Secretary General in a language the servant did not understand but believed to be French. The Secretary General had seemed very perturbed. He had sent his servant out for some medicine obtainable only in a special pharmacy. The errand had taken about forty-five minutes. When he came back, he had knocked on the study door and receiving no answer, had entered—to find his master dead on the floor.

The search of the house yielded at first only a cache of pornographic pictures. The wall safe behind the Indian tapestry was open and completely empty. But the man in the shabby suit kept coming back to a wide, massive wardrobe which contained innumerable pairs of silk pajamas in the brightest colors. The little man sniffed around the wardrobe, repeatedly tapped it, and finally declared that the sound on the left side differed from that on the right. Once more the wardrobe was emptied, and this time the specialist discovered a spring on the inside. When he pressed it, the left side wall slid open. By now the number of persons in the room had swelled considerably; General Baderescu, Rananu and Rozescu had turned up, as well as Barbulescu and other high officials of the Sigurantza and the police. What was revealed inside the wardrobe made them all gasp. Not only was there a fortune in dollars and gold coins heaped inside the hidden compartment; on the very top lay a packet of brand-new British hundred-pound notes to the tune of £83,000 sterling.

The morning newspapers reported noncommittally that the Secretary General of the Ministry of the Interior had been found dead in his home. The police were investigating the possibility of murder.

General Baderescu read this terse account at seven o'clock in the morning. Rananu and Rozescu were already in the office. "Well," he said, removing his reading glasses and swinging them lightly in his hand, "that was a fast solution. Your shot in the dark hit the mark, Rozescu."

"Sheer good luck that none of us actually fired," Rananu said. "I came very close to doing so before your eyes, sir. But tell me, Rozescu, where did the shot come from?"

"There's hardly any doubt that Danghu was shot on orders from the Germans."

"Explain that to me, philosopher," Rananu asked.

But the General took it upon himself. "The man who came to see him is undoubtedly an old hand and had his instructions. They'd learned somehow that Danghu was working for the English, and sent someone to take care of him. The idea was to have him shoot himself. But time was pressing, the servant might be back at any moment, and Danghu showed himself an utter coward. So the mysterious visitor had to press the trigger."

"How do you see it, Rozescu?"

"As I see it, this murder was not only a punishment, but a terroristic threat. The thing was meant as a warning: anyone who betrays us will be shot. Leaving the pistol beside the body was a hint to the authorities to represent the death as suicide. At the present moment the Germans don't want to intimidate the masses, but to win them over, and murder is bad strategy. They have their hands full as it is, combating 'atrocity propaganda,' as they call it."

"I see why you insisted, sir, on having the newspapers put it as a simple murder case," Rananu said to the General.

"That was just a start," the General replied. "Before the day is out, Bucharest—and by tomorrow the whole country—will know the political ramifications of this episode. Not to speak of all the embroidery that will be added to the tale."

"Yes," Rozescu agreed. "There'll be a great deal of talk, which is all to the good. The man in the street will draw the right conclusion: it's dangerous to do business with the Germans."

"The man in the street—if only he had more to say in our country!"

"And if only we had more philosophers like Lieutenant Rozescu," Rananu said, laughing.

Nagy's telegram to Rundberg from Arad had read, "Suitcase shipped by car via Bistrita." There could be no question about its meaning. Eisner had decided to bring the Polish noble back by car. There must have been some compelling reason for this, for who would venture to drive over bad roads and a dangerous mountain pass at this season, unless it was absolutely necessary? Rundberg, who had imagined that he could now breathe easier, was profoundly disturbed, and remained uneasy until Eisner drove up to his door. Eisner had come straight from Candomireni to see him.

"What happened, Mischa?" Rundberg asked as soon as they had shaken hands.

"Here, read the letter. This one's for you; the other is for Candomir."

"But you've just come from him; why didn't you give it to him?" Rundberg asked as he opened his envelope.

"Didn't get a chance to. Read first; then I'll explain the rest." He stood up, went to the cupboard for the bottle of cognac, and poured himself a drink. Then he lit a cigarette. He had taken only a few puffs by the time Rundberg laid the letter on the table.

"The Baroness writes that we must be careful about Bilinski, that he's unreliable. She suggests that we accede to his demands, or at least pretend to do so, and not cross him in any way, because he might be dangerous. He's threatened to spill."

"So he has. The Baroness is right, the man *is* dangerous. You know, Karl, when we rode over the Magura—God, how he carried on, wet his pants out of sheer funk—I thought, if I bash him on the head and toss him into a ravine, he could lie there till—"

"Mischa!" Rundberg exclaimed, horrified.

"It would be no loss. He spoke of going to the Sigurantza."

"What happened? All this is news to me. And let's have no more talk of—of violence. You're a Jew, Mischa."

"You're right there, Karl; the Jews exist to be killed, not to kill." He ground out his cigarette in the ashtray. "Ah—" He shrugged.

"Yes, the man can do a lot of harm. Though I don't believe the fellow knows where Alda is. Still, he knows enough to make trouble for us. We're all in danger. I'll—" He paused. "It was a bad mistake not to give Candomir the letter. Why didn't you?"

"I thought I'd better consult with you first. If you thought the Baron ought to have the letter, then you could give it to him."

"Why did you think that he shouldn't?" Rundberg said with a frown.

"Well, the way I saw it was this: the letter probably tells only half the story. A lady wouldn't want to write about such filth. And she's a lady, Karl! So I would have to fill Candomir in on the juicy details. But a baron is a baron, Karl—they can't help themselves. Maybe he'd throw the bastard out because he wouldn't want such a creature under his roof, and then the fellow would run straight off to the Sigurantza and tell them God knows what."

"You're right, Mischa. The Baron will have to be given some preparation. Hm . . . I think I can arrange it."

"We're practically at Candomireni already!" Schajeh pointed with his whip. The first houses of the small town were already in sight.

Rundberg crossed the road and set out on a footpath in the direction from which they had come. He pursued a cart road for a short distance across an open field to the woods which formed the continuation of the Candomir park. He turned into the lane of ancient beech trees, and chose the turning that led to the paddock. Radu Candomir was coming from the paddock, and they caught sight of each other almost at the same moment.

"Good morning, Domnule Rundberg, good morning," Candomir saluted him cheerfully.

"Good morning, Baron." Rundberg lifted his fur cap and, like Candomir, removed his right glove. The two shook hands.

"Wait a moment, here he comes!" A groom was leading a horse toward them; he held the lunging rein and the whip in his left hand. "Just look at him. A son of Bucur. He was three years old in November."

"A beautiful horse, Baron." It was a golden chestnut, with a flaxen mane and tail. "Yes, Bucur—and the dam?"

"Oglinda. Noble stock, if it weren't for the color. But I imagine you have more important things to talk to me about." He waved the groom away. "What brings you here?"

In lieu of reply, Rundberg handed Candomir the letter. "From Baroness Martha."

"Aha—let's go into the house." Candomir put the letter into the pocket of his fur jacket. "I suspect its contents will not be pleasant."

"Not at all pleasant, Baron, I'm sorry to say. I've had a similar letter from the Baroness."

"She's safe, I hope?" Candomir paused and stared at Rundberg.

"For the present—but let's wait till we get into the house. It isn't advisable for me to be seen here, Baron. Even by Pan Bilinski."

"He's in bed, sick—the trip took a terrible toll of him. He even had to have the doctor. It's no picnic to come by car all the way from Arad. It's a wonder the accident had no worse effects than it did."

"Oh yes." So Bilinski had pretended that he had been smashed up in an automobile accident en route!

They sat in Candomir's study. Candomir read Martha's letter. "But this is fantastic—what does it mean?" he exclaimed. "She tells me Bilinski is dangerous, totally untrustworthy, and must be handled with extreme caution. What in God's name has happened? Do you know anything about it, Domnule Rundberg?"

"Bilinski told her that if we crossed him he would betray Lutz's whereabouts to the Sigurantza; he claims he knows. I don't believe that Lutz confided his plans to anyone, but even false information might lead to terrible difficulties for Lutz."

"No!" Candomir was stunned. "He does know where Lutz is! But how can he . . . ? That would be—"

"He knows?" Rundberg's face resembled a grinning death mask. "How does he know, Baron?"

Candomir stood up and approached Rundberg's chair, his head bowed. "I must think this over calmly. I simply cannot understand it; it makes no sense at all. It—" He broke off.

"Can you tell me how he knows where Lutz is and—do you also know?"

"I—not I!" Candomir was deeply perturbed. He shook his head violently.

"Baron," Rundberg said resolutely, "I know where Lutz is, and it would not surprise me if you knew also that he—has crossed the border. You're his friend, after all. But why should Bilinski have been told?"

Candomir sighed with relief. He threw a grateful look at Rundberg for having spared him the necessity of abrogating the promise to his friend. Then he drew up a chair and sat facing Rundberg, so close that their knees touched. "Oh, you're in on it. Thank God," he said. "Now I may tell you how Bilinski knows. Lutz went on his account."

"Baron Candomir," Rundberg said with a sternness that seemed alien to him, "you will have to tell me the purpose of Lutz's—trip. This is most important; it may hold the clue to the entire situation."

"Lutz went to hunt up Bilinski's wife and, if he finds her, to bring her here."

There was a moment of oppressive silence. "No," Rundberg said, "it doesn't make sense. There's something wrong. Very wrong." He shook his head. "Lutz is risking his life to save this fellow's wife, and this fellow threatens to betray him to the Sigurantza. Can you figure that out? You know him better than I do."

Candomir rubbed his brow with a tormented expression. "Are you positive that he made the threat? Couldn't there have been some misunderstanding? How did it come about?"

"I suppose I must tell you the whole story, although I didn't intend to. But there's too much at stake."

Candomir listened to Rundberg's anecdote with mounting relief. "So that was it?" He grinned. "A lady-killer's hard luck. It really isn't serious. Bilinski was balked, humiliated, and said something that could easily have been misunderstood."

"No, I don't see it that way. Baroness Varsany didn't exaggerate, and the man who drove Bilinski here is also sensible. The threat was made in earnest; there's no doubt about that."

"What if it was? Granted that he said something in a state of anger that sounded like a threat—can't you understand that, Domnule Rundberg? Here we are all doing our best for him, a man is risking his life to help him, his wife is in terrible danger, and he's caught fornicating with a servant girl. Of course he was mortified. I'll handle him with kid gloves for a while. By and by he'll forget the episode."

Rundberg looked at Candomir with an expression almost of pity. "It may be that I have no proper understanding of aristocrats. The aristocrats I have known were men like old Baron Neagoe, or your father, or you and Lutz, and a good many others. They weren't the kind of people who made threats. They might have lost their heads, taken a shot at someone, done God knows what—but they never would have blackmailed anybody—or even dreamed of it."

"That's true, Domnule Rundberg," Candomir admitted. "But don't you think we can keep him neutralized if we give him no pretext?"

"What do you call a pretext? Tomorrow, the day after or next week he'll find himself another pretext, and then he will threaten blackmail again. He has become a link in a chain—involuntarily, because the situation created it. And he's a thin wire between links of hardened steel."

"You exaggerate, Domnule Rundberg. I can't believe it—he's a nobleman." And as if the word had restored his strength and confidence, he repeated firmly, "He is a nobleman, a coane."

"I haven't come to slander the man, but the situation is a good deal more dangerous than it was a week ago. I intensely regret having sent him on that trip to Satul Turnului. Even then I didn't really trust him."

"What did you know about him a week ago?"

"I wasn't going to mention this, but it's best for you to know the whole story. Read this letter, please." Rundberg produced a sheet of letter paper from his pocket.

Candomir read it and returned the letter to Rundberg. "You have risked nothing, Domnule Rundberg," he said stiffly, rising. "I recommended Pan Bilinski and therefore I am his warrant. I shall order Domnule Hasler to have the money sent to you today."

"Baron," Rundberg said very quietly, "you have read the letter but not noticed the date. It arrived a month ago."

"I didn't notice, that is true. But what is the significance of that?"

"If I had been concerned about the money, I would have called on you last month."

"And why didn't you?"

"Because I wanted to give Pan Bilinski time to settle the matter. After all, he too must have been informed that the money wasn't paid out."

"He mentioned the matter, I recall, the very day he went to Oradea. He said he had received no news, but that if the sum had not been paid, you would have let him know. I cannot share your view that he did not behave correctly in this business matter." Candomir spoke coolly and formally.

But Rundberg refused to be put in his place. "Julius Zwick in Zurich is a highly respected firm. Herr Zwick knows Lutz very well. Countess Elizaveta Voronovska told Zwick to communicate with her son-in-law and financial administrator, Prince Roman Bolgurski. Bolgurski declared that he knows no Countess Janina Voronovska and knows nothing of any demands or claims which she might legally have upon him or his mother-in-law."

"This doesn't prove that Bilinski acted in bad faith, but that his wife's relatives did. His wife is a Countess Voronovska by birth, a niece of Countess Elizaveta, and is entitled to a share in her grandfather's estate. It's a large fortune, and more than a fourth of it must accrue to Bilinski's wife."

"If I understand you correctly, then, Pan Bilinski attempted to discount an unconfirmed claim on the part of his wife."

"I'm not so familiar with the terminology of these matters, Domnule Rundberg," Candomir said coldly. "Your reasoning strikes me as farfetched, to say the least. What connection is there between this financial matter and a remark made in anger or shame? It may be that in his inexperience or credulity Bilinski did not proceed as would a businessman. What can he possibly know about business? He is a nobleman; he undoubtedly acted in good faith. Be easy." He laid a hand on Rundberg's shoulder. "I know you're afraid for Lutz. But your fear is unjustified."

"Afraid?" Rundberg raised his head. "Yes, Baron, I am afraid. And there are connections between all these things, although I cannot see them clearly at the moment." With sudden resolution, he stood up. "We must have a talk with Pan Bilinski."

"Then come along, Domnule Rundberg. We'll go up to see him."

"Fine. And I assure you I'll deal gently with Pan Bilinski, very gently."

Anatol lay in bed. When Candomir entered, he laid his book aside. He did not seem especially surprised to see Rundberg.

"Good morning, Anatol," Candomir said. "How do you feel?"

"Thank you, not too bad." He responded to Rundberg's bow with a slight nod.

"Forgive our barging in on you like this," Candomir said courteously. "But Domnule Rundberg has something important to tell you."

"I hardly know—" Bilinski sat up in bed and turned his face toward Rundberg. The bandage had been replaced by several wide strips of adhesive tape, and these transformed his insolent, supercilious mask into a grotesque grimace. "To be candid, I've had enough of Rundberg and his associates." He dropped back on the pillow, but kept his eyes on Rundberg.

As if he didn't recognize the snub, Rundberg drew a chair up to the bed and sat down. "You must forgive my calling on you when you aren't well, Pan Bilinski," he said. "But—business is business. I'm sure you'll understand. Here, the letter from Zurich has come." Rising from his chair, he handed the letter to Anatol with a bow.

"Well, what of it?" Anatol, with a contemptuous gesture of disgust, let the letter flutter to Rundberg's feet.

Rundberg took it, folded it, and placed it in his breast pocket. "Nothing," he said with a grin. "I have no claims; Baron Candomir has volunteered to make good any arrears. No doubt you haven't spent the entire sum; the larger part of it must still be in your possession. Two and a half million lei—that's a fortune in Romania."

"Oh!" Anatol turned to Candomir. "How can you expose me to such impertinence in your house, Radu?"

"I'm sorry, Anatol. I haven't fully understood what Domnule Rundberg means. Won't you explain yourself?" he said sternly, turning to Rundberg.

"Pan Bilinski understands me perfectly. To his mind it is an impertinence if I request him to return my money. Maybe it is. I bow to that. Therefore I shall make another proposal. Pan Bilinski keeps the money, the entire sum, as remuneration for his services. For the hardships he was exposed to, and for the anxiety, as compensation." Rundberg spoke with his usual matter-of-factness. He seemed not to notice Candomir's horror, and gazed stolidly at Anatol, who was again sitting up in bed.

"As hush money, you mean!" Anatol said. He turned to Candomir. "Too little, far too little, my dear Radu. After all, a miserable five thousand dollars!" He turned back to Rundberg. "That is an even greater impertinence." He smiled spitefully.

"Too little? How much did you have in mind, Pan Bilinski?" Rundberg asked, undeterred.

"Enough of such talk!" Candomir commanded, loudly and sternly. "Or I must ask you—everything has its limits, Domnule Rundberg!"

"Quite right, Baron Candomir." And to Anatol: "You understand, Pan Bilinski, everything has its limits! Name the sum you want for keeping quiet. What will you settle for?"

"Twenty-five thousand dollars."

Candomir sat there as if he had suffered a stroke. He struggled for breath. But Rundberg pretended not to notice. "That's a lot of money, Pan Bilinski, a lot of money. I doubt that I can raise it. I offer you fifteen thousand. My proposition is this: consider the five thousand as a down payment, and if you keep your mouth shut until Alda returns safe and sound, another ten thousand is forthcoming. In cash!"

"But—but—" Candomir groaned. "What is going on here?"

"Don't you understand, my dear Radu? But how could you? Rundberg knows that I've seen through the whole farce. And he's your fine friend Alda's partner—Alda, the rescuer and knight-errant —Alda the Bolshevist agent, the chief of the whole gang."

"Why, you're insane!" Candomir sprang to his feet and towered menacingly over the man on the bed.

Rundberg gazed calmly from one to the other. "Don't upset yourself, Baron Candomir," he said. "There's nothing we can do. Every deal has its risks. . . . So you won't accept my terms, Pan Bilinski? You stick to your original request?"

"Have you both gone mad? Anatol!" Candomir pleaded, almost weeping. "What is this all about?"

"It's somewhat painful to explain, Radu. The man whom you have given your affection and your trust is in the employ of our mortal enemies. He's a Bolshevik. He hadn't the slightest interest in rescuing my wife. That was a convenient pretext, an alibi that came to him like a gift from heaven. Or else he would have been back long ago."

"A bit too much for you to absorb all at once, Baron Candomir," Rundberg said, grinning. "How long have you known Lutz Alda? And my modest self? You would never have thought it possible, would you, now? But the pitcher goes to the well once too often. Now we are unmasked. And let's be thankful that money at least can save the situation. For twenty-five thousand dollars, then, you'll keep this to yourself? Forever?"

"I will keep silent," Anatol said with dignity, "not for money, but for Baron Candomir's sake. He is a man of honor and an aristocrat. The money is a contribution you must make. It is Bolshevik money. You people have stolen more than that from me, far more."

"I take it, then, that you would keep silent—for Baron Candomir's sake, of course—even if you did not receive the money? Didn't you understand it that way, Domnule Baron?" Rundberg asked naïvely. "Or does Pan Bilinski mean something else?"

"I understand nothing at all. This is ridiculous and I've had enough of it!" Candomir bellowed.

Rundberg stood up and went over to the table. He took a cigarette from Candomir's case, and took his time lighting it. His back was momentarily turned to Anatol, and he looked hard at Candomir. Then, just as he was about to turn, he winked very swiftly at him. "The question is," he said deliberately, "whether Baron Candomir will accept your silence. If I know Baron Candomir, he himself will go to the police. He hates the Bolsheviks, and he cannot be bought. It's hard luck for all of us, Pan Bilinski."

"Baron Candomir will not betray Alda, or any of you!" Anatol spoke with great self-assurance. "You have no conception of what a friend is, nor of how a gentleman regards his reputation."

"How right you are, Pan Bilinski; how cleverly you put two and two together. Yes, I guess there's no help for it; we must pay. You will then receive twenty-five thousand American dollars, in one-hundred, five-hundred and thousand-dollar bills, and on the following basis: ten thousand today, and fifteen thousand on the day Coane Alda returns."

Anatol tried to interject something, but Rundberg went on: "However, the return must not be delayed beyond March first of this year. If he is not back by then, you will receive payment of the remaining fifteen thousand. The money will be deposited with Baron Candomir. Are you agreed, Pan Bilinski?"

Bilinski waved his hand airily in Candomir's direction. "If Baron Candomir confirms the agreement."

Candomir gasped. If up to this point he had believed, had hoped, that the whole affair was a cruel practical joke, he realized at this moment that Bilinski was an utter scoundrel. He could not speak, could not even move.

Rundberg stood up quickly. "Of course the Baron agrees. He would have to. If only to protect your 'reputation,' eh, Baron Candomir?" He looked firmly at Candomir and again closed his left eye in a lightning wink.

"Yes, of course," Candomir managed to say.

"Then everything is settled!" Rubbing his hands, Rundberg turned to Anatol. "And now, speed is of the essence. Give me the lei, as much as you have left—there must be more than two million, I would think."

"But why? You need only add five thousand to them and the first installment is paid."

"These are two separate accounts, Pan Bilinski. True, I only have to obtain an additional twenty thousand, but do you imagine I can shake such a sum out of my sleeve? I'll have to strain my entire credit. In such transactions down payments are customary, to cover possible exchange differentials; other people don't handle things as informally as we do, between ourselves. I need your lei. It's a complicated transaction; but what does a nobleman know about business? So please hurry; it's a pity to waste time."

"I don't understand." Anatol's distrust was undisguised.

Rundberg took a deep breath. It was the first time during the conversation that he showed any feeling. "What are you worried about? We're in your hands, after all."

"True." Anatol left the bed, went to the wall safe, and took out a leather folder. He opened it with a tiny key that hung on a gold chair around his neck along with his medallion. "There. The whole sum minus three hundred thousand lei."

"You're very thrifty, Pan Bilinski." Rundberg said commendingly. "Then I shall deduct six hundred dollars from your total. Strict accountings make good friends. You will remain here until the final settlement of our transaction, Pan Bilinski. In Baron Candomir's house." And as Candomir made an unmistakable movement, he repeated, "In Baron Candomir's house. So that you can be more easily watched."

"Watched? What new impertinence is this? I give my word of honor—"

"Word of honor? Excellent! Except that in this kind of agreement that's too weak a guarantee. What would *I* know of words of honor? Am I a nobleman? We will settle that part of it right now: you are staying here. You will not be allowed to write or to telephone, and you are allowed outside only so long as you remain in sight of the house. One of our men will keep you under constant observation. You know him, Pan Bilinski. He came with me and is within call. He is Feri, the chauffeur of Baron Nagy of Arad."

"Why, he—" Anatol screamed.

Rundberg continued without change of expression and without raising his voice. "Yes, he is a member of the gang, our Feri. You may as well be forewarned, Pan Bilinski. We will be instructing Feri that if you make a single movement which looks suspicious, he is to"—Rundberg made a grotesque gesture of twisting a neck—"finish you off. He will do so with the greatest pleasure. He says he has a private score to settle with you. But of course that part of it doesn't interest us. Now I take my leave. I shall return later today."

Rundberg tucked the folder under his arm and bowed low. With a respectful inclination of his head, he turned to Candomir. "Baron, let us not disturb Pan Bilinski any longer. I'm sure he needs his rest. I hope you're satisfied with me. Have I not treated him very gently?"

Candomir stood up with some effort. His face was stony, his eyes blank. He painfully avoided looking at Anatol, who now lay outstretched, eyes fixed on the ceiling. With stiff footsteps he preceded Rundberg to the door. As his hand touched the latch, Rundberg said slowly and clearly, *"Gość w domu, Bóg w domu."* Anatol reared up in bed, turning his plastered face, distorted still further by fury, toward Rundberg. Candomir too looked questionly at him. "A Polish saying, Baron Candomir," Rundberg explained. "It means: Guest in the house, God in the house. You have the Heavenly Father himself in the house, Baron Candomir." And then he said to Anatol, "Yes, I happen to know Polish too."

He took two long strides past Candomir, opened wide the door and said, "After you, Baron," and with a last look at Anatol, who stared malignantly at him, "I am at home here."

* * *

"What next?" They were in the study once more, facing each other. Rundberg had made no comment. He had waited for Candomir to come to terms with what he had witnessed. It had been too much all at once; the Baron could not cope with it, and was still less able to come to terms with what must necessarily follow. Rundberg himself felt emotionally drained. "We will think of something," he said.

"Then you have nothing in mind, Domnule Rundberg? I thought you already had a fixed plan."

"Plans are worthless, Baron, at least in cases such as this. What good would the finest plans have done me if it hadn't occurred to me at the last moment to try this—this experiment? He seized the bait; he wanted money."

"And he's got it," Candomir said bitterly.

Rundberg looked at him in surprise. "Do you think I intend to hand twenty-five thousand dollars over to Bilinski?"

"I see no other recourse. Naturally I am prepared—"

"To give money to a blackmailer? That would be selling your soul to the devil. No, Baron Candomir, on the contrary, I've stripped the fellow. As you saw, it was not easy." He gestured at the folder which lay beside him. "Here." And he took a wallet from the outside pocket of his jacket. "And here."

"How did you get that?"

"While you and he were talking. A simple trick quite common among pickpockets. He is helpless now, without money and without papers. That was the point of it. Won't you please lock up the wallet?"

"No, I won't touch it." Candomir watched as Rundberg pocketed the wallet again. "The episode I have just witnessed suffices me." He stood up resolutely. "You can leave all the rest to me, Domnule Rundberg."

"But, my good Baron—" Rundberg said in a creditable imitation of Bilinski's light disdainful tone. The implication was clear.

Candomir started and looked at him. "I suppose I can't order him out of the house, for he would go straight to the Sigurantza. To have him stay on here, sit at my table, with my wife, my children —a lucky thing my family is away at the moment. I was going to run down to see them—the children have measles."

"I hope they recover quickly," Rundberg said with warmth. He thought of his own children, so far from him at present. Who could say when he would be seeing them again? "Yes, the children! For their sake, Baron Candomir, put rash actions out of your head. It is truly fortunate that the conitza is not here. The family is in Bucharest?"

"Yes, in Bucharest."

Rundberg looked at his watch. "It is half past eleven." He reflected. "Does your wife know Lieutenant Colonel Rananu or Lieutenant Rozescu?"

"Rananu is a relative of hers, and we are good friends."

"Excellent. Please telephone your wife. Ask after the children, of course; tell her that you won't be able to leave until tomorrow; talk about the weather, the farm work, and in the midst of this ask her once, and afterwards once more, to have the Lieutenant Colonel telephone us here. Ask her to call him at once, imply that it's about a horse, the son of Bucur and Oglinda. After all, Rananu is a cavalryman, isn't he?"

"Yes, but—"

"Please, Baron, no questions," Rundberg implored. Shrugging, Candomir went to the telephone. When the chat was over, he reported, "My wife will make every effort to reach Rananu. But what do you hope for from him?"

"If the Lieutenant Colonel—and if possible, Lieutenant Rozescu —can be made to appear here before the day is out, we will have won."

"If we can get in touch with him, he'll surely come. But what shall we tell him?"

"Naturally you can't go into details on the telephone. Say he must come for his horse—his horse, please don't forget that—and that it would be fine if the Lieutenant could come, too. I hope the Lieutenant Colonel will understand—I know the Lieutenant will."

"I think I too am beginning to understand," Candomir said. He laughed. "Yes, that would be a way out. Good, Karl Rundberg, very good." He pressed a button, and told the servant that Domnule Rundberg would be staying to lunch.

They had scarcely finished their drinks when the telephone shrilled once more. Both men sprang to their feet. Candomir reached for the telephone. The conversation darted back and forth for minutes. The problem seemed to be that Rananu had been up all night and had just been on the point of going to sleep. Candomir's tone became more and more urgent. It sounded as if there were some obstacle. Finally he hung up. "There has been a murder in Bucharest, a political murder, apparently. How slow news is to reach us out here! Not a word about it on the radio. The Cabinet Chief or Secretary General of the Interior has been shot."

"Someone shot?" Rundberg's lips quivered with excitement. "Of the Interior Ministry? What is his name?"

"Danghu. Is that such an astounding piece of news? You seem quite overwhelmed."

Rundberg stared into space. "Dead," he whispered. And then: "It isn't right that we rejoice in the downfall of our enemies." He looked at Candomir. "My father always says that—and also, that God knows what He's about."

"Was this Danghu an enemy of yours?"

"I never met him. He was Lutz's enemy. He's the one who was after Lutz. The charges, the investigation, all the alarm and confusion and despair, came from Danghu's hatred."

"It seems odd that he should have hated Lutz."

"He hated him out of sheer instinct. At least that's how the young doctor of philosophy explained it to me. There is hate at first sight just as there is love at first sight, he said. I didn't understand it at all, because it's not in me to hate. Is that a failing, Baron?"

"You mean, you don't even hate the man upstairs, Domnule Rundberg?"

"Not a bit. I've only been defending myself. He was dangerous."

"Was? Isn't he still?"

"Not nearly so dangerous, no, although we must still take our precautions. Danghu would have found him an ideal tool. The harm that man might have done is almost inconceivable. But now. . . . All Bilinski wanted was to lay his hands on money in an easy way."

"We can't be so certain of that, Domnule Rundberg. There's hatred there. . . ."

"Hatred which can be expressed in a round sum? No, I don't believe in his hatred. He conceived a plan. In his fury at its failure, he will lash out at all of us—but it all comes down to money. Real hatred is bent on tasting blood, not on making a profit."

"And you're not going to let him have his profit."

"His whole plan revolved around money, nothing else, and you were to be the victim, Baron."

"I? How so?"

"He was counting on two factors: your friendship with Lutz, and your concern for your reputation. You're wealthy; you're a man who would pay dearly for your honor. If I hadn't brought the subject so rudely to the fore, he would have made his touch in some more delicate way. Whereas talking to the Jew Rundberg, he didn't have to beat about the bush. He came right out with it. Now you know where you stand."

"Yes," Candomir said gloomily, "I know where I stand. What will you tell Rananu when he comes?" Hesitantly, he added, "Perhaps there's no point in his coming. Why don't I telephone him and call it off on some pretext?"

So Candomir had changed his mind. He was deeply reluctant

to expose himself in an unfavorable light before his friends. Hadn't Rundberg implied that Danghu's death changed the whole affair? Perhaps they could get out of this mess without involving B II. For Candomir was an aristocrat through and through, and it came hard to him to deviate from the traditions of his class. He would have liked to settle this problem privately and not disgrace another aristocrat, even if the man had proved himself a scoundrel.

"If you were to settle up with this fellow on his own terms, Baron," Rundberg said, speaking very slowly, "you would be making a great mistake. I feel it my duty to say this. I understand your motivations . . . they do you credit. But we must not allow this blackmailer to think that we fear him."

"But what in the devil's name are we going to tell our friends?"

"You couldn't do better than to call them in. A nobleman would have to do so. You are a boyar, a pillar of the state, a guardian of morality and legality. Do you want to make common cause with an extortioner? Yes, Baron, common cause. For if you bought him off, as he expects you to, you'd encourage him to think you're afraid of him. From this he'd conclude that there really is something to his diabolic fiction, which up to now he himself hasn't believed in. You'll start him on a new career of slander."

This was heavy artillery. It was rather embarrassing for a nobleman to have to be guided by a Jew in matters of right conduct. But the Jew Rundberg was incontrovertibly right. "All right, then," Candomir said resolutely, "we will seize the bull by the horns. Come to think of it, that's really more my style."

"Of course," Rundberg grinned. To himself he thought, as he had repeatedly on this day: a baron is a baron.

It was well after dark when they heard the tinkling bells of a sleigh. Candomir went out to meet the guests. Rananu had Rozescu with him. They had also brought along a soldier.

"We thought we'd better have the Corporal along," Rananu said to Candomir. "If I buy this horse of yours, he'll supervise its transportation."

Neither Rananu nor Rozescu showed any surprise at the presence of Rundberg. It reassured Candomir considerably to see the easy friendliness between the Jew and these two noblemen. At table Rozescu had a lively talk with Rundberg about yarn, thread, wool, the economic situation and the effect of the war upon it, but nobody asked any questions or made any allusions to the purpose of the journey.

They sat over cognac and coffee, cigarettes lit. The servants withdrew, and a silence fell over the group. Candomir went to the door and turned the key.

"The problem is as follows," he said resolutely. "A gentleman from Poland whom I have known for many years, who recently escaped from his unhappy country and whom I took into my house, this morning asserted—in Domnule Rundberg's presence—that Lutz Alda is a Bolshevist agent, the chief of a large gang of spies and"—he inclined his head politely in Rundberg's direction—"that Domnule Rundberg is, as it were, Alda's deputy." He cleared his throat. "He warned me that if a certain—hm—sum were not placed at his disposal, he would make a denunciation to the Sigurantza. I prefer to inform the authorities myself. The matter would fall within your province, wouldn't it?"

Rananu had swiftly recovered from his surprise. He seemed to take the revelation in his stride. "Yes, we are much occupied with Alda these days. But the gentleman, whoever he is, is out of luck. He comes too late with his news. The man to whom it would have been worth a sackful of gold is dead. You might inform your Polish gentleman that anyone who tries to injure Alda will be shot. Forgive my joking, but I'd sooner laugh than weep. It really is getting to be too much—what the devil do they want of Lutz?"

"In this case," Rozescu spoke up, "it's not so much a question of getting Alda as of getting money. There seems to have been a strong intent to blackmail, wouldn't you say, Baron Candomir?"

"A strong intent, certainly."

"Then you acted very correctly, Radu," Rananu said. "This is a case for B II. We'll investigate; let him tell us what he knows. . . . And would you just write us a short statement of your view of the case, as you've just told it to us?"

The deposition was written and Rananu began reading it. Immediately he started. "Prince Anatol Zbyszko Guninski. Prince Guninski?" he repeated interrogatively.

"That's his name. He called himself Bilinski here, as a precaution. I've known him for twenty-five years."

"Come here, Fanica—I think we have a surprise for the Old Man. Here, fill out this form—and you, Radu, will be receiving a decoration, I think."

With this all three—the Lieutenant Colonel, the Lieutenant and the Corporal—donned their holsters. "Show me his room, Radu," Rananu said.

"It's the guest room where you always stay when you're here," Candomir said.

The door had barely closed behind the three when Candomir turned to Rundberg in high excitement. "Do you know what this is all about?"

"Hardly. But I suspect that Bilinski did not give himself that name by chance. Why should a man be a prince and degrade himself voluntarily, so to speak? A prince! One thing is clear: If what the Lieutenant Colonel thinks is true, the Prince will have no time or inclination to throw his mud at Alda. He'll have enough to do trying to save his own skin."

"In that case, his conduct is inexplicable."

"No, it begins to be explicable. The Prince needed money. After all, he must have thought, there was a limit to what he could borrow from you. He can't stay on here indefinitely. Sooner or later his incognito would have to be lifted. And so he built up a story. First he told you that song and dance about his wife's inheritance. How could you possibly fail to believe a prince? After all, you've known him twenty-five years and he was somebody, undoubtedly he was somebody—you can tell that by looking at him. My dear Baron, I've grown up among gentry. After all, my grandfather was here with the Aldas. You develop a nose for it, a sensitive nose, until after a while you can smell the difference between a noble and a gentleman. Now my nose has been telling me that the Prince is no gentleman. He pretends to be, but only a gentleman would be fooled by him, not one of our kind. It's not a question of the number of notches in a coronet, or of uniform, manners, bearing, wealth, even education. That stuff doesn't matter to us, only what remains when all those externals drop away and the man is left. We've observed these people, observed and studied what makes a man a coane, because it was important, vitally important to us. To us Jews, I mean, Baron."

"Yes, the Jews are sharp observers. They have that over the gentry."

"They've had to be if they were to survive. Only now not even that will help us Jews."

"You are pessimistic, Domnule Rundberg."

"It is going to be hard, unbearably hard, and not only for the Jews, Baron."

"For the gentry, too, you mean?"

"For the true, the genuine, gentry. Not for those who turn in every wind."

"I think the Jews have some practice in doing that."

Rundberg's grin was very sad. "But where are they to turn now? To whom are they to turn? Who will take them in? What gentleman is going to protect them? We are outlaws."

"You will think of some expedient or other," Candomir said lightly, and instantly regretted having said it. But the subject seemed to him a futile one. Pessimism always made him uncomfortable.

"Yes, some expedient or other," Rundberg said. "But to get back to our friend the Prince," he added diplomatically.

"Yes, yes," Candomir hastened to say. "How will that turn out, do you suppose?"

"Hard to say anything definite," Rundberg said, trying to master his feelings of depression. "The affair has taken an unexpected turn. For the better, I *hope*." He leaned back in his chair and half closed his eyes in an attitude which struck Candomir as disrespectful, insolent, challenging. He was on the point of showing his irritation, but stopped short as he took a better look at the man. That troubling, deceptive grin had vanished from Rundberg's face. The man was suffering. His face expressed nothing but suffering. And the suffering communicated itself to Candomir, overwhelmed him; he shared it, was filled with sympathy which left no room for any other feeling. He went close to the chair in which Rundberg sat slumped and sat down on the hassock beside him. Placing his massive rider's hand on the other man's nervous, thin fingers, he said softly, "These are hard times, Karl Rundberg, I know."

Rundberg turned toward him that familiar, shrewd grin once more. He laid his free right hand on the hand which held his left hand. "Hard, but—we'll think of something, Coane Radu." How many years had passed since he had called Candomir that!

The jingle of spurs was heard. Candomir sprang to his feet, and the officers entered. "When is the next train to Bucharest?" Rananu asked.

Candomir, barely concealing his suspense, replied, "There's one at seven thirty-five tomorrow in Adancata. But how did it turn out?"

"All in due course, Radule," Rananu said, putting on his most official expression. "Seven thirty-five—but that one's not an express. It won't bring us in until late afternoon. That won't do."

"There's the former Warsaw-Bucharest Express that leaves from Cernauti at three o'clock in the morning," Rundberg said. "But it doesn't stop in Adancata. You would have to—"

"Thank you, Domnule Rundberg. That's the one for us. Excellent. Fanica, you telephone Tarnovietzchi and tell him to arrange for the train to stop. On orders of the General Staff. Have him reserve two compartments. If there are no Pullmans, let it be first class."

"Very well, sir," Rozescu said. But he made no move to carry out the order, and when Rananu looked inquiringly at him, he said, "I think it wouldn't be advisable to telephone from here—better from the post office."

"Do you know where that is?"

"If you'll permit me, Lieutenant, I'll take you there," Rundberg said.

"That's very kind of you, Domnule Rundberg. Let's go at once."

As soon as they were out of the room, Rananu turned to Candomir. "At the moment, I can tell you no more than that Alda's name didn't even come up. Your Prince hasn't admitted anything, but I'll eat nothing but polenta for the rest of my life if I haven't guessed right. He gave B II a hard nut to crack, but that was long before I was in the Bureau. Our Major Burda knows your Prince personally. He was the—hm, you know, Radu, even old friends that we are, it doesn't feel right to me to talk official business to you."

"I can well understand that, Alecu."

"Just this much, then—you acted very wisely, very correctly, Radule, in calling us. He hadn't counted on that, apparently. He takes it for granted that someone else called us in, not you. And even if my hunch proves wrong, he'll be kept under wraps until Lutz turns up."

"Let's drink to that, Alecu." Candomir filled their glasses.

"Right! Here's to Lutz!"

"To Lutz!" They drank, and Candomir sensed, though he could not have said how, that Alda's whereabouts were no mystery to Rananu, either.

Rananu was anxious to lead the conversation away from confidential topics. "I suppose what Florica said about a horse was only a pretext, wasn't it?" he said.

"It was. But the horse exists. A fine animal, only—"

"Didn't Florica say he was a son of Bucur? Could I see him, I wonder?"

"Would you like to?"

"What a question!"

They went to the stable.

When they returned, they found Rozescu and Rundberg in lively conversation. Rozescu reported that he had carried out his mission. The train would stop, and Major Tarnovietzchi would see about the two compartments.

"Thanks, Fanica, and you too, Domnule Rundberg," Rananu said. "Meanwhile I've been indulging in some private pleasure. Looked at a horse, a beautiful creature. Pity I can't buy him. But I have no time for horses any more, and besides his color is a little on the fancy side for me—if you'll forgive the comment, Radu."

"What color is the horse?" Rozescu asked.

"A golden chestnut—really better for a lady. He has a fabulous pedigree; the sire's Bucur—"

"Bucur?" Rozescu interrupted excitedly. "Bucur out of Polka by Belami?"

"The very same. Since when have you been so interested in horses, Domnule Philosopher?"

"If Baron Candomir considers the horse for sale, I'll gladly buy him," Rozescu said.

"Of course the horse is for sale—that's why he sent for us in the first place," Rananu laughed. "All the rest was just by the by. But why do you want a horse? So you can take a bit of a canter occasionally?"

"To relieve you, Alecu. So you won't be worrying yourself sick about Pluto."

"Aha, for Aglaia. Oh, these young folks." He whinnied softly.

"Yes," Rozescu said without embarrassment, "for her. She'll be overjoyed to have him—a grandson of Polka. What's his price, Baron Candomir?"

"Why, we have an expert here." Candomir nodded in Rananu's direction. "What does an officer pay for a good horse nowadays, Alescu?"

"Officer? Horse? In the first place he isn't an officer, but a philosopher; in the second place this isn't just any horse, but a son of Bucur; and in the third place the philosopher is named Rozescu. Anyone that rich has to be plucked till the feathers fly."

"By all means," Rozescu said, laughing.

"I don't know how to pluck." Candomir mimicked despair.

"If you'll permit me, Baron Candomir," Rundberg volunteered, "I'll help you out as an honest broker. I've seen the horse and know his pedigree."

"I'll be extremely grateful to you, Domnule Rundberg," Rozescu said.

Candomir thanked him with a look. "So will I. We'll rely on you."

"Then," Rundberg began in a highly businesslike manner, "I suggest the following: a horse of that caliber used to cost twelve hundred gold crowns or gold francs. That would be two hundred and forty dollars in gold. According to the official New York rate of 1937, that comes to three hundred and sixty-three paper dollars, which by the black-market rate in Bucharest as of yesterday would be about a hundred and seventy thousand lei. That is what the horse would be worth. But we must consider first of all that there is no demand corresponding to the supply, and secondly that the purchasing power of the buyer is excessively high. The price therefore is one hundred thousand lei, exclusive of my commission."

Rananu had listened open-mouthed. "Blast me if I've understood that rigamarole, but the price is about right. Did you understand, Radu?" And when Candomir shook his head: "What about you, Fanica?"

"Every word," Rozescu said, doubled over with laughter. "If the price suits you, Baron Candomir."

"Agreed; the horse is yours. I'll pay the commission. That's customary."

"No, I will," Rozescu said.

"No, I will!" Rananu exclaimed.

"There are no limits to generosity," Rundberg decided. "Each of the gentlemen will pay ten per cent and . . . one moment, I'll be right back."

Rananu meanwhile filled their glasses. "A Jew's a Jew," he said, laughing. "Pockets his profit where he can. I have no objection, but twenty per cent seems steep."

Before any of the others could reply, Rundberg was back in the room. He had three bundles of fifty thousand lei in his hands. "I take the liberty," he said with a bow to Rozescu, "of advancing the purchase price for you." And when Rozescu nodded his thanks: "Here, Baron." Counting rapidly, he took twenty-five hundred-lei bills from one bundle and handed them to Candomir, together with a full bundle. "Here is ninety thousand." He put the ten thousand into his pocket and then produced Anatol's wallet. "Here." He placed fifty thousand lei in the wallet and handed it to Rananu. "This belongs to—to the Baron's guest."

"The Prince?" Rananu stared blankly at the wallet.

"Domnule Rundberg," Candomir explained, clearing his throat, "took the precaution of—safeguarding the wallet. So that my guest would have no documents. You see, I had obtained a residence permit for him. Without money and without papers, he would—"

"Very wise," Rananu said. "Then the fifty thousand is his money?"

"No." Candomir could not explain and looked at Rundberg.

"We must be just, Lieutenant Colonel," Rundberg said. "But for our friend the Prince, the whole deal wouldn't have taken place. The baron has sold a horse, the Lieutenant has purchased an excellent one, and he hardly cares whether it costs him ten thousand more or less. As for me—the Polish gentleman still has a large credit outstanding with me."

"I understand, Alecu," Rozescu intervened. "Just as well not to leave the Prince entirely penniless. He will in any case be shut off from contact with the outside world for quite a while."

"He will, he will, you can be sure of that. But I wouldn't have given him any money, not I." Rananu looked at Rundberg and shook his head.

"It's better so, Alecu—let it be; Domnule Rundberg is right," Candomir said.

"You and my philosopher are brothers under the skin." Rananu raised his glass to Rundberg. "To philosophy," he said jovially.

"To the true gentry," Rundberg responded to the toast.

Rananu looked at his watch. "Radule, would you have two sleighs here at half past two? And you, Fanica, go up now and tell him to pack."

Rozescu returned after some time. "The gentleman has become somewhat refractory," he reported. "He warned us that we would find ourselves involved in highly embarrassing complications. And when that made no impression upon me, he switched from threats to remonstrances. Finally—" Rozescu laughed so hard he couldn't go on.

"Well, what did he say?" Rananu was growing impatient.

"Pardon me—it was really too funny."

"Funny?"

"Yes, funny. He suggested that I drop a hint to the Lieutenant Colonel. He had observed, he said, that I was on an easy footing with him. A great deal of money could be made here, and he knew how; he'd already struck up a bargain. Candomir could be bled, and the Jew—forgive me, Domnule Rundberg, he meant you—would bring up cash by the bushel. He had the impression, he said, that the Lieutenant Colonel was amenable to reason, even though he put on such proper and official airs. Yes, he meant you, Alecu. In short, we three—you, Alecu, he and I—were to form a league for the exploitation of the two gentlemen here. A priceless opportunity, he declared. What do you think of that?"

Rananu had turned pale; he had tears in his eyes from sheer fury, and the others could hear him grinding his teeth. "And you laugh at that!" he burst out. "You laugh!" he roared. "Why didn't you shoot the dog down then and there? Are you an officer? Is your name Rozescu?"

Candomir, far more upset by Rananu's outburst than by its cause, tried to calm him. "Come, come, Alecu. I was very close to doing the same myself today. But I'm grateful to Domnule Rundberg for restraining me."

"He's another—another philosopher like Rozescu!" Rananu bellowed. "Goddamn your philosophy! Here!" He went to the table where his pistols lay and pulled one from its holster. "Here is my philosophy!" He turned to Rozescu. "And what did you answer?"

"Answer? Not a word. I ordered the Corporal to stand by, watch in hand, and see to it that the gentleman finished dressing and packing in exactly fifteen minutes."

"That was all?"

"The boy is strong as a bull and highly intelligent. He understood me. He will see that the gentleman is ready on the dot."

When the bells of the sleighs rang out, all four men were relieved that the strain of waiting was over. Rananu stood up quickly, beckoning to Rozescu. "Better for you two to stay here," he said. "No need for him to see you. Good-bye, Radule." He embraced his friend, and shook hands with Rundberg. "It was a great pleasure to get to know you better. Good luck," he said.

Rozescu, too, bade a cordial farewell to the two men.

Candomir had sent the servants to bed much earlier. But old Mishu had been roused by the sleigh bells. He stood in the vestibule, head trembling slightly, watching the departure. In the dim light his old eyes only dimly observed the scene of the three soldiers and the civilian, and his old mind utterly refused to fathom the fact that guests could leave the house without being seen out by the master and the servants. He was still wagging his head disapprovingly when the sound of the sleigh bells was fading away down the road.

BOOK SIX

THE PEASANTS AND THE POWER

Russia, whither are you rushing?
Give me your answer!
But Russia does not answer.
NIKOLAI GOGOL, *1842*

THE MEETING HAD BEEN SCHEDULED FOR SEVEN O'CLOCK. BY eight the audience was still sparse. None of the top chiefs was there yet. Maximenko was chatting with some of the younger leaders about soccer; his was the only group in which the talk was lively. The others seemed unable to initiate any kind of conversation, nor did anyone pick up a newspaper, book or pamphlet. Furthermore, no one even glanced at the walls thickly clustered with pictures—portraits of dead and living heroes of thought and action.

The room in which the workers of the power plant sat so apathetically had formerly been the hall in which directors' meetings were held. In those days it had been forbidden territory to the workers; now it was their club, their "culture home." And just as in the past they had not been allowed in, now they had no desire to be there. They were tired and sleepy. They constantly looked up at the clock or asked one another the time.

Workers were straggling in by twos and threes, followed by a sprinkling of office employees, many of whom were women and girls who carried chairs with them. The room was nearly full when the sound of wagon wheels became audible. The *khoziaistva,* someone said, and soon the farm employees entered the hall—a far larger complement than usual. For the farm workers had numerous good reasons for staying away from meetings, such as the distance from town, and were apt to take full advantage of their reasons. But this time the organizers of the meeting had insisted on their turning out. The leaders wanted as large an attendance as possible.

Director Mermelstein grabbed a chair and sat down with a group of girls. The gardeners, the blacksmiths and the harness makers took one of the benches toward the rear; the bookkeeper and the milkmaids occupied another two benches. The stablemaster and the drayman completed the farm contingent. They made a sizable party, although they were by no means the whole personnel of the farm. Some were absent for reasons of political prudence. Their "capitalistic" background was offensive to many of the class-conscious workers, or those who pretended to be such.

The workers of the power plant had every reason to be satisfied with the performance of their farm. Of course there were grumblers and troublemakers, know-it-alls, oppositionists and gripers everywhere, who out of sheer negativism refused to admit the merits of the farm and criticized the leadership at every suitable and unsuitable opportunity. The leaders, however, had no intention of changing anything. They had not expected the farm to be of any practical value, but it was functioning miraculously; it was producing and showed no deficit.

The hall was now crowded, and at last the director and his deputy entered. Both took seats on the platform. Fyodor Ivanovich Lavrenenko laid his cap on the table in front of him, rose, and said, "Comrades, before we proceed to the serious, the highly important, subject of our present meeting—the speakers who are to discuss this point have not turned up yet—I should like to ask whether any of you has anything to say on other topics. Does anyone wish the floor?"

A few spoke up, bringing up trivial matters. There was little enthusiasm, and no real debate developed. The director, at once relieved and disappointed, was about to turn to Saposhnik. But Saposhnik, who had been staring indifferently into the hall, called his attention to the fact that someone had raised his hand. "Comrade Krzankovski has the floor," Lavrenenko said softly. A man in his mid-twenties, with light blond hair, pale blue eyes and almost white eyebrows, stood up. Over a black sweater he wore the blue smock of a mechanic. Before he began to speak, he took off his cap. He spoke Polish, but also employed Ruthenian and Russian words and tried his best to make the two officials understand him. "Comrades, I believe I speak for all of you when I take the liberty of inquiring"— what a bourgeois phrase! Lavrenenko twitched—"why there has been no butter ration this week."

Someone administered a vigorous nudge to Mermelstein, who had been whispering with one of the girls. He heard the word *maslo*—butter—and instantly deduced what issue was being raised. At once he put on a superior smile, and quickly glanced at Saposhnik. But the man's face told him nothing. Then his eyes sought out the bookkeeper, who sat far to the rear, among the milkmaids. But her expression likewise conveyed no message. Whereupon he stared at the speaker, who was gradually warming to his oratory. The miserable devil had left the subject of butter behind and was ranting about the bourgeoisie, their practices, their tricks and weapons. Carried away by his own words, he was launched on an endless stream of slogans and quotations, and might have gone on and on if he had not been called to order by a shout of "Butter!" Krzankovski was not disconcerted. "Yes, comrades," he perorated, "inside the prison walls of the bourgeoisie and imperialism there was no butter for class-conscious workers. The bosses ate it themselves. But now the workers are the bosses and they have the sole right to butter. I ask Comrade Mermelstein: Has our butter, the butter of the class-conscious workers, by any chance been sold on the market to the burzhui, at speculative prices, so that they can fill their bellies and have strength to continue their campaign against the working class? Are we to feed them with our own butter? We will never concede that! We will fight it! Director Mermelstein, report to us: Where is the butter?"

The speaker sat down with aplomb, and several men in the audience, carried away by the speaker's words, called out in chorus, "Where is the butter?" A number of others took up the battle cry, until in a moment nearly a hundred men, chiefly for the pleasure of making noise, were shouting, "Where is the butter?"

The racket angered Lavrenenko. He did not like the speaker in any case. Krzankovski was not a bad workman, but he was a conceited chap and a mischief-maker. Here he was stirring up the people, when they were just beginning to grasp what the discipline of a meeting should be. Director Lavrenenko stood up, cast a chiding look at the crowd, and called out, "Quiet!" Then he reproved the speaker, who was sitting there exuding self-satisfaction. "Comrade Krzankovski, you wanted to ask why the butter ration was not available this week. That is no reason to deliver such a long speech. A Soviet man respects brevity. May I also remind the other comrades that they must preserve the dignity of the meeting. Comrade Mermelstein will explain why no butter was distributed this week."

While the director was speaking, Mermelstein had repeatedly appealed to Saposhnik, with desperate glances, for help. But Saposhnik had looked away, indicating that no help might be expected from that quarter. And so Mermelstein began, "The butter—well, you see, it was this way. . . ." He groped for words, sweated, took out his handkerchief and wiped his brow. The audience stared at him hostilely.-Here stood this man Mermelstein, whom few of them had known before, who had suddenly turned up as director of the farm, who rode in a carriage, flirted with the office girls, put on airs with the workers, and sold their butter on the black market (there seemed every reason to believe this) to line his pockets and have himself a merry time. A wave of malice and hatred rolled in Mermelstein's direction and took his breath away. He sat down, without looking at Saposhnik or Lavrenenko. Krzankovski was already on his feet, triumphant, ready to recapitulate his successful speech. But Lavrenenko signed to him that he did not have the floor yet, and looked to Saposhnik for guidance. Saposhnik was staring straight toward the back of the room, where Bookkeeper Linhan sat. His glance slid away from her and was caught by a mustache, Stablemaster Vassily Khomniuk's mustache. Vassily, slowly and deliberately in his peasant fashion, raised his arm to ask for the floor.

"Comrade Khomniuk, can you explain why there has been no butter this week?" the director asked.

"I will—the comrade in charge of the buttermaking isn't here," Vassily said, rising to his feet.

"Please go ahead," the director said. He was glad for several reasons that this slow-spoken peasant wanted the floor. Comrade Khomniuk never said much, but what he said had substance. The director could also understand his language, mélange of Russian and Ruthenian though it was, much better than the boneless Polish with its twisted Russian slogans.

"Comrades," the stablemaster said, "Comrade Mermelstein can't explain this thing to you because he is just as much of a city man as most of you." The whole audience had turned to look at him. "There is not enough milk because many of the cows are about to freshen, and have been dried off. And when there is no milk there is also no butter. After the cows have calved, there will be enough milk and we will make butter again. Then you will be getting more butter than before. But until the cows have their calves, they will be dry. A cow is not a machine."

Many nodded, smiling, as did Lavrenenko. He turned to Krzankovski. "Have you any further questions?"

"I have," Krzankovski said. "How is it that in one week all the cows have stopped giving milk?"

"Not all the cows, comrade. Only the ones that are close to freshening."

"Funny," Krzankovski said. "Unbelievable."

"If you don't believe me, comrade, come along back to the farm with us and talk to the cows yourself. Maybe they'll explain it better."

Lavrenenko and Saposhnik laughed, each for his own reasons, and the crowd laughed with them. A roar of laughter filled the room, and continued while three men entered the hall—two strangers and behind them Arkady Samuelovich Feingold.

Both Lavrenenko and Saposhnik had risen. The two strangers seemed to be important men. The bigwigs on the platform conferred for a few minutes, Saposhnik evidently explaining the cause of the laughter, for he pointed to Vassily who sat quietly twirling his mustache. Feingold waved cheerfully to him. Meanwhile chairs had been brought and the new arrivals sat down. Lavrenenko alone remained standing. He tapped his palm lightly against the table, and as the noise gradually subsided he said, "Comrades, the Deputy Chairman of the Party Committee, Comrade Tarashchenko will now speak."

One of the two strangers slowly rose and went over to the table. Everything about him was long and lean—his body, face and cropped head with its lusterless, dark-blond hair. The movement with which he placed his long-brimmed cap on the table was like that of an automaton. But as soon as he began to speak, everyone gazed at him spellbound. Most of them did not understand him fully, for he spoke Russian, but they responded to his voice, which vibrated with a passionate determination to convince.

"Comrades, I am here to have a talk with you about three deserters. The workers of Power Plant II know whom I am referring to, and I want the others to know also. Master Machinist Ignatiuk and the two mechanics Filopowicz and Niedzielski did not come to work this morning. Everything points to the fact that they have fled. You will think, comrades, that that is nothing new; it happens every day; how many men have run away in the past few months! Why the fuss, then? Why should we call meetings about it? You would be right, comrades, if it had not been these three men in particular, or rather two of them. If they wanted to risk being arrested at the border and given some years of imprisonment, just to reach a place where slavery awaited them—the slavery of capitalism, of fascism—that is their business. They were unteachable men who have abandoned their work, their native land, the cause of progress, and have thrown in their lot with reaction, with slavery." His voice grew more vibrant still. "But in the case we are discussing now, the deserters alone are not to blame. You are all to blame. Ignatiuk was the chairman of the workers' committee and Filopowicz the secretary. You, comrades, unanimously elected traitors to the working class as representatives of your interests.

"But we, who regard ourselves not as your commanders but as your teachers, we members of the Communist party, the party of the Bolsheviki, must refuse to take the responsibility. We took your word for it when you told us: we have known Ignatiuk for many years; we have worked together with him; he is the right man to represent our interests. No one attempted to put any pressure on you; your choice was acknowledged and accepted. It is bad enough that Ignatiuk and his accomplices are placing their labor power and their skills at the service of capital and fascism; but they will in addition betray a great many things that they have seen and heard among us. You, comrades, have therefore helped them practice espionage. It may be that the three have reached their destination alive; it may be that after spending some time in jail they will even be permitted to work. Do not think they will have an easy time of it. Not among the fascists, not among the capitalists! As Ukrainians, they will be considered sub-humans by the fascists; they will be given just enough to keep them going, so that they do not collapse under the hard labor they will be assigned to. The bourgeoisie accept them only because they will work cheaply.

"Do not think, comrades, that conditions are better and easier elsewhere. Every day hundreds come across the border to us because of their conviction that life is better here. They risk their lives to come to us. For if anyone on the other side is caught trying to cross the border, he is shot. But now hear this: although up to now those who have secretly attempted to leave the territory of the Soviet Union have risked only their liberty, not their lives, from today on, comrades, the border guards have been instructed to fire at anyone who appears suspicious, at anyone who wants to go over to the fascists, to the capitalists."

He sat down and the director gave the floor to Comrade Feingold. Feingold spoke Ukrainian—literary Ukrainian, in fact. But he did not make a speech; he chatted. He did not underline his points, but dropped them casually here and there. For a while he talked straight from the shoulder; then his smile reappeared, that winning, magnetic smile of a fair-haired demigod. He gave political dogmas a wide berth and instead stressed common sense. He pointed out, by various examples, how foolish it was for a Slav, especially a Ukrainian, to leave his brothers and run off to those who had always despised and persecuted Ukrainians. What could he hope for from the Germans, the Hungarians, the Romanians, if not misery and hunger, abuse and shame? "Is that worth risking your lives for, comrades?"

When he had finished, there were minutes of silence in the hall. Then a murmuring and whispering began. Men talked over the case in small groups. And naturally they agreed with the speakers. A good many, however, sat silent; they bitterly regretted having waited so long to make their getaway. For many had been thinking of flight. Now there was the danger of being shot.

The director opened the discussion: "Who would like the floor?"

A number of arms were raised. Always the same ones, Lavrenenko thought, and they always say the same things. A mechanic from each of the two main power plants spoke; someone from the bookkeeping department, two administrative clerks, and of course Krzankovski. They spoke Polish and Ruthenian, mixed with fragments of Russian they had picked up, with quotations they had learned, with slogans used in the wrong places. They talked loosely, railed, threatened, uttered prophecies of evil. And for the most part they did so out of envy. They envied those who had succeeded in doing what they themselves longed to do; they hated the runaways for having had the courage to act where they themselves had deliberated too long. Perhaps those others were already in lands of freedom. For out there, across the border, there was freedom; of that they were firmly convinced. But not a single one of these men mentioned the reasons for the wholesale exodus. No one so much as hinted at what was wrong here, what was bad, why so many had run away.

The men on the platform sat sober-faced watching the speakers, listening to the phrases they had heard a thousand times before. As long as no one at the meeting spoke his real thoughts, as long as they did not deviate from the line, as long as they pretended obedience and submission, all was in order. When the atmosphere in the room was soaked through with class-conscious, hate-filled, menacing words, with forecasts of terror and death, and when no more workers offered to speak, Lavrenenko prepared to say a final word. But Feingold whispered something to him, and Lavrenenko said, "Comrade Feingold has the floor."

"Comrades," Feingold began, "you have all spoken as Soviet citizens and workers should. Someone from each division of our organization has expressed his opinion, except for one: the khoziaistva. Does not the khoziaistva belong to our organization? Has none of its workers anything to say about this incident, which concerns all of us and therefore them too? How is that, Vassily Vassilevich Khomniuk?" He turned sharply toward Vassily. "What is your opinion? What have you to say on this subject?"

Vassily had listened attentively to each of the speakers, had watched each carefully all the while, as was his habit, stroking his mustache. Now he stood up slowly. The workers, office help and administrative officials gazed at him with a certain mild spite. He had come out on top in the tiff with the griper Krzankovski; but now the subject was not butter and cows. This was a serious matter; the peasant would stumble and make himself a laughingstock.

Vassily ignored the spiteful feeling in the air. In his slow, deliberate, peasant manner he said, "We workers of the khoziaistva belong to the plant just as much as every worker at a machine. We help the others by our work. But speechmaking has to be learned, and I have not learned it. Still and all, I've listened to all the comrades speak, and I am certain the other workers have paid attention and understood what was said, since they repeated it often enough. If you'll permit me, I'll tell you a story." He made a pause, with a kind of village courtesy, so that the audience might indicate whether they wanted a story or not.

The tall, lean man kept his pale, lifeless eyes fixed on Vassily, and nodded to him. Except for Feingold, who gave a friendly smile, the other men on the platform also nodded, although they were somewhat chary of such stories. Stories that were not censored and approved might contain dubious points, could be given tricky interpretations. But if Tarashchenko approved, then he took the responsibility, and the stablemaster could go on.

And Vassily told the following story:

"I was very young at the time. It was long before the war—the whole country still belonged to Austria. I worked for a baron. In the stable, with the horses, of course. On the estate—it was very big—there was also a dairy where a Jew was the foreman. Everybody called him Shlomko. He was a good man at cheesemaking. All day long, till late at night, he worked in the dairy. He had to work hard, because he had many children at home. And Shlomko wanted them to learn something so they'd be better off someday than he was. He sent them into town, the girls to learn to be seamstresses or hatmakers, the boys to be apprenticed to a locksmith or a carpenter. They were good obedient children; they learned well, and when they started earning on their own they would send their parents a little money now and then, or something to wear. All except the oldest son, Simon. He never liked any trade and never stuck at anything. First he'd have an idea he'd like to try this, then that. So he got to be twenty-three or twenty-four and hadn't amounted to anything, though he could have. Then one day he took a new notion into his head. He didn't want to be a Jew any more. He decided he'd go over to the Orthodox Church. That was a misery to poor Shlomko. He had always been a wizened little man; now he seemed even more shrunken, and his wife wept, but it was no use. Simon had himself baptized. Now in the village there was another Jew, a devout one, almost a rabbi. He had always got on well with the priest, but one day he met him and didn't greet him; he turned his head away. You can imagine why. The priest stopped him and asked the reason. Then the devout Jew reproached the priest because he had baptized Shlomko's son and so helped him give up his religion. The priest looked at the Jew for a minute and then he said: 'We've got the worst of the bargain. You Jews have lost a lump of dirt and we Christians have picked it up.' "

With seeming innocence and fearlessness Vassily had ventured into the forbidden territory of religion. His simple words, his mixture of Russian and Ruthenian, had been understood by nearly all. Everyone had enjoyed the story, with its roughly humorous point, but no one dared to show it. For the five men on the platform had not yet indicated whether it was all right to enjoy a story mentioning a landowner—a baron, to make matters worse—a rabbi and a priest. That depended on the five men, or no, rather on one of them, the tall, gaunt man. He did not speak until Vassily started to sit down. Then he said, "A good story, but you have not said what lesson we must draw from it, Comrade Khomniuk."

Vassily stood up again. "Deserters are liked nowhere; nobody trusts them. Wherever they go they are treated like dirt. They have a miserable life. People do better to stay where they are. That is what I meant." Then he sat down.

"*Pravelno!*—Right!" The relief in this exclamation was unmistakable. To the other men on the platform, the word was a signal, a command. They repeated it several times, and rang the changes on the story with happy alacrity. It was appropriate; it was useful. But Vassily did not seem to bask in the success of his story. The applause, the expressions of agreement, the verbose affirmations seemed to pass over him. He sat still, not even smiling.

They rode home in silence. The light farm buggy with its attachable leather double seat was drawn by two medium-heavy brown mares. Mira set beside Vassily; Antek and the smith Baczynski, a taciturn man, sat back to back with them. The night was foggy and damply cold; the springless wagon bumped on the bad pavement. The roads were barely illuminated, and it was difficult for the driver to avoid potholes. They made slow progress. After a ride of nearly an hour, past deserted small farms, they saw the lights of Jiusefovka. Vassily stopped at the entrance to the village and Baczynski got out.

The wagon stopped again in front of the office. Mira jumped down, and said, "You might come up to the office for a few minutes. There are several things to discuss."

"I'll be a while. I have to unharness and had better wait until the other teams come in," Vassily replied.

"I have work to do anyhow," Mira said.

Antek stayed in the wagon as Vassily drove slowly toward the stables. He jumped down with Vassily and stood, cigarette in his mouth and hands in his pockets, as Vassily unhitched the horses and led them into their stalls. He followed him in, watched as he rubbed the horses dry with a handful of straw and provided them with hay. Then Vassily sat down on a low bench, and Antek sat beside him. "Why did you go to so much trouble to get that idiot out of trouble?" he asked. "You were quite a star tonight anyhow —ought to apply for a job as a propaganda man." He spat the stub of his cigarette into the drain gutter.

"What good would it have done if I'd left Mermelstein in the lurch? He would have tried to put the blame on Saposhnik. Mermelstein would have been fired, and Saposhnik would be reprimanded. Then a new director would be sent here who'd stick his nose into everything and find out a lot of things this idiot will never see. And Saposhnik would be scared and instead of closing his eyes would come inspecting every day. I'm sure he's racking his brains anyhow trying to figure out how we do it."

"Yes, how we do it. That girl Mira. . . ."

Vassily nodded. "She's organized it well; that's why it works. But how long? If I hadn't thought of that gag about the cows—"

"What did happen to the butter?"

"The President of the Trust came here from Kiev, you remember. He came to see us too—the bald fellow with the Order of Lenin —and praised our work highly. Before he left, Saposhnik said to Mermelstein that if possible he should be given some butter to take with him—meaning three or four pounds, of course. Mermelstein promptly came driving up with his own driver, went directly down to the dairy where the butter had just been packed for the canteens —a hundred and ten pounds of it. He took it all before old Meerblum could say a word, and was gone. The President took some twenty to thirty pounds—no more, I'm sure, and paid four rubles and forty kopecks per pound for it. Mermelstein, instead of bringing the rest back, sold most of it on the market, or else his driver Rudnicki did it for him. He brought back ten pounds, for the sake of appearances. Sixty pounds of butter will bring in more than a thousand rubles—you know that, Antek. Even though he paid the official price to our bookkeeping department, that left him more than eight hundred rubles for—"

"For his whores. Rudnicki provides them. But that's his business. I know that guy from way back. But go on about the butter."

"Mermelstein drove the President to the station. He came back and reported to Saposhnik that he'd given him the butter—a hundred pounds of it."

"He sure is walking on thin ice!"

"He's a fool—does he think Saposhnik believes him? But what can Saposhnik do? Ask the President in Kiev how much butter he took? By letter or telephone? Even if the President took a measly twenty or thirty pounds, he had no right to. Not even one. Buying the workers' butter, eh! Saposhnik had no right to empower Mermelstein to give the butter away, any more than the President had a right to take the butter and Mermelstein to sell it."

"O sure—no right to, no right to, no right to. What has anybody got a right to do? But we have butter on reserve, our blackmarket butter, Vassily. Wouldn't it have been more sensible to send the usual amount to the canteens, rather than take a chance of being questioned?"

"But Saposhnik knew the butter was all gone. How would we have accounted to him for the new supply?"

"Hm—hm—right, a complicated business. If any of that ever

comes out, Vassily!"

"There's nothing we can do. But the way Mira runs things, we're pretty well covered."

"What a head that woman has! She could put ten men in her pocket. And yet she hardly ever says a word."

The sound of wagon wheels could be heard, and the other wagons rolled into the yard. Vassily gave terse instructions for the next day's work and then went to the office, accompanied by Antek. Mira scarcely looked up from her account books when the two men entered. "In a minute," she said, and went on noting down her figures. The white light of the high-powered bulb fell directly upon her face, which had aged considerably in these past few months. With practiced movements she at last placed the books and accounts in various drawers, locked these carefully, and put the keys into her bag. "After eleven," she said, "and we must be in town by seven tomorrow, Vassily."

Vassily nodded. "Kreisel has already prepared the meat. We can take it along for the office canteen. Jurko will take care of it for Number I and Metro for Number II. Give me the slips; I'll give them to the drivers."

"Here," Mira said, handing him two vouchers. "And here is a notice for the wall newspapers." Vassily pocketed the page. "The butter ration that was omitted this week will be replaced by lard. Antek, you'll see that one more pig is slaughtered. So—I guess that's all for a moment." She fell silent, then said, "Would you be so kind as to give me a cigarette?"

Antek hastily brought out his pack. He still had Egypski. He offered the pack to Vassily also, and lit a cigarette himself. For a while they smoked in silence. "We just squeaked through tonight," Mira said. "That was an inspiration, Vassily, about drying off the cows—we must tell Kornhaber so he'll back up the story."

Natan Kornhaber was the chief milker. He was a Jew and nearly sixty. Most of the cows on the farm had been his property. Antek had discovered him and had persuaded him not to wait to be expropriated, but to allow his cows and all the equipment of his dairy to be "taken over" into the khoziaistva. This was highly profitable to both sides, for to Kornhaber the official prices for livestock were found money. Naturally he had mobilized all his relatives and acquaintances to appear in the contracts as owning the cows—otherwise he would have been exposed as a kulak. What was more, his spravka as chief milker entitled him to a regular identity card, not to a "thirty-sevener." (By the law of 1937, members of the former capitalist class were given special cards—and found themselves in due course candidates for transportation to the northern regions of the Soviet Union.)

Now Kornhaber was just a worker, like Ruben Meerblum, who formerly had run a butter plant. At Kornhaber's suggestion Meerblum had likewise sold his machines to the farm and joined it. He had set up a quite respectable dairy in one of the large concrete cellars near the stables.

Those cellars, those spacious cellars of the former German colonists, built for eternity, were a chapter in themselves. They were turned into machine rooms and storehouses. The best workers of the power plant had vied with one another to equip the cellars with modern lighting and power installations. After all, they had been incessantly told that it was *their* farm, that everything raised on it would benefit them and them alone. They were already deriving advantages from the farm, although barely half its produce ultimately reached them. The other half was sold, in free trade—on the black market, to be blunt about it—to speculators who in turn passed on these goods at considerable profit. For the burzhui were still around; thousands upon thousands of them were still in the city. Though so many had succeeded in escaping, and so many others had been "resettled," many more had stayed on in their big, empty apartments with bare walls devoid of pictures, mirrors, hangings or rugs. No comfortable furniture, no silk coverlets on the beds, no clothing in the wardrobes, no pianos, radios, phonographs, typewriters or sewing machines were left to them. They had no watches on their wrists or in their pockets. For everything had been sold for chervontsy, for rubles. What could they buy with all those rubles? What was available? Who wanted to eat poor food when you could get good food for money? And so they bought and consumed butter, cheese and meat in the corners of their big, bare, melancholy apartments. They consumed the precious food hastily, terrified of being surprised at their feasts, hearts pounding; for any minute the bell might ring, and two, three or four men in uniform might begin asking questions and taking notes.

Mira's bold but simple plan was based upon the fact that these people would buy. The plan had arisen out of a conversation with Saposhnik from which it became apparent to Mira that if she stuck strictly to the law, mounting deficits were inescapable, and hence the farm would not be able to function. She raised a purely theoretical question—and the answer to it brought relief and illumination. What, she had asked, would be done if there were surpluses? The farm, she learned, could then deliver its surpluses to other organizations or, if these did not want them, might sell produce at the bazaar, on the free market. Of course this applied only to fresh fruit, fresh vegetables and similar highly perishable products.

In her terse manner, Mira had explained to Vassily and Antek —whom she felt to be allies from the first day they started work— that the farm must aim for surpluses. And she had explained how these could be produced. Thereupon Antek brought in Kornhaber, and Kornhaber brought in Meerblum. Meerblum enlisted his brother-in-law Wagner, who had formerly been a supplier of forage to the Polish army. Wagner assumed the post of warehouse director. As soon as transportation was available, he saw to it that the repaired barns and granaries were filled with thousands of sacks of oats, barley and corn from secret stocks.

Vassily provided the wagons and horses. He went to neighboring villages and in his deliberate peasant fashion, which won the confidence of the peasants, he persuaded young farmers to resettle in Jiusefovka. They came with their wives, their own teams and the whole household gear, and moved into the houses, which were better than their own. They were paid for their teams, their plows and harrows, their chopping machines and beet cutters. They could count themselves fortunate on a number of scores, for one of Mira's first acts had been to set up a canteen in the former community hall where tasty and generous meals were served at very low prices. The men worked as drovers, the women as milkers. They earned good money and saved their rubles, for what was there to buy?

Vassily obtained thirty-four horses as a virtual gift. Some two miles from Jiusefovka was a Red Army horse hospital run by a veterinary who ranked as a captain. The farm did not yet have a blacksmith of its own, and Vassily went to the hospital with a request from the power plant management that eighteen of the farm's horses be shod. Six Red Army men did the shoeing in an incredibly short time. Vassily was loud in praise of their skill, and the captain and his subordinates were highly pleased. The Captain showed him many of his four-legged patients, most already on the road to recovery. Then he led Vassily across the garden to an open field. There, shivering in the cold, heads drooping, was a group of horses so emaciated that their bones stuck out everywhere. They scarcely had the strength to rub up against one another. Vassily thought they had mange, but the Captain explained, "Lice. Salves, tinctures— nothing does any good. The lice seem to thrive on our medication; you can watch them multiplying. It's a pity—they're good animals, Polish artillery horses. Some of them are really first-class."

Vassily had already observed that. They were strong-boned, well-built and still young animals. "It certainly is a shame. Can't anything be done for them, Comrade Captain?"

"Maybe you can. I'll give them to you for your khoziaistva," the Captain said, laughing.

"We wouldn't be allowed to take them as a gift, of course, but perhaps we will buy them. What would you want for them?"

"Nothing, nothing at all. I'd be glad to have them off my hands."

"I understand that, but still they have to be paid for."

Finally they agreed on fifty-three rubles per horse—what the hides would be worth according to the official tariff.

Next morning, well before six o'clock, Vassily turned up with his men and a wagon loaded with dry wood, brush, and huge pots. On the top of the heap lay a half-filled sack. He handed the veterinary Captain a check on the Gosbank for 1802 rubles. The Captain was delighted, not so much at having got rid of thirty-four troublesome lice-ridden horses, as at the opportunity to show the "natives" what fools they were. But by noon he realized that he had been the fool. True, the ten men had worked like slaves at a filthy job, scrubbing the horses all over with the brownish-black tincture that was kept boiling in the big pots. The horses were just being washed a second time and rubbed down with straw when the Captain came out to see the results. He could not believe his eyes. The day before, he would not have dared to go close to the horses; now he went right up to them and inspected their hides, manes and tails. "Not a louse." He shook his head. Then he looked into the pots, sniffed the odor, and started. "Why, that's—"

"A secret, Comrade Captain, but I'll let you in on it. Makhorka. Tobacco. Lice don't like tobacco."

These horses were the occasion for the first open clash between Mermelstein and Vassily. Rudnicki, Mermelstein's driver, who had balked at Vassily's order to help wash the horses, had gone running to Mermelstein with a story of Vassily's idiotic deal. The Director came into the stable and raised a great storm about the miserable skeletons Vassily had bought. He inveighed against Mira, who had tricked him into signing the check, and threatened to denounce the two of them. Vassily let him rage on until he used the word "swindle."

"Mermelstein," Vassily said then—not Comrade Director, or Comrade Mermelstein, but simply Mermelstein. He spoke German, and there was no one around who understood it. "Mermelstein, if you, of all people, say anything more about swindle, I'll hold your head in the liquid manure until you stop breathing."

Mermelstein preferred to remove himself from the scene. But he had a partial revenge by reporting to Saposhnik that the purchase had been made over his head by the stablemaster, with Mira's collusion. Comrade Saposhnik had given the bookkeeper too great powers, he said, when he ordered him, Mermelstein, to sign whatever checks she presented to him.

Saposhnik let Mermelstein finish his story. He had his own thoughts about it, but still it was upsetting, and four days later he paid a visit to the farm. By chance he arrived at the time the Captain from the horse hospital was visiting the stables. The Captain was astonished at the condition of the animals, who looked clean and spruce, standing at their mangers and eating with hearty appetites. An honest man, he did not conceal his thoughts. He told Saposhnik about the miracle cure that the stablemaster had effected before his eyes, and topped it all by saying that the power plant had made fifty thousand rubles at the expense of the army, for the horses would be worth that, and perhaps much more, in three weeks at the latest.

Friendly and neighborly relations developed between the farm and the horse hospital.

Where pigeons are, other pigeons come. Baczynski, the blacksmith and wheelwright, came to join the collective. He was followed by the harness maker, a fat little old man with steel-rimmed glasses who set up his shop in the adjoining building. Farm members received visits from their home villages, showed off their houses, the barns, the land. Word got around, and since conditions in the countryside were almost unendurable, new recruits came pouring in. The complement of drivers and milkers was soon complete. Wagner, the warehouse director, brought in one of his former business associates, a pig breeder, who moved in with his livestock and equipment. A few days later a sausage plant was installed in a house with a big cellar. A barn was converted into a primitive but relatively hygienic slaughterhouse. All the new workers who came brought machinery and tools, and everything was paid for in cash.

Soon the houses were all occupied. In the stables stood fifty-three strong, well-nourished horses. The cow barns held a hundred cows; more than two hundred pigs grunted in the sties. Buttermaking proceeded smoothly; the sausage plant worked in two and sometimes three shifts. In the orchards Antek with his two helpers, Tadek and Freddy, busily pruned trees and bushes, and a big square was dug up for the establishment of cold frames. Taciturn Baczynski and his two assistants presided over the smithy. The little harness maker, Josef Radetzky, sang cheerfully the whole day long. In the canteen two sturdy women cooked great stews in monster kettles. All in all, the farm was a model enterprise. Everyone had his job, everything ran smoothly—and there was no deficit!

How did they do it? How had they managed it? Lavrenenko asked Saposhnik; other party men asked him; the nachalniki of the big organizations, who had also received permission for farms, asked most urgently of all, for their projects were all on the rocks.

Saposhnik explained it this way: "First of all there is the transport business. There are twenty-five teams working every day. The farm has made contracts with many organizations. It charges only the regular rates, of course, but these have been high. The teams have brought in thousands of rubles, leaving a surplus which covers the temporary deficits from the production of food and the supplying of the canteens. But the predominant factor in our success has been the spirit which dominates the farm. There is order, thrift and cleanliness everywhere. The workers on the farm are satisfied, they like to work, and no one has left his job so far. Productivity has been mounting steadily."

That was Saposhnik's official story; it was partially true, and it satisfied the questioners. But it did not satisfy him.

Somewhere, he knew, there was a buried rat. But why exhume it? He was fairly sure that no one on the farm (unless it was Mermelstein; sooner or later he must find a pretext for getting rid of that fellow) was putting anything into his own pocket. But he also suspected that most of these exemplary, industrious workers were hiding a past, a past of forbidden, parasitic lives. Was the whole farm nothing but a nest of stinking bourgeoisie, a sinkhole of capitalism?

Those drivers—you could see at a glance that they were kulaks. Not to speak of Kornhaber, Meerblum and Wagner. You could smell the dealers, the entrepreneurs, the speculators, even though their autobiographies glossed over these facts and they all pretended to have been humble officials and clerks. Oh well, that much was all right with the higher-ups; they were no longer demanding that people have virginal pasts. Feingold, during that significant first conversation, had indicated that there would be time later on to separate the chaff from the wheat. But who would pass that ultimate scrutiny? The bookkeeper Linhan, the stablemaster Khomniuk, the gardener and his two helpers—they were workers all right, of working-class stock. Maybe one or two of the others had been too. But the great majority of the others? Suppose they were sent packing—what would happen to the farm? Who could replace those competent and hard-working people—doubly competent and hard-working because they were afraid, afraid of "resettlement." Well, the time had not come yet. For the present the farm was functioning magnificently. So the rat had better stay buried.

Mira had similar thoughts as she stepped out on the street with the two men. They walked in silence as far as her house, and bade her good night.

Antek and Vassily still had a long way to walk to the small cottage where they lived with Tadek. It was the smallest in the entire village. Tadek kept it spotlessly clean. When they reached home, he was already fast asleep. The fire was still burning; a caldron of hot water stood on the stove; washbasins glistened on small stands; soap dishes and neatly folded towels lay on the windowsill. They took off their boots and polished them. Vassily's were already in wretched condition, the soles worn through and the tops badly cracked. "They're done for," Antek said. "I have a few pairs laid by, brand-new—I'll pick out a pair for you in the morning."

"No, thanks. I could easily buy myself some, but—"

"But?"

"It might attract attention if I had new boots."

"How so?"

"Where would a koniukh who gets barely two hundred rubles a month find the money to buy new boots? Do you think they don't know what a pair costs? Besides, the ones you have are far too good."

"What a lovely life." Antek was angry. "But you can't go on slogging around in those, in all this wet. What are you going to do?"

"I'll apply to Saposhnik tomorrow. There are factories where boots and shoes are made in this glorious Soviet land. I'm a worker. I want boots at the official price. After all, I have a right to them."

"Saposhnik will laugh himself sick. The shoes are only for the big shots—you know that. He himself couldn't get a pair."

"I can't go barefoot—maybe he'll give me an advance on my pay."

"Sure! What with your big hit tonight."

Vassily did not answer. He stood stripped to the waist over the steaming washbowl and thoroughly soaped his face, neck and ears. Antek realized that he was in no mood to talk. He washed also, and then they both shaved in front of the small, crude wall mirror which made their faces look distorted and green. While they were cleaning their razors, Antek said, "Razor blades are disappearing. No more Gillettes to be had, and the others aren't worth a damn."

"The farm has applied for a permit to install a barbershop and a health station."

"We'll get them. But then we'll also have to have a manicurist."

"Manicurist!"

"Haven't you heard? The milkmaids have to have their

hands manicured—newest order from above. For hygienic reasons. And they must wear white smocks and caps, and the tails and udders of the cows have to be washed in some antiseptic before milking."

"Not a bad idea."

"No, that's all we needed to make our happiness complete," Antek sneered.

"Are you so unhappy, Antek? I've watched you at your work. It seems to me you like it."

"Yes, I like the work, but when I think that if I'd swotted this way in the past—when we had the damned burzhui—I'd have been a millionaire, not had one foot in jail all the time."

"The bark is worse than the bite, Antek. Only morons and hard-luck boys land in jail. And over there"—he made a vague gesture—"it isn't any better."

"You've made that point once before tonight—when you told your story."

"I meant that. There's no sense running to the Germans. It wouldn't be any better with them, that's for sure."

"You don't know everything, Vassily," Antek answered. "As far as I'm concerned, nothing is worse than the pen, and what we have here is one big pen."

He fell silent abruptly and watched Vassily out of the corner of his eyes. He waited for a reply, and when the stablemaster, boots in hand and clothes over his arm, stepped silently out of the kitchen, he followed him.

At the door of his room Vassily said, "Good night, Antek."

"Good night, Vassily. And—don't mind what I say. I won't be bolting. It's all bullshit anyhow."

The light wagon rolled along the country road. To the right of the road were the farm's fields, flat as a table. It was rich, black earth, steaming with mist, soaked with melted snow. Vassily drew the smell of the soil deep into his lungs; he looked up at the sky, where the sun lurked behind gray walls of cloud, too feeble to pierce them with its rays. The whip clicked over the big hindquarters of the shaft horse, a caress rather than a command. "Well, now!" Vassily said. But the words were intended in the same way as the gentle tickling with the whip, for the two chestnuts were already moving at the proper tempo, a deliberate, distance-eating trot. Nor was Vassily really addressing the horses; he meant to rouse the woman who sat beside him.

But Mira's face remained stony; her eyes stared fixedly ahead and her lips were firmly compressed.

"We ought to start plowing this week," Vassily said. "In fact, we should start tomorrow."

"I don't know how we can manage it. I've hired the teams out for the next two weeks. Their time is completely taken up. We have contracts we must meet. I can't keep things going without that money, Vassily. Don't forget that we are delivering too much to the canteens. We cannot make up for it any other way."

"Then," Vassily said slowly, "we must simply—produce more." He looked as if he had discovered something highly interesting on the horses' ears.

Mira gave him a short, sharp look. "I can't go on with that. It has to stop. My nerves won't stand it any more. One of these days our swindles will come out and then—" She sighed. "Do you think it's true, what they said last night about shooting people at the borders? You never know whether they're telling the truth or not."

"You can well believe that when they say it," he said without looking at her.

"I suppose so." She fell silent, and Vassily gave the horses their head. As they approached the city and the road became a paved one, he walked them again. Only then did Mira speak of what was really on her mind. "Vassily," she said, "I've been thinking the matter over for a long while. There's something I've wanted to discuss with you. Perhaps ever since I met you, when you gave me that loan. You or Antek—I don't even know which of you to thank for it. I've only repaid a small part of it. But I still have the stones." She became acutely embarrassed. "You can have them whenever you want them."

Vassily laughed. "Diamonds—yes; I've long had it in mind to order a tie pin, or cuff links for an evening suit." He looked down at his battered boots. "They'd go so well with my footgear. No, I don't need diamonds, or money either, Mira. Why add that to your worries? We're friends, you know."

She showed no surprise at his mentioning matters which should have stood outside his experience. Nor did her usual acuteness stand by her, for she did not realize that he had planted these references. She only asked, "Are we friends, Vassily?" and looked at him with an air of suspense that he could almost physically feel.

"Why, of course," he said lightly, gazing straight ahead at the road as if the potholes required his full attention. Under his breath he hummed the old army song: "The light and the heavy, the whole damned cavalry. . . ."

But Mira did not know how to construe this either. She felt only the reassurance, the sense of protection, that always emanated from him, that came to her even when she merely thought about him. She did not probe her feelings, did not try to analyze. It was a good and a comforting feeling. He sat there with his mustache, which completely concealed his mouth, with his blue-gray eyes fixed on the road, reins held lightly in callused hands, feet in their battered boots braced against the footboard, no different from the other drivers—a peasant like the rest, and yet different from the others. He worked as they did, but harder, more intently, and also with greater assurance, resolution, determination. He walked, sat and talked like the others—but they took his leadership for granted. He had organized the farm's one really profitable business, the hiring out of the teams, and never once had he alluded to the fact that the whole enterprise was due to his experience, his farsightedness and his energy. She had explained to him why the farm had to have a surplus, and he had understood. Without needing to, without deriving the slightest advantage from it, he had put his head in the noose; he had helped work out and carry out the plan. Sixty per cent of the farm's produce—the butter, fresh meat and sausage—went by secret routes to "private" consumers who paid many times the official prices. The extra money covered the losses the farm incurred from delivering produce at official prices to the workers of the power plant. Only Vassily, Antek, Kornhaber, Meerblum and the warehouse director, Wagner, were in on the fraud. It was a dangerous business that required a great deal of caution and adroitness. Mira kept many books in addition to her official bookkeeping. The latter, of course, was always exact to the kopeck. Kornhaber had to fix things at the milking so that even the milkmaids had no idea of the total quantity of milk produced; and Meerblum's assistants could never say how much butter, cheese or cream the dairy actually supplied. The sausage factory often produced four times the actual needs of the power plant and farm and was the most difficult item in Mira's accounts to conceal. But she had left herself some room for maneuver by insisting on the advisability of keeping a varying quantity in reserve. For purposes of exchange, so to speak. "Up above" they understood that and approved of it—all the more since certain bars frequented by party functionaries weekly received considerable quantities of fine sausages at trifling premiums above the official price—these were imposed largely for the sake of form. This favor was highly appreciated and netted the directors of the power plant, and Saposhnik in particular, considerable praise.

For this and other reasons Saposhnik was eager to keep the farm alive and viable, and to shield it from adverse winds; for he knew far better than his subordinates how faint a breeze could sweep away the favor of the upper hierarchy. Overnight their good will could disappear as if it had never existed, and be re-

placed by the strict application of doctrine and dogma. Saposhnik
knew, too, how easily such a contrary wind could arise out of envy,
when one group accomplished far more with the same means that
were at the disposal of all others. Nachalnik Saposhnik had witnessed that all too often, and he had dropped clear hints to Mira to
be careful. Mira, for her part, had passed on the word. Everyone
did his best, for their very lives were at stake. If the farm was a success and offered so few weak points for attack, it might provide a
certain justification, in the eyes of the men in power, for the existence of the burzhui.

Like all the others on the farm, Mira herself worked furiously.
Everyone was haunted by the fear of being exposed, everyone sustained by the delusion that by their labors they could prove their in-
dispensability and so forestall "resettlement"—for they shunned calling it by its right name: deportation. Mira's sense of jeopardy never
slept. She had carried the others along by her own fear and her
own enthusiasm. Most of them understood her and worked as they
had never worked before. They made nothing of overtime, never
claimed their days off; they worked for the farm because the farm
was working for them—that is, providing them with a livelihood.
They worked in fear and trembling, without comforts, without
diversions, without the most modest amusements. All they wanted
was to stay here, in the land where they had always lived. The mere
thought of Russia's arctic regions chilled their blood.

Mira sensed all this, and utilized their fear. She understood
those who were afraid, because she herself was afraid; but she did
not understand this man Vassily. Had he not always been what he
now was? A worker laboring for others for scanty wages? Always
in the stables, always with the horses? As a matter of fact, he knew
far more than the ordinary peasant—that was apparent. How
quickly he grasped business matters; how calmly and self-assuredly
he spoke; how reliable he was. Reliable—yes, that was it. You
could always trust him. But why, why did he go along with her
scheme? Why did he voluntarily assume guilt? It would be understandable if he were making some profit out of it, if he had been
concerned about money; peasants loved money. But he did not care
about it; seemed even to despise it. She had observed that more than
once.

They were already in the center of town, passing overcrowded
streetcars and hurrying pedestrians. All were hastening to work,
anxious not to be late. Mira looked at a clock; it was a few minutes
before eight. "Let's drop in at the Textile Trust, Vassily. I must
squeeze two hundred yards of linen out of Sumkin."

"For work smocks? Do you have a sausage or a good piece of

bacon with you?"

Mira nodded. "That too. But I have a more effective weapon. If he won't give me the linen, I won't renew the contract with him. Then let him look for vehicles to transport his goods."

"Fine—and don't forget we must start spring planting, Mira." They stopped in front of the Textile Trust building. "Perhaps there'll be a miracle. I'm going to the office. Wait until I'm finished and then we'll drive to the bank and from there to Panya Jadwiga's."

Mira stepped down onto the shaft, supporting herself with her free hand on Vassily's shoulder, while her other hand held her bag. Vassily could not help observing, as he had often done before, that Mira had lovely legs, though they were disguised by heavy stockings and clumsy boots. She stepped to the pavement. "Well, then, I'll see you in an hour or so. Make sure the meat is weighed in your presence, and don't forget the receipt. So long, Vassily."

"So long." A few minutes later Vassily drove into the courtyard of the Elektrostantsia's office building. He hoisted the canvas bag of meat over his shoulder and went down to the canteen in the basement. Priesner, head of the canteen, had formerly owned a small restaurant. He too had been "taken over" with his equipment. His wife cooked; he and his niece served the food. All three were employees of the power plant.

Priesner weighed the meat, praised its quality in German—he had worked as a waiter in Vienna for two years—and wrote out the receipt. Vassily pocketed it, picked up the empty sack, and set out to see Saposhnik.

The Deputy Director received him with great friendliness. "How are things at the farm, Comrade Khomniuk?"

"We're working, Comrade Saposhnik. This time I've come to see you on a personal matter—with a request."

"A request of your own—fine, fine." Saposhnik was plainly pleased. "Of what sort?"

"I need some new boots," Vassily said.

Saposhnik looked down at Vassily's boots and remained for some time lost in contemplation of them, as if he were determining whether the stablemaster's claim was justified. He shook his head slightly. This was no refusal, rather a gesture of embarrassment, of astonishment at such naïveté. Where were boots to be obtained? But it would not do to tell this man with his childlike faith in the new regime that he might just as well place his hopes in Santa Claus as in the Deputy Director of the power plant. It would be a crying shame to shatter a faith like his. But what could he, Saposhnik, do to preserve that faith? "Write a petition. Address it to me. I'll pass it on. It will take a little while, but I am sure—" Saposhnik did not have the courage to say what he was sure of. The lie would have been too blatant. As for the truth—how could he explain it? "We have everything!"

"Thank you, Comrade Saposhnik." Vassily smiled blissfully. As though he were already wearing the new boots, Saposhnik thought.

"Here are pen and paper." Saposhnik got up from the desk. "Sit right down in my chair and write."

Vassily sat at the desk, the paper in front of him and the nachalnik's fountain pen in his hand. At last he looked up. "Comrade Saposhnik, I've never written a petition before. How do you go about it? Besides, my Russian isn't so good, especially when I try to write it down."

"Write: 'To the Deputy Director' and so on. 'I request the allocation of a pair of boots,' and then put your name down. Write it as best you can. A koniukh is not a professor; they know that."

The stablemaster laboriously drew letter upon letter on the yellowish paper. Not all the letters were of equal size and they did not line up in a neat row. Some hung in the air; others clung timorously to one another. Meanwhile Saposhnik stood at the window smoking and looking out into the courtyard. He had not turned down this good fellow's request, had not disappointed him. Vassily could hope. He had given him a few drops of the medicine with which millions of human beings had been put off for decades. The name of that medicine was *budet*—it will be!

"Lavrenenko will also recommend it; let's go right in to see him. Come along, comrade."

While Saposhnik talked with Lavrenenko in a whisper, Vassily stood discreetly in a corner of the luxurious office. He could not hear what the two were saying, but it was clear that Lavrenenko was reluctant to support the petition. Lavrenenko liked Vassily and didn't want to hold out this empty soap bubble to him. If the man still believed, he of all people ought not to be duped.

"Vassily Vassilevich," the Director called out finally, "come over here, sit down." He cleared his throat. "I have a proposal to make you: we'll give you a loan. What does a pair of decent boots cost at—hm—at the bazaar?"

"An awful lot, Comrade Director."

"More than four hundred rubles?"

"For four hundred you could get some—Polish boots, of course."

"Very well. You will receive a loan of four hundred rubles. You could pay that off easily in two years, couldn't you, Vassily? A few rubles every month—you'd hardly notice it. It would be taken right out of your wages—all right? Your petition will also be passed on, you'll be put down for boots, and when your turn comes you'll have another pair of boots. That means you'll have three pair, if the ones you're wearing can be repaired."

"That's fine. Thank you, Comrade Director."

"You write the petition for him, Mark Lvovich." Lavrenenko stood up. Just then the door opened and Feingold strode beaming into the room. He nodded to Lavrenenko and Saposhnik and promptly turned to Vassily.

"I saw the wagon and was looking for you everywhere, Vassily Vassilevich. So here you are. How are things?"

"Good, thank you, Comrade Feingold—in fact, very good." He nodded in the direction of Saposhnik, who sat writing. "I'm being given money." His whole face was wreathed in smiles.

Lavrenenko explained the situation to Feingold, whose happy look gave way to reflective gravity. Then he smiled heartily once more. "Mark Lvovich, no doubt you have a good many farm problems to talk over with Vassily Vassilevich. Why don't you two go along to your office? I'll be with you in a few minutes."

Saposhnik understood. He rose and beckoned to Vassily, who followed him.

Saposhnik was deeply troubled. He had spent the past few nights at the bedside of his sick wife. The local doctors, too, had given up hope, and he was in despair. With a sigh, he sank into a chair. "Sit down, Comrade Khomniuk. Life is hard, hard. My wife, you know, she's very sick. Tuberculosis."

"Yes, I know. What do the doctors say?"

"That it's too late. Something should have been done sooner."

Vassily looked thoughtful. "Yes, it is a terrible disease." Then he said very slowly, "You ought to try Dr. Feuerberg."

"Feuerberg? Who is he? Where does he work?"

"I don't know where he works; I've only heard his name. He is supposed to be a specialist in lung diseases."

"Let me take down his name, in any case. It can do no harm."

They fell silent. The mention of the doctor who was said to be a specialist had kindled a spark of hope in Saposhnik. Vassily, for his part, was trying to come to terms with his own conscience. For he had played a trick on Saposhnik, taking advantage of the man's distress. What he as a simple stablemaster could not do, the nachalnik could: discover whether Dr. Feuerberg was anywhere in the region called the "Western Ukraine." For in spite of enormous difficulties, Vassily had made his way to Czeravna, only to learn that Dr. Feuerberg had disappeared a few days after the Russians marched in. This information had been given him by the Catholic priest of Czeravna. The worthy pastor had told him a good deal more, which had had no bearing on his search, and which his mind had scarcely registered at the time. Now, however, these stories sprang to his mind, and somewhat assuaged his feeling of guilt. It seemed that Dr. Feuerberg, guided by the priest, had taken the path of salvation, and that he, the pastor, took pride in bringing to the Church a man of such great human and professional qualities. Dr. Feuerberg was a great physician, he had said, and with the help of God and the Blessed Virgin had performed a miraculous cure upon the wife of the former (and surely future) owner of Czeravna. He had healed her lungs after far-better-known doctors had given her up for lost.

After a short while Mira appeared in the office, followed almost at once by Feingold.

"I wonder if you could let me have the use of the wagon for an hour," Feingold said to Saposhnik.

"Of course!"

"Then come along, Vassily Vassilevich, we'll start at once."

"If you're driving into town, I have some business there too," Saposhnik said.

"I'm going to the Secretariat," Feingold replied.

"So am I."

"If you don't mind, I'll come along as far as the Gosbank," Mira spoke up.

"Konechno!" Feingold said.

Although there was a long line at the window at the Gosbank, Mira was finished very quickly. She had won the friendly cooperation of a teller, one of the "natives," by small offerings of highly desirable foodstuffs. As soon as he caught sight of her, he called out loudly, "Elektrostantsia!" She repeated the word just as loudly, and the crowd in front of the window, all "native" officials, respectfully made room for her. In a few minutes her business was completed and she stepped outside, considering what she had to do next. Suddenly she found herself surrounded by five or six bright-faced young men in the simple uniform of Red Army officers. "What do you wish, comrades?" she asked.

"Nichevo," one of them said. "We're strangers here and wanted to ask you to kill time with us a little, citizeness. We want to go to a restaurant, eat, drink, maybe take in a movie or the theater. *Nada she guliat*—we have to amuse ourselves!"

"It sounds lovely," Mira said, though she had not the slightest sympathy with the young men's plans. "But, Comrades *Kommandiry* [officers], I can't go with you—work to do. If it were my day off, I'd be happy to. Thank you for your invitation." She shook hands with each of them in turn. "Good-bye, comrades!"

"Good-bye, comrade!" the men replied in a loud chorus. Mira walked away, but not so quickly that she failed to hear one young soldier's exclamation: "*Shayil, khoroshaya baba—*too bad, a fine-looking dame!"

Those three words gave quite a lift to Mira's spirits. Still smiling, she found herself stopping in front of a big shop whose sign in antique script, Salon de Beauté, had been only lightly covered with whitewash. Above it, in Cyrillic letters, "Parikmacherskaya No. 3" had been painted. She entered as if the shop had been her destination all along, with an air of assurance and unconcern. And as the characteristic atmosphere of the beauty shop surrounded her, her smile deepened.

After almost two hours Mira left, her hair well shampooed and skillfully set, her face massaged, her hands manicured and feet pedicured. She was wearing a lipstick that had come from "former" stocks and carrying in her purse a sinfully expensive bottle of Chanel cologne.

She had looked at herself in the mirror without a twinge of conscience over so much lost time, and had observed an image utterly different from the Mira of these many months past, these months of fear and hard work. Now she looked much more like that other Mira—when had that other Mira existed?—than the Mira of two hours ago. And she was content.

It was eleven o'clock when she emerged on the street. High time. Vassily would surely be waiting impatiently for her. Fortunately it was only a short way from here to Antek's little house. Panya Jadwiga opened the door after Mira had given their private signal: two short raps with the knuckle, a pause, and then one rap with the palm of her hand. "You're late today," Panya Jadwiga growled, and picked up the glass which she had set down while opening the door.

"Has Vassily been here yet?"

"Not yet." The gigantic woman took a sip from her glass of brandy and drew on her cigarette. "I've got to leave. Fresh goods?"

"Can you use more?"

"Are you joking? Would you like a decent meal?"

"I'd sooner wait for Vassily. He ought to be here soon."

"Brandy?"

"Brandy? Yes, thanks."

Mira followed Panya Jadwiga into the kitchen. "So, here's some brandy; and there are cutlets in the warming oven." She untied her apron. "I must go." She remembered Mira's peculiarities.

"There's hot water. Would you like to bathe?"

"Konechno!" The word had made the rounds, was the rage on the farm. It was used most of all by Tadek and Freddy, for it had established their friendship.

"Konechno," Panya Jadwiga growled in her deep bass, and took her leave.

When she returned three hours later, Mira and Vassily were sitting at table, deep in talk. Panya Jadwiga could observe only the outward changes in the two. She had already noticed the results of Mira's visit to the beauty shop. Now her eyes lit instantly upon Vassily's boots with their soft, short, wrinkled tops. "Russian boots," she growled contemptuously.

"We take what we can get, Panya Jadwiga. These are much cheaper," Vassily said apologetically.

Panya Jadwiga refreshed herself with alcohol and nicotine. Then she said, closing the matter, "A peasant is always a peasant." She undid the buttons of her blouse and produced a fat package of hundred-ruble notes. "Here. Eighteen thousand three hundred. Worthless paper!" Picking up her glass, she marched into the kitchen.

Vassily sat watching her. As soon as she closed the door behind her, Mira stood up and went behind his chair. She took his head in her hands and drew it against her breast. Bending, she brushed her lips lightly and tenderly over his forehead and eyes.

Vassily took her hands and kissed each one. "Sit down, Mira; she may be back at any moment."

"What if she is?" But Mira obeyed. Seated once more, she propped her head in both hands and gazed fondly at him. He twirled his mustache. "Have you had it long—the mustache, I mean, Vassily?"

"It feels as if I've had it forever," he said, avoiding her eyes. "Why? Don't you like it?"

"Like it?" She looked at him and shook her head. "It has nothing to do with liking."

He rose, went to the window and stood looking out in silence for a moment. Then he turned to her once more. "We must go, Mira. Put the money away."

She did not move. "And what about me? Do you like me, Vassily?"

"You know you are a woman any man would like, Mira."

Khoroshaya baba, she recalled. "I'm glad you like me, Vassily. I—I think"—her voice was hoarser than it normally was—"no, I know it: I love you, Vassily!"

"Do you, Mira?" He smiled his customary smile. "Then it is good." He went up to her, placed his work-callused hands under her arms and raised her to her feet. He put his arms around her and kissed her. "Good," he repeated, and he hummed "But one does not speak of love," the words of a new Soviet tango which one of the Red Army men had recently sung in the canteen.

"One must, Vassily, one must speak of it."

"And now"—he laughed and kissed her again—"we'd better start. Saposhnik is waiting."

"The boots our Vassily is wearing—a colonel or a party secretary could envy him for them!" Maximenko said, not without a touch of envy himself, but flashing his teeth in a big smile. Saposhnik nodded. Mira had tied her kerchief over her head to conceal her new coiffure, and she kept her manicured hands in the pockets of her jacket.

Saposhnik turned to her. "So, Mira Isakovna, would you come into my office, and you too, Comrade Khomniuk? We have to discuss the plan. Mermelstein ought to be here—where in the world is he? He is supposed to sign for it. This isn't, strictly speaking, the business of the bookkeeping department or the stables. Mermelstein is responsible for seeing that the plan is fulfilled. Oh well, he'll certainly be along shortly. You'd better be informed about it, Mira Isakovna, so that you can explain it to him. . . . Pavel Pavlovich, will you outline the plan to the comrade?"

"Here is a point-by-point list of what the farm must perform." Maximenko handed Mira a long sheet of figures. She promptly began to study it. At a glance she saw that these were production quotas which could never be achieved. It was all pure theory, and Mira did not know whether to laugh or cry out in fury. Nevertheless she said very quietly, "The plan is not complete, Comrade Maximenko. The most important thing has been forgotten."

"Forgotten? Nothing has been forgotten. This is precisely the quota established by the People's Commissariat for Agriculture, and it applies to the whole Ukraine."

"Nevertheless such a plan has to state precisely how much feed and what kind of feed will be needed in order to achieve the required production. If the plan requires a cow to give a minimum of sixty pounds of milk of a given fat content per day, the cow must have adequate feed—not to speak of the fact that such yields are only possible with cows of the highest breeding. Even so, the feeding is crucial. If a horse is to travel a certain number of miles with a prescribed load every day, it must get the proper quantity of energy feeds. In the past three months we have had assigned to us a total of eight tons of feed for three hundred fifty-nine farm animals. That is less than half a pound per day per head. We can realize the plan only when the necessary basic investments and equipment are provided for. But what are they, where can we get hold of them, and what will they cost?"

Maximenko listened to all this without blinking an eyelash. "The plan must be signed, stamped and sealed by the Director of the farm before twelve o'clock tomorrow," he said to Saposhnik. "It must then go to the party." He turned to Mira. "As bookkeeper, comrade, you bear no responsibility for all this—only the Director. He must sign. And whether he fulfills the plan or not is his business."

That was true, and no further remonstrance was possible. The Director bore the full responsibility. Mira knew that, but she saw no way to avert the threatening danger. For the fool, the *shubiak,* would sign, and the plan simply could not be carried out. In her brief service as bookkeeper Mira had leared a good deal—among other things that the bark was generally a good deal worse than the bite. These people were fond of playing with figures, data, statistics, building castles in the air, and didn't give a damn about reality. But Mira's respect for obligations undertaken, for contracts and signatures, was too deep for her to be able to regard this absurd plan merely as an empty formality. And indeed she knew that it would remain a formality, remain a scrap of paper in the documents, only as long as it suited those "up above." Given a change in the situation, it would be fetched out to provide a pretext for a charge of sabotage.

Vassily also recognized the danger and attempted to intervene. "I understand, Comrade Planovik, you say that only the Director is responsible. But we on the farm—all the workers, I mean—share the responsibility for meeting the plan. Everyone has to fulfill his quota if that is to be done. That is why we are concerned about the additional equipment."

But Comrade Planovik had nothing to do with that. The plan he had presented was not the product of his own brain; it was an arbitrary assortment of figures and data set down by someone much higher up. He had only had it copied. But he had to say something now, something that would not commit him to anything. What else was there to say, if not "Nichevo"?

With that, and a cheerful greeting, Maximenko left the room, leaving the others in thoughtful silence. Saposhnik felt that Maximenko's parting shot was hardly an appropriate answer to "natives." But he suspected that the bookkeeper, whom he regarded both as his discovery and his pupil, as well as in a certain sense his confidante and in another sense—though this was rather hazy—his own, had already gained enough insight into Soviet ways to make the game considerably easier. The stablemaster, too, was sensible and dependable. He had proved that. And he was also important—no doubt about it. Probably he himself was not entirely aware of what those boots he was wearing signified. How could he know that Feingold had conferred with the party Secretary for the whole of the Western Ukraine on their account? Lavrenenko, who had heard the telephone conversation, had passed the word along to Saposhnik. Khomniuk was Feingold's discovery; he had made the man his protégé, and the boots were in themselves dramatic proof of how much Feingold's protection counted. Ridiculous—a koniukh could wait a whole lifetime before he obtained a pair of boots from one of the factories which worked exclusively for the verkhovki—the top echelon —and at government prices. But the thing that came out was not so much the importance of Comrade Feingold, but of Khomniuk himself. It was clear to Saposhnik that those "up above" needed the koniukh Khomniuk. For Vassily had received not only the boots, but stockings, two shirts and a cap with a broad brim to take the place of his lambskin cap in the summer. And all that for eighty-three rubles, which price included the repair of his old boots. None of this was anything he had a claim to, nor was it acknowledgment of past accomplishments. Those precious articles of clothing, precisely what a peasant needed and wanted, were an advance, a promise, a lure. To men in the know, like Saposhnik, these items of clothing spoke a plain language: we are available, but only to those who do what is asked of them.

A further conclusion could be drawn: if this koniukh did what was asked of him, and did it well, he would not remain a koniukh; he would move up into spheres where it would become a legend that he had once rubbed down horses, carted dung and cleaned out stables. For such a past was no drawback "among us"; on the contrary. The lower a man's origins, the swifter his rise could be, assuming that he had the ability. And this man Vassily had demonstrated all sorts of abilities. Had he not mentioned the name of Dr. Feuerberg who, as Saposhnik had discovered in short order, was a surgeon and working as deputy director of the only tuberculosis sanatorium in the city? A position which no "native" would hold unless he were otherwise acceptable on all counts. By way of recompense, and because it was pointless to continue discussion of the unfortunate plan for the farm, Saposhnik said, "You know, Comrade Khomniuk, I've already found this Dr. Feuerberg. You are right—

he is a specialist." He took a slip of paper from his pocket. "Here is the address of the hospital. I've tried to reach him by telephone but haven't had any luck. I want to call on him personally; perhaps I could persuade him to come with me right away. The sanatorium is very far from my home, at the other end of town."

"I'll be glad to drive you, Comrade Saposhnik," Vassily replied eagerly. "Just say when."

"Thank you, comrade. Let's make it five o'clock tomorrow afternoon. Now, there remains the question of spring planting. High time to begin that." He looked across at Mira. "That's a difficult problem. We can't spare the teams, but the planting has to be done. If only"—he faltered, and then began again—"if only we could get hold of a tractor."

"That's right, a tractor!" Vassily exclaimed enthusiastically.

"There is a tractor station about forty miles from here. Fairly near Khodorov. If a tractor were free there, maybe—" He paused. "You see, it's this way. We cannot demand a tractor from them. They don't have to rent us one, because the station doesn't belong to our district. But if we could come to an agreement with the na-chalnik—on a comradely basis, so to speak—over a bottle of vodka."

"I'll go on horseback," Vassily said. "That will take less time than if I try driving the truck over those bad roads."

"Splendid," Saposhnik said.

"What is the name of the village, Comrade Saposhnik?"

"Soniewicze."

"Soniewicze. . . ." There was a strange note in Vassily's voice, but Saposhnik did not notice. Instead he felt a surge of hope, and promptly scribbled down the *komandirovka,* the authorization that was required whenever an employee had to go some distance on a mission from his plant. Then he himself took it to the typist's room to have it typed out.

"What was it struck you about Soniewicze, Vassily?" Mira asked as soon as Saposhnik was gone.

"Oh, old stories." Vassily started as if roused from a dream. He heard, as though it had been only yesterday, only an hour ago. "Take six uhlans," his Captain had said. They had been garrisoned in Khodorov. "Take six uhlans and ride toward Soniewicze. There's a shortcut to it—take that. Keep your eyes open and ride as far as you can. Take care of yourself and your men, Ensign. Dismissed!" On that patrol he had ridden as far as Lvov. He had brought eight Cossacks back with him, and a "ticket home"—a bullet through his left bicep. And received his first decoration for that ride. The estate had belonged to a Prince Baraniecki; years later he had been the Prince's guest. And tomorrow Koniukh Vassily would ride over to the same village to make a deal with a nachalnik over a bottle of vodka. Oh well, why not?

Saposhnik had returned to the room without Vassily's noticing. Vassily was standing at the window looking out on the street. The irregular, rapid clatter of hoofbeats on the pavement had attracted his attention. He stared tensely in the direction of the sounds. The heads of two roans appeared. Rudniki sat on the box, swinging his whip furiously, each time striking his horses' necks. He did not stop at the gate. It would not have been possible for him to stop; by now the horses could not be checked. They swung sharply around and, lashed by the whip, leaped over the little ditch that separated street from courtyard. The well-sprung carriage bobbed. Mermelstein, who was sitting in the rear, laughed aloud. Rudnicki pulled the horses back with a cruel jerk. They reared up; once more the whip cracked about their ears and necks, and then they stood still, quivering, covered with sweat, flanks heaving, struggling for breath.

Every blow of the whip had struck Vassily too; he felt the brutal pull at the horses' mouths as if it were his own pain. When he turned, deathly pale, fists clenched, Mira was terrified. She did not know the reason for the change in him. Saposhnik was reading through the travel permit and was too absorbed to notice. Wide-eyed, Mira watched Vassily stride angrily toward the door. He already had the latch in his hand when she cried out, "Vassily!" Saposhnik started up. "What's happened?" He saw Mira sitting numbed, staring at Vassily. In a moment he had leaped up from his desk and was moving toward Vassily. Nachalnik Saposhnik, the little man with hamster cheeks and comic gait, had, during the many years before he became a nachalnik, done nothing but kill and keep himself from being killed. He recognized that expression on Vassily's face, having seen it thousands of times. But now Saposhnik was no longer a fighter; he was a nachalnik, a Bolshevik, who stood for law and order. And so the little man, who was a good head smaller and not half as broad as Khomniuk, blocked the koniukh's path. "Sit down again, comrade," he said quietly and firmly. "We still have a good many things to discuss."

Vassily stopped. The voice was calmness, reason, command, and his rage subsided. Saposhnik went back to his desk, and indicated the pass. "We must wait until Lavrenenko comes; he has the stamp and seal. Did you want to say something, Comrade Khomniuk?"

Vassily had returned to his seat, and once more became the worker speaking to his nachalnik. "Yes, Comrade Saposhnik. I want to tell you that Rudnicki must be taken away from the horses; he's killing them." He stood up and led them over to the window. "Look out there." He pointed to the team. "Horses that were worth three thousand rubles, and now they're done for, good for nothing."

That was something Nachalnik Saposhnik understood. To damage state property was a crime. He returned to his desk and pressed a button. The courier came in. "I want to see Comrades Mermelstein and Rudnicki," he said.

In a few minutes the two men appeared. "Mermelstein," Saposhnik said, "from tomorrow morning on Rudnicki will be working as a courier in Plant II. He will also help in the canteen kitchen. Tell him that." Saposhnik spoke Yiddish.

Mermelstein stared blankly. He looked at Mira and Vassily and finally at Rudnicki, whose small, bloodshot eyes were impudently surveying Mira. Saposhnik repeated his statement. "He is free to refuse this work if he wishes," he added this time.

"But why?" Mermelstein stammered. "He's a fine driver."

"Tell him what I said," Saposhnik insisted.

Mermelstein turned to Rudnicki and repeated the order in Polish.

Rudnicki thrust both hands into his pockets. "Who is sending me to the kitchen?" he demanded insolently. "I'm a driver, not a cook." He laughed harshly.

"Comrade Director has given the order, not I," Mermelstein apologized.

"Comrade Director?" Rudnicki jerked his head in the direction of the desk. He thrust his chin out toward Saposhnik, who looked back at him indifferently. "Director? Is that a director? That lousy, stinking Jew, that mug?"

"Rudnicki!" Mira cried out in horror.

"Shut up, you red-headed whore," Rudnicki said coldly, and then he addressed Saposhnik in Ruthenian: "So you'll understand me better, Comrade Director, you can kiss my ass, you and your whore of a mother."

Vassily had already sprung to his feet when Rudnicki began insulting Mira. He raised his clenched fist. Mermelstein had slipped behind the stove.

"Comrade Khomniuk," Saposhnik called out, without especially raising his voice, "see to it that Rudnicki does not leave the room. Block the door." He reached for the telephone and without haste asked for a number. The connection went through with surprising speed.

While Saposhnik began telephoning, Rudnicki had begun moving toward the door. He approached with a light, almost prancing motion. "Get away from the door, Rusniak," he snarled. "You son of a bitch, get away, I say."

Vassily stood leaning against the door, scarcely looking at him.

"Get away or else—" His right hand flashed into his trouser pocket and flashed out again with a knife, its point directed at Vassily's stomach. Mira screamed, and Saposhnik, who had just set down the telephone, leaped over the desk and rushed toward Rudnicki's back. He was too late. Vassily's left hand had shot forward and gripped Rudnicki's wrist. A tug, a crack, and Rudnicki was writhing on the floor, howling. Vassily picked up the knife, studied the honed blade and the needle-sharp point. Then he laid it on the desk. "Nasty thing to have in your belly," he commented.

Saposhnik was looking down at the man writhing and groaning on the floor. "Is his wrist broken?" he asked quietly, returning to his desk.

Vassily took a cigarette from the breast pocket of his woolen jacket. "He'll never beat another horse," he said. "And he may remember not to call names." He lit the cigarette.

Saposhnik was once more seated at his desk. He looked at the knife as if it had stirred recollections. Then he sought Mira's eyes, as though he meant to ask her, "Do you understand now what I told you, about the pogrom and all the rest. That's what they were like, that's what they're still like." Mira, for her part, had eyes only for Vassily, as though she had to keep reassuring herself that the knife had not harmed him. Mermelstein came creeping out of his corner looking anxiously at Rudnicki, who was sitting up now, his left hand clutching his right.

That was the way the militiamen found him. There were three men in uniform and one in civilian dress. The latter shook hands with Saposhnik. "What was going on here?" he asked.

Saposhnik explained tersely. The officer nodded. "Pick him up," he told his men. They were not very gentle about it, and Rudnicki bellowed with pain. The civilian ignored that; he took over the desk and began to write. The report was then read aloud, and the witnesses confirmed it with their signatures. A Polish-speaking militiaman translated the document for Mermelstein, who also signed. "With charges like that," the officer said, standing up, "he won't die of old age. We take care of that kind."

It was not much later than eight o'clock in the morning when Vassily halted his horse in front of the Traktornaia Stantsia. The gate stood open. He could count six tractors, but saw nobody around. He rode into the yard, dismounted and tied his horse to a broken wagon. It had been a long, hard ride. He loosened the saddle girth and examined the horse; he showed no signs of fatigue, but the road had been fearfully muddy in spots. Vassily touched his legs and fetlocks and was pleased to note that they felt cool. Next he removed the saddle, examined the horse's back for pressure bruises, found none, and proceeded to rub and massage the place where the saddle had rested—its outline was plainly marked in the damp hair. From one of the saddlebags he took a collapsible canvas pail and brought water from the pump. He removed the snaffle and let the horse drink, taking care he did not drink too fast.

"Right," he heard a man's voice say, and when he turned he saw the man standing on the wooden porch; he had evidently been watching for some time.

"Good morning," Vassily said, going to the pump for a second pailful.

"Good morning," the man replied. He jumped down the few steps of the porch and came over to the horse. With eager attention he studied the animal. He was a rather short man with a round face which gauntness had rendered oblong. His sinewy, small hands expressed intense tenderness as they caressed the horse's mane and neck, forehead and nostrils. "What a horse," he crooned, "what a horse. He has intelligent ears—what's his name?"

"Golodnyi—Hungry," Vassily replied. "So you like him, comrade?"

"I am a Circassian, brother," the man said in explanation. "And you?"

"A Ruthenian."

"Do you work in the kolkhoz? You know how to handle horses —I was watching you. Take him into the stable." He looked rather shamefaced. "All I can offer is a stall for him, nothing to eat."

"I have his oats with me," Vassily said, indicating a bag strapped to the back of the saddle.

The Circassian nodded. "Very wise. Have you come far?"

"Quite a way. The farm where I work is near Lvov. It belongs to the Elektrostantsia there."

"You certainly must have started early. Have you business here?"

"Yes, right here. I'd like to speak to the nachalnik of the tractor station."

"I'm the nachalnik," the Circassian said.

"What luck. I'll take the horse into the stable and then we'll talk." Vassily smiled over the horse's withers at the nachalnik.

"Yes, come into the house and have tea with me. I imagine

you haven't had breakfast yet," the Circassian smiled back.

"I've brought my breakfast with me—and something to drink with it as well."

Later they sat at the table. Except for this there were only a doorless cupboard and two crude beds in the room, which served as office and living quarters for the nachalnik and his deptuy. The deputy, Vassily learned, had gone to see the director of the kolkhoz to discuss the work plan for the tractor station. "They don't have any seed, you see."

Vassily nodded. "We have seed and no tractor."

The nachalnik stood at the primus stove, waiting for the water to boil. From the cupboard he took a little packet of tea, a paper cone of sugar, half a loaf of bread, a bowl of puckered, gray-green pickles, and a tin can containing a chunk of raw bacon. He placed all this on the table and then poured the water, which had begun to boil, into a large metal teapot. He emptied half the packet of tea leaves into the water.

"A guest deserves strong tea," he said, placing the lid on the pot.

"Thank you." Vassily brought out his canteen and added a sausage wrapped in a clean cloth to the pathetic array of victuals. "If you don't mind, before we drink the tea let us celebrate our meeting with something stronger." He poured vodka from the canteen into the tin cups.

His host, however, seemed more interested in the canteen than its contents. He picked it up and studied it carefully before replacing it on the table. "Foreign make, very practical," he said. "We don't have that sort of thing yet, but the time will come, rest assured, brother. Well, then." He picked up his cup. "Health!" With one toss he gulped down the vodka and ate a morsel of bread. When Vassily started to refill his cup, he covered it with his hand. "Enough! Let's leave some for my assistant Volodia. He likes to drink too, and maybe he needs it more. You see, he's very poor."

"Poor?" It was the first time Vassily had ever heard this word applied by one Soviet worker to another. He suspended his slicing of the sausage and looked questioningly at the Circassian.

"Yes," the nachalnik said, "he's a good boy and a first-class worker. But women, you see; he's been married four times and has children by all the women. Seven head all together, and none of them more than six years old. He's still a child himself—well, you'll see him. They deduct from his wages for the seven children—contributions to their support. You can figure out for yourself what's left for him. But it's his own fault. A man doesn't always have to buy a cow when he wants a glass of milk, does he? Are you married? Have you children?"

"No, no wife and no children."

"That isn't right either. A man ought to have one wife and some children. I'm married. My children are both in Moscow. My son is a movie projectionist, already a member of the party, and my daughter is in the Komsomol, learning nursing. My wife—hm— she's in Tiflis. It's very good to be married when your wife is in Tiflis and you yourself are in the Ukraine, don't you think?"

"Yes," Vassily said, laughing, "it's quite bearable that way." He pushed the sausage, which he had cut into thick slices, across the table. He himself ate with good appetite. He had started his ride before dawn.

"Where do you get this?" the tractor man asked. "This is fine quality." He smelled the slice of sausage. "Hm, first-rate." His strong widely spaced teeth took a bite. "Bought on the free market?"

"No, comrade, we make this sausage on our farm."

"Really? Well, there you are. What I always say. All that's needed is the will, and you can do anything. For years they've groaned over these auxiliary farms and never gotten anything out of them. And now they're making sausage like this. Ah!" He took another hearty bite and chewed it with gusto. "Even old Nikolai never ate better. Or sat a horse better than you, brother. What is your name, anyhow?"

"Vassily."

"Vassia, good. My name is Grisha. As I was saying, the Russian people, Brother Vassia, the Russian people, once they take something into their head, nobody can stop them. What sausage!" He reached for a second slice. "But we'll leave some for Volodia. Let him see for himself. He's a griper, you know. Nothing suits him; everything is better elsewhere. But when he eats this sausage, he'll understand that it's only a matter of patience. Only patience, Vassia."

"That's right," Vassily agreed. "But won't Volodia be here soon? I'd like to ask you a favor—it's about our farm." And he explained directly what they wanted.

Just as the Chief of the tractor station was beginning to answer, a slight young man entered the room. His worn and patched clothing scarcely detracted from the grace of his appearance, and in spite of his rapid stride his movements had distinction.

"This is Volodia, my *zamestitel*," the Circassian said, introducing his assistant. "And this is my friend Vassia." The two men shook hands. "Here, Volodia, I've already had breakfast—take my chair." He sat down on one of the beds. "Vassia's brought along a sausage they make on their farm. But first have a drink."

Volodia's frown vanished. His tip-tilted nose sniffed—he looked like a rabbit being offered a fresh leaf of lettuce—and his blue eyes twinkled cheerfully. "Vodochka," he said tenderly, taking the full cup. "You have a grand friend, Grisha. Health, Vassily!" He drank the cup slowly, savoring each sip, and then reached for the bread and sausage. Suddenly he stopped eating and regarded the piece of sausage he still held in his hand. "This is the life," he said. "Vodka and sausage." He looked Vassily over from head to foot, his gaze lingering on the boots. "I suppose you're the head of the farm?" he asked. "And no doubt a party member, eh? I've been suspended for a year. Still five months to go."

"He didn't do anything wrong, Vassia," Grisha explained. "It was on account of all those women."

"I am not the head of the farm," Vassily said quietly. "I'm the starshi koniukh. And not a party member either."

Volodia made no attempt to hide his incredulity. "Not either, and you wear such boots, ply us with sausage and vodka—you bought everything at the bazaar, didn't you? Out of your hundred and eighty-seven rubles a month!"

"The vodka was bought at the bazaar, but long ago, before prices went up. The sausage is made on our farm. The farm distributes almost two thousand pounds a month to the workers, at government prices, of course. As for the boots, comrade, I bought them yesterday. In the promtorg shop, along with three pairs of socks, two shirts and this cap, all for eighty-seven rubles."

"A stablemaster! A likely story."

"There are stablemasters and stablemasters, Volodia," Grisha said. "You haven't heard everything yet."

"I've heard enough, Grisha, I've heard plenty," Volodia said spitefully. "I know what I know."

"Then keep it to yourself and don't insult honest men. If Vassia says it, it's true."

Volodia changed his tone. "When we have troubles, it all comes out." He looked at Vassily with a winning smile. "And we have many troubles, Vassily, if you only knew. . . ."

"Nothing ever goes as smoothly as we'd like," Vassily said deliberately.

"True enough. But we have enough with our own troubles and shouldn't take on the troubles of others." He addressed his superior. "Nikiforiuk doesn't know what to do. The courier has brought a letter from the agricultural sector. Seed won't be along for two weeks; once it comes, the kolkhoz must arrange about transporting it. And the plan must be sent in, everything has to be planted—the usual stuff. Meanwhile we can play balalaika on the tractors."

"That's rotten, for Nikiforiuk and for us too," Grisha said gravely. "Meanwhile others have everything ready, only no tractors to plow up their patch of ground."

"Who do you mean by others?"

"Well, the farm where Vassia works."

"How big a place can they possibly have?" Volodia said contemptuously.

"Still and all, eighty-three dessiatin," Vassily said. He took cigarettes from his pocket. When all three had lit up, he said, "I've told Grisha what we're up against. If only you could help us out."

"Ah," Grisha said, "nothing to it. Only, Vassia, you must realize that Lvov is not in our district. What is your farm called?"

"Jiusefovka."

"One moment, I'll get the map." The tractor men bent over a crude sketch map, trying to find the village. But they could not, for it was not marked.

"The village is about seven miles southeast of Lvov." Vassily took the map from Volodia's hand. "About here." He indicated a point with his fingernail. As the two studied the map again, Volodia remarked, "Your friend is the only koniukh in the whole Soviet Union who can read a map. Don't you understand, Grisha? Seven miles southeast of Lvov—southeast."

Grisha looked embarrassed and confused. But Vassily explained quietly, "I served under the Austrians for four and a half years, and became a noncom. You couldn't get a promotion in that army without reading maps. And once you've learned something, it sticks, doesn't it?"

Grisha was pleased. "You see, Volodia," he said, "why shouldn't there be a starshi koniukh who knows more than he has to know? And if he weren't a capable man, they wouldn't have sent him."

"How do I know they sent him?" Volodia carped.

"Just to shut up this griper," Grisha said, "let's see your komandirovka, Vassia—we have to have some kind of document if we're to sign a contract."

"Konechno," Vassily said, and produced his identity card, spravka, military pass and finally his travel permit. The two fell upon the documents. They read them thoroughly from beginning to end and compared the photos with the original.

"Well, all right," Volodia conceded. "Everything seems in order."

Grisha rebuked his zamestitel. "I told you Vassily is all right. We'll draw up the contract right away—eighty-three dessiatin." He went to the cupboard and brought out a form, which Volodia filled out and Grisha and Vassily signed.

"Better get started right away, Volodia," Grisha said, "and ask your way, or you'll end up plowing the streets of Lvov."

Out in the yard, Volodia busied himself with the tractor. He was all ready to go when he stopped in front of the gate. "Hey there, Vassia, give me a few cigarettes," he called. "I haven't a crumb of tobacco." He laughed gaily. Vassily handed him half of his supply, nine cigarettes. These were all the provisions Volodia took along on his journey.

"Let's stop by to see Nikiforiuk," Grisha said as Vassily led out the horse, already saddled. "It's just as well if he sees you—though you don't have to tell him where your farm is. He doesn't have to know it isn't in our district. A fool asks more questions than twenty wise men can answer. Have you anything left in your canteen? You know, it's easier to talk over a little vodka."

"There's still a third of it left. Why don't you take it?" Vassily handed Grisha the canteen. "It's yours. You like it, don't you?"

"You're giving it to me?" The Circassian took the canteen and once more examined it carefully. Then he slung it by its strap over his shoulder. "Thank you kindly, Vassia. I'm very glad. A canteen like this is always useful."

"Come, Golodnyi," Vassily said, taking the horse by the reins. He didn't want to have Grisha walking alongside while he rode.

"Why is he called Golodnyi?" the Circassian asked. "What an odd name."

Vassily told him about the deal with the veterinary hospital. The stallion had been one of the hospital horses. While the other horses had begun to eat almost as soon as they were rid of the tormenting parasites, this stallion had been slower to recover. For days they had had to feed him warm cereal by the spoonful, like a sick child. But when at last he was on his legs again, he had become insatiable; no matter how much feed they gave him, he ate everything and was still hungry. "And that is why we call him Hungry," Vassily concluded.

"Just like men, brother, just exactly," Grisha said. "If fellows have been hungry for a long time, they can't eat when at last food is offered them. But once their appetite comes back, they eat more than they can stand. Ah yes, hunger! What do you know about it? What do any of the people here know? If you'd seen them, puffed up, with swollen bellies, thousands and tens of thousands of them. The peasants didn't want to enter the kolkhozes. The party went about it wrong. The peasant, brother, the peasant is the most important man in the country. If he's satisfied and healthy, the state is healthy. The party has finally got around to realizing that. Stalin's taught them that. Everything rests on the peasant; he's the one has to be relied on. In war, too. He's a good soldier when he has something to defend, his own land, the soil that feeds him."

"War?" Vassily asked. "Who would we be fighting a war with?"

"You haven't been a Soviet citizen long, Vassia; you don't understand these matters. You work on your farm, keep your gear in order, and that's enough. You'll learn about the rest in time. They're all waging war against us; they've never stopped. We, brother, don't want war; it would do us no good. But it is coming, it must come, and then we'll see!"

The big wrought-iron gate was open and hung askew on its hinges. Through the bare trees a muddy lane, littered with rotting leaves, led to a rambling one-story building. Near the entrance lay all sorts of trash. Rotting boards, boxes without lids or bottoms, blocked the front steps. The glass panes of windows and doors were broken or opaque with dirt. "This isn't the entrance now," Grisha said. They walked around the building. There wasn't a soul in sight; no dogs barked. "There," Grisha said, "tie your horse to this post. We'll see whether Timofey Porfirovich is around."

They found the Director of the kolkhoz sitting on an unpainted kitchen chair in front of a gilded Louis Seize ladies' desk. He was chewing a fountain pen and obviously so absorbed in composing some document that he barely noticed his visitors and answered their greeting with an inaudible murmur. Grisha went up to him and took the pen from his hand. "Why wear yourself out with more letters?" he said. "Go to Stanislava; you have to put your case in person. If you don't pound on the desk, you'll get nowhere."

The Director of the Pobeda (Victory) Collective Farm pushed his cap farther back on his neck and looked up at the tractor man out of childlike brown eyes. "You're right, Gregory Mikhailovich, writing's no use. What can I ask for? Seed? Suppose I had it. Who would help with the planting? I've got nothing and nobody, not a soul. They've all scattered, run away. All of them, gone to the cities or across the border. They're frightened of the kolkhozes; they'd sooner work illegally or leave the country." Then, as if he had just caught sight of Vassily, he asked, "Who is this comrade?"

"This is my friend Vassia," Grisha said. "He works on a farm fairly near here. He's hired a tractor. Volodia has already left. That job will take only two or three days; they don't have much land."

The Director looked at Vassily, and then back at Grisha. "That means that somewhere else people are working, plowing and—that was what you wanted to say, wasn't it, Gregory Mikhailovich?"

"They work, and how they work! But wait, taste this sausage they make." He took the remainder of the sausage from his pocket and offered it to the Director. "But first have a drink." He made an elaborate procedure of unscrewing the canteen cap. "Here."

The nachalnik sniffed the canteen, raised it toward his guests, and put to his lips. When he set it down on the table, it rang rather empty. Then he bit into the sausage without taking the trouble to slice or peel it. His gloom had vanished. "Come with me, please," he said. "There are chairs in the club." He swallowed. "You must answer a few questions," he said to Vassily.

"Gladly," Vassily replied. From a pocket in his woolen jacket he took a huge nickel watch that Antek had given him. "But it's getting on eleven and I haven't much time."

Canteen in one hand, the end of the sausage in the other, the nachalnik proceeded them down a long corridor, past many doors. "Two people lived here in twenty-two rooms," he said. He kicked open one of the doors, revealing a large salon, its parquet floor gouged and grooved under a thick film of dirt and mud. On the walls, whose paper was torn and soiled, hung portraits of revolutionary heroes. Along the walls and scattered through the room were chairs in a wild variety of styles. There was a platform for speakers, with a table and three easy chairs. The nachalnik led his guests to it. "So," he said when they were seated, "now we can talk. So you work in an agricultural organization. What kind is it, what do you need a tractor for, and how come you make sausage? For whom?"

Vassily told him as much as he thought proper about the farm. The two men listened with the most eager interest. "Do you understand it, Gregory Mikhailovich?" the Director asked the tractor man.

"What's so mysterious about it?"

"I'll wait to hear what account Volodia brings back. Thank you, comrade," he said to Vassily.

Vassily stood up, glad that the man had not kept him too long. "Dosvidania." He extended his hand to Grisha.

"I'll go with you, Vassia." He reached for the canteen, but the Director was faster. He seized it and finished the rest of the vodka before he returned it.

Vassily examined the girths, reins and saddlebags. He glanced once more at the neglected, empty house and the huge, empty yard. Then he turned to Grisha, who was scratching the horse's forehead. "Good luck, Grisha!"

"Good luck, Vassia. Keep up the good work. We need people like you."

Vassily mounted and rode off. When he reached the path that led to the woods, he checked his horse and looked back at the house. Two people in twenty-two rooms, the nachalnik had said, with hatred, scorn and vindictiveness in his voice. What kind of expression would you have had, nachalnik, if you had known that I was once their guest; ate, drank and slept in those rooms, sat in that big salon hung with the portraits of their ancestors, danced with beautiful, cultivated, alluring women? Would you, Grisha, still have said, "We need people like you"?

"Comrade Khomniuk," Saposhnik said, "there's a party meeting today and I can't get away. But I've written a letter to Dr. Feuerberg. Will you take it to him? I've got a recommendation from the head of the Public Health Section; the doctor will surely come to see my wife. And will you put in your word, too? You have such a way with people."

"Gladly, Comrade Saposhnik—I'll drive over at once."

Half an hour later the wagon stopped in front of the sanatorium. The doorkeeper, a one-armed invalid, told Vassily that Dr. Feuerberg had left at four o'clock, but lived nearby. The second street to the right and the third house on the left side.

Vassily drove off again. He knocked on the door of the cottage —the electric bell was not functioning. It was some time before he heard the lock chain rattling. The door opened on a crack. Vassily had Saposhnik's letter in one hand, his whip in the other. The crack widened. A desperately gaunt man, slightly bowed, appeared; he looked around forty. "Good evening," Vassily said, smiling, "does Dr. Feuerberg live here?" He had tried to speak Polish, and had probably made mistakes, for the tall, lean man smiled. The smile wrought a transformation on his thin, grave face.

"I am he," he said.

"Then this letter is for you."

"I take it you are not a Pole," the doctor said, accepting the letter in a somewhat gingerly fashion. He stood irresolutely in the doorway. Then he came to a decision. "Come in, please." He spoke Russian.

This time Vassily smiled. "But you're also not a Russian," he said.

"You can tell at a word, can't you?" Both men laughed. The doctor switched on the light in the narrow vestibule, and Vassily put his whip in a corner and hung his cap on the clothes rack, above the mirror. A woman's blue coat hung on another hook. Meanwhile the doctor opened a door. "Please, go right in!"

"We might both get along better in German, Herr Doktor," Vassily said.

"There are no longer any *Herren,* Herr—what was your name?"

The doctor spoke perfectly correct German, but with a touch of the soft Polish accent.

"Vassily, without *Herr*. As you see, I'm a driver."

"I wish I were one, Vassily. A very sound occupation." The doctor was still holding the letter in his hand. Now he studied the address. "I can read the address, might even be able to write it. I've been practicing writing my name. But if you could tell me what the letter is about—in its general outlines—"

"I can—in its general outlines."

"That would be wonderful. Then I wouldn't have to wake my wife. She's just lain down, came home from work only an hour ago. My wife knows Russian."

Vassily told the doctor what he knew of the contents of the letter. "A visit from you would mean a great deal to the poor woman, Dr. Feuerburg," he concluded.

"Ah!" The doctor struck the edge of the envelope against his palm. His eyes narrowed to small slits; tiny wrinkles formed in their corners. A moment later he opened his eyes wide and the wrinkles disappeared. It was hard to tell which was truly Dr. Feuerberg's face—the wrinkled, frowning, troubled and contemptuous look, or the smooth, firm, attentively listening expression. "Oh well," he said, "I'll go with you, Vassily, although I shouldn't. No, I shouldn't. I am not honest; I am a liar and a cheat to go with you to examine this Comrade Saposhnik's wife, to pretend to be a doctor and to act as if there were any sense to my coming. But I must, you understand; I must lie and cheat because they insist I do it. I can see the woman; I've already examined her; I know her case and I know she cannot be saved, because I've seen and examined hundreds of such cases in these past months, although that really isn't my field. I'm a surgeon, you know. When the lung specialists decide that surgery might possibly help, that there's a glimmer of hope, then I cut, and sometimes it works. Which doesn't mean, even if the operation is successful, that the patient is really any better off. It's very complicated, you know."

"Not so very, doctor."

"We have two hundred and twelve beds in the hospital and, at the moment, three hundred and eighteen patients. That's all wrong. And the majority of them are in the last stages. Because these people, you see, they don't come as long as they can still crawl, as long as they can get about at all. Rightfully speaking, tuberculosis is a disease for rich people. They can go to Switzerland. For mountain air. People die there too, but still—"

"But mostly the poor have it."

"Everybody has it in him—possibly—no, certainly—you and I.

But there's no sense brooding about it. Can you read Russian?"

"I can manage."

"Then would you kindly read and translate the letter for me? I must know what's in it, after all. Your director is a party member, I take it?"

Vassily nodded.

"Then he probably has a recommendation from some superior—?"

"Yes," Vassily said.

The doctor carefully opened the envelope. "You see, I know everything. It's always the same. They think they have to put pressure on you. As though a doctor wouldn't be glad if he could help. But please read it, you strange driver."

Vassily read the letter and translated it literally. At the mention of the recommendation from the doctor's highest superior, he smiled. "You see, it's all there. I could have spared myself that whole lecture. Why in the world did I tell you all that? But sometimes we have to get things off our chest, and you struck me as—oh, well." He stood up and began pacing the room, at the same time flexing his long, strong fingers. "I know what we'll do. First we'll drive over to the hospital. Perhaps I can free a bed—a patient died today, a seventeen-year-old girl."

"You want to take in Saposhnik's wife?"

"That's really the only thing I can do for her. Make her dying easier for her and her family. Let's drive over there."

It was half an hour before Dr. Feuerberg came out again, waving a slip of paper. He took his seat in the wagon. "It was a battle," he said. *"Ochered*—wait your turn—you know how it goes. But I suspect that head nurse of cheating. She's found herself a source of income—horrible thought, isn't it?" As they stopped in front of the doctor's house, he paused for a moment in front of the wagon. "A very spiffy farm wagon," he said. "Practically a carriage. How smoothly it rides, and everything so clean and well-kept. You're an excellent coachman, Vassily. Perhaps we ought to take my wife along. A little fresh air would do her good, don't you think, Vassily?"

As they entered, they were met by singing. The doctor rubbed his hands contentedly. "My wife," he said. "She's slept well and it's done her good; she's in good spirits when she sings." He hurried, still in his overcoat, down the long, narrow hallway, knocked gently on a door, and waited with visible eagerness to be asked to enter. But he was not; only the singing stopped abruptly. "Jeanne," the doctor said, speaking French, "we have an opportunity to take a lovely ride. In a nice carriage with fine horses and a unique coachman. Yes, really unique." The two men returned to the room in which they had sat before. Both waited in silence. Then Jeanne entered.

Dr. Feuerberg was standing by a table, and Vassily in a corner, screened by the open door. He could not be seen by the woman, but saw her plainly, though only from behind. He saw the slender legs in carefully mended silk stockings, the graceful feet with the high insteps in old but very carefully polished shoes. He saw a green skirt, barely reaching below the bend of the knee, a skirt that had been cleaned and ironed very often, and through it he saw the lines of slender hips. He saw a lithe, straight back and soft round shoulders through the thick cloth of a light-brown homespun jacket. And he saw a finely shaped head, hair close-cropped in the Russian fashion, supported on a neck like the bending stem of a precious flower. He heard a silvery, singing voice, and he knew that it was she, the woman he had been sent to find: Janina.

"Jeanne," the doctor said, "I'm going to see a patient. It would be nice if you were to ride along. Vassily here"—he gestured, and Vassily rose—"will drive us."

The woman turned slowly. "Ah!" Vassily took a step forward and bowed. "Vy Russki?"

"*Nyet,*" Vassily said, looking squarely at her. It was Janina, though she had little left of the radiant madonnalike look of the portrait in the locket Anatol had worn around his neck. Nor could he detect any of those traits that had been described to him time and again in Radu's romantic effusions.

She must have been used to the fact that men looked at her longer and more keenly than at other women. And she looked at him in the same way. Probing, without embarrassment. And she saw that his chivalrous bow no more suited his dress than his mustache and horny hands suited the shape of his head or his gray-blue, intelligent eyes. "I am very pleased to meet you, Vassily," she said in Russian.

He responded, breathing the hint of a kiss upon her hand. "It is a great honor to me."

Dr. Feuerberg had lifted his fine, patrician head from his instruments, and his warm brown eyes lingered upon the two of them, upon their courtly greeting, their movements—all so measured and so natural—and he said, "*Mais oui. . . .*" That was all.

"You will need your bag," Jeanne said. "I'll bring it."

"Thank you, *chérie.*" As soon as she was out of the room, he said to Vassily, "I hope you don't also understand French, Coachman Vassily?"

"I'm sorry to disappoint you, doctor—I do."

"I thought so."

"I've been knocking around Europe all my life. Here and there. In my occupation you meet all sorts of people."

"And what is that occupation, Vassily?"

"Horses, doctor, always horses. Nothing but horses."

"Coachman—always a coachman? People haven't been using coachmen for a long time, you know."

"No, doctor—always a rider. Thoroughbreds. I've been a jockey, trainer and stableman for more than twenty years, in different countries. That's why—"

"Aha—oh, well. No offense meant, Vassily."

"None taken, doctor."

Jeanne returned with the doctor's bag. While he checked his instruments, the doctor said, "Our Vassily—he also understands French, by the way—has been a great man with horses. All over Europe, he's always been with horses—isn't that odd, Jeanne?"

"It's a bit hard to realize. But we—weren't we all over Europe too? And now we're here. Fate, my love. But why waste words on it any more?" She turned directly to Vassily. "About how long will the expedition take?"

"You should be back in two hours. Unless the examination is a lengthy affair."

"Still, two hours. . . . You should have something to eat before we go, Léon."

"Something to eat? What about you, chérie? And friend Vassily?"

"Of course," Jeanne said. "I'll fix a snack for us."

Vassily cleared his throat with some embarrassment. "This is the time to mention another part of my mission. I have something I was supposed to give you." He went out to the wagon and returned with a package. "We raise all this on our farm." He handed the package to the doctor.

Feuerberg shook his head. "Aha—so that's it. To put it bluntly, you're bribing me."

"Bribing? No, certainly not. This is a completely official gift, put down in the books, if that makes you feel easier. Comrade Saposhnik gave the farm a written order; he is paying for the things and has taken the responsibility. He regards it as—uhm—as part of the fee. All on the up-and-up, doctor."

"He takes the responsibility. Well, well, then everything is all right." The doctor shrugged and laid the package on the table. Jeanne took it and carried it off to the kitchen.

In a short while she was heard singing, "*À table, mes amis, à table, à table.*"

"That tune, for a change, is not of her own composition," the doctor remarked.

"Meyerbeer," Vassily said thoughtlessly.

"Yes. *The Huguenots*. The things people learn from horses!"

"Why not? After all, you know a few things outside of medicine!"

They sat in a room containing nothing but a table, four odd chairs, and a huge, three-door wardrobe. They had herring salad and ham and eggs, conjured up from the "honorable nachalnik's fee." There was a pat of butter and a plate of cheese. The tea was brewed in a chipped stoneware pot.

"Why, this is princely," the doctor said. "Real ham and real eggs. And butter, if I can believe my eyes."

"Yes, such things exist, as you see," Jeanne said.

"And the patients—no butter or milk for them, while we are reveling here."

"Eat and don't be gloomy," Jeanne said, placing a slice of buttered bread on his plate. "You at least must stay alive, or the patients won't even have a doctor. Incidentally, there was a slip of paper along with these priceless gifts."

"Yes," Vassily said with embarrassment. "Receipt has to be acknowledged. For the bookkeeping."

"Isn't that . . . ?" Jeanne frowned.

"Not a bit risky," Vassily said. "Since the order comes from our own superior. His name is on the slip."

"Right," Jeanne said, and went on eating with good appetite, the while pressing food on the doctor. There was no sugar with the tea, but some confectionery smelling vaguely of kerosene.

"Let's leave the dishes," Jeanne said. "I can wash up when we return."

"I'll help you," the doctor said.

It was already going on eleven when Vassily turned into the road that led to Jiusefovka. The sturdy chestnuts leaned into the harness and set a fast pace. They wanted to reach their mangers, and their driver did not try to slow them down, for he himself was tired, utterly exhausted. Hard as he tried to order his thoughts, he could not keep them from flying in all directions. It had been a hard day. He had been up since four o'clock in the morning; after the long ride and the hasty work in the stables he had had to drive to town again. And now it was eleven, with chores still awaiting him when he reached home. If only one of the other drivers were up to help him. There were the lights of Jiusefovka. The sausage plant was still operating, and a light was still on in the house opposite it, where Vassily lived. Undoubtedly Antek was waiting up for him. From the canteen came the sound of singing. The office was also illuminated. Mira was working there. Still working, Vassily thought. The horses halted in front of the stable. He jumped stiff-leggedly down from the box and stretched his tired body. He had just started unharnessing when Metro, one of the drivers, entered the stable, an old hunting rifle over his shoulder. He stood the gun against the wall, took off his *serdak*—a peasant coat of crude, handwoven wool—and began on some of the chores that normally would have been Vassily's. "Thanks, Metro. I'm worn out. A tough day."

"What day isn't?" The young peasant hung up the harness and rubbed the horses dry.

Out of habit Vassily ran his eyes along the stalls. "Where are the two grays?" he asked.

"Ivan drove into town with the Director," Metro said.

"No teams are to go out in the evening. One pair ruined is enough." He went over to the two roans. They lay with their legs plastered to the knees with a thick layer of mud which had been made by kneeding earth and vinegar. "I'm afraid they'll never be any good again. A pity. Good night, Metro. Thanks for helping."

"Nothing to thank me for—I'm glad to do it. Good night, Vassily."

Mira was waiting out in the street. "I heard your voice," she said.

"Yes, Mira." He continued walking. She took his hand and pressed close to him. They walked on slowly, hand in hand. "I'm as tired as a beggar's dog," he said.

"Poor Vassily. It's terrible how you wear yourself out."

"But I'm going to sleep now. Like a stone. I'll take an extra hour, too. If I get to town by nine, it will be time enough." They had reached the house where Mira lived. "Good night, Mira." He touched his cheek against hers. "I don't know how I'm going to get home," he said, laughing, "I'm that tired."

"And I wanted to ask you to come with me. I have something to talk over with you. Really important."

He heard the anxiety in her voice. "What's wrong, Mira?"

"Mermelstein," she said. "He's been immobilized—you understand—since that incident with Rudnicki. He's in the vilest possible mood and is going around raging and complaining, making trouble everywhere. And besides all that, he has it in for Freddy. They're carrying manure for the cold frames. Tadek and Freddy. And Antek—" She was beginning to digress, contrary to her habit, as if she were reluctant to get to the heart of the matter.

"What does he want of Freddy?" Vassily asked.

"He—" Mira hesitated. "He threatened Freddy and cursed him. Such language—O God—Freddy scarcely understood half of what he was saying. But what he did understand is horrible. Mermelstein said he'd show us all up, expose the lot of us, the redheaded whore first of all—by that he meant me, Vassily."

"Don't pay attention to it, Mira." Vassily tried to calm her.

"You can't just ignore him, Vassily. It isn't just his filthy mouth. It's too dangerous to give way to him. I've found out that he owes money to Kornhaber and Meerblum. Owes isn't the word for it—he's been blackmailing them. Thousand of rubles, Vassily."

"We'll have to think the thing through, Mira. But I'm simply not capable of thinking now. My head is heavy and altogether empty, I'm so tired. Tomorrow—all right?" He pressed her hand.

"I'll walk you part way, Vassily. I wanted to look in on the sausage plant anyhow," she added quickly. They walked in silence as far as Vassily's house. "Sleep well and—" She did not finish the sentence, but rapidly crossed the street.

Vassily went in. Antek was in the kitchen, sitting at the table and reading. "So here you are at last. How can you stand it, Vassily?"

"I can't stand it." Vassily smiled sadly. "I'm dead with weariness." He sat down on a chair and began pulling off his boots. Antek clapped the book shut, stooped, and helped him. He also pulled off his trousers, and Vassily let him help. Then he stood in his shirt and underwear, indifferent to the clothes scattered around him. He turned to the door. "Good night, Antek," he mumbled.

"Vassily, you've forgotten to wash!"

"Too tired. Tomorrow." He was already at the door of his room. He fell into bed and was instantly asleep.

He awoke at his accustomed hour. Admonishingly, tyrannically, the sense of duty penetrated the depths of his sleep. Today the tractor work was to begin. If he was not there to get things started, the prearranged order might be upset and total confusion follow. Vassily went into the kitchen, still dazed and drunk with sleep. Antek and Tadek were already at breakfast. Vassily drank a cup of hot, almost black tea; only then did he wash and shave and dress. Clean clothes had been laid out for him; his boots shone as if for a parade.

"Thanks, Tadek," Vassily said.

"Not Tadek, Antek," the giant said in his high-pitched voice. Vassily raised two fingers to his forehead, saluting Antek.

"Have a decent breakfast," Antek said, pushing the platter of fried bacon toward him. He poured another cup of tea for Vassily, this time adding milk. They ate silently and heavily. Antek was finished first and lit a cigarette. Vassily soon followed his example. Then Tadek stood up, cleared the table and washed the dishes in almost scalding water. The other two helped him dry. They worked with practiced speed, and in a few minutes they were outside on the foggy street. Tadek peered through the morning mist. Suddenly he thrust his fingers into his mouth and gave a piercing whistle. Vassily looked inquiringly at Antek.

"The eye of love; he must have spotted Freddy." Antek peered. "Yes, there he is." Tadek said, *"Do widzenia"*—Polish for good-bye —and trotted ahead. Freddy, spade over his shoulder, had stopped and was waiting for Tadek. They greeted each other warmly and turned off on a shortcut to the gardens.

"They're certainly great pals," Vassily said.

"Tadek is all worked up over Mermelstein. He says that if the bastard doesn't ease up on Freddy, he's going to finish him off. He's figured out the perfect crime. Hit him over the head with the pickax and drop him into the pit that's been dug for the hotbeds. There'll be a lot of manure on top anyhow, and then earth on top of the manure—not a soul will think of looking for him there. We'll all be better off without Mermelstein."

"Just talk," Vassily said.

Antek smiled. Vassily knew that smile only too well.

"I'd been wondering whether I ought to tell you all this, Vassily. On the whole, it's better if you know. So you can be more careful." He cleared his throat; he obviously found this a hard subject to discuss. "I have it from the woman Rudnicki lived with. The old slut knows you broke her sweetheart's arm. And they say it's your doing that he's gone to jail. Probably she's got that story from Mermelstein. Now the whole gang is mobilized."

"Gang? What kind of gang?"

"Don't play dumb, Vassily. Rudnicki was a pimp all his life, nothing else."

"I see, Antek. Is it still going on?"

"Everything is still going on. Where do you think they've gone to, the whores and pimps and thieves and burglars? There are more of them than ever, and they're not afraid of anything. And they're eating, too, eating damned well without working. Seems they haven't learned that those who don't work are not supposed to eat."

"That's their business, Antek," Vassily said. "If they want to risk it. But why are you telling me this?"

"There's something else, Vassily. While Mermelstein would be having his fun with one girl, Rudnicki would use the farm team to bring customers to other girls."

"Impossible! How did he dare?"

Antek tapped his forehead. "Are you really so naïve? What could possibly be safer than one of our teams and wagons? What militiaman would stop it? They'd take it for granted that a big-shot nachalnik was riding. And Rudnicki had his regular customers who trusted him. He'd been taking care of them for years. Men with money. And *that* is just as important as eating, more so for some people. He was doing better business than ever before."

"And you knew so much about it, Antek?" Vasily asked, a certain bitterness in his voice.

"Are you crazy?" Antek snapped. "I only heard about it yesterday afternoon. They're laying for you, Vassily, and if they catch you—"

"Then the same thing will happen to them that happened to Rudnicki," Vassily said. "I can take care of quite a few. The bigger question is what part Mermelstein is playing."

"I don't know. For the present he's the nachalnik who's doing some business on the side and leaving his profits with the women. Besides paying for the liquor and bringing good food with him. Without Rudnicki—without the team and wagon, I mean—he can hardly do anything. I know for certain that he also used the wagon for transporting stolen goods. If I'm not mistaken, they'll use Mermelstein as bait and he'll lead you into their hands, maybe without being in on the plot himself. And then—"

"And then?"

"Vassily," Antek said angrily, "once you're up against this crew, boxing or jujitsu won't help; they use knives or a rod. They'll murder you, Vassily!" He almost screamed the words into Vassily's face.

"Then," Vassily said quietly, "I'll be murdered." He smiled. "Who cares?"

"Who cares? Who? Maybe you don't. But I do, Vassily. I don't want you murdered, not you."

"All right, all right, Antek, take it easy. I'll be careful. But you warn Tadek: no violence, and not a word. Only have him remember exactly what Mermelstein says, the exact words of abuse he uses, and not answer, not answer at all. Freddy too. Tell them to go on working quietly and let Mermelstein shoot his mouth off all he pleases. We'll get rid of him without his realizing what is happening. We have to outsmart these people, Antek. As for you, just keep your ears open. How come you're so thick with Rudnicki's woman, anyway?"

"You'd hardly understand that, Vassily," Antek murmured. "As far as she's concerned, I belong to the gang; she knew my father and she knows me from those days. They have it in their blood—I mean, they don't know anything different. They think that once you're in that game, you're in for good. And"—he spoke very slowly and hesitantly—"if it hadn't been that you were involved, Vassily—"

"So that's how it is. I'm grateful to you."

"Never mind the gratitude. You know—" He didn't finish the sentence. Volodia, singing loudly, came charging into the stable-yard. He leaped over the shafts of a wagon that stood in his way and ran with arms outspread into Vassily, almost pulling him down in his exuberance.

"Greetings, Starshi Koniukh." He pounded Vassily on the shoulders. "You're a wonder and the farm is a paradise. To think an outfit like this exists! Who is this comrade—the Director?"

"No, Volodia, this is the Starshi Ogrodnik."

"Fine." He extended his hand to Antek. "I'd like to see the gardens during the noon break, all right?"

Antek had not understood, but he said "Da" and smiled. His usual smile. Then he said, *"Robota—work,"* touched his cap and left.

"Robota, right. It's time for me to get started. Where are the men who are going with me? Is everything laid out? Where's the Director? Will he be supervising the plowing?"

"Everything is laid out; the Director is busy in his office. Just get your tractor ready."

"It's all ready, Vassia. I wish I were stationed right here. I wouldn't get sick of things."

"I'm glad you have such a good impression of our farm. One moment, I'll see where Ivan is. He knows all about the fields." Vassily went into the stable. The white horses that Ivan drove and which were supposed to be used for bringing up the seed today lay on their bedding. Ivan had not been there yet; the horses were not curried and the stalls were filthy. Vassily felt anger mounting within him; he ran out of the stable, past Volodia, across the big yard and into the cow barn. The milkmaids were already at work. Kornhaber came down the aisle toward Vassily. "Good morning, Kornhaber," Vassily said. "Where is Paraska?"

"Here she comes." The little man with timid eyes pointed to a woman of about thirty who was approaching them, carrying a full milk pail.

"Where's Ivan?" Vassily asked her curtly.

The woman hardly paused. "Asleep," she said, and made as if to pass Vassily.

"Look, Paraska, won't you go and wake him?" Vassily said.

"Ivan's the only one who knows what was decided about the plowing. He has to be out there. That's how it is with field work."

"Field work, Vassily? You want Ivan for field work? In that case, he shouldn't be kept up all night long, driving that stinker to town, waiting around for him till four o'clock in the morning. Now His Honor the Director is snoring. He'll sleep half the day, then get up and come sniffling around after the women to see whether he can't feel one of them up. Let him try it with me, the swine; he'll get a milk pail in his face."

"Did I make him director, Paraska? If the work doesn't get done, who'll be in trouble? All of us, Paraska, all of us. So please wake Ivan, and meanwhile I'll get everything ready, hitch up, load up; he'll only have to drive. Go on, Paraska!" He took the pail from her hand. "As a favor to me."

"Only because it's you that's asking, Vassily." She started to say something else, but Vassily had already rushed off toward the stable.

Volodia was sitting on an overturned pail in front of the stable, whistling under his breath. "We'll be all set in a few minutes; two of my men are missing," Vassily called out. He plunged into the work, curried and cleaned up the two mares he usually drove. He threw the work harness over them, led them to the pump, let him drink, and hitched them to the heavy wagon. "The man will be along soon, Volodia. I'm going to get the seed." He drove over to the storehouse and carried bag after bag—each one a hundred pounds—to the wagon, meanwhile conducting a jagged conversation with Wagner. He drove back to the stable. Ivan was already there, although somewhat groggy with sleepiness. "I've heard what happened, Ivan," he said, forestalling explanations. "We'll discuss it later. I appreciate your coming. Stay on the job till noon. Then you can tell Metro what we want done and catch up on sleep."

"It's all right, Vassily," Ivan growled. "Since I'm up, I'll work straight through. I see you've hitched up your horses?"

"Yes, yours were worn out. I'll use them later when I have to take the light wagon into town. That will give them a chance to rest for a while."

"They've worked, the poor devils—more than twenty hours. What kind of lousy deal is that, Vassily?"

"It's going to change, you can depend on that. . . . Volodia!" he shouted. "Come, we're ready. Take the two boys from the smithy along, Ivan—they know they're to help."

Vassily returned to the stable, cleaned the stalls, renewed the mud packs on the legs of the two horses that Rudnicki had treated so mercilessly, watered them and the two grays, rubbed them down, washed his hands at the pump, lit a cigarette and looked at his watch. Seven-thirty. The day had barely begun and weariness was already seeping into his bones. Lucky everything was going well. He even had half an hour to spare, and so he sauntered over to the gardens to watch Antek and his two helpers for a while. He helped Freddy shovel manure from a cart and asked him in a low voice, "Where is your brother Gus now, Freddy?"

"Why, in New York for sure—where else would he be?" Freddy saw nothing strange in Vassily's interest in an unknown brother. Mira had warned him to keep absolutely silent about the past, but that didn't apply to Vassily; he and Mira were good friends, after all.

"Do you know his address, Freddy?"

"Not of his place on Long Island—can't keep that in my head. But you can always reach him at the First Diamond Club in New York."

"Fredziu," Tadek called out from some distance away, "robota."

"Konechno," Freddy said, and jumped down into the pit. Vassily went straight to the farm office. Only Mira was there, poring over her books as usual. "Good morning, Vassily," she said, looking up at him. "We're getting a late start today."

"I don't have to be in town until nine. I'll be taking Saposhnik's wife to the sanatorium. Won't matter if I'm a half hour late or so. Are you ready?"

"In a few minutes. Sit down while I finish."

"There is something else I wanted to tell you. Since today is payday. Don't pay Mermelstein a kopeck; keep his week's salary as an installment on his debts. What's more, make him write out a slip for yesterday's drive. Seven hours, two horses, night rate, and overtime for the driver, also night work. Figure it out to the ruble and kopeck. That's one thing. Talk with Wagner, Meerblum and Kornhaber and make them promise that they won't give Mermelstein any money. Warn them that they'll be in hot water along with him if they do. If Mermelstein gets tough—here in the office, I mean —if he so much as speaks one loud word, telephone Saposhnik. Tell him whatever you like, but give Mermelstein the impression that you're lodging a complaint—remember, he can hardly understand a word of Russian. The milkmaids are to report every attempt of Mermelstein's to molest them. We're going to scare the living daylights out of him."

"We have to try to, at any rate—things can't go on like this. Saposhnik is only waiting for the right moment, but I have the impression that he's afraid of Mermelstein, too. And if we do get rid of him"—she sighed—"what will we do with a director who really knows his business? But we have time to talk it over; I'll be ready in ten minutes."

"I'll hitch up meanwhile."

As soon as they had driven out of sight of the village, Mira climbed up on the box beside Vassily and pressed close against him. "Vassily," she said, "we must get away from here."

Vassily looked straight ahead. The horses were trotting along at a lazy pace. Only their hoofbeats made any sound; the wagon rolled almost noiselessly along on its rubber tires. "Well, Mira," he said, "where do you want to go?"

"We must get across the border. Romania would be best."

"Romania? Have you relatives or friends there?"

Mira smiled. "I haven't told you everything, Vassily. You don't know who we are, or were. And it doesn't matter. But once we're there, we'll be all right. Have you ever been in Romania? Do you know the country at all?"

"Pretty well. I've worked there."

"Do you know Ilie Rozescu?"

"Of course! I mean, I know he's a very rich man; everybody in Romania knows that."

"Will it do if I tell you that I have unlimited credit with Rozescu? He'd let me have any sum I ask for. I have a brother-in-law in London and his nephew is in Romania, in the oil fields. Danny Linton is Steve Rozescu's friend. I used to see Steve often in London at—oh, Vassily, if only we were in Romania right now!"

"Steve is not a Romanian name," Vassily said.

"It's what Danny calls him; they went to school together in England. His name is Stefan. Dr. Stefan Rozescu. A great scholar, Danny says. And Danny must be in Romania now, and we're practically related. If only we could get there, Vassily! Do you think there's any chance?"

Vassily twirled his mustache and smiled. "Why shouldn't there be a chance? We only have to be on the lookout for one, Mira."

"And will you be on the lookout, Vassily?"

"I promise you I will, but—"

"You'll do it, Vassily," she said joyfully. "You—yes, you will!"

He looked at her profile. As she sat there, her face radiant with hope, she was very beautiful. He shifted the reins to his right hand, put his left arm around her shoulders, and then he stooped and kissed her on the mouth. In a moment he released her, tightened the reins and cracked the whip. The horses pricked up their ears and went into a rapid trot.

* * *

Saposhnik opened the door for Vassily. "We are ready," he said. His wife, already bundled up in her coat, sat in the big upholstered chair. Her mother was on her knees in front of the sick woman, tying her shoelaces. Without fully straightening up, she brushed past her son-in-law, eyes cast down. She did not want to see him. Since yesterday she hated him more than ever. Now she would not even be able to take care of her Rifka, for Saposhnik was sending her off to the hospital. No doubt he had fixed it up with the doctor. Hospitals and doctors were anathema to old Ruchele. Still this doctor was different. He was a Jew; he had spoken to her in Yiddish and tried to comfort her. Ruchele Boim had a keen ear; she could tell true from false, and this doctor was true, a real doctor, a fine man. Had he not said to her, "God will help"?

God, the physician of the sick poor, the support of the fallen, as it said in the *Shmone Essrey,* the Eighteen Prayers. *"Reboinu shel Oilom,* Lord of the World, help my Rifka. Help, Adonai Melakh, God is King." Her heart wept, but her eyes were tearless and her face stony as she shuffled out of the room. But at the threshold her daughter's weak voice called her back. *"Kum aherzu, Mome."*

"Jo." The old woman went up to her daughter.

"Mother," Riva said, "I want you to shake hands with Mark."

"Rifkele!" the old woman groaned.

"Mark." Riva spoke Russian. "Shake hands with Mother, I want you to."

"Nu ot, Schwigger." Saposhnik held out his hand.

Vassily wished he could leave the room. He should at least look away, but he could not. He was too fascinated by the sight of this wrinkled old Jewish woman engaged in a struggle between love and hate. For an entire minute she was torn between these conflicting impulses, and when at last she laid her hand in that of her hated son-in-law, it was only a temporary compromise, an untruth, a sin that she was committing for the sake of her daughter who had not long to live. She overcame her true feelings and pretended to make the peace which her dying daughter had longed for throughout all those years of dissension and hate. *"S'is schoin gut,* Rifkele." She pressed her daughter's head to her breast, her eyes fixed on the ceiling and seeing through it to the Rabenu shel Olam in the sky who must read the prayer in her eyes.

Vassily went up to the chair. "Come, comrade, I'll carry you," he said. And before she could object, he had picked her up. He was startled at how light the poor thing was. Carefully, he carried her out and made her comfortable in the wagon.

"Thank you, comrade," she said, as he draped the blanket about her legs. Saposhnik sat down beside her. Vassily sprang up on the box.

They had a long wait at the hospital before Riva was accepted. Although Dr. Feuerberg had made all the arrangements, the woman in charge of reception invented difficulties. Dr. Feuerberg was operating at the moment, and she refused to acknowledge the admission papers which she herself had made out. Dr. Feuerberg had taken the patient out of turn on his own responsibility, she said, but he was only the Director's deputy. The woman spoke Russian fluently; she was a refugee from German-occupied Poland, rather plump, with thin, straw-blond hair and a greedy and domineering look. From her tone it was evident that she was counting on her superior's support. But he was not in the hospital. Saposhnik was feeling thoroughly defeated and was resigned to taking his wife back home when Vassily, who was waiting in the corridor, caught sight of Dr. Feuerberg and told him what was happening. Dr. Feuerberg went straight to the admissions office. "Room sixteen, bed five; everything is ready. Bring the patient in," he said, speaking Polish and permitting no demur. Vassily carried Riva in. The woman made the necessary entries reluctantly, deliberately taking her time about it. Saposhnik did not say a word; he gave no sign that the receptionist's resistance troubled or angered him. But when Riva had been taken away on the wheeled stretcher, Saposhnik turned to the woman. "You are a bad worker, citizeness," he said. That was all.

Dr. Feuerberg saw them to the front gate. "We'll take X-rays tomorrow if—"

"I understand. If you have current. It isn't our fault. Too few technicians. But it will be better soon; we've applied for specialists. Good-bye, and thank you, doctor." Saposhnik got into the wagon.

Dr. Feuerberg took leave of Vassily. "Come tomorrow evening if you can," he whispered in French, as they shook hands.

"Dosvidania," Vassily said loudly, jumping up to the box.

They had driven barely a hundred yards when a woman who was also leaving the hospital waved to Vassily. For a moment he did not recognize her. She had pulled her beret down almost to her eyebrows and was wearing big, ill-shaped dark glasses. Her high black shoes and heavy black stockings made her gait awkward. Only the graceful motion of her arm recalled the Jeanne he had seen. He stopped and asked Saposhnik whether it would be all right to give Dr. Feuerberg's wife a ride. Saposhnik nodded, and Vassily called out, "Come along, comrade."

"Thank you, comrades," Jeanne said, agilely climbing into the wagon.

"Are you on your way to work?" Saposhnik asked when she was seated. It was already after ten o'clock.

"I am."

"Where do you work, comrade?"

"In the Conservatory. I give piano lessons."

"Aha—that's why you go so late. Fine work, cultural work," Saposhnik said.

"So it is," Jeanne replied. She took a score from her worn briefcase and began studying it.

Saposhnik had Vassily stop at the Party Committee office. "Go ahead and take Comrade Feuerberg to the Conservatory, Khomniuk," he said as Jeanne prepared to get out.

"Thank you very much, comrade."

They drove off. "When must you be at work, and where is the Conservatory?" Vassily turned to her.

"I still have an hour to spare, and the Conservatory is just a few blocks away. Why do you ask?"

"There's something I must discuss with you." He drove as quickly as possible out of the busy streets and drew up at a gate in a quiet lane. "Please get out and wait for me here," he said. "I'll be back in five minutes."

Jeanne got out. Vassily drove off. He returned on foot through the gate at which she was waiting. "So—now we can talk. But—if you don't mind, please take off those glasses."

She did so. "I don't need them. They're only part of my armament." She walked at his side along the quiet lane.

"I understand. But I must be able to see your eyes—to know whether I may go on with what I have to say."

"What can it be?" she asked wearily. "Certainly nothing good. I'm accustomed to the bad and innured to it."

"You'll judge for yourself whether my message means anything good to you. Certainly not anything bad. I wish you would trust me. Can you?"

"*J'ai confiance en vous,*" she said.

"*Et moi aussi en vous,*" he said gravely. "Do you know Radu Candomir?"

Her step faltered. "I know him," she said at last. "He is a dear memory, one of my dearest. A fine man, and a good one, but it is many years since I have seen him or heard from him."

"Radu Candomir has commissioned me to search for you and to help you."

"How does he know I am here?"

"Your husband is with him and informed him that you were last in Czeravna. He also gave us the name of Dr. Feuerberg as someone who would know your whereabouts. Neither you nor Dr. Feuerberg were in Czeravna; I found you here by chance."

"My husband, did you say? My husband can't be here and simultaneously asking favors of Radu Candomir in Romania. I don't understand."

"This is hopeless, Jeanne," Vassily said reproachfully. "You have no faith in me. Dr. Feuerberg is not your husband. I know."

"Dr. Feuerberg *is* my husband, Vassily. We've been married twice, in fact. Once in a Catholic and once in a Soviet ceremony." She smiled. "Two links are better than one."

"Then would you mind telling me what your relationship to Prince Guninski is?"

"Oh," Jeanne said, not especially disturbed. "If you want to know the truth, he is my worst error, the most stupid mistake I ever made. I was married to him. For three months, two of them the most frightful in my life—and when I say that, I should add that I haven't had an easy life in general, Vassily."

"So I've gathered, Janina," Vassily said.

She threw him a radiant smile. "You call me Janina—that's my right name. Radu used to call me that, but hardly anyone has since."

"Anatol used to call you Rêve."

"You know a great deal, Vassily."

"That was the password I was to use, so that you would know that I had really come from Anatol."

"If anything in the world would put me on my guard, it would be something connected with that man. Keep that in mind, Vassily. What do you know about Anatol?"

"He served in the Austrian cavalry and cut the finest figure among the young officers."

"Cut a fine figure—that was it. But what was behind that figure! Were you an officer too, Vassily—perhaps one of his friends?"

"No, I was with Baron Candomir; I worked for him. For many years. We knew each other very well. I took on the job of finding you for his sake. Entirely for him."

"Yes, people would do things for him. Radu is a—a noble man, and a good friend."

"But you didn't want to do anything for his sake, Janina," Vassily said, smiling.

"Because I didn't want to marry him? How could I? I didn't love him. How unhappy he would have been if one fine day he'd found out that I had married him only in order to have a comfortable berth. God, how poor I was at the time! And then"—she paused

—"I'd already met Léon, my husband, only I wasn't yet aware that I loved him. I wasn't quite certain. Do you understand that, Vassily?"

"I understand. Only I can't see how it happened—forgive me, Jeanne—that you married Anatol in the interval. That could only have been—"

"We were divorced about a year ago, in Cracow. Oh, I was fascinated by him, spellbound. Didn't you say yourself that he cut a fine figure? Why shouldn't a woman fall for him? Especially when he was bent on making a conquest. My best years were past, and Léon was not in Paris. I was so lonely, so far from him, and my father had just died. It was like a dream—*un rêve,*" she repeated. "But the awakening was frightful. That's a long story, and I must be at my class on time. Punctuality—you know. Come to see us tomorrow evening, won't you? My husband's already asked you, hasn't he? Then you can tell us more, you strange stablemaster. Au revoir, Vassily." She held out her hand, adding, "I go to my virtuosi and you must get back to your horses!"

"Yes, Janina. I'll come tomorrow evening. Au revoir!"

He hastened down streets and lanes and across many courtyards, not realizing that in his haste was an intensity of longing to see Mira again, to embrace her. He felt a surge of pleasure when she and not Panya Jadwiga opened the door. "Where is the circus lady, Mira?" he asked.

"Left, less than ten minutes ago. Where have you been, Vassily?"

"With a beautiful woman," he teased her. "Really, Mira."

"You shouldn't, Vassily, and if so, don't tell me," she said earnestly.

He took her into his arms and kissed her.

Vassily was up by four in the morning. Sausage, ham, bacon and beef were to be delivered to the canteens and to private buyers. The canvas bags had been sealed and labeled—including the two large bags which contained wares for the black market. The "bills of lading," in duplicate, were in the charge of Wagner, who rode along with Vassily. If they should be stopped en route, these bills of lading were 100 per cent perfect. So far they had never run into such a checkup, but their caution had not slackened, nor Wagner's fear. His teeth chattered audibly every time a militiaman's cap bobbed up out of the morning mist. When at last the two bags were unloaded at Panya Jadwiga's and they rode on with the "kosher" produce, Wagner was a changed man. He laughed, cracked jokes, and poked fun at himself. "Take a good look at me, Vassily. Maybe you've seen fools before, but you've never seen one like me. In 1937 my

brother was here from Kansas City. You know where that is? In
America. Brother, he said, what are you hanging on in the old country for? Do you want to wait till Hitler cuts your throat? Come back
with me, he said, I've got enough to take care of you. Do you call
this a business, what you've got here? And I, fool that I am, I says,
brother mine, you go back to Kansas City; this is my America. How
do you like my America, Vassily?"

"But it is America. Aren't the two of us gangsters?"

"We're gangsters like this is America. What do we get out of
it? We work like slaves, scared stiff all the time, and if we're caught
—Siberia. Night before last a shipment was sent off—more than
three thousand people, they say."

"If we go on making the farm a success, we won't be deported."

"Yes, if. But are we allowed to? If only we could make a contract with them: We provide the plant with so and so much at government prices, and the rest is none of their business. But as it is?
Sooner or later we're sure to be caught, especially when we've got
the *soine*—the enemy—in the house."

"You mean Mermelstein?"

"Yes, Mermelstein. I don't think much of Mira's idea. I've got a
better one. Kornhaber and Meerblum agree. We three will give up
our wages in his favor. That means he'll have nearly fifteen hundred
rubles, counting his own salary, and can live pretty well. He doesn't
have to drink and whore every single day."

"Stick to Mira's instructions. You'd be taking a terrible gamble
playing along with him. When they finally get him—and they will,
sooner or later—it would mean Siberia for the rest of you, Wagner.
If he tries to blackmail you, threaten him back with denunciation.
Does he owe you money too?"

"Don't ask such dumb questions, Vassily. Owe? He doesn't
even say "lend me," but "give me." He's the Director, and he keeps
reminding us, 'Did I check your official records? Didn't I just go
ahead and sign, even though I knew exactly who you were?' You
mean to say you don't know that, Vassily? He has us in the palm of
his hand; he can get us shipped off any time."

"And himself along with you—if he ever dares report it. He
had nothing to do with the official records; he didn't sign anything;
they weren't his affair at all. Don't think the nachalniki were born
yesterday. They know perfectly well that you weren't workers in
the old days. But our farm is going well, better than any of the others.
So unless an order comes from way up above, nothing will happen
to any of you. And if that order does come, nothing will help."

"That may be right. Maybe—" He broke off, his jester's face
furrowed with anxiety. "How do you know that for sure, Vassily?"

Vassily stopped the horses. "I've figured it out, Comrade Wagner." He smiled. "You get out here, don't you?"

" 'Figured it out' is good. Go on figuring!" Wagner climbed cautiously out of the wagon.

Vassily drove on to Plant II. On the way he picked up four workmen. The sacks in the wagon gave rise to a lively conversation. "What are we getting today?" an elderly worker asked.

"The best. Sausage and ham, a pound and a quarter for every man. In addition the married men are receiving a pound of beef."

"And butter?" one of the others asked, laughing.

"Day after tomorrow there'll be butter, a quarter of a pound apiece. Six ounces for the married men."

"Bravo, Vassily. That's the life!"

"Don't laugh; others have nothing at all," the older man said. "It's a big help. Try to buy stuff at the bazaar sometime and see what it costs."

"I want to live like a human being."

"Forget that! Stop a moment, Vassily, there goes our engineer. Let's give him a lift."

But the man in a tightly buttoned overcoat, well-polished boots, and cap drawn down low over his forehead, strode on, ignoring the fact that the wagon had stopped. One of the workers called to him, but he waved aside the invitation and walked even faster.

"I thought so," one worker said. "He won't ride with us."

"What's the matter with him?" another asked.

"How should I know? He's at the machines all day and speaks only when he absolutely has to. One or two words, no more. But he knows a lot."

"Party?"

"No—the opposite, I think. Rudnenko, the master machinist over at Plant I, says he did time for eight years. Used to be a White."

"Then how come he has this job? It carries a lot of responsibility."

"Sassnikov, the chief engineer with the Order of Lenin, is the one who has the official responsibility."

"Sassnikov's never around and doesn't know a thing about the work. What did he get the decoration for?"

"Certainly not for working in a power plant. He turns up every so often, signs a document and says to the typist, 'I'm at the Party Committee if anyone needs me.' But nobody ever needs him. Kirilov takes care of everything."

Vassily made quick work of delivering the rations. When he came out again, he collided with the engineer Kirilov. He made his excuses, which the other man accepted with a curt nod. For a brief moment they looked into each other's faces; then Vassily leaped up on the wagon and drove out of the yard, while the engineer turned the corner and went into the machine shop.

As long as he was within sight of the plant, Vassily drove as if the devil were after him. Once he had put some distance between himself and it, he let the horses slow down to a walk as he began searching his memory. He had seen the engineer Kirilov somewhere. That face, cracked as congealed lava, with dead eyes that looked only inward, and that nose like the beak of some bird of prey. . . . *I know him, I know him, but where have I seen him and when?* The two chestnuts moved at a deliberate pace through the empty, early-morning streets; they knew the way and stopped of their own accord in front of Plant I. Vassily, startled out of his thoughts, set to work carrying the sacks into the canteen. He was just pocketing the receipts when Master Machinist Rudnenko, a man in his late forties with heavily grayed hair and a mustache, entered the canteen. "Good morning, Vassily," he said. "Lucky I've run into you. My wife arrived yesterday. Now it's really serious. Have you found a place for me?"

"Congratulations," Vassily said. "I must make a note of it right away. You're entitled to another pound of beef and more butter."

"Good, that's fine. But the chief thing is: have you found a place for me? Living in a hotel with a baby isn't so pleasant."

"There is a cottage halfway to Jiusefovka that might do for you. But it's in pretty poor condition."

"That doesn't matter. You'll see how I can repair it. Will I need much material? Is there a barn with it? Garden? Water? I'd like to keep chickens, a pig, maybe goats too; I have a little money."

"It's a pretty nice place, Dmitri Alexevich, only very neglected. As for building material, if Saposhnik will give you an order, you'll find all you need at the farm."

"He'll give me one; you can depend on that. I'll take a day off and run over to see the house with my wife. There's a woman for you—works as hard as two men. Thanks, Vassily." He shook hands.

"You're welcome. Just give me a note that you claim the supplement for your wife. Like this one. I need it for the bookkeeping, you know." While Rudnenko was writing, he asked, "It just occurs to me—I forgot to ask, but perhaps you know. Is the engineer at Plant II married? Does he have his wife here?"

"Sassnikov is married and has two kids," Rudnenko said.

"I know that. But the other one—he's been here six weeks, and if it turns out he's not been getting his full family ration, he'll probably file a complaint."

Rudnenko handed the slip to Vassily. "There won't be any complaints from that one; he'll keep his mouth shut. I wouldn't give him any sausage or butter either—I'd give him cyanide. Him and others like him. Enemies of the people, Vassily. They should be stamped out, all of them."

"What has he done?" Vassily smiled incredulously.

"You can't understand that—how could you possibly? But I can. I've been in the movement since 1905. When I was only fourteen and an apprentice at the Putilev Works, I fought on the barricades. Kirilov—the devil only knows if that's his right name—was a White. And there are thousands like him. No matter how well they work, they carry that inside them and they're only waiting for the chance to stab us in the back."

Vassily shook his head soberly. "Then I don't understand why they're allowed to work."

"You don't? Because they're needed. They've had an education; they know how to run things. We must advance, industrialize, build up, produce. And so they've been fetched out of their corners, out of the jails and camps and even from abroad. But we'll settle with all the enemies of the working class, with all of them, depend on that! Well, I'm off to work now. When could you take us out to the cottage, Vassily?"

"I'll be bringing butter day after tomorrow. At about the same time as today."

"Fine. And what I said to you about those people—better if you don't have to mention it to anyone. It's easy to talk to you; you're all right, Vassily."

But Vassily, driving toward Jiusefovka about an hour later, did not feel all right. When he unhitched at the stable, he did the work very slowly and unhappily. A single thought haunted him: where had he met the man Kirilov before? Undoubtedly it had been on the other side, but when? On what occasion? He stood leaning against the manger staring at the legs of the two injured roans when Mermelstein appeared at the stable door. "I must drive in to town, Khomniuk," he said. "Hitch up."

"I have no horses," Vassily said.

"I see four and need only two, so snap into it!"

"Two are laid up, as you see, and the others have gone more than twenty-five miles today."

"I order you to hitch up a team," Mermelstein screeched. "And you are going to drive me!"

"Which ones am I to hitch up?"

"The two chestnuts you always use."

"You must give me the order in writing and the bookkeeper must sign it; otherwise it would seem as though I were doing it on my own responsibility. I have to go out and help with the tractor and have no time for driving."

"Tractor? What tractor?"

"A red one with black stripes painted all around it."

"What's going on here? I know nothing about red tractors. What is the tractor doing?"

"Churning butter." Vassily entered the stall and washed the caked mud packs off the legs of the roans.

Mermelstein trailed after him. "Why won't you do me the favor?"

"I don't do favors; I obey orders. But when I don't feel that I can take the responsibility, I have to cover myself. Give me a written order and I'll drive you whenever and wherever you like."

"You'll regret it, you—" Mermelstein left the stable.

Fifteen minutes later Vassily had finished his work and went to the office. Mermelstein, hands in his trouser pockets, was standing in front of Mira's desk talking to her in some agitation.

"I wanted to ask you whether you still need the team or whether I could use the horses elsewhere," Vassily said, pausing in the doorway.

"I'm not going, and you get out of here!" Mermelstein roared.

"At once. I just have to give the Comrade Bookkeeper some receipts. Here."

"What receipts are those?"

"We delivered our quota of sausage and fresh meat to the canteens today," Mira informed him without looking up from her books.

"We throw away thousands of rubles that way. The bastards could do without sausage for a while," Mermelstein sneered.

"May I have my pay, comrade?" Vassily said. "I didn't get around to coming for it yesterday."

"Of course. Here's your account. Fifteen days and thirty-four hours overtime." She counted out his money, which he carelessly thrust into his pocket.

"Overtime—what's this about overtime? He doesn't get overtime; I won't sign that," Mermelstein bellowed.

"You signed it three days ago," Mira said.

"Well, then," Vassily said, "I'll finish unhitching and go out to the field to help the tractor man."

"Stay here!" Mermelstein shouted. "It's high time I found out what this tractor business is all about."

"But you signed for it," Mira said patiently. "We've hired a tractor for the spring planting."

"What planting? What is being planted? Who is planting? I'm

not told about anything; all I do is sign. I have to know what's going on."

"So you do," Vassily agreed. "Here!" He went to a bookshelf, took several agricultural pamphlets from a stack, and gave them to Mermelstein. "Here, these tell you everything you need to know. You can study up on spring planting and tractors."

He was already out of the office when the association struck him with all its force. Among the pamphlets on the shelf was one dealing with Kiev—at least the word KIEV had been printed in large letters over the photograph on the cover. And suddenly Vassily remembered where he had seen the engineer with the hooked nose. It had been in Kiev, twenty-two years before, at a reception given by General Skoropadski, the hetman of the Ukraine, to the German and Austrian officers of the Army of Occupation.

"Take a look at that nose," Alex Röhmer had said, pointing discreetly to a man among the Ukrainian ruler's colorful retinue—a man who looked very spruce in his Russian uniform with the insignia of a captain of the engineering corps.

"What language is that you're speaking, Lieutenant?" the Captain had asked in correct German when they were introduced.

"It's sometimes called Ukrainian and sometimes Ruthenian."

"Ah, very interesting. If it's Ukrainian, I could offer you a highly paid job. The hetman of the Ukraine is looking for a tutor —you see, he doesn't know Ukrainian. But what nationality are you, Lieutenant?"—

"What would I be? An Austrian, of course."

"Let's hope that we both remain what we are, you Austrian and I Russian."

Four months later, the bubble had burst. The hetman of the Ukraine was a refugee somewhere in Germany, the Lieutenant was no longer an Austrian, and the Captain with the hooked nose. . . .

Here he is, I know it, Vassily said to himself. He stood in the yard, leaning against the wagon, feeling not the slightest desire to go ahead with his unhitching. The hell with the whole thing. He went to the garden and shouted, "Tadek, Freddy, the horses are here for you." Then he continued on, toward the fields. And the past walked alongside him in the form of the Captain with the hooked nose. And Vassily heard him talking: "So this is what we've come to, Lieutenant! This is my Russia, and where is your Austria? Did you recognize me? I recognized you, too. I have my place; I'm bound to it with chains of iron. But you—what are you doing here, Lieutenant? Weren't you an aristocrat? They'll ferret that out, and then you'll be done for. They'll make things tough for you in ways you can scarcely imagine. They have a shortage of trained engineers;

they need them, so they're not killing them at present. Better let
them work themselves to death. But there are plenty of stablemasters.
Too many. They know everything about me; there's no hoodwink-
ing them. But you put something over on them, for otherwise how
would you have become a stablemaster here? I'll tell them that you
aren't an honest laborer, but a lieutenant and an aristocrat. I have to
—it's a way of raising my miserable credit. Then they'll let me
breathe a little more freely; they understand treachery—and reward
it, too."

"Go ahead and tell them, Captain Hooknose; you can't scare
me. Then at least something interesting will happen. This playing
at stablemaster—it's pretty boring. I still don't know much about
them, and I want to find out what they're really like. Go ahead and
denounce me, Captain Hooknose."

"You fool, you stupid adventurer. You're playing with your life.
What are you risking it for? You have friends and a woman you
love, who loves you. . . ."

"Martha," Vassily said aloud, "Martha." Whereupon Captain
Hooknose's shadow vanished from his side.

Mermelstein was in the dumps. He had tried to borrow from
everyone, and failed. That redheaded bitch had even refused to pay
him the lousy few rubles of his salary. Meerblum had given him the
runaround, and Wagner had offered him twelve rubles—all the
money he had in the world, he maintained. Well, he would get even
with them all, with the whole lot of them. And most of all with Vassily. That peasant blockhead! He had put Rudnicki away! Well, he'd
get his.

Mermelstein yawned, turned over on his other side and looked
at his watch. Only three. Still an eternity till evening, and what
could he expect when evening did come? No transportation, and
even if he had it, no money. Without money he couldn't get at
Manya. A crazy piece, that girl could drink for three, and in bed—
terrific, but terrific! Mermelstein shuddered at the prospect of a
dreary evening, eating in the canteen, holing up in his bare room.

Once more he looked at the watch, not as a timepiece but as an
object of value. What would they pay for a watch like this nowadays? Ah, a few months ago—those had been the days. Then he
could have got twelve or even fifteen hundred rubles for it. But today—who would lay out cash for a watch? He'd let it go for a thousand or even eight hundred if he had to. Mermelstein yawned, and
forgot to close his mouth. A thought had come to him; he knew a
customer for the watch. He'd have money soon. Then he could go

off and have a little fun.

Antek, with his two helpers, was sifting black loam. All three were so busy with their work that they did not see Mermelstein approach the garden plot. They scarcely noticed him even when he stood right in front of them; they went on working. "Comrade Gorecki," Mermelstein said pleasantly, "I'd like to speak with you for a moment—privately."

"What about, Comrade Director?" Antek walked a few steps up the damp garden path with Mermelstein.

"Here," Mermelstein said, handing Antek the watch. "Runs fine, good as new. I need money."

"If you're out of money, what about me? Your salary is nearly twice what mine is. Sorry, but I can't help you out, Comrade Director. I'm not buying and selling; I have my work." Antek returned to his helpers. Mermelstein, furious, pocketed the watch and slowly walked back. Perhaps if he offered Antek the watch for five hundred. . . .

Vassily was standing on the road, waiting for the teams which would soon be returning from town. The first of them appeared, and the drivers stopped. "We still have to cart a few loads of manure for the garden," he said to them. "No way out, we'll have to work a little longer tonight. Metro, you stay here and tell the others as they come in what we're doing. I'll take your team and bring in a load; the forks are over there. It will go fast." Metro clambered down from his wagon and Vassily took the reins. He called Antek, who laid aside his sifting screen and started toward him. But Mermelstein blocked his way. "Comrade Gorecki," he said plaintively, "give me five hundred rubles for the watch—four hundred—I need money— I have to have it."

"Not ten. I'm not buying," Antek said, and ran toward the manure heap. Mermelstein was left alone. What now? Hang around home, not go to Manya, nothing to drink, no fun—what a stinking life.

As Freddy passed by, Mermelstein vented his rage on him. "Goddamn bastard, standing there and grinning. Go to work, you feeble-minded idiot!" he snarled at him.

"I am working," Freddy said, with a look of appeal toward Tadek, who stood at the other end of the long trench. Mermelstein did not notice the look, nor did he see Tadek bearing down on him. "Working," he said, mocking Freddy's uncertain voice. "You fool, you son of a bitch with your whore of a wife. Your Mira's a whore and your mother's a whore. . . ."

Freddy bowed his head. Tears spilled from his eyes. Tadek had reached them by now; he saw Freddy's tears, heard his sobs, and charged forward. Mermelstein started to beat a retreat. He took one step; before he could take another he had landed in the trench and was flat on his back in the manure.

Tadek crouched beside him, pushing one handful of horse manure after another into his face.

"There," he squeaked, "that's for you, you goddamned shit. You'll choke in shit." He pushed Mermelstein deeper and deeper into the manure.

Vassily and Antek, when they came back with the first load, found Freddy standing at the edge of the trench, smiling through his tears, looking down at Tadek, who had heaped so much manure on Mermelstein that only the tips of his boots were visible.

Horrified, both men leaped into the trench. "Tadek!" Antek cried. "Have you killed him?"

"Of course not," Tadek said grumpily. "You said I mustn't." And then he went back to Freddy. "All right, Fredziu?" He took out Freddy's handkerchief and wiped his tear-stained face.

"All right, Tadek, you're a good friend," Freddy said. He gave a simpleminded laugh. "Robota! Come on!"

"Robota," Tadek chirped. They jumped up on the wagon and began pitching off the manure.

Vassily and Antek meanwhile had got the almost unconscious Mermelstein to his feet. He looked ghastly. They lifted him out of the trench and began scraping him clean. He stood dazed while they drew his sweater and shirt over his head. Vassily held him and Antek poured a whole watering can of water over his face, ignoring the fact that he shivered under the icy stream. Antek wiped him dry with the more or less clean shirt, while Vassily pulled the sweater back over his head.

Mermelstein spat. "You wait, you murderers! The whole lot of you will go to Siberia! Starshi Koniukh, take me to town at once, at once. I'm going to the head office! To report you all for sabotage, attempted murder!"

"Take it easy," Antek said, smiling. "What's a little dirt? You aren't even wearing your good suit. If you calm down, maybe you can still do some business with your watch."

Mermelstein instantly grew calmer. "I haven't anything against you, Comrade Gorecki, but—" He fell silent, his eyes fixed on the entrance to the garden plot. A group of men, led by Saposhnik, was just entering. Mermelstein walked slowly toward them. Vassily and Antek jumped into the trench. Meanwhile another wagon had driven up and was being unloaded.

The group stopped, and Saposhnik introduced his farm director. Mermelstein made the best of impressions, dung still clinging to his sweater and beret, and a ripe smell emanating from him. "This," Saposhnik said to Nikiforiuk, "is our farm director, Comrade Mermelstein."

The visiting deputation shook his hand warmly. They then moved in a body toward the trench, where the work was going forward at a furious pace. Here was a scene such as they loved. More and more wagons rumbled in; the manure was unloaded by Tadek and Freddy, aided by the drivers. In the trench Vassily and Antek distributed and leveled it. Everything went smoothly, without a pause. The nachalniki stood at the edge of the trench and watched reverently.

"What are they here for?" Antek asked when he came close enough to Vassily.

"Probably to inspect the place. The small fellow with the red face is director of a kolkhoz—his name is Nikiforiuk. He must be wondering how it is our farm does so well."

"And now Mermelstein is telling him! A lot he knows!"

"Saposhnik won't let Mermelstein shoot off his mouth—he knows the situation. Knock off now, Antek, and send the two young ones away." The last load had been pitched off. Freddy and Tadek drove off with the last team. Vassily and Antek climbed out of the trench, shouldered their manure forks and rakes, and started away also.

"Where to, Vassily Vassilevich?" Feingold called out.

"Feed the horses."

"Shall we take a look at the stable?" Nikiforiuk asked.

The drivers had hosed down the wagons; they stood in a row, still dripping, clean, their metal parts gleaming. In the stable the horses were being rubbed down while they plucked hay from the full racks. Vassily went directly to the massive grain chest, got his measure ready, and waited until all the horses were clean and dry. Then he unlocked the chest and tapped his measure against its side. A neighing, stamping and rattling of chains broke out, as if the animals had only been waiting for a signal. The drivers stood one behind the other; each was given his allotment of grain, and looked close to make sure that his horses were not being scanted. After handing out the grain to the others, Vassily measured out five rations for himself and fed his chestnuts, the sick roans and the stallion. Hardly a word was spoken. The routine was simple enough, yet the six men gave it their full and serious attention. This was their work, and every detail of it mattered.

In the cow barn the evening chores had not begun; the cows

stood in their stalls, chewing their cuds. Kornhaber was busying himself with the milk pails at the end of the long barn. Saposhnik hurried his visitors through the place. "We can't linger," he said, "if we want to see the whole farm." The butter plant was closed; it went into operation only after the milking. But the meat-packing plant was functioning, as were the smithies and harness workshop, and the pigs were being fed. Nikiforiuk became increasingly quiet and more thoughtful. More and more frequently he glanced at Mermelstein, who did not understand the warmth of his looks.

The inspection tour was to end at the office. Saposhnik found a moment in which to whisper to Mermelstein, "Go and wash up now and change your clothes. Today is a holiday for you; you're going to receive a high honor." Mermelstein did as he was bidden, and the commission repaired to the office, where Mira was still at her desk. She stood up and shook hands with each of the men in turn. Saposhnik explained that the comrades had just made a tour of the farm and wanted to see something of the bookkeeping.

The comrades looked into the books, very thoroughly and carefully. The records were all so clear and comprehensible that they had very few questions. Everything Nikiforiuk wanted to know was down on paper in Mira's small, neat handwriting. Tarashchenko asked Mira for one account or another, glanced through it expertly, and silently handed it back. His expression was impassive, but all the others knew that he was thoroughly satisfied. With a calm *"No da,"* he gave the signal for departure. Nevertheless Nikiforiuk ventured one question. It was a real catch question, the kind of question a bookkeeper might not be prepared for and which could unearth the buried rat. "Comrade Bookkeeper," Nikiforiuk said, "Vassily, the starshi koniukh, rented a tractor at the tractor station in Soniewicze—is that right?"

"He did," Mira said.

"On that occasion he plied three men, including myself, with sausage and vodka—is that right?" And without waiting for a reply he continued, "No doubt the koniukh did not pay for the sausage and vodka from his own pocket—is that right?" He and the others waited for the reply with bated breath.

Mira's answer was utterly unconcerned. "The organization pays for those things."

"And do you keep a record, or . . . ?"

"Naturally, it is right down in the books." She took a small volume from the file. "Here it is, under 'Tractor': two pounds, five ounces of sausage: nine rubles, fifty-four kopecks; one quart of vodka: thirteen rubles. We reckon all that as part of the rent for the tractor."

Nikiforiuk was effectively stilled, but Mira continued her explanation. "Under pig feed, for example"—she produced the requisite items as she talked—"you will find certain items that have nothing to do with the feeding of pigs. A bottle of vodka here and there, some sausage, or a few meals in the canteen. The Red Army men of the vicinity send us their kitchen scraps. We do not pay for these things, but invite them to the canteen. They have fun with the workers, sing and dance with the girls and boys, and of course it is our treat. A sandwich, a bit of sausage or cake, a glass of vodka. This entertainment accomplishes various purposes. First of all, the farm gets food which would otherwise go to waste—our pigs practically subsist on these scraps, along with the scraps from our canteens. In addition, and this is highly important, our young people meet young men their own age from the Soviet Union; they not only have a good time but learn the language and ideology."

"*Yasno*—right," Saposhnik said.

"What is your mother tongue, comrade?" Tarashchenko asked.

"Yiddish, comrade. But I also know German and Polish and as much French and English as a person learns in school. Every language you speak makes you that much more of a man."

"Stalin," all of them said in chorus. The conversation could not have wound up on a finer note. Tarashchenko looked at his watch. "I think," he said to Saposhnik, "it's about time. Probably there's a club here."

"A very handsome one, Sergei Ivanovich."

"Then tell all the workers to assemble there, as soon as possible." He left the office, followed by the others. Mermelstein was standing in the yard, still hopeful of selling his watch. In gleaming high boots with well-cut breeches and close-fitting, dark jacket, a white handkerchief at the collar, he was his old self once more. He stood among the nachalniki, listening to their talk and catching only a word now and then. Saposhnik was just about to ask him to pass on Tarashchenko's order, but seeing Vassily come out of the stable, he applied to him instead. A moment later the siren screeched, calling everyone to a special meeting in the House of Culture.

Everyone came, including those who usually shirked such affairs. Somehow, word had got around that it was to be a festive occasion, and all came washed, shaved, in clean clothes, polished shoes or boots, the women in brightly embroidered blouses with wide, gathered skirts and silk kerchiefs. The mood was one of joyous expectancy, although no one could have said what was being celebrated.

"Comrades," Sergei Ivanovich Tarashchenko said, "we are assembled here for a joyful occasion. I give the floor to your nachalnik,

Comrade Saposhnik."

Saposhnik stood up, took a sheet of paper from his pocket, and began to read: "Order No. 167 of the Elektrostantsia." He then read several paragraphs of routine announcements, racing through these so quickly that everyone shared his impatience to get to the important point. At last he paused and let the hand in which he held the paper drop. "This, comrades, is a matter for your closest attention. Comrade Oswaldowicz Mermelstein, director of the Podsobnyia Khoziaistva of the Elektrostantsia, is herewith relieved of his present post. In consideration of his organizational abilities he is being assigned to the Pobeda Collective Farm as deputy director. The decision has also been made to award him the distinction of *otlichno.*" This was the highest rating below that of stakhanovets.

Mermelstein still did not know what had happened. Saposhnik came down from the platform, went up to him with outstretched hand, and said in Russian, "Congratulations." He briefed him in Yiddish: "You've gotten a big post; you've been made zamestitel at the Pobeda Kolkhoz—nice work, too." Dumbfounded, Mermelstein accepted the congratulations.

As soon as Saposhnik had returned to the platform, Feingold stood up and spoke in Ukrainian, "Comrades, perhaps some of you did not understand what Comrade Saposhnik said to you, and my Ukrainian is different from yours. Comrade Vassily Khomniuk will come up here—yes, up here to us," he said, speaking directly to Vassily, "and explain it all to you. He will also explain what the difference is between now and the old days. You understand what I mean, Comrade Khomniuk. Could anybody under the old regime have been valued according to his abilities and given such opportunities as are possible here in the Soviet Union?"

Despite the invitation, Vassily forbore to mount to the platform. Nor did he stand in front of it directly. Rather, he took a step forward, past Mermelstein, who sat in the first row, so that he had his back both to Mermelstein and the nachalniki. He looked at the auditorium and then, in his habitual gesture, brought his hand to his mustache. As he did so, he pointed his forefinger at his audience as a signal: everybody look at me. And then he placed the finger over his mouth. And that clearly meant: keep quiet and look serious. Those who saw the bit of pantomime understood plainly, and those who did not were informed by kicks and nudges of Vassily's order.

"Comrades," he began, "I want to tell you what has happened." He spoke Ruthenian, intoning it quietly and deliberately, a peasant having something important to communicate to other peasants. "Up here"—he jerked his thumb backwards over his shoulder—"is sitting a nachalnik whom you are seeing for the first time today. He is

Comrade Nikiforiuk, the director of the Pobeda Kolkhoz. A few days ago he ate some sausage—good sausage, and he liked it. And when the nachalnik learned that this sausage was made on our farm, he knew right away that it must be a good farm, that other things about it would be all right too. And if that's so, he reckoned, who sees to it that a farm is good—who if not the Director? We are an organization, comrades, and an organization is like a fish—if the head is good, the whole fish is good; if the head stinks, the whole fish stinks."

A good many in the audience grinned with satisfaction. The men on the platform also liked the image. "Our farm is a good healthy fish from head to tail. I ask you, who originally found this place? To whom do we owe the good houses, the good outbuildings, the canteen, the workshop, the whole farm, if not to Comrade Mermelstein? He looked for it and found it, and we have only had to work. That is not hard, that's something we've learned how to do; we've been used to hard work since we were kids. We have—but what about the Director? I ask you, if a year ago, when the burzhui, the capitalists, were still in power here—if Comrade Mermelstein had turned up and wanted to be the director of a farm, would he have been able to become one? But Comrade Mermelstein himself did not know that he had it in him to be a director. Not to speak of the burzhui! Wouldn't they have asked, 'Where are your papers? Where have you worked?' Comrade Mermelstein would never have become a director under the burzhui! But now? One, two, three, and he was a director; he located this marvelous place, organized it, and one, two, three, everything was in tip-top order.

"Why, you will ask, is our wonderful director being taken away from us? I will tell you. Because Comrade Mermelstein is a good organizer. He must go on organizing. We here with our few hundred acres—what are we to a collective farm with twenty times that much land and more? There Comrade Mermelstein can really organize; there he has a real chance to show what he can do.

"Like everybody in the beginning, he will have a tough time of it. But let him think of Comrade Stalin's words: 'Difficulties exist to be overcome'!" The men on the platform nodded happily. "Therefore, comrades, long live the great teacher Stalin; long live the Soviet Union; long live the nachalstvo; and also long live our former director, Comrade Mermelstein. Let's give him three cheers!"

Everyone joined in the cheers till the windowpanes rattled. Vassily went up to Mermelstein with outstretched hand and said in German—under cover of the general racket—"You're a lucky bird, Comrade Mermelstein. You can easily become a People's Commissar for Agriculture." Then others thronged around him; everybody wanted to shake the Director's hand to bid him good-bye.

Saposhnik jumped from the platform. "Mermelstein," he said in Yiddish, "get ready and pack your things. You're going with Nikiforiuk at once. By tomorrow you'll be in charge of the kolkhoz."

"Yes, yes, at once," Mermelstein said. He was stunned by the cheers, by the boisterous congratulations. At last he had grasped what was happening. He gave no thought to the reasons or the consequences, or the possibility that he might not be able to cope with his new tasks. But where was Antek? Ah, there he was, coming. Mermelstein beckoned to him to follow. Once outside, he pressed the watch on him once more.

"Keep the watch," Antek said cheerfully. "I don't have cash enough to pay you what it's worth. Here are two hundred rubles; I give them to you as a loan. Your salary will be larger now, so it won't be hard for you to pay it back. I'm in no hurry. And if you have any messages"—Antek smiled—"for Betka or Yusia or Janka or Manya, I'll deliver them gladly."

"Manya, if you like. Tell her I'm getting a big job and that I'll come to see her as soon as possible."

"All right, for Manya. That means you must know Josek too."

"Of course, a fine boy. Give him my regards too. Thanks a lot, and good luck, Comrade Gorecki."

A fine boy, Josek, Antek murmured under his breath as he returned to the canteen. I'd like him best six feet under. Lucky we're getting rid of this crook; maybe things will ease off now. But what a fellow Vassily is. Not afraid of anybody and turns everything to advantage! Antek entered the club and looked for Vassily. He caught sight of him talking to Mira. As he went up to them he heard Mira say, "In two days we'll have him back."

"That was quite a line you handed them, Vassily," Antek said, laughing.

"You caught on, Antek? I didn't tell a single lie. Did he find the farm or didn't he? And he brought Mira—after that, the rest was easy. And would he have become director of a farm anywhere else in the world? So then—"

"But what about Saposhnik?" Mira said. "Once they have Mermelstein at the kolkhoz and see what he's really like, it will all come down on his head."

"You can rely on Saposhnik. I bet he told Nikiforiuk Mermelstein is no good, and he probably told the party that he refuses to take any responsibility for what happens after the transfer."

"Then why has Nikiforiuk taken him? He seems a pretty clever chap."

"Because he doesn't believe Saposhnik. He thinks that Saposhnik only said that in order to hold on to Mermelstein. Comrade Nikiforiuk is clever, all right—too clever for his own good. But—" Vassily had to stop. Saposhnik was walking toward them.

"Mira Isakovna, you take over stamp and seal from Mermelstein. Until we get another director for the farm, I'll do the signing. To-morrow we'll go to the notary and the bank, confirm your signature and your powers. It may be quite a while before we find a director, so for the time being we'll have to—uhm—manage this way." He moved away, followed by Mira.

Tarashchenko and Feingold were still sitting on the platform, talking. "What do you say to our koniukh, Sergei Ivanovich?" Feingold asked.

"I like him better and better. But the more important thing is that the workers like him. They understand him and go along with whatever he says; it's obvious that he's popular with them."

Saposhnik and Mermelstein, with Mira and Vassily behind them, reappeared in the hall. "Would you come and have a small snack?" Saposhnik said to the three nachalniki.

"Gladly," Tarashchenko said, and Feingold smilingly nodded.

In one corner of the dining room bowls of herring, ham, sausage and cheese had been pleasingly arranged on a spotless table. There were baskets of sliced bread, and two bottles of vodka.

Feingold lit a cigarette. He beckoned to Vassily. "Here, Vassily Vassilevich, you take one. If I offer them around to everybody, there'll be none left." He smiled conspiratorially.

"Thank you," Vassily said. He wiped his mouth and mustache before he reached out for the papirosa. "I really shouldn't. After I smoke one of yours, my own don't taste good," he said, laughing.

"Nichevo, you can indulge in them for a while. I received five cartons today. Here"—he reached into his breast pocket—"here's a pack for you, Vassily. But put them away quickly or I'll find I have too many friends here."

Vassily slipped the pack into his trouser pocket. "Thank you very much, Comrade Feingold. Today is a real holiday!" He beamed. His pleasure was genuine, for he would be able to pass on the cigarettes to Janina this evening. Strange world, he thought, when Feingold was called away by Tarashchenko and he remained standing alone for a moment. The former Princess Guninska, a countess by birth, would smoke the cigarettes which the nachalnik had given to the koniukh who was really. . . .

Vassily was so lost in thoughts of the events of the day that he would have let his horse canter past the cottage, his destination, if

Jeanne had not been standing at the door. "Hello, cavalryman!" she hailed him.

Vassily rode across the street and dismounted. "Greetings, lady!"

"Welcome, comrade. What a splendid horse! Come around into the yard through the back gate; there's room for him there." She led the way. "Here," she said, "under the overhang of the roof. Oh, what a fine animal. Thoroughbred; I know horses. Where did you get him? What is he doing on a farm?"

"He's my favorite. Later he'll be at stud—in a few weeks."

"For those heavy, common mares? What a pity!"

"I don't think he'll mind," Vassily said, laughing. "And he'll sire fine horses."

"He surely will—but I would have wished him a fine, aristocratic bride of his own kind."

"I still don't think he'll mind," Vassily said. "But you're right, he is a thoroughbred. In fact he comes from a noble stand, to judge by the coronet. Look here, Jeanne." She came over to his side. It had grown darker, meanwhile; he switched on his flashlight and focused it on the horse's rump. The brand of the stud farm had been burned deep into his left hindquarter. There was a coronet with an R to the right and a B to the left. "I've been racking my brains, but I don't know the brand."

"I do," Jeanne said. "The stallion comes from the stud of Prince Roman Bolgurski. How small the world is. But come in now."

Vassily followed her. Dr. Feuerberg rose and greeted Vassily like an old friend. "Jeanne has fallen in love with a horse again, it seems," he said.

"Sit down now, Léon, and be quiet for a while. And you, too, Vassily. I want to read a letter to you. Do you understand Polish? Never mind, I'll translate as I read. You see, this letter was the beginning of the end, and it explains a great deal. It is addressed to Prince Anatol Guninski and the sender is, as it happens, Prince Roman Bolgurski."

"Good old feudal times," the doctor growled. "But the contents—"

"Are nothing but lies," Jeanne said, completing the sentence. "Are you listening, Vassily? Here it is: 'I hasten to clarify your error. As I gather from your letter, you believe that your wife, as the daughter and heiress of Count Basil Voronovski, who died in Paris, has a claim to part of the inheritance of my mother-in-law, Countess Elizaveta and her two children, my wife Marenzia and my brother-in-law Vladislav. This, however, is not the case. The woods mentioned in your letter were mortgaged down to the last twig and overburdened with borrowings from the house of P. R. Linkhand of

Warsaw. The company which is exploiting the former Voronovski property, and in addition other, far larger properties, is an English firm which has enlisted the Voronovski family as partners for financial and above all for political reasons—old personal relationships to the house of P. R. Linkhand having been the decisive factor. As representative of the family, I am the only one who has invested capital in the enterprise—a fact which can be proved at any time if you should choose to take legal steps, as you hint in your letter that you will. I regret to have to disappoint you and ask you to give my regards to my unknown cousin; my relatives, too, had no notion of her existence. Sincerely yours.' Signature. All that, of course, is a crude lie on the part of Prince Roman Bolgurski. The forest belonged to my grandfather; he had three sons, and each of them had a share in the inheritance. Incidentally, there is still my Uncle Cyril. I wonder if he's still alive, though; he stayed in Paris."

"Don't confuse things, Jeanne. I'm sure Vassily has no doubts about your rights, have you, Vassily?"

"Certainly not. But didn't you say that the letter was the beginning of the end? What beginning of what end, Jeanne?"

"Of my rêve, Vassily. That was my awakening. It didn't take me as long to put two and two together as other countesses. I realized that Prince Guninski had married me only because I was an heiress. He knew about the forest, of course, and the huge fortune. And that was why he'd made such a tremendous play for me. How enamored of me he was in Paris! He lay at my feet, became a poet. The same man who five weeks after the wedding told me I was a beggar and did I think he had tied himself down to an obscure exile just because she had a pretty face? If I did not give him a power of attorney to conduct the suit against the Voronovskis, I could go to the devil. Yes, Vassily, that was Prince Guninski for you!"

"One moment, Jeanne," Vassily said. "Guninski was very wealthy, wasn't he?"

"His father had already lost everything. He himself was very clever about preserving appearances, although in fact he had nothing. The estates were mortgaged to the hilt, and he was eternally traveling, visiting, welcomed everywhere. He did cut such a fine figure, had so much charm, was an intermediary in discreet affairs, highly skillful and experienced in spinning intrigues—political as well as social ones." She fell silent, musing. After a while she said, "If I only knew why he thought up this scheme of having me searched for. . . ."

"Did Anatol know of your relations with Candomir?"

"Certainly. How could he help knowing? I told him everything." She blushed slightly. "I—I wanted to prove that I preferred him to all my other admirers; there were quite a few of them in the old days, you know."

"I see. Did you often talk about Candomir?"

"Quite often. I showed him my album—I still have it—with the photos Radu used to send me, of his house and park, and horses. Would you like to see them, Vassily?" Without waiting for a reply, she flitted out of the room, came back with a thick, leather-bound volume. "Here is all of Candomireni."

Vassily was not conscious of the eagerness with which he took the album, nor of the fact that he became completely absorbed in the snapshots. Yet there was nothing new in them. Among all those pictures of countryside, buildings, people and animals, there was nothing and no one he did not know. The last page was a much-enlarged photo. "St. Hubertus, 1926" was written under it. It showed a cavalcade starting out for a steeplechase. There were splendid horses, smart women, riders in uniforms and pink coats, and in the van, Radu Candomir. It was a remarkably good and clear picture taken in the lane of ancient beech trees. Right behind Candomir was a woman, flanked by two men. That was Nadejde Rananu, now dead for many years; to her left was her husband. And to the right, who was that? Could he still recognize himself?

Jeanne took the album from his hands and studied the picture she had seen so often before. She doesn't recognize me, Vassily thought, eying her closely. Ah yes, a mustache, and fourteen years are a long time, he thought, with mixed feelings, and could not suppress a small sigh. Regret? Sadness? Relief? "So Anatol knew that Candomir had loved you and wanted you to be his wife?" he asked matter-of-factly.

"Of course!"

"That's a key point in this mystery. All right: let's retrace the steps; when you realized that Guninski's great passion was a passion for money, you broke with him. You had also refused to give him power of attorney to sue for the inheritance. Why?"

Her husband answered the question. "Out of pride," he said.

"No, out of spite," Jeanne corrected. "I wanted to disappoint him. Because he had so bitterly disappointed me."

"You stuck by your refusal, with the result that he divorced you. Was that so easy? You're both Catholic, aren't you?"

"We had a civil marriage in Paris. The church wedding was supposed to follow here. But you are certainly well-informed about me—even to knowing that I am Catholic. Yes, my mother had entered the Greek Orthodox Church, for my father's sake, but she remained a Catholic at heart. After her death I myself became a

Catholic in Paris; to honor my mother's memory, and out of conviction."

"And you, doctor—did you also become a Catholic out of conviction?"

"You do know everything, Stablemaster Vassily—one has to be careful with you. No, I became a Catholic out of lack of conviction. You see, I have no real concern with what I do not believe in, if you know what I mean. My wife made all the arrangements with the old priest. I saw no reason to obstruct."

"Yes, Prince Guninski left me without any money at all. Aside from the fact that I couldn't afford a ticket back to Paris, I also didn't want to return to the surroundings in which I'd become involved with him."

"And then," the doctor interpolated, "when my wife was left alone and abandoned, she had a wonderful idea, the best in her life. She knew I was in Czeravna—how close it used to be to Cracow!— she telegraphed me, and in a few hours I was with her."

"You see, we're old friends, Léon and I. We've known each other fifteen—no, sixteen—years. We've quarreled often, but we've always come together again."

"Yes," the doctor said, "a long illness is sure death—and now we're married."

"And you're sure that Guninski knew it?" Vassily asked.

"I'm absolutely certain of it," Jeanne said.

"Then I simply don't understand; I cannot find the clue. What did he really have in mind in sending me—"

"I think you are puzzling over that in vain. Anatol lies for the sake of lying," Jeanne said.

"Let me put my Talmudic mind to work, Vassily," the doctor said. "I was a confirmed dialectician at the age of twelve. Well, then. . . ." His face tensed; he turned his chair toward the table, propped his chin in both hands and his elbows on the table, and for a while looked as if he were rocking his lean body backward and forward. "Anatol is a liar; he lies about everything and on all occasions. He is not Jeanne's husband, but he says he is because that is to his advantage. He is base and cruel and takes advantage of goodness and decency; he is quick to recognize these qualities in others, and quick to exploit them. Perhaps he didn't count on chivalrous Candomir's sending his faithful Vassily to find Jeanne; Anatol wouldn't have known about Vassily's special qualities, and the idea first occurred to Candomir. But once Candomir took it into his head to send someone to rescue her, could the Prince oppose his plan? So Vassily sets out to find Dr. Feuerberg and of course finds

Jeanne, Janina. 'Princess,' Vassily says, 'your esteemed spouse has sent me to rescue you.' What does Jeanne—Janina—say? 'My esteemed spouse is Dr. Feuerberg and I am no princess.' What must Vassily think? She's afraid to say she's a princess; being a doctor's wife in Poland is better than being a princess in Siberia. So Vassily brings or sends word that Princess Guninski is not in Czeravna or won't admit that she is. Anatol registers sadness and despair, but goes on living the good life. That's one possibility. Or else Vassily is unable to locate the doctor or the Princess—the chances are very good that he should not. Vassily reports: no trace of them. Sadness and despair, but life goes on. And then there is the third possibility." The doctor turned to face the two of them, and spoke very slowly. "Vassily finds the doctor and his wife Jeanne. She sees her chance to escape from a life of grim poverty to one of ease and wealth. It is only natural that she leave the Jew Feuerberg and go along with Vassily, who will take her to the fine castle with its park and servants and horses. That's your mission, is it not, Vassily? Prince Guninski must imagine that all those comforts would exert a powerful lure for Jeanne. So, my dears, I know Prince Guninski's mode of reasoning very well, even though I've seen him only once in my life. But is it not written: 'By their deeds shall you know them'?"

Once more there was an interval of total silence. Jeanne sat with her eyes fixed on the window. Vassily stared at the floor, and the doctor looked in turn at his wife and their guest.

Jeanne was the first to speak: "You've reasoned that out very well, Léon chéri," she said, smilingly. "But thinking and talking make people hungry. I'll bring us some refreshment." She stood up.

"Can I help you?" the doctor asked.

"Stay. I have everything ready." She hastened from the room.

The two men remained sitting in constrained silence. The doctor stood up, glanced at Vassily, and proceeded to clear the table of its books and papers, which he transferred to the windowsill. "There," he murmured under his breath, "now we have room." Vassily nodded abstractedly, but said nothing. When Jeanne appeared carrying a large tray of sandwiches, a bottle and glasses, he stood up and helped her. The doctor filled their glasses, raised his to his wife and then to Vassily. "Health!" he said, and they drank the red cherry brandy at one draft.

"Ah, that's good," Vassily said, putting down his glass. The doctor filled all the glasses again and they nibbled their sandwiches. "These are still courtesy of your nachalnik," Jeanne explained.

"Yes," the doctor said, "my fee. Saposhnik's wife will die very soon."

"Is there no hope?" Vassily asked.

"None. I knew it, even without the X-rays. Still a young woman." He reached out for his glass. "Sometimes alcohol is very useful." He finished his glass, stood up and began pacing the small room. Jeanne sat with lowered eyelids, smiling faintly in an ironic and grief-stricken way.

The doctor sat down again. "Now that we have analyzed the Prince's motives," he said, "let us consider the nature and purpose of your mission, Vassily. It seems that you are to offer my wife aid and rescue in the name of Baron Candomir. Is that right?"

"That's right," Vassily said tersely, making a great effort to conceal his discomfort.

"This can mean nothing else than that you propose to take my wife out of reach of Soviet power to a place in which the Baron's money and influence can assure her a comfortable life. Jeanne, chérie, this is a great opportunity, and Vassily seems to be the right man to reduce the dangers of crossing the border to a minimum. You would accompany my wife, wouldn't you?"

"My task is to see to your wife's safety, Dr. Feuerberg," Vassily said. "But before you pursue your questioning any further, I want to make something clear. What applies to your wife applies to you. Precisely. I would be in charge of both of you. Baron Candomir was misinformed. He had no notion of the changed situation. You will be highly welcome to him; he will receive you with the utmost friendliness. This is not an offhand promise; I guarantee it." A smile flickered across Vassily's face. "Absolutely."

"A most magnanimous offer, Vassily."

"Let him finish, Léon," Jeanne reproved her husband.

"There's one more point I want to make," Vassily said. "I understand your scruples, doctor. You wouldn't want to be obligated to Radu Candomir. You would feel in a false position. But you must see the situation as it is. Although Candomir was once deeply in love with your wife, and suffered greatly when she refused him, he is now a happily married man, with two children of his own. You can be sure that Radu Candomir is doing all this out of respect for the dreams of his youth."

"Then he is a romantic, and you are the oddest stablemaster on the face of the earth."

The doctor's face was once more a network of folds and wrinkles. Vassily shared the man's suffering, and the suffering of his wife with her husband.

"Léon, chéri," Jeanne said after a long minute of mute struggle. "We are staying—of course."

The doctor's face suddenly smoothed. "Thank you, my darling." He turned to Vassily. "You have heard, my friend. We're staying here." He sighed with relief.

"Léon is a Communist," Jeanne explained. "In spite of everything."

"In spite of everything," the doctor repeated. "Jeanne means, you see, that by now we should be thoroughly disillusioned. After what we see all around us." He made a sweeping gesture. "She doesn't understand it."

"Yes," Jeanne said smilingly, "he will not be swayed by any arguments."

"And yet," Vassily said with a kindred smile, "the doctor sees the faults of this system only too well, and finds them just as painful as—"

"As?" The dctor poked a forefinger in the direction of Vassily's chest. Then, shaking his head, he withdrew it. "Of course," he went on, and Vassily knew that he had intended to say something else, "of course there are abuses everywhere, abuses which arise from all this unnecessary childish formalism. But where is there an army without drill, discipline without punishment? And how they multiply mistakes! Let them—mistakes are educational. We have to suffer from mistakes; otherwise we'd repeat them forever."

"Ah yes," Vassily said, "you're a Bolshevik, doctor. And I thought you were a bourgeois who had tentatively and tremblingly reconciled himself to a hated situation. Do you remember your first —hm—critical remarks?"

"I spoke to you as if you shared my viewpoint. We are entitled to criticize, even urged to do so."

"Commanded to do so. Criticism and self-criticism. Or does self-criticism come first? Those words are part of the terminology and are the same kind of empty slogans as so many of the others. Who really dares to criticize?"

"Those who do dare. There is something about you that inspires trust. That partly explains why I spoke to you as I did. I don't regret having misjudged you; I only regret your being different from the man I took you for."

"And what do you take me for now?" Vassily asked. Asked too quickly, and secretly chided himself.

"For a faithful servant of his master—an antiquated phenomenon."

"Antiquated! How you pin your labels on everything! What do you know about it? Have you ever been either a master or a servant?

If you only knew how much fine humanity there can be in the relationship between master and servant!" Jeanne spoke more loudly than was her wont.

The doctor seemed to overlook her protest. "I am one of those who are fighting against a world of masters and servants. There must be no masters; then there will also be no servants." But he added placatingly, "Forgive me, Jeanne."

"There will always be masters and servants," Vassily said quietly, "though they may be called something else in the new terminology. That is normal—as is faithfulness, doctor. If that should be wiped out, how frightful it would be. Because you said before: a faithful servant of his master."

"I honor faithfulness and loyalty between individuals, but only so long as it doesn't endanger a man's loyalty to the cause. If faithfulness to another human being begins to become ballast, it must be thrown overboard."

His face was hard in its tension, and his eyes, too, took on a harsh gleam. Jeanne's expression was blankly horrified. Her hands were clenched in her lap, and her eyes were lowered. Vassily sat still, feeling confusion and deep sympathy.

"Of course that's only theory, doctor," he said, forcing a smile of incredulity.

"No," Jeanne said tonelessly, with a gentle, terribly mournful shake of her head.

"Jeanne knows that," the doctor said. "I've made my position perfectly clear to her—although in the relationship between man and wife the lines cannot be so clearly drawn. Our beliefs must be unshakable, but we can make concessions. I'm a Marxist, you know, and Marx recommends concessions. I am now busy relearning to be a Bolshevik. A dogma here and there must be dropped, it is true, but the essence of the idea remains—and the essence is what counts."

"I should think so," Vassily said thoughtfully. "But how much of that essence will remain? And will it ever be recognizable again— what with all these pacts and alliances . . . ?"

"Aha!" The doctor's exclamation was almost triumphant, as though he had only been waiting for this. "So that's it. The Pact! You talk just like the others, Vassily, who always bring that up whenever they want to take a poke at the Bolsheviki." The doctor stood up and posted himself in the middle of the room, shaking his finger. "Do you see, out there"—he gestured toward the window— "there is fire, and here"—he swung his arm toward the door—"is water. And there"—he pointed with one foot to a crack in the floor —"is a wall. Not of iron, not a thick wall, a thin partition of wood or better still of paper. Can it divide fire and water, or keep water from the fire? Either the fire consumes the wall or the water will wash it away. Then the fire and water will mix. If the water is stronger, it will put out the fire; otherwise the fire will evaporate the water and will rage on, finding new fuel, flaring higher and higher. But the evaporated water will also rise, gather into clouds, discharge in tremendous cloudbursts, and with its torrents beat down upon the fire until at last the blaze is extinguished. The others—the Nazis, the Fascists, the reactionaries—are the fire, and we—the Bolsheviki, the whole Russian people, all those who believe in progress, in the right to live—are the water. And, Vassily, that thin partition wall is the Pact. It is an emergency measure, just sufficient to keep the water away from the fire for a few minutes, from the stupid fire that does not know of the fresh, healthy, genuine streams of water that are flowing together to form a mighty torrent, while the fire itself is being artificially fed. Yes, Vassily, that's how it is." The doctor went over to his chair and sat down again.

"Ah yes, doctor—a figure of speech, and I shall try to see it the way you do, for whatever you may think of me, I too am fighting against the fire to the last."

"Drop of water," the doctor said, laughing. "Let us drink to that, Comrade Koniukh!"

"Yes, let's, Comrade Doctor." This time Vassily poured the drinks.

"Bring us your piano substitute and sing something for us," the doctor asked his wife. Jeanne went out and returned with a guitar. They toasted one another. Jeanne touched the strings and sang *"Pit budim*—Let us drink"—an old Russian song about singing and reveling in gay company to the last breath.

"I'll go along," Antek said next morning while Vassily was hitching up. "The sashes for the coldframes should have been ready long ago. It's high time we finished that project."

"Fine," Vassily said. "We're leaving right away. Here's Mira now." He climbed up on the box. Antek waited until Mira had taken her place and then sat down beside her.

"Everything finished on time," he reported with pride. "Field work one hundred and thirty per cent complete. Vegetables, three hundred per cent."

"Three hundred? What does that mean?"

"It's just a way of reckoning," Mira explained. "Instead of the prescribed forty, Antek has set out one hundred and twenty beds of early vegetables. You can't imagine the struggle I had to get the sash and the seed."

"You are a regular stakhanovets." Vassily turned his head swiftly so that Antek would not observe his smile.

"Who cares what I am? Those vegetables will be a help. You know how vegetables sell when they come in early!"

"Yes, and there's no rule against selling them at the bazaar," Mira said. "Go to it, Antek; everybody will help with the work."

Antek got out at the center of the city. "When will you be driving back, Vassily?"

"Around three, I think. Where do you want to wait for me?"

"If I don't get a ride sooner, I'll be at my house. Drop by and look for me there."

When they were alone and riding through quieter streets, Vassily turned smilingly to Mira. "How do you feel, Mira?" he asked.

"Better, Vassily. Much easier in my mind."

"Because you're rid of Mermelstein?"

"Oh, him! Who knows what we'll get in his place? We may go along by ourselves for a while, but then? Saposhnik tells me it's against regulations for the bookkeeper to be also the cashier. That may become embarrassing. Luckily the nachalniki passed over that matter yesterday. But we'll have to hire a cashier, and there's no telling whether he'll understand, or whether he'll want to cooperate. And there'll be another director before too long—this time not a 'native,' so Saposhnik says."

"For a while we'll swing it, and then—"

"Then, Vassily?"

"I've not forgotten, Mira. I'm beginning to look around."

"I thought you'd already begun. Because you came home so late yesterday."

"I've already begun, Mira—you're right," he said quietly, as though he hadn't heard the note of bitterness in her remark. No doubt she had hoped to spend some time with him, and he had ridden off without a word and returned to the farm very late. Who knows how long she may have waited for me, he thought—and felt her waiting as a burden.

At the entrance to the Electrostantsia office he was able to smile again. "Just a little while longer, Mira—a very short time. I'm exploring every avenue. It will work out; it's as good as certain."

After leaving Mira at the bank, he stopped opposite a row of bookstalls. Old men and women were trying to sell books, but there were no buyers. A small man with a white goatee greeted him in Polish, then, when he saw him hunting among the German books, asked him if there was anything special he was looking for.

"I've already found it." It was a school edition of Schiller's *Wilhelm Tell.* "How much?" Vassily asked.

"Take a few more. Here, Bert Brecht, Ilya Ehrenburg, Alexei Tolstoi, Leonid Leonov, Maiakovsky—we have everything." But Vassily declined all this literature. "Here, take this," the old man said at last, reaching into a compartment on the side of the stall, "so I'll make a few kopecks. Historical miniatures, very pretty, interesting, piquant, from the old days—the two books together, ten rubles." Vassily took the book because the old man was so persistent.

He went and sat down in the back of the buggy, took out the *Wilhelm Tell,* and began to read. Anyone watching would have assumed that he was studying the book and taking notes, for he kept a sheet of paper alongside the book and a pencil in hand. But instead of transferring his notes from the book to the paper, he was doing the opposite. As he read the paper, he underlined certain passages in the book.

Mira arrived. She had several other errands in town and arranged to meet Vassily and Antek in two or three hours at Panya Jadwiga's. The two men drove straight there. The buggy was put under the shed roof, and Vassily surreptitiously pocketed his *Wilhelm Tell.* He also produced the other book and gave it to Antek as a present. Antek didn't even thank him or glance at the book, although he was ordinarily irresistibly attracted to anything in print.

"I'll be walking back into town," Vassily said.

"Come into the house for a moment," Antek replied. "I need to talk to you. It's been all my nerves can stand to hold out this long."

"What's the matter?" Vassily asked. Panya Jadwiga opened the door and they went in.

"Listen closely now, Vassily, and don't play tough guy. I've just come from Rudnicki's girl. It's all fixed up; they're going to kill you. . . . Let me finish!" he shouted abruptly, as Vassily made a gesture of reassurance. "They had a job planned for yesterday. They wanted to clean out a warehouse full of chocolate, cigarettes and liquor. They had it all planned. Mermelstein was going to pay them a visit. They would have invited his driver in for a drink, given him some knockout drops, and taken the wagon. They would have made their haul, then come back and unloaded while Mermelstein was with Manya. Neither Mermelstein nor the driver would have known a thing."

"A nice piece of work," Vassily said.

Antek reproved him with a savage look and went on. "Mermelstein didn't come, and so one of the fellows—his name is Josek and he's a dangerous boy—handles a knife better than you do horses—Josek biked out to the farm. Halfway there he met the car with the nachalniki. You remember, the driver was wearing a cap like a militiaman's. Josek recognized Mermelstein and reported to the others that he'd been arrested. So a council of war took place right away in Rudnicki's dump, with the new chief of the gang presiding. His name is Ossip—he's a Russian—and Josek's a baby compared to him. Rudnicki's woman says they're all scared stiff of him; he's bumped off half a dozen men already. They all obey him like they were a bunch of children, the men and women both. Now they've figured out that if you were responsible for Rudnicki's arrest, you must have squealed on Mermelstein too, and probably you know his old hangouts and will start poking your nose into their business. Ossip said you had to be eliminated because you're a stool pigeon and because you ruined their jobs. But apart from that, he'll kill for the sake of killing. There are people like that, believe me, Vassily."

"I know there are, Antek," Vassily said. "But why didn't you set the woman straight on what's really happened to Mermelstein?"

"Of course I thought of that, Vassily. But getting her to believe me is another matter. I promised I'd bring her Mermelstein's new address. It seems he boasted that he'd appear as a witness and get Rudnicki out."

"Mermelstein! What a string of troubles we've had on his account," Vassily said.

Antek shook his head furiously. "Is that all you have to say?" he snarled.

"What else should I say?" Vassily asked. "I promise you I'll watch out. Do you want me to run to the militia?"

"Militia? A fat lot of good they'd do, or the police either. Never since this city's been standing, not under the Austrians and not under the Poles either, has there been as much thieving, burglary and murder as there is now. Good Lord, have you been asleep? They're pulling jobs in broad daylight—and ask the militia how many thugs they've caught! No, Vassily, you can't count on any protection from the forces of law and order. I've got a pistol I can give you—I have it in Jiusefovka. I'll show you how to wear it so it doesn't show and yet is handy for when you need it. You'll keep it on you, won't you, Vassily? For my sake?"

"For my sake too, Antek," Vassily said. He gave Antek a rough pat on the shoulder. "All right, Antek, I'll watch my step. I'm going into town now and I'll be back soon. Meanwhile, you read a bit. So long." He gave Antek a military salute and hurried out.

Number 8 was a three-story tenement house. The façade and the stairwells were dirty and neglected, the walls gray and battered, the windowpanes cloudy, and the steps had not been swept or washed for months. They were littered with scraps of paper, burned matches, cigarette butts and the husks of sunflower and pumpkin seeds. The landings were rank with the smells of many kitchens and poorly functioning toilets.

Vassily stopped a boy of about sixteen. "I'm looking for someone in this building. This street used to be called Kilinskiego, didn't it?"

"Yes, this used to be Kilinskiego. I don't know everybody in the house any more, but if it's one of the old tenants and he's still here—" The boy smiled.

Vassily stepped closer to him and lowered his voice. "I'm looking for a man named Besselmann—Yossel. Do you know him, young man?"

"Oh, Yossel Besselmann?" The boy's head bent as if he were trying to remember. His eyes lingered on Vassily's boots, then slowly rose to his mustache. "Are you a 'native'?" he asked.

"Of course," Vassily said.

"Then why don't you speak Polish?"

"My Polish isn't very good. I'm Ruthenian."

The boy's face tightened. "I don't know anybody by the name of Yossel Besselmann," he said. He turned away and began mounting the stairs.

"*B'li pahad*—Don't be afraid, young man," Vassily called in Hebrew.

"*Eyn li pahad*—I am not afraid," the answer was returned. The boy turned around on the staircase and probed Vassily's face. "Why do you say the word without even knowing who you're talking to?" the boy asked sternly.

"Oh," Vassily replied, laughing, "I knew very well." He pointed to the notebook under the boy's arm. "There's your name; Arye Besselmann. So I'm fairly safe. If you don't know the password, no matter; if you do know it, fine and dandy."

"Right. One-to-nothing for you. You don't have to tell me anything more. I know who you are. Come on."

"I'm Vassily."

"That's what you call yourself. I've said I know who you are."

He stopped in front of a door on the second floor and unlocked it. The hallway into which they stepped was completely empty; that much could be discerned even in the almost total darkness. "Arye?" a woman's voice called.

"Yes, Mother. Is Father home yet?"

"He will be any moment." The mother spoke Yiddish with her son.

"We have a guest, Mother." The boy opened the door to the kitchen. The woman at the stove turned toward them. At a glance

Vassily saw her close resemblance to the boy.

"Guten Tag," he said in German.

"Guten Tag," the woman replied. In a low voice she asked her son, "Who is this?"

"Vassily," the boy replied. "Come into the parlor," he said.

The parlor was large and bright and sparsely furnished. Arye went into another room and returned with cigarettes, Egypski. He offered them to Vassily.

"Thank you," Vassily said, taking one. Arye held a light for him. "I suppose you don't smoke yet?"

"I probably never will. My father smokes enough for two and coughs for three—there, you can hear him." A key had turned in the lock, doors were opened and closed, but all the sounds were accompanied by a hacking cough.

Yossel Besselmann was a man of average height with a full beard. He tried to control his cough but didn't succeed, and tears welled from his eyes. He kept bringing a large handkerchief to his mouth and then to his eyes.

"Here's a man who wants to talk to you, Father."

"Sholom aleichem," Besselmann said, extending his hand.

"Aleichem sholom."

"He's not a Jew," Arye said.

"So what if he's not a Jew? Can't I give him sholom? You heard, he answers fine."

"Yes," Arye said, "he answers fine." He turned to Vassily. "Speak German with my father. He knows it and so do I."

"Yes," Besselmann said, "what Jew doesn't know German? Where do you come from and what brings you to me?" He removed the sportsman's cap he was wearing; underneath it he had on a small velvet cap which suited his face much better. With two swift movements he pulled forward his hair and twisted it into temple locks, and became a Jew, a Hasid. "The comrades don't like to see hair worn this way, but at home, you know, I'm the nachalnik."

"My father works as a watchmaker in an artel," Arye explained quickly.

"Who has sent you?" Besselmann asked gravely.

"Karl Rundberg of Cernauti."

"I know no Karl Rundberg, and Cernauti is very far nowadays."

"Then," Vassily said, "I'll go. If you don't know Rundberg—"

"Did I say I didn't know a Rundberg? It's Karl Rundberg I don't know."

Vassily shook his head in bafflement. Then his glance fell upon Arye's laughing face.

"You have to get used to my father. Why make it simple when

you can make it complicated? He only wants to know how well you know Rundberg, whether you know his Jewish name."

"His father—and his mother, when she was living—called him Chaim."

"That's what I mean. Chaim. Right. You can never be too careful in times like this."

"I understand," Vassily said. "But my time is limited."

"All along you've been very leisurely, friend Vassily, and now all of a sudden you're in a hurry. Chaim has asked three times whether you've come to see me yet."

"Asked. How could he?"

"He seems to be worried about you. He doesn't say anything about any Vassily, but I know now that he means you. He also asked in Snyatyn, asked—" He seemed to have forgotten the name.

"Birnberg?"

Besselmann sighed with relief, and his son laughed with gentle mockery.

"Yes," he said, twisting his temple locks, "he asked Birnberg. In fact, Birnberg came here to find out if anyone had come. And for him such a trip isn't a simple matter; he isn't kosher, you see."

"Did Rundberg indicate what he's uneasy about?"

"Does he have to say why? Isn't it enough he's worried? If Birnberg came all the way here, Chaim must have told him it was urgent. He wants to know whether you're still alive at all. Probably"— Besselmann looked sharply at him—"you're an important person to him. Chaim is waiting for news from you or about you."

"That's why I've come to you. I want to send Rundberg news. Is that possible?"

"Possible, impossible, why not possible? If news goes from there to here, why not from here to there?"

"We can get a message through, Vassily," Arye said incisively.

"He's made up his mind, the *huzpenik,* fresh boy. You deal with him; I talk no more."

Arye was not discomposed in the least. "A letter to Rundberg will reach him in three days. By tomorrow a week you'll have an answer," he said.

"Who takes care of it?" Vassily asked with pretended casualness.

Besselmann flashed a meaningful look to his son, a look of astonishment, question and command. But Arye ignored it. "Maybe you know him. His name is Motje Platzer, and he comes once or sometimes twice a week," he replied.

"Rundberg has mentioned him. But he certainly takes risks!"

"Not so many." Arye dismissed the matter. "He's covered on both sides. And he's earning big money. He smuggles people now.

Motje isn't cheap. A thousand dollars per head. Others do it cheaper but aren't so reliable. I know the route. If I want to cross, I won't need anyone; I'll go alone. From Hersch Birnberg's house I'd be in Romania in two hours."

"Then I don't understand why you two don't go," Vassily said, half jokingly.

"What kind of life awaits Jews in Romania?" Besselmann asked. "Here, bad as it is, we can keep under cover, and we aren't penalized just for being Jews. But there it gets worse every day. The Germans are tightening their hold and the evildoers are living it up."

"We wouldn't have to stay there," his son said softly.

"Aha!" Besselmann exclaimed. "From there to Eretz Yisroel, that's your plan!"

"And why shouldn't you go to Palestine?" Vassily asked in some surprise. "Rundberg's father wanted to emigrate there."

"He's been there for months, and Chaim's two children also," Arye said sorrowfully.

"Really?" Vassily asked. "I didn't know that."

"Yeshieh Rundberg is an old man. He's gone there to die. That is allowed, is prescribed even, but we will return to the homeland only when Meshiach comes. He hasn't come yet." Besselmann spoke gravely.

"I don't want to wait till he comes," Arye said darkly.

"Because you with your fifteen years don't believe, you're an apostate—what am I saying?—you're a huzpenik, and a childish one at that."

"Apostate—bah, I'm a Komsomolets, a member of the Young Communists. I'm given no choice. And how did you feel, Father, when Olga Gregorevna—that's our teacher, Vassily—stood up at the parents' meeting and announced, 'The teaching in our school is based on absolute atheism. We cannot tell the parents what to believe, but we must warn them against working against the school. If they do, they will have only themselves to blame for the consequences'? Did you enjoy hearing that, Father? You know what they mean by consequences."

"Let me alone with your foolishness. What does your Olga Gregorevna know about it? Others have rebelled against God before her, and we Jews have been threatened with worse things."

"Enough of us have died as helpless victims. If we're going to die, let's do it for a reason, for our own country," Arye said sternly.

"The time is not yet, not yet!"

"It's never been closer than now, Father! Now, today, tomorrow —soon."

"I'm not keeping you—go," Besselmann said angrily.

"You know perfectly well what would happen if I went without you. If I didn't come to school for two days, they'd look for me at home, and if they didn't find me they'd take you and Mother."

"As God wills," Besselmann said.

"I don't quite follow," said Vassily, who had been listening in silence to the quarrel. "What do you mean, if they don't find you they'll take your parents? Why should they?"

"You don't know everything, friend Vassily. What do you think happened to Birnberg? He was on the list; he's the richest man in town. So he went into hiding. Then they took his oldest son, and he was the very one who never could get along with his father, because his father was a capitalist—between you and me a *protzentnik,* a usurer—and the son was a socialist. But what did that matter? Blood is thicker than water and so the son was deported, and the father, who has more thousands than hairs on his head, stayed on. He works, has a spravka and a good passport. That's the way they are. The quota has to be filled."

"That's how it is," the elder Besselmann agreed. "They don't care so much whether they take the right one. I know thousands of cases. And things can be arranged with them, if you have the connections."

"In a lot of things," Arye said slowly, "they're no different from the Poles."

"Shush!" Besselmann tapped the table commandingly with an angry look at his son.

Arye flared up. "Don't be so timid, Father. Vassily is on our side. Chaim sends him and worries about him like one of our own! Why shouldn't I say it?" He turned to Vassily. "There are some of them who are just as much anti-Semites as the Poles," he said.

"But they don't show it," Vassily said.

"Oho! They get around it with dialectics, but in their hearts— they'd drown us all in a teaspoon of water if they could. The teachers too. You can sense it."

"Oh well," Besselmann senior said, twisting his temple locks, "in their hearts. Where do you think they've disappeared to, all those thousands and tens of thousands of Jew killers, the Black Hundreds and the Petliurozets? Of course they're still around, even if they pretend they never existed. But some of them are the sons and grandsons of *rabbanim* and *gaonim,* of Jewish teachers and scholars who knew nothing but the Torah. That can't be put off like a suit of clothes—oh no! And if they're atheists a hundred times over, those big nachalniki, they stay Jews, they can't help it; the blood lives and cries out and defends itself in them. But—"

He was interrupted. His wife appeared in the doorway and said,

"Come eat. You both have to be back soon."

"Would you do us the honor to eat with us?" Besselmann said to Vassily. "Good things. Thank God, there's always a chicken for the pot."

"Thank you, but I've already eaten. I'd like to write my letter now, and for that I need an old arithmetic notebook with two or three blank pages at the end. Do you have one, Arye?"

Arye gave him a notebook. "I'll be done by the time you've eaten," Vassily said. "A pleasant dinner to you."

Left alone, he took the copy of *Wilhelm Tell* from his pocket and began setting up arithmetic problems, following the words and sentences he had previously underlined; he took pains to make his figures look like Arye's in the other pages of the notebook. When he was finished, he tore off the cover of the notebook, wrote the address in code, and by the time father and son had knocked and re-entered the room, the *Tell* was back in his pocket and he himself was sitting quietly smoking. "Here, give this to Motje Platzer. If he's caught with it, he can say it's—hm—toilet paper. And on the other side there's no danger."

"Don't worry about a thing; in a week you'll have an answer," Besselmann said.

"I hope so."

"And if you want anything," Arye said, "just send someone to ask for me at School Number Twelve." He went out of the room and returned with a tin of a hundred Egypski. "Permit me, friend Vassily. The Russian cigarettes aren't so good."

"Thank you, I'm glad to have these. Good-bye, Arye." He shook hands with the boy and his father, and left.

Yossel Besselmann got ready for work. He brushed the temple locks behind his ears. His son tucked his school books under his arm, and together they descended the stairs. Before they stepped outside, they kissed. On the sidewalk, Arye paused for a moment. "Father," he said, "have you considered who this Vassily is?"

"Who should he be? Vassily, Chaim's man. What's to consider?"

"Vassily isn't just Vassily, Father. I know who he is: the Uden." He turned and strode rapidly away.

"Him?" Yossel Besselmann wanted to call his son back, but time was short; he had a long way to go to his place of work. He set out, his walk somewhat pigeon-toed, swaying the upper part of his body slightly, his back bent and head lowered. His bearded chin almost touched his chest. There was an odd contrast between his appearance and his short pea jacket, bright sports shirt and above all the brown, checked English sportsman's cap.

* * *

The sash was delivered in the afternoon. Antek could not contain his delight; he happily nudged Vassily, who helped to unload the frames. "One hundred and twenty cold frames, my friend—a record. We'll show them all!" He had other reasons for his cheerfulness, and soon found a chance to explain to Vassily. He had gone to meet Josek that morning and brought him convincing proof that Mermelstein had not been arrested but had moved on to another and much better job. Moreover, Antek had intimated, he would now have not only horse-drawn wagons, but trucks and automobiles at his disposal. Josek had "bought" it—all the more since he himself had seen Mermelstein in a car—and had run off to report to the chief of the band. "I think that's straightened out, but safety first; keep the rod with you for a while. Who knows whether this fellow Ossip will believe Josek? When a thug like that gets something into his head, it's hard to get it out again. Anyhow, I feel easier."

As Vassily was undressing that night, the bright yellow paperback edition of *Wilhelm Tell* fell to the floor. He picked the book up and for a while held it indecisively in his hand. His first thought was to destroy it, but then it occurred to him that he might still need it, and he decided to keep it; Rundberg would undoubtedly use it for the key to the code in his return letter. Therefore he put it among the books and pamphlets which lay on his table—shaking his head, even as he did so, over his own exaggerated caution. Reading was not prohibited, and the book would arouse no suspicions if found among his belongings. I'm no longer myself, he thought. They've gotten me down, made me the way they want me, obedient, cringing, super-careful.

Antek looked up from the *Historical Miniatures,* which he had been reading with absorption. "What things there are in here!" he exclaimed. "You have to read this book!"

Vassily took the book from him and glanced through it. "You like it?"

"Those old kings and emperors and their wives—the way they acted! Much worse than ordinary people. And when I read about Catherine and Potemkin—what a deal!"

"Potemkin was not only a prominent statesman but a capable one, as well as a good general and an effective colonizer."

"A fine colonizer! That's described here too. He put up stage sets and drove the Empress past them in a sleigh, pointing out everything from a distance and telling her they were all fine farms—what's the phrase in the book?—flourishing villages. Potemkin villages!"

"I imagine he did that famous trick not as a colonizer but as a statesman, the minister to a capricious ruler who was his mistress besides. She probably thought that all she had to do to establish colonies was to give the order. Potemkin villages existed hundreds of years before Potemkin. They still exist and will as long as anyone in power tries to force the people to create something which is beyond their capabilities."

"If you look at it that way, practically everything is a Potemkin village."

"If you didn't have your autocratic Catherines demanding the impossible, so that others have to pretend they've done it, simply out of fear, you wouldn't have these fakes."

"Simply out of fear," Antek repeated thoughtfully. "Yes, everything's a Potemkin village. Certainly this farm of ours is. If they ever find out how we keep the whole thing going, and if they look closely to see who's in charge, we'll be on our way to Siberia."

"As long as they don't want to look closely because it suits their books, there's no danger. But any day the wind can change and blow down the stage sets."

"Potemkin village," Antek mused. "But the devil take them. Why should I worry my head about that? Though when I hear how the other farms are getting nowhere and producing practically nothing, I wonder about our being so efficient. They must envy and hate us and want to put a spoke in our wheel."

"Right you are, Antek. But I'd better hit the sack now. Tomorrow's butter day. When I get back from town, I'll help you with the sashes. Good night."

"One moment, Vassily, I have something for you." Antek checked to make sure that the curtains were drawn and the door locked. Then he took a pistol from his pocket. "Here," he said. "A little one, isn't it? Fits in the palm of your hand. Take it, whether you think you need it or not. Something may still come up."

Vassily went into the garden, where a frenzy of activity reigned. Everyone who had managed somehow to take time off from his own work—the butchers, the smith, the harness maker, even the two oldest men on the farm, Kornhaber and Meerblum—were helping to set the sash. Vassily pitched in, too. By noon the greater part of the work was done, and everyone trooped to the canteen. Antek, in high spirits, ordered a round of vodka at his expense.

"As though we'd been helping you in your own garden," Vassily teased him.

"What's the difference? The main thing is, we're getting it done.

By tonight it will be all finished. That's efficiency for you! Cheers, Vassily!"

"Your health, Antek!"

By five o'clock the job was in fact finished. Vassily had to make a quick trip to town, and Tadek asked to go with him to visit his mother. Antek lingered by the cold frames with Freddy, explaining to him what had been done and what this meant for the future of their farm. Freddy listened politely, but when he began to feel hungry he slipped away. Antek, unable to tear himself away from the sight of the completed beds for early vegetables, remained alone in the garden.

Freddy was just going into his own cottage to wash up when he heard a man's voice call out, "Hey, grazhdanin!" A cyclist in a quilted jacket, and sporting a military cap, jumped down in front of the cottage. Freddy had understood the call, but he had no idea what the man was saying to him. Nor could he guess what the cyclist meant when he pointed to Antek, who was slowly and wearily tramping toward his house on the other side of the street. Freddy nodded to the stranger and pronounced his all-purpose Russian word: "Konechno."

The man jumped into the saddle of his bicycle, and Freddy went into the house. He had just taken off his shoes when two reports in quick succession startled him. "Funny the way the tractor backfires," he muttered to himself. "Doesn't sound at all like a car."

Kreisel, the butcher, who was cleaning up in the slaughterhouse, also heard the noise and also connected it with the tractor. Then it occurred to him that the reports had not been followed by the usual clatter, and he went outside to look. He saw no sign of the tractor and was about to return to his house when he caught sight of Antek lying in the roadside ditch across the street, face to the ground. He rushed to help him up, and saw to his horror that he was handling a corpse.

Volodia, the tractor man, was the only one who kept his head. He must have had experience with such affairs; he knew how to act. Antek, he determined, had been killed by two shots in the back. Mira, who was called to the scene, quickly assumed control of things, implementing all Volodia's orders. When Freddy told her of his meeting with the cyclist, she guessed the connection and cautioned him to say nothing to the militiamen. If they questioned Freddy, there were sure to be complications. It was no longer possible to help Antek, even if the murderer should be found. And the risks of involving Freddy, simpleminded as he was, were far too great. She would tell Vassily and no one else.

Nearly two hours passed before the militiamen, accompanied by

Saposhnik, Lavrenenko and Feingold, arrived in their truck. A few minutes afterwards Vassily drove up, his horses dripping with sweat. As he leaped down from the wagon, the farm workers moved aside, and he strode between a lane of silent figures to the place where his dead friend still lay with his face pressed against the ground in the wet mud of the ditch. Vassily knelt down beside him and stared at the two patches of blood on Antek's jacket. Ignoring the policemen in uniform and mufti, the nachalniki, and all the others who stood there, he took his final leave of his friend. At last Feingold stepped over to him and helped him up. "Come, Vassily Vassilevich, the comrades of the militia must take over." He led Vassily away from the group. "You were his friend, weren't you? A good worker—it's a great pity."

Vassily only nodded. He took the cigarette that Feingold offered him. While he stood beside Feingold, smoking silently, the body was lifted onto Vassily's wagon. Kreisel followed slowly along behind, with two of the investigators. "We must locate those bullets, you understand, Vassily? Who can have killed him—in broad daylight?"

"He had no enemies," Vassily said.

Mira had brought the payroll to the canteen, where the workers were gathered. Their names were called out, and they were divided into as many groups as there were militiamen present. Vassily explained the reason for Tadek's absence. The questions that were put to all were the same, and so were the answers. Antoni Gorecki had been a good, extremely industrious worker, had almost always been good-natured and given to jokes. He had treated women politely; as far as anyone knew, he had not been particularly close to any of them. No one could conceive of any motive for his murder.

Vassily was questioned by the head of the investigating commission, the same nachalnik who had arrested Rudnicki. Lavrenenko and Saposhnik sat at the table with him; Feingold stood leaning against the wall, smoking. Vassily's first impulse had been to tell them what Antek had been afraid of. But then he remembered Antek's own admonition. "Militia?" Antek had said only yesterday. "A fat lot of good they'd do. Ask the militia how many thugs they've caught. If you don't protect yourself, nobody will help you." Antek had looked out for him and been killed himself. If the militia drove the cart, who could say where they would stop? No, he would have to handle it himself!

"Take a seat," the nachalnik said. "You lived with Antoni Antonich Gorecki?"

"Yes."

"For how long?"

"Ever since we've been working together. We used to be with the Meat Trust. He and Comrade Tadeus Zembrinski and I shared lodgings."

The nachalnik began taking notes. "What kind of person was Gorecki?"

"He was an excellent worker and liked his work. The fruit trees were pruned at the right time, and instead of forty hotbeds and cold frames he set out one hundred and twenty. He'd just finished that today."

"One hundred and twenty beds!" The nachalnik was astonished. He looked at Saposhnik and Lavrenenko, who nodded confirmation. "Three times the quota!" he exclaimed. "What a loss!"

He removed his cap and scratched the back of his head. "Comrade Khomniuk," he said, "you are a serious and capable man. Listen closely and give me a straight answer. What kind of man was Gorecki—I mean, what do you know about his past? What was he—politically?"

"I can only tell you what he told me," Vassily said slowly. "He had a very unhappy boyhood. His mother died, his father was brutal and negligent. He was a grown man before he began to learn anything. As for politics, ever since he learned to think he was against the burshui, against their officials and the priests. He supported the persecuted, contributed to revolutionary causes, and gave shelter to revolutionaries who were being pursued by the police. He fed them and helped them escape. Just today he treated everyone to a round of drinks because he was so happy that the project was done ahead of time."

For a while there was a silence. Vassily and the others stared at the floor. At last the nachalnik said to Feingold, "Now, do you know where the rat is buried, Arkady Samuelovich?"

"I have a good idea," Feingold replied. He went out with the nachalnik. Lavrenenko and Saposhnik followed them, and Vassily brought up the rear.

The militiamen in the mess hall were almost finished with their interrogation when the doctor came in. He placed two bullets in front of the nachalnik. The nachalnik picked them up. "Nine millimeters," he said to the others, "not our caliber. I knew it." He stepped close to Feingold. "The same gang," Vassily heard him say.

Saposhnik called Mira and Vassily over. "We've decided that Gorecki will be buried here on the farm—preferably in the garden. Look for a suitable spot, Comrade Khomniuk. The funeral will be at five tomorrow afternoon. We'll need all the wagons at Plant I to bring the workers over. Mira Isakovna, will you draw up a list of Gorecki's personal belongings and have his things placed in the storeroom. Does he have relatives?"

"No," Vassily said. "He has no one, aside from Zembrinski and Zembrinski's mother; he lived with them for seventeen years."

At ten o'clock the car with the militiamen and the nachalniki left. The workers stayed in the canteen. Some of them lined up for food, but they ate without appetite. Vassily sat in a corner with Mira and Wagner. None of them talked.

Baczynski came over to the table. "If you'll give me a few boards, I'll make the coffin tonight," he said to Wagner.

Wagner stood up at once. "You must drive out to see Tadek very early tomorrow morning," Vassily said to him. "I haven't the heart to tell him."

"I'll go." He left with Baczynski.

When they were alone, Mira said, "Don't feel so unhappy, Vassily. And don't stay by yourself in that house tonight; come to us. There's something I must tell you about." He looked questioningly at her. "Later."

Volodia came over to their table and sat down. "They seem to suspect something definite, did you notice that, Vassia?" he said. Vassily only nodded. He was not in a mood to talk. But Volodia had something on his mind. "Vassia," he began, "I'm through here; I'll be going back to the tractor station tomorrow. There's something I'd like to ask you. Look at the state of my shoes. . . . If I could have the gardener's boots—he doesn't need them any more—and I'd be glad to pay for them out of my overtime here. You could arrange it, you and the bookkeeper. It isn't against the law—there's still a lot of wear left in those." He did not see the despair, the horror, on Vassily's face. When Vassily did not answer, he turned to Mira.

"Take the boots, comrade, on my responsibility," she said. And Volodia left in a happy frame of mind.

"Come, Vassily," Mira said in a low, insistent voice. She looked around. Freddy was no longer there; he had gone home. When they reached the house, they found him fast asleep.

When Mira told Vassily about Freddy's encounter, he became intensely agitated. All the pieces of the puzzle were dropping into place. He knew who Antek's murderer was. The bicyclist in uniform must have been Ossip.

Mira brought in sandwiches and a pitcher of milk. They ate, then smoked, and Mira told Vassily about her life. Much about her had perplexed him hitherto. Now he understood why she did not fit into the pattern of the Linkhand women—some of whom he knew personally—and how she had become a member of the family. She spoke in her usual dry manner; she did not embellish and she did not boast of her successes or her riches. "Have confidence in me,

Vassily," she concluded. "I'm a good judge of people. You could go far. You're capable, intelligent and energetic. You would learn in weeks what takes others months. And once we're outside—I have the means to give you a proper start."

Vassily made no comment. What could he have said? He did not want to lie to her, and as for the truth . . . why should he burden her with it? Her own cares and her own fear were heavy enough for her to bear. No, he would remain Vassily. As long as they were here, he was committed to that role, and once Mira Linkhand was outside, would they ever meet again?

Mira had set up a bed for herself in the kitchen; Vassily was to sleep in her bed. It was long after midnight when he lay down. Later, Mira came in; she was in her nightgown. She closed the door, slid the bolt, switched out the light and slipped into his bed.

When Vassily stepped outside at four o'clock in the morning, a cold, driving rain struck his face. He set to work at once in the stable. First of all he watered and fed the two brown mares that Wagner would use for driving to town for Tadek. Undoubtedly Panya Jadwiga would also come back with them.

Wagner entered the stable a few minutes later. "Break the news as gently as possible to Tadek," Vassily said to him after the mares were hitched up. "You know how he feels about Antek."

The other drivers came in, watered, fed and curried the horses, cleaned the stalls, then scurried through the rain to the canteen. Vassily went into Golodnyi's stall. After he had tended the horse, he looked over the partition to make sure the stable was empty. Then he dislodged two bricks from the wall beneath the manger, reached into the hole and took out the pistol. It and the cartridges were wrapped in a thick cloth, and although the cloth was still dry, he wrapped a second around it and returned the package to its hiding place. "Stay dry. I'm going to need you," he murmured.

The drivers returned from the canteen. They were not as boisterous as usual, but inevitably there was a good deal of calling and shouting until the horses were harnessed.

"All ready?" Vassily asked. "Come here for a moment. You'll drive to Plant I and wait there. The workers are coming to the funeral. Don't take more than six people. Remember that the horses will have to make the trip twice today and be in condition to work tomorrow. Ivan, see to it that order is kept. Don't strain the horses. Trot and walk! Mikhailo, you drive in the lead and set the pace. When you get back here, unhitch but leave the harness on the horses. When the time comes to drive the workers home, take them no farther than the tram station. Don't let anyone give you orders. If anyone tries to, demand them in writing. You know how to handle that, Ivan—you say it's because of the bookkeeping. Stefan, you take the meat for the head office and Plant I, and you, Gregor, for Plant II. That's all."

"What a tough customer that Vassily is," Mikhailo said to Ivan as they were hitching up. "Antek was his best friend, and there he stands, on the job, giving orders—"

"You don't understand that," Ivan replied; he was ten years older than Mikhailo. He drew the reins of the shaft horse through the rings. "My father always used to say, the harder the shell the softer the kernel. I saw Vassily yesterday and—" He changed the subject abruptly. "This rain has come just in time. The planting is done—let it rain."

The wagons rolled out of the yard. Vassily stood at the stable door, gazing into the rain. He wanted to smoke and had no cigarettes. Perhaps Mira was up already and he could get some from her.

She opened the door before he knocked, as though she had been waiting for him. "You left without breakfast," she said.

Freddy thrust his head in at the door. He was still in his pajamas. "Hello, Vassily," he called in the best of spirits.

"Good morning. Have you any cigarettes?"

"Plenty." He ran back into his room and brought a handful. "So you'll have some for later," he said, laughing.

"Thanks. Get ready, Freddy. Tadek will be along soon, and it will help if you're waiting for him."

"I'm dressing now—Tadek—konechno."

"You musn't say 'konechno' all the time, Freddy," Vassily said darkly. Mira plucked at his sleeve. "All right, all right," he murmured unwillingly.

She withdrew her hand. "You'd best have something warm to drink now," she said quietly, and led the way into the kitchen. "There's no sense. He doesn't understand you, and you only make yourself unhappy for nothing."

"You're right, Mira. But I must try to find out something. I must," he said tormentedly.

"I hope you can." She turned toward the stove. Both of them were silent until Freddy entered the kitchen.

"Freddy," Vassily said, "after you've had breakfast, go to my house and wait until Tadek comes. And, Freddy, it's better not to tell him about the man on the bicycle, understand?"

"Not tell Tadek. Konechno."

Vassily twitched. "Don't say 'konechno, ' Freddy," he said nervously.

"But it's Russian; Tadek taught it to me. The two of us always say it." Freddy's voice was already tearful; ever since his accident he had wept easily.

"I don't mean to scold you, Freddy." Vassily put a hand soothingly on his shoulder. "But 'konechno' doesn't fit all occasions. What did the man on the bicycle ask you?"

"I don't know."

"What did you think he was asking you?"

"Nothing." Freddy beamed.

"Now, listen carefully, Freddy. Maybe he said something that sounded like An-ton?" Vassily pronounced the name as a Russian would. "An-ton, Freddy?" he repeated.

Freddy reflected. "I'm sure not, Vassily. No, I'm sure he didn't say that, but—" He shook his head in perplexity.

"Well, did it sound anything like kon-iukh, Freddy? Kon-iukh?"

"How do you know that, Vassily? Kon—wait a minute, wait!" His babyish mouth pursed under his small beard. "Koniukh, that's it. I could swear he said that." He stood up. "Give me your key now—I'll go and wait for Tadek."

Vassily let him go. There was nothing more to be got out of him.

Mira's face was frozen in horror. "You think it was you he wanted to kill, Vassily?"

"Not really. I was just asking, because I can't figure it out."

Her features relaxed. "You mustn't pay attention to anything Freddy says. That's the way he is."

Vassily left the house with Mira. "I have to choose the place for Antek's grave," he said to her. He avoided the path that led by the cold frames. At the far end of the garden, where a dense hedge of lilac bushes divided it from the open fields, stood an ancient, high, wild pear tree with unusually wide-spreading branches. It was still bare and dripping with rain. The tree would bloom soon; here under the tree where the pear blossoms would fall upon the grave, here he would lie. Antek, his friend Antek. "I don't want you murdered, Vassily." And he had been killed instead. . . . The murderer was after me and killed Antek. . . .

He was back on the road in time to meet Wagner's buggy coming from town. Panya Jadwiga and Tadek sat in the back. The big, heavy man huddled against his mother like a child, and she had both arms around him.

Vassily went up to the buggy and took hold of the dangling hand, the wide, hairy, stubby-fingered paw of a huge animal. He stroked it. "Don't cry, Tadek, don't cry. . . . Antek—" He could not go on; he swallowed and sobbed, and Tadek raised his head and looked at him and said, "Vassily, brother. . . ." Then his head dropped back on his mother's shoulder. Vassily went forward to where Wagner was sitting with a dismal face and reddened eyes, rain-soaked and shivering, nervously toying with the reins. "Drive to my house, Wagner," he said, "and tell Freddy to take care of Tadek."

By early afternoon the walls of the Culture Home and the dining hall were draped with black-and-red cloth. Only the portraits of the revolutionary heroes and the platform with its lectern were undecorated. The black coffin stood on a crude stand draped in black and red. Saposhnik arrived long before the others, approved the funeral decorations, and ordered that special streamers should be hung around the portrait of Stalin. He wanted as many chairs as possible to be placed on the platform; a great many officials would be attending the funeral. Vassily had found time to wash and shave; he was wearing a clean shirt and trousers. Soon the wagons and buggies began driving up in quick succession to the Culture Home.

Just as the Red Army artillerymen from the nearby barracks marched up, led by their band playing "Esli zavtra voĭna"—if war comes tomorrow—a large sedan arrived. Tarashchenko, Feingold, the small gray-haired man who served as interpreter, and another man got out of it. This stranger seemed greatly impressed by the presence of the soldiers. He turned to Saposhnik, Lavrenenko and Maximenko, who had come forward to meet the group, and asked a question. Apparently the answer was not satisfactory, for Saposhnik hurried to call Vassily over. "Why are the soldiers here?" he asked.

"Because they are our neighbors," Vassily replied. "We're on good terms with them. They knew Antek and want to pay their last respects to him."

"Fine, fine," said the stranger. He had a dark, weather-beaten face, small, piercing black eyes, and unusually thick, coal-black brows which gave him an expression of unbending sternness. He scrutinized Vassily sharply, then turned toward the Red Army men, who were lined up in two rows, and raised his hand in salute. The Starshina signaled to the band. The new arrivals were on the way to the platform, but had to stand still, for the first bars of the "Internationale" rang out. They had barely ascended the platform and were about to sit down when the anthem began again, for the Elektrostantsia band had been instructed that it was to be the first item on the program and no one had informed them what would be played by others.

All the windows were wide open, because the hall was too small for the crowd that had come, and the people outside too must be able to hear what was being said. For the speeches were important. The man with the weather-beaten face and the piercing black eyes spoke, and he was the most important man in the whole district, in the whole of the Western Ukraine. Saposhnik introduced him as Fyodor Fyodorovich Potapenko, president of the Party Committee.

He spoke, and his words reached every corner of the room, flew out through the open window—words that thundered, that struck like bolts of lightning. There was no regret, no sympathy, no mourning in his speech. He was using the occasion to prove one thing: we are on one side, the others are on the other side. Our enemies lie in wait for us and strike us wherever they can; they have done so ever since we arose and with our own strength shook off the yoke. Because we would no longer be their slaves, because we fight for our rights, we must pay with our blood. "Yes, comrades, you must understand that: Starshi Ogrodnik Gorecki was killed on orders from our enemies, like so many before him who did their work well. For, comrades"—his voice soared and roared—"reaction is our main foe! But we know the enemy and know not only how to guard against him, but how to meet him. For we are strong, comrades. The best weapon against our enemies is our work, and in our defensive struggle the workers are as important as our glorious Red Army.

"And where in the whole world is the worker so highly honored as in the Soviet Republic? Behold, here is Antoni Antonich Gorecki, a worker! And is he not being accorded honors such as elsewhere, among the burzhui and the fascists, only generals, ministers and priests receive, and all the other parasites who live on the sweat of the workers? We shall always preserve the memory of our comrade, Stakhanovets Antoni Antonich Gorecki. As we remember him, so will all workers of the great Soviet Union, who will learn of his accomplishments and his death, and so also will our Comrade Stalin, who knows everything that happens in our Soviet land."

The speaker sat down, but stood up instantly, for the cry "Long live Stalin!" rang out. No one could have said who started it. It was taken up by many in the crowd, and soon everyone was joining in the cheer, both inside and outside the hall. As soon as the noise subsided, Lavrenenko, Maximenko, Feingold and Saposhnik took the coffin on their shoulders. Once again the army had an edge on the factory band. The Starshina had evidently been watching closely, and as soon as the coffin appeared at the door he signaled to his wind players, who quickly formed up in front of the pallbearers, began the Chopin "Funeral March," and led the way down the driveway and across the big paved yard to the garden gate. At the hotbeds and cold frames the procession stopped, and the coffin was put down.

The artillerymen's band finished playing the march and Saposhnik spoke a few effective words, calling attention to the deceased's extraordinary achievement. From this point to the grave the farm workers and the plant workers took turns as pallbearers. They thronged forward in their eagerness to honor Antek, and the procession moved very slowly because of the frequent changes. At last they reached the grave by the old pear tree.

Lavrenenko spoke in Russian, Feingold in Ukrainian and the small, gray-haired man in Polish. They spoke briefly, repeating the same speech in the different languages.

Spades were leaning against the pear tree. The Chairman of the Committee and his deputy Tarashchenko each took one, and the men who had last carried the coffin removed the drapes preparatory to letting it down into the grave. But Feingold, who had whispered something to Potapenko, motioned to them to wait. He himself stepped back a few paces and called, "Comrade Khomniuk!" The call was relayed to the last row, where Vassily stood beside Panya Jadwiga, Mira, Tadek and Freddy. He didn't hear his name, although it was being called out to all sides, and had to be pushed forward until he stood in front of Feingold, who requested him to speak in the name of the farm workers. With slow, heavy step, Vassily walked up to the coffin and motioned to the bearers to pick it up and let it down into the grave. He did not see the crude, ill-painted box; he saw only Antek, who was no longer there and whose presence he felt, whose voice he heard: "I don't want you murdered, Vassily." And he answered Antek: "We are bidding good-bye to you, Antek, we workers of the farm. We respected you and loved you, as you deserved. Your life was very hard and your struggle was an honest one. You knew what injustice was and hated it; you wanted what was good and true, and you strove for it, worked for it and fought for it. You were a friend, a good companion. You have been murdered in cold blood. You can no longer work, no longer help anyone. We will always think of you, hold you in our love and avenge you."

Vassily stooped, took two handfuls of the damp earth and threw it on the coffin. Then he turned and walked back to his place. The nachalniki reached for the shovels.

It was still fairly light, and the press photographers could get good pictures.

Almost two hours passed before all those who had come for the funeral returned to the city. Many of the bigwigs had taken the opportunity to inspect the farm while they waited for their turn to be driven back. The high party functionary stayed with his suite, to which the reporters also attached themselves, and Saposhnik acted as guide. The cars which transported Potapenko and his companions drove away from the farm just as the first of the teams were returning from town.

Vassily offered to drive Panya Jadwiga back to town. However he did not park the buggy on the street; he drove it around into the small yard behind the cottage.

Panya Jadwiga was sitting at the kitchen table with her son and Freddy. They were drinking brandy and smoking. "A fine funeral!" Panya Jadwiga growled. "Lots of people, but—no priest, no crosses, no candles, no bells. . . ." She sipped her brandy.

"It doesn't make any difference to Antek, Panya Jadwiga."

"Don't say that," she growled angrily. "It does make a difference." She emptied her glass and refilled it.

Vassily said no more. He lit a cigarette and went into the other tiny room. Next door, Mira was making a list of Antek's personal possessions. "What's to be done with the books?" Mira asked, pointing to the heap. The *Historical Miniatures* lay on top.

"Oh, put them with the other things." Vassily picked up the brightly bound volume. "I'd like to keep this one, as a memento."

He had had less than four hours' sleep the night before and was utterly exhausted. He stumbled across the threshold into his room and threw himself down on the bed. Mira followed him. "Forgive me," he said. "I want to lie down for a few minutes; I still have to take Panya Jadwiga home. If only I don't fall off the box."

"How you manage to bear up—"

"One has to, Mira."

"Yes, one has to, and now it's going to be even tougher—getting the garden work done without Antek." She stopped abruptly.

Vassily had sat up and was staring at her with a kind of horror. He wanted to say something sharp, but forbore when he saw her dismayed look. Instead he brought his hand to his brow with a nervous, hasty movement, covering his eyes. "Oh," he said, quietly and in a friendly tone, "we'll manage, Mira."

She probed his face for some sign of the horror that had hurt her so deeply. Seeing that it was gone, she said only, "Yes, Vassily."

There was a knock at the front door. They started and looked at each other. "Who can it be?" he asked. "Go into the kitchen and clear away the brandy." Mira tiptoed out of the room. He waited until she had closed the kitchen door behind her before he went slowly to the front door. "Who is it?" he asked before sliding the bolt.

"Come, let me in, Vassily Vassilevich." It was Feingold at the door.

Vassily led him into his small room and offered a chair. "You are still in Jiusefovka, Comrade Feingold?"

"As you see, I am." Feingold laughed. "I've just come back. We were barely out of Jiusefovka when I discovered that I'd lost my keys. Imagine, I found them right where I stepped into the car. That's luck, isn't it?" He triumphantly rattled a bunch of keys on a key ring.

"Really a stroke of luck," Vassily said.

"Yes, but now I am here and must get back to town, because I walked back, of course. The comrades have an important meeting tonight and couldn't wait for me. You're not going to make me walk twelve miles, are you, Vassily Vassilevich?"

"It's only eight, Comrade Feingold," Vassily said. "Of course I'll drive you into town. Perhaps I can take Comrade Zembrinski's mother along, if you don't mind."

Feingold thought for a moment and then said reluctantly, "I guess it's all right."

Vassily slipped into his short fur jacket. "We'll be ready shortly, Comrade Feingold," he said, and went out to the street. He circled the house to the yard, softly opened the kitchen door and beckoned to Mira. "It's Feingold; he lost his keys and found them again. Now he wants a ride to town. Tell Panya Jadwiga to get ready. I must pretend to go and get the buggy. We'll leave in fifteen minutes."

Mira returned to the kitchen and Vassily sat down in the buggy. He tried to penetrate the reason for Feingold's visit, for he didn't believe the story of the lost keys. But his fatigue, which came not only from his limbs but from his brain and heart, produced a dull indifference against which his will fought in vain. And so he sat still, his legs outstretched, head pressed against the leather of the seat, staring at the night sky. At last he got down, shivering, lit the wicks in the buggy's lanterns, and drove to the front of the house. "All ready to go, Comrade Feingold," he said, entering the room.

"Good." Feingold closed the book he had been leafing through. "Where is the woman?"

"Waiting outside."

Panya Jadwiga and Tadek beside her cast huge shadows on the street. Feingold said good evening and clambered onto the box.

"Do you want to sit with me?" Vassily asked.

"I like to chat while we go along, and she probably doesn't speak Russian."

"No, she doesn't speak Russian—and if you sit with me, her son can sit next to her. He doesn't understand Russian either. Hop in!" he said to Panya Jadwiga and Tadek.

They were already some distance out of the village when Feingold asked in a low voice, "Are you sure those two don't understand Russian, Vassily Vassilevich?"

"Hardly ten words, and besides, they're too grief-stricken to listen."

"What about you, Vassily Vassilevich? Do you feel no grief for Gorecki?"

"He was my friend, you know—how could I help feeling grief?" The horses shied at a pool of water that glittered in the light of the lanterns. Vassily calmed them. "Yes, Comrade Feingold, I feel very bad about him."

"We cannot bring the dead to life, but—" He fell silent and waited. But Vassily said nothing; he paid close attention to the horses and the road, so that Feingold had to continue. "But we must avenge them. Didn't you say that today, at the grave? Remember? Comrade Potapenko was very much impressed. He—how did you mean that, Vassily Vassilevich, when you said, 'We will avenge you'?"

"How did I mean it? I really can't explain."

"I understood it this way: if someone kills my friend, I must try to kill the murderer."

"Then you misunderstand me," Vassily said. "I didn't mean that, Comrade Feingold. There are plenty of others whose job it is to enforce the law."

Vassily gathered the reins tighter. The roans raised their heads and sharpened the pace of their trot. He let them run. He felt a violent desire for movement, for speed. The damp wind was reviving him; he no longer felt tired and indifferent. His head was clear now, and he could feel his muscles swelling and his heart beating strongly.

"Drive slower; we have time." That was not the tone Feingold usually used with him. It did not sound friendly and familiar, but neither was it a command; rather, it was as if Feingold himself were troubled and needed quiet in order to think how best to meet an unexpected turn in the conversation. Vassily obeyed. He called out a soft, tender "O-ha," followed by a humming whistle, and the horses slowed.

Feingold began again, slowly. "If you knew who had shot your friend in the back, would you kill him?" He did not sound very sure of himself.

"Kill him? Certainly he deserves the death sentence. But should *I?*"

"He deserves the death sentence," Feingold repeated. Again he paused before he went on, hesitantly and cautiously. "The gardener is not the only person he has killed. We know of three victims. A weaver, a metalworker, and now—" He fell silent again. "And tomorrow it might be you or the bookkeeper or any other good worker. That was not just a random murder."

"Yes," Vassily said, "Comrade Potapenko said that."

"Fyodor Fyodorovich—yes, he knows what he is talking about." Feingold flashed a look over his shoulder and saw that Tadek was fast asleep. In a very low voice he went on, "We must protect the good workers and punish the murderers. We must, and that is why Comrade Potapenko liked the way you said, 'We will avenge you.' That was speaking like a real Soviet man, Vassily."

"But what can I do?"

"You can do it, you of all people. If only you want to, Vassily Vassilevich; if you have the courage."

Vassily shook his head. "I don't understand."

"Suppose it depended upon you. Suppose you could do it—would you?" Feingold whispered.

"But I don't even know who he is. And with what? Fists against pistols, or whatever weapon it was."

"It was a German submachine gun. All three victims were killed with the same weapon—and all shot in the back. The man's task is to create confusion, to sow panic by killing our workers."

"It's just one man?"

"It may be he has gathered a number of criminals around him. They are enemies of society."

"All very well. If you say so, Comrade Feingold. But what can I do—a single man against a whole gang?"

"You can do a great deal—you can settle it, if you only want to. Do you want to, Vassily Vassilevich?"

"I don't know what you have in mind—but how should I go about it?"

"You can do it, Vassily. And now speed up! Potapenko expects us."

Vassily stopped on a street fairly close to Antek's house. He jumped down from the box and helped Panya Jadwiga wake Tadek. As he did so, he whispered to her to wait up until he returned. Then he drove Feingold to the party chairman.

He found himself confronting a small conclave who watched him narrowly at every step of the interview. Opposite him sat Potapenko, to his right a youngish man in uniform with brass stars on his epaulets, to the left Feingold. Behind Vassily, leaning against the wall, stood a man in spectacles and Western clothing: a dark-gray

suit, tie, low shoes. He kept his hat on, its brim screening his face.
Potapenko's incisive sentences were deliberately emotionless. They
ruled out any objection and any question. The murderer was a
saboteur, an enemy of the people and the government. He had to be
found—if possible, apprehended alive. Finally Potapenko asked,
"You understand your task, comrade?" Without waiting for a reply,
he beckoned to the man in uniform. This man gave Vassily a slip of
paper on which was a list of names and telephone numbers. "Telephone only if it is very urgent. Do your best to capture him alive—
that is extremely important." He then took several pistols from a
briefcase. Pointing to the smallest, a Browning six-gun, he said,
"This one is the best; it will fit easily into your pocket. Here are
extra cartridges and here"—he produced two typewritten forms,
stamped and sealed—"are your permits." He entered in one of the
forms the serial number of the gun and quantity of cartridges. "That
is all."

"When will you begin on this job?" Potapenko asked.

"I've already begun," Vassily replied, getting up.

He went out, got on the box, guided the horses through the
dimly lit streets, and when he reached the rear of Antek's house put
the team in the shed and blew out the lanterns. Then he sat for a
while in the back of the buggy, staring into the black sky and going
over his past life, searching his memory for any similar experience.
He was searching for himself and could not find himself, for never
before had he been so torn, so perplexed, so despairing. Only two
hours ago he had had a firm resolution, and now he had lost his
stomach for the whole thing. He was allowed to hunt, but he could
not shoot to kill.

Why were they sending him, him of all people? Did they not
have thousands of men who were trained for this thing? Since they
already knew who the murderer was. . . .

Then have they hit on the fact that you're special, Vassily—an
odd stablemaster? If that's the case, you haven't played your part
well. You should have lost yourself in the mass, been one among
thousands, just one more Vassily with nothing noteworthy about
you. And now—who are you, what are you? Someone slated to
avenge the death of Antek and who no longer wants to? Who am I,
sitting here in this buggy and not knowing what to do?

You must carry out their orders, Starshi Koniukh Vassily Vassilevich Khomniuk, with your spravka and Soviet identity card. A
Soviet citizen and a Soviet man. You've played your part too well
—you are Vassily, a special Vassily whom they have chosen for
special tasks.

But I—no, I won't retrieve for them; *I am not Vassily!*

I was Vassily; but I am no longer and never want to be again.

With that, he leaped from the buggy so vigorously that the springs creaked and the horses, which were dozing with lowered heads, uneasily pricked up their ears

Then he sat in Panya Jadwiga's kitchen, drinking a great deal of brandy and smoking. Tadek sat beside him, staring at the floor, sobbing intermittently and muttering again and again in his falsetto voice, "I've got to kill him! I've got to kill him!" At each of these outbreaks Panya Jadwiga took a sip of brandy, drew on her cigarette, and comforted Tadek with "He'll be killed, son." Suddenly she stood up, went into her room, which adjoined the kitchen, and returned with a letter. She handed it to Vassily. "This is from Antek," she boomed. "I haven't had a chance to give it to you up to now."

The letter was written in German. It read:

Dear Friend Vassily:

I am going to look for Josek so that I can explain everything to him. You don't understand how dangerous they can be, because you don't know those thugs. I'm afraid they'll do you in, so I'm going. And because I do know them and know how easily they can go off the deep end and maybe do me in, I'm writing this. I'm leaving it to you to divide my stuff. Let Tadek and Panya Jadwiga have the house and the furniture, since you don't need it, but you take more of the gold and the jewels—especially the two rubies; there was once a high reward on them, but that was a long time ago. Maybe you'll want to get out of here, and in that case jewels are handy, also the dollars. So you take them and leave the rubles for Tadek and Panya Jadwiga. Here is a drawing of how you find the hiding place.

Affectionately, your faithful friend,

Antoni Gorecki.

"Your faithful friend . . . ," Vassily whispered hoarsely. "Your faithful—" And sobs shook his whole body. "What does the letter say?" Panya Jadwiga demanded.

"It's Antek's will," Vassily said. "He left everything to us, Panya Jadwiga, to you and Tadek and me. Antek—"

"Antek, Antek—kill them, kill them!" Tadek whimpered. "Who did it to him, Mother? Who?"

"We'll finish them, son," Panya Jadwiga growled reassuringly. "We'll find out. . . . Vassily, will you help?" And when Vassily gave no answer, she demanded, "Are you scared shitless, peasant? If you'd been the one, Antek wouldn't have sat there; he would have found him and given him what he deserves. He was a fine fellow, Antek was."

"He was a fine fellow," Tadek repeated.

"He was." Vassily stood up. "Do you know where Rudnicki's woman lives, Panya Jadwiga? Or do you, Tadek?"

"I know," Panya Jadwiga said. "What about her? What has she to do with it?"

"Do you know a man named Josek?"

"Josek! Of course, Josek did it." Tadek stood up and reached for his cap.

"Good you know him," Vassily said. "No, Josek didn't do it. The man we want is someone named Ossip—a Russian. But Josek knows where he is. We must find him."

"We'll find him," Panya Jadwiga said. "Come, boys."

She stood up and took her leather jacket from the hook.

It was pitch-dark. The streets were deserted. Panya Jadwiga walked ahead, taking enormous strides and leading Tadek by the hand like a child. Vassily followed close behind them.

"There," Panya Jadwiga said, tempering her deep bass and stretching her arm out into the darkness. "Another fifty paces." Vassily tried to see what she was pointing at, but it was too dark.

"Can you handle a pistol, Tadek?" he asked.

"He has his knife," Panya Jadwiga replied for her son. "I can shoot, but I don't need the thing. Just let me get my hands on him—Josek doesn't use a gun."

"But the other man has one, and a dangerous one; you can't fight it with bare hands. Here, Panya Jadwiga." He drew the small Browning from his trouser pocket.

She took the weapon doubtfully and her fingers felt for the safety. Then she decisively thrust it into the side pocket of her leather jacket. "What about you?"

"I have one."

"So you came prepared. Good. I'll lead the way; you follow me and let Tadek stay a few steps behind." She dropped her cigarette into the mud of the street. "Let's go," she commanded, and strode ahead. After about thirty paces, she stood still. Vassily did not realize she had stopped until he collided with her—it was that dark. When Tadek reached them, she said, "Let me talk to her. I can handle her; she'll talk. If Josek is there, keep your eye on him; he loses his temper fast and is quick with the knife. Uses it with his left hand, and throws it too. Don't kill him or we may never find the Russian."

"Right, Panya Jadwiga," Vassily said. "And if we do find the Russian, leave him to me."

"Whichever of us gets at him has the killing of him," Panya

Jadwiga growled angrily. "Now, you two wait here until I call you." Panya Jadwiga glided away, her huge, heavy body moving without the slightest noise. Tadek was breathing audibly; Vassily drew him closer. He heard Tadek testing the mechanism of his switchblade knife. There was a light clicking sound, like a snapping match. Vassily reached under his armpit, loosened the pistol in its noose, drew it out, cocked it and then uncocked it again and put it back, leaving his jacket open. The cold, damp air penetrated through his shirt to his skin. He shivered, but ignored the cold; he was in a new, exhilarated, state of mind. Thanks to Panya Jadwiga, who had shown him how Antek would have acted in this situation, he had recovered the resolution which he had almost lost in his bout with the officials.

He and Tadek stood close together, pressed up against the thin wall of the house. Then Vassily thought he heard a sound. He laid his ear against the wall and detected a low, muted sound, a rustling, as if someone were moving cautiously on a bed of straw.

"Do you know the way, Tadek?" he whispered. "We'd better not wait any longer."

Tadek led, groping along the wall. Vassily kept close behind him. It was only a few steps to the door, but they seemed to take forever. They reached it and slipped into the front hall. The floor was merely hard, dry, tramped mud. "The door to the right," Tadek whispered. Vassily pulled quickly and the door yielded. The room was dimly lit by the feeble, flickering flame of a small kerosene lamp that stood on the floor in one corner.

In the dimness they could make out only the outlines of the woman standing near the table. Panya Jadwiga stood before her in all her bulk. As the door opened, she turned briefly, recognized the two, and turned back to the woman. "Toiska, where is Josek?" she asked.

"How should I know?" The voice was cracked from nicotine and alcohol; the woman sounded drunk and spiteful.

Vassily had glanced quickly around the room. There was a wide couch covered with several horse blankets, a table, a few rickety wooden chairs. In one corner stood a ramshackle kitchen cupboard. The windows of the room were boarded over. In addition to the door through which they had entered, there was another, which led to another room.

"You won't say? You won't?" A fearful slap followed Panya Jadwiga's words, and then another. Toiska lay moaning on the floor. "Get up, you bitch, and if you don't talk I'll twist your neck. Where is Josek, I asked."

A key turned rapidly in a lock; simultaneously a bolt was slid back, and a man leaped through the open door into the middle of the room. "Here's Josek, Panya Jadwiga. What do you want with him?" Suddenly he saw that there were others in the room. His left hand darted into the pocket of his short jacket.

"Take your hand out of your pocket and leave the knife in it," Vassily said quietly.

"Who are you?" Josek snarled. Tadek, standing a step behind him, reached out and clamped his enormous paws around the man's neck.

"Take your hands out of your pockets or you're done for!" he squeaked.

Josek obeyed. Vassily reached into the pocket and found a switchblade knife and a pair of brass knuckles. Further search revealed no other weapons. "Let him go, Tadek," he said. He stood looking at Josek, who was rubbing his throat to restore circulation.

"All right, now you've got nothing to worry about. What do you want and who the devil are you? You with the mustache, I mean." He spoke brashly, challengingly, as though he were master of the situation. He was a slender, wiry man who moved with a dancer's grace. His face, as far as Vassily could make it out in the poor light, was thin, with a wide, deep scar running from temple to chin. The scar gave him a fierce look.

"Why did you kill Antek?" Vassily asked quietly.

Josek started. "Kill who? Antek? I don't know a thing about that, not a thing. Something happened to Antek? Is he dead?"

"But you know who killed Vassily, the koniukh, don't you?"

Josek looked at him tensely. "Who the hell are you?"

"I am Vassily."

Toiska, still lying on the floor, sat up. She croaked hoarsely, "Vassily—he's the one, Josek. He's the one who put Stasek—" She got to her feet. "You dirty bastard, you—"

Josek leaped toward her. "Shut your mouth, you bitch!" he snarled at her. "She doesn't know what she's talking about," he said to Vassily. "And neither do you."

"Tell me where Ossip is," Vassily said quietly. "I mean to find out if I have to break every bone in your body."

"So you're a bone specialist, Rusniak. The hell with you. I don't know no Ossip."

Tadek approached him again, gripped him by the back of the neck and raised his fist. Josek writhed and slipped out of his grasp. He dropped to a chair and cradled his head in his hands, shielding his eyes. It looked as if he had collapsed and was trying to gather his strength. But his eyes were fixed commandingly on Toiska. Vassily caught the look and understood. He moved slowly toward the hall door and opened it. The cold, moist air came in; the lamp in the corner smoked. "Too much smoke in here," he said, and returned to the corner near the lamp. Toiska slid along the wall behind Panya Jadwiga's back, crept to the open door, and vanished through it, apparently unnoticed. Josek could scarcely conceal his sense of triumph. He looked at Vassily with a spiteful smile. And Vassily, as if he had only been waiting for this signal, drove his fist into the man's chin. Josek sagged. "Quick, Tadek, drag him in here." Vassily kicked open the door to the other room. "You get in here too, quick, quick. Tadek, if he makes a sound, choke him, stab him to death!" Vassily struck a match. There was no door to the room, only a single boarded window. "Panya Jadwiga, you stand here, covered by the wall. If a man in uniform comes in, fire at him; don't wait, shoot." He bent over Josek; Tadek was sitting on the man with drawn knife. "Don't let him stir," he repeated. "If you hear one word, cut his throat. And you shoot, Panya Jadwiga, but keep in cover, keep in the dark."

In three leaps Vassily was by the cupboard in the corner. He crouched down, shielded by its wide side. It was so still that he could distinctly hear Tadek's breathing in the next room. But only for a few seconds. Footsteps approached, cautious, creeping. He heard them on the hard floor of the hall and then they entered the room. Almost simultaneously, two shots were fired in quick succession. The bullets struck the wall, and the rattle of a submachine gun instantly answered. But the firing stopped, the weapon fell to the floor, and the shadow in the doorway collapsed with a fearful scream. Vassily dashed forward and reached the front door just as Toiska was about to escape into the darkness. He gripped her mercilessly, pulled her back and pushed her into the room. There Panya Jadwiga stood over a man lying in a pool of blood. She held the lamp to his face. It was a young face, thin, with sunken cheeks and full, girlish lips. The Russian military cap had fallen askew, and long, light-blond hair dangled down over the man's forehead.

"I wouldn't believe he could be the one if this thing weren't here," Panya Jadwiga growled. She touched the submachine gun with her foot. "Is he done for?"

Vassily stooped until his ear touched the man's chest. The heart was beating feebly. "Done for," he said. "We'd better clear out."

Tadek pushed Josek into the room. "What's to be done with these two?" Panya Jadwiga asked.

"Kill them," Tadek piped.

Panya Jadwiga stood with head bowed, both hands in the pockets of her leather jacket. "Give me the pistol, please, Panya Jadwiga," Vassily said quietly.

She handed it to him reluctantly. "Let's have no more killing, son." She stared at the floor. "This is enough. What should we do with them, Vassily?"

"Tie them up. They'll be found—if they're lucky. Go on, Tadek. There must be a rope or a chain in the shed. Hurry!"

Tadek moved slowly and unwillingly. At the open door he paused, turned, and looked at Vassily and then at his mother, who nodded encouragingly. He went into the hall, and was suddenly caught in a bright beam of light. A roar of motors filled the house. Tadek took a step back. The light intensified; automobiles stopped, voices rang loudly. "Here! From here—I heard it—this house!" Three, four, eight men, pistols and carbines in their hands, stood in the narrow hallway. And one of them, a small, stocky man with close-set eyes and a huge, long-barreled revolver in one hand, a brilliant flashlight in the other, entered the room. He looked around, saw the man lying in his blood and the gun beside him. "A Red Army soldier!" There was grief and furious menace in the words. "Take them away, all of them!"

They stood with faces to the wall, the barrels of carbines inches away from their backs. The two women stood thus, and a yard away from them the men: Josek, Vassily and then Tadek. They held their hands clasped behind their backs and waited. Vassily leaned his head against the wall. That helped him stand. He was very weary; his knees threatened to give way and his ribs ached so from the blows of the militiamen's rifle butts that he scarcely dared breathe. He wanted to try to relax, to shift his weight, but he did not stir, although it was unbearable to continue standing this way.

Somewhere footsteps became audible, a chair was shifted, and a man's voice sounded behind the partition wall which divided the room in two.

The militiaman standing behind Vassily gave him a shove. "Move!" he barked. Vassily walked slowly to the other side of the partition.

The official had a longish, pallid face with sunken cheeks and deep-set eyes of some indefinite light color. His cap was pushed back on his head; a strand of hair fell over his forehead. He barely looked up at Vassily. "Your documents."

Vassily produced his identity card, spravka, military card and finally the permit and special pass he had received a few hours before. He laid these on the table. The official examined the cards and the spravka, opening them, comparing, noting down the data. "What are these?" he asked when he was finished, indicating the two other documents.

"Read them!" Vassily spoke softly but emphatically. As he did so, he placed a finger on his lips and jerked his head toward the wall.

The official unfolded first one document and then the other. He read them word for word, once and then again; he bent over the stamps and the signatures, raised them to the light, studied them letter by letter. He took the identity card and spravka and compared them, then looked up at Vassily in amazement. "You're the man, but—"

"Don't talk so loud," Vassily whispered sternly. "The others mustn't know. Send me back and report everything to the nachalnik and"—he reached into his watch pocket—"call this number." He laid the slip with the telephone numbers on the table. "Comrade Potapenko—yes, the Chairman. Understand?" To the militiaman he said, "Lead me back now. Let us sit on the floor. Permit us to smoke and don't interfere if I talk with the other prisoners. Tell the other men that, understand?"

The official stood up slowly. While Vassily was speaking, he had been exchanging glances with the militiaman. "Yes, but—"

The militiaman slung his rifle over his shoulder and reached for the two documents, then for the identity card. He looked hard at the photo.

"No doubt about it," he said. "Where is the gun?" He spoke loudly.

"Here." Vassily reached under his armpit and produced the small Browning. Antek's pistol lay under the kitchen cupboard in Rudnicki's hovel. The two men eagerly compared the number of the Browning with the number in the permit.

"Right," the militiamen said to the official. The latter stood up and gathered together the documents and the gun.

"Do as he says. I'll go to the nachalnik."

The official was already at the door and the militiaman had once more tucked the rifle under his arm. Vassily took a step, but the militiaman clutched at his sleeve. "Who killed the Red Army man?" he whispered in Vassily's ear.

"He isn't a Red Army man and he isn't dead," Vassily whispered back.

The militiaman started. He was a small fellow with a hard, sly face. Now he was beaming, happy. "Not . . . oh. But who is he?"

"That's what I want to find out. So take me back to the others. And pretend I'm still a prisoner."

"All right, that's enough. Move along!" the militiaman barked.

For one or two minutes they stood against the wall, as they had before. Then Vassily heard the militiaman's commanding voice roar, "All of you, about face!" Vassily did so, but the others had not understood and remained as they were. The other militiaman turned them around. "Sit down!" Vassily sat down on the ground, and the others followed his example. Only Panya Jadwiga continued to stand. She didn't even lean against the wall, but stood like a tower beside the group on the floor. Josek had moved close to Vassily. He sat with bowed head, whispering something which Vassily couldn't make out. He let his head droop, lower than Josek's, so that his ear was almost at the other's mouth.

"You can get us all out of this, Rusniak. Say you knew he wasn't a Russian."

Vassily drew up his knees and propped his chin on them. Josek interpreted this movement correctly; he went on whispering. "Came from over there, get it?"

Vassily raised his head until his mouth was close to Josek's ear. "What for?" He let his head droop again.

"What do you think for, you dumb peasant?"

"Tell them everything you know," he whispered to Josek.

"The hell I will," Josek replied.

Vassily leaned back against the wall. He looked at the militiaman. "Can we smoke, Comrade Militiaman?" he asked.

"I'm not your comrade," the man bellowed, and gripped his rifle as though inclined to shoot all of them. "All right, smoke if you want." And to the militiaman who was guarding Panya Jadwiga he said, "Bring the *babushka* a chair." He's all right, Vassily thought. Thank God.

They all smoked, including the militiamen. They smoked incessantly. An hour, two hours, passed. What was happening to the horses, Vassily thought. He threw a reassuring look at Panya Jadwiga and whispered to Tadek, "Nothing to worry about."

At last the door opened on the other side of the partition and a voice called, "Vassily Vassilevich Khomniuk." Vassily rose heavily to his feet and went out, followed by his militiaman. In addition to the official with whom he had dealt before, there was a man in a tunic, blue trousers and low boots. He led the way through the second door and a number of empty rooms. He ignored Vassily until they came to an iron winding staircase. Then he stopped and said, "You go ahead."

Vassily had to cling to the railing. He climbed slowly, a step at a time. "I'm hurt," he said apologetically, but the man did not change expression. When the stairway at last came to an end, he said, "The door straight ahead." Vassily opened it. He found himself in a room with one window, dimly illuminated by a single bulb and empty except for a high-backed sofa covered with oilcloth.

"Wait!" the man said, and went into the next room.

Vassily sat down on the sofa and felt along the aching ribs on his left side. There were bad swellings, but nothing was broken. He could breathe without pain now. He reached for his cigarettes. But with his hand halfway to his pocket, he fell asleep.

He could not have said how long he had slept, whether it was hours or only minutes. Nor did he know whether a sound or a touch had awakened him. When he opened his eyes, the man who had brought him there was standing in front of him saying in an expressionless voice, "In here." He motioned toward the door he had previously entered.

"Yes." Vassily was wide-awake now.

In the glaringly bright room stood a big table with Potapenko and Feingold at one end, at the other end the man who had given him the documents and the pistol. By the wall opposite the table stood the man in the gray suit and the felt hat.

Precisely at the center of the table sat another man, still as a statue. His white, oily face with its broad, plump cheeks billowed out of the tight collar; his chin passed without transition into fleshy dewlaps, so that it looked shapelessly wide. Even the slightly hooked nose was so embedded in the soft white flesh of the cheeks that it scarcely emerged; and the thin upper lip was almost covered by the heavy, puffy lower lip. His hair was a thick mass of tight black ringlets that grew almost to his eyebrows.

Vassily had paused at the door. In one glance he took in the five men sitting immobile and sensed, as if it were something tangible in the smoke-thickened, stale air, the atmosphere of danger.

"Good evening," he said. His greeting, spoken with calm friendliness, engendered nervousness. Potapenko raised his black eyebrows, and Feingold compressed his lips even more tightly. He stood in the doorway, waiting for an answer to his greeting, and when none came he took his big watch from his pocket. "Oh, four o'clock! The horses—" And pretending not to notice the horrified disbelief that distorted the faces of the two men who sat close together at the end of the table, he went blithely on. "I didn't figure I'd be held up so long." He leaned against the door. "And then I have—"

"That's not important." The fat man at the table spoke in a low, glassy voice. "We are not here to talk about horses. I take the responsibility for them." There was no human note in his tone.

Vassily turned with a gesture of perplexity to Feingold. "Do you say that too, Comrade Feingold?" Feingold didn't reply; he only threw a look at Potapenko and the fat man. "After all, Comrade Feingold is from our organization and I don't know you." Vassily looked at the fat man with a disarming smile. The man's

expression and bearing did not change, but the thumb and forefinger of his right hand—a small, smooth, grayish-white child's
hand—rubbed rapidly against each other, as if he were testing cloth
or crumbling something. This Buddha is not so calm as he likes to
appear, Vassily noted. But why not? What had happened?

"I am the Nachalnik NKVD, Western Ukraine, citizen; I take
the responsibility for the horses." His thumb and forefinger were in
violent movement now.

"Oh!" Vassily made his voice sound deferential. "But it's not
just a question of responsibility," he persisted. "The horses have
been in harness for eight hours. They're standing in a cold shed. If
I've got to stay here to report, Comrade Zembrinski and his mother
could be released. He'll take care of the horses—and she's seventy
years old. Both of them helped me a great deal." He looked ex-
pectantly at them, especially at Feingold, as though everything depended on him.

"Come over here, citizen, up to the table." The glass in the man's
voice had developed a crack.

"I'm sorry but I can't, Comrade Nachalnik. I have to lean against
something. My ribs are aching something awful. Unless—but there
aren't any more chairs."

The fat man threw a brief glance at the man with the brass star.
The latter stood up and placed his chair so that it was opposite the
nachalnik. "Sit down," he said. Vassily thanked him and made a
business of sitting down.

"You received your assignment at nine-thirty," the nachalnik
said softly. "Is that right?"

"I didn't look at the clock—but I'll gladly answer all your questions if I know the horses have been taken care of. Horses are not
cars; you can't park them and let them stand. Please send the other
two home and then you can keep me here as long as you like. I
must pull my thoughts together; what I have to report is very important, and I can't think while I'm worried about the horses."

A voice suddenly roared close to Vassily's ear. He started, but
instantly regained his composure. The man in the gray suit had
crept up to him and was shouting, "Don't be so sly, koniukh, and
cut that comedy about the horses. Talk when you're asked questions,
or else—"

Every syllable was fired at Vassily like a shot, till his eardrum
ached.

Vassily stood up. He moved slowly, and turned just as slowly to
face the man. "Don't shout. I don't know who you are and I don't
care, but don't shout at me. I am not your servant, I'm a worker in
the Soviet Union, not among the fascists. *They* shout at people; here

a worker is spoken to decently." He raised his voice. "And don't threaten me. I'm not afraid of you. I have nothing to be afraid of; I've done my duty." He turned to the others and said, "I beg your pardon." Then he sat down, ignoring the man behind him.

Nothing happened; the incident had no consequences, nor did it produce any surprise that he could observe. The man who had shouted returned to his place; the man with the brass star let his head droop; Potapenko's piercing eyes were half shut, and Feingold sat with legs crossed and exchanged a rapid glance with the fat man. The fat man fumbled at the collar of his tunic, opened it and his shirt collar as well, and made a sound. It might have been a gasp or it might have been a giggle smothered before it could penetrate through the compressed, puffy lip. "No da," he said, and gazed down at his hand.

Vassily took his keys from his pocket and placed them in front of Feingold. "Here, one of these is the key to the feed bin; it will be feeding time soon. The keys must be sent out to the farm. Koniukh Ivan Petriuk must give out the feed. Wagner should go for the team and drive them back to the farm at a walk. Please have that taken care of—it must be done."

The keys lay in front of Feingold, but he sat motionless, his face devoid of expression. Vassily turned his head toward the nachalnik and gave him a look meaning "All right, you tell him; you see, he doesn't dare speak up; you seem to be the strong man here."

The fat man looked at the man in the gray suit, who promptly opened the door. Meanwhile Vassily was feverishly trying to put two and two together. The fat man had not said a word to either Potapenko or to Feingold. Therefore they were also in disfavor, along with him. All the others, including the man with the brass star and the bespectacled man in Western clothes—although they seemed only supernumeraries—clung together like bits of iron attracted by the same magnet. The fat man wanted to pin some guilt on him. But the only way he knew, the only method he had, was the old game of *We know everything*. And he had already lost the first round; the peasant had refused to be disconcerted. Vassily sat more comfortably and smoothed his mustache. The man who had brought him here appeared. "Tell him what you want done at the farm," the fat man said.

"Is he driving there himself?"

"Tell him what you want done," the man repeated, and once more his two fingers rubbed against each other. Vassily, taking his time, explained to the official what orders were to be given at the farm and what had best be done about the horses. He spoke easily, unconcernedly, as if he were back at the farm stables issuing his instructions. After the man had left, he promptly turned to the Buddha. "All right," he said. That was all.

Once again there came that bubbling sound of a suppressed chuckle. "You received your order at nine-thirty, is that right?"

"Must be about right. We left the farm before eight."

"Where did you drive after you received the assignment?"

"To the home of Comrade Zembrinski's mother. He's gardener at the farm and was to ride home with me."

"And then?"

"We ate and drank some, and talked."

"About what?"

"The murder," Vassily said quietly.

"You told the two that you had been entrusted with the task of catching the murderer?"

An almost pitying smile appeared on Vassily's face. "Do you think I'm stupid?"

The fingers rubbed. "Answer properly."

"Very well. I didn't say a word about it."

"Then what?"

"I thought it would be a good idea if I had one or two assistants, because I had nothing to go on. Actually all I knew was what I'd been told, that the murderer had been hanging around the infantry barracks. Zembrinski and his mother are not exactly heavy thinkers. My documents were sealed and stamped by the NKVD. To them, that's the police—and from the old days they're afraid of the police. If they'd ever learned that the stablemaster was in cahoots with the police, they would have been suspicious of me."

"And they wouldn't have helped you?"

"They might not have."

"Among us everyone must help."

"I know that; Comrade Feingold explained it all to me. But those two wouldn't have understood. It was enough for me that they hate the murderer."

"And you yourself don't hate the murderer?"

"I hate all murderers, and certainly one who killed my friend."

"So you were out to liquidate him and would have done it even if you hadn't been ordered to track him down?"

"You misinterpret what I said. I only said that I hated the murderer. It's a long way from hating to killing."

"You must answer my questions. Had you revenge in mind? Did you intend to kill him, you personally?"

"No." Vassily did not himself know whether he was telling the truth or lying. "Anyhow, I didn't kill him. I was careful not to; that was my assignment. He was still alive before the militia came."

The Buddha raised his hand to his chin, and fingered his dewlap, pulling at the loose flesh and letting it snap back. He did this several times, and then fixed his eyes on the man with the brass star. "Bring a chair for yourself," he said. After the man had left the room, he turned to Vassily again. "You spoke at Gorecki's grave?"

"Yes. Comrade Feingold called on me to speak."

"Do you remember what you said?"

"The things you say at a comrade's grave—that he was a good—"

"I mean your last words: 'We will avenge you.' "

Vassily's attention sharpened. If they were bent on proving that he had been out for personal vengeance, they would have a difficult time. Apparently it had been a mistake to give him the assignment; something had gone wrong, and he would be the scapegoat. They wanted to get themselves out of a pickle. But—that much he knew—to have him in their power they needed a confession. This was what they were after now.

They were all ganged up against him! All? He looked over at Feingold, quite openly, and as he did so he smiled. "Comrade Feingold"—he searched for the word—"also chided me for that. Comrade Chairman had also noticed that I said, 'We will avenge you.' "

Feingold continued to look impassive.

"So you intended to take vengeance?"

"Because I said that?" Vassily smiled broadly.

The fingers rubbed. "We're not at the club here—it's no laughing matter. If you said that, it meant something."

"Meant something. I said *we*. The fact is, I said it just because it suddenly came to me. It's something I've heard very often—on similar occasions."

"Similar occasions?"

"Yes, at the front. Maybe you don't know that I was a soldier. When we buried fellows, an officer always made a speech. And it always ended: 'We will avenge you.' I guess, seeing the flags and the soldiers, and Gorecki with those two shots in his back, I felt as if I were at the front again and burying a buddy. So the words came to me—though to be honest about it, I wasn't really thinking of anything in particular."

"Not thinking of anything in particular?" The Buddha lapsed into a brooding silence. The room became very still, as if all the men were holding their breath. The man with the brass star broke the silence. He came in carrying a chair and placed it quietly at the end of the table. But he could not avoid making a slight noise, and that made the nachalnik nervous. Thumb and forefinger began moving. Then his hand lay still, his eyelids rose, and his eyes probed Vassily, who sat up straighter. "Thinking of nothing in particular? And when you were asked when you would begin—on the job—do you remember what you said?"

"Yes, Comrade Chairman asked me that as I was leaving—you mean then, don't you?" Vassily smiled.

This time the fat man ignored his smile. "Yes, then." His glassy voice had an undertone of uncertainty. "What was your answer?"

"Oh, I remember that. I said I'd already begun."

"And you said that, too, without thinking anything in particular?"

Vassily laughed with a good imitation of peasant slyness. "I thought a good many things, and I was right. But—I don't know whether I can explain all that so exactly." He twisted his mustache thoughtfully and hitched his chair foward. "Do you want me to retrace all that?" he asked trustfully, looking squarely at the fat man.

The hand reached for the fold of flesh under the chin; the chuckle bubbled and was absorbed by the puffy lower lip. "Of course."

"When Comrade Chairman asked me that question, I already knew how to go about getting at the saboteur. I mean, I didn't exactly know, but I had a plan. I'd been thinking about something, you see. Figured something out." His stubbly face radiated satisfaction.

"Figured out? What do you mean?"

"Well, you know when that thing with Rudnicki happened—you know about that—"

"Who is Rudnicki?"

"The driver who had to be put in jail. He went at me with a knife."

"I know, but what has that fellow to do—to do with it?"

"Plenty," Vassily said.

"How?"

"I did some thinking about that. How would such a man dare to cuss out a nachalnik in his own office, draw his knife? He wasn't drunk; I could see that. Somebody must have told him something; he'd been talked into believing something. Somebody must have said to him, 'Don't crawl; if one of them ever crosses you up, tell him off; you don't have to take any crap from the Bolsheviki and the Jews.' That sort of stuff. Don't you think so? That's why I said I was already started on the job. Thinking is work too, especially for someone like me. I doped out where to look for him." Vassily's face was grave as he deliberately repeated, "I mean, I had a plan."

"What was the plan?"

"To look for somebody who knew the murderer, who was taking his orders, somebody like Rudnicki. That was the only way to get at him. You see, I knew a lot more yesterday than I did when that business with Rudnicki happened. The comrades had explained some things. Comrade Chairman said straight out in his speech that the murderer was in the pay of our enemies. I may not think so quick, but once I get an idea into my head—"

"In what way were the gardener and his mother connected with this?"

"Oh, hardly at all. But I just happened to mention to them that I wanted to talk to Rudnicki's woman. They knew where she lived and took me there. And so then we caught the man, not that that was so easy."

"Whom did you catch?"

Vassily leaned back in his chair. "The saboteur who killed Gorecki and the two others. And I got him alive, just as I'd been told to do."

The fat man gave him a searching look. Then he said very slowly, "You fired at a Red Army man and wounded him badly. Not a saboteur, not a murderer." He opened the drawer and took out the big submachine gun and a green pay book. "Do you recognize that?"

"The gun? That's the one he fired."

"He fired and didn't hit you or the others; he alone was wounded, wasn't he? The gun is German and the man is a Red Army soldier."

"Gorecki was killed with that weapon; the bullets were found and can be checked. That fellow isn't a Red Army soldier."

The fat man took the green book and opened it to the photograph. "Here," he said. "Ossip Pavlovich Faberov."

"What is that supposed to prove?" Vassily said quietly.

"What do you mean?"

"That fellow isn't a Red Army soldier. He comes from Germany." Why in the world were they all so bowled over, as though they had been struck by lightning? Or were they only pretending? Perhaps they really didn't know. Impossible to tell what they were all afraid of—the Buddha, too. His fingers fluttered; in a moment he would reach for his dewlap. Vassily's guess was right; the nachalnik snatched at his throat and said, "You shot at a Red Army man. You have admitted that."

Hopeless, Vassily thought; there's something behind this that I can't figure out. "What makes you think he's a Red Army man?" he asked.

The fat man stabbed his finger at the green pay book.

So the document was genuine. "But he's still alive," Vassily said. "You'll be able to question him, tomorrow or the day after.

You can confront us. After all, there were five people in that room. They all know he fired without provocation. He was the one who killed Gorecki and the others—I'm sure of it."

Not a word, not a sound, not a movement. All of them sat as if they had been turned to stone. All. How could he fathom them, make out where they stood? It occurred to him that they didn't care whether the murderer had or had not been captured. The only point at stake was whether he was a Red Army man or not. And what evidence did Vassily have aside from Josek's assertion that he was neither a soldier nor a Russian?

"Downstairs there's a man who knows for certain that he is not in the Red Army, that he's nothing but a saboteur, a murderer," Vassily said.

There was no response, nothing but the same wave of the hand, only wearier, more indifferent this time. There was nothing more to be done, Vassily told himself; he had given up.

"Ah," the fat man said softly, with a glance at the man by the door. The latter seemed to have been waiting for the signal; he stood up and opened the door. Vassily eyed Potapenko and Feingold. Potapenko showed no change of expression, but Feingold's handsome young face was marked by grief and horror. Vassily felt that this was a reaction to the opening of the door. He heard the man in Western clothes murmur a name, with deliberate indifference. Now they're coming for me, Vassily thought. Once I leave this room, I'm done for.

The official who had brought him here appeared briefly in the doorway. He stepped aside, and three Red Army men, a captain and two noncoms, marched into the room. The Captain, square-set, blond, still quite young, with a round, pimply face, strode up to the nachalnik. He pushed his cap back on his head. "Are you the nachalnik?" he asked the fat man. And in response to a silent nod, "Here is my identification." He showed it and placed a document on the table. "I've come about the shooting affair tonight. We've checked and discovered that the man is not *voennyi*, never was in the army. Only his boots and cap are government issue, the rest of his clothing is not. Would you please confirm receipt of this information." He spoke in official phrases, but with an unmistakable note of reprimand in his voice. "The Colonel is surprised that he had to hear of all this only by chance. If a soldier is involved, we must be informed."

No one in the room said a word. Had the fact that the man was not a soldier no bearing on the case? Vassily expected the fat man to produce the pay book. But he did nothing of the kind.

"We were not finished with our investigation," he said.

"You've been very long about it," the Captain remarked laconically. He lit a cigarette.

Without a trace of expression, the fat man folded the document the Captain had brought. "Come into my office!" he said to the officer. "The others will wait here until I return." He went out with waddling step, followed by the three Red Army men and the silent official.

The door had barely closed behind them when the man in the gray suit said, "The Army doesn't like it." Potapenko glared at him, and Vassily, although he did not look, had the feeling that the man in the gray suit was biting his tongue.

The fat man returned alone. He had no sooner sat down than two men in NKVD uniform entered.

"How does it look?" the fat man asked them.

"He will certainly pull through," one said. "The knee is shattered, the hip bone injured but not too badly." He turned to his companion. "Show the photos."

The other man had a map case slung on a strap across his chest. He took from it a folded newspaper. Between the pages of the paper lay photographs. "They're still damp," he said, and laid one after the other, six in all, carefully on the table in front of the nachalnik. Vassily caught a glimpse of the photographs. Two showed Ossip lying with his eyes closed, one showed the back of his head, but three were photographs of a swastika with writing inside the arms and above and below it.

The nachalnik scrutinized each of the pictures. "A swastika," he said. "What language is the writing? Where did you find this?"

"That is a very large tattoo on the left side of his chest," the man replied.

"Tattooing? A Finn?" (The swastika is also a traditional sign among the Finns.)

"The writing is certainly not Finnish," the NKVD man said.

"What is it?" Receiving no answer, he turned his head toward Potapenko and Feingold and said, "Arkady Samuelovich, you know languages. Wouldn't you like to take a look at this?"

It was the first time the nachalnik had addressed either of the two directly, and Vassily would have liked to see their reaction. But they were concealed from him by the backs of the two NKVD officers. The fat man's voice sounded different now, almost human. Evidently he was in a propitiating mood. There had been an exchange of roles; the Chairman of the Party—and with him his man Feingold—had the upper hand once more.

Potapenko answered sternly. "This affair is now completely a matter for the People's Commissariat for Internal Affairs," he said.

"The party abrogates all further responsibility. We have helped as much as we could. Our men have worked well and effectively. I expect a report by twelve o'clock tomorrow, and wish to be kept informed of any further developments. Arkady Samuelovich and you, Comrade Khomniuk, come with me now." He stood up. Feingold rose quickly and hurried over to Vassily, who was slowly getting to his feet.

"Come, Vassily Vassilevich," he said. His ordinarily clear, high voice was low and hoarse. He put his arm under Vassily's shoulder as though to support him. "There's nothing broken, is there?"

"It'll be all right in time for the wedding." Vassily had quoted an old Ruthenian proverb. He smiled. The quotation and smile were intended as reassurance to Feingold. But the effect of his words was surprising. The two uniformed men turned almost simultaneously and stared at him. The man at the door growled, and the man with the brass star sighed. Potapenko, making a great effort to appear unconcerned, pulled his cap forward. Feingold, however, returned the smile, though with an effort. He was about to say something, but the fat man intervened.

"Fyodor Fyodorovich," he said, wagging his heavy head back and forth, "I don't think that this matter concerns NKVD alone. It concerns all of us. You cannot take such a stand. I must proceed according to regulations. If it had by any chance turned out that the man was a Red Army soldier—"

It didn't bode well, thought Vassily, that the dispute should be conducted so candidly in front of him. No, it didn't bode well at all. Either they were abandoning all discretion because he would be unable to tell anyone what had gone on in this room, which meant that one way or another he would shortly vanish, or else they already counted him as "belonging"—and that was hardly more pleasant a prospect. A new plot was thickening here, a highly dangerous one. If the two chiefs parted in anger, there were bound to be victims. Chips would fly—and Vassily did not want Panya Jadwiga, Tadek or himself to be among the chips. He acted quickly. The movement he made and the words he spoke gave the effect of spontaneity and naïveté. He stepped away from Feingold, innocently picked up one of the photographs of the swastika and said, "Finn? Why, that man is a German." He looked closely at the picture. "There, you can see it, right at the top. It says 'Heil Hitler!'"

"The writing is German." Thumb and forefinger rubbed. "How do *you* know that?"

"Comrade Khomniuk speaks, reads and writes German, and Romanian also. That is in his official record," Feingold said informatively.

"Official record?" The fat man opened the drawer; then, as if realizing that the action was pointless, closed it again. "Can you read that?" he asked, pointing at the swastika.

Vassily cleared his throat and said quietly, "If I had a magnifying glass."

"Bring one," the fat man said. The man who had earlier shouted at Vassily raced out of the room and returned breathlessly. He laid a huge magnifying glass on the desk.

Vassily drew his chair up to the desk and sat down again. Potapenko and Feingold moved forward with him; the two uniformed men and the shouter lined up behind him. "May I have pencil and paper," Vassily said with heavy courtesy. The man with the brass star hurried to give him what he wanted. Vassily held the thick round magnifying glass over the photograph and wrote slowly, taking great care to make his script clumsy. Word by word, he copied the writing on the photograph. He did not make it easy for himself, nor for those who were watching him. The fat man's face, which was close to him now, was beaded with sweat. Potapenko and Feingold were breathing audibly behind him. He could feel the tension of his audience. When he was finished, he read the text aloud, slowly, in German.

"Can you translate that into Russian, Comrade Khomniuk?" Potapenko asked.

"I think so," Vassily replied quietly.

"Go ahead!" Potapenko commanded, and once more there was utter stillness in the room. "Comrade Feingold," he said, "it would help if you'd take this all down."

Vassily began on a slow word-for-word rendering. When he couldn't think of the Russian word, he said it in Ruthenian. He made a laborious process of it, but even so he had ventured far, had shown far more knowledge than a koniukh ought to possess. And so he contented himself with reading a crude translation of the rhymed German text: "Hang him on the gallows where he ought to be. The people and the ravens have been waiting long enough. We'll have the brute on our necks until there is a rope around his neck."

"Enough," Potapenko said with a piercing look at the fat man. "Quite enough for a Finn. I think you realize"—he dropped his voice and whispered hoarsely—"what is meant by—who the brute is. That's fairly clear, isn't it, Comrade Nachalnik?" The "Comrade Nachalnik" sounded very barbed.

"I'll have a proper translation made," the fat man said very feebly. "I can't quite make this out."

"Go ahead—I'm satisfied with this one. Arkady Samuelovich,

take the copies," Potapenko said. "And you"—he spoke with deliberate discourtesy to the fat man—"give instructions for the release of the people who helped Comrade Khomniuk. They've been held long enough. That is not the Soviet way, Comrade Nachalnik."

"By all means." The fat man beckoned to the shouter. "What are their names?"

"Jadwiga and Tadeus Zembrinski," Vassily said tersely.

"But there are four of them," the man with the brass star said. Those were the first words he had spoken.

"There were only two who helped me," Vassily said, feeling utterly wretched. Fortunately, that seemed to pass unnoticed.

"What about the two others?"

Vassily composed himself. He must not let them see the struggle within himself. His reply was clear, calm and deliberate: "The others were on the killer's side. And—I'm convinced there are a good many more in the city who belong to the gang. Perhaps you can track them down, now. They must be stopped. Otherwise"— with an effort he pulled himself to his feet—"otherwise there will be many more innocent people shot or stabbed in the back. . . . May I have my documents, if they are here?" No one saw Vassily's despairing expression or heard the sigh he uttered. The fat man opened the drawer and placed Vassily's papers on the table. Vassily pocketed them. With peasant courtesy he made a slight bow and said, "Good night, all."

Vassily was ill. Tadek plied him with food, renewed the compresses on his side, changed his bedding. Mira came as often as she could. They hardly talked to each other, for Vassily kept his eyes closed even when he was not asleep. He was too exhausted to speak. Two doctors had come to see him; once he had been taken to the hospital for an X-ray. But there were no broken ribs. The doctors attributed his weakness to exhaustion and shock.

The story given out at the farm was that Vassily had been hurt when the wagon went into a hole in the dark and turned over. Tadek and Panya Jadwiga had not needed to be cautioned to say nothing at all about the events of the night.

Feingold came to see the patient every day, sat with him for a while, and then drove back to town. Lavrenenko and Saposhnik also visited him, as did workers from the plant. All were friendly, all concerned.

Vassily lay still, resting and thinking. The physical pain was almost gone by now, but his mental pangs were more intense. He had seen life from so many aspects. Yet always he had kept his own integrity, like the proverbial bird whose feathers stay clean even though it builds its nest in a swamp. But now he, who had been free, had become a tool, a spy, a killer, in the service of a system which he understood less and less and feared more and more.

How would it have turned out for him if they hadn't found the tattooing on Ossip, or whatever the man's real name was? It was lucky that so many of those fanatical killers had their brand pricked into their skin, out of pride that they were serving insane murderers.

Compulsively Vassily lived over every moment of that fearful night; he heard every word that had been spoken, he saw every shade of expression on his captors' faces. Could it be that all of them—the nachalniki and the bosses of the nachalniki—were marionettes dancing on wires pulled by the same puppet master, Fear? If so, the wire from which the Buddha hung was not the same kind as the others, and he dangled in a different direction. Up to the very last he had been unwilling to grant that the murderer was a saboteur, a Nazi sent out to create confusion by assassination. His attitude could only be explained by the support of stronger men in the background. Which meant that there were some who regarded the Pact as more than a feeble paper partition; there were men who believed in it and were ready to go along with the Nazis. The NKVD man had tried to prevent the party stalwarts from obtaining one more proof of their new ally's dishonesty. Potapenko, like all the old party men opposed to the Pact, had won the game this time; but who could say whether the next and more important round would not be lost?

It was horrible to imagine those two totalitarian powers, each sustained by fear, sending masses of men hurtling against one another because they could not exist side by side, because one had to destroy the other. How much more horrible to picture what it would be like if they formed a true alliance, fought together against the world. Humanity would drown in its own blood.

Vassily gave up. His imagination would not stand the strain; he escaped into the life he had chosen and became once more what he was pretending to be—Vassily. And since Vassily was a peasant with robust nerves, he could not lie still and torture himself with thinking. He was a worker and his place was at work, in the stable, with the horses. And so, after nine days in bed, he got up and returned to his work.

There was plenty of it, and that was good. Good, too, was the joy with which everyone greeted him. Mira took his hand in hers and pressed it against her cheek. But before they could say anything, Wagner came rushing into the office and embraced Vassily.

"Vassily, Vassily, thank God you're up! How I worried about you, seeing you lie there all limp. Thank God," he repeated. "When you're around, all's well; I'm never afraid when you're around." And then he began a rather incoherent account of his experiences during the days he had driven to town alone to make the official and unofficial deliveries. "You can imagine what I went through; they were stopping me four or five times a day. Since yesterday it's calmed down somewhat; not so many patrols any more; not so many red, blue and green caps on the street. But you should have seen it at the outset, Vassily—a regular campaign. Raids and arrests going on day and night; trucks, wagons, every vehicle checked, even pedestrians carrying stuff. But I guess it's blown over for a while."

Lavrenenko showed satisfaction when Vassily reported to him, and Saposhnik, ordinarily so undemonstrative, beamed over his whole broad hamster's face as he welcomed Vassily in his office and congratulated him on his recovery.

Vassily called on Feingold last of all.

"Ah, Vassily Vassilevich!" Feingold exclaimed. He rose and strode forward to shake hands. "I'm so glad—back at work—that's fine. Wonderful that you're well again. Nothing wrong with you now, is there?"

"I've taken it easy long enough, Comrade Feingold. Yes, I'm back at work and feeling pretty well."

They chatted about one thing and another, but not a word was said concerning the events of that night. Only when Vassily was leaving and already had his hand on the latch did Feingold, back at his desk and apparently once more absorbed in his work, say without raising his head, "Oh, I forgot to tell you—Igor Borissovich is no longer here; there's another man in his place. You can tell the difference too—perhaps you've heard about it. The new man's put all suspects behind bars." And then, with no apparent transition, "You worked very well indeed, Vassily Vassilevich—excellently."

Vassily, who was hearing the name Igor Borissovich for the first time, realized at once that this was the Buddha. But he pretended to be pondering the connection between arrests, raids and praise of his work. It was only after a considerable pause that he said, "No da, Comrade Feingold, everyone works the way he can. Dosvidania." He was on the point of opening the door when it was thrust open from outside, and a young woman marched into the room stiffly, stopped at the desk, waved a sheet of paper and said in a rapid-fire, half-mocking official tone, "Comrade Nachalnik, here is my official record!" And as Feingold took the sheet of paper, she added with a sudden shift to intimacy, "You really ought to know it by heart by now, Arkashka." She reached out for the box of cigarettes on the desk, and produced a match from the pocket of her mannish jacket.

Vassily was so struck by this scene that he remained standing at the door. Now he remembered that he no longer had any business here and said one again, "Dosvidania." But Feingold called him back.

"Comrade Obadieva will be working on the farm as cashier. This is Comrade Khomniuk. He'll take you along in the buggy, comrade."

So this was the cashier Saposhnik had spoken of. No "native." That was going to present quite a problem to Mira and force a change in the farm's practices that would hardly be welcome.

"I suppose you'll live out at the farm, comrade?" Vassily asked the young woman when they were out in the hall.

"If there's a place for me. . . . How far is it from the farm to town?"

"From where we're standing right now, just about eight miles," Vassily said smilingly.

"Then I'd better live there. I'll fetch my rags—they're in the canteen—and then we can go. No, not yet; I must speak with the zamestitel. Can you wait a few minutes?"

"Certainly. I'll be in the buggy; it's in the yard."

Ten minutes later she reappeared with a large suitcase. When she propelled it into the buggy with a vigorous heave, it sounded hollow. "A remarkable suitcase, isn't it? But what is inside isn't so remarkable." She got into the buggy, moving with natural grace.

Vassily was struck by the odd manner of his passenger, but he wasted no thought on it. The request to drive her to the farm had complicated things for him. He had intended to take care of two important errands, to Panya Jadwiga and Besselmann, but now he couldn't very well, with her along.

"How would it be if you were to offer me a cigarette, uncle?"

"Fine," Vassily replied laconically. He took out his cigarettes. After the first puff she said, "Not Uzbek."

"The main thing is they smoke. People always would rather have what they haven't got."

"And do what they aren't doing. For example, there are any number of things I'd rather do than count up money and write up figures. I'm so bad at arithmetic."

"Our bookkeeper is very efficient. She'll teach you soon enough."

"Never!" The exclamation sounded convincing. "I haven't learned a thing in the course I took."

"Then why have you been sent to this work?"

"I was a student, but there wasn't any work for me at the university. What is your name, anyway? Mine is Tatiana Nikolaevna—Tania to my friends."

"Happy to meet you. My name is Khomniuk, Vassily Vassilevich."

"Vassia!"

"No one calls me that. I prefer Vassily."

"I give people the names I prefer," she declared, making a clownish grimace. "So then I wanted to be a dancer, but I broke my ankle." She raised her left foot and showed him the place. She had lovely legs and wore good, new silk stockings which contrasted oddly with her clumsy battered shoes. "It didn't heal right. The specialists"—she grimaced again—"said they would have to break it and set it once more, and since I didn't want to end up a total cripple I gave up the idea of dancing. But I was pretty good at it —better than at arithmetic, anyhow."

"I can well believe that," Vassily said. "But it isn't so hard to learn arithmetic if you want to."

"If you have to. Is the bookkeeper very strict? I can't help it that they sent me here, can I, uncle?"

"She won't bite."

"At any rate I didn't learn anything in the course."

"I'll put in a good word for you with the bookkeeper." Vassily smiled. They were already entering the village. Vassily stopped at the office. "Here—I'll take your suitcase." It was in fact exceedingly light.

Vassily introduced the girl to Mira—speaking Russian, of course. "I'm going over to the stable," he said in conclusion. "I must ride out and see how things look in the fields." Mira nodded; she understood that he wanted to talk with her privately.

Half an hour later—by that time Golodnyi was already saddled—she entered the stall where Vassily was standing beside the horse. Peering over the partition wall, he kissed her hastily. "I have to go back to town," he said to her. "It's important. Make out some kind of document for me as an excuse, in case I'm stopped."

"You could look for a band saw. I'll make out a request to the Metals Trust. Is it on account of—"

"Yes. I hope I'll be able to tell you something definite today."

"Oh, Vassily!" She composed herself, but with difficulty. "What do you say to the new recruit?" she asked with patent nervousness.

He shrugged. "What is there to say? We always have to be cautious anyhow. She isn't so Soviet-minded. Plays around." He said no more; he didn't want to upset Mira.

"I noticed a number of things. She's been sent here without ever having worked at such a job before. She doesn't understand a thing and I don't think she'll ever learn."

"You mean she's stupid?"

"I mean I'm afraid she's too clever."

He led the way out to the road and thrust his foot into the stirrup. Something stirred in him when he felt the warmth of the horse. No sooner was he in the saddle than Golodnyi began turning in a circle. Vassily gripped him hard with his thighs. The stallion stopped short, his ears twitched nervously, and he hurled his splendid body through the air in a tremendous arching leap. Mira cried out in alarm. "What's the matter with him, Vassily?" she asked breathlessly when he had the horse under control again and it stood with bent neck, pawing the ground.

"It's spring, Mira," Vassily said, laughing, and rode off.

Golodnyi was wet when Vassily tethered him in the shed. He had traveled by devious routes, but nevertheless had not taken more than half an hour. With rags and blankets from the house, he rubbed the horse dry and covered it well.

Panya Jadwiga brought him a snack and brandy, then sat down with him. "Got your strength back, Vassily? Good. How's Tadek?"

"He's working, Panya Jadwiga. With Freddy. I help them when I can."

"Good that you can do that. It's hard for him without Antek."

"For all of us, Panya Jadwiga."

"At least we finished off that Russki. How is it they let us go? Can you figure it out, Vassily?"

"They were looking for him themselves. Antek wasn't the only one he'd killed."

"They nabbed the whole lot of them. Josek probably talked, or that slut Toiska." Panya Jadwiga took a sip of brandy and waited for Vassily to comment.

But Vassily had had enough of the subject. "Panya Jadwiga." He found it hard to speak. "Here is Antek's letter. He sort of knew it was coming. Do you understand German—a little, anyway?"

Silently, she took the letter from his hand, read it, and laid it on the table. She reached for the brandy glass, drank, and lit another cigarette. "There aren't many like Antek was." She spoke Polish. "Do you know where the hiding place is?"

"He's made a diagram." He showed her the sketch on the last page of the letter.

"I can't make it out," she growled. "Can you?"

"It's clear enough. Come along, Panya Jadwiga."

She quickly emptied her glass and followed him behind the house to a decrepit shed that had probably once been a stable. All sorts of junk lay about. Vassily pushed aside a battered bathtub, shifted the boards on which it had been standing, and shoveled away earth and stones from a fairly large hole. He took out an iron chest nearly two feet long. It was heavy, but he hoisted it to his shoulders, feeling a stab of pain in his ribs for a moment.

In the chest were four bundles of ten thousand rubles each. There was a leather bag containing nearly six thousand American dollars. In addition there were some two hundred gold coins, sovereigns, napoleons and louis d'or. There were four gold bars, and a quantity of gold rings, brooches and watchcases. Several pillboxes were filled with small diamonds, colored precious stones, loose pearls. In a blue-enameled powder case lay the two rubies, each almost the size of a hazelnut.

"Did you understand all of the letter, Panya Jadwiga?"

"Are those the red stones he meant?" she asked, evading his question. "Take them, and this bag. And how much of the gold do you want? Half?"

"I'll take the red stones as a remembrance, and half of the dollars; the rest is for you and Tadek: the house, the rubles, the gold, all of it."

"But that isn't what the letter says," she boomed, reaching for her glass.

"I wouldn't take that much if I weren't going to need it. That is—"

"You want to get out, Vassily?" There was a note of anxiety in her rumbling voice.

He smiled reassuringly; he knew that she was concerned about who would look after Tadek. "Not for a long while yet. Things are all right for me at present. But I may need the money sometime, and Antek wanted it that way. My advice, Panya Jadwiga, would be for you to turn all the stuff into money. Your best bet is American dollars. They'll keep their value and they're a lot less weight."

"Yes. You're all right, Vassily. Here, take yours so that I can put this thing away." She lifted the heavy iron chest as if it were a cardboard carton and put it in the pantry, where she kept kindling and potatoes. "Don't look so surprised, Vassily, my boy." Suddenly she was speaking German. "Elmira, the world's strongest woman, the big number in circus and variety shows. Medrano, Paris; the Winter Garden, Ronacher's—you weren't even born yet." She finished her glass and drew deeply on her cigarette.

"And then?" Vassily asked.

"What else?" she growled angrily. "A stinker in a pair of pants, of course. The catcher in the trapeze act. We got married, I was pregnant, he started chasing a slut with a trained dog show—cheap stuff. I caught them; she got away, but he croaked on me three weeks later." Hatred half a century old thickened her voice.

"What happened then, Panya Jadwiga?"

She considered, looking at him out of the corners of her eyes and shaking her head as if surprised at herself. "Do you have to know everything?"

"No," he said, embarrassed, and reached for his cap.

"Have another; here." She filled both glasses. "They called it manslaughter. I got three years, on account of he was my husband. But it was only two years and four months with time off for good behavior. That was in Graz—you know where that is? In Austria, 1898 to 1901. Tadek was born there. Afterwards—"

"Afterwards it must have been hard," Vassily said.

"It was. I couldn't get an engagement anywhere. All the newspapers had been full of it. Circus people are strict about that sort of thing. I traveled around, small towns, villages, local fairs. In a green wagon, Tadek with me all the time. It was no life. Then I got sick of it and came home to Zimnawoda. My mother was dead, both brothers in Canada, father a drinker. Drank up what land we had, nothing but the garden left. How I slaved! At home, working for strangers—for Tadek. I wouldn't have given a damn for myself—drink, Vassily." She thrust the glass across the table to him. Vassily finished it and lit a cigarette, careful not to look directly at Panya Jadwiga.

"Tadek got to be sixteen—couldn't hold a job anywhere—would always be getting into fights with the other men or with the boss. He lost his temper too easy. I always had to smooth things over, sometimes pay damages, but I didn't want him landing in jail." She paused, reached for the bottle again; but this time, instead of pouring more, she pushed it away with an angry look. "You understand, Vassily?"

"Of course, Panya Jadwiga."

She nodded. "They didn't take him in the army on account of his eye. So we stayed together all through the war. You know how it was in Lvov—one time the Austrians, then the Russkis—though they were different then. But things weren't too bad for me and Tadek. Except I had my worries about Tadek. Bad company. Though he's a good son, you know, Vassily."

"I know. But things were better, weren't they, after Antek met him and the two of them teamed up?"

"Yes—Antek. You didn't know him the way I did. Antek was

the best, the most decent man I ever met in my life. All those years we were together, never a loud word from him. Always polite. He knew how to make that gang respect him. He was smart. And like a brother to Tadek. And now"—she gestured vaguely in the direction of the pantry—"he's taken care of us for good. And Tadek works. That's good. That's the one good thing you can say about these Bolshies. You have to keep an eye on him, Vassily, the way Antek did."

"He'll be all right; don't worry about him."

He stood up. "I must run into town, Panya Jadwiga." He went to the shed, gave Golodnyi a crust of bread to munch on, and then hurried on foot through the many courtyards with their mounds of rubbish. He wanted to catch the streetcar before the noon break, when the crush on the trams became unbearable.

The Besselmann family was at table when Vassily arrived. "Where have you been all this while, Vassily?" Arye asked. "Your mail arrived punctually—four days ago. Works pretty well, doesn't it?"

"Go get him the letter," the boy's father commanded.

As Vassily started to tear open the envelope, he realized that there was no need; it was unsealed. And when he took out the letter, it was smooth and white, without as much as a single inscription on it. But neither he nor Besselmann senior or junior showed any surprise.

"Milk or alcohol?" Arye asked coolly.

Vassily went to the window, held the sheet against the light, smelled it, and said, "Alcohol."

Arye brought the bottle and a sponge. Vassily moistened it with a few drops of alcohol and dabbed the letter paper. "Only talks when drunk," Besselmann senior commented.

"How have things been, Hābhēr Besselmann?"

"Not too quiet. Quite a few arrests in the last few days. This time no politicals. Instead—" He looked over at Arye, who was intent on the gradually emerging writing.

"Yes, so I've heard—from the underworld," Vassily said.

"Very few Jews in the lot." Besselmann cleared his throat. "As a matter of fact, only one that I know of. When it's our people that are being deported, we manage to supply them with things, a little money, food, blankets. Some are taken just as they are, you know. We find a way to get things to them. But this time, praise be His name, only one Jew is involved. And he's no one to be sorry about, I must say—as you have to be sorry for the thousands who've been deported before, Jews and Christians both."

"Who is this man you know?" Vassily asked, largely out of politeness.

"Mermelstein is his name. Between you and me—we shouldn't say bad things about people—but between you and me, it's no loss to anybody."

"Ready, Hābhēr Vassily," Arye called out cheerfully.

Vassily took the letter slowly. He was disturbed by Besselmann's information. God knew what new complications might come out of Mermelstein's arrest—undoubtedly he'd been implicated by Josek. He also felt a certain pity for the man; the fool was probably being punished too harshly. . . . But here was Karl's letter!

The paper was covered with minuscule writing. Karl had contrived to convey everything important in words and phrases which —even if the letter should fall into hostile hands and be treated with alcohol—would have sounded like a doctor's confidential report to a colleague. Medicines were mentioned, possible treatments suggested—such as change of air. Dr. Stefan, at the writer's personal request, was administering the Stangman cure (*stânga* is Romanian for *left, mâna* for *hand;* i.e., Linkhand). But if no improvement was registered within three weeks, it might be best to call in Dr. Bringer, whose method usually achieved amazing success. The patient Sany was in the best of health, but suffering frequent psychic depressions. The Chief of the Internal Medicine Department had died suddenly.

Only one sentence was something of a puzzle to Vassily: that the doctor's patient Radmir had been cured of tolemia by *la răcoare.* On rereading the passage, however, even that became clear: tolemia stood for Anatol; and răcoare, Romanian for *coolness,* was used in its colloquial sense of the cooler, jail. *That* would be news for Janina! If he decided to tell her.

"Good," Vassily said. He went to the stove. The alcohol-soaked paper instantly caught fire. When it was reduced to ashes, he sat down at the table again.

"Are you satisfied, Hābhēr Vassily?" Arye asked.

"I most certainly am. Many thanks to both of you."

"We also have had a verbal message for you," Besselmann said. "You have been accorded unlimited credit."

"Very good. But at the moment I want to give and not receive." He took out the bundles of dollars. "Here are three thousand. Keep two thousand. In about three weeks, there may be two persons to take that little trip with Platzer—pardon, I mean Bringer. As for the remaining thousand, would you change it into rubles? I'll let you know what is to be done with it. And then there's one more thing. You mentioned Mermelstein—did the committee help him?"

"A Jew's a Jew, Hābhēr Vassily; that's taken care of in advance. He'll receive what's due him in the train. We have—hm—our connections. You might be surprised at how well informed we are. The transport leaves at five tomorrow morning."

"Then please add five thousand rubles to the gift for Mermelstein and charge it to my account. You might also send him some winter underwear, perhaps a heavy fur coat, blankets, felt boots and tinned foods, if you can get hold of any. Please," he said, in response to Besselmann's look of utter astonishment, "I have my reasons for wanting to help him."

"As you wish, hābhēr," Besselmann said.

"I'm much obliged. Now I must run. Robota!"

Arye collected his pile of school books and went along.

Outside, Vassily had some further words with the boy. "If I don't come to see you again within three weeks," he said, "take that thousand dollars' worth of rubles to Comrade Janina Feuerberg. She is a piano teacher at the Conservatory and works there from, I think, eleven to five. Make a nice package of the money and tell her she's not to open it until she gets home, that it's from Vassily. And tell her also that if she needs anything else, or is ever short, she should come to you. Any money you may advance her is to be placed on Rundberg's account. Will you do that, Arye?"

"*Ken, adoni!*"

"What does that mean?"

"Yes, my master—in Hebrew."

"There are no masters, Arye," Vassily admonished him, laughing.

"That's what you say!" Arye retorted.

As Vassily rode into the yard, he saw Mira just coming from the stable. She ran toward him. "Thank God you're here," she said. "The new Director's come."

"Already?"

"You'd barely left when he arrived. How is it you didn't meet him? He came on foot."

"I rode through the fields."

"He's already asked for you."

"He can wait," Vassily growled. "What's he like?"

"Twenty-five years old, party candidate, a sailor for eight years. Every second word is 'nichevo' and he holds the world's record for spitting. I would never have believed it possible. Now he's sitting in the canteen with that Obadieva girl. She's flattering him and he loves it. He's telling her stories about storms and fishing, and she keeps saying, 'Remarkable,' and he keeps saying, "Nichevo,' and spitting. This is just about the end—how can we go on with our work?"

"Is he so smart?" Vassily asked, smiling. Mira was most attractive when she was in a temper. "If this will ease your mind any, you'll have to carry on for three weeks more at the most. Is that possible?"

"Vassily!" she whispered hoarsely. "Oh God, if only—"

"Virtually a ninety per cent certainty, Mira."

"If there were only one chance in a hundred, we'd gladly risk it. And if you're with us—"

Vassily stooped and felt Golodnye's hocks. He did not want Mira to see his face because he hated to deceive her. The patient Sany's (Varsany's) psychic depressions—Karl had thrown that in on purpose, he was sure—had greatly increased his longing to return. When the time came, it would be a parting of the ways with Mira. But until than he wanted to stay with her, to help her. Once she was across the border and could rejoin her family, once she was breathing a different air, once she was embarked again on the life for which she was meant, she would forget Vassily the stablemaster, who had played such a role in her strange adventure in Poland. Vassily straightened up slowly and looked around the yard. There was no one else in it. "Could you hold the horse, Mira?" he asked. "I need to get a watering can."

"He's perfectly gentle, and I can handle riding horses, you know." She reached for the reins.

"Talk to him, tell him something!" Vassily hurried into the stable and returned with the watering can. "Hold him a little longer." He filled the can and directed the spray against Golodnyi's legs. The stallion stood quietly. Vassily took the reins from Mira's hand. "You've never really looked at this horse, Mira," he said. "I don't suppose you've seen his handsome brand. Here!"

Mira's eyes followed his pointing finger. "One moment," she said, and leaned forward to study the brand. When she straightened up, her face was pale. "I know the monogram."

"Do you? You must be something of an expert. That happens to be the stud brand of Prince Bolgurski. He has, or rather had, property around Warsaw."

"Warsaw," she whispered almost inaudibly. Her face was tense; two deep furrows appeared between her brows. Then she regained her composure. "How old is the horse?" she asked quietly.

"I would estimate about five. A fine animal."

"I know, I know. . . . Take him in; I'll wait here until you come back."

Vassily unsaddled the horse, feeling somewhat guilty at having so cleverly staged the incident which had unsettled Mira. Ever since Janina had mentioned the house of Linkhand in Warsaw, he had thought of sounding Mira out and learning the true story of the inheritance—perhaps it would help him to understand Anatol's behavior better. Mira would surely know the ins and outs of the affair.

When he rejoined her, she said, "Vassily, you are very fond of horses?"

"Very." He nodded soberly.

"There's something I must tell you, Vassily. Come to my house this evening, will you? Come tonight—no questions now."

In the canteen they found only the Director and the cashier. She was standing in a casual pose against the wall, and he was sitting astride a chair, separated from her by the whole length of the room, waving his arms. He seemed to be completely taken up in what he was describing, and was demonstrating rowing movements, a boat in a storm, or something of the kind. His round sailor's cap sat askew on his close-cropped hair, and the sleeves of his heavy blue sweater had worked up to his elbows. His forearms were covered with tattoos. "That was the way it was, Tatiana—no cinch, but— nichevo!" He spat almost as far as his listener's toes.

The sailor had seen Mira and Vassily enter, but had told his story to the end. Now, however, he was all sobriety and dignity, as befitted a director. He introduced himself as Ignat Ilich Gorbatenko and at once outlined his program to the bookkeeper and the starshi koniukh. For the present everything was to go on as it had been going, until he had a chance to acquaint himself minutely with the operations of the farm. But he could say in advance that he would place great stress on certain points: discipline, hygiene, and political education. "Well then, I must get to work," Vassily said. "Comrade Bookkeeper will show you your quarters."

Vassily went to the garden and worked for an hour with Tadek and Freddy, telling them the latest news of the farm. "Director, cashier—a fat lot of use they are," Tadek piped. "We need at least two more people to handle the garden. Things are sprouting already—you can see that, Vassily."

From the garden he went to the stable to meet the teams, which would soon be returning. He had intended to prepare the drivers and advise them to be careful, but the Director was already in the stable, a list in his hands. Under the circumstances Vassily could only make a short announcement before he handed out the feed. "Listen, fellows," he called. "The comrade standing here is the new director of the farm. His name is Gorbatenko, Ignat Ilich."

The drivers seemed disinclined to break into cheers. The Director took occasion to say a word: "Comrades, as you have heard, I am the new director. And so you'll know right from the start, I look for three things in particular: discipline, hygiene and political training." He spat and was about to go on talking, but his pause was too long; Vassily tapped his bowl against the grain bin, the horses began their neighing and stamping, drivers lined up for their rations. As they filed past the grain chest, they had time to give their new chief a close scrutiny, and size him up. His remarks had scarcely registered on their consciousness. Most of them knew what the word discipline meant, but none of them understood hygiene (*gigiena*), and political education was, in their minds, a phrase straight out of slogans. Vassily would tell them later how to behave. For the present they poured out the oats for their horses and stood by until they had eaten, making sure no horse took more than his proper share.

Meanwhile Ignat Ilich Gorbatenko walked with a swaying gait, as if on the deck of a ship in a heavy sea, down the stable aisle, counting the horses and comparing the count with his list.

"Five sections, ten horses in each," Vassily explained. "The last stall takes only four. The two horses used for carting manure stand separate as you see, and the stallion is kept on the other side of the partition. None missing. Fifty-seven in all."

"Fifty-seven in all," the Director repeated. He looked at the list once more. "And where are the cows? A hundred and one head?"

"Cows." He felt considerable misgiving. Kornhaber would not be able to cope with the sailor's questions. Who could say what might come of this inspection? "In another barn," he said. "They're just milking now. Let's go."

The milkmaids were at work in the barn, sitting on their low stools, talking to the cows softly or admonishingly. Kornhaber, who had evidently been warned of the arrival of the new Director, had withdrawn to the end of the barn and was busy with the milk pails. But he could not escape, for Gorbatenko entered demanding, "Who is the starshi here?"

"Comrade Kornhaber!" Vassily called out loudly. "Quiet girls," he added, "this comrade is the new Director of the farm."

He went no further, for Gorbatenko pushed him aside, eager to introduce himself. By this time Kornhaber had presented himself. Gorbatenko gave the starshi a look of astonishment that quickly changed to anger. "You are responsible here?" he asked sternly.

Kornhaber, not understanding Russian, looked as Vassily. At Vassily's nod, he said, "Da."

"And what is that?" the Director said scornfully, pointing to the cakes of manure.

"Cowflop," a woman's voice called out so loudly that Gorbatenko turned sharply.

"I am speaking to the starshi *korovnik* [milker]; he is to answer me. Why is cowflop lying around?" he demanded of Kornhaber.

"Because the cows have just shit." It was the same woman's voice.

"Who said that?" Gorbatenko took a step in the direction of the mocking voice. When no one answered, he turned back to Kornhaber.

"No hygiene, no discipline. You are responsible. I am the Director now. This must not happen." He pointed to the manure; the cows, tails raised, were at the moment steadily adding to the quantity in the gutters, with loud splattering noises. "Filth. That's got to stop!" The order having been given, he went to the end of the barn and began counting the cows.

"Don't be afraid of him," Vassily said to Kornhaber in an undertone. And he called toward the voice, "Be careful, Vasilena!"

"Starshi Korovnik!" Gorbatenko's voice rang out. Kornhaber started off at a run, but Vassily restrained him. "Go slowly and show no anxiety at all." He too strolled toward the director.

"You must see to the strictest hygiene; I'm making you responsible for it. Tomorrow I'll make a full count. See to it that no cows are missing!" He swayed down the aisle, to the accompaniment of the milkers' crooning to the cows and the steady splat of dung into the gutter.

As soon as he was outside, he said to Vassily, "This starshi korovnik is a *zhid!*"

Vassily pricked up his ears. This was the first time he had heard a Russian use this term. Only the term *evrei* was legitimate; anyone who said *zhid* was throwing himself open to a charge of anti-Semitism, and could be tried for it.

"Yes," he said slowly, emphatically changing the word, "Comrade Kornhaber is a evrei."

"I spit on him!" Gorbatenko illustrated his pronouncement; the missile did not strike Kornhaber but the hatch of the cellar entry, a good twenty feet from where he stood.

Vassily growled something about an urgent errand and strode off rapidly.

Late that evening—Freddy was already asleep—Vassily and Mira discussed the events of the day in her room. "This Obadieva girl," Mira said. "I don't know what to make of her. She's altogether different from the Russians I've met up to now. The clothes she's wearing are no longer new, but they're good and were custom-made for her. That suit and that blouse. . . . Either she's been the protégée of someone high up, and they're punishing her by sending her out here, or—"

"Or else she was sent to us specially, and not just as a cashier." Vassily finished the sentence.

"That's what I think. She came from Kharkhov. By plane. She has a mission here—what it is God only knows. She's a spy, Vassily."

"Everybody is, or everybody has to be, in the end. Don't worry, Mira. The books are in order. We'll lay off the free-market trade for a while. Have you a decent surplus?"

She nodded. "Forty-six pigs and about seven thousand rubles. Besides, we've had favorable action on our petition. Ten tons of feed grains at government prices. We can work on the up and up for a month or even more."

"It won't take that long before you're over the border, Mira. I can guarantee it. But what about the others? Wagner, Meerblum, Kornhaber, and a good many of the drivers." Mira looked at him in some wonder, but refrained from questions. He went on, "You see, the Director is—well, he doesn't seem to be fond of Jews."

"What proof have you of that?" She watched him tensely while he told his story.

"It doesn't surprise me that he is an anti-Semite," she said. "They all are, more or less, but that he shows it and even says it—"

"Yes, that's exactly it. There remains the possibility that he's a *provocateur.*"

"That idiot?" Mira shook her head violently. "I don't believe that for a moment. He doesn't like Jews and assumed that you wouldn't either. He didn't feel he had to be careful with you. Or else—" She broke off and gave him a searching look.

"Or else? What did you want to say?"

"Say? First I must ask something, Vassily."

"What are you afraid of?" He smiled reassuringly at her.

"Do you hate and despise Jews—and Jewish women—too?"

He stopped smiling. "What makes you ask that, Mira? Have I ever given you cause to think so?"

"No, no!" She shook her head vehemently. "On the contrary!"

"All right, then. Once and for all, Mira: I see no difference." He spoke with unwonted sternness.

"Don't, Vassily, don't be angry. Please don't. The idea's been haunting me since this afternoon. Ever since I saw that monogram —of Bolgurski." Her feelings were dark and chaotic, even to herself. She groped for words. "The whole thing was dead, as though it had never been, and these past few hours it's been tormenting me so—because of you, Vassily."

"I don't understand, Mira. Tell me about it, if you can."

And Mira told him. Told him everything, from her first meeting with Count Voronovski to that horrible and grotesque scene which had marked the end of her dream of love and happiness. "And your horse Golodnyi," she said, "is Vladek's Slim—one hair of whose tail is worth more than a hundred thousand redheaded Jewesses."

Vassily nodded mutely. "If it had been a real gun instead of a cigarette box, would you have fired?" he asked.

"Would I have fired? Perhaps—I don't know. If I had, it would have been only because I felt his hatred and his scorn, not because he rejected my love. It was terrible. From that moment on I've known what it means to be hated just for being Jewish."

"Oh," Vassily said contemptuously, "his hatred was worth no more than his love. Forgive me, I don't mean to hurt you."

"I know his love was worthless," she replied. "But the hatred— it must have been there all the time—that hatred for the Jews. And yet how could he have embraced me hundreds of times, called me by all kinds of endearments, accepted everything from me? I can't understand it, Vassily."

He took her hand and stroked it. "It isn't easy to understand, Mira. And yet that paradox exists; you've experienced it." He could have said a good deal more if he had not been Vassily the koniukh. "And how many are experiencing just the opposite? Especially now, Mira. How many men stick to their Jewish wives, how many wives to their Jewish husbands? They submit to suffering and want in order to stay together. Not everyone is like His Excellency the Count."

"You certainly are not. I must apologize—but—it was seeing the way you handle horses, the way you love them—and then, finding out that the horse was Slim. It made you seem so like him, and suddenly I was terrified, wondering whether perhaps you too. . . . Do you think he's still alive? And how would this horse have fallen into the hands of the Russians?"

"It's possible to love horses and still to love people more," Vassily said gravely. "The one thing has nothing to do with the other. And I am not a count, I am Vassily. . . . There was a war fought here. Perhaps he's a prisoner, of either the Germans or the Russians—who knows? Or perhaps he's crossed the border."

"You're worth more than a hundred thousand counts, Vassily," Mira said.

"There are decent counts, too. I know a lot of them. And you must be my sensible Mira and not make yourself unhappy with needless brooding." He took her in his arms and kissed her. During the next few hours they spoke very little.

Within the span of a few days Gorbatenko succeeded in making himself generally unpopular. He bellowed, he repeated his piece about discipline, hygiene and political education, spat, nichevoed, and paid endless inspection calls on the workshops, garden, dairy, stable and especially the cow barn, where he took sadistic pleasure in seeing the small, weak Jew Kornhaber scurrying up and down the aisle to remove manure as fast as it was deposited, or toiling out with the heavy dung cart.

He had a run-in with the Red Army soldiers who, as was their wont, came to spend their free evening at the canteen. Self-importantly and rudely, Gorbatenko began to interrogate them, which resulted in a long debate over whether he had any right to do so. One of the veterinaries, a sensible young man, finally managed to smooth over the quarrel and establish a kind of armistice, but the usual gaiety was dampened, and instead of singing and dancing with the farm girls, the Red Army men soon left.

Vassily heard about the squabble next morning, and while he was driving Mira and the cashier to town, he thought it over carefully. Although everything he had seen and heard of the new Director marked him as a stupid, rude, arrogant and reckless fellow, there was simply no explaining this latest episode. For the Red Army was the pride—the coddled favorite child—of all Soviet Russians without exception. Out of the ragged, anarchic hordes of the Civil War's Red Guard there had developed a regular army whose equipment the Russians were wont to describe with wild exaggeration, but whose organization and appearance were undoubtedly unique and impressive.

Anyone who had ever belonged to an army could not help but be struck by the quality of the Soviet soldier, from the ordinary soldier to the *kommandir*. There was none of that heel-clicking spit-and-polish discipline which results from crushing the individual's spirit and will. The men moved lightly but rhythmically, taking short, easy steps; they were never bawled out for getting out of step during drill. No Red Army soldier was obligated to salute a superior. Food was the same for enlisted men and officers. And there was as much concern for the entertainment of Red Army men as for their physical welfare. Three-quarters of the audience at movie houses consisted of soldiers. Any ensemble of artists that came to a town for guest performances invariably set aside one or two evenings for playing for the army.

In those April days of 1940, when Vassily was puzzled by the new Director's foolish behavior toward the Red Army, the soldier had a special status within the framework of Soviet society. Surprisingly enough, this seldom made him arrogant. Rather, he was inclined to display a certain dignity, a grave friendliness and candor. An observer like Vassily, who based his conclusions only on personal observation and carefully avoided discussing the matter with soldiers or those who might be better informed than himself, could plainly see that the army stood outside the sphere of anxiety which enclosed everyone else. If a serious dispute developed between a Red Army man and a civilian, the Red Army man could be sure of winning. Hence Vassily's astonishment at the behavior of the new Director was all the greater, and he wondered whether he should not drop a hint to Saposhnik or Feingold. He decided, however, to keep quiet about it. If Mira, who was irreplaceable, departed, and if he himself took off, as he intended to do, the farm would lose all backbone anyhow, and would soon go hurtling down the same track as all the other farms of the vicinity.

At headquarters Feingold saw Vassily coming from Saposhnik's office and beckoned to him. Smilingly, he offered Vassily one of his cigarettes and chatted amiably with him for a few minutes. Then, abruptly, he said, "Did you know that the former Director, Mermelstein, has been resettled?"

"Resettled? What does that mean, Comrade Feingold? He's already been transferred, from Jiusefovka to Soniewicze."

"Now he's going to travel a little farther. He was caught in a raid, in a prostitute's apartment."

Vassily showed extreme astonishment and naïve wonder. "But he has no wife; under such conditions, was it a major offense for him to go to one?"

Feingold laughed. "That isn't the reason for his resettlement. He had no komandirovka, had come to the city illegally, and so the NKVD sent an inquiry to Nikiforiuk. He answered that he would be happy if they sent Mermelstein away—as far as possible—that the man was no use to them at all. Mermelstein wasn't such an agricultural genius, was he, Vassily Vassilevich?" Feingold asked, winking.

"That's a director for you—where has he been sent?"

"Where people live, and work. And how they work! I myself worked for two years in the north—see this?" He held out his left hand; the little finger and the ring finger were mutilated. "Frozen, and almost all my toes too."

There was a knock at the door. Feingold said, "Da!" A man entered. Vassily had time to observe him, for Feingold, who obviously had no prior acquaintance with the man, went forward to meet him, talked with him for a few minutes in a low voice, and checked his documents. Vassily was struck at once by the neatness of the man's appearance. His dark-blue jacket was spotlessly clean; his trousers did not have the usual comic puffs at the thighs. His knee boots, too, did not sag or flap, and they were carefully polished. His dark-brown hair was not close-cropped as most Russians wore it, nor did it fall in locks or strands over his forehead; it was parted carefully on one side and brushed back. As Feingold finished his conversation and invited the man to sit down in the chair at his desk, Vassily saw a pallid oval face, a rather protruding brow, deep-set brown eyes, pinched lips, and a weak chin.

"This is Comrade Ivanchuk," Feingold said. "He speaks Romanian and seems to doubt me when I tell him that you know it too."

The good-natured smile with which Vassily received these words was a miracle of hypocrisy. Not only was it strange that Feingold should suddenly be interested in his knowledge of the Romanian language, but there was something highly enigmatic about the man who had been called in to test that knowledge. Vassily's life might well depend on the results of this little examination. What was more, Vassily had the strongest feeling that he had met this man before. And while he puffed at his cigarette, he strained his memory to the utmost—and was successful. He knew the man.

Eleven years ago the man sitting opposite him had been a lieutenant in a field artillery regiment garrisoned in the well-known town of Sadagora, five miles from Cernauti. The son of a Ruthenian village schoolmaster, Ivanchuk had changed his name to its Romanian equivalent, Ionescu, and joined a Romanian nationalist student group. He had been called up for military service, and after his two years were done had remained in the army. Shortly after being promoted to his lieutenancy, he had deserted and made it known by letter that he was crossing the Dniester to join the Bolsheviki. The incident in itself was grist to the mills of the nationalist newspapers, but what had made a real sensation was the romantic background of the affair. Ionescu-Ivanchuk had been twenty-six at the time of his desertion and was engaged to a beautiful Jewish girl of barely nineteen, an orphan who lived with her brother, a businessman in Sadagora. Even as the girl suffered the first pangs of heartbreak at the loss of her fiancé, the Sigurantza descended. The whole family was suspected of connections with the Bolsheviki. Their house was searched; as bad luck would have it, letters from the deserter were found. These were so childish and idealistic in content that they could not be taken seriously; nevertheless they were considered damning evidence of complicity. The girl was sentenced to four years' imprisonment, her brother and sister-in-law to two years each. The latter were reduced to penury, but were at least able to emigrate and begin a new life; the unfortunate heroine of the romance left the prison half demented, and with a case of acute tuberculosis—an old woman at twenty-four. Soon after her release she died miserably.

But the man Ivanchuk had evidently done well in his elected homeland. He must have even become a party member—for only as such could he hold the responsible post of interpreter. And here he was to test Vassily's knowledge of Romanian.

Vassily's anxiety vanished almost as soon as the conversation began. He had only to remember to give his mother tongue a slight Slavic accent, and that was easy enough, for he just needed to imitate Ivanchuk himself.

"How do you know Romanian?" Ivanchuk asked, as Vassily had expected. "Are you from Bessarabia or Bucovina?"

"Neither," Vassily replied with complete composure. And he told an involved story about a village named Ovsyechleb which had been cut in two when the border between Romania and Poland was adjusted. He himself, because his grandfather's house stood behind the mill, became a Polish subject. The estate where he worked as a schoolboy later became Romanian.

When Vassily mentioned certain villages in Transylvania, his examiner guided the conversation, not very skillfully, back to places in Bucovina, especially the northern part, and finally, after much beating about the bush, he brought up a landowner named Mustatza. Vassily could feel that he was driven by an impulse stronger than all caution.

"Mustatza?" he asked. "Do you mean Baron Mustatza?"

"Was he a baron?" The interpreter injected the maximum of contempt into his tone.

"I know one who was a baron; he was an officer in my regiment under the Austrians. In Romania there are no barons, though in Bucovina and Transylvania too they still use the title."

"To hell with them!" the former artilleryman said dutifully in Russian and Romanian. "You didn't by any chance work for him?"

"Not for him, but for a relative of his, Grigorcea was his name. Mustatza didn't keep any horses—any thoroughbreds, I mean. But

I once called on him with a stallion, a heavy Norman horse that belonged to Grigorcea, for stud service. For Mustatza's work-horses."

"I see. Where was his property?"

"In Sadagora, a small town near Cernauti."

"Were you there long? And when?"

"I can tell you exactly—for three weeks in November, 1932."

"Then you must have been in the town too, weren't you?"

"Of course. It isn't far from the estate, and I had plenty of time to kill. It's a dull place, movies only once a week."

"Did you know any people there?"

"Know any? I talked with some of them in taverns or at the market—there are many Ruthenians there."

"Many Jews also?"

"They outnumber the Ruthenians. There's a famous rabbi in the town, in fact. Many Jews come to see him, even from far away. He has a whole estate of his own, with a manor house and a good many outbuildings. Lives like a boyar, because people come to him for help and advice, and the rich Jews pay heavily. Not only Jews come to him."

There was a long pause, so long that Feingold began to wonder. He looked up inquiringly, and the interpreter seemed uneasy. He had used, or rather abused, the examination for his own ends; he had not stuck to the prescribed pattern of questions, and therefore had not received his quota of answers. His guilty conscience made him insecure. He did not dare to go deeper into the subject that really concerned him. And so he asked Vassily sternly, "Have you ever belonged to any political organization?"

"Never," Vassily truthfully replied.

"Can you read and write Romanian?"

"About as well as I can Ruthenian, I think."

The examiner took a printed sheet from his pocket. He handed it to Vassily, who quickly saw that it was the Stalin Constitution, in Romanian. "Read this aloud and translate it into Ruthenian or Russian, whichever you like."

Vassily read carefully and slowly; he made a few mistakes, of course, and once asked the meaning of a difficult word. But when he had finished, the examiner looked over at Feingold and nodded. The former Lieutenant stood up and shook hands with Vassily. Feingold accompanied him to the door, and returned obviously pleased. "You acquitted yourself well, Vassily Vassilevich," he said.

"Oh well," Vassily said, "Comrade Ivanchuk knows it all much better. I've only learned by ear, you understand, Comrade Feingold."

* * *

"Bookkeeper," the Director said to Mira as he rummaged among the pamphlets on the shelf, "give me the books on milk production for the past few months."

Without a word, Mira placed the material on the desk and resumed her work. The folder was a fat one, for she had taken pains to set up a separate sheet for each cow. Aside from the fact that not a single one of the animals had yielded the officially prescribed quantity of sixty pounds a day, a good part of the actual production had been subtracted to be made into the butter which was sold on the free market. They had already prepared a plausible explanation in case of any check: the totally inadequate "official" feed supplies, which scarcely would have sufficed even to keep the cows alive. Since Mira, in view of the new Director and the hopeful prospect that she would soon be leaving, had put an end to all free-market dealings—much to the relief of everyone involved—the yield had automatically increased. For that, too, there was an adequate explanation: the assignment of feed at the ridiculously low government prices, which had made possible an increase in the cows' rations.

In any case Mira was not responsible for milk production, only for keeping careful records of the same. Moreover, she had taken the precaution of protesting repeatedly to Saposhnik about the shortage of feed. At the inspection by the highest party functionaries the whole farm had come off very well. Consequently, she was scarcely troubled when the Director, roaring with laughter, pounded his fist on the desk and roared that he had found "where the rat is buried." Even when he started ranting about "the Yid work" and "the zhidok Kornhaber," she scarcely frowned. Bent over her books, she went on with her computations.

Not so the cashier. For once Tatiana Nikolaevna Obadieva did not exclaim "Remarkable," as was her wont when the Director put on one of his exhibitions. Instead she raised her voice in a surprising accusation: "What you have just said, citizen, is provocation, anti-Semitism, and a violation of the Stalin Constitution. Every pioneer is supposed to know those things. You are actually a party candidate and must be perfectly aware of these statutes. As such you also know that I am required to file a denunciation against you. Comrade Bookkeeper, may I have a sheet of paper, please. You, too, are required to make a report. Required, you understand!"

Mira was greatly disturbed. Those words had not been spoken by the "playgirl" whom she mistrusted anyhow; the tone and the matter-of-factness were those of a genuine partinyi. Although Mira had accepted the girl's ignorance and incompetence, and did not even feel contempt for her, she was repelled by Tatiana's whole personality, and still more by her way of making advances to Vassily. Mira was suffering—for the first time in her life—from the torments of jealousy, which were all the more burning because her reticent nature forbade her from voicing these feelings. But now the cashier was placing Mira in a dilemma which she had so far managed to evade. Rather than attract attention to herself by a written denunciation, which might entail her appearing later as a witness, she would meekly have put up with far worse insults than those of this blustering sailor. But the words had been spoken; the cashier had left her no alternative; she must take the step which might lead to unknown complications. What did this otherwise feather-headed and—if she discounted her own distrust and jealousy—distinctly droll and amusing little creature have in mind? To whom was the denunciation going to be sent? What would come of it? Mira was seized by sheer terror—by the fear that the cashier's correct sovietski behavior might start an avalanche which would come crashing down upon the farm and smash the façade she and the others had built up so painfully with so much physical and mental toil. And while she glanced covertly from the altogether unabashed Director, who went on contentedly spitting and grunting "nichevo," to the cashier who was absorbed in the composition of her denunciation, she fervently wished that Vassily were here to advise her.

The cashier finished writing and asked, "Are you done with yours, Comrade Bookkeeper?"

Mira had not even begun. "I have no experience in writing denunciations. If you would show me your—letter. . . ."

"My letter goes to a different address, but I'll gladly write your statement for you and you need only sign."

"I would be very grateful," Mira said.

"Here—it's good to know how to do these things too. Upper left, your name—Mira Isakovna, isn't it? And the surname—Linhan. Then Bookkeeper, then the organization, and the date. And then: 'To the Comrade Director of the Elektrostantsia: I, the undersigned, hereby inform you that the Director, etc., today at 10:35 o'clock in my presence said *zhidok.*' Then sign it." She read what Mira had written at her dictation. "That's all there is to it. We'll go right away." And she said to the Director, who was standing at the open window, spitting, "I need transportation. I must go to the city."

Without turning around, Gorbatenko replied, "I am not a koniukh; the starshi has ridden out to the fields, and when he returns I will forbid him to drive you. It isn't so far; you can easily

walk that distance. During the noon recess or after work, of course!
I am the Director and I came out here on foot."

The cashier did not reply. The Director sat down again at his
table and started reading his pamphlet, his lips moving as he did so.
At twelve o'clock Mira began clearing her desk, and when she was
done she left the office. The cashier followed her, and with a
curt "So long," began tramping in the direction of town. Heavy-
heartedly, Mira went to the garden and picked up Freddy; they always ate lunch at home. The Director ate alone in the canteen. The
few others who came to the canteen to lunch—the main meal was
served in the evening—sped through their eating and went home
for a brief nap.

When Vassily rode into the yard around one o'clock, noontime
repose had spread over the whole farm. He took care of Golodnyi
and set out for the canteen. On the way he saw Mira standing at the
door of her house beckoning to him. From the very way she stood
there he knew that something disturbing had occurred. And when, sitting with her in the kitchen, he heard her story, he grew thoughtful.
Mira had good reason to be concerned. The cashier's denunciation
might well upset the whole applecart. But the first thing to do was
to reassure Mira, and so he pretended to take the whole matter
lightly. He succeeded in dispelling her anxiety, although he himself
could not reconcile the cashier's rigorously Soviet conduct in this case
with her ordinary attitude, which was the very opposite of Soviet
strictness. "Anyhow," he said, reaching for his cap, "the bureaucracy
is usually pretty slow to act on these things. She's probably sent
her report in to the party. It'll take a while for them to decide
whether or not to do something. Don't forget, he's not the only one
to be denounced. And each has to take his turn. By the time his turn
comes, you'll be—" He whistled cheerfully.

His good humor and his optimism were infectious. *"We,* Vassily!" She took his head in both hands and kissed him—Freddy, in
the next room, was sleeping his deep, childlike sleep.

"Yes, we, Mira—I'm coming too. Whether it will be at the same
time, I don't know. I can't decide that." Her face clouded. "You see,
I'm not arranging it. The man won't take more than two persons at
one time. And Freddy can't manage without you."

"But what about you? Without you, Vassily?" She was deeply
distressed.

"I'll follow right after you—with the next shipment." He
laughed. "Ochered—then it'll be my turn. You have my word, Mira."

"I'll be very anxious about you, Vassily."

"I wish you were out of this already."

He stood up. As he laid his hand on the door latch, she threw her arms around him and kissed him ardently on the mouth and eyes. "Vassily," she whispered hoarsely, "Vassily, I can't imagine life without you."

As he approached his house, Gorbatenko appeared at the door of the sausage plant. "Starshi Koniukh, where the devil have you been?" he roared.

Vassily took his huge watch from his pocket. "It's not yet three, Comrade Director—fifteen minutes before."

"You and your watch! The zamestitel of the Party Chairman— Tarashchenko—has called. The carriage must go to the Party Committee headquarters at once!"

"At once?" Vassily repeated. "All right, I'll go hitch up. Telephone them that I'll be there in an hour. They'd better wait downstairs for me, because I can't let the horses stand in the street."

"Nichevo," the Director said.

Only the cashier stood at the side entrance when Vassily brought the roans to a halt. The carriage he was driving looked very elegant, which fact the cashier dramatized in her own fashion. With both hands she grasped the sides of her knee-length sports skirt, vividly mimicking the gesture of gathering up a train. Haughtily squinting and drawing down the corners of her mouth, she clambered into the vehicle. When she had taken her seat with exaggerated dignity, she crossed her legs, pretended to be tucking a monocle into her eye, and put on the bored expression of a roué of the hated old regime.

Vassily laughed so heartily that the frozen face of the guard at the entrance dissolved into a look of alarm; he shook his head in perplexity as he watched the departing carriage. Tania leaned forward, propping her elbows on the back of the coachman's seat. "I've fixed him, our sailor," she said. "Drive faster, Vassinka, so we get out of town quicker." Then she sat back and amused herself by nodding graciously to pedestrians who looked up, startled, at the sight of the equipage. As soon as they reached the end of the streetcar line, she scrambled over to sit beside Vassily and commanded sternly, "Cigarette!" When it was lit, she said, "Remarkable," and began trilling in imitation of an opera star. Between notes she took puffs of the cigarette, and when the song was finished, she fell silent. The roans, which by now had recovered completely from Rudnicki's mistreatment, trotted along gaily on the wide, dry road; the afternoon sun spread its glow over all the fresh green growth in the fields and along the roadside. Vassily enjoyed the landscape and the movement, and evidently his pleasure was mirrored in his face, for Tania, who was scrutinizing him closely, said, "Beautiful, isn't it, Vassinka? Hard to believe that people, seeing all this beauty, can remain stupid and wicked and always be trying to kill each other." She sighed—a real sigh from the heart.

"Yes, people. . . ." Vassily said, without turning his head.

"Look at Gorbatenko—that idiot, that boor. Running amok out of sheer stupidity. Do you know what it means, to run amok?"

"Amok? No, I don't know the word."

She gave him a crude explanation; he dutifully expressed wonderment and asked how this applied to the Director.

"Apparently the fellow's stupid and arrogant enough to go in for provocation. As though he didn't know exactly where it leads. Is it worth it?"

"I don't understand much about that, but—in a big pond there are all kinds of fish."

"Suppose you leave the business of quoting proverbs to others, Vassily! Fish have one advantage: they can't talk. Men's own tongues are their worst enemies, I might tell you, but I won't."

"You're right." He laughed. "You have such an enemy in your own mouth."

"In my pretty mouth you mean, don't you, Vassily?" she asked with exaggerated coyness. "Oh, in my case it doesn't matter; they don't take me seriously." And as if she meant to confide a great secret to him, she twisted and turned, looking around as if to make sure no one was spying, and with darkly frowning brow whispered into his ear, "They think I'm cuckoo." She twirled her finger with an eloquent gesture at her own forehead. "It's very pleasant; it makes things a lot easier sometimes. Understand, Vassily?"

He let the horses drop from a trot to a walk. "When I consider it—you told the bookkeeper that we're required to send in a report when we hear anyone saying things, saying any"—he pretended to be trying to remember the long word—"provocations and anti-Semitism. Didn't you?"

"That's a word you ought to know! And since you're so fond of proverbs—eat or be eaten!"

"Well, then, I should report you. I'm not supposed to realize that you're—cuckoo. Or am I?"

"Can't you tell right away?" She laughed, and then abruptly turned deadly serious. "If you hadn't realized it up to now, then of course you're supposed to report me. Absolutely! But what would you bring up against me?"

"Well, you don't always talk like a real Soviet citizen. Sometimes it sounds very much like—provocation."

"Then you shouldn't have waited so long before reporting me. Eat or be eaten," she repeated, laughing.

"How was I to know? I always take a while to think things over. But don't you think it would be better if you stopped playing games and didn't go on with your—provocations? What's the point of it? One of these days you'll run into someone who doesn't consider so carefully, and he'll run off and denounce you, and then you'll be in hot water. Or else you'll run into someone who chimes in with what you say, but means it, and then you'll have to denounce him. It will be your duty."

"Oh. You see, Vassily, if I hadn't denounced the sailor and made the bookkeeper do the same, it might easily happen that fellow would denounce us. When people talk that way, it isn't always genuine. Sometimes they do it only to find out what the other man thinks. And then if you don't act the right way, if you don't denounce, you're denounced for not having made a denunciation. Get it, Vassily?"

He shook his head vigorously. "No, I don't get it. What in the world is the good of it? No, Tania, I think you really are—"

"Cuckoo. . . . Another cigarette, please."

Vassily gathered up the reins, and the roans trotted. But not for long, for Rudnenko stood by the road, waving. When the carriage stopped, he shook hands with Vassily, ignoring the passenger. "Ah," he said. "I have to ambush you if I want to see you. Can't you come into the house for a moment? You ought to see it now, and have a plate of borshch with us. My old lady's a damned good cook, I tell you!"

"Thanks," Vassily said, "I can't just now. I have to take our cashier home and be at the stable at feeding time. The teams ought to be on their way home about now—haven't you seen them?"

"Oh well, then I suppose you can't. May I ride with you? There are some things I want to talk over."

"Get in, Dmitri Alexevich. You can ride home later with one of the Red Army men; they always come for bread around this time."

"Fine. In that case I'll bring Vanka. One moment." He ran into the house.

"The master machinist from Plant I," Vassily explained.

Tania was obviously annoyed to have their tête-à-tête interrupted. Then Rudnenko came out, the baby on his arm, his bulky wife trailing after him. "A baby!" Tania exclaimed delightedly. When everyone still ignored her, she sprang down from the box and went up to Rudnenko. "A boy—oh, how sweet! How old is he?" she bubbled, taking the baby's little hands and kissing them.

"Oh, give him to me. You want to talk with Vassily anyway, don't you? Sit with him—I'll take care of the baby. I—"

Hesitantly, Rudnenko held the child out to her. His wife, however, her big round face beaming, said, "I suppose you have no children?"

Tania did not hear the question; she was too taken up with Vanka, who was exultantly pulling her hair. "Good-bye." And as the carriage started up again she waved to Rudnenko's wife. "I'll take good care of him, I will."

As they drove, Rudnenko explained to Vassily what was on his mind. He intended to make use of a piece of fallow land that adjoined his garden. But he lacked a plow, harrow and horses.

"I'd like to be able to help," Vassily said. "But we have a new Director. If you could bring an order from Saposhnik. . . . Anything I can do personally, I'll be glad to do."

"I know that. So you think the new Director might make trouble?"

Tania, who was absorbed in the game that she or Vanka had invented, nevertheless was eavesdropping on the men's conversation. "The Director will make no trouble," she remarked. "Don't worry about him. But as for Saposhnik—he was just at the Secretariat. His wife, it seems, will not live out the night."

Vassily and Rudnenko both turned around. "Has it come to that already?" Vassily asked.

Rudnenko exclaimed with some surprise. "At the Secretariat?" "Are you a party member?"

"Don't look it, do I, little father?" Tania said pertly. She turned back to Vanka, who reached both hands out for her nose. Rudnenko shrugged imperceptibly and faced around. Vassily urged the horses on.

He stopped at the office and both got out. Tania gave Vanka a last kiss and handed him over to his father. "I'll come to visit him," she said to Rudnenko, and without waiting for his reply skipped up the stairs to the office. Vassily drove slowly into the yard, the master machinist following with his offspring in his arms.

Vassily unhitched quickly and let the horses into the stable. Rudnenko followed him and when Vassily was finished he accompanied him to the gate. They discussed Rudnenko's plan once more. Vassily was willing to bring out the plow and harrow, but without an order from Saposhnik he would not dare supply the horses; even with the order, it would be hard to free a team for a day.

"If I get a chance tomorrow," Rudnenko said, "I'll go to Fyodor Ivanovich. He'll give me a note; he has authority to. I wouldn't like to bother Saposhnik with my business now. He has troubles enough with his wife. Poor woman—she's had such a hard time of it for so many years—it would be a release for her."

"Do you know her, Dmitri Alexevich?"

"I was the machinist in the Grishino sugar refinery. How we worked until we had it repaired! And she—she was as thin as a finger and weak as a straw. And with those infected lungs besides. We didn't have any easy time of it, Vassily, none of us. And now a snotnose like this sailor comes swaggering along, and is apt to knock everything to bits, with his stupidity. He's got to go! At the next party meeting I'm going to bring it up. We need somebody in charge who knows farming and likes it—somebody like you, Vassily."

"There are better men."

"I don't know many. Wouldn't you like to be the director, Vassily?"

"Director? Me? I wouldn't do for the job—positively not!"

"Well, well, I'm a better judge of that than you, you pigheaded peasant. What's the matter? Won't there be any more wagons to-day?" As if he had conjured it up by these words, a wagon came into view and stopped at once when Vassily hailed it. The Red Army man amiably made room for Rudnenko, helped him in, chucked the baby under the chin, and drove off.

Vassily started to cross the road to go to the canteen. At that moment Mira called to him from the window. "There's just been a telephone call," she reported. "Saposhnik's wife has died. The funeral is at four o'clock tomorrow. Whoever can get off should be at the Jewish cemetery. And the coffin is to be made in the shop here, and there's to be a wagon at the hospital at two o'clock, to serve as hearse."

Lavrenenko was in the chapel at the cemetery to deliver the eulogy. He extolled the deceased woman as a class-conscious worker, a pioneer of the Revolution, a self-sacrificing fighter. Employees of the plant and the farm carried the coffin down a long, extremely dirty and neglected lane, muddy and full of puddles. The hedges on either side of the lane were unpruned. The flower beds around the fenced-in vaults were overgrown with weeds, and spring flowers grew rankly over the graves marked by stones carved with Hebrew inscriptions. Behind the pallbearers walked Saposhnik and his children; then came the bearers of flags, portraits and streamers. Lavrenenko, Feingold and Maximenko were next in line. Tarashchenko was there as deputy to the party Chairman; the heads of various state enterprises and a number of Saposhnik's personal friends followed. Mira, Wagner, Meerblum and Kornhaber were together, and far behind them, propelled rather than led by a small group of miserable, ragged, extremely old Jewish men and women, came the deceased woman's mother, Ruchele Boim. Her feeble, dry sobs were punctuated by the heartrending howls and wails of her entourage.

That wretched, wailing, shuffling little group had nothing in common with the others who were grouped around the portraits of the bearded, mustachioed and beardless heroes of the Revolution, and around the streamers which roared slogans of threat and exhortation in huge red letters.

Gusts of wind suddenly whipped the trees and shrubs, the high grass and the weeds that surrounded the gravestones and monuments. The sun vanished behind the black wall of cloud, and rain began pattering down. The pallbearers walked faster, almost ran, and those behind them followed at a rapid pace, for they were afraid of getting wet and even more afraid that the portraits and streamers would be soaked. But the old men and women around Ruchele Boim ignored the rain and wind; they did not modify their creeping and shuffling or limping steps; they did not look at the sky or the trees or the stones. They saw only the mother, felt only her grief, for she was one of their own. Now those ahead also slowed their tempo. The wind and rain had desisted as suddenly as they had begun. At a solemn pace they reached the freshly dug grave and stood around it; the portraits and streamers were held high in the damp air, and when Rudnenko, one of the few who had known Riva Saposhnik, stationed himself in front of the grave to say a few words about the departed comrade, the sun shone down once more upon the gathering and the stones, upon the crude coffin, the trees, the shrubs and the high grass.

The coffin was let down into the grave, and Rudnenko spoke. He did not say the things he had learned and repeated countless times, but instead quietly and thoughtfully recalled a period whose symbol Riva Saposhnik had been—the woman "thin as a finger and weal as a straw, with infected lungs" who had toiled and labored, done men's work, sacrificed her young life for progress—Riva Saposhnik, one among millions of quiet, unknown, nameless fighters, who was now going to the rest which she had honestly earned.

When he had finished, he reached for the shovel. But as soon as the first clods of earth thumped down on the coffin, a piercing cry cut through the clear spring air—a cry uttered with uncanny force, with a concentration of the will that could only have come from the wildest grief, the most frantic despair. The wrinkled little Jewish woman had uttered the cry. She had reached her daughter's grave with her retinue just as the unbelievers were about to close it. And the same strength which had brought that scream from her old lungs poured into her withered limbs. Like a swimmer breasting a wild sea, Ruchele Boim parted the compact mass of people holding the portraits and streamers. They gave way before her pushing and opened a path for her to her daughter's grave. She rushed upon Rudnenko, who was stooping to the pile of earth, tore the shovel from him and held it tightly in her two hands. Her kerchief had slipped aside, her wig was displaced, and gray-white strands of hair fell into her pale-gray, dim eyes. From her contorted mouth, in a wild mixture of Yiddish, Russian and Ukrainian came a howled plea, a wail of indignation: "No, no! I won't allow it! You can't! A sin, sin, sin! Sirs, nachalniki, comrades—you can't—God, God! God! kaddish! No kaddish—her soul will not find rest! kaddish—kaddish—kaddish!"

Ruchele Boim stood alone, abandoned by her companions, who had shrunk back into the shrubbery out of fear of the booted and capped party stalwarts: out of the fear in which their forefathers had been born and died, in which they themselves would live and die— the fear that was stronger, not than their belief in the One, the Almighty, but stronger than their courage to stand up for Him and His commandments against men in boots and caps, who had always oppressed them, no matter in whose cause or in whose name.

The nachalniki and their underlings stood numb with bafflement, their eyes all fixed on the highest representative of power present at the funeral, the Party Chairman's deputy. Tarashchenko, leaning against a tree, had his eyes fixed on Saposhnik, who stood immobile between his two children, his broad, pallid face and swollen eyes no longer expressing grief, nor hatred for his old adversary, but only sternness. It was an expression as hard and inexorable as the toneless voice in which he said, *"Men tor nit, Schwigger*—It isn't allowed, Mother-in-law."

But she did not hear, did not understand, did not want to hear or understand him, the apostate. Ruchele Boim's head dropped to her chest, her knees gave way; slowly, like a dying animal, she fell across the grave. And panting, whispering, but in a voice clearly audible to everyone, and utterly unable to believe that so simple a request might not be granted, she asked, "Without kaddish? A Jew —*buried without kaddish?"*

Vassily stood between Mira and Kornhaber and suffered acutely. No one noticed, because everyone was spellbound by the terrible scene before them. He felt extremely weak, because he saw no solution, could think of no way to help the old woman racked by her tremendous grief. His eyes caught hold of Feingold's. Only for the fraction of a second. Feingold dropped his; then he took a step aside, to where Tarashchenko stood, and whispered something to him. The Deputy Chairman looked at the portraits and streamers, as though calling them to witness or asking their forgiveness. He went to Saposhnik, and taking little Boris by the hand to lead him away, said, without slowing his pace, "Let her pray, Mark Lvovich." Saposhnik promptly followed him, drawing his daughter along behind him.

Vassily, however, caught Feingold's eye once more and thanked him with a look. Then he stooped over Ruchele Boim, raised her to her feet, and beckoned to Kornhaber. "Pray, Kornhaber!" he said.

And as though God Himself had called him, Kornhaber, the feeble, timid and anxious little man, stepped to the graveside, stood erect and proud, and in a strong voice began: "*Yisgadal V'yiskadash* —Extolled and hallowed by. . . ."

The ancient prayer, which in Aramaic words praises the One and Eternal but never once mentions the departed, drove off the bearers of portraits and streamers. They hurried to catch up with Tarashchenko, Saposhnik and the others, thus proving their clean ideology. But the same prayer, heard and spoken thousands of times, lured the old Jews from behind the shrubs, trees and gravestones; shuffling and limping, they hurried forward, the men to fortify and round off the prayer with long-drawn-out amens, the women to join in the wails of the mother as Meerblum, Wagner and Vassily shoveled the loose earth into the grave until it arched in a firm mound above it. One of the old men, snuffling and gasping for breath, sang "*El Maleh Rahamim*—the Lord full of mercy."

And then the small congregation broke up. The members of the farm went ahead, followed by Ruchele Boim and her cronies. Ruchele Boim, in fact, was never seen again by her son-in-law, the partinyi, nor by her granddaughter who was a member of the Komsomol, nor by her grandson, the pioneer. From that day forth she went and lived with the wretched old people who still maintained their ties to Yahveh, the All-merciful, the Omnipotent.

Although comparatively few had attended the funeral, the drivers with their teams had remained in town to take the Elektrostantsia workmen to and from the cemetery, and it was nearly evening when they returned. The drivers attended to their horses, washed their hands at the pump, and went straight to the canteen. Kornhaber found milking already in full swing, and Meerblum arrived just in time to receive the milk. The Director was not in the cow barn, much to Kornhaber's relief; Kornhaber finished his work as quickly as possible and made off. He and his wife lived in a cottage which they shared with Meerblum and his wife. Both couples' married children lived in town, as did Kornhaber's unmarried daughter, a nineteen-year-old student. Wagner and his wife—they were childless—had moved into a nearby house. Both places were some distance from the farm, and so when the farm siren sounded to announce a meeting at the Cultural Hall, Kornhaber and Wagner were last to arrive. The Director, who seemed to have been waiting for them, threw menacing glances at Kornhaber, who slipped into a seat in the last row and cowered there behind the broad backs of the drivers. Meerblum sat beside him. The summons to the meeting had caught him midway in his work; he had been forced to turn off the separator and leave the milk standing in the cans. Now he was troubled not so much by the prospect of working until long after midnight with his tired and reluctant helpers, as by the possibility that hundreds of pounds of milk would spoil. Of course he would be considered responsible.

The Director evidently had something special in mind. He proceeded at once to take the roll. The bookkeeper had to read out the list, and each member of the farm raised his hand as his name was called. Gorbatenko fixed his eyes on each in turn, forcing the person to keep his hand up as long as the insulting stare rested upon him. The roll call and scrutiny were done so thoroughly that it lasted more than an hour; the Director lingered for several minutes on Kornhaber alone. At last he asked, "Is that all?" Mira replied, "Da," and he responded, "No da." He thereupon laid his round cap on the lectern before him and began his speech.

It went on and on and seemed as if it would never end. For he had worked up his findings of the past seventeen days, and what he now produced was a methodical collection of all the nonsense he had uttered at odd moments during that period. The only good thing to be said for his oration was that most of the audience scarcely caught the drift of it. But Tania, Mira and Vassily understood Russian, and the effect of the speech upon them differed according to their temperaments. The cashier writhed in her chair as if someone were stinging her; her face twisted as if she were suppressing an impulse to weep or laugh convulsively. Mira, sober and pessimistic, sat with her eyes fixed gloomily on the sailor as he bellowed on in a rapture of smugness, tearing down everything she and the others had built up with such incessant physical and mental labors, trampling on it all in his boundless stupidity and incredible ignorance.

Not so Vassily, who sat in one of the last rows, a smile around his lips and in his eyes. The loud-mouthed fool amused him. But suddenly Vassily's smile vanished. He became coldly earnest, for the sailor had placed a finger on the single factor which all those in the know had so far carefully concealed.

Ignat Ilich Gorbatenko took out the directives of the People's Commissariat for Agriculture, which set forth the amount of milk a cow was supposed to give. And he compared these norms with the figures he had copied from the books, or rather with the figures on a single sheet, which he had studied very carefully: the production of Mayorka, cow No. 5, during the month of January, 1940. Anyone who could add two and two could understand it, he declared. If the directives stated that a cow's production must be sixty pounds, and cow No. 5 had given only twenty-six pounds, and often less—here it was in black and white in the bookkeeper's records—then there was a rat buried somewhere. And he, the Director, had exhumed this rat. It was clear as glass that Kornhaber must have stolen millions of pounds of milk, that Meerblum had turned it into thousands of pounds of butter, and that the bookkeeper was in league with them and had falsified the entries in the books. And although no one had seen through the racket up to now, he, Ignat Ilich Gorbatenko, had uncovered it. He would bring those three, and the others who had helped them, to judgment. That was his duty, his task as director and Soviet citizen—nichevo!

And now he proceeded to the official business of the meeting: the classification of the workers. For it seemed everything leading up to this had only been by way of preamble. In bringing all this up, Gorbatenko had been following a deliberate strategy. If he could play upon the feelings of the audience and induce them to give the rating of *plocho* [bad] to the three Jewish members of the collective whom he had accused of cheating, he would have won his point. That would be enough to make them outlaws, prime candidates for the next "resettlement." But he would have to bring the matter to a vote. The farm workers would have to ratify his motion that Kornhaber, Meerblum and the bookkeeper be given the rating of plocho. Only then would the plocho be set down in the minutes of the meeting; then the stigma would be ineradicable, and fateful in its consequences.

However, it did not happen as he wished. Before he could rush through his vote, the verkhovki marched into the hall: Feingold in the van, with his Apollo smile, and following slowly behind him, stony-faced, came Tarashchenko. Saposhnik too was there, a sterling example of self-discipline: he had gone directly from the funeral to the party meeting. Bringing up the rear, his steel spectacles slipped down to the tip of his nose, came Rudnenko, the machinist.

Saposhnik mounted the platform. "Comrades," he said, "we have only a few days to the First of May, the holiday of all workers. We in the Soviet Republic have, as you know, the custom of classifying work. At our previous meeting we discussed the significance of this and the procedure." He drew a list from his pocket and began calling out the names alphabetically. "Anastasiuk, Ivan Ivanovich, koniukh. Exceeded the norm by thirteen per cent. He has worked very well; I propose the rating of *otlichno*. All in favor raise their hands." He himself raised his hand, as did all the farm workers, taking their cue from Vassily. And so it went: norm fulfilled, good; exceeded, very good. Not a single "plocho" was meted out.

When the name "Khomniuk, Vassily Vassilevich" was read out, Tarashchenko rose and said, "Comrades, the starshi koniukh, Vassily Vassilevich Khomniuk, should be specially honored. He has not only exceeded his norm by more than one hundred per cent, but has also demonstrated organizational talent and, most important of all, a genuinely Soviet, collective spirit. Starshi Koniukh Vassily Vassilevich Khomniuk is worthy of the rating of stakhanovets. All in favor raise their hands!" He raised his, Saposhnik and Feingold theirs; Rudnenko smilingly shook his finger at Vassily. Gorbatenko twisted his cap in his hands; all the others raised their hands and turned to look at Vassily, who sat quiet. The hands dropped and the voting proceeded without interruption to Starshi Korovnik Kornhaber. He, Saposhnik stated, had not fulfilled the prescribed norm. Various factors could be considered as extenuating circumstances; still a certain lack of initiative had been shown. He moved, therefore, that Kornhaber be given the rating of good—all in favor raise their hands—but a reshuffling in the management of the dairy would soon have to be undertaken. Meerblum was rated good, without comment; Tarashchenko made a short speech about the bookkeeper, who was then declared a stakhanovets. Her husband, Alfred Arturovich, and his fellow gardener, Tadeus Karlowicz Zembrinski, were rated "otlichniki," as were all the other men and women with the exception of Wagner, who came last and received only a "good."

It was eleven o'clock when the meeting was adjourned. Only the verkhovki, Rudnenko, Mira, Vassily and Gorbatenko remained behind. Tarashchenko retired to a corner with Gorbatenko and had a brief but evidently serious talk with him. Gorbatenko sat scowling for a while afterward. He then bethought himself of the brochure, and brought it out, as though to clear himself. He had only made his "un-Soviet" utterances because he had got wind of something rotten going on in the department of milk production. Rudnenko was about to make an angry retort, but Vassily kicked the machinist's ankle. He had realized that the nachalniki were not so concerned with enlightening this stupid and unteachable party candidate as they were with avoiding the fuss that Gorbatenko could raise if he felt himself unjustly treated. If he pursued the mat-

ter of the milk too far, he could still wreak a good deal of mis-
chief—for the facts were there; the dairy had not fulfilled its quota.
And so Vassily turned with a modest, eager-pupil air to Gorbatenko,
and said, "Comrade Nachalnik, would you mind telling me a few
things about ships that I've always wondered about?"

He began plying the man with questions. Gorbatenko took
the bait and self-importantly began discoursing on the construction,
capacities and speeds of various types of ship. After a while Vassily
asked what was done on the high seas when oil or coal ran short. It
was not supposed to happen, Gorbatenko said, but of course if it did,
because of bad weather or bad planning, then you had to slow down
until you reached a port; high speeds required far more fuel
than low speeds. Vassily listened with close attention, as did all
the others except Mira. When, at the end of Gorbatenko's lecture,
he said, "You see, comrade, it's exactly the same with cows," everyone was greatly surprised at the turn he had given the thing.

The sailor was the first to recover. "You may be a stakhanovets,
but you can't make a fool of me. I know what I know." He pounded
his fist on the brochure. "Here it is in black and white, nichevo." He
spat.

"But you yourself made the very same point. There are ships of
different types, right? Those are the different breeds of cow. And
when a ship runs short of fuel, it has to slow down, it makes fewer
knots. With cows, their fuel is the feed. Less feed, or feed of
poorer quality—fewer knots, that is to say—less milk or none at all.
Why didn't you study the latest figures, Comrade Director? Lately
we've had more fuel—that is, more feed—and so there's more milk,
and the workers have been receiving nearly twice as much butter! Is
that right, Comrade Saposhnik? Is that right, Comrade Rudnenko?"
The two nodded vehemently. Gorbatenko looked at each of them
in turn, then at Tarashchenko, and finally threw a look of be-
wilderment at Vassily. He had been outflanked, found it terribly hard
to admit it. There was no further objection he could raise. Or was
there? "But lately there's been another captain on board here, too,
nichevo!" He spat, and the missile landed somewhere in the next
room.

Vassily readily admitted that the new Captain had adapted
himself with amazing speed to rural life and agriculture. Only it was
a pity, he said, that so much energy was being squandered on an unsuitable object. What did eighty dessiatin of land amount to for a
man of so much insight and vigor? Gorbatenko swelled, Feingold
gave the faintest of smiles, Rudnenko returned Vassily's kick, in the
shin this time; fortunately Vassily's new high boot softened the blow.

Tarashchenko, face expressionless, stood up, and the others followed suit. He extended his hand to Gorbatenko. "Come to the Oblispolkom [District Executive Committee] at half past seven tomorrow morning," he said. "Take your stuff with you; you'll go to Stanislava, to the agricultural section, and will be assigned as zamestitel at the Pobeda Kolkhoz. They have nearly two thousand dessiatin and authorization for four hundred cows. Here"—he turned to Saposhnik—"Comrade Khomniuk will be zamestitel. I know, there's no such position in the table of organization, but you'll remain responsible anyhow. I'll put the thing through." He went out, followed by the others.

On the way to their car, Feingold asked, "Satisfied, Vassily Vassilevich?"

"What more do we want than to work in peace, Comrade Feingold?"

The four got into the car, Tarashchenko, Feingold and Saposhnik in the back, Rudnenko in front. While the chauffeur was taking his place, Rudnenko told Vassily that he hoped the work on his plot of land could begin soon. He would bring the necessary orders tomorrow—and after all, Vassily was zamestitel now.

Vassily nodded. He had hardly listened, for his attention had been caught by an exchange in the back seat. Feingold had said to Tarashchenko, "A divan must be sold."

"Several, in fact," the Deputy Chairman had replied, and then the car drove off.

There were many vital matters for Vassily to think over that night. He had first to extract the most important from the less important, but even after this, it was no help—certain mysteries persisted.

It was only a minor enigma that Tania's and Mira's denunciation of Gorbatenko had seemed to go ignored. Perhaps the Party Committee had not even conferred about it, or perhaps decided that an oral reproof was enough; Vassily had noticed Tarashchenko's private talk with the Director, and had observed the sullen look on Gorbatenko's face. Perhaps, too, his counterrevolutionary and reactionary remarks would figure as a black mark on Gorbatenko's record later on—when, say, the question of his final acceptance into the party came up. Gorbatenko's crude and undisguised anti-Semitism was, obviously, not taken so seriously as the fat NKVD man's attitude. It was possible, too, that enough power had been accruing to those who were "for" so that the others did not want to provoke them over a casual "zhid" on the part of an idiotic loudmouth. Rather than make an issue of it, they had shut him up and flattered his stupid vanity. Gorbatenko, who by tomorrow would no longer be swaggering around the farm, no longer counted.

But there was that other matter, tormenting because inexplicable. What was that strange remark about selling the divan? Not one but several. Feingold's remark, with its eerie cynicism, and Tarashchenko's reply, with its note of decision, were riddles which must be solved. The phrase boded no good. And so he sat in his long, coarse peasant's nightgown by the bed, brooding vainly, coming to no conclusion. At last he crawled under the blanket.

The sleep he fell into was not relaxing. A gaudy-colored top spun slowly in his brain, with a tormenting hum. A faulty machine hissed and creaked somewhere. Di-van, di-van—two long-drawn-out syllables—trickled like black heavy drops into his unconscious, multiplied, spun like liquid in a centrifuge; broad sofas covered with Oriental throws, grotesquely distorted designs, wild colors. Striped turbans were wound about invisible heads; curved scimitars were swung by unseen hands. Blare of bugles, neighing of horses, laughing—a wild cacophony out of which rose a signal that hovered solitary over a boundless plain. Mount! Astride divans, Austrian uhlans in long-brimmed Russian caps galloped in a circle around Major von Rist. He bellowed, "Walk! Ensign Schlick to me! All right, Ensign, tell your joke." Feingold. What was he doing here? What did he want here? He knew no jokes. But all the same it was Feingold telling a joke in Viennese dialect mixed with Yiddish: "So a feller named Feiglstock, he comes to the rabbi and he says to him, 'Reb, you've got to help me—I come home and who do I find on the divan. . . .'"

Vassily was wide-awake. His hand reached mechanically for the light switch above his bed; the small room blazed with illumination, and so did his brain. He dressed frantically, and by the time he had finished and looked at his watch—it was half past three—his mind had worked through to the end of Ensign Schlick's—or rather, Feingold's—joke, the ancient saw about poor Feiglstock who catches his wife *flagrante delicto* with the bookkeeper on the divan, and rushes to the rabbi to ask him what to do. The rabbi considers the case from every angle. Feiglstock had better not divorce his wife, or she'll take her dowry out of the business. It wouldn't do to discharge the bookkeeper, either, because he knows too much about various manipulations. Yet action must be taken in such a situation: the only thing to do is to get rid of the divan!

Why, Vassily asked himself as he strode through the dewy grass in the gray pre-dawn, am I so certain that Feingold was quoting the punch line of that old anecdote, and why am I so disturbed? It might have been a perfectly innocent private allusion. But no, there was no doubt about it: they needed scapegoats. Had not Wagner, usually well informed, said that there would be no deportations until May? But how much longer would they put them off? May was almost here. And who on the farm would be the divan that had to be sold? Not one divan but several!

Who were they, the appointed scapegoats? Vassily tramped over the wet spring grass. He felt the dampness up to his ankles, and it occurred to him that it was time the cows were sent out to pasture. Why wasn't Kornhaber taking care of that? Kornhaber, the head of the dairy, who lacked initiative and would therefore have to be replaced. No initiative—in spite of the rating of "good." Another man in his place would. . . .

Then Vassily knew who Feingold had meant by the divan that would have to be sold.

But Tarashchenko had said *several*. Who were the others? Who could they be? Whom had Gorbatenko named along with Kornhaber? Who was accused of converting the "stolen" milk to butter? Meerblum: Meerblum, corpulent, sluggish, hard of hearing but tireless, who had sold his excellent new machinery to the farm for a song, just as Kornhaber had sold his cows and Wagner his huge quantities of feed, only a percentage of which was listed on the books.

They were the ones—the divans that would have to be sold: the most readily identifiable burzhui on the farm, who had set the farm up and maintained it by their contributions, and now for their pains. . . .

No deportations until May. But it was not yet May, and he was still here. Until Mira was across the border, he could not go. He had given his word. But aside from his word, there was his determination. To help the others—to help those three: Wagner, Meerblum and Kornhaber. Vassily broke into a run, although he was only a few hundred feet from Wagner's cottage. And as he ran he thought with intense pleasure, I'll drop a few hairs into your soup, verkhovki!

It was 4:15 A.M. when he entered Wagner's cottage. Soon afterwards, Wagner called Meerblum and Kornhaber in for consultation. It was ten minutes to six when Vassily sat down in the canteen to a breakfast of bacon, bread and hot milk, and then strolled off toward the stable, smoking his morning cigarette. Until his promotion was announced in the *prekaz,* the order of the day, he was still the starshi koniukh and did a koniukh's work. He had already selected for his successor to that post Mikhail Yeremczuk, the oldest and most astute of the drivers.

Toward eight o'clock Vassily got the buggy and the roans ready. Mira and the cashier had to go to the bank and to headquarters. The horses were already harnessed, and Vassily stood waiting in front of the stable door. He did not wait in vain. Vasilena, one of the milkers, came rushing from the cow barn in a frenzy of anxiety. "The old man has collapsed!" she shrieked. "He's in terrible pain—he's dying!" Vassily rushed to the barn and found Kornhaber doubled up on a pile of straw. With the aid of the milkers, he carried the old man to the wagon; Mira and Tania were called, and Vassily drove Kornhaber to the clinic that was responsible for medical treatment of the farm personnel. The doctor, a "native," diagnosed Kornhaber's case as an emergency, kidney stones, and sent him to the surgical ward. Kornhaber was at last to undergo this long-overdue and repeatedly postponed operation. He really needed it, Vassily knew. And dangerous though the operation was, in the circumstances it was a real blessing, for the hospital was off limits even to the agents of the NKVD.

Saposhnik received a report of the incident without comment and instructed Vassily to find a capable successor, preferably a woman. Vassily named Big Maria. Saposhnik also took occasion to say that two gardeners would be arriving next day. Since there were no local men available, they were being brought in from outside.

At three o'clock that afternoon Vassily met Wagner and Meerblum in the warehouse, as arranged. The plan had to be described down to the last detail. Vassily sketched it out, and Wagner bellowed the details into Meerblum's deaf ears. Meerblum asked no questions, and agreed to everything without demur. They settled on May 1 as the day for their action. Meerblum left, and Vassily lingered with Wagner for a while.

"What made Kornhaber decide to have this operation?" he asked. "He was always so scared of it."

"It's on account of his youngest daughter. He's had a hard time with her these past three years. She's an ardent Communist, you see. Young as she is, she was jailed twice under the Poles and beaten black and blue by the police. Now she's attending the university, is a member of the Komsomol—and is one hundred per cent for the new order. Kornhaber can't bring himself to leave forever without saying good-bye to her, and he wouldn't dare tell her what he had in mind because the crazy girl might up and denounce him. Hard to believe, isn't it, Vassily?"

"I can believe it. Oh well, for three months at least he'll be let alone, and then—he's already sixty, isn't he?"

"Thereabouts. He'll manage. They'll let him keep his spravka, won't they?"

"If he's lucky, he'll be given an invalid's certificate. They don't check very closely on those. He won't have to work any more, I think, and will just have to keep out of sight for a while, not attract attention. He'd better move to some other town when he goes out of the hospital. Suggest it to his wife. He has other children, hasn't he?"

"Yes, a son and a daughter, and grandchildren too. God will have to help him."

Next morning Vassily drove into town with the first team. He instructed the driver Yeremczuk to call at the office later; perhaps the bookkeeper or cashier would need transportation into town. He himself would be at headquarters around nine o'clock, he said.

Long before eight o'clock he was loitering outside Besselmann's house; he did not go in for fear of attracting attention from any of the other tenants who might be leaving for work. In a few minutes Arye came out with his pack of books under his arm. As if by chance, Vassily fell into step beside the boy and explained the plan to him.

"May Day. But Platzer's coming sooner; I don't know whether he'll want to wait that long," Arye objected.

This wasn't a job for Platzer, Vassily said; he would be needed for the two others, the Linhans. The four newest candidates were to go to Hersch Birnberg. The question was whether he would be able to send them across.

"No trouble at all. But who are they? Do you know their names, Hābhēr Vassily?"

Vassily told him. Arye didn't know Meerblum. "But Eliezer Wagner? He dealt in grain, didn't he? He's an acquaintance of Father's. Does he know the password?"

"No, and I don't intend to tell him. But have your father send them along to Rundberg. If they haven't enough money, I'll take care of it."

"Everything will be arranged, Hābhēr Vassily." School No. 12 loomed before them, and Arye waved good-bye.

On the way to the Elektrostantsia office, Vassily passed the promtorg shop, and remembered his boots. The repairs must have been completed long ago. He went in, and saw his trusty footgear standing in a corner, covered with a thick layer of dust, but soled and mended. "Your new ones won't last as long as these," the proprietress—a "native"—said. "The way those are made—there was such a thing as quality once upon a time."

"I bought them secondhand," Vassily said. He asked for a rag, wiped the boots as clean as possible, and since there was no wrapping paper, he bought a *Pravda* outside, glanced through it, and then wrapped the boots in it.

He had a long talk with Saposhnik, who wished to know what part the farm would play in the coming May Day celebration. The nachalnik had been nurturing the plan of having all the farm animals join the May Day parade. Without appearing to contradict, Vassily soon made him see that transporting the cows into town would not only be terribly time-consuming, but dangerous as well. The animals had been in the barn all winter, he pointed out; their hoofs were soft and would not stand up to the stones of the highway, let alone the pavements of the city. There might be difficulties enough even driving the cows out to pasture, an operation which they intended to begin this very day.

Vassily took his leave and went downstairs to the canteen. Priesner, the former Viennese restaurateur, snatched away his bottle as soon as he caught sight of Vassily. Vodka was obtainable only at the farm canteen—though in restricted quantities. That was due to Wagner, who had long ago bought them a large supply at extremely low prices.

"Some bird's been hanging around," Priesner said, wiping his mouth and putting on the heavy Viennese dialect he reserved for Vassily, "who, I don't know—he's been in here a couple of times asking for a bottle of vodochka, and doesn't understand or won't understand that I can't sell him any." He paused, listening. "There he comes, the creep. Sit down, Vassily. I'll bring you a glass of milk. You like milk—I don't!" He flounced into the kitchen, and Vassily, although he hadn't heard a sound, obediently took a seat.

Priesner's hearing, sharpened by caution, had not betrayed him. It was a mystery to Vassily how he could have heard the "creep," for Vassily himself didn't become aware of the man until he appeared in the doorway: tall, stooped, with a hairless, wrinkled, stalklike neck on which a small head swayed as though it did not belong there and had been only loosely attached. A ruddy, shapelessly swollen nose protruded from a leathery face, above a big, broad-lipped mouth. Nose and mouth were divided by a wisp of mustache, its feeble substance complemented by the hairs sprouting from his nostrils. The bulging eyes, of the palest blue, were filled with the tears so characteristic of habitual drinkers. The man wore an almost new suit, of a grayish-brown stiff cloth, and a pair of brand-new sneakers, the rubber soles still white. "No vodka," he said hoarsely, and it sounded as if he were asking and answering simultaneously. As he spoke, he pushed back his cap and ran his hand over his sweaty, bald pate.

"Milk," Priesner said, pointing to the glass he had placed in front of Vassily. He well understood the other's plight, and somewhat sympathized, but fear kept him from infringing regulations.

He doled out vodka only to the very few persons he trusted completely. Even then, he did so not to make a little profit but solely out of good nature. Now his eyes flickered toward Vassily, asking advice and aid. The peculiar guest caught the look, and also turned to Vassily for help. "Tell him, milk drinker, to sell me a drop of vodka."

"Milk is good too." Vassily took a sip.

The stranger reached his table with two soft steps, and sat down. "Good for children and nursing mothers. I'm neither." His Adam's apple rose and fell. "I wouldn't think you were, to look at you. You've got a mustache like Budyenny. You look like a man, and you drink milk!" He gulped, and shook himself.

"I like it," Vassily said.

"I don't," the man croaked. "I like vodka, and he has some. You're not a 'native,' are you?"

"Yes, I'm a 'native.' "

"Then you ought to know where to get vodka. I have money. Come, we'll go kill a pint—my treat."

"Work, comrade."

"Work, comrade," the man repeated derisively. "How can you work without vodka? Speaking of work, where is the Elektrostantsia farm?"

"I'm the head of the farm, and you're the new gardener, I suppose."

"Yes—I'm the gardener." His eyes wandered. "If you're the Director, how come you speak Russian? I know Polish too. Come from Kamenets—they sell vodka at the bazaar there."

"Here too, but it costs a lot. If you're with the farm, you're entitled to a hundred grams a day at the canteen. Very cheap—government price."

"A hundred grams—not much, but better than nothing. If you drink milk, maybe you'll let me have your ration. Or have you made a deal with some other guy? I'll pay premium prices, twice, three times, you name it. Then you'll see how I work! Can we go now?" He had dropped into a whining tone.

"Have you already reported?"

"To the polit-worker and the zamestitel. Let's go. Is it far?"

"A wagon from the farm may be along soon. Another gardener is supposed to be coming."

"I know, from Bar. Where is the son of a bitch? Come, let's go!" He stood up.

"Where's your baggage?" Vassily asked.

"Baggage? What do I need baggage for? Baggage!" He shook his head at the concerns of the "natives."

As Vassily left the building, the "creep" at his side, the farm buggy turned into the street. Only Mira was in it, aside from the driver Yeremczuk. "Well," Vassily said, "we're in luck. We'll be able to ride out to the farm shortly."

The buggy stopped and Vassily went up to it. "The new gardener," he said to Mira.

Mira hardly gave him a glance. "I've just this one last errand. Then we can drive straight home."

It was some time before Mira reappeared, accompanied by a young man. His long-brimmed cap sat jauntily on the back of his head, and a tuft of black hair fluttered around his brow. He wore glasses and had a considerable squint. "The other gardener," she said tersely. She got into the buggy and sat down in the back. Vassily saw that she was upset. She pressed her foot against him to indicate that she had important news for him. It couldn't be good news, for the furrow between her brows persisted throughout the ride. The two gardeners sat up front with the driver. Only the younger one talked. He launched into a discourse on the cultivation of fruit trees, to which none of his fellow passengers paid attention.

In the office, Mira handed the two gardeners their assignment cards, which Saposhnik had signed. The vodka lover was called Benderski, the young theoretician Chalev. Benderski was given a room in the headquarters building, and Chalev was assigned—on his own demand—the room of the deceased head gardener. He was a party candidate and a graduate of the school of gardening in Melitopol.

Vassily took the two new arrivals and introduced them to their fellow gardeners. Chalev declared that he knew nothing about cold frames and hotbeds; his specialty was fruit trees, and he promptly devoted himself to them, leaving the rest of the work to Benderski. Despite the poor impression the alcoholic made, he quickly showed that he knew nursery gardening.

Vassily gave Wagner a quick summary of his meeting with Besselmann, learned that Kornhaber was to undergo surgery on May 3, and then went to the office.

Mira had received travel passes for Wagner and Meerblum from Saposhnik, she told him. Vassily had arranged for the two men to make a trip to Kolomea District to buy a bull for the farm.

They prolonged their talk in the hope that Tania would be bored and leave, so that they would be alone and Mira could tell Vassily what was worrying her. But the cashier refused to abandon the field, and so in the end the three left the office together. Vassily could not let Tania see him going home with Mira, and so he went to the canteen. The cashier joined him, sat down with him, and attacked her supper of sausage, bread and tea. She seasoned the meal with her customary jumble of talk, one moment deadly serious, the next bubbling with laughter. There was no doubt that her interest was concentrated upon him alone, of all the workers at the farm. He had already speculated on the reasons for this. Undoubtedly it was her mission to ply the verkhovki with information about people and incidents, and especially about him. Hardly an agreeable thought. But then, was there really anything to worry about? The whole farce could not go on much longer. Mira was "due" in two days, and he himself would wait only until she and her husband were safely across the border. Perhaps, too, he'd wait for the departure of Wagner and Meerblum and then he himself would be off. His plan was ready.

But while the cashier chattered on, he came to the conclusion that even for the short time remaining, Tania's interest in him constituted a danger. Mira, too, had learned something disquieting in her morning's talk with Saposhnik. Anxiety, or at least tension, was a permanent state around here. A deep moroseness settled upon him. He made no attempt to keep up with Tania's volubility, and even ceased to listen.

Suddenly he noticed that she was looking at him quizzically. She must have said something that called for an answer. "Pardon me," he said. "My thoughts were elsewhere."

Her sportive expression changed to a look of deep earnestness. "Be on your guard with the young gardener," she said in a lowered voice. "I don't like the looks of him. He has other things to do around here than prune the fruit trees."

Vassily smiled skeptically. "What should I be on my guard about? And what sort of things are you referring to? He seems a nice young man, with lots of spirit and ambition."

"I'm cuckoo, I know. But I can't help myself. I have to tell you; I would never tell anyone else. Never, understand? Be on your guard with him—watch every word, every expression. He wants to make his mark, but not with onions and radishes, or fruit trees. Besides, he's an idiot, and that's even worse. Of course you can't understand—how could you possibly? But take my word for it and watch yourself—only don't let him know that you're on your guard!"

Vassily had listened with close attention. But he answered with a good semblance of indifference. "I don't see what you're driving at, Tania, but I'll be careful. Even though I don't know what to be careful about."

"Oh, you dumb ox," she said with a grimace halfway between tears and laughter. She scratched the back of her head in imitation of Gorbatenko. Then she puffed away a strand of hair that had fallen over her forehead, and repeated, "You're a dumb ox, zamestitel—I'd put that in writing and stamp, seal and sign it. But I'll look out for you; nothing will happen to you. And if—" She stood up, struck one of her ballet poses—the room was empty by now—and pirouetted across the room and out the door.

Vassily sat over his tea for a while longer. Then he went out through the back of the canteen into the garden, crossed through the hedges that surrounded the potato fields into the tiny back garden of Mira's cottage, and knocked on the kitchen door. She had been waiting for him.

"What did the cashier have to say?" she asked when he had sat down.

"She warned me against the gardener," Vassily said lightly.

"She ought to warn you against herself, the spy!"

Vassily smiled. "We are warned against her, Mira." He caressed her hand reassuringly. "Anyhow, it doesn't matter. It won't go on much longer."

"It better not go on much longer, Vassily. It just better not."

"What's up, Mira?"

"If I understood him rightly, Saposhnik proposed marriage to me today."

"He certainly is in a hurry. But—you're already married. Or has he overlooked that?"

"Divorce is easy in the Soviet Union, he gave me to understand— dialectically, of course, in a roundabout way. And besides, he said it isn't legal for married couples to work in the same enterprise."

"We have a total of seventeen married couples working on the farm."

"I didn't bring that up; I only pretended that I didn't see what he was getting at. I let him talk, and luckily the new head gardener came along, and so I was spared the necessity of replying. But what in God's name are we going to do if he seriously pursues the matter?"

"Don't let that worry you, Mira. You and Freddy will soon be on your way. Besides, Saposhnik isn't the sort of man to abuse his power to further an affair of the heart. Or is it that for you too, Mira?"

"It's nothing to joke about, Vassily! There's no man in the world I see but you. And I'll never, never abandon Freddy."

"Then don't let it bother you, Mira." He drew her close and put his arm around her. "By the night of April 29 you'll no longer be here, and by May 3 at the latest I'll be across the border too, and then this whole crazy episode will be behind you. You'll see how quickly you forget all about it."

She put her own arm around his neck and spoke in a voice

scarcely her own. "I don't want to forget everything, Vassily, not everything. If—if only I could be certain that you'll be crossing too."

"I will, Mira, depend on it. But now I must look around—as long as I'm here, I don't dare cut any corners. Everything must be done in orderly fashion. Good-bye, Mira." He left by the way he had come, and stepped out on the street near the sausage factory.

The new head gardener met him at the door of his house. "Where have you been, comrade?" he inquired.

Vassily scrutinized him from top to toe. He was wearing no jacket, and the black, sleeveless undershirt under a moth-eaten sweater revealed thin arms and a puny body which had seldom seen the sun. His hands, too, were hardly those of an outdoor worker, and certainly not the hands of a gardener. They were thin, soft-boned and hairless, the pallid white hands of an invalid. His glasses gave his sharp features the expression of a spiteful and inquisitive old woman.

"What makes you ask that, comrade?" Vassily asked, slowly puffing out the smoke of his cigarette.

The gardener removed his glasses and forced his features into stiff, resolute lines. "That's my own business," he said.

"And where I've been is mine," Vassily retorted. He looked into the room. Tadek lay on his bed, but he was not snoring, as he normally was at this hour of day. He lay awake, his glance moving from Vassily to his new boss.

"Tadek," Vassily said to him, "you can stop at the smithy tomorrow and take the two helpers along with you to the beds."

"I've been to see them already. They're coming and Baczynski will be along later. The old drunk knows what's what, but the professor here never saw a hotbed in his life."

"What language is that you're speaking?" Chalev asked Vassily. "Polish."

"You must speak Russian—or Ukrainian."

"I'm quite aware of what I must do, and you don't give orders here—certainly not about what language we can speak. In the Soviet Union everyone can speak whatever he likes, and we happen to know that too." Vassily turned to Tadek again. "I'll be along around three and help out a little. Lucky the old fellow can garden, anyhow."

"Konechno," Tadek piped. He turned his back to the head gardener and promptly fell asleep—or pretended to.

Vassily went into his room and closed the door behind him. He thought he detected an alien smell. Someone had surely been in the room. He made a hasty survey of the place. The bed was untouched; the books on the table lay in the order in which he had left them. He glanced into the wardrobe—it, too, seemed unmolested. Looking into the wardrobe reminded him that he had forgotten his old boots in Golodnyi's stall and that he must buy brown shoe polish for them. He opened the window and lay down.

One day passed and then another, filled to the brim with work and errands. Vassily was so busy that he didn't have a chance to think. Nor did he try to. Wagner's and Meerblum's wives were already in town—they had each taken a few necessities along in their shopping bags. Their husbands were participating in the preparations for May Day. The garden work moved along; everyone who had any free time did volunteer labor in the vegetable fields. The "old drunk" had taken command as a matter of course; he was having a happy life, for Tadek and Freddy were letting him have their vodka rations. The head gardener stayed away from the forcing beds; whenever anyone was in sight, he was counting the fruit trees and listing them according to type and age; otherwise he disappeared, and no one paid any attention.

Mira did not go to town, and when Saposhnik turned up on the afternoon of April 28 to see how things were going, Vassily so arranged matters that he didn't have a moment alone with the bookkeeper. Saposhnik didn't become aware of this; he was intensely interested in all the operations, and went back to town late that evening, highly satisfied.

As soon as he was gone, Vassily and Mira, who had been in the sausage plant with him, strolled slowly toward the canteen, reviewing once more what was to take place next day. Vassily would ride to town during the noon break and take with him their two small suitcases, which Mira had packed with a few necessities. The man who was to take them across the border was already awaiting them. Mira was not to tell Freddy what was about to happen until after they had reached town; otherwise he might babble about it to his friend Tadek.

Mira listened attentively to Vassily's exposition. "To think I must go without you. . . ." She sighed.

"It's better that way, Mira. There would be a terrible rumpus here if all three of us were to disappear at once. Besides, I can't arrange it any differently."

"I understand that, Vassily. But follow us soon. You know where to find me in Romania—Rozescu will always know where I am."

As they looked around for a table in the canteen, they saw Tania in animated conversation with the head gardener, Chalev.

Tadek and Freddy were sitting with the drinker, who had apparently tanked up on all available rations and was now in high good humor. At a long table in the corner of the canteen, the young boys and girls of the farm sat with the Red Army soldiers and veterinaries. A balalaika, a guitar and an accordion promised music and dancing.

Vassily and Mira joined Tadek, Freddy and Benderski. The three had already eaten, and Tadek was passing on to Freddy, in their private language, what Benderski told him in Polish.

While Mira and Vassily ate, they listened to the story of the gardener's life. Stimulated by the triple vodka rations, he was recounting stories from the distant past, when he had been his father's helper on the estate of Novo-Bakhmutovka, which had belonged to a Baron Hülsen. "Those were the days," he said, raising his glass. "Those *pomeshchiki* had their four or five thousand dessiatin of land! In the Ukraine, mind you—that soil—you could grow what you liked there—poppies, hemp, anything. And among the Germans—this Baron was a German, you see; his great-grandfather was born in Russia but still they all spoke German at home—things weren't slipshod like with the Russians. These folks had money. There was the young Baron Grisha, served with the Alexandra Hussars. When he was home on leave, he would say to my father, 'Hey, Jozef, I'm going here or there tomorrow, I want to take flowers with me.' Roses or carnations or chrysanthemums, whatever was in season. And then my father came with the bouquet—the Baron already sitting in the troika, an Orlov in the middle and two flashy mares on either side—and my father says, 'Here, Your Grace,' or 'Here, Your Excellency'—not grazhdanin or tovarishch; he wouldn't have dared anything like that. 'Here are the flowers,' my father would say, and the Baron would only glance at them. 'Fine, Jozef,' he'd say, and then a bird would go flying through the air, a golden bird, a five-ruble gold piece, right into my father's cap! And how you could stretch that—you could drink on it for a month. And you didn't have to go looking where you could get vodochka, or beg anybody to let you have a little glass. You went to the village, you bought as much as you wanted—no rations!" He took a swallow of his vodochka.

"Yes," Tadek commented, "my grandfather was fond of vodka too. He drank himself to death, my mother says."

"That's fine, that's the best!" Benderski said elegiacally. "Drank himself to death—rot! You have to die anyhow, so why not enjoy it? We always used to say, in the old days, the good old days, being drunk is the best life."

"Konechno," said Freddy, who had not understood a word.

"You're mistaken, Comrade Ogrodnik," Vassily said with a grave expression. "The phrase is '*Half drunk* is the best life.'"

"Half, half. Never do things halfway. If you do anything, do it right. Working or drinking—put all you've got into it. That's what my father used to say. My father fought with Makhno—the Austrians hanged him in the summer of 1918."

"In Gulai-Pole, I suppose?" Vassily asked.

"Where else? That was the life—under Papa Makhno. Everything went—that was anarchy, he said. Those were the days when I really learned how to do it—drink, I mean. And then the Germans and the Austrians came along and hunted us. Hunted down the whole lot of us—Papa Makhno's band. But we gave them a few nuts to crack all of them—the Bolsheviki too. How do you know about Gulai-Pole?"

"I've heard about it. He was a bandit, your Papa Makhno."

"Depends on how you look at it. It depends. He was an anarchist, so he said. But what did we care? It was a jolly life. My throat's dry. You're not drinking your ration, or the bookkeeper either. Mind if I get it?"

Vassily nodded, and Benderski went to the counter to moisten his throat. Vassily thought of Gulai-Pole. Two squadrons of his regiment and an infantry battalion had been posted there. It was true—they had had quite a few nuts to crack. How many of his comrades Makhno's men had shot from ambush, how many of them butchered! They'd concentrated on the officers. And the Austrians had hung many a jolly "anarchist" from the telegraph poles—quite possibly Benderski's father had been among them.

The gardener returned to the table, thanked Vassily and Mira courteously, and prepared to go on with his story. But he didn't get far. Music sounded, loud and gay; the young folks were singing, "*Kalinka, kalinka, kalinka moia*—little rosebud, little rosebud, my little rosebud." The singing soared, louder and louder. It was impossible to hear yourself think.

Nevertheless, Tania and the gardener bent toward each other, talking. On Tania's face were none of her usual expressions of boredom, irony, mockery or exaggerated gravity, none of her "faces" and grimaces. She was—or was convincingly playing the part— concentrated, all ears, intensely interested in what the party candidate Chalev was telling her with more and more loquacity and vigor—for he had to outshout the music and singing in order to make himself heard. His struggle was reflected in the fierce looks from his small, squinting, myopic eyes at the table of young people.

They, however, did not even notice. They kept their instruments and voices fortissimo, and when several couples rose and began to waltz, the noise was augmented by the thumping of feet and cheers from the non-dancers.

Tania Obadieva leaned forward and said something to the gardener. Then they both rose; he pushed his cap back on his head, put his right arm around the cashier's waist, and holding her as far away as possible, waltzed off with her. Or rather, she waltzed and he hopped along beside her, frequently changing pace in an attempt to get into step. But he evidently enjoyed it. Probably he had never tried to dance before, and was now finding it pleasant and scarcely as difficult as he had imagined. When the music stopped, he released his partner reluctantly and sent a pleading look to the musicians. But they continued to ignore him, and took a rest.

Benderski stood up, went over to the young people's table and asked for the guitar. His small, swaying head tilted to his left shoulder and remained there. In a hoarse baritone he sang "The Black Hussars," plucking the strings in accompaniment. Each time he came to the refrain, he raised his head and looked around the room; then, after this pause, he sang with dramatic emphasis, *"Marsh v period, marsh v period, tsernye gussary*—Forward march, forward march, black hussars!"

After the second stanza the Red Army men joined in the "forward march"—they were much taken with the "new" song. The singer was applauded with an enthusiasm which any stage star would have envied. Benderski, confident that no one in the canteen understood what the song meant, or knew anything about the hated era from which it had sprung, began a new one.

Chalev stooped toward Tania and asked her something. Vassily noticed this; he rose and went over to the young people's table. He thought he would invite Benderski to a ration of vodka and so put an end to his "counterrevolutionary" activities. But Tania was quicker. She casually took hold of Benderski's hand and cried in the properly brisk, jolly tone, "Come, I want to dance for you! Kozachek! Hopak! Davai—let's go!" As she spoke, she carefully took the guitar from Benderski's hand and returned it to its owner.

Tania was wearing new shoes and stockings; her feet and legs showed to fine advantage as she danced through the room, arms folded, hips swaying, facial mimicry expressively suiting her movements. She tossed her head, inviting a partner to join her; her face expressed astonishment and regret when no one did so. At last she placed her arms akimbo and mimicked intense indignation. Benderski, aroused from dreams produced by alcohol and music, sprang toward her with a bound that no one would have thought him capable of, and fell into step with her. The old drinker was an excellent partner, in spite of his grotesque appearance. His effective leading, his pleasure in complicated steps and leaps, inspired his partner. She followed him intelligently, and when the pair began —alternately at first and then together—leaping into the air, then crouching and throwing their legs out straight ahead or to the sides, the rhythmic clapping that accompanied their performance became one storm of wild applause.

Mira alone did not clap, but no one noticed, for she had stayed in her place while Vassily, Tadek and Freddy had joined the ring of onlookers around the dancers. Vassily found her still looking gloomy when he returned to the table. He was left alone with her; Tadek and Freddy were steering their gifted colleague to the counter, to reinforce his pleas for another ration. "They're pretty good, aren't they?" Vassily said, laughing in an effort to cheer Mira.

"I've seen better." Mira shrugged.

"They make a wonderful couple. I enjoyed it anyway."

"Did you? That crazy chit will do anything to show off. It's all meant for you, Vassily."

"Now, what kind of foolishness is that—meant for me? Who can figure out what she's after? I can't, and I'm not going to worry about it."

She ignored the reproof. Looking away, she said, "I'm terribly worried, Vassily, and I feel sick at the thought of going away and leaving you here. That"—she fumbled for a word and then went on lamely—"girl is dangerous. Couldn't you come with us after all?"

"Do you think I wouldn't, if there were any way to do it? You're ordinarily so sensible, Mira. I'll be across the border very, very soon. By the day after tomorrow you'll have forgotten all this." He quickly changed the awkward subject and looked over at the counter, where the cashier was touching glasses with her dancing partner, for she had coaxed Chalev into giving up his ration for him. "Look at them," he said. Tania was raising her glass with such a clever travesty of drunkenness that Vassily could not resist laughing.

Mira had not looked, and Vassily, thinking that she was deliberately angry, turned toward her again. His expression sobered, and he was overcome by feeling. Mira's golden eyes were swimming with tears. But she quickly regained control of herself because Freddy, Tadek and Benderski were returning to the table. "Time we went to bed, Freddy," she said quietly. He nodded docilely. Tadek, too, was tired, and Vassily, who judged that Benderski had had just about enough, suggested that he, too, should get himself some sleep. "Tomorrow's another day."

"You're a smart man and a nice one—very smart and very good,"

Benderski said. "But you won't stay that way long. All right, I'll come." He went along, staggering a little. On the street their ways parted. At a gesture from Vassily, Tadek and Freddy took the drinker between them and led him to his house. Halfway, he stopped, lifted his cap, and with liquid courage and pathos sang, *"Ya Sibiri, Sibiri—ya nye boyus—Sibir tozhe russkaya zemlya—*I am not afraid of Siberia—Siberia is also Russian soil!"

Next morning Vassily went to the canteen for breakfast with Tadek. Since Antek's death they had stopped breakfasting at home. Chalev, the head gardener, still lay curled up in his blanket, his jacket bunched under his head for a pillow. He had come home last night much later than Vassily and Tadek. There was still a good hour before the workday began.

Vassily had given instructions for the milking to be started earlier, so that the milk would reach the dairy in time—the dairy had a heavy schedule these days—and the cows could be driven out to pasture immediately after milking. In view of the coming celebration, all the milkers were to accompany the cows to pick meadow flowers and gather branches in the pinewoods; these would be used for wreaths and garlands to decorate the horses and wagons for the May Day celebration.

In spite of the early start, it was a good while before the cows were out on the road. They left behind a courtyard splattered with the signs of digestive activity stimulated by fresh green grass. Meanwhile, the teams had ridden out; Wagner had left among the first with the dairy and pork products.

Vassily summoned the three gardeners, and all four set about cleaning the big yard. Just as the dung cart was about to set out with its first load, Chalev turned up. "What are the gardeners doing here?" he asked challengingly, without so much as a good-morning. He punctuated his question with several explosive sneezes.

Each time he sneezed, Tadek said in Polish, "I hope you burst." Benderski went on sweeping unconcernedly. Freddy said, "Cheers!" and Vassily called out gaily, "Good morning, comrade. Our climate seems rather hard on you."

"My business." Chalev sneezed several more times. "I asked why the gardeners are not at work."

"Whom are you asking?" Vassily said. He knew quite well why the party candidate was sneezing. Yesterday, along with his shoe polish, he had bought a package of sneezing powder and scattered its contents among his clothes, under the blanket, into his sheepskin and into the tops of his other boots. As Vassily had suspected,

Chalev had searched his belongings and inhaled the powder. Tania is right, he thought; he's out to check on me. But what does he want? Who has sent him?

Whatever indignation the starshi may have felt at this answer was somewhat lost in a new fit of sneezing. Moreover, he completely lacked a bourgeois handkerchief. "The gardeners must stay at their work," he finally spluttered. "Cleaning is not their specialty."

"It isn't my speciality either," Vassily said. "But on a farm, everybody has to help out. Are you so busy counting trees that you haven't noticed the others helping to set out the vegetables? By the way, you can continue your counting next fall; right now the vegetable beds are the main thing. You are to start work there immediately."

"Who? Me? Ha—not my—" He had to stop the sneeze. "Not my specialty."

"Then I'll apply today for a starshi who knows something about vegetables, which are one of the farm's main crops. And you are going to start in on the forcing beds at once. Won't do you any harm to learn another specialty; you're still young."

"Ah—hm—in the forcing beds." He had another fit of sneezing, and made no further protest. Later, when Vassily went to the forcing beds, he found Chalev there. Reluctantly and making a great show of clumsiness, but obeying Benderski's directions, he did unskilled labor, frequently interrupted by bouts of sneezing

Vassily had a few words with the "anarchist" about the wreaths and bouquets which would have to be made after work. "It will all be done,—so long as I have my rations." And when a wink from Vassily reassured him on this important point, he went back to work, humming contentedly.

In the office the bookkeeper and cashier were at their desks. Tania was just locking her drawer when Vassily entered. "I'm going to town alone today; the bookkeeper isn't coming. Can't you drive me, Vassia?" she asked.

"I'm not going; I must see to the cows. Yeremczuk will take you."

Tania, piqued, put on her jacket and pettishly slid her beret on her head. After she had gone, Vassily asked, "Did you send her away, Mira?"

"Yes. She is to go to the bank for money."

"Fine, Mira. Do you have everything?"

"I'm ready." She looked up at him. "All is in good order here. Whoever comes to take over will have no trouble. Our little secrets are carefully covered up. No one will find them out. Of course, once the surpluses are used up, there will be holes, and how they're going to fill those—"

"They'll manage. Are you sorry to be leaving the farm, Mira?"

She looked at him wonderingly, then grew thoughtful. "Sorry? I've worked hard, God knows, and not done too badly. We could have done much better if we'd been allowed to go our own way. How hard it's been sometimes. And it would have been unendurable if it hadn't been for you." Her eyes filled with tears. "You are the farm for me; that's why—"

"Don't, Mira, you mustn't! Why cry? Tomorrow you'll be breathing free air." He glanced at the door, listened to make sure no one was coming, and then took her head in his hands and kissed her on the forehead, eyes, mouth. "Keep hold of yourself, Mira; don't lose your nerve. This noon I'll take your things into town. Now I have to ride out to check on the cows."

Vassily lingered with the cows longer than he had intended, and also took a look at the flower pickers and gatherers of pine boughs. It was nearly half past eleven by the time he rode back. As he approached the farm, he saw almost all the farm workers on inside duty gathered in the yard, talking excitedly and waving their arms wildly. Even the cooks from the canteen were there. Tadek came running toward him. "Vassily, brother!" His voice broke into its highest falsetto. "Fredziu, Mira, arrested. Two cars—Fredziu's gone!" He waved in the direction of the city and clapped his hands over his eyes in despair. "Jesus Maria, Fredziu!"

Aghast, Vassily leaped from the horse. He was surrounded and pelted with questions and scraps of information. Everyone had a different version of the incident and a different opinion. Chalev alone watched the tumult in silence. "Quiet!" Vassily thundered at last, almost out of his mind with worry. That took effect. He asked precise questions, and was able to put together some picture out of the fragmentary accounts. About fifteen minutes after he had ridden away, two automobiles had stopped in front of the office. Three uniformed men and two "civilians"—one of them was the small, gray-haired man who had spoken in Polish at Antek's funeral—had got out of the cars and gone directly into the office. They stayed there for about half an hour. Then the small gray-haired man and two men in uniform had come into the garden, where everyone was working at the forcing beds. They had fetched Freddy and gone with him and Mira to their house. After about an hour they emerged, Mira and Freddy very warmly dressed and each with a suitcase in hand. They had been allowed to say good-bye to the workers. Mira had been very pale, with tears in her eyes, and Freddy had repeatedly embraced Tadek and wept. Then one automobile had driven off with Mira and Freddy, the gray-haired man and two uniformed men following in the second automobile.

As he listened to the various accounts, Vassily felt somewhat calmer. There was a good deal about the story that struck a re-assuring note—the casual manner of the "arrest," the fact that Freddy and Mira had been given time to pack and dress. At the same time, the excitement of the others had infected him, and, like them, he feared the worst. But he said nothing about his fears, and did his best to encourage the others by his manner and soothing phrases. While he was talking, he was struck by Chalev's mocking expression. "You seem to be familiar with these matters, Comrade Starshi Ogrodnik," he said. "What do you make of it?"

"That's my business," Chalev replied.

Benderski came up to Vassily and croaked, "I'll drink milk for the rest of my life if they've been arrested. That was no arrest; I've seen arrests before. I know Podgorski, the little gray-haired fellow, too. He's from the *Spetz Otdel,* the Secret Service. God knows what they want with Fredziu and his wife, but they weren't arresting them."

Tadek had heard only the name Fredziu. He raised his head. "Fredziu—now he's gone too." And he growled a curse in his treble voice, which, more piping than ever in his misery, greatly detracted from the fierceness of the words.

"Go ahead and curse, Tadek, but don't let others hear you at it. I've been cursing the whole damn thing a long time," Benderski said.

"*Psiakrev cholera*—goddammit!" Tadek repeated several times, itemizing the various nachalniki he knew, and throwing in the name of the new head gardener as well, for good measure.

"All right, now, Tadek," Vassily said, trying to soothe him. "Damn the whole lot of them. And now be a good fellow and bring me a pail from the stable." The giant obediently trotted off.

"What should we do, Benderski?" Vassily asked the "anarchist." "If anything."

"Well, you might go ahead and report the latest development, and also see if I can't get credited for their two vodka rations at the canteen." Vassily led the horse to the pump and let him drink while he listened to Benderski. "That other civilian who was with the party was definitely not a Russian," Benderski went on. "That suit. And that tie. You could tell at a glance he was a foreigner. Now tell me, what would a foreigner be doing at an arrest? Hey, how about that vodka?"

The reasoning was sound, Vassily thought. "Tadek," he said, "see if you can't get a ride into town after work with some of the soldiers. Then you can pay a visit to your mother and bring back a bottle of cherry brandy for Benderski. You'll see, you haven't tasted stuff like that for a long time, Comrade Benderski."

"All right," Tadek said, greatly heartened by Vassily's good humor and big grin. "What do you think they're doing to Fredziu, Brother Vassily?"

"Nothing bad, Tadek—I'm certain of it. No need to worry." He tightened Golodnyi's girth and mounted.

Vassily gave Golodnyi his head. Although the stallion kept to a fast trot, he was amply able to reflect. Benderski was right, of course—he should have known at once. Rozescu and Linton, or rather the many alarmed relatives in England and America, had succeeded, by virtue of their connections, in reaching out to Soviet Poland to rescue Mira and Freddy. His message to Rundberg had worked, and the problem had been solved in the best possible way, without the dangers of an illegal border crossing. It would be a waste of time and energy to try to find out what means the family had used. The clever old Macedonian proverb had once more proved true: donkeys laden with gold can surmount the highest walls. The donkeys need not have been laden with gold; the exchange might have involved diamonds, industrial diamonds, indispensable for making airplane motors. An honest swap: each party gave what he had and what the other party needed. . . . But now it was vital to decide what attitude he should take in reporting the thing to the nachalniki. Much would depend on his strategy. He drew in on the reins, rode into town at a quiet trot, and reached the Elektrostantsia headquarters.

Saposhnik was still in his office. In contrast to his usual slow, deliberate pace, Vassily rushed in and immediately blurted out his story. He did not express his own opinion—he had not been there, after all—but told Saposhnik what the others had told him: Mira and Freddy had been arrested. Saposhnik's face turned a chalky white; he struggled to preserve a look of superior knowledge, but failed miserably. When he stood up, his hands gripped the edge of the desk for support. "One moment," he said, and left the room.

He returned ten minutes later with Lavrenenko. If the latter had been violently upset, he showed no signs of it; in any case, he was not personally concerned. Still and all, the arrest of two exceptionally highly rated workers was perturbing. Saposhnik ran his hands through his tousled hair, and Lavrenenko took off his cap and also ran his dark-skinned hand over his close-cropped hair. Both officials grappled with this new problem in silence. They had nothing to say, did not dare to ask questions, or express an opinion. This was a normal part of their life; it was an inevitable aspect of the power to which they had submitted, of the vast machine in which they were tiny cogs. Questions were not tolerated. "Da."

Saposhnik said, and his voice sounded almost normal. And, "No da," Lavrenenko said very softly.

"What do you think, Fyodor Ivanovich? Perhaps we can transfer an assistant bookkeeper from the plant, until a replacement turns up?"

"I think we'd better apply to the Committee. After the May Day celebration, perhaps. Meanwhile we'll have to ask Comrade Khomniuk and the cashier to manage somehow."

"They certainly don't have a bookkeeper to spare. We'll have to find a local."

"After May first," Lavrenenko said. He turned to Vassily. "It isn't so complicated, Vassily Vassilevich. Weigh everything carefully and put the figures down. In two or three days someone will be out there."

"I'll do my best, Comrade Director, but I can't take the responsibility—I really don't know a thing about keeping records. I need a gardener also—or rather, two. Definitely two gardeners."

"Why two?" Saposhnik asked. "There's no provision for more than three gardeners."

"I know that, but Comrade Chalev is a specialist in trees. He says he knows nothing about vegetables."

"That's impossible!" Lavrenenko exclaimed in astonishment. "What does that mean, he knows nothing about vegetables?"

Vassily merely shrugged. Lavrenenko was on the point of saying something to Saposhnik, but at that moment Feingold pulled open the door and strode rapidly into the room, followed by Tatiana Obadieva. "Well," he said, turning smilingly to Vassily, "you're sitting there like a shepherd without his pipe. So they've taken your bookkeeper away and one of your gardeners. That's pretty rough on you, Vassily Vassilevich."

Tania had taken a seat without more ado and sat looking indifferently across at Vassily. "So you've already heard of it," Feingold said to the others. He also sat down. "They're gone, on the plane already." He looked at his watch. "Kharkov, Moscow, Stockholm, and from there, New York. That's how it goes, comrades!" He looked triumphantly around the circle to observe the effect of his news. Only Vassily did him the favor of registering surprise. Evidently he had not expected the others to, for he went right on. "Paliev came in person, in a special plane, went for them and is taking them all the way to the border. Yes, my friends, I'd like to see anyone match us in efficiency! Podgorski says they both cried when they said good-bye—a pity, they were both fine workers, but nobody is indispensable." He produced a package of Uzbek and offered them around.

"So that's it?" Vassily asked.

"What did you think?" Feingold grinned.

Vassily caught a warning look from Tania before he answered. "I knew only what the others told me," he said stolidly. "I was out in the pasture looking to the cows when they were taken away. Two cars, I hear." He laughed. "Everybody figured they'd been arrested and so I thought so too, dumb ox that I am. But"—he frowned abruptly—"Comrade Chalev, the starshi ogrodnik, was there at the time; he's a party candidate and should know about such things, shouldn't he? I asked him first what he thought about it and he—you know what he answered? 'My business,' he said. What did he mean by that, Comrade Feingold?"

A small furrow appeared between Feingold's handsome eyebrows, only to be promptly dispelled. "Does he know gardening —Chalev?"

"Seems not," Saposhnik said. "Comrade Khomniuk has just asked us for two gardeners because Chalev claims he's a specialist in fruit culture and knows nothing about vegetables."

Feingold nodded and veered away from the subject. "We must explain the matter to the farm workers. It won't do to let them go on thinking that two people who worked so well have been arrested. Why should they be? That isn't good, isn't healthy. . . . Comrade Obadieva, you go out and talk to them today, and someone will translate what you say into Ruthenian. Perhaps I'll come out myself. When is the farm workday over?"

"Do you want to call a regular meeting, Comrade Feingold? We have such a heavy load right now—don't take it amiss—I mean, if you'd just give a short speech to the people when they're in the canteen, right after eating . . . you understand, we have to get the garlands and wreaths ready—there's so much to do to prepare for May Day. Would it be all right if I send the buggy out for you at six? Then you'd be with us around seven. Where should I send it, Comrade Feingold?"

"To the Party Committee, Vassily Vassilevich. But come yourself."

Feingold swung into the buggy with a lithe, gymnast's leap, and sat down beside Vassily. "Learned that from Maximenko," he said, laughing. "*Fisicultura*—highly important. Fine horses these are, the ones you saved, Vassily Vassilevich."

"Hm," Vassily murmured. He had to drive with more than usual care; most of the city's factories shut down at six o'clock, and the streets were crowded. It was some time before they reached the end of the streetcar line, where the open highway began. But Vassily was glad of the excuse not to make conversation. He was in a black mood as a result of a fresh incident on the farm. The tree specialist had come upon the wild pear tree by Antek's grave, pronounced it useless, and wanted it cut down. What was more, he had committed the ultimate indiscretion of asking Tadek to do it. When the starshi showed him the tree he meant, Tadek simply laid down the tools and went back to the forcing beds. The head gardener went after him. When Benderski attempted to intervene and explain what lay behind Tadek's attitude, Chalev dismissed it all as *burzhuiskaia sentimentalnost*—bourgeois sentimentality. He repeated his order: Tadek was to cut down that tree. Whereupon Tadek had piped at his highest pitch, "Psiakrev cholera!" Chalev had walked away in a huff. No doubt he would file a denunciation, and things would go badly for poor Tadek.

Feingold himself gave Vassily a chance to broach the subject. "What's your impression of the new head gardener?" he asked abruptly.

"I don't know much about gardening," Vassily replied, "but on a farm as small as ours no one can afford to limit himself to fruit culture alone. At this season there's hardly anything to do in that line anyhow. This morning he put in a few hours at the vegetable beds, but in the afternoon he took it into his head to cut down the tree by Gorecki's grave. And the way he went about it! Maybe that's how he was taught—but to want to cut a tree down with a carpenter's saw and a hatchet. . . ." Vassily went on to tell the whole story of the afternoon's incident. "Of course Tadek should break himself of the habit of cursing, hard as it is," he concluded.

"What do those words mean?" Feingold asked.

"It's just something you say, not an insult really; it's not directed against anybody—just a way to let off steam. Psiakrev cholera—it's nothing. But when a man doesn't understand it—"

"Then someone should have explained it to him."

"Of course. But he ran off. Dropped everything and disappeared. What do you say to that, Comrade Feingold? Is it right to let your temper interfere with your work? Besides, Gorecki was a stakhanovets, and the farm workers wanted to take up a collection for a plaque with a picture of Stalin, and underneath they wanted to write that here was a good worker and so on—and they'd planned on fastening the plaque to the pear tree. Is that allowed or isn't it?"

"Konechno! It will be done; you'll have the plaque and it will be fastened to the pear tree. You can depend on that. The workers mustn't take up a collection for it—we don't allow that—but the collective will pay for it, don't worry! But this man Chalev." He looked at Vassily, and then he said something that seemed wholly unrelated to the conversation. "Gorbatenko was an idiot—that's been proved—just a plain idiot." He dropped into a meditative silence, which lasted until they'd almost reached Jiusefovka. Then he said, "You are the head man, Vassily Vassilevich; you're in command. The head gardener must obey your orders. That applies to the pear tree, too. If you need him in the vegetable beds, set him to work. He cannot be starshi, but at the same time we can't put him under another gardener's orders. It's a complicated business. And something else: you're living in the same house with him. It would be a good idea to find out what kind of bird he is. I mean—you understand me, don't you?"

The buggy stopped in front of the canteen. Feingold leaped to the ground. As he turned toward the entrance he said very softly, "Watch carefully, Vassily Vassilevich. Watch very carefully." And with his customary radiant smile he added, "It may be that the bird comes from a strange nest."

He marched into the canteen and Vassily drove into the yard. The horses would remain in harness, since they would be needed soon to drive Feingold back. As he slowly crossed the yard, he speculated. Chalev obviously had been assigned to spy on him, Vassily. He had gone to the length of ransacking his room. Now he, in his turn, was supposed to spy on Chalev. The bird had come from a strange nest. What nest? He reached the canteen without solving that riddle, but he had come to a resolve: once Wagner and Meerblum were in safety, he would waste no more time. He'd get out without stopping a moment.

In the dining room the farm workers, under Benderski's direction, were weaving garlands out of pine twigs and red ribbons, making wreaths, and tying flowers into bouquets.

Feingold sat down at a table with Tania and Vassily. He ate hurriedly and was already smoking when the others had barely begun their meal. He sat lost in thought until Tania returned from the serving window with tea for all three of them. Vassily thanked Tania for her thoughtfulness, deliberately speaking somewhat louder than was necessary, and so roused Feingold from his musings. "Where are the two gardeners?" Feingold asked as they drank their tea. "I see neither Chalev nor Zembrinski."

"I don't know where Chalev is," Vassily replied. "Zembrinski drove into town with me to collect some clean clothes. His mother does his laundry. He'll come back in one of the army trucks."

"No da," Feingold said. He turned to the cashier. "Now's the time to begin, Tania. Let them go on with what they're doing—don't stand up. Just tell them—you know what to do."

Vassily observed that Feingold had dropped the official tone and formal address which he used at other times toward the cashier. This meant that he himself was being admitted to a circle of intimacy. But he had no time to reflect on that, for Tania had called out in her loud, artificially jesting tone, interrupting the hum of general conversation, "Comrades!" He paid close attention, for he would be called upon to translate her speech when she was finished. But he would never be able to reproduce it, as he had to admit to himself after her first few words. For she did not make a report; she acted out a skit, and there was no need to understand her Leningrad Russian. Her pantomime told the whole story. There sat Mira over her books, reckoning and making notes, intent on nothing but her figures; and there was friendly Freddy, toiling with shovel and rake and watering can; and there were the parents in America, longing for their son and daughter-in-law, appealing to the representatives of Soviet power and asking them to send them their children! Then petitions were written and read, telephones rang, inquiries were made and orders issued. Propellers hummed at the Moscow airport; a plane rose into the air. Nachalniki with the stamped and sealed documents sat in the plane. It landed in Lvov. Automobiles tooted, and then they were stopping in front of the farm's office, and the two Linhans, totally ignorant of what this was all about, had to bid tearful good-byes to their place of work and their workmates, to leave the land of freedom and progress. Soon they would be on the ship sailing toward the uncertainties and insecurity of a land whose people, bowed under the yoke of the capitalist system, waited for liberation. And Mira and Alfred would tell them—shedding tears of nostalgia—what a good and beautiful life they had had in the Soviet Union, on the Elektrostantsia farm!

"Was that all clear to you?" Feingold asked the audience in his literary Ukrainian. A joyful, unanimous "Da" rang out. "All right, then," Feingold told Vassily, "no need to translate." But Tania nudged Vassily under the table. "That's how it was, wasn't it, Vassia?" she asked, a mocking light dancing in her eyes. "Yes, my friend, telling a story properly is something that has to be learned."

Vassily put on his look of peasant wonder. "Learned?"

"Yes," she said, abruptly changing from self-congratulation to bitter sarcasm. "To each according to his abilities."

"Could we drive back now, Vassily Vassilevich?" Feingold said. "They need me at the Party Committee. Work—May Day."

But he was to get back much, much later. For no sooner had Vassily stood up than three militiamen, the youngest wearing the insignia of a second lieutenant, all with large pistol holsters strapped on their right sides, entered the noisy hall. "Who is the starshi here?" the Lieutenant demanded loudly.

"You handle them, Vassily Vassilevich; I'll come if necessary," Feingold whispered.

Vassily went up to them quietly and deliberately. "Good evening," he said to the militiamen.

"You the starshi here?" the Lieutenant asked. His subordinates had responded to the greeting; he did not.

"I'm the zamestitel."

"No da." He dropped his voice and consulted a slip of paper he had taken from his pocket. "You have a gardener by the name of Tadeus Karlowicz Zembrinski. Which one is he?"

"He isn't here just now," Vassily said; he had surmised, only too correctly, whom the militiamen were looking for.

"Not here? Where is he, then?" the Lieutenant demanded.

"He finished his work at six o'clock in the evening and until half past six tomorrow morning he can go where he likes. I can't ask everyone what he does in his free time—and they wouldn't tell me if I asked."

"Well, then, you come along, citizen," the Lieutenant said softly.

"Where to?" Vassily asked loudly. Feingold rose and sauntered slowly toward the group, followed by the cashier.

"What's the trouble?" he asked the Lieutenant amiably.

The cold official expression did not change. "My business."

"Mine too," Feingold said quietly. And Tania added, "The business of all of us."

"I am the political officer of the Elektrostantsia," Feingold went on. "If any worker in our organization is involved, I'm supposed to be consulted. You know that or you would not have reached your present rank. Here are my documents." He held out his party card. The cashier also presented hers.

The Lieutenant took the documents, studied them, and handed them back. "My assignment is—"

"Not here," Feingold interrupted. "We'll discuss this in the office. Come along, Vassily Vassilevich."

Tania led the way, unlocked the door and switched on the light. They were barely inside the room when the lieutenant said, "I am to arrest the gardner Zembrinski. Those were my orders."

"The gardener Zembrinski is not on the premises. What else were you to do? Show me your documents and your orders, please," Feingold said sharply.

The Lieutenant presented them in silence. Feingold glanced over the identification, compared the photograph with the owner, and handed it back. Then he read the arrest warrant. "In the first place, only Zembrinski is mentioned here," he said, "and in the second place, you belong to the Stalin District; the Elektrostantsia is in the Lenin District. It was your duty to point that out to the informer. You should know that better than I."

"The denunciation was not delivered to me but to the nachalnik," the Lieutenant replied. "I am only to carry out the order."

"And were you to arrest the head man if you didn't find the gardener?" Feingold asked casually. The militiaman shrugged and did not reply. Feingold did not press him for an answer; instead he turned the crank of the telephone several times. The line went through the plant headquarters, but within a comparatively short time Feingold had the number he had requested—a number which compelled the Lieutenant to strained attention. It was the number of the Lieutenant's superior, who greeted Feingold in a friendly fashion. Feingold pointed out the breach of form. Apparently objections were made at the other end of the wire, for the conversation went back and forth for some time until Feingold convinced the other man that the charge against Zembrinski for "slandering the mother" of Party Candidate and Head Gardener Chalev should be transferred to the militia of the Lenin District. He himself had received a report on the very same incident at six that evening. Apparently no one's mother had been insulted, as was alleged. The phrase used was only "psiakrev cholera," a mild remark which didn't warrant immediate arrest. By the way, even the insult which Chalev reported did not warrant immediate arrest, did it? These regulations were the same everywhere, were they not? Well, then. Feingold refrained from mentioning the attempted arrest of the zamestitel. He handed the telephone to the Lieutenant, who was officially instructed to drop the matter, and the militiamen left.

The three sat for a while in the office, smoking in silence, until Feingold stood up and strode out of the room. The others followed him. But on the street he stood still a moment. "Nichevo," he said with a sigh. "It seems you were right, Tania. Vassily Vassilevich, you filed that denunciation against Zembrinski. Have Chalev report to me at eight o'clock tomorrow morning."

Tadek turned up at the canteen much later, an interesting package under his arm. Vassily told him of the little adventure with the militiamen. Everything would be all right, Vassily said, but he must avoid getting into any hassle with Chalev. It might be wise for him not to sleep in his usual place tonight. There was a spare bed in Benderski's room. "He'll give you a hearty welcome," Vassily said, laughingly indicating the package. Tadek agreed; he found Benderski, and the two made off together. To Vassily it looked like an auspicious beginning of a new friendship for Tadek, a friendship he needed.

Tania and Vassily were among the last to leave the canteen. Their houses lay in the same direction, and they walked along together. Neither spoke until they reached Tania's house. "Mind if I walk you home?" she said, with somewhat less than her usual pertness. "It's a wonderful night."

They had almost reached his cottage when Tania broke the silence. "Listen closely, Vassia." She leaned against the fence, over which hung the branches of an old nut tree. "You go in now. If Chalev is at home, switch the light on, switch it out, then switch it on again—very fast. If he isn't there, come back. I'll wait here—go ahead, and hurry."

He forbore to ask questions and did as she told him. Chalev was not there, and he returned to Tania. At once she began further instructions. "Stand here, look to right and left. When you see him coming, go toward the house, whistling. Whistling, understand?"

"Yes, but—"

"I'll be in there. Which is his bed? Where are his things?"

"What do you have in mind? It's not allowed—"

"No time. I'll explain later." After he had pointed out which room was Chalev's, she slid along the fence up to the house and disappeared inside. Vassily stood watch, keeping a close lookout toward the left, the direction of town, and toward the right, the direction of the main buildings of the farm. No light showed in the house. The moon shone, bathing everything in silver.

He stood for about half an hour, tense and watchful for he knew that something vital was at stake. At last Tania came out. She crept cautiously along in the shadow of the wall and the fence. "That's all," she whispered. "Come along with me part of the way and I'll tell you—" She broke off and listened in the direction of the city. "A motor, you hear it?"

He listened. "Yes, it's a car," he agreed in surprise.

"It is either bringing Chalev or—they're coming for you," she whispered, greatly keyed-up. "Run into the house; lie down in bed fully dressed. I'll stay here. If they've come to take you, I'll hold them at bay. If you hear me talking, beat it out the back door and run for all you're worth. Hide. In three hours come to the garden, near the cold frames; I'll wait for you there. If it's just Chalev, he won't drive right up to the house with the car; he'll get out at the road. It's important that he find you at home. Hurry, run—there are the headlights already."

Vassily leaped through the door in three long strides, locked it from inside, withdrew the key, threw himself down on his bed and pulled the blanket over his head. He strained his ears to hear whether the noise of the motor was coming closer. Nothing happened—for endless minutes nothing at all. After about fifteen minutes the key turned softly in the lock of the front door. He heard the door being locked again, the door to the other room being opened very softly—and then he heard nothing more.

Vassily lay, blanket pulled up to his chin, eyes closed, as though he had been sleeping for many hours. He lay motionless, drawing deep breaths like a sleeper, and waiting for some suspicious noise outside the window, in the narrow hallway, or in the other bedroom where the enemy lay in Antek's bed. Chalev—the enemy? Why? What do I know of him? Do I know his intentions, who sent him, what for? "You seem to have been right, Tania," Feingold had said. Tania, who had warned him from the start: "Vassia, Vassinka, you dumb ox Vassily!" What had she warned against? What had she known? What did she know now? Was she too acting on orders? Was she too playing a part in a game? What kind of game? Who were the players, what were the stakes? . . . Again he listened. Not a sound. But the night was passing, dawn approaching. He could feel it, although it was pitch-dark in the little room with the narrow, curtained windows. It would be normal for him to be awake now, to turn on the light, open the window, move about, smoke.

The air poured into the room, brisk and fresh. The stars were paling against the gray sky. Fifteen minutes after three. Vassily put his blanket out to air and detected patches of dirt on the edge of the sheet. He stripped it off, got out a clean one, took the soiled sheet into the kitchen with him. He moved quietly, but not too quietly; let the man know that the head of the farm was already up. There was a great deal of work to be done today, April thirtieth, one day before May Day. In the sausage plant they were already starting work at four, and not much later in the dairy—to have the double rations ready for the holiday.

Vassily made a fire in the stove, put on water for washing and tea, polished his boots and brushed his clothes. Now and then he listened—would this habit of anxious listening stay with him for the rest of his life? But nothing stirred in the house.

"Enough," he said aloud, hurling his cigarette butt into the stove. "I've had enough!" He would clear out, he would run for it! And even as he thought this, he realized that he would not run, for curiosity had taken root in him. He had to know what the game was, and what was at stake. His part had already been assigned to him; that was clear. He must play it to the end to find out what it was. If the sport was dangerous, so much the better.

He washed and shaved, drank several glasses of hot tea, went back to his room and made the bed, deliberately wrinkling the fresh sheet—perhaps Chalev would make another search, in which case here was a little way of letting him know that someone was aware of his activities. As Vassily lifted his thin mattress to tuck in the ends of the sheet, he had the impression that the mattress was heavier than usual. Could it be? Perhaps his nerves were playing tricks on him. But no, there was something the matter with the mattress; it crackled softly—an eerie, almost inaudible crackling. In one leap he reached the door, slid the bolt. His callused fingers felt the ticking, pressed into the horsehair, here, there, slid along the seams. Here! Here the mattress had been opened and sewed again; the seam was fresh, and a hand seam, not sewed by machine.

He reached out for his shaving kit, took a razor blade—then changed his mind. No, not here. Chalev might come and surprise him. He tossed the mattress out the window, jumped through after it, picked it up, and ran at top speed through the gardens to the back door of the stable. Golodnyi scented him and whinnied softly. Vassily opened the door, carried the mattress into his horse's stall. He threw it on the pile of straw in the corner, strewed it with straw, took a deep breath and lit a cigarette. "You seem to have been right, Tania," he again heard Feingold saying. Tania would be alone now. He ran back through the gardens. The other women in her house would all be at the canteen, preparing breakfast. He reached the garden, the kitchen door of her cottage. It was not locked. A narrow hall, a door to the right, one to the left—it would be the door to the left. Vassily knocked. "Tania, it's Vassily."

"Yes," he heard her saying, "come in, it isn't locked."

In two minutes he had told her. "I'm sure something is in the mattress," Vassily said.

"How right you are! Go on, Vassinka, my clever Vassinka, run and bring the mattress. But not here—where?"

"Do you know the pear tree by Gorecki's grave?" She nodded. "I'll meet you there. Bring thread and a big needle."

She was there almost as soon as he was, and took over the whole task. She worked as though she had done it all her life, Vassily thought. She fished about in the horsehair and drew out a motley collection of paper: pamphlets, leaflets, newspaper clippings, cartoons, in German, French, English. All stuff directed against Soviet Russia, against the Bolsheviki, against Lenin, Stalin and the other Soviet heroes. "What an idiotic old trick! No one swallows this stuff any more. And all of it's antiquated—look at the dates, Vassia—1923 . . . the latest is 1927. But still it could cost you your pretty mustache, my clever ox Vassinka. . . . There, that's the lot."

She stuffed the horsehair back. The opening in the mattress gaped like a black wound.

"Sew it up, Tania—do you know how to?"

"I'll sew it up as good as new. Don't you wonder what he has against you?"

"You warned me to look out for him. The devil knows what he has against me!"

"We'll be rid of him soon. But you won't always have Tania to look after you, or Arkady Samuelovich either. He has your interests at heart—sincerely. Incidentally he's always sincere; he—oh well, you're still too dumb to be told that yet."

She bundled up the printed matter. "Return the mattress to your bed, then go to see Arkady Samuelovich." She gave him Feingold's home address. "Say I'll be coming afterwards, with Chalev."

Half an hour later Vassily dismounted in the yard of the house where Feingold lived. He tied the horse to a solitary acacia tree. In ten minutes he had told Feingold the whole story. "A good thing you're so observant. Tania knows what to do. We'll have this whole thing settled by this evening. Ride back, Vassily Vassilevich."

Yeremczuk had already hitched up when Vassily, after bringing the stallion back into his stall through the back door, came out into the yard. Chalev was standing by the buggy and waiting for Tania. She appeared, carrying the big briefcase Mira used to use, and sat down beside the driver. Chalev took the back seat, and the buggy rolled away.

Toward twelve o'clock Vassily had a last conference with Wagner and Meerblum. He wished them good luck, and they set off in the wagon that was bringing the extra rations to town. They would never return.

Vassily headed for the canteen. As he crossed the street, a small truck drove up. Tania, Feingold and Chalev got out, followed by five others—three men in uniform, with red caps, and two in civilian dress. "There is Khomniuk over there," Feingold said loudly. "Come here, citizen!"

Warned by the impersonal, official tone, Vassily approached. He greeted the group and waited. "Perhaps we ought to go to the office," Feingold said to the men in uniform.

Tania led the way. In the office, the stage was instantly set for an interrogation. Two men in uniform seated themselves at the desk where Mira had been working only the day before; one asked for Vassily's personal data, the other wrote down the answers. After all this had been recorded, one of the two civilians took up the questioning. "You have been denounced for possession of counterrevolutionary propaganda writings of foreign origin," he said. "Is that true?"

"I don't understand what you mean," Vassily said, wanting to test their attitude.

"You possess written material that tells lies about the Soviet Union, the Soviet power, the party, and various leading personalities in the Central Committee," the official explained patiently.

"I have only the books I've bought recently. All were published in Moscow: the history of the party, books by Marx, Lenin and Stalin, and some novels of Ehrenburg and Tolstoi. Oh yes, I also have a book by Friedrich von Schiller—a play called *Wilhelm Tell*. I can bring them and you can see for yourself."

"No need," the official said. "Where do you have them?"

"In my room."

"Let's drive over there." They all got into the car. Vassily sat between two uniformed men. Feingold sat opposite him but there was never a look or a word.

The books lay in two piles on the table. The German books bore the imprint in Russian: "Published by the Foreign Literature Publishing House, Moscow." All except the *Tell*. "What is this?" the official asked.

"I bought it on the street, near the theater." The official leafed through it; he evidently could not read the text, but the marked passages caught his attention. "And why are these lines underlined?"

"I wondered, too," Vassily said, smiling, though he could have kicked himself for his carelessness. "I bought the book secondhand, at a stand, as I told you."

Tania took the slim volume from the official. "Friedrich von Schiller," she read aloud. "Permitted—he's the one who wrote the revolutionary play *The Robbers*," she added. She didn't hand the book back to the official, but laid it on the table.

"Konechno," the official said. "Have you any other books?" he asked Vassily.

"None."

Chalev, who had remained outside in the hall—there was not space enough for so many people in the tiny room—now pressed forward. The search was about to begin. It was undertaken by one uniformed man and one civilian. They proceeded slowly and methodically. They looked through the wardrobe, going through Vassily's small stock of shirts, underwear, socks and bed linen, tapped the sides of the wardrobe, examined the walls—fortunately the floor was cement. There remained only the bed, a big, wide wooden bed.

They felt the pillow, sheets, blanket, neglected nothing that was a fraction of an inch in thickness. Finally there was only the mattress. They had left that to the last, as the stage magician saves up his best trick to make a good finale, Vassily thought. He observed them narrowly, trying to decide whether the men knew they were looking for something that had been planted there. For he could draw no conclusions from Feingold's or Tania's manner. At any rate, the men proceeded to attack the mattress with zeal. They felt it, shook it, even smelled it before they slit open one side. Handful after handful of horsehair was taken out, and examined; Chalev, who stood staring at the mattress with rising desperation, sweated profusely. Vassily could see the head gardener was obviously suffering.

"That's it," the official said to Feingold. He got up from the floor where he had been rummaging through the horsehair as if in search of a needle.

Feingold nodded. "Who lives in the other room?" He directed the question at Vassily.

"The head gardener and Zembrinski," Vassily answered.

"Who knows?" Feingold said. He left the room, followed by the NKVD men. Tania, who had whispered something to Chalev— something unpleasant, evidently, for the man made a gesture of despair—beckoned to Vassily, who stood contemplating the scene of the search. In the hall, one uniformed man posted himself at the front door and one civilian at the kitchen door. The head of the investigation had made an important discovery at first glance. On the windowsill beside Tadek's bed lay, in addition to his shaving things and soap, a book. It was the *Historical Miniatures*.

He turned to Vassily. "What kind of book is this and whom does it belong to?"

"It belonged to the head gardener Gorecki. I can't say what it is—I don't understand such things."

"What is it doing here?"

"Zembrinski likes to look at the pictures. He can't read it, since it's written in German."

"Have you read it?"

"No," Vassily said truthfully.

"Too bad," Tania said under her breath. She handed the book to Feingold and commented primly, "These are historical anecdotes that have nothing to do with history," and with a slight wink only he and Vassily could see, "The book should be confiscated." Her suggestion evidently fell in with the wishes of the head investigator, for he agreed heartily, and promptly wrapped the masterpiece in a sheet of newspaper.

Meanwhile the NKVD men were searching Tadek's bed; fortunately it had no mattress, only webbing covered by blankets. It was a simple matter to sort through his humble possessions, which yielded nothing of the smallest interest. Oddly enough, they then turned to Chalev's things. Chalev remonstrated, but the chief only said, "Those are the rules," and Chalev had to open even his suitcase, which was fastened by a heavy padlock. It was largely empty but for a suit of long underwear, several pairs of bathing trunks, and a few books. The NKVD man examined these books very closely, despite the fact that they were products of the State Publishing House. He found them highly rewarding, for as he leafed through *Lenin's Works,* several thin sheets of paper fell out, covered with purple typewriting. "Hectographed," the nachalnik said. He glanced over the sheets and thrust them into his pocket. "Shouting stop thief, eh?" he said to Chalev, who stood numbed. "It's an ancient trick."

"I never put those papers there; they don't belong to me!" Chalev cried hysterically. "I don't even know what they are!"

"I do," the NKVD man said. "They all say the same thing." And he ordered his subordinates, "Go on with the search!"

They went on. Nothing was found in the kitchen, cellar or attic. It was nearly three o'clock when the nachalnik, who still held tightly to the *Miniatures,* said, "Finished. Both of you come along!" He indicated Vassily and Chalev.

Chalev was ordered to take his belongings, which must have struck him as an ominous sign, for he sat mute and downcast between the two men in uniform. As they rode toward town, Feingold said to Vassily, "You'll be brought back to the farm by car, so that you won't lose too much time." The remark was obviously intended to reassure him. Evidently with the same intention, Tania nudged him as they got out of the truck in the yard which he still remembered very well. They stopped in a room on the second floor. A report was drawn up and signed by Feingold and Tania. Search of the premises of Vassily Khomniuk—no suspicious findings. Writings of a counterrevolutionary nature found in the possession of Head Gardener Chalev. What the contents of these writings might be was not mentioned. Nor was anything said in the record about the confiscation of the *Historical Miniatures.* That was all there was to it.

Or rather not quite all. For Feingold, who left the room with Tania and Vassily, led the way upstairs rather than out into the yard, where the car was waiting to drive Vassily back to the farm. He beckoned to Vassily to follow him. Not a word was said until they reached a door where Feingold paused just long enough to say, "Nothing to worry about, Vassily Vassilevich." He opened the door.

A uniformed man looked up from his newspaper. "Ah yes," he said. "He's waiting for you."

Vassily followed Feingold through a door on the right. Feingold addressed the man at the desk. "Maxim Danilovich, this is the zamestitel of our farm."

"So this is the man?" He gestured to chairs in front of the desk. "Sit down, all of you." Vassily found himself in the middle chair, directly opposite the nachalnik. The man put on his glasses carefully and repeated in a mild, unctuous tone, "So this is the man—good." In spite of the military cut of his tunic—which bore no insignia—his whole manner radiated gentleness and carefulness. He had the air of a minister, and as he rubbed his fleshy, extraordinarily white hands and raised his small, light-blue eyes, Vassily half expected him to begin, "Dear brethren and sisters in the Lord." But instead he had some words with Feingold about somebody named Kolia; was it certain that he would be coming to the celebration tomorrow? "Almost a certainty unless he is detained at the last minute," Feingold said. There followd a rather pointless and mysterious conversation about this "last minute," to which the nachalnik put an end with a final "No da." He reached for the telephone, murmured something into it, listened with a devoutly patient air to the reply, hung up, rubbed his hands, lowered his eyes, and asked gently, "So you've worked in Romania, have you? Could you explain to me what kind of holiday May Tenth is there?"

What was this now? Vassily wondered nervously. Why were they interested in May Tenth? What should he tell them? What did they want to hear? Even as his mind raced over these thoughts, he answered in a simple, bumbling way, "It's what they call the Day of Independence; there are big parades, usually with the army, and schools and athletic clubs marching too."

"Big crowds?"

"I saw one only once; the sun was shining and everybody was out."

"What does it depend on?"

"The weather."

They all laughed, Feingold loudest of all, who asked, "Then there's no independence when it rains?"

"I didn't bother going in rainy weather."

Again they laughed, and the "pastor" said, "No da." He looked at the door, took a watch from his pocket and laid it on the table. "Eleven minutes," he complained gently. "Punctuality!"

Tania shook her head sympathetically.

"Is Cernauti a big city? How many inhabitants?" he asked.

"I didn't work in the city—I always worked in the country," Vassily replied. "But I've been there a few times. There are big houses, a streetcar line, lots of automobiles, fine shops and restaurants. I don't think it's as big as Lvov, though."

"Do you have any acquaintances there?"

"In the city? None at all." What was he after, this soft-voiced "pastor"? Vassily stared straight ahead, looking neither toward Feingold on his right nor Tania on his left. Nor did he try to read that bespectacled face; it was hopeless. The Buddha had been easier, he thought.

A uniformed man entered the room and silently laid a number of typewritten sheets of paper on the table. The nachalnik said in his low, unctuous voice, "Seventeen minutes late. Punctuality!"

"Not my fault." The uniformed man paled.

"Mine," the gentle voice said. "I'll call when I need you." The man went out. "Comrade Khomniuk, do you know what a sketch map is?"

"I do."

"How do you happen to know?"

"I learned in the army."

"Aha—good." He took up a sheet of blueprint paper, which lay on top of the others, and examined the sketch; the lines were in green ink. "Nichevo." He sounded resigned. "Comrade Khomniuk, what do you see in this map?"

Vassily took the thin sheet of paper in his callused hands and studied it. "Easy enough," he said. He made a long pause. "But—"

"What is it?" the nachalnik asked. Vassily stood up, laid the sketch on the table, and pointed to a line. "If that's the main highway, then there are many villages and even a small town between it and the other highway. But they're not marked."

"Konechno." The nachalnik gave him a look of gratification. He turned to Feingold. "Of course," he said plaintively, "nobody is reliable. Nobody knows anything." He glanced down at the map. *"I knew it. Sit down, Comrade Khomniuk."* He looked over the typewritten sheets, reading a line here, a paragraph there. "Good," he said in conclusion. He held out a stamped and sealed quarto sheet. "Here, Vassily Vassilevich Khomniuk—this is for you. You know what the Spets. are, don't you?" He paused. "They are our specialists. The most special workers of all. From now on, Vassily Vassilevich, you are one of them. If any of the NKVD workers should stop you—but only in that case—show them this document." He cleared his throat. "No one has the right to call you to account except me, konechno." He smiled, gently, sanctimoniously.

"Thank you, Comrade Nachalnik," Vassily said.

"Arkady Samuelovich will give you your instructions," the nachalnik said. He shook hands all around. The interview was over.

At nine o'clock in the morning on May 2, Tania and Vassily sat in the office going over the receipts for the produce that had been delivered to the canteens. "The bookkeeper ought to be here by now," she said, yawning. She had returned home from the city after midnight.

"Yes," Vassily agreed, continuing to set down figures. "I hope he comes soon. I don't do it right."

"Better than I do." She pushed away her sheet of paper. "Fyodor Fyodorovich said yesterday that our farm made the best showing in the whole parade. Are you glad, Vassia?"

"I'm glad. A fine parade, wasn't it?"

She yawned heartily. "Cigarette!" He gave her one and she put it lazily between her lips. "Light!" she commanded, staring fiercely down at the paper on her desk. He patiently struck a match for her, and resumed his work. She stood up and came over to his desk. "Tell me what you think about the business with Chalev. Talk, for once!"

"I don't think anything about it. I can't figure it out anyhow. A fool. Now he's in trouble himself. What did they find on him?"

"I haven't any idea. Who cares?" She turned toward the open window. The street lay still and empty in the sunlight. From the dairy came the low hum of the separator.

Vassily got up. "So—I'm going to the garden now and then to the dairy. If you need me—"

He was at the door before she said, without removing the cigarette from her mouth, "What the devil would I need you for?"

"You haven't had enough sleep, Tania. Take a nap during the noon break."

"My business," she said; she tossed the barely lit cigarette out the window and stuck out her tongue at him.

"That was Chalev's favorite expression, but he didn't have as pretty a tongue as yours." He had opened the door. Laughing, he waved to her.

With one long leap she reached him and seized the edge of his jacket. "Stay here a while, won't you?" She closed the door and nudged him in the ribs. "Sit down. I want to talk with you—even if it costs me my neck."

"Your pretty neck," he laughed. He sat down. "Be quick about it, Tania; I have all sorts of things to attend to. There's no one to look after the storehouse either."

"All that bores me. I want to know what you think of me, Vassia."

"Well, I like girls like you, Tania. You dance, tell stories, do pantomime, and you're smart; cuckoo but smart. Besides, you know so much! You've learned a lot already, and you're still so young."

"In spite of which I sit here over these idiotic milk figures and meat figures—doesn't that make you wonder?"

"It does. But what other job could you have, since you can't dance any more? If the doctors said you couldn't, it's so. I know how that is, once you break something. In horses—"

"Don't give me that again. I don't want to hear about horses and cows and butter and sausage, not a word! When someone talks too much about something, he wants to put something over. I wasn't born yesterday, Vassily."

He looked at her with amusement. "You forget that I'm the man in charge here. You can't order me around, and I can only talk about what I know. You don't have to listen."

Tensely, she studied his smiling face. "I know that a man can be dumb from sheer cleverness, but I didn't know that anyone could be clever from sheer dumbness. Not till now."

"It's never too late to learn."

"I'm supposed to learn—to learn from you! By the devil's grandmother, what else am I supposed to learn? I know plenty—too much, believe me! But you—I have a hunch." She fell silent. Instead of pressing her to say more, he looked at his watch. "Don't make me nervous; you'll have time for everything," she shouted, but then once more fell into a quiet and friendly tone. "Vassinka, believe me, I mean well, I have your interests at heart—honestly."

"I know that, Tania—I saw that with Chalev. There's no doubt I would have had lots of unpleasantness if it hadn't been for you." He patted her hand. A thin hand with long, limber fingers.

She caught hold of his hand and held it. "Unpleasantness—how you put it! Do you really have no notion of what was going on?"

"Absolutely none. I've thought about it, don't think I haven't —about how you went into Chalev's room and how you were afraid they were coming for me—of course, I'd be a dumb ox not to think about it. But—what I don't know won't hurt me."

"You and your proverbs. It could hurt you, Vassia. They have you in their grip and won't be letting you go! If I only knew why they're so bent on having you. What the devil have you managed to do with the horses and the cows, that you've become so important to them? Tell me, are you scared to answer me if I ask you questions? You're absolutely safe with me, believe me!"

"What kind of questions, Tania?"

She turned on her heel once more and went over to the window. From the street rose a roar of motors; a heavy truck stopped in front of the entrance. "An army truck with a cow on it," she said.

"Our new bull!" Vassily cried out delightedly. "Come along, Tania." He rushed out the door. She followed him, shaking her head.

He was coal-black with a white vest, broad of head and short of horn. He stood in the body of the truck, his rope halter fastened to the side wall. But the only men in the truck were two Red Army soldiers. There was no sign of Meerblum or Wagner. "Where are our men?" Vassily asked the driver, with a fine show of astonishment.

"Are you the starshi?" asked the other man, a Sergeant who sat beside the driver.

"He is," Tania said pertly.

"We've brought the bull—as a favor. We don't know a thing about your men. Unload him; we're in a hurry."

"Yes, at once, but—" He wanted to question them, but the driver raced the motor. The noise drowned out speech, and Vassily could do no more than wave his hand toward the loading ramp in the yard. The truck backed toward it, while Vassily fetched Benderski and Tadek from the garden. With their help he managed to unload the bull, made fractious by the long drive. The Red Army men did not lend a hand; they were flirting with Tania, and when the tail gate was at last clapped shut, they parted from her reluctantly. "Ask them what happened to our two men, Tania," Vassily prompted as she bade the soldiers good-bye.

"I've already asked. I have the receipts, too."

The heavy truck rolled out of the yard. Vassily and Tadek dragged the bellowing bull to the box stall at the far end of the cow barn. Tania was still standing in the yard when Vassily came out. "Two men the less again," she said.

"Two men the less?" Vassily asked dazedly.

"Don't worry—they're out of the running for a while."

"Out of the running? An accident?" He pretended to be horrified. So the plan had worked perfectly.

"The idiots took their wives along as though they were going on a picnic—and the women had no documents, of course. They were cavorting around in another district, having a good time. All four have been arrested. It will all come out in the wash," she added, bored. "It doesn't matter."

"How do you know?"

"The Red Army men."

"They saw it all? How did it happen? We must do something about it; I'll go to see Saposhnik."

"What can he do? Do you think he's going to make a fuss about it? If anyone sends an inquiry, he'll answer; otherwise he'll keep quiet. He signed their travel documents, didn't he? Naturally, the less he has to do with it the better."

"But—"

"No buts, Vassinka. Those boys had hard luck, that's all." Seeing how wrought-up he looked, she added, "All right, calm down, I'll telephone Saposhnik."

"Do, Tania. How do the soldiers know about it?"

"A little bird told them." She laughed. "Somebody by the name of Ivan Ivanovich Ivansky. My, but you're naïve. It was nice of them to bring the bull."

"It was. And so now I'm supposed to handle everything all by myself. Storehouse, dairy, bookkeeping—how can I possibly?"

"It will all turn out—you have me, after all. I'll pitch in. All right, come on back to the office."

He went along with her, shaking his head in seeming perplexity and all the while rejoicing that the trick had worked and that Tassya, for all her cleverness, had not found a single hair in the soup he had cooked. What she had said about Saposhnik's probable reaction fitted in with his expectations; he had based his plan on that. It had succeeded, and he himself would soon, very soon, be gone.

In the office she went to the window once more, a sign that she would be trying to pump him again. "Please make your call, Tania —it takes so long to get a connection anyhow."

"Do you want to bet it doesn't?" She would have lost, for it was nearly ten minutes before she reached Saposhnik. The call itself, however, took very little time. Tania gave her report tersely; Saposhnik merely heard her out. The bull was there, the receipts were in good order. Very well. "You see, he isn't the least bit upset," she said as she hung up.

"But I am. I have five workers missing—how can I possibly manage?" As he spoke, there was a knock at the door, and an apparition entered: a withered little man in knickerbockers, sport socks and heavy-soled shoes, with a bright sweater under a worn brown sports jacket. He held a beret in his hand and had a briefcase tucked under his arm—identifiable at a glance as non-Russian. His big bald spot was ringed by a tonsure of flaming red hair; he wore large horn-rimmed glasses on a knobby nose; and behind these glasses darted mousy eyes. "Dr. Weidenfeld," he introduced himself.

"I have been hired by Comrade Deputy Director Engineer Saposh-nik."

"I suppose you're the new bookkeeper?" Vassily asked, extending his hand. "My name is Khomniuk; I am the head of the farm. This is Comrade Obadieva, the cashier. Are you a bookkeeper by profession, comrade?"

"I am," the man said, with a little gasp of nervousness. He tried very hard to speak Russian, but it remained Polish.

"What are you a doctor of, comrade?" Vassily asked in German.

"Doctor of laws and business administration, graduate of the Commercial Academy of Vienna, at your service." Vassily translated this information for Tania's benefit.

"Wonderful!" Tania made a show of enthusiasm. "Then he can certainly figure. Here." She pointed to the pile of receipts. "You can start right in adding those up."

Weidenfeld nodded and bowed low. "Certainly, gladly, if Comrade Director would show me the books!"

Vassily showed him the two sections of the file and the shelves of ledgers, and he at once sat down and became absorbed in them. "Marvelous, absolutely marvelous," he murmured. "A joy to see." He was evidently enormously relieved. "I'll have them brought up to date before the day is over. Comrade Engineer Saposhnik has informed me of what has happened."

"I hope you'll be able to manage," Vassily said. "Our former bookkeeper was very orderly."

"A genius!" Dr. Weidenfeld exclaimed, his eyes fixed to the books.

Vassily turned toward the door. "I must get to work now."

"I'll go along—maybe I can help you," Tania offered.

In fact Tania was underfoot everywhere, and her skittish ways got on his nerves. The two women in the dairy had previously worked only under Meerblum's direction, but had learned so much from him that with one assistant they were now perfectly adequate to the job. Vassily checked the work, gave orders, and submitted patiently to the running fire of jokes from Tania. It was not until they got to the warehouse, where he weighed out feed for the horses, cattle and pigs that she quieted down. The supplies would last a good three weeks more, he saw. But what then? "How long can Meerblum and Wagner be held up? What do you think, Tania? Should we wait for them or ask for replacements?"

"Saposhnik will take care of that—don't wear your brains out on it, Comrade Director."

"Wearing my brains out wouldn't do an ounce of good. I'll

speak to Saposhnik today."

She fell silent and looked on as he carried sack after sack to the scale and noted down the weight. When he was finished, she said softly, "You won't be doing that much longer anyway, Vassia."

"I hope not," he replied. But he knew what she meant.

"It would be better if they left you at it. You love this work, don't you?"

"It's what I know."

"You seem to know other things too, but—"

"I must go to the vegetable beds," he interrupted.

"Me, too," she said. But now she was very subdued.

At the beds the two blacksmith's apprentices and the harness maker were helping out. They did so gladly, for it was a perpetual circus to work with Benderski. "Well, things seem to be going along fine," Vassily said, and started toward the office again.

"Let's look at the tree Chalev wanted to cut down."

He looked at his watch. "Why?"

She didn't answer. Silently, they walked as far as Antek's grave.

"He was your friend, wasn't he?"

"He was. I was very fond of him. You should have known him. A fine fellow—it's very sad. And what a worker—a stakhanovets."

"Yes, yes, I've heard the whole story." She pointed to the cut at the base of the tree. "That wasn't Chalev's own idea," she said, speaking to herself rather than Vassily.

"A dumb idea, anyhow. You can't cut a tree like that with a handsaw!"

"Handsaw or not, not so dumb. You just don't understand —you don't, do you?"

"What is there to understand?"

She pursed her mouth, looked at the tree and then at him, and walked slowly toward the hedge of lilac bushes that separated the orchard from the fields. "Vassily," she called, "come here!" He followed her; she sat down in the grass and gestured to him to sit beside her. "I'm not nosy; you musn't think that," she said. "But I have to know."

He laughed. "Not nosy, but you have to know."

She remained in deadly earnest. "You know perfectly well what I mean. Only you don't trust me, and perhaps you're right not to. But if you don't speak out, I can't either—and what I have to say is important."

"Then say it. I'm not being cagey."

"And you haven't been wondering about all that has happened? What about the pass that Maxim Danilovich gave you?"

"That was awfully decent of him. Now nobody can come along and bother me over every little trifle. He's certainly an important nachalnik, isn't he, Tania?"

She looked at him. Contemptuously and pityingly. "An important nachalnik—yes, he's important. But you haven't wondered why he gave it to you—to you of all people?"

"Oh well, I'm a stakhanovets, so they think pretty well of me, and if tomorrow another of these Chalevs came along and stuck something into my mattress—"

"Maxim Danilovich—of course he's terribly impressed because you're a stakhanovets!"

"I beg your pardon—I know something about such matters too."

"Rot! Give me a cigarette."

"We haven't time to take a smoke now, Tania. Let's go to the canteen and have some lunch."

"Give me a cigarette!" When he did not comply, she reached into the pocket where he kept his cigarettes. In jest he held her hand fast, and then the other, and they tussled a bit—all in jest—and as they did so they came closer and closer, very close, too close. . . .

"Those are the regulations," Saposhnik said, concluding his exposition. "If they let Wagner and Meerblum go, good; if not, intervention won't do a speck of good. That's the militia's affair; they have the responsibility. If Wagner and Meerblum don't turn up by tomorrow, we'll have to appoint a starshi for the dairy and a magazinshchik."

Vassily got up to go. "We'll have to have a gardener and two drivers also."

"I'll see to that. One moment, Comrade Khomniuk. Since you spoke of gardeners—" He rummaged through his papers. "Here, a summons for Tadeus Karlowicz Zembrinski. May seventh, Court Number Eight, nine o'clock in the evening. You know where that is, don't you?"

"I know." Vassily took the sheet of paper. So Tadek was to appear in court for swearing at Chalev. "It may be," he said slowly, "that we'll need two gardeners."

Saposhnik shook his head. "Not a serious charge. But it will be better if you go along—as his nachalnik. Is Zembrinski a good worker?"

"First-class." Vassily left. He had failed. He would have to think of some other way to swing it. He had hoped that Saposhnik could be induced to send him out to search for Wagner and

Meerblum. But the zamestitel did not dream of doing that. Had his theory been right, that the three had been slated for "shipment"? Or had he been wrong and only sounded a false alarm? Well, at any rate those two were already across the border. But what about Kornhaber? He was to undergo surgery today—if only that went off well. Vassily stood in the yard, reflecting. How do I reach the border without documents? The railroad is out of the question; I can't even buy a ticket without a komandirovka. I ought to go soon—right away, if possible. Ride? A hundred and fifty miles will take two or three days, and if they catch me it's an extra stiff sentence on account of theft. On foot? A good five days—and I'm not Meerblum or Wagner; they'll send a posse out after me. They need me. Need me.

And Tania. What is she so bent on knowing? Is she supposed to feel me out? You're dangerous, Tania, even though you've been a godsend at times. Thinking doesn't help. I must get away, far away. A hundred and fifty miles. Across the Ceremus—back! Besselmann? Platzer—a thousand greenbacks per head. Dependable, absolutely safe.

"Vassily Vassilevich!" It was Feingold's clear voice. Vassily saw his sunny face at the window. "I've been watching you quite a while. You've been standing by your horse, shaking your head, shrugging your shoulders. Are you talking to yourself or the horse?"

"The horse, Comrade Feingold—I've got too much on my mind, too much for one man," Vassily called back, laughing. "I was just sharing my troubles with Golodnyi here."

"It will all straighten out. I know, you're pretty short-handed on the farm. Saposhnik will take care of it."

"Yes. So long!" Vassily mounted.

At the entrance, Feingold was waiting for him—how fast the man was, and what did he want now? He seemed to be in high good humor. "I," he said, "or rather you, filed a denunciation against Zembrinski. Regulations. But nothing will happen to him. Podgorski will be there—you know him—the interpreter."

"I remember, Comrade Feingold."

"He'll do the interpreting." He winked. "Everything must be orderly."

"Konechno," Vassily said cheerfully. "I appreciate it." He picked up the reins.

"One more thing. Wait for me at six o'clock in the evening on May fifth. Party Committee, side entrance."

"All right, Comrade Feingold."

"So long, Vassily Vassilevich."

Tadek did not understand why he was supposed to go to court.

Chalev was no longer there, and besides that, he hadn't done a thing to him. Just on account of a "psiakrev cholera"! Vassily tried to explain it; failing, he left it to Benderski. But Benderski couldn't manage to get it across, either. So right after work, without even bothering to wash, Tadek caught a ride into town on one of the army trucks. He wanted to consult his mother. I only hope Panya Jadwiga understands, Vassily thought. He gave out the feed, checked the stable, stayed with the milkers for a while and saw that everything was done properly in the dairy. As he walked across the yard, he became aware of how tired and hungry he was. He must eat quickly and get to bed. His last night on the farm. By tomorrow at this hour he would be at the border. He had discussed the plan with Besselmann, father and son, that afternoon. Platzer would "bring" him. They would leave tomorrow afternoon at four o'clock. Vassily already had the "sign." A hundred and one per cent certain, Arye had assured him as they parted. Good that you still believe in certainties, Arye, he thought; I used to once, but that was long ago.

"Comrade Director—" The little bookkeeper sidled up to him. "Yes?"

"I've brought everything up to date in the books."

"Fine! But you shouldn't have worked so hard and long. How are you going to get home? At this hour there are no more army trucks. I guess there's no help for it—I'll send you in one of the farm wagons."

"Oh—that's too kind of you. I wouldn't expect such a favor. I can walk to the station."

"No, no, it's too far, and it's late. Come to the canteen; I'll have a bite to eat and take you in myself."

"Excellent food," Weidenfeld said as they stepped out into the yard again after eating.

"And cheap. You should arrange to take your main meal here, Dr. Weidenfeld."

"Hm, yes, I could at that. Though in some respects. . . . You see, Comrade Director, I have a family—just my wife and my mother, now. That is—my two sons are prisoners of war in Germany and—hm—we always eat together. They wait for me—you see, once a day we like to be together. My mother particularly, she would—"

"I see," Vassily said. Odd that the Weidenfeld family should be so concerned with preserving its own style of life.

He hitched up quickly and went to the stable for his whip. When he returned, Tania was standing by the buggy.

"You're off again, Vassily?"

"Yes, I'm driving Comrade Weidenfeld to the tram station."

"You're driving—oh. Nichevo. I'll go along." She plumped herself down beside him. "One of these days you'll do one good deed too many."

Vassily didn't answer. He rebuffed her various attempts to strike up a conversation. Weidenfeld got out at the station and, with many a bow, bade them good-bye. It appeared that Tania had only come for the drive and was ready to ride back. Vassily was just turning around when someone shouted his name. It was Panya Jadwiga in her leather jacket and felt hat. Tadek ran up to the buggy. "Mother wants to talk to you, Vassily. Can she come back to the farm?"

"All right, get in. Good evening, Panya Jadwiga." He drove rapidly. Tania smoked and held her peace until the buggy stopped in Jiusefovka.

Panya Jadwiga and Tadek got out and waited for Vassily to take care of the horses. Tania waited too. "I must talk with you," she murmured.

"Can't it wait, Tania? The old lady has something she wants to discuss. We'll talk tomorrow."

"All right," Tania said sadly, "talk to her first. But your conference can't take forever. I'll wait up for you." She tripped off toward her house.

Panya Jadwiga was sitting in the kitchen with Tadek. They were drinking cherry brandy and smoking. "What's this story Tadek tells me?" the huge woman growled. "What's he done that he has to go to court?"

"It's nothing serious, Panya Jadwiga. He'll just appear, be given a lecture and be fined a few rubles."

Panya Jadwiga stared into space. "I want you to be there, Vassily. Please—I beg you." She began to speak German. "I've done my damnedest to keep him out of trouble. Up to now, in all his brawls, I could always step in; he never had anything to do with the police or a court. And now—with these Russkis—on account of a 'psiakrev cholera.' . . . But they don't give a damn why or what for. They'll send him off for God knows how many years in jail. It'll break my heart, Vassily!"

"No, no, Panya Jadwiga. You're upsetting yourself for nothing. Besides, what good would I be in court?"

"I've asked you, Vassily, and I want your word that you'll go along. That's what I came to see you for." She drank and smoked, and waited for his promise.

Come to think of it, Vassily remembered, Saposhnik also said it would be good if I was there, as his nachalnik. But I don't want to be a nachalnik any more. I'm through. "It wouldn't help any, Panya Jadwiga," he said. "They don't like anyone interfering."

"Maybe yes, maybe no. All I say is, Tadek will feel better if you're there. Antek wouldn't have abandoned him. I want your word that you'll go with him." She held out her hand. "You'll go, Vassily?"

He took her hand. "Certainly, Panya Jadwiga—since you want me to." You're right, Tania, I'm a dumb ox. He had a glass of brandy, then several more, and offered Panya Jadwiga his bed. He could sleep in Wagner's or Kornhaber's place; he had the keys.

And so he went out once more, wrangling with himself. What about his plans? But he would keep his word. Feingold might think the court order nothing but a joke . . . but you never knew. They needed a scapegoat, didn't they? Once Tadek was in their clutches, they could build up a big case on the basis of a "psiakrev cholera." . . .

"You're talking to yourself, Vassinka!" Tania suddenly accosted him as if she had risen from the ground.

"One ox to another, Tania."

"Where are you going, Vassily?"

"Didn't you say you'd wait?"

"I was tired of waiting so long. I was on my way to you."

"What for? What's so pressing?" he temporized. They were in front of her house, the very one that had been Mira's so short a time ago.

"Come in," she said gravely. He looked around. "What's all the caution for?"

"It seems a little caution might be in order—this late at night," he growled.

"You mean, you don't want anyone to see you visiting me?" They were already in the room which Vassily knew very well— the room and the bed. "Why not?"

"The whole farm will be talking by tomorrow morning."

"Suppose they do?" she asked in astonishment. "What does it matter? Who cares?"

"If you don't care . . . I only thought—"

"What?" She shook her head. "Oh"—she laughed and imitated Gorbatenko—"spit on it."

She offered him vodka; she had a bottle of liqueur also. They drank, joked and laughed, and Vassily experienced the strangest night of love in his eventful life. For Tania, Tatiana Nikolaevna Obadieva, told him a great deal about her life. And when Vassily left her house at dawn—by the back way—the strange girl was no longer a mystery to him.

Tania's father had been a university professor. In 1917, he had died at the hands of the Ochrana. Tania was then a child of three. Her mother, a Frenchwoman, had brought up the child alone, taking charge even of her education. The child learned quickly and was an avid reader. As she grew up she clung to the image of her father as the brave idealist. By fourteen she was disillusioned with the Bolshevik system. She had enrolled at the university but was more attracted by the stage, and so she studied dancing. But no field satisfied her; everything, everyone, seemed soiled and stupid. Until Alexei, an engineer, had come along. That had been three years ago. Tania was pregnant, in her seventh month, when Alexei was arrested. He was involved in the big Yagoda show trial. He was innocent, as it later developed, but he was liquidated along with thousands of others. Tania had been on the brink of suicide; her baby was born prematurely, and didn't live. But for her mother's sake she hung on, pretended to recover, tried to work at her dancing. She found herself incapable even of hatred. Who was there to hate? That was the way revolution was. There was no such thing as a bloodless revolution; people were either lucky or unlucky.

Then Feingold had come into her life—Arkady Samuelovich. No, not as a man, not like other men. Feingold was idea and action personified; he was dedicated to the Revolution. He had no private emotions . . . would have put his own mother to death if she were an enemy of the Revolution. In his thirty-eight years Feingold had been everything, had worked everywhere, in Russia —as a Red Guard, party man, Spets., NKVD. "Tatiana Nikolaevna," he had said to her, "we must place all our abilities at the service of The Cause." And he had convinced her. Or had she been too torpid, too tired, too indifferent, to withstand his arguments? Why not become a "special" worker? And she had even been declared a stakhanovets—like Vassily with his horses. She had been sent to check on Vassily. She just returned from abroad. Oh, she had been everywhere in Europe, for she spoke English and French and could dance and cut up like a regular burzhuika. And she knew how to handle men—men were so dumb and betrayed all their secrets in bed. Oh, she had tripped up many counterrevolutionaries, who had paid for their naïveté in prison, in Siberia—or in the NKVD cellars. But Vassily—with him it was different. Actually, she didn't quite understand what they wanted of him. Her instructions were rather vague: was he really what he seemed, or was he putting on some kind of act? She was supposed to find out, one way or another. That sort of thing was her *spetsialnost*. But Vassily—he was different from other men. She'd felt sorry for him, the dumb ox—because . . . but of course that was strictly against regulations.

No private emotions. Only she sometimes had them—nothing you could do about it. And she didn't want the same thing to happen to him that had happened to so many others. Not him. And so she'd reported right away that he was an ox and good for nothing but horses and cows and field work. No intelligence. Maybe they needed some like that, the simpleminded type. Be that as it might, they hadn't taken her report as final.

Instead, Chalev had been sent in by another bureau. Apparently these others were also interested in Vassily, but from another angle. For Chalev had been sent in to make so good a case against him that his superiors would no longer be able to support him: not Potapenko, not Maxim Danilovich, not Feingold. Not even Feingold, who had a lot of influence, and had taken a shine to Vassily. Not out of liking or friendship; he didn't give way to such emotions. But Feingold was known to be against the Germans. It followed that Chalev must have been sent by those who were for the Germans. At least this was Tania's deduction. She was fairly sure of it; but of course the true situation could be otherwise— one could never tell for sure. That was what the system was like —you never knew. But if it was as she thought, as she feared, then Vassily would soon become a spets. too. Or was he one already? He had the spravka, after all. In that case they would send him on a job that was dangerous, very dangerous. And Tania didn't want that, because. . . .

Vassily had listened, smiling incredulously, playing the part of Vassily to the hilt—dumbly cunning Vassily who knew no better. He had listened and said nothing. What could he say? He was touched and grateful, but couldn't show his gratitude. Or did he? Perhaps she had sensed it; after all, she was a woman.

Vassily drove Panya Jadwiga to town in the morning. "See that nothing happens to Tadek," she said in parting. He went on to School No. 12 and waited there for Arye. Since it was a good half hour before school would begin, he busied himself with the wagon, removing a wheel and fussing with hammer and screwdriver. As Arye passed by, he beckoned to him as if asking for help. Arye understood, and positioned the wheel for him. Under cover of this enterprise, Vassily passed along his message: his trip would have to be postponed for a few days. "All right," Arye said tersely. As he was leaving, he murmured that there was talk of more resettlements.

Vassily drove back to the farm and plunged into the work there. He lost himself in it so completely that he didn't realize it was noon until he was suddenly hungry. Tania was sitting in the canteen with the bookkeeper. They ate sausage and cheese, drank tea, and chatted. Weidenfeld was gaining confidence by the hour, as he saw that his job was within his powers. He had checked the inventory and was acquainting himself with his other duties. It was obvious that he would be pedantically precise in everything. Good luck to him, Vassily thought as he rose to go home. He napped for a few hours, rose refreshed and rode out to the fields and then the pasture, where he stayed until the cattle were driven home. It had been a quiet day.

At the agreed hour, Vassily was waiting in the buggy at the side entrance of Party Committee headquarters. Feingold appeared, and Vassily drove him to his house. True to form, Feingold joked with Vassily, and invited him in. Once in his room he produced the list of farm workers. "You know all of them well, don't you, Vassily Vassilevich?"

"I've worked with them long enough. Good workers, Comrade Feingold."

"Let's leave that aside for the moment. What I want to talk about is their reliability."

"There's not one that's a thief, I'm dead certain of that."

"That, too, is beside the point. What I want to know is their political reliability."

"Political? What do they know about politics?"

"Isn't there one or another who grumbles that he has a harder time of it than in the past?"

"But all of us on the farm are satisfied. Why not? Meat every day, living in stone houses. Do you know how the peasants used to live in these parts? Sixteen and seventeen hours of work a day. And under what conditions? Meat at Easter and Christmas, the rest of the year corn, sour skim milk, barley bread. And ten months out of the year they went barefoot."

"All of them, Vassily Vassilevich?"

"Most of them, Comrade Feingold."

"Some of the workers on the farm don't strike me as that type. Do you know them from the past?"

"Well, no. I was working for the landowner. But I don't have to have known them; it's clear enough that they all feel they're better off, today. You can tell right away."

"You mean there are no kulaks among them?" Feingold asked.

"Kulaks? There's hardly a man on the farm who had more than a hut with a thatched roof and a bit of a garden."

"None of these fellows used to be rich?"

"Rich?" Vassily laughed. "You ask them whether they'd like

to go back to the way things were. No, Comrade Feingold, we
don't have any kulaks here, don't worry."

"You're our liaison man. You know what that means—you
have the responsibility!"

"For all who are on the farm right now, Comrade Feingold—
that is, all our present crew. I've watched them at work, the
drivers especially. A fine bunch—not a kulak among them. And
the craftsmen—they work their heads off for the collective, they
love it so. But there are a handful who didn't fit in—it was hard
on them being workers like all the rest. I saw that right away. Even
so—they did a great deal for the farm."

"Which ones, would you say?"

"Wagner, Meerblum and Kornhaber. Well, Kornhaber is more
or less out of the picture, from now on. After that operation, he
won't be able to take over the cow barns. But the other two—
I really don't like to say this—after all, the militia will probably
let them go soon—but I would feel a lot easier if they didn't come
back to us. You understand, those men just aren't honest-to-goodness
workers. Even though they try to be. But we can manage by ourselves. The cow barn and the dairy are functioning fine; we don't
really need a starshi for those—maybe one more woman worker.
But in the warehouse there ought to be an older man, steady,
who can manage the scales and handle figures."

"I suppose you're deeply attached to the farm, aren't you, Vassily Vassilevich?"

"Attached to it?" He put on an excellent show of looking
abashed. "How do you mean that, Comrade Feingold?"

"Well, would you be sorry if you had to leave?"

"Why would I have to leave? Oh, you mean if a director comes.
That wouldn't bother me too much. I can just as well be the stablemaster again, if only I stay on the farm. I know the work, and
I've helped build the place up from next to nothing. And the farm
is doing all right, isn't it?"

"It certainly is! That isn't the point at issue. With us—you
see, Vassily Vassilevich—with us, men are used where they fit in
best. Where they can serve society the best. You understand?" Vassily nodded silently. Feingold laughed. "We can't always leave it
up to the individual's own choice. Anyhow, with you I'm certain
that you will do whatever is asked of you and do it well. I'll
drive back to town with you. And everything remains the same on
the farm—for the present."

"That's fine." Vassily nodded contentedly. On the way back
to the Party Committee he didn't talk much, although there were
a number of questions he would have liked to ask Feingold. But

he knew a great deal already, and had plenty to think about. He felt little desire to continue the discussion—especially when he would have to go on maintaining that Vassily manner. Still, the manner had proved its worth; the workers on the farm were safe, for the moment anyhow. So what Arye had said was true. A new wave of "resettlements" was beginning. Arye? It was Wagner who had said that there would be no more deportations until May. Now it was May, and Wagner was in safety. Safety? What about himself?

Another twenty-four hours passed, and Vassily had barely noticed. At seven o'clock in the evening on May 7 he drove to town with Tadek. He left the buggy in the shed. Panya Jadwiga, who had been drinking heavily, went along to the court.

There, beside a man with a long, pale face and sleepy, infinitely bored blue eyes, sat a woman whose oily braids were wound tightly around her head. She had a round, well-nourished face, a turned-up nose, a wide mouth with a good-natured, peasant smile, which grew broader when the sentences were heavier. A thin volume lay on the table: the law book. Or rather, it was a price catalogue. Listed in it were all the misdemeanors and crimes with which a Soviet citizen could be charged, and opposite them the penalties proper for each fault. Some misdemeanors called for fines, but in most cases a prison term was meted out: so many days, weeks, months or even years. The most common crimes were lateness, absence from work without excuse, and infliction of damage on tools or machines. The citizen came half an hour late to work: reason immaterial, six months in jail. Theft: two years; if of state property, six years. Podgorski, the small, gray-haired interpreter, appeared. He went up to the judge's bench. Evidently "psiakrev cholera" was not listed in the book. There was a brief consultation between the braided woman and the bored man. Tadek was fined a day's wages, to be turned over to the fund for the support of political prisoners abroad. That was all.

Panya Jadwiga reclaimed her son. Hand in hand, they walked toward the door. Vassily started to follow them; the two had already reached the street, when in the doorway he met Jeanne Feuerberg. She was pale as death, her face rent by despair. "Oh, Vassily!" she sobbed. She clung to his arm while she told him what had happened. Three days earlier Dr. Feuerberg had been arrested. For theft. He had been accused of stealing a syringe and five ampoules of morphine. The director of the hospital had denounced him— out of revenge. The receptionist, who had made such difficulties at the time Saposhnik's wife was being admitted, was the director's mistress. She had been dismissed, no doubt on a complaint from Saposhnik. There was no proof aside from the fact that the syringe and morphine were missing. Dr. Feuerberg had one key to the cupboard, the director the other. Léon was to come before the judges at ten o'clock.

"Léon is ill," Jeanne finished, in a voice soft with utter despair. "He will never endure it—the prison and the disgrace and the disillusionment. Oh, Vassily!"

Vassily could not speak encouraging words. His one hour in the courtroom had taught him that Dr. Feuerberg had no chance; he could expect a long sentence—many, many years.

"Have you hired a lawyer?"

Jeanne nodded. "But what's the use? The statutes call for four to seven years. Oh, God!"

At that moment Podgorski passed by. "Wait a moment," Vassily said to Jeanne and hurried off after the interpreter.

Panya Jadwiga and Tadek were waiting outside for him. "Go home, I'll come later," he said. But they lingered. He caught up with Podgorski at the streetcar stop. "Good evening, comrade," he greeted him. "Do you remember me?"

"How could I forget? Lost one piece of shit, picked one up." Smilingly, he shook hands with Vassily. "Well, are you pleased? They haven't taken away your gardener."

"Yes, thank you for the way you handled it, comrade—he's a good worker."

"It wasn't anything serious. All of us sound off sometimes." The streetcar was coming along. Podgorski was about to board it. Once more he extended his hand to Vassily.

Vassily retained his hand. "There's a favor I want to ask of you, comrade. If you can give me a bit of time."

"What is it?" Podgorski let the streetcar pass by, but not without a regretful look. "Is it so urgent?"

"Perhaps not. But Comrade Feingold has been instructing me— you understand, I'm still a beginner. Still, I thought I'd better tell you before it's too late. Because I've just heard a story about another trial coming up this morning. I don't know much about the law, but this isn't being done the Soviet way."

The small, gray-haired man smiled, probably at such zeal and naïveté. "I'm listening," he said.

It was important to tell the story in the tried and true Vassily manner. But Vassily gave way to genuine indignation as he described Feuerberg's personality. Here was a convinced and enthusiastic Communist, a great doctor, happy to be able to contribute his work for the Soviet Union. Perhaps he was telling the story too clearly and too eloquently, Vassily thought, as he continued to the end. The charge that such a man would steal state property was false, he said. It was a frame-up!

The little man listened without interruption. Still without saying a word, he turned and headed toward the courthouse. Before they entered, he asked, "Have you already been to see Maxim Danilovich?"

"Yes," Vassily replied in some astonishment, "but not in connection with this affair."

"That doesn't matter," the interpreter said smilingly.

Vassily had no chance to reflect on his words, for Panya Jadwiga towered before him. "Come along, Vassily," she bawled. "What are you hanging around here for with the filthy Russkis?" Her black hat was askew, and the neck of a bottle protruded from the pocket of her leather jacket.

"Go home, you and Tadek, and look after the horses," Vassily said severely. The interpreter, standing at the entrance, must have heard, but his face was noncommittal. Nevertheless he asked casually, as they reached the second floor, "I suppose the old drunk is the gardener's mother?"

"Right," Vassily said, smiling. "I guess she's had quite a few to celebrate her son's release."

"It happens."

Feuerberg was sitting on a bench, unshaven, in rumpled clothing, without a hat. A militiaman was on guard beside him. Jeanne stood at some distance with a man in boots and army trousers, a pinstriped black jacket, and a bright red tie.

"Wait here," Podgorski said softly. He nodded toward Feuerberg. "That's the doctor, I take it? I'll see what can be done." Vassily nodded to Feuerberg and smiled in Jeanne's direction. She came over to him. "I've been talking to the lawyer. He'll try to do his best. Thank God I had your money. How could I have paid him otherwise? I want to thank you very much, Vassily. Though I have so little hope. Oh, God—Léon."

"Don't lose heart, Jeanne," he urged. "The verdict doesn't always go against you. One of the farm workers was acquitted today. That's what brought me here. And I happened to meet a nachalnik, an important nachalnik. Perhaps—"

"But they don't give you a chance for a defense."

"Don't lose heart, Jeanne!" he repeated. He looked over at Feuerberg. The man's face was as wrinkled as his clothes. He hardly dared even nod to Vassily. Then Podgorski reappeared. He beckoned to the lawyer and stood talking with him in a corner for five minutes. Then he stalked down the stairs and back to the streetcar stop, with Vassily beside him. "I've explained the situation to the judge," Podgorski said. "He'll get off. But keep in mind that prison isn't so bad with us as under the burzhui. A man can have done time for years and still receive an Order of Lenin. Sometimes it's only there that a man's real worth is seen. That's how it must be, understand, comrade?" He jumped into his street car.

The trial of Feuerberg was summary, to say the least. The lawyer pointed out that proof was lacking that any theft had actually been committed, and the charges were dismissed. Feuerberg embraced his wife and, in his joy, Vassily as well. "I knew it!" he exclaimed. "That is Soviet justice! What do you say to that, Vassily?"

Jeanne was about to speak, but Vassily stopped her with a light touch on her arm. Instead, he offered the doctor and his wife a ride, and went to fetch the buggy. Tadek and Panya Jadwiga were still waiting for him outside the courthouse. Jeanne sat beside him, the doctor beside Tadek, who was in the best of spirits and told the doctor at length the story of his crime and the outcome. Vassily had a low-voiced conversation with Jeanne in Russian and recommended that she keep the real story of the acquittal to herself.

"But why?" she wondered. "I don't quite understand."

"Don't you? It would be such a shock to him, that's why. There's no sense inflicting such a blow on his faith."

"That's true," she said softly, "it would be very hard on him. And he would be thrown into a new quandary about you. Because you see, Vassily, he's been through a lot of soul-searching over you. According to his principles, he ought to have denounced you. Because you're working against the Union if you tempt Soviet citizens to flee."

"But he decided not to?"

"We talked about it a great deal. I made him see that there are relationships between human beings, like yours to Candomir, which really matter more than political abstractions. Also that you could be a faithful servant of your master and still contribute to the building of socialism."

"Was he convinced?"

"Not quite, no, not quite. But denunciation doesn't come naturally to him. It's against his whole nature to make trouble for anyone."

"Then he will never be a real Bolshevik," Vassily said, laughing. "Loyalty to the cause—"

"No, he'll never be," she interrupted, also laughing. More seriously, she asked, "How did you get him off, Vassily?"

"By telling the truth. Nothing but the truth. I told the little nachalnik the whole story. You saw him, didn't you?"

"And he took your word for it and intervened?"

"So it would seem."

She sighed heavily. "Well, I must take your word for it. Because if I doubted you—that would be frightful!"

"Don't, please don't doubt me. I'll arrange to come to see you tomorrow night, or the day after tomorrow. Perhaps I'll be able to explain the whole thing, and set your mind at ease. You do trust me, don't you, Janina?"

"Janina!" She smiled at him. "I trust you. Come the day after tomorrow. Tomorrow Léon will probably be on night duty."

"All right." The buggy stopped.

"Good night, friend Vassily!" Feuerberg called out.

"Good night, doctor."

"Day after tomorrow, Vassily," Jeanne said.

The day after tomorrow was the ninth of May. And it proved a day of reckoning. The eighth was Tadek's day off and he had gone to stay overnight at his mother's. He should have been back by eight at the latest; by eleven he was still not at the farm. Vassily, although he had a great deal to do, kept going to the garden to check. Tania and the bookkeeper had left for town at seven, to go over accounts with the canteens. Vassily hated to leave the farm with no one in the office. Still, he had intended to call on Besselmann and make new arrangements for his "departure." By eleven he felt he could delay no longer, and deputized Benderski to handle any unexpected contingency.

His first stop was Panya Jadwiga's cottage. As he was about to tie the horse in the shed, he noticed two men at the front door. Both were Russians. They had just finished nailing several boards over the entrance. One of them pasted a large notice on the door. Vassily went up to them. "Is the old woman no longer living here?" he asked. They didn't answer, and he glanced at the notice. It stated that the house was the property of the state and under the supervision of the housing bureau of the Lenin District. It was clear: Panya Jadwiga had been arrested, was being "resettled." There was no point in questioning the men further. Even if they knew anything, they wouldn't talk.

And Tadek? Had they taken Tadek also? If not, would he not have come running to Vassily with the awful news?

Vassily reached the office just as Saposhnik was closing up to leave for lunch. "There you are, Comrade Khomniuk. I tried to get you by telephone."

"I was in the fields and then—I suppose I have to report it: Zembrinski had his day off yesterday. He wasn't back at eleven o'clock today."

"Yes, Zembrinski. That's what I wanted to talk with you about. Zembrinski—hm—he's being resettled."

"What?"

"Yes, we heard two hours ago. With his mother. So I'll have to put in a request for another gardener." He turned the key in the door. "This is my lunch hour."

Vassily walked along with him for some yards. He held himself in check and said only, "I hope the gardeners come soon, Comrade Saposhnik."

"It will be all right; everything will be all right," Saposhnik said, and waddled down the steps.

The farm buggy was standing in the yard. "How is it you're still in town?" Vassily asked the driver, Yeremczuk.

"This new bookkeeper isn't Mira—it takes him forever. And the cashier—each errand takes her hours. We've just got here. God knows how long they'll stay. At Plant II I waited nearly three hours. Have you heard, Vassily? They've arrested four on the textile farm. Siberia. They're deporting again."

"Tadek too."

"Tadek! Why him? On account of a couple of lousy swearwords?"

"Maybe, who knows? Who can figure them out?"

"So you weren't able to help him, Vassily?" Yeremczuk was the sagest and the most taciturn of the drivers. "We know you're keeping us afloat. Everybody knows where we'd be without you, Vassily."

"Me? Don't say that, Mikhailo. You're keeping yourselves afloat."

"You know how to talk to them; they believe what you say. If it weren't for you. . . ."

"I'm not so sure. Tie my horse behind the wagon and take him back, will you? I'll be in town most of the day."

"All right. I'll pick you up at the tram stop later . . . just say when."

"It won't be necessary. I'll get back one way or the other." He took a small package from the saddlebag and pocketed it. "So long, Mikhailo."

He walked slowly, as though he were carrying a heavy load. It was true, what Mikhailo had said—he was the guardian of the farm workers. If he left, they would be resettled the next time, or the time after. And even if he stayed, what could he do to stave off the inevitable? Who could do anything to stave off the inevitable? He was already at the gate when he heard voices behind him. It was

Tania, talking quite loudly to Feingold. It was she, too, who called out to him.

Vassily pulled himself together. No need for them to see how despondent he was, how worn out. "Yes?" He turned slowly, with a conscientious look at his watch. Feingold came up and shook hands with him. Tania hung back a few steps.

"The telephone operator is having fits—I've tried so often to put a call through to you," Feingold said with his most charming smile.

"There was no one in the office, and I was in the fields for a while and then rode straight out here. To report that Zembrinski hasn't come to work."

"Zembrinski is being resettled."

"So Comrade Saposhnik has just told me. Now I have just one gardener." He shook his head forlornly.

"It will be all right, Vassily Vassilevich. No great matter. But Zembrinski—it took a long time; there was a battle, I hear. They resisted the NKVD people, both of them. The mother too. The men nearly used their guns."

"You don't say! I suppose the old woman had been drinking. She goes off the deep end when she's tight, but she's useful and not a bad sort. Now she's cooked her goose for herself."

So it took a long time, Vassily thought; then at least they may have hidden Antek's money on themselves, and with it, somehow, they'll make out.

Feingold started, then said urbanely, "Yes, we must have order. This sterling character drinks herself pie-eyed and then goes at the filthy Russkis with her fists."

"Who can read a person's mind? Now her son is gone too, and I'm left with a single gardener. He was a good worker." Feingold made no comment. "I'll look around at the bazaar. Maybe I can find a couple of men—there are always a few lounging around hoping for a job. Benderski can show them what to do."

"Yes, Benderski." Feingold sounded as if he had swallowed something bitter. "Does he work well?"

"He really knows his stuff. Of course, he's fond of the bottle, too," he added, sensing that the nachalnik wanted to be fed a little information.

"And wags his tongue, doesn't he?" Feingold said.

"He sings more than he talks, and he's a first-class dancer," Tania put in. "Oh, he doesn't matter. . . . Are you walking, Vassily?"

"Yes, Yeremczuk is taking the horse back." He looked at his watch. It would be one o'clock soon.

"We'll walk as far as the streetcar stop," Feingold said.

They set out. The next car didn't even pause at the stop, it was so jammed. As Vassily shook hands, Tania said lightly, "You'll be getting a new cashier for the farm, too. I'm leaving tomorrow. Another assignment. No great loss, eh, Vassily?" She smiled through tears.

"It'll work out," Feingold said abstractedly. He had gone ahead a few paces while Tania had her last words with Vassily. "It will all work out. When will you be back at the farm tonight, do you know?"

"Hard to say, since I'll have to look around for a couple of loafers. It's too much, Comrade Feingold."

"Things will change, will change a great deal," Feingold assured him blandly. "But you'll be back around six, won't you?"

"Bound to. I'll pick up a ride—the Red Army men drive by around that time."

"Good luck, Vassily Vassilevich."

"Good luck, Comrade Feingold."

"Good luck," Tania called from the tram stop, and each went his way.

It wasn't far to Besselmann's apartment. This time Vassily ignored precautions. He bounded up the steps—only to stand petrified in front of the door. The white notice gleamed in the semidarkness of the hall. Nationalized. The hand of Fate had descended on the Besselmanns, too.

Mechanically, Vassily reached for a cigarette. He had barely lighted it when he heard footsteps on the stairs. "You are looking for someone, comrade?" a man of about fifty asked in Polish. He had a sharp, long-nosed face and bristly hair. Vassily lingered in the dimness of the hall.

"Are you the *upravdom*—the superintendent? I've heard there's an apartment available here. On what floor is it?" He spoke Russian.

"You're standing right in front of it," the man said in broken Russian. "Do you have an authorization from the housing bureau?"

"In time," Vassily growled. "So far they've only given me the address. Listen, citizen"—he gave the man a cigarette and a light from his own—"I'm the director of the Meat Trust. I'll make it right with you. If any of the comrades come, say the apartment has already been taken." He took a fifty-ruble note from his pocket. "How big is the apartment?"

"Two large rooms and one small, and they've been kept in very good condition."

"Who's had it up to now?"

"A Jew and his family. They used to be very rich—no loss. To hell with them—psiakrev cholera!"

"Had he a son?

"The son was going to school. What the hell! You can't get rid of those Yids too soon—psiakrev cholera!"

"Did you fix them?" Vassily asked in a confidential tone.

"Who else, comrade?" The superintendent grinned. "I hope they all croak, the scum—the more of them the better. Psiakrev cholera!"

Abruptly Vassily became a nachalnik. "You'd better watch your language, citizen!" he said gravely and sternly. "Day before yesterday a worker was given two years for using that swearword. And you are counterrevolutionary—an anti-Semite, and you also take bribes. Maybe you'll be on the next shipment up north; unfortunately it's too late for this one." He walked away with the pleasant feeling that he had left the informer shaking with fear.

But the feeling didn't last. As soon as he reached the street corner, other emotions overpowered him with such force that he had to lean against the wall. What next? He didn't waste time over the thought that with Besselmann's disappearance he had lost his most important connection. How was he to reach Platzer, since he didn't know the man? But—Arye. At the moment the boy was more important than anything else. The poor kid was also being deported. If only he could help him. Or at least see him once more, say a few words to give him courage, wave to him. "Burzhuiskaia sentimentalnost," Vassily said under his breath.

He scarcely noticed that he had set out at a rapid pace, and he became aware of the direction he was taking only when the police headquarters building loomed before him. What do I want here, what can I do here? he wondered. Perhaps—but what harm? What can they do to me? If I lie my way through, good; if not. . . .

"*Propustka*—pass!" the militiaman called, putting his head out of the unpainted wooden sentry box at the entrance.

"I'm looking for a starshina," Vassily said. "Maybe you know him—he comes from my village. His name is—"

"I've only been here for a few days and don't know anybody. Most of them are at the railroad station—for the resettlement, you know." The young soldier took a cigarette from the pack Vassily was offering.

"Oh, then I'll find him there for sure. Thanks very much." Vassily walked away; he had learned that the deportees had been taken straight to the trains. He boarded a streetcar and rode to the railroad station. The entrance to the station was guarded; everyone who entered had to show a pass. They can't possibly send them straight from here, he thought. But then from where? Whom could he ask? No one would answer. He observed the faces and clothing of the few persons admitted into the station; they were all Russians.

He went to the freight station. There was a double guard there too. He showed his documents, was admitted, and saw some of his own farm teams standing in front of a shed. The drivers were delivering produce, and working straight through without a noon break —in compensation they would be finished with their day's work around three. Jurko was the last in line. "What brings you here, Vassily?" he asked. The other drivers also noticed him and started strolling toward him.

He motioned them to stay away. To Jurko he replied, "They arrested Tadek last night. I'd like to see him once more. Have you any idea where the deportation train is?"

"Tadek too? The hell with them! I don't know—it may be over there, down the line. A whole company of the militia went that way."

"Has it left yet?"

"Couldn't say. I came last. Maybe some of the others know."

"Better not ask. Is there a street behind the fence over there?"

"I guess so. But it might be guarded."

"Should we risk it, Jurko?"

"If you want to, Vassily. Climb in." Jurko turned his horses and drove around the freight sheds to the street. After about fifteen minutes along a high board fence, he stopped the wagon. There were few houses here, and these seemed empty. Jurko drove up close to the fence. Vassily stood on the back of one of the horses and peered between two pickets. Yes, there was the train, an immense line of freight cars, their sliding doors closed except for a narrow crack. On the side toward the station was a cordon of armed men. At a table some distance from the train sat men with red and blue caps, papers piled before them. Now and then someone got out of a car and was led by a militiaman to a wooden shack, evidently a latrine. "Turn around," Vassily said. They drove for about five minutes. "Stop here and pull in close to the fence again." Once more he mounted the back of the horse. "You drive back," he called, and swung himself over the fence.

He dropped into grass and weeds. For a moment he lay there, peering toward the train. He had not been seen. Slowly and cautiously he rose to his feet. He stood there a while with his face toward the fence, fingered his clothing, and with his hand still at his trousers he turned and headed straight toward the table. He lit a cigarette, walking still faster, and by the time he came close he seemed to be hurrying in a businesslike manner. He did not wait for questions, but demanded imperiously, "Who is the starshi here?" A red-capped man with the insignia of a lieutenant stood up. Vassily took three steps away from the table, beckoning, and the Lieutenant followed him. "I need one of them," he said, nodding his head toward the train. Without waiting for a question, he held out the spravka that Maxim Danilovich had given him. The NKVD man did not look at the name; he saw only the signature, the stamp and the seal.

"Certainly," he said readily. "What's the name?"

"Arye Besselmann. A boy of fifteen or sixteen. Want me to write it down for you?"

"I can keep it in my head. Besselmann—there are very few boys in the shipment anyhow," the Lieutenant said. He was a most cooperative sort. "We have the B's right behind the engine."

"Bring him." Vassily looked gravely at the man. "I'll wait behind the train. And—" He brought his finger quickly to his lips.

"Of course." The NKVD man hustled away, and Vassily went around behind the train. On that side the car doors were locked. There were no guards. After a ten-minute wait, Arye appeared, escorted by the officer. The boy's face glowed as he caught sight of Vassily. Vassily looked distant and cold, and Arye's face changed also. "It will take a while—maybe he'll have a story to tell. When are you leaving?" He looked at his watch.

"Between eight and nine, I hear."

"Time enough. Thanks."

"No trouble at all." The officer went back to his table. Vassily remained along with Arye.

"How did you know, Vassily? They came for us last night."

"How is your father bearing up—and your mother?"

"Father's all right. But Mother—she's sick."

"Do they have enough clothing, blankets, money?"

"We're not too badly off. The men who came for us were decent. They let us take things. We have bedding and fur coats, and fifteen thousand rubles besides."

"But I thought your father had a 'connection.'"

"Maybe the man doesn't know, and even if he does, he might be powerless, this time. It seems they haven't filled their quota, because otherwise they wouldn't be taking boys. It's wonderful of you to have come, Vassily—how did you manage it?"

"Arye, I'll get you out, if you're game for it."

"Game?" the boy smiled, and the smile gave his face an expression of manliness and superiority. "I'm game enough for anything. But my parents—who'll help them?"

"Don't you think they would prefer to have you free?"

Arye reflected. Then he nodded. "They might prefer it, yes. But how would they find out? And suppose we're caught? Then you'd be in for it too, Vassily."

"We'll come through, Arye. B'li pahad!"

"Eyn li pahad!" Arye had tears in his eyes. "Father didn't want to listen. Remember, Vassily? They won't survive it!" he cried out suddenly.

The NKVD man peered around the corner of the car. He was curious to know what the Spets. man wanted of the boy. When he saw the boy crying, he nodded with satisfaction. "They always cry," he said.

"Nichevo," Vassily replied. He went up to the man. "Any exit nearer than the main one?"

"Two hundred yards from the engine, to the right. There's a guard there. Do you want to take the kid with you?"

"I've got to try." He bent down and whispered this, with a crafty glance toward Arye. The Lieutenant was flattered by so much confidence from a superior. He could only nod significantly. "Though maybe I can get it out of him here. A stubborn customer." He turned to Arye again. "When was the last time you saw him?" he demanded sternly.

Arye shook his head. "I don't remember," he sobbed.

"You'll remember soon enough. Come!" Arye followed him, and they walked slowly toward the locomotive, Vassily pretending to be berating the boy.

"I can't leave. I can't desert my parents, Vassily. What will they think if I don't come back? It will kill them."

"There must be some way to inform them. Here's paper and pencil. Scribble a few words. That you're free and going to Chaim."

For a moment Arye hesitated. Then he wrote. Vassily could not read the writing; it was in Hebrew.

"Which car are they in?" he asked.

"The second behind the engine."

When they reached the car, Vassily looked around. There was not a soul in sight on this side. Only sidings on which were parked a number of empty freight cars. Vassily pointed to one of them. "Jump in there and don't make a sound. I'll call you." He wrote the name Besselmann in Cyrillic letters on top of Arye's note, walked boldly around to the other side of the train and hailed a militiaman. He flashed his spravka, and handed the note to the man. "Second car," he said. "Deliver at once."

The man trotted off, asking no questions. Vassily returned to the car in which Arye was hiding. "It's done," he said softly. "Come."

By now he felt that he had stretched his luck as far as it could go. They did not go to the guarded exit, but squeezed through a gap in the fence and found themselves on the street. "Do you know where we are, Arye?" Vassily asked.

"I've never been here. The station is over there." Arye pointed.

Vassily looked at his watch. They were walking by small, tumbledown houses with neglected gardens. The whole area looked uninhabited. "A sad neighborhood," Vassily said. "And yet people were living here not so long ago."

"Of course," Arye said. "Who knows where they are now?" He fell silent.

Vassily, too, was silent. There was a great deal to consider. Above all, how could Arye be taken over the border? Reach Birnberg. Who could say—perhaps Birnberg was being "resettled" also.

At last they came to less deserted streets. The people were unquestionably "natives."

Once on top of a hill, Vassily had his bearings again. Yes, the hospital where Dr. Feuerberg worked wasn't far from here. Perhaps he could persuade the Feuerbergs to hide Arye for a day. What would he tell the doctor? And how would Feuerberg, with his unshakable faith, react? But whom else could they go to? It was fifteen minutes to five—he must get back to the farm. "Come along, Arye. Janina Feuerberg lives near here. You remember, you brought the money to her. Perhaps you can stay there overnight."

"Fine, Vassily."

A few minutes later Vassily unlatched the gate. It was only a few steps to the front door. The big white notice stood out sharply against the dark brown paint of the door. Although Vassily knew at once what it must say, he went closer. Nationalized! Arye watched him timidly. Vassily looked awful. Pale, his teeth grinding, his fists clenched in helpless, despairing fury. The boy touched his hand. "Come, Vassily, there's no help for it."

"No, there's no help for it," he moaned. They set out, not knowing where they were going.

The street descended steeply. From this point, by cutting across the fields, it was not too far to the farm. "Come with me, Arye. You mustn't fall into their hands again. Come, my boy." He put his arm around Arye's shoulder.

"Yes, Vassily."

"The fellows are all stirred up," Jurko said. They were standing in one of the stalls; Jurko was rubbing his horse dry.

"What about?" Vassily asked.

Jurko did not look up. "They're scared. If I didn't have two kids myself—who can go on living like this? Did you see Tadek, Vassily?"

"No luck." He had a guilty conscience. "Tell the others they didn't see me at the railroad station."

"You can depend on that, Vassily. But the young fellows—I know they want to skip out."

"Where are things any better?"

"If you don't know from what quarter trouble is going to strike—"

"We ought to have a few months' peace now, anyway."

"Peace? That's something you never have with them. Nothing but fear. Don't you feel it, Vassily?"

"Who doesn't? But what's the use? After a while you get used to it—as you see."

Wasn't it madness for him still to be here? Suppose the Lieutenant of the deportation detachment began to worry and made an inquiry. He had played a dangerous game. . . . But no, the man wouldn't pursue the matter; the responsibility was his and he shouldn't have delivered a deportee without a receipt. The train would depart without Arye Besselmann, and no one would give it a thought. One prisoner more or less didn't matter. The quota was still unfilled, apparently. Vassily left the stable and started toward the dairy. The bookkeeper came running into the yard. "Telephone, Comrade Director."

Vassily didn't hurry. What can they want now? he thought grimly as he lifted the receiver. But it was Tania. "Would you do me a favor, Vassia? Just gather up my rags and throw them into the suitcase? It may be I won't have the chance to come out for them. The key to the house is in my desk drawer. I'm leaving today. Would you do that for me? Keep well and good luck, my darling ox!" Her laughter tinkled over the telephone.

"Good luck, Tania. Good luck and thanks for everything." Then there was nothing but a clicking sound on the line.

He hurried to the warehouse first. The bundle of Antek's possessions still lay there. He quickly selected several articles of clothing, put them into a bag, and hid the bag in the bushes.

There were quite a few dresses in Tania's wardrobe that had belonged to Mira, so the suitcase was soon a good deal heavier than it had been when she arrived. Vassily removed the rubies from the blue enamel compact and tucked the compact into one of Tania's shoes. For a moment he held the rubies in his hand. They gleamed like great, heavy drops of blood. He put the gems into the pocket of his work pants which was covered by his belt.

Most of the farm people were already at the canteen. Vassily made sure there was no one on the road and recovered the sack from the bushes where he had hidden it. He went straight to his house. Antek's work clothes did not fit Arye badly. The boy ate and drank tea while Vassily packed him a knapsack with clothing and food. He sketched the route the boy was to follow. "How long will it take you to reach Khodorov?"

"Oh, I'm pretty good at walking. I've gone on lots of hikes. How many miles is it, by your route?"

"About sixty to Khodorov. Maybe more. I'll take you as far as I can."

"Why don't you come with me, Vassily?"

"It would attract attention; they'd start looking for me. No, you must go alone. Come, now. Here's three hundred rubles—it's all I have." They walked along behind the houses. About thirty yards beyond the smithy they crossed the highway and came to a path. "Follow this path for half an hour to a small brook. Then hide in the bushes. If I don't come by dusk, start walking till you reach the railroad tracks. You can't miss them." He turned quickly, and Arye set off.

Vassily went to the stable. Yeremczuk followed him. "Stay around the yard, Mikhailo," he said. "If anyone asks for me, the stallion has colic. Understand, Mikhailo?"

"Right—you're giving him a workout."

"Just so. And tell the bookkeeper that if anyone calls, give the same message. And he's to wait until I come back." He tightened the saddle girth.

"Till you come back?"

"Till I come back, Mikhailo," Vassily said gravely.

"All right, Vassily."

As soon as he reached the path where he had left Arye, Vassily let the stallion run. At the brook, the boy stepped out of the bushes. "Have you ever ridden a horse, Arye?"

"Oh yes."

"Good. Get up behind and hold tight to my waist."

"Like Indians."

For a minute or two Golodnyi was indignant at the extra burden; then he began going like clockwork. Ten minutes at a gallop, five minutes at a walk. They went on this way for almost two hours. At last they reached the railroad. "Here we are," Vassily said. "Follow this country road on to the woods. Keep to the road. It leads to Soniewicze. Don't go through the village; you'll see a path that cuts back to the railroad track. That takes you to Khodorov, and from there—"

"Why won't you come with me, Vassily?"

"Because you're safer alone. Good luck, Arye." He embraced and kissed the boy. "Forward march!"

"Till we meet again, Vassily." Arye threw his arms around his neck.

"Yes, till we meet again!"

The horse was covered with sweat when Vassily rode into the yard. It was ten o'clock at night. Yeremczuk came out of the stable. "I'll take care of him—the bookkeeper has been asking for you. Go along, Vassily."

"Yes. Lead him around until he's dry, Mikhailo. Thanks."

Weidenfeld gave a sigh of relief when he saw him. "You're to call this number, Comrade Director—I think it's the comrade cashier. And twice another comrade asked for you. He gave the same number."

And there was Tania's pert little voice: "Please take my suitcase to your house—it will be picked up there. One moment—Arkady Samuelovich wants to have a word with you."

"How is the horse, Vassily Vassilevich? Better? Glad to hear it. And you'll be turning in soon? You've had a long day, haven't you? So long."

Vassily turned to the bookkeeper. "Thanks so much for staying, Dr. Weidenfeld. Yeremczuk will drive you out to the streetcar stop. I hope you've had some supper?"

"Thank you, I have; very kind of you."

Vassily collected Tania's suitcase and went home. He checked the rooms to make sure there were no telltale traces of Arye's having been there. Needless anxiety, he thought, as he looked over the kitchen and his room. If they'd missed him and suspected that I had him, they'd have been here by now. Arye will make it. But what about me? What am I still doing here? It isn't true, what I've been telling Arye and—and myself. He looked at his watch. Twenty minutes to eleven. They would be on their way by now: Panya Jadwiga and Tadek, Besselmann and his wife, and Janina and Leon Feuerberg. No, he must not think about all that, *must not.*

Must not think, must not think about anything. Not about Feingold's call either. Time to turn in, Vassily. Did you call just to wish me good night, nachadnik? . . . Get some sleep.

He had barely gotten under the blanket when there was a knock at his front door. Already? he thought as he went to open it. He had expected Feingold, but not the second man. It was the "pastor," Maxim Danilovich in person. "We've come to get Tania's suitcase," Feingold said, laughing.

"Here it is." Vassily pointed to it. The "pastor" was already in Vassily's tiny room. He checked to see that the window was well shut and that the heavy curtains were completely drawn. Vassily stood there in his peasant's nightshirt, his legs bare. "I didn't expect you to come for the suitcase yourself or I would have waited up," he said.

"Nichevo, nichevo," the "pastor" said gently. "If you could clear the table—"

"You can go into the other room. There's a large table there, and nothing on it."

"This one is good enough." He looked toward the window. "And if you would lock the doors—"

When Vassily returned, the books had been dumped on the bed. He carried in a chair for Feingold and slipped into his trousers. They all sat down, and Maxim Danilovich explained the "work" that he wanted Vassily to do. He spoke no more than twenty minutes, in his low, unctuous voice. He asked no questions and evidently expected none. "Get dressed now and come along," he concluded.

"I'll put on my old boots," Vassily said. "I'd better not be seen in these on the other side. A pity to have to leave them here. I'll need a different cap, too."

"Of course," the "pastor" said. "Let's see those old boots of yours." Vassily brought them out. "Perfect," he said. "A cap?" He reflected. "We'll find you one. Take your old one along for the time being."

Maxim Danilovich left. Feingold remained. Vassily dressed, took Tania's suitcase and his short fur jacket. When they were outside, he asked Feingold; "What's to be done with the key?"

Feingold took it. "Tomorrow I'll pack up your things and take them to my house," he said.

"Don't forget the boots, Comrade Feingold."

"Certainly not, Vassily Vassilevich."

The car was waiting about a mile outside Jiusefovka. Maxim Danilovich was already seated beside the chauffeur. They drove to Feingold's house, where he put vodka and cigarettes before them. "Take Khomniuk's cap and bring one of the same size, local make," the "pastor" said.

Feingold returned in about an hour with a large cardboard box. "He gave me all he had in that size," he said. There were three caps, but all of them with wide brims. However, there were also hats. Vassily chose a plush hat of a poisonous green color. It fitted him.

"Ready," Maxim Danilovich said, getting up. He looked at his watch. "You can start now."

They drove into Snyatyn around six o'clock in the morning. Once in the car, Vassily pretended to be sleeping. He wanted to think over this sudden turn of events. Why—for what purpose—was he being instructed to cross the Ceremus. Why should he find work in one of the Romanian villages between the Prut and the Siret, and stay there until . . . ?

Until what? The "pastor" hadn't told him that.

Vassily walked, fur jacket under his arm, the hideous green hat in his hand, beside Feingold through still deserted streets. "Why don't you put the hat on, Vassily?"

"It's all right for over there, not for here, Comrade Feingold."

"Like the boots." Feingold smiled.

"Yes. I feel sorry about my new ones. They were so comfortable."

"They won't be lost, nothing is lost. I'll take care of all your things for you."

"But how am I going to reach you? When the rains start, I'll have only these, and they're already so old and—"

"By the time the real rains start, you'll have them back. Sooner, much sooner than that. My word of honor, Vassily!" He laughed. "Now let's have some tea."

"Something in Vassily stirred. He remembered a long time back, an old general who had said, "Find out. . . ."

They returned to the car and drove to the railroad station. But there was no breakfast to be had in the restaurant as yet. They returned to the car. "The buffet at the Committee is open by half past seven," Feingold said. They drove there, and after a short wait, received an ample breakfast. Afterwards, they smoked and chatted. "The boots are pinching me," Vassily said. "My feet aren't used to them any more. A pity I couldn't have worn the others."

"Yes. But Maxim Danilovich saw they wouldn't do." Feingold reflected. "Once you've crossed over, you can buy yourself a pair. I'll give you money. Though in any case you'll have your boots in a couple of weeks, Vassily Vassilevich." He got up. "I'm going to make a telephone call."

Vassily sat alone thinking. In a couple of weeks I'll have my boots. In a couple of weeks . . . there . . . without an order to return. Stay there until—the boots will be brought to me? How will I be found? In one of the villages between the Prut and the Siret. There are a great many villages between those rivers.

Feingold returned. He kept looking impatiently from his watch to the door. At last a man entered, went to the counter, took vodka, ham and bread, and sat down at their table. He did not greet them. He downed the vodka, bit into the ham, and chewing hastily, mouth full, he said; "At ten forty-five."

"But not by day?" Feingold said softly.

The man shook his head. He chewed again, disclosing wide,

white teeth. His face was round and pockmarked; his small gray eyes held a sly look.

"It's all settled," he said hoarsely. "He'll be across before midnight." He bit into a large piece of ham and said, chewing, "Come along. There's no need for him to be seen around town." He got up.

At the station close to the border they led Vassily into a big room with large windows. The windows were open and looked out over the ragged field. "Can you use field glasses?" the nachalnik asked Vassily.

"I've never tried."

The man nodded as though he had expected this reply. He unlocked a cupboard and took out an old pair of Zeiss field glasses, the kind used for hunting in the mountains. "Try, then. Don't go too close to the window. Here, turn this screw until you see clearly."

Vassily slowly picked up the glasses, applied them to his eyes several times, and experimented a while before he said, "Now, now I see fine." He removed the glasses from his eyes and looked in the same direction. "This way I see nothing, and with them everything: a house, a garden, and that must be the Ceremus."

"It is," the nachalnik said. To Feingold he murmured, "An intelligent man."

"He is that, our Vassily," Feingold said proudly. He laughed. "My discovery!"

Vassily brought the glasses to his eyes again. "Now look carefully," the pockmarked man said. "A little to the right, a little more—there, you must have it now. What do you see?"

"Do you mean the trees?"

"Yes. How many do you see?"

Vassily counted. "Five. They're oak trees."

"Right. Look to the right of the oaks. What do you see?"

Vassily looked and said, "A house with a chimney; I can even see the smoke rising."

"Right, and to the left of the trees?"

Vassily swerved a bit. "A small house with a garden, many smaller trees, probably fruit trees."

"Right again. Now listen: what you have seen is the other side of the border."

"I understand."

"Look in the direction of the house with the garden. Do you have it?"

"Yes."

"Do you see the small stream?"

"I see it."

Almost directly opposite the house—on this side of the border—there is a ditch. Do you have it?"

"Yes, not very deep."

"Deep enough. Now listen carefully. You will be led to the ditch. Lie in it and keep looking at the small house. Until you see a tiny flame—the flare of a match. That's the signal. You'll crawl out of the ditch and down to the water. It isn't deep, barely up to your knees. In all this area, it's the place where the Ceremus is easiest to cross. On the other side you'll come right into the garden. A man will be waiting for you. You'll say, '*Nash brat* [our brother]'; he'll say, '*Bez voprosa* [without question].' He'll hide you until tomorrow morning and then take you into a town, Vishnitza. That is all."

"Easy," Vassily said.

"Yes," the nachalnik said. He gave Feingold a look and nodded. Then he led them into a room with a bed and sofa.

"You can lie down a while, Vassily Vassilevich," Feingold said. "Stock up on sleep. I'm going to the Secretariat. I'll be back toward evening."

Vassily removed his boots, rolled up his jacket for a pillow, and stretched out. Sleep—yes, that was best now. But he seemed to hear Karl Rundberg's voice: Go to Jivan Bes; the Ceremus flows behind his garden. Between the five oaks and the distillery. Yes, Bes was reliable!

It was around six o'clock that Feingold woke him. "Had enough sleep?" he asked. "You must be hungry."

"So I am," Vassily said cheerfully.

They had hot, fatty borshch, pork, and a small bottle of vodka. The nachalnik ate with them. Then he left, and Vassily remained alone with Feingold.

"Your new boots, Vassily; I'll bring them to you myself." He laughed.

"I'm not a child, Comrade Feingold. I'll buy a pair over there. I've worked there before; I'll find work again."

"Fine. But only this side of the Siret. You heard what Maxim Danilovich said."

"Heard but not understood, Comrade Feingold."

"Just do as he says. You'll understand later—perhaps in five or six weeks." He winked. "Oh yes, we'll see each other again before very long, Vassily. And here—you know what this is?"

Vassily took the envelope and looked into it. "Of course I know. American dollars."

"Right. They're for you."

Vassily pushed the envelope aside. "No good, Comrade Feingold. If they catch me over there and find dollars on me—that's a great deal of money over there—what laborer would have it? Lei would be better, a thousand or fifteen hundred, that's all. They have the Sigurantza over there—they're no people to fool with."

"I know, we know all that." Feingold mused. With sudden resolution he thrust the dollars into his pocket. "Lei—yes, I have some." He left, and soon returned. "Here are three thousand. But what can you buy for that amount? Not even boots."

"No, but you say I'll get my own back soon. Although if you're going to bring them yourself"—he winked—"then you musn't be dressed the way you are. Not in that outfit. Or the Sigurantza would have you in the first half hour."

Feingold laughed heartily. "When I come, there won't be any more Sigurantza." And then he left the room.

Vassily opened the window that opened on the yard. At a long table the border guards were cleaning their guns and singing along with the music from the radio. Then the music stopped, and a woman's voice reported the latest news from abroad. In England Churchill had been asked to form a cabinet. German troops had crossed the borders of Belgium and Holland. The Belgians and the Netherlanders were offering resistance. Then marching music began, and the soldiers sang along: *"Moskva Moia* (My Moscow)"! And Vassily walked with dragging footsteps to the table and dropped into a chair. Frightful images, underscored by thundering music, filled his mind: torn bodies, smoking ruins, bursting shells, roars of cannon, shrieks of pain. And into the still-vivid memories of the past war surged a vision, unbearably clear, of what was to come. ". . . have crossed the border." Now it had really begun.

Have crossed the border. And I too am going to cross a border now, a border that soon will be erased.

For the ally must have his share. Only a bit of Bucovina in exchange for the Netherlands and Belgium? And what about Bessarabia? Hadn't that once been Russian?

Feingold entered the room, followed by the nachalnik. "Vodka, Vassily Vassilevich?"

"Thanks, gladly."

Then Feingold extended his hand. "Keep well, good luck and success!"

"Good luck." Feingold left the room. Vassily remained with the nachalnik. "No da," the pockmarked man said. "I'll have to blindfold you now."

The march lasted half an hour. The blindfold was not very tight; the man who led Vassily wore no uniform. "Lie down with your face to the ground," he ordered finally. "There, that's right."

He removed the blindfold. "Stay where you are." He dashed away. "Now," Vassily heard him calling, and raised his head. Only a step in front of him was the ditch. The idiots, he thought as he crawled in. Then he lay there, peering over the top. Close by he could hear the Ceremus flowing. Not thirty paces away was his own country. For how long would it be that? Five or six weeks. I'll bring you the boots. . . . ("There'll be no more Sigurantza.") Oh yes, I've come back with important news. You'll be content with me, General Baderescu, Old Man. They're coming, they're already on the march, and I am their advance guard. How many like me have they already sent?

From the other side of the river he heard a peasant song. A young, vigorous voice—undoubtedly it was a border guard singing. Vassily rubbed his eyes. Suddenly his callused hand was wet with tears. Calluses on the hands don't remain, but on the soul. . . . Soul—"bourgeois sentimentality"! But one suffers, doesn't one, when others are in pain, and their suffering becomes one's own? And one helps; sometimes almost helplessly one is gripped by the compulsion to help others.

The strong young voice sang:

> Lord God, give me seven hundred sheep,
> And I will climb up, up to the green stone.
> Although tonight without a girl I sleep,
> With seven hundred sheep I'll not be alone.

Not be alone, any longer not be alone. Martha, Karl, friends. And the weak and the helpless must be helped against the strong and powerful.

I'll not be alone.

Then the match flared.

GLOSSARY

Romanian

boyar	member of the gentry; landowner
coane	sir (usually used with given name)
conitza	aristocrat (fem.)
Doamna	Mrs., Madam
Domnule	Mr., Sir
nene	uncle; term of respect for an older man
turceasca	Turkish; Turkish coffee

Polish

Pan	Mr.
Panya	Mrs.

Russian

burzhui	capitalists
Chekist	member of Soviet secret police
chervonets (pl. chervontsy)	monetary unit: ten rubles
dessiatin	measure of area: about 3 acres
grazhdanin	citizen
khakhol	Ukrainian (abusive term)
khoziaistva	aggregation of farm employees
komandirovka	travel permit
Komsomol	Soviet Youth
konechno	naturally
koniukh	stableman
korovnik	milker
kulturno	"high-class"
nachalnik (pl. nachalniki)	chief; big shot
nichevo	it doesn't matter
no da	yes, of course
ogrodnik	gardener
partinyi	party member; Bolshevik
perekupshchiki	middlemen: buyers
planovik	economic planner

politruk	political adviser
robota	work
spravka	permit: work permit
starshi	chief; principal
starshiletenant	first lieutenant
starshina	sergeant
verkhovki	leader; top echelon
zamestitel	assistant; deputy
zhid, zhidok	Jew (derogatory terms)

J. Klein-Haparash

Born in Romania in 1897, J. Klein-Haparash was
raised there and in Vienna. During World War I
he fought as an Austrian. Later he made illegal
trips into the Soviet Ukraine to inform American
newspapers of the pogroms. He has crisscrossed
Europe many times, sometimes on horseback, and
has worked as a political journalist for German
and Romanian newspapers. After 1940, Klein-
Haparash lived under the Soviet system, where his
life included times as a carriage driver, a community director and a prisoner. He escaped to his
birthplace, through both Russian and German lines,
only to be arrested again. He escaped once more
and became active in an underground movement
to rescue children from Eastern Europe. Since 1946
he has been living in Israel.